BLIND HOPE

Kristy Shelton

innovo PUBLISHING

Published by
Innovo Publishing, LLC
www.innovopublishing.com
1-888-546-2111

Providing Full-Service Publishing Services for
Christian Authors, Artists & Organizations: Hardbacks, Paperbacks,
eBooks, Audiobooks, Music & Film

BLIND HOPE

Scripture marked NIV taken from THE HOLY BIBLE, NEW INTERNATIONAL VERSION®,
NIV® Copyright © 1973, 1978, 1984, 2011 by Biblica, Inc.®
Used by permission. All rights reserved worldwide.

Scripture marked NKJV taken from the New King James Version®. Copyright © 1982
by Thomas Nelson, Inc. Used by permission. All rights reserved.

Scripture marked NASB taken from the NEW AMERICAN STANDARD BIBLE®,
Copyright © 1960, 1962, 1963, 1968, 1971, 1972, 1973, 1975, 1977, 1995
by The Lockman Foundation. Used by permission.

Library of Congress Control Number: 2014934278
ISBN 13: 978-1-61314-201-1

Cover Design & Interior Layout: Innovo Publishing, LLC

Printed in the United States of America
U.S. Printing History

First Edition: March 2014

Dedicated to my son, Ty.
I could always see your heart.

Acknowledgments

Chuck Swindoll once said, "Everything that comes to you has first come through the hands of God."* I wholeheartedly agree. Every part of this book has been a gift from the Creator. So to Him be all the glory and honor.

I have to admit, writing a sequel to *Blinders* was not on my radar screen until Janice Stroud and the sweet ladies of Burnt Hickory Church invited me to their book club meeting. I laughed when they asked for a sequel. Hopefully, I didn't hurt their feelings. Incredibly, a week later an entire scene came to mind. School was out for the summer, and I got the urge to write again, so I poured out that scene on my computer. My daughter, Alex, was home from college and asked me to read it out loud to her. When I was finished, she said, "Oh, Mom, you have to write that book." So thanks to her encouragement, I did. And that first scene I wrote turned out to be chapters 9, 10, and 11—an unusual way to start writing a book, I know.

I want to thank Dr. Bart Dahmer of Innovo Publishing for believing in me yet again. His high principles and deep sense of morality are a light in this dark world. I count it a great privilege to be a part of the Innovo family.

Darya Crockett, you inspire me to be a better writer. Thank you for your long hours of editing. Your sweet spirit and love for the Lord draw my heart to yours. I have a big hug reserved for you!

Catrina White, Darcy Huber, and Allison Anderson—friends, colleagues, book lovers, precious women of God—thank you for taking the time to read each chapter as it was being written. I feel so blessed that you shared your insights and ideas with me throughout this long journey. I am truly honored by your loyalty and dedication. Each of you had such a unique perspective that encouraged me greatly—even when our opinions differed.

Tammy Hughes, English teacher extraordinaire, thank you for taking time out in your summer, once again, to help clean up my manuscript. As you can see, I still need that lesson on commas! I appreciate your friendship of thirty years now.

---

* Chuck Swindoll as quoted by Mark Gregston, Parenting Today's Teens, "Dealing with the Cards You've Been Dealt,"
http://www.heartlightministries.org/blogs/markgregston/2013/05/10/dealing-with-the-cards-youve-been-dealt/

Mom and Dad, thank you for your constant encouragement and unceasing prayers on my behalf. You are my heroes!

Cliff, I'm grateful for our rock of a marriage and for the incredible ministry of teaching and coaching that God has given us. I hope you have time to read this book!

And finally, to my son, Ty, *my Will*—many of the prayers Annie uttered in this novel were my exact words for you as you were growing up. There were times I wondered if we were going to make it through this journey together. But I could clearly hear God saying, "I gave him to you because you can handle him." I'm sorry for the times I didn't do a very good job of it. But please know there was never a moment that I did not love you. I pray that you will never fail to see your worth in God's eyes. You are such a mighty man of God, and I am honored to be your mother. Thank you for making me a stronger person!

Prologue

Eugene's eyelids grew heavy, but sleep was an unwelcome foe. He had been deprived for three straight nights, two of which had been forced upon him, the third—his choice entirely. He sat up a little straighter in the chair, rubbing weary hands across his face. A slow, deep breath filled his lungs, and immediately he regretted taking in so much air at once. His brow wrinkled into tiny lines of anxiety. The smell all around him was unmistakable—it was the smell of death.

Breathing out another prayer, Eugene leaned toward the bed, begging for mercy. The doctors had done everything within their power. Now he relied solely on the beneficence of God.

Trust in the Lord with all your heart, and lean not on your own understanding.[1]

Trusting God had never really been an issue with Eugene. The longer he lived, the more he realized a trusting heart had been one of his gifts from above. Even as a child living with an abusive stepfather, he had always believed God would provide a way out. That provision had come in the way of a godly man and woman who had shaped and molded him into the man he would become. They had protected him with their very lives and restored his hope for living. More importantly, they had taught him how to love others unconditionally.

But now, something terrible had wrapped itself around his heart. His chest grew tight as he wrestled with an unexpected darkness. Doubt and fear seeped in through any opening they could find. It felt like even the pores in his skin were clogged with uncertainty.

Eugene reached over and caressed the face of the one he loved—silent pleas spilled unceasingly from his heart. He would stay at this bedside as long as it took, and he would try to hold on to the hope in his heart, as feeble as it seemed.

He allowed his mind to wander to the war he had fought as a youth, a war Eugene had been dragged into against his will, and yet God had protected him and taught him perseverance. He was reminded of the life he had lived following the war—what others had intended for evil, God had intended for good. The Lord had blessed him with a wife and family far beyond his hopes and dreams.

Now he reached for the immovable hand in the bed and brought it to his lips. A tear spilled onto the once-vibrant skin. He laid the hand down on the crisp, white sheet, gently wiping the moisture away.

---

[1] Proverbs 3:5, NKJV.

Eugene sat back and chanced leaning his head on the back of the chair. With no intention of sleeping, he now occupied his mind with the passage of time since the Great War. No doubt about it, he had been blessed. Even though mistakes had been made, love had always triumphed—without fail.

PART ONE

We have always held to the hope, the belief, the conviction that
there is a better life, a better world, beyond the horizon.

~Franklin Delano Roosevelt

For everything that was written in the past was written
to teach us, so that through the endurance taught in the Scriptures and the
encouragement they provide we might have hope.

~The apostle Paul (Romans 15:4, NIV)

Chapter 1

February 1924

Annie quietly opened the front door, meeting head on the chill of predawn. She felt her body rebel against the cold and noticed her breath escaping into the grayish light. Hardly visible and perched on the top step of the porch was the outline of her husband, bare to the waist, taking in deep gulps of frosty air.

Eugene felt the quilt engulf his shoulders and gladly accepted Annie's warmth as she nestled up close to his side. As always, she laid her warm hand on his chest, and he reached up to hold it there tightly. Feeling her hand over his heart seemed to bring him back to reality—a beautiful reality that morning would soon wash away the terrors of the night. Her hand could somehow will his heart to slow down, could somehow bring warmth back into his body, could somehow chase away the fear.

He knew she wouldn't ask, that she would stay by his side as long as he needed her—his sweet Annie, so full of life and joy. Eugene took in a deep breath and looked out over the pasture in the dim light. Today, for some reason, he *wanted* her to ask. He had an overwhelming desire to tell her the truth, but it seemed impossible unless she asked it of him.

A whimper came from inside the house that soon turned into an all-out cry for Momma. Annie felt her milk coming in, so she eased out from under the blanket and pulled it tight around Eugene's shoulders. Just for a moment they locked eyes, and Eugene felt incredibly blessed to have this woman in his life. She stood on a lower step and put her hands around the back of his neck, drawing his mouth to hers. When she released her hold, he took her left hand and brought it to his lips, as was his habit, then let her go.

"I love you, Eugene Wyatt . . . with all my heart, I love you."

Annie reached into the bassinet to rescue her one-month-old son from his hungry outburst. "I'm sorry little Jake, but we have to get your diaper changed first."

She turned on the lamp beside the changing table and went to work as fast as she could to get her youngest son dry and ready for his early morning feeding. As soon as Annie started talking to him, Jacob calmed to the sound of her voice and patiently endured the task until it was done. She propped up her pillow along with Eugene's and slipped back into bed with her little bundle.

Suddenly startled, Jake momentarily pulled away from his mother at the sound of a noisy *thunk* on the floor in the next room. Annie sat completely still for a moment wondering what she had just heard, until a loud wailing filled every corner of the house. Easing out of bed with Jake, Annie rushed into Will's room. At just over two years old, her eldest son had managed to find a way to climb out of his crib. But judging by the look on his face, and the sound she had heard previously, he had just learned a tough lesson.

When Annie reached out to her son, he quickly backed away and yelled, "No!" as if he were somehow blaming her for his tumble. She tried not to take it personally, but Will was beginning to show a stubborn streak that was a bit disconcerting. Lately he had bristled in her arms whenever she tried to comfort him. She knew part of his problem concerned this new little baby she now cradled in her arms. She and Eugene tried to reassure Will every day just how much they loved him by spending extra one-on-one time with him. Nothing, however, seemed to work when he was angry.

Thankfully, Annie heard Eugene come inside the house. He appeared in the doorway of Will's room as he was pulling a t-shirt over his head.

"Come 'ere, Son. Let me see what's the matter."

Instantly little Will's arms reached out for his daddy, and once again Annie tried to squelch the hurt feeling that wrapped around her heart.

Eugene worked his fingers into Will's blonde hair trying to feel for any lumps on his head. "Just as I thought, you've got a thick skull just like your momma."

Annie playfully rolled her eyes at her husband and headed back to their bedroom with Jake. As soon as she was situated in the bed again, Eugene crawled around the corner with Will riding his back gleefully calling out, "Giddy up, Daddy! Giddy up!"

Eugene dumped him onto the foot of the bed and rolled him over so he could blow on his stomach. Will giggled at the funny sound, then hopped off the bed and ran into the other room to find his favorite stuffed animal—a sock bear named Knucklehead.

With Will out of the room, Eugene sat down on the side of the bed facing his wife and youngest son. He lovingly cupped Jake's little head in the palm of his hand, bending to kiss his soft, fuzzy hair. Even as he was eating, Jake started to smile, and milk gurgled from his mouth.

Eugene grinned at Annie. "What do you think? Is it safe to say our two boys are total opposites?"

Annie let out a soft laugh, but her words to Eugene were lost as Will came running around the corner yelling that he was hungry.

Eugene tweaked Annie's cute nose, then swooped Will up into his arms again. "Come on, fella. How about we make some French toast for me and you and Mommy?"

*****

This morning, Eugene stayed around the house a little longer than usual. He wanted to make sure everything was going all right with Annie and the boys before he started to work on their horse and cattle farm. It was a small acreage compared to some of their neighbors, but it was theirs.

When he and Annie exchanged marriage vows three years ago, they were both barely twenty. Eugene had been working as a horse trainer for Annie's father, Nathan Harrison, and living with his hired hands in the bunkhouse. After the wedding, they had moved in with her parents up until a year ago. They had finally saved enough money to put a down payment on a small piece of land just outside of Louisville, not more than five miles from Annie's folks.

Eugene owed a lot to Mr. Harrison, more than he would ever be able to repay. As a gift, Nathan had given the young couple several head of cattle to get a good start on their farm. He told Eugene that buying and selling thoroughbreds was a fickle business, but the cattle business was altogether different. "Everyone wants beef—you'll always have an income raising cattle." Still, Eugene loved his thoroughbreds, and Annie was downright crazy about them.

Despite the lateness of the morning hour, Eugene stopped at the outer fence overlooking their bluegrass pasture. He put his foot on the bottom rail and leaned his forehead into the back of his hands on the top one. It had been several months since he'd had a night terror—this one most likely triggered by the sounds of his newborn son in the bassinet beside their bed. And this terror, just like all the others, left him plagued with doubts and a feeling that something wasn't right. It was a feeling that would probably follow him the rest of the day.

Scrunching his eyes tight, Eugene tried not to let the haunting images enter his mind. They came anyway. Images of tiny bodies in his arms, their little limbs dangling loosely, their heads tilted back, no breath in their lungs. In the light of day, none of them had faces. But at night, they bore the faces of his sons.

"Lord, when will it end?" He kept his head bowed, praying that this would be the last one.

Eugene had been just seventeen when he hit the fields of France along with the 357th Infantry. The horrible acts of war he had witnessed and participated in had tormented him for a long time. Most of it he would never be able to talk about—not as long as he lived. He had carried a load of guilt the size of Kentucky back home with him. If it hadn't been for Rachel Hawkins, the woman who had adopted him when he was eleven, he might have lost his mind and soul. With her help, he was able to unload his burden to the Savior. Now the only remnants of the Great War were the debilitating nightmares.

There had been a bright spot in his army days, however. His deep friendship with Sergeant William Gano had been the most incredible blessing during those two years away from home. Will had been as close as a brother, sharing his wisdom of life and faith with Eugene freely. He never would have survived without him. But Will had paid the ultimate price in the cause of human liberty, and now Eugene tried to live his life in a way that would honor Will's sacrifice.

Naming his first son William was the least he could do as a tribute to his dearest friend. Eugene's heart lightened just a bit as he remembered Will's pleasing smile, even when the machine gun fire was thick and shrapnel was flying.

"And the peace of God, which surpasses all understanding, will guard your hearts and minds through Christ Jesus."[2] Eugene quoted the passage from Philippians out loud. It was time to get to work, and he would be relying heavily on that peace the rest of the day.

That evening, after the boys were asleep, Annie breezed into the front room and settled on the couch beside Eugene. He had been trying to read his Bible but was ashamed that his chin kept hitting his chest. Annie brought him fully awake with her characteristic cheerfulness. Setting his Bible on the table beside the lamp, he pulled her close to his side. Eugene ran his fingers through her thick hair, loving how its caramel color framed her pretty face.

"Tell me what you were reading," Annie said, as she sat back so Eugene could pick up his Bible again.

"I was in the book of Hebrews chapter twelve." Eugene began to read, "*. . . since we are surrounded by so great a cloud of witnesses, let us lay aside every weight, and the sin which so easily ensnares us, and let us run with endurance the race that is set before us, looking unto Jesus, the author and finisher of our faith, who for the joy that was set before Him endured the cross, despising the shame, and has sat down at the right hand of the throne of God."*[3]

Looking up he said, "Those words meant a lot to me during the war."

Annie drew her knees up to her chest and looked intently at her husband. "Eugene," her blue eyes were disarming him, "tell me what you saw."

He didn't consciously act, but he realized he was now standing on his feet—heart beating a reckless rhythm. Gently, Annie reached for his hand and pulled him back onto the couch, moving her body up close to his.

"It's all right. There should be no more secrets in the night." Her soft hand caressed his face. "Let me help you carry this burden."

Eugene felt his taut muscles relax as her hand moved to his chest. Holding it there with his own, he pressed his lips together and took in a deep breath through his nose. Slowly, he nodded his head and let Annie's hand go.

"Toward the end of the war, when the Germans realized they were losing, they did something so heinous—so despicable . . ." Eugene's voice broke slightly, and he cleared his throat before continuing. "They used poisonous gasses on two of the towns near our position. Annie," he looked at her, shaking his head, "they were *civilians*—innocent people just trying to survive with their families. Families just like ours."

"How could they do such a thing?" The look on Annie's face was one of genuine outrage.

---

[2] Philippians 4:7, NKJV.
[3] Hebrews 12:1–2, NKJV.

"I don't know," he said, rising to his feet again. "I wondered if they actually had hearts beating inside their chests."

Eugene began to pace the room, rubbing the back of his neck. "My unit was assigned to the town of Mouzay the night the gas was released. We went from house to house trying to rescue the citizens before it was too late. We were protected by our gas masks, but most of the people in the town had no protection."

Now Eugene turned to Annie with tears welling up in his eyes. "There were little children lying in their beds, little babies I tried to save. I held their precious bodies in my arms, praying I could get them to safety before it was too late." Eugene's legs seemed to give out on him, and he went to his knees right there in the middle of the floor. "I couldn't save them . . . some of them took their last breath while I held them."

Annie's face was now flooded with tears. She dropped down on her knees in front of her husband and began to gently kiss his face. Then she took both of his hands and led him back to the couch, crawling onto his lap for him to hold her as he had held those ill-fated French citizens. Again and again she uttered, "It's over now, sweetheart. It's over."

Eugene shook his head. "It's not over at night."

Annie forced him to hold her tighter in his arms and softly breathed, "Those babies are with the Lord, Eugene. You'll see them again someday with Jesus. It's over."

Gradually, Eugene's body relaxed as he pictured those children with God. They would never have to endure the sorrows of this life; they were happy with the Creator of the universe. Maybe it truly was over—there was no way of knowing. He bent his head and kissed his wife, tasting the salt from their tears. Only time would truly tell.

***

"Eugene, we're going to be late for church again."

Baby Jake was contentedly bundled up in Annie's arms as she waited at the door for Eugene and Will. They found it easier on Sunday mornings for Annie to take charge of the baby while Eugene took care of their eldest son.

Patience was one of Eugene's strong suits, but even Will could sometimes push him to the limit. "Son, if you take your shoes off again, I'll have to carry you to the car."

Annie finally moved to the back of the house to peek into Will's room. He was standing defiantly with arms across his chest, his shoes nowhere in sight.

"Eugene, where are his shoes?"

"No clue," Eugene responded as he began to search the room. He finally got down on his hands and knees and found them underneath the crib, next to the wall.

"Okay, buddy, what'll it be? Do you want to walk out of here or be carried?"

It took another five minutes before Eugene walked out of the house with Will struggling in his arms and the shoes dangling from two fingers. By the time they made it to Oak Hill Church, the congregation was deep into their first hymn. Verses of "What a Fellowship" swirled enthusiastically amongst the brethren, bringing a feeling of joy to the Wyatt family as they snuck into a pew near the back.

Eugene and Annie loved this church. It was one of a kind, an oasis in a desert of prejudice and racism. This was the church where the two had reconnected after the war. Every pew was filled with blacks and whites all mixed together praising the Lord who had fashioned each one in His image.

When the service was over, Eugene was pulled into a conversation with Brother J. W. Hobbs, a kind old soul who lived in a small shack not far down the road. J. W. cleaned the church building from top to bottom every week. His meticulous work far exceeded the small salary he was paid by the church. Eugene had seen Annie's father slip extra money into J. W.'s dark, weathered hand many a Sunday. J. W. always responded with a "God bless ya, kindly, Mista Nathan," humbly dipping his head.

Annie was busy with a cluster of ladies trying to get a closer look at little Jake. Finally, one of his most devoted admirers was able to push her way through the crowd. Claudia Harrison leaned over, kissed her daughter, and took her new little grandson into her arms.

"Oh, there's my precious boy." Claudia kissed his forehead, asking Annie how he had slept last night.

"He slept a full six hours for the first time!" Annie's exuberance brought a cheer from the passel of dear ladies standing around her.

In search of Will, Grandpa Nathan joined the ladies. He hugged Annie tightly, kissed little Jake on the cheek, then reached over and gave his son-in-law a friendly nudge.

"Where's my boy?"

Nathan loved Will's energy and spent hours playing with him whenever Annie brought him to the house.

Eugene looked down at his feet, but Will was nowhere in sight. Both men began to scan the crowd until they spotted the toddler run onto the platform at the front of the sanctuary. Eugene started to head that way, but Nathan held him back. "I've got him," he said with a laugh as he made his way down front.

At that moment, a gentle hand took hold of Eugene's arm, and he turned to see Rachel ready to pull him into her embrace. Holding her close, he was reminded how much he owed this incredible woman. He had been so busy with the farm this week that he hadn't seen her since last Sunday, although he had spoken to her several times on the telephone. Normally, he and Annie would've picked her up for church at her house in town, but since the arrival of the baby, Annie's parents gladly gave her a ride.

"Mama, you look pretty today."

At sixty-six, Rachel was still a beautiful woman. She had worked hard for forty-five years on the farm near Winchester with her beloved husband, Franklin. Wearing hats and long sleeves in the sun had preserved her creamy complexion. The only telltale signs of her age were the sunspots on her hands and the silver threads working their way through her dark hair.

"And you look so handsome," she said with a smile, then added, "although, just a bit tired."

Eugene grinned. "Jake's been making sure we get to see more of the stars lately, but I'm fine."

"Well, hang on tight, Son. I can't believe how fast Will is growing up."

At that moment, Claudia moved to Rachel's side and asked if she would like to hold their mutual grandson. Without hesitation, Rachel took the precious bundle into her arms. She had never been blessed with a baby of her own—never known the feeling of having a child at her breast—and regretfully had not known Eugene as an infant. There were times while holding her grandsons that she thought her heart would literally dissolve with affection.

Eugene loved watching his mama hold their sons. Her deep love for them was obvious. He put his arm around her shoulders as they made their way to the door. Annie came to Rachel's side and pulled the blanket up around Jake's face before they stepped out into the crisp February afternoon.

Instantly, Eugene's senses snapped to full alert. His family had not been the first to exit the building; a hushed crowd was already standing motionless in the churchyard. It gave Eugene an eerie feeling, and his first impulse was to rush the women back inside. But all he could seem to do was stand rooted with the rest of the congregation, transfixed by the object across the road.

The sputtering flames in the breeze made a devilish hissing sound, sending a stab of fear throughout the crowd. A large cross was fully engulfed in flames—a sight that many had never before witnessed. Even more alarming was the presence of a dozen hooded men—ghostly figures—unmoving, staring directly at the mixed congregation from across the road.

It seemed like long minutes had passed in silence, although Eugene knew it had only been a matter of seconds. None of the brethren moved, fearful of a confrontation. Finally, Jeffrey Swanson emerged from the building, taking in the sight for only a moment before speaking to the congregation. Jeff was the church's white minister; Edwin Jones was the black minister. "Folks, please get in your automobiles and head on home." He opened his arms wide as if he were sweeping them all toward the gravel parking lot.

"What are we gonna do about this, Preacher? How's this gonna be handled?" With Devon Watson's questions out in the open, others began to murmur their thoughts and fears.

Quietly, Jeff reminded the congregation that the Lord would take care of this situation. "There's no need for worry. We have a mighty God who protects His people. Go on home now and put this right out of your minds."

Edwin Jones began to work among the crowd as well, reassuring the people that God was in control. He put his hand on Eugene's shoulder and said, "You and Annie take your boys on home. God bless ya, folks."

Taking his hand Eugene said, "God bless you too, Edwin."

Annie and Rachel had already moved to the car with the boys and were getting settled inside when Eugene opened his door. Annie was in the front holding Jake, and Rachel had gotten in the back seat with Will in her lap. Eugene noticed his mama's expression and suddenly realized how unnerving this situation must be for her. Exactly half a lifetime ago, she had witnessed a brutal slaying at the hands of a racist mob. His heart went out to her as they drove past the faceless menace lining the road. Eugene said a silent prayer on behalf of Rachel and their congregation. He knew in his heart, this was only the beginning.

Chapter 2

Two weeks passed without incident, although three members of the Oak Hill congregation suffered harassment in the form of rocks thrown through their windows at home. Most suspected it was the work of the Ku Klux Klan, which was beginning to flourish in many Kentucky towns and cities. Eugene had heard talk in the city about the Klan. While most were considered to be upstanding members of the community, it was still a secret society of sorts. Klansmen considered themselves to be defenders of traditional morality and true Americanism. It was difficult to understand how they could direct their acts of violence against fellow human beings just because they were different. Even more difficult to understand was how they could carry out their deeds in the name of God.

It was now mid-March and blustery winds were still holding the sun's warmth at bay. Annie made sure Jake was well covered and Will's coat was buttoned as she followed Eugene into the lobby after the morning worship service. Before they could make it to the door, the sound of a loud commotion came from outside the building. A scream rose up from Miss Ruby, one of Oak Hill's most prominent church members.

Eugene turned to Annie with a hasty command. "Stay right here with the boys. Something's going on; let me check it out." Rachel walked up, and Eugene repeated his instructions. "Mama, stay with Annie and the boys."

A hot puff of air hit Eugene in the face as he stepped outside the door. Miss Ruby cried, "Lawd, have mercy. They's burnin' down the old church."

The sight before him was frightening to say the least. The old meetinghouse across the road, where the black congregation had once worshipped, was now fully engulfed in fire. Worse yet, the wind was carrying a thousand tiny sparks across the road. Some of the dry grass and bushes near the Oak Hill Church building were beginning to catch fire.

Nathan Harrison threw off his suit jacket and grabbed Eugene's arm. "Come on, we've got to soak everything down on this side of the road." He then yelled over his shoulder, "Someone call the fire department!" Oak Hill Church was on the outskirts of Louisville, so it would take them a while to get here.

Brother J. W. Hobbs came flying around the corner of the building with an armload of cleaning buckets and met Nathan and Eugene at the pump. A line of men began to form, old and young, standing shoulder to shoulder ready to receive the buckets of water. A police officer had already arrived, joining the men as they passed the splashing buckets hand to hand. Several long minutes passed before the siren of the fire brigade could be heard speeding down the highway.

Finally arriving on the scene, several firefighters jumped from the outside of the truck where they had been hanging on precariously. Edwin Jones met them on the other side of the road to show them where the old cistern was located. Working at a furious pace, the fire brigade was soon pumping water onto the inferno. They bravely battled the blaze for the better part of an hour.

When it appeared that the fire had been contained, the remaining church members came pouring out of the Oak Hill building. Eugene and Nathan joined their family as they watched the flames grow weaker. A collective gasp echoed through the crowd as the smoking timbers collapsed into a gigantic, charred heap. Many of the black members hugged each other and sobbed; they were losing a part of their heritage.

Eugene noticed Rachel was in a state of distress. "Mama, are you all right?" He moved to her side, trying not to get her wet. His shirt and trousers were soaked through to the skin.

She continued to stare straight ahead. Eugene wasn't sure she had heard his question, so he laid a gentle hand on her elbow. At her son's touch, Rachel began to slowly shake her head; she wasn't all right.

"Claudia?" Eugene turned to his mother-in-law for help. "Can you take Mama back inside? I think she needs to sit down."

A concerned look wreathed Claudia's face as she wrapped her arms around Rachel and began to speak to her softly. She turned her friend gently toward the door, and the two women disappeared inside.

Annie immediately turned to Eugene. "I need to be with her too." She had an anxious look on her face, no doubt worried about Rachel's well-being. Eugene reached down to take charge of Will so Annie could join the women.

"Come on, buddy, whaddaya say Gramps and you and I go for a walk." Eugene started to get a bit chilled from the wind, but he wanted to give his mama time to talk if she needed to.

"Wanna see fire. See fire, Daddy?" Will reached for both of the men's hands, hoping they would take him across the road.

Eugene looked down at his son, "No more fire, Willie. It's all gone."

None of the church members had gone home yet. Everyone remained, talking in hushed voices, scattered across the churchyard. Eugene and Nathan walked around the building with Will hoping to keep him occupied. Preacher Edwin Jones looked up from the pump where he was washing his hands and called out to the men.

As they approached, Nathan laid a sympathetic hand on Edwin's shoulder. "I'm really sorry about the building, Ed. I know that place meant a lot to you and your folks."

"Thank you, brother. This has been a tough afternoon for all of us." He looked longingly across the road, then back to the soaked men. "I appreciate how hard you two worked to keep this place from goin' up in flames too."

At that moment, two Louisville police officers approached. These were not just any officers, at least not the older one. This was the Louisville Chief of Police himself, Cecil Redman. Eugene couldn't imagine why such an important man would be concerned with an abandoned church fire.

The younger officer, nodding toward the preacher, inquired, "Are you Edwin Jones?"

"Yes, sir," he replied, taking off his hat.

"We've got some questions we need to ask you."

Before Edwin could respond, the chief jumped in. "Which one of your parishioners do you believe set that fire?"

Edwin shook his head back and forth, his brow deeply creased. "Sir, I don't believe a one of our church members would've done such a thing."

"We'll need to make sure everyone was accounted for. Someone from your church must be holdin' a grudge."

Eugene could see where this was going, and he had to fight a fierce desire to get involved in the conversation.

Edwin kept his voice calm. "No sir, like I said, I don't believe this was the work of someone in our congregation."

The police chief spread his legs a little wider and folded his arms across his chest. His eyes were dark and narrowed. "Then what's your theory? I'd sure like to hear what you think was happenin' here today."

Little beads of sweat broke out on Edwin's forehead despite the crisp breeze. He seemed to be wrestling with himself on how he should answer. But just as he opened his mouth, Nathan broke into the conversation.

"Officer, my name is Nathan Harrison." He dropped little Will's hand and stepped forward. "I'm certain I know who was responsible for that fire. It's the same group who burned a cross on that property two Sundays back."

"You stay out of this, Mr. Harrison. This is none of your business." Even though the chief's words were strong, he moved into a less threatening pose.

Nathan Harrison was nothing if he wasn't authoritative. He had a dynamic personality that was hard to overpower, and he wasted no time in pressing his point. "Officers, you and I both know the Klan is responsible for this egregious act. They're nothing but cowards hiding behind white hoods. I suggest you go about questioning some of our fine, upstanding Louisville citizens instead of implying that the good people of Oak Hill Church are responsible for destroying their own property."

A dark, purplish color began to creep slowly up the chief's neck and spread onto his broad face. Eugene feared there would be trouble and wondered if he should take Will inside. But to his amazement, the chief turned to the younger officer and said, "Let's get goin', Miller. Obviously they don't need our help."

Silently, the three men watched the officers stride away. Edwin Jones wiped the sweat from his brow with his sleeve, and a slow smile relaxed his features. "Nathan, I don't know whether to thank ya or admonish ya. But I think I'm inclined to say *thank ya kindly.*"

Nathan returned his smile, taking Edwin's outstretched hand. "In that case, I'm inclined to say *you're welcome.* But I *am* sorry if I chased off the law. We could use their help if this goes any farther."

Eugene chimed in. "I don't think they were exactly looking to help our situation. I just hope this is the end of it."

"As do we all," Edwin agreed.

Inside the sanctuary, Rachel sat between Claudia and Annie on the back pew. Jake was sleeping soundly beside his mother, utterly oblivious to the day's excitement. Rachel felt incredibly blessed to have these two women in her life. It was hard to believe she had gone nearly thirty years without another woman to share the joys and sorrows of life. Who knows what her life would have been like if it hadn't been for the tragedy she and Franklin had been a part of in Winchester. After that horrible incident, they had never stepped foot into town again—at least, not together. She would always be thankful for the loving relationship she had shared with her husband, along with the adoption of Eugene into their family, but the lack of a heart friend had been dispiriting.

"Thank you both for your concern. I truly am better now."

"Rachel, I think it would do you good to talk about how this is affecting you." Claudia held her friend's hand sympathetically.

Rachel appreciated the way she and Annie cared for her during such a frightening turn of events. Both women were aware of her racial heritage, but neither was aware of the brutality she had suffered as a young woman at the hands of an angry mob. She felt compelled to share it with them, especially since she had never had the luxury of working through the experience with a close friend. Maybe that's what was happening to her now. Maybe she couldn't get over it because she had never been able to confide in another woman.

Breathing deeply, Rachel made the decision to bare her heart. "I have something to tell you that I've never really talked about with anyone before. After it happened, I was never able to discuss it with Franklin because it made him angry that he hadn't been able to protect me. I didn't want to make him feel worse than he already did." Rachel now reached for Annie's hand, and all three women clung to each other.

"Eugene knows about the incident, but he has no idea what was done to me." She looked at Annie, dark eyes brimming with tears. "I don't want him to know. You have to promise me that we'll keep this among the three of us."

Annie responded passionately. "You have my word; this will stay between *us.*"

Taking in a slow, deep breath, Rachel began her story. Both Annie and her mother were horrified that a gang of white men had killed two black men from her church in Winchester over thirty years ago. The violence had stemmed from their prejudice over Rachel and Franklin's seemingly mixed marriage.

"Their deaths, of course, were the worst of it. Franklin and I never got over the pain we caused at our little congregation. But those men did something else to me that I've never been able to fully get over." She let out a nervous laugh. "You'd think by now I would've been able to put it behind me."

Rachel stared down at her lap and breathed out a soft, agonizing sigh. She wasn't sure how to share the graphic details with these two dear women.

Claudia spoke lovingly to her friend. "Take your time, Rachel. Only tell us what you feel you can."

"I need to tell you everything, but I don't want you to think badly of me."

"Oh, Mama," Annie spoke up. "That would never happen." She lifted Rachel's hand to her heart. "No matter what you say, I will always love you."

"Thank you, darlin'. You have no idea how much that means to me."

Rachel felt Annie press closer to her side, giving her the courage she needed to finish the story. She revealed how the men had passed her around, touching her any way they saw fit, exposing her to intense humiliation. She had been molested in front of her entire congregation and, worse yet, in front of her beloved husband.

"I kept thinking I should be fighting back, but I couldn't. Every time I fought them, Franklin grew intensely angry. I was so afraid they were going to kill him. So I didn't . . . I didn't resist." A sob escaped her throat, and she covered her face with her hands. "I *let* them have their way, praying they would grow tired of me and leave."

Eventually they *had* grown tired of her and had run out of vile names to call her as well. Leaving her lying on the ground weeping, clothes torn, they had mounted their horses and ridden away with cruel laughter echoing in their wake.

Though Claudia was nearly young enough to be her daughter, she pulled Rachel into an embrace, holding her as if she were her mother. Annie caressed Rachel's back, waiting her turn and quietly crying.

When Rachel was released, she turned into Annie's waiting arms. The two women clung to each other fiercely as Annie conveyed her love and told her how sorry she was. Unbelievably, at that very moment, Rachel felt her burden lifted, almost as if an invisible hand had reached into her heart and wiped it clean. It was an incredible feeling. The dark cloud from the past had finally been lifted; she knew she was free.

Rachel let go of her daughter-in-law and reached up to wipe a tear from Annie's cheek. "You are so dear to me." Then looking at Claudia with a smile, she added, "You have no idea how unburdened I feel."

Instantly, Annie exclaimed, "We need to pray!"

So right there in the back pew of the Oak Hill Church building, all three women poured their hearts out to God, thanking Him for His mercies, praising Him for His Spirit of peace, and loving Him with all of their hearts.

As the three women walked out of the building with baby Jake in Annie's arms, Rachel was reminded of a passage from the Psalms—*I waited patiently for the Lord; he turned to me and heard my cry.*[4]

"Thank you, Lord," she breathed. "Your timing is perfect."

Nathan, Eugene, and Will joined the women as they emerged from the building. The wind had finally dried their clothes, and both men were wearing their jackets. Eugene was concerned about his mama and immediately went to her side. "Are you all right, Mama?"

Nodding her head and smiling brightly, Rachel replied, "Better than ever."

He didn't know what to think about the smiles on the women's faces, but whatever had happened in there, he was thankful for it.

Nearly all of the black members of the congregation had moved across the road to survey the wreckage. The fire brigade was still present, sitting on the side of the long red truck, drinking in gulps of water. They would remain for another hour or so to make sure hot spots didn't reignite the fire.

As the former members of the church across the road circled together in prayer, Rachel exclaimed, "I need to be with them."

Eugene watched her cross the road and take the hands of her brothers and sisters. Those were her people, and they didn't even know it. Soon the entire congregation had crossed the road, and the white members surrounded their black brethren, encompassing them in the arms of love and protection.

The following Sunday afternoon, the people of Oak Hill had come to their wits' end. During their closing hymn, a huge rock came crashing through one of their stained-glass windows, narrowly missing the two Jackson children. Some of the women and children screamed, and "Oh Victory in Jesus" came to an abrupt halt in mid-sentence. Some of the men immediately ran outside, but to no avail. Not a soul was in sight. Edwin Jones and Jeff Swanson stood at the front of the sanctuary deep in discussion. Finally, it appeared they had come to some sort of decision.

"Folks, let me have your attention please." Jeff was motioning with his arms for everyone to sit down. "Please, everyone take your seats for just a moment." Eventually, the murmur of the crowd died away, and the pews moaned and creaked as everyone collectively sat down.

"Church," Edwin Jones bellowed in his deep, rich voice, "let us not be afraid. Let us continue to love one another, even in the midst of strife." A few strong *amens* rose up from the crowd, and the preacher continued. "Brother Swanson and I have come to a conclusion about these disturbing events. It's time for us to come together as a congregation to discuss our current problems. We would like for all of those interested to meet here next Saturday morning at nine o'clock. We'll still see you at midweek Bible study, but at the end of this week, let's come together for a time of discussion and prayer."

---

4 Psalm 40:1, NIV.

Jeff Swanson then stepped forward and led the people in a closing prayer. As soon as the amen was spoken, the church was all abuzz again, marveling that no one had been hit by the flying rock or breaking glass.

Claudia had prepared a wonderful Sunday lunch for the family that day. The women had just finished cleaning up the kitchen and joined the men in the living room of the Harrison's beautiful home. Nathan sat in his chair cradling little Jake in his arms while Eugene and Will wrestled on the floor. Claudia took the chair next to her husband and reached for Jake. Rachel and Annie made their way to the sofa, trying not to trip over the boys on the floor. No one had spoken yet about the events at church; they didn't want to put a damper on their Sunday meal.

Nathan was the first to bring up the subject. "I'm a little concerned about where this is all heading. The violence seems to be escalating by the week."

Eugene scooted up against the couch and pulled Will into his lap. Annie reached out and momentarily rubbed her husband's shoulders, then smoothed Will's hair back into place. Surprisingly, Will reached up for his momma, and she gladly took him onto her lap, planting a big kiss on his cheek. It wouldn't be long before he would need to go down for his afternoon nap.

Eugene picked up where his father-in-law had left off. "Brother Jones told me that we were supposed to have a police officer outside the building today during worship, but for some reason, he didn't show up."

Nathan shook his head. "I wonder if someone paid him off."

"Nate, surely you don't mean it," Claudia gasped.

"Eugene and I saw how the police chief himself treated Edwin after the fire. I wouldn't doubt that a few of Louisville's finest have a white hood stashed away in their closets."

Annie posed a question of her own. "Then who can we trust, Daddy? We can't keep going like this. Sooner or later someone's going to get hurt." Her maternal instincts were on high alert. She would do whatever it took to protect her young sons.

Leaning back in his chair, Nathan clasped his hands behind his head. "Let's pray it doesn't come to that. Maybe by this Saturday we'll have some answers."

Will began to rub his eyes and fuss a bit in Annie's arms. Eugene hopped to his feet and said, "I guess we'd better get the boys home before the floodgates open." He stepped across Annie and kissed Rachel on the cheek. "We'll see you soon, Mama."

Rachel ran her hand across his face before he rose up. "I love you."

"I love you too, Mama. Do you need a ride back to town?"

"No thanks, Claudia and I are going to visit a while."

Annie leaned over and kissed Rachel, then allowed Eugene to take Will while she kissed her parents and lifted Jake out of her mother's arms.

Nathan followed Annie and Eugene onto the porch, making funny faces at Will all the way. He opened the car door for Annie and waited until she was situated in the front seat with her two boys. "Try not to worry, honey. This will all blow over soon."

He closed the door and waved as Eugene turned the car down the road. He hoped his daughter hadn't noticed that he was the one worried about the situation. Deep down, Nathan felt certain they were all about to come face to face with evil.

Chapter 3

On Saturday morning, Oak Hill Church was packed with members. It seemed no one stayed home to sit out this meeting. Eugene and Annie took a seat near the front with the rest of their family, and instantly, the boys were taken from their arms by doting grandparents.

Elders of the church stepped forward and led the congregation in prayer, beseeching God's wisdom for how to proceed. When they were seated, the two ministers, Jeff and Edwin, came to the front, remaining on the floor level so that they could move among the congregation.

"Now folks, we want to do this in an orderly manner, so we're going to ask if you have a comment, please raise your hand to be called on." Jeff looked a little different dressed in his everyday casual clothes. "Everyone will have a chance to be heard."

Edwin, who was dressed in his best suit, added, "Let's be quiet and respectful while each one speaks; that way, every voice can be heard—young or old. And all questions are welcome." He looked at the front row of six elders. "We'll try to answer them the best we know how."

With that said, hands began to rise. Many in the assembly had been waiting for an opportunity to be heard on the matter. For the next half hour, troubling questions were presented to the church leaders: "Do you think the situation will get worse?" "How can we protect our church?" "How can we protect our families?"

Eventually, the questions died down and the brethren began to voice their own opinions on the matter.

"Maybe we need to go back to the way it used to be," Carl Montgomery, a long-time white member of the congregation spoke boldly. "I'm not sayin' I want it to be that way, but maybe it's best for now."

One of the black members raised his hand and asked, "Where would we go? Our buildin' was done burned to the ground."

Another white member spoke up without being called on. "We could help you rebuild."

With that comment, the place erupted with whispers and muttering. Everyone had turned to their neighbors and started voicing their opinions. Rachel took hold of Eugene's arm, shaking her head. How could anyone suggest such a thing?

Jeff finally got the crowd settled down just as someone made a loud suggestion. "Maybe we could both worship in this buildin', just not at the same time."

Another murmur rippled through the crowd. "Folks, please." Jeff threw his arms up in the air again. "Let's not talk unless you're called on; that way, everyone can be heard. But let's remember too, we're a unified body of people."

Carl Montgomery came to his feet then. "Why don't we take a vote? Let's just see where everyone stands on separating our two groups for a while."

"Brother Carl, I don't believe we're to that point yet," Edwin countered. "Let's have some more discussion on the matter."

For the next few minutes, the church batted the idea around, some for separating the two congregations, others adamantly opposed. Finally, Brother L. J. Sweeney, one of the elders, stood to face the congregation.

"Brothers and sisters, I remember the day the Lord brought our two fine people together back in 1913. Here we were worshipping the same heavenly Father, separated by a wide road. But when elders from both churches got together and started talking about the possibilities of coming together, that old road out there didn't seem to be so wide anymore. I know for a fact my life has been blessed for the last eleven years by being in this church. We've been showing our community that unity *is* possible, that all men truly are created equal."

At that moment, Abraham Cook stepped up beside his fellow elder and asked permission to speak. L. J. nodded his head, indicating that he was done, and Abraham cleared his throat. "I've been an elder for nearly twenty years, and I've never seen anythin' like what happened with our two peoples. I echo what Brother L. J. is sayin'; this has been the greatest blessin' to my life and my family's life that ever could be. And I say, glory hallelujah to our merciful Savior for bringin' us together."

Still, after the men were seated, many in the congregation felt like separation for just a while would put an end to their persecution. Carl Montgomery continued to head the charge, ending a long-winded speech by saying, "Bottom line is, none of us white folks know what it's really like to be a black person, and none of you black folks know what it's like to be a white person. We are different, whether we like it or not."

An unexpected silence permeated the sanctuary. No one, including the two preachers and six elders, knew how to respond.

Rachel immediately locked eyes with Eugene. Fully convicted, she began nodding her head slowly. She also noticed the worried look in her son's eyes.

"Mama, are you sure?" he whispered.

"I'm sure, Son. It's time for me to speak." She knew she was about to uncover her past in front of a large crowd, but these were her brothers and sisters in Christ. If she could help them through this crisis by revealing her heritage, then she would do it—even if it cost her.

Rachel stood in the third row, her back straight, holding onto the pew in front of her. "May I say something, please?"

Edwin Jones nodded his head in her direction and replied, "Certainly, Sister Rachel. The floor is yours."

When Rachel stepped out into the aisle, Eugene followed her to the front and stood by her side as she faced the congregation. She briefly looked at her son, and he offered her his elbow. So grateful for his loving support, she put her hand through his arm, and he covered it with his own.

Turning to the audience she bravely said, "I have something to tell you that I think is important for all of you to hear. You see, I know what it's like to be a white person, but I also know what it's like to be a black person." Rachel noticed the puzzled glances of the congregation.

"I was born into slavery on the Hawkins plantation of Lexington in 1858. My mother was a Negro slave, and my father was the owner of the plantation." Rachel could feel the warmth rising into her cheeks, but still she continued.

"I was raised among the Negroes on my father's plantation. In my heart and in my soul . . . I am a Negro woman." The stares she received from the congregation nearly unnerved her. It was obvious no one in the crowd had ever considered such a possibility—that she had been passing as a white woman all these years.

"I know this may be asking a lot, but if you're willing, I'd like for all of us to walk outside to the grave of my beloved husband, Franklin."

Everyone stayed seated, looking back and forth at each other. But immediately Annie rose to her feet and made her way to the front, holding Will's hand, with Nathan right behind his daughter and Claudia following with Jake. Miss Ruby jumped out in the aisle and nearly broke into a run to get to Rachel. She enveloped her in a loving embrace whispering, "Child, I know'd there was somethin' about you from the beginnin'."

Soon, the entire congregation was on their feet and began pouring outside. It was only a short walk to Oak Hill Cemetery just off to one side of the building. Rachel led the way to the giant oak tree at the heart of the cemetery and stopped before her husband's grave.

As the congregation circled around Franklin's grave, many of them read the stone marker. Rachel could see it beginning to dawn on them by the look on their faces. The name Hawkins was the name of the plantation owner; Franklin had taken that name. A few heads snapped up, their eyes staring right at Rachel. They knew at that moment that Franklin had been a slave.

Rachel spoke with a strong, clear voice so everyone could hear her. "This is where my beloved Franklin is buried. We were married for forty-five wonderful years. As many of you have now realized, Franklin was a Negro, born into slavery and freed from those bonds at the age of thirteen." She smiled then. "And he is buried right here—right in the middle of our *whites only* cemetery."

Eugene spoke up then. "He was an amazing father who taught me how to be a man of God." His voice broke slightly as he added, "He would've loved this church."

A spattering of amens traveled through the crowd. Black and white arms began to encircle one another. New hope was beginning to rise inside their hearts.

But that wasn't all that Rachel had in mind. Slowly she worked her way through the crowd and started walking down the hill toward the graveyard of *her* people.

As the congregation gathered beside the dilapidated stone wall separating the two cemeteries, Rachel said, "I used to think this was where *my* people are buried, but I was wrong." Laying her hand on top of the old wall, she exclaimed, "This is where *our* people are buried!"

"Praise God!" someone shouted from the crowd.

Then L. J. Sweeney stepped up on top of the wall and opened his Bible. A hush came over the people as he began reading from the book of 1 John. Before he was done, he had read all five chapters. But throughout his reading, he emphasized many phrases: *"if we walk in the light, as he is in the light, we have fellowship with one another, and the blood of Jesus Christ, his Son, cleanses us from all sin . . . do not marvel my brethren, if the world hates you . . . we also ought to lay down our lives for the brethren . . . He who is in you is greater than he who is in the world . . . if we love one another, God abides in us . . . God is love!"*[5]

After he had finished, he went back to one passage and read it again, boldly. *"There is no fear in love. But perfect love drives out fear . . ."*[6] He looked up at the people he loved and proclaimed, "We are not afraid! God is with us."

Carl Montgomery now weaved his way through the crowd until he was standing right by Rachel's side. His face was red and his eyes were burning. Rachel feared there would be a confrontation. Instead, he took a large stone from that old wall and held it high in the air. A tear slid down his cheek as he shouted, "Let no wall divide us—not in death . . ." he paused, looking directly into Rachel's eyes. "And not in life!"

This time, a cheer rose up from the church, and everyone began praising the Lord without restraint. The rest of the morning was spent clearing off the graves and dismantling the old wall. One by one, stones were removed by young and old and were thrown into a heap at the edge of the cemetery, all except for twelve large stones piled where the wall had once stood.

Edwin Jones came forward then, speaking in a loud voice. "Just as the children of Israel set up a monument of stones to the Lord God when He led them into the Promised Land, so we have made our own monument to the Almighty. And when our children ask us, 'What do these stones mean?' we will tell them about the day God preserved the unity of His people, both black and white, at Oak Hill Church."

After a time of prayer, future plans were made to add grave markers and plant trees in the lower cemetery. Eventually, the church folks began to move back up the hill. They were determined to continue to worship together and love one another without fear. They were trusting that God's love would be sufficient.

As the congregation emerged from the cemetery, they realized sooner than expected that they would have to defend their newfound courage. The way to the

---

[5] 1 John 1:6–7, 3:13, 3:16, 4:4, 4:12, 4:8, NKJV.
[6] 1 John 4:18, NIV.

parking lot was completely blocked by a long line of men in white robes and hoods. One man stood out in front, presumably their leader.

Brother L. J. stepped forward and faced the Klan. "What business do you have with us?"

What proceeded from the Klansman's mouth was nothing but foul language and putrid racist comments. He made it clear that their purpose was to break apart this congregation.

Eugene held little Jake up close to his chest, and Annie was doing her best to hang on to Will, but he was putting up a struggle to get out of her arms.

"Eugene, you're going to have to take Will. He wants down."

Rachel stepped forward then. "Here, let me have Jake so you can take care of Will."

"Thanks, Mama." Eugene laid the baby in Rachel's arms and before he had a chance to turn back for Will, he heard his wife cry out.

"Annie, where is he?"

There was a look of panic on her face, and she started to run toward the Klan. Eugene grabbed her arm to stop her. "What are you—?" The rest of his words got caught in his throat. Will had run right up to the leader of the Klan and had taken hold of his robe.

To Annie and Eugene's horror, as well as that of the congregation, the Klansman let out a sinister laugh and reached down to pick Will up off the ground. "Now this is a pure child—blonde hair and blue eyes." He held him high in the air. "We are the superior race!"

Eugene and Nathan sprang forward, ready to get Will back by any means necessary. But the Klan moved into a defensive position, blocking their path to the child. Screams of panic rose up from the congregation, and for a few tenuous moments, it looked as if there would be a violent confrontation. That is, until Will unveiled the leader of the Klan.

Seconds ticked by as no one moved. Only Nathan and Eugene were able to see what was happening behind the wall of Klansmen. The leader's face had turned a dark shade of purple, and he appeared to be panicked. Finally, he put Will on the ground roughly and snatched the hood out of his hand. With shaking hands, he tried to get his hood on as fast as possible. It was almost comical to watch him try to line up the little holes with his eyes.

"Let's go!" he yelled.

None of the Klansmen moved.

A string of curse words followed before he yelled, "Now!"

Without a word, the white-robed men backed a few steps away, turned on their heels, and headed into the trees across the road. Eugene grabbed Will into his arms as fast as he could to keep him from running after the white robes.

Annie came flying to Eugene's side, not an ounce of color left in her face. "Will, what are we going to do with you?" She kissed his little face and hugged him in Eugene's arms. "Eugene, I'm so sorry. I just couldn't hang on to him. He wiggled right out of my arms."

Annie stopped talking when she noticed the look that passed between Eugene and her father. If her instincts were right, and she felt certain they were, both men had just recognized the leader of the Louisville Ku Klux Klan.

Chapter 4

It wasn't often Nathan Harrison withheld anything from his daughter, but this was a different matter altogether.

"Annie, honey, please. I don't think it would be wise for me to say."

"But Daddy, if Eugene knows, then I have the right to know too."

Claudia sat down on Rachel's sofa beside her daughter and reached for Annie's hand.

"Do you know, Mother?"

"No, honey. If your father thought it was safe for us to know who the leader of the Klan was, he would tell us."

Annie just couldn't let it go and looked intently at her mother. "Aren't you the least bit curious?"

"Well . . . yes." Claudia sheepishly glanced at her husband. "But I respect your father's decision."

Annie stood up and paced around Rachel's living room, trying not to start an argument with her father. But for obvious reasons, she couldn't let it go. That evil man had picked up her son and used him to spread his malicious propaganda.

Eugene and Rachel entered the room with glasses of iced tea. They had all stopped for lunch at a café in town and Rachel had invited them in to let Will and Jake take their Saturday afternoon nap.

Eugene handed Annie a glass and said, "Here, maybe this will cool you off a little." He grinned at her and she nearly came unglued.

"Eugene, this is not funny. There's no telling what that man might have done to our son. We need to call the police."

Both men immediately made eye contact. All three women were oblivious to Nathan's imperceptible shaking of his head.

"Honey, trust me," Nathan urged, "Eugene and I are not trying to keep you in the dark; we're trying to protect you. Just let it go for now. I know a few people in high places. First thing Monday morning, I'm driving over to Frankfort to make some contacts."

Exasperated, Annie finally gave up. She decided to sit down and try to enjoy her iced tea. Claudia discreetly changed the subject, and finally, Annie's mood lightened. But before she could finish her tea, Jake began to cry in the next room, so Annie excused herself to take care of her son.

Nathan also rose to his feet and motioned for Eugene to follow him. "Ladies, if you can do without our company for a little while, Eugene and I are going to sit out on the front porch and talk."

When Annie came back into the room a few minutes later holding Jake, it was all she could do not to head out onto that porch. Even on the way home later in the afternoon, she tried one more time to get information out of her husband, but to no avail.

Arriving back at the farm, Eugene still had a lot of work to do before his day was over. He'd risen from bed long before sunup this morning just so he could take care of the horses and livestock and make it to the meeting at church. After changing his clothes, he found Annie in the kitchen washing the breakfast dishes she had left on the counter this morning. Jake was lying in his bassinet nearby as Will stacked blocks on the floor.

Eugene moved up behind his wife and put his hands on her waist. After a little kiss on Annie's neck, he rested his chin on her shoulder. "I'll probably be in after dark tonight. You can go on to bed without me."

Annie laughed. "Not on your life, buddy. Is there anything I can help you with?"

"No thanks. Not tonight. I think it'd be better for you and the boys to stay in the house this evening. As a matter of fact, I'm taking my key. I want you to lock the doors."

"Eugene?" Annie immediately went back to worrying. She turned from the sink to face her husband, drying her hands with a towel.

"Sweetheart, everything's gonna be fine. I just think right now we need to be a bit cautious." He moved in a little closer and kissed her warmly, then reached for her left hand. Eugene's tenderness seemed to melt Annie's anxieties into a little puddle right there on the kitchen floor. She had half a mind to tell him to forget about those old cows out in the pasture, but she knew how hard he'd have to work to get everything done. Someday, it was their hope to hire a farmhand or two. But for now, it was all Eugene. Annie couldn't wait for the boys to get a little older, so she could pick up some of the slack.

Eugene headed for the back door and slipped into his boots. Annie followed her husband. "Do you want to take something to eat? You're going to get hungry."

"Naw, I ate so much in town today I think I could last another week or two." Annie laughed as she closed the door behind him. Then she did something she had never done before; she locked it.

Late that night, Eugene was so exhausted, he didn't even hear Jake crying. Annie quickly got out of bed and threw on her robe before picking her son up and heading for the living room. She wanted to give her husband as much uninterrupted sleep as possible.

With Jake in a dry diaper, Annie made herself comfortable on the sofa and reached over to turn off the lamp. It would make it easier for Jake to go back to sleep after nursing if the room remained dark. There was just enough dim light for her to see his little form in her arms. Lightly taking his tiny hand in hers, she thanked God for blessing her with this sweet child. Then she cupped his soft head in the palm of her hand. Amazing how much he already looked like Eugene. A full head of dark hair and a mini-sized dimple right in the middle of his chin.

Eugene had hoped for a little girl this time around. But for some reason, Annie wanted another boy. Not that a little girl wouldn't have been wonderful, but just the thought of boys brought her joy. She anticipated the fun they would have together as well as the challenges she would meet as they grew up. Annie wasn't the kind to ever back away from a challenge; she met them head on. She reminded herself that there was a mighty *challenge* asleep in his crib in the back room. A smile passed her lips just thinking about the tests they had faced with him already—and he was only two years old.

Jake began to slow down until finally he stopped nursing altogether. He was fast asleep with a full belly. Annie laid him on her lap while she covered herself and gently lifted him onto her shoulder. She began patting his little back, listening for the all-important burp. Instead of a belch from her son, however, an utterly frightening sound reached her ears.

Nerves of steel, she told herself, *don't panic.* Annie sat perfectly still, not daring to move, listening intently as another creak on the boards of the front porch fractured the night silence. She turned her head toward the door just in time to see the glass knob slowly move, first to the right and then to the left. Thank goodness Eugene had locked the house up tight before he went to bed. They *never* did that— *oh thank you, Lord.* She waited, petrified as a man's shadow passed by the window behind her, the sheer curtains protecting her from sight.

The creaking of the porch suddenly stopped, and she was certain the man was making his way around the back of the house. Annie knew that was her cue. She sprang off the couch and hurriedly tiptoed back to the bedroom, laying baby Jake quietly in his bed.

"Eugene!" she whispered and grabbed him by the arm. He rolled over, blinking at her in the dim light.

"Is it Jake?"

"No." Annie was nearly breathless. "There's someone outside; he tried to get in the house."

Eugene was out of bed in an instant. He went straight to the wardrobe and took out his shotgun. "Annie, take Jake into Will's room and don't come out until I tell you to."

"Eugene, you can't go out there. Please." She thought her heart was going to jump right out of her chest.

"Get Jake now, Annie." Eugene waited as she gently removed their sleeping baby from his bassinet and, putting his hand on her lower back, guided her to Will's room.

"I mean it, Annie, stay with the boys. Don't come out of this room until I tell you."

Annie knew that no amount of pleading would keep Eugene in the house. Her only choice was to stay with her sons and pray.

Eugene rapidly went to the kitchen door, knowing he would be less exposed on the backside of the house. He didn't bother to put his boots on—besides, he would make less noise barefooted. Slowly he turned the lock on the door, barely making a sound, and took his time partially opening the wooden door. He waited only a moment as he looked for movement outside, then he painstakingly opened the screen door and stepped onto the back porch just in time to see the shape of a man disappear around the corner of the house. Letting the screen door come to a silent rest, he leapt from the porch and took off at a sprint, coming to a halt at the corner. Quickly he peered around the house, then ducked his head back. The man was standing still, trying to look inside their bedroom window.

Adrenaline shot through his body in a matter of seconds. He was no longer relying on his brain for information; Eugene's body had completely taken over his every move. This was not his first encounter with such a thing—his experiences in France had given him more adrenaline rushes than he cared to count.

Without thought, Eugene stepped around the end of the house and raised his rifle at the intruder. "One move, mister, and I'll drop you where you stand."

Slowly, the man raised his arms into the air. "Eugene, don't shoot; it's me."

"Nathan? What on earth?" Eugene lowered his rifle and gulped in a deep breath.

"Eugene, I'm so sorry. I know this must have been a shock."

"You have no idea. Annie's holed up in the back of the house with the boys, scared to death."

Nathan moved quickly to Eugene's side and gave him a little shove. "Get back in there so you can put her mind at ease. I'm right behind you."

As the two men stepped inside the kitchen, Nathan said, "Go get Annie, we need to talk."

Seconds later, Annie rushed into the lighted kitchen and threw herself into her daddy's arms.

"Honey, I'm so sorry about this. I really didn't mean to frighten you. I thought I'd be able to get into the house and wake Eugene first."

Annie tried to get her nerves under control just so she could make sense of what was going on. She stepped out of her father's arms and looked intently into his face. "Daddy, it's two o'clock in the morning. What are you doing here?" Suddenly, her heart took off like a shot. "Is something wrong with Mother?"

Nathan took hold of his daughter's shoulders and returned her gaze reassuringly. "Your mother is fine, just fine."

"Then what—"

Eugene briskly entered the kitchen wearing blue jeans and an unbuttoned work shirt. Alarmingly, his rifle was still in his hand.

"Eugene?" Annie looked at her husband in shock.

Eugene cocked his head to one side. "Nathan?"

Nathan instantly turned his gaze toward his son-in-law. "We don't have much time. You need to get Annie and the boys over to Rachel's house right now. Claudia is already there."

"Is it the Klan?" Eugene asked.

"Yes, they came to our house tonight just after midnight. I thought our house was on fire, but I looked out to see a cross burning on the lawn. Unfortunately, that wasn't all. They butchered one of my cows and used the blood to paint racial slurs on the front of the house."

"That's it; we're calling the police right now." Annie made a move toward their telephone in the hallway, but Eugene put his arm out and pulled her up short.

Exhaling loudly, he said, "Annie, we can't call the police."

"Well for heaven's sake, why not?"

"Because the head of the Louisville Ku Klux Klan is Cecil Redman—the police chief himself."

Annie felt a wave of nausea pass through her body. *Hopeless* was the only word that penetrated her mind at the moment. She stood dumbfounded.

"Sweetheart," Eugene said quietly, "go get dressed and get Jake's things together. I'll take care of Will."

Nodding to his children, Nathan added, "Make it quick."

***

Rachel and Claudia met their family at the door and nearly yanked them into the house.

"Where's Eugene?" Rachel asked in a panic.

"He'll be fine, Rachel," Nathan quickly replied. "He decided to stand guard at his farm. I'm heading back right now to help him."

Claudia put her hand on her husband's arm and spoke softly. "Don't let anything happen to him, Nate. And you better come back to me."

Nathan smiled at his wife and kissed her. "Don't worry, Claudia. We won't risk our lives over a cow or even a house for that matter. I seriously don't think they'll do anything at this late hour. We just want to make sure."

Thankfully, the rest of the night turned out to be uneventful, but when none of their family showed up for church later that morning, the Oak Hill congregation was worried. After everything they had been through on Saturday, it just seemed odd that neither the Harrisons and Wyatts nor Rachel Hawkins had shown up for services. So throughout the afternoon, the three women received a steady stream of visiting church members who dropped by Rachel's house to see if everything was all right. It was nice to know how much everyone cared.

That evening, Rachel prepared dinner, and Nathan and Eugene came back into town. They both looked tired but planned to stand guard again tonight.

After a quiet meal, Nathan got down on the floor with Will for what he called playtime. Claudia insisted on Rachel spending time with baby Jake while she finished cleaning up the kitchen, and Annie followed her husband out onto the porch.

"You feel like sitting in a swing with your fella?" Eugene grabbed his girl by the hand and pulled her down beside him.

Annie squeezed as close as she could to her husband. "Mmm, you feel good."

He lowered his mouth to hers. "And you taste good," he said.

Annie giggled, but the mood didn't last long. She raised herself up slightly to look into his deep brown eyes. "I'm worried about you."

Eugene didn't patronize her. He knew how anxious she must be right now, and he wasn't exactly feeling too good about the situation himself. "I want you and the boys to stay with Mama for the next few days, just until all of this blows over."

"Eugene, we can't stay here forever. Something's got to be done about the Klan."

"Your dad's driving over to Frankfort tomorrow. He's got a friend in the state legislature that has some pretty high connections. Let's just give it a little time."

They fell silent for a while, and Eugene rested his head on top of Annie's. He wasn't looking forward to nightfall. Something in his gut told him that Cecil Redman wasn't finished yet. Earlier in the day, Eugene had helped Nathan with the clean up around his house. Not all of the words written in blood had been racially motivated; they had been threatening words aimed at their family. Both men had agreed to spare the women the disturbing details.

All too soon, Nathan stepped out onto the porch to see if Eugene was ready to go. Claudia and Rachel were close behind, each of them with a grandson in her arms. As Eugene and Annie joined the others, the family naturally drew in close and put their arms around each other. Nathan led them in prayer asking God to protect his family through the night. Before the men could get away, they were hugged and kissed by everyone in the gathering, including little Will. He reached out for his daddy, so Eugene held him tight for a few moments while Nathan shared their plan.

"I've got two farmhands working a night shift tonight. They'll make sure nothing happens out at our place. Eugene and I will be guarding his place."

"Daddy, if you're driving to Frankfort tomorrow, you'd better get some sleep," Annie said with concern.

Nathan laughed and said he'd try to get a little sleep on the couch. Turning to Eugene, he clapped him on the back. "We best get a move on before it gets dark."

As the men headed for the car, Claudia called out, "Be safe."

"We'll be fine as long as my son-in-law doesn't try to shoot me!" Nathan quipped.

Everyone laughed, but it was nervous laughter. No one in the family had a good feeling about tonight.

Chapter 5

Eugene and Nathan put on dark clothes and turned off all the lights in the house. It was nearing midnight, and they now sat silently against the back wall of the front porch, side by side in kitchen chairs. Each of them had their hands on a shotgun lying across their lap. They had agreed to stay together until one o'clock, then take two-hour shifts while the other one slept on the couch.

At half past midnight, four cars stopped on the highway not far from the farm and several men in white emerged.

Nathan breathed, "Steady now."

"I'm fine, Nathan," Eugene whispered.

"I wasn't talking to you."

Eugene breathed out a quiet laugh and noticed his father-in-law's heavy breathing.

The Klansmen, fifteen strong, looked like ghosts floating silently up the road to the farmhouse. It was a hair-raising sight to say the least. But Eugene's heart remained slow and steady. For some unexplained reason, he felt a calmness overtake him. Maybe it was the fact that he had faced a far worse enemy than this during the Great War.

Nathan and Eugene had agreed to remain still until the Klan reached the drive in front of the house. At that point, they planned to fire a warning shot into the air before leveling their weapons at the mob. Neither would actually shoot at the men. They just wanted to scare them away.

The Klansmen were now within a few yards of the drive. Eugene noticed some of the men carrying weapons and cans of gasoline. Evil intentions filtered into the night air as they menacingly made their way toward the house. Nathan and Eugene silently rose to their feet. The time had finally come, but what happened next would be the subject of many family conversations for years to come.

***

Rachel lay half asleep in her bed when she felt someone tap her on the shoulder. Immediately, she sat up in bed to see who it was. No one was there; she must have dreamed it. Suddenly, she had an overwhelming urge to pray for Eugene and Nathan. She climbed out of bed and went to her knees, pleading for God to put a mighty hedge of protection around them. As she was praying, she could hear a stirring in the next room where Claudia and Annie were sleeping. She rose up off the floor, put on her robe, and looked inside their room. Both women were on their knees at the side of the bed praying.

***

As soon as the Klansmen stepped onto the gravel driveway, they stopped dead in their tracks. Every single one appeared to have been startled by something.

***

Rachel didn't hesitate to join Annie and Claudia. She dropped to her knees again, and both women encircled her with their arms. They didn't dare get off the floor. Each one of them sensed there was a spiritual battle being waged and their intercessory cries and pleas were necessary to turn the tide.

***

A shriek rose up from the throats of more than one Klansman.

***

There were times the women were all praying out loud simultaneously; other times, just one was praying. Still other times, they were all pleading silently. Wherever the Spirit led them, they went.

***

Pandemonium broke loose. All fifteen Klansmen began to yell and scream, slapping at their robes as if they were on fire. Suddenly, they turned and fled down the road toward the highway. Nathan and Eugene watched in amazement as the men fought desperately to throw off their hoods and robes as they ran.

***

Gradually, the women's prayers began to turn from cries and petitions to joy and praise. They were overcome with an urge to worship their heavenly Father in prayer.

***

Doors slammed, tires squealed, and all four cars sped down the highway out of sight. Eugene and Nathan stood on the edge of the porch, completely stunned. They hadn't even raised their shotguns into the air.

***

The women were exhausted. All three sat down on the floor breathing deeply. No one spoke; it was almost as if they had used up all of their allotted words for a lifetime.

***

In the light of the moon, Eugene and his father-in-law slowly walked the road of his farm, picking up what the Klan had relinquished. Weapons, gas cans, hoods, and robes were strewn all the way from the house to the highway.

***

Rachel finally pushed herself up off the floor. Annie got up and came into her arms, and the two women held each other for a long moment. Then Rachel turned to Claudia for a strong embrace before heading back to her room. None of them spoke.

***

Nathan prodded the robes with a pitchfork as he tended the fire. Eugene walked up and threw a white hood into the flames. "I found another one down by the highway." The men's faces were illumined as they watched the robes of the Klan go up in smoke. They had emptied one of the cans of gasoline on the pile of robes before setting it ablaze.

Eugene stepped away from the fire and gazed up into the night sky. He would never grow tired of looking at the incredible display of stars. He wondered what that roaring fire must look like from heaven. When he tried to imagine it, he suddenly felt incredibly small. Something had happened here tonight that was so unbelievable, so inexplicable, he was utterly awestruck.

"Nathan, are you okay tending the fire for a while?"

"Sure, what's up?"

"I just gotta take care of somethin' real quick. I'll be right back."

Eugene headed around to the back of the house, but before he could get to where he thought he was going, his knees hit the dirt. Nothing on earth could've stopped him from praising the Almighty. It felt good to release his emotions to God and thank Him humbly for whatever it was that had happened here tonight. He would never be able to fully understand it, but somehow, he didn't think he was supposed to. After a few minutes, he took in a deep breath, rose to his feet, and unashamedly wiped the tears off his cheeks.

The fire was finally dwindling down to a charred heap. Nathan watched his son-in-law for a while after he rejoined him at the front of the house. He hadn't readily accepted Eugene when Annie first broke off her engagement with Benjamin Martin. Benjamin came from a prominent banking family in Louisville. She would've been financially set for life. But it hadn't taken long before he could see how happy Eugene made his daughter. Nathan had never raised a boy of his own, but if he could've had his choice of one now, Eugene would be his pick every time.

Nathan's relationship with his own father had been tenuous at best. Growing up with an alcoholic father had robbed him of a decent childhood. His life had pretty much been a wreck until Claudia came along. She had been the one who introduced him to the Lord. It had taken him a long time to dump his enormous pride and allow the Savior into his heart. Now, if he was being honest with himself, he was actually learning from Eugene what it meant to be fully committed. The young man had a way of relying on God that almost made him jealous.

"What should we do with all these weapons?" Eugene asked, as he moved over to the porch. There was a sizable collection of pistols, shotguns, and even a few knives.

"Let's put them in the back of my car. I think I'll lock them up in a shed at my place for the time being."

By the time they had the weapons stashed in Nathan's automobile, an ugly pile of gray ash remained on the front drive.

"Nathan, why don't you go on home and get some sleep. You've got a long day if you're heading over to the capitol."

"I don't want to leave you here alone," Nathan responded, concerned about how Eugene was holding up.

"No, seriously, I'd feel better knowing you were able to get a few good hours of sleep. I'll be just fine."

Nathan nodded his head and leaned the pitchfork up against the porch. It would feel good to clean up and crawl into his own bed for a while. He reached over and pulled Eugene into a brief hug. "I'm proud of you, Son."

Eugene returned his hug. "Thanks." Then he grinned and said, "I'm proud of you too, Gramps."

Nathan gave him a slap on the back and laughed all the way back to his automobile. Oh yeah, he would pick Eugene every time.

That Monday morning, Nathan met with his friend in the state legislature and eventually ended the afternoon in the office of Nicholas Cranfield, the state's attorney general. He couldn't go much higher than that if he wanted to get something done. Nathan had been surprised to learn that the police chief was already under investigation by the attorney general's office. Providing an account of Redman's illegal Klan activities just added a little more fuel to the fire—a slight nudge to get the ball rolling.

That night, he drove straight to Rachel's house to pick up Claudia. He was glad to see that Annie and Eugene were still there with the boys. Rachel invited the family to sit down in her living room to hear about Nathan's trip to the capitol before they all left for home. As he explained the day's events, it was obvious his news brought a welcome relief. Still, something was hanging in the air that had yet to be discussed.

Nathan leaned forward in his chair and looked at Eugene through tired eyes. "Did you tell them what happened last night?"

Eugene hesitated for a moment before quietly answering, "Not entirely."

Nathan's brow wrinkled. "What did you leave out?"

"Well," Eugene said sheepishly. "Just about everything."

"I knew it!" Annie remarked loudly. "Would you two please tell us what really happened last night?"

Nathan leaned back in the chair and rubbed weary hands across his face, wondering where to start. How could he possibly explain what they'd witnessed last night? He was beginning to wonder if it had just been a dream.

As he started recounting the strange events, Nathan noticed the women's puzzled glances. They each sat up a little straighter and looked at one another intently as he told them how something had caused the Klansmen to flee in panic.

"I'm convinced they didn't even see us on the porch. They just started running like their robes were on fire. It was the craziest thing I've ever seen."

"What time did the Klan reach the house?" Claudia asked, turning her animated gaze toward Nathan.

He looked over at Eugene again. "What would you say, twelve thirty or so?"

Eugene nodded his head. "That's about when they pulled up on the highway."

The women were in an obvious state of excitement or agitation. They started conferring with each other about what time something else had happened last night.

Nathan was so exhausted he didn't have enough energy to figure out their babbling. "What's going on?" he finally asked.

Claudia's eyes were ablaze with emotion. "Last night, at just past midnight, each one of us was jarred awake by something . . . something that caused us to get down on our knees and pray intently for the two of you."

"All three of us ended up together," Rachel interjected.

"I've never prayed so earnestly for anything in my whole life," Annie added passionately.

Claudia picked up where her daughter left off. "We had no idea what was going on out at the farm, but the Spirit led us to intercede for you in prayer. When we finished, we were absolutely laid to waste but satisfied that the Lord had intervened." The three women shared a heartfelt smile.

When Nathan glanced over at Eugene, he was touched by the emotion he saw on his son-in-law's face. Eugene reached up and wiped his moist eyes. At that moment, Nathan actually felt ashamed of himself. Every single person in this family had recognized the power of God at work last night except him. He envied them for it, but his pride kept him from acknowledging the fact that he had missed out on it. *Lord, forgive me for that, but I see it now, and I believe.* Nathan hoped his silent plea would make up for his spiritual ignorance. He knew he still had a long way to go in matters of the soul.

Following a lively discussion, which wove the previous night's two events more tightly together, Claudia turned to Nathan and asked, "Honey, would you lead us in a prayer of thanksgiving?"

Nathan's throat constricted. He was the only one in this room not worthy enough for such a task, but he knew he shouldn't refuse. He cleared his throat and stood, reaching his hands out to the rest of the family. They intertwined their fingers, just like the intertwining roots of a tree, running deep into the ground, anchoring the tree in the soil, while keeping it straight and secure. Then with awe and meekness, Nathan poured out a beautiful prayer of thanks to God for revealing His mighty power to their humble family in a time of need.

By the following Sunday, there was excited talk flying through the Oak Hill fellowship. "Did you see Thursday's headlines?" "Can you believe it was the chief o' police hisself?" "Do you think we're gonna be left alone now?"

Nathan and his family joined in the conversations, even commenting on the newspaper articles concerning Cecil Redman's indictment on charges of fraud, gambling, and arson. However, the bizarre events that had transpired on the Wyatt farm remained a private matter among their family.

While Redman languished in jail, Frank Curtis was sworn in as the new chief of police. He immediately made it his business to clean up the corruption in the Louisville police department. More importantly, for the reenergized fellowship at Oak Hill Church, the hostile activities of the Ku Klux Klan came to an abrupt halt. With the head of the local Klan cut off, so to speak, the rest of its membership tucked tail and remained at home licking their wounds. Besides, over a dozen of their members had mysteriously lost their robes and hoods.

Even though the Oak Hill fellowship still suffered at times from cruel remarks and insensitive criticism, they continued to pour out their compassion on all people without regard to color. They were determined to bring up their children in a fellowship of love and acceptance. And when adversity arose, they would remember those twelve stones piled upon one another in the cemetery and refuse to let anything divide them ever again.

Chapter 6

It was now the first of June, and Eugene had devised a plan whereby Annie would have the opportunity to be with her beloved horses three evenings a week and some Sunday afternoons. She loved raising her boys, but it had been hard on her since Jake was born last January to be away from her horses for so long. Most mornings, she took the boys down to the barn for a while just so she could give her thoroughbreds a little lovin'. But she couldn't wait to get back in the saddle again after more than ten months off.

"Eugene, I'm about to pull my hair out. He is *so* stubborn." Annie dried the last dish from their simple supper of fried ham and beans and put it in the cabinet.

Eugene sat at the table finishing his tea and gave his wife a half grin. He knew she struggled with spending her days in the house, trying to take care of the boys and still figuring out how to cook. "Is it really that bad?" he asked.

"Oh, you don't know the half of it. Today, he yanked the cushion off the couch and stood right there and deliberately wet on it before I could stop him." Annie plopped down in the chair across from her husband and dramatically put her head on the table. "Potty training is going to be the death of me."

Eugene wisely suppressed a laugh. He knew they had a strong-willed child on their hands. "So do we need to stop trying for a while?"

That comment brought Annie's head up from table. "He's two and a half, Eugene. Mother said I was potty trained before I even turned two."

"Well, maybe he's telling us he isn't ready."

"Oh no, he's ready. I think this is Will's way of trying to control me. And it's not going to work." Annie had a pretty strong will of her own. Eugene could only imagine the battle going on in their house while he was working.

He stood and took his glass over to the sink, then reached up underneath his wife's arm. "Come 'ere, *feisty.*"

She stood up reluctantly and went into his arms. "Very funny, Eugene. You have no idea what I've been going through."

"Well, I guess I'm about to find out." Eugene released her and gave her a little slap on the backside. "Daylight's a wastin'; you'd better get out there and ride."

Annie headed to the back door entryway next to the kitchen and slipped into her boots.

"Just don't forget to come back," he teased.

Annie gave her husband a playful smirk. "You never know."

This evening, Annie felt like trail riding. Lately, she had spent her evenings in the arena working with Conquering Hero, a two-year-old thoroughbred that had come with them from her daddy's farm. But Hero possessed a stubborn streak, and Annie didn't want to be reminded of what she had been dealing with all day. For now, she chose Anne's Amazing Grace for a relaxing ride. Annie had practically grown up with Gracie on the Harrison's farm. The fifteen-year-old mare had been born there when Annie was nine, and they had formed a special connection from the very start.

Annie walked down the row of stalls and into the paddock out back. Gracie's head shot up when she heard her shrill whistle. The beautiful pinto mare broke into a trot when she saw Annie stretch out her hand with a sugar cube.

"Hello, my sweet girl." Annie reached up and rubbed the white blaze on the mare's muzzle. "What do you say we hit the trail together?" She hooked a lead rope to Gracie's halter and led her inside the barn to be saddled.

Annie loved Gracie's coloring. She was a fifty-fifty mix of bay and white, with a dark head and four white legs. But more than that, she loved her spirit. She had just a bit of mischief in her that pleased Annie. She knew she'd have to stay alert trail riding with Gracie. Sometimes the mare would purposely take her under a low tree branch, then cut her eyes around to see what Annie thought about it. Most people wouldn't associate teasing with a horse, but Annie and Gracie teased each other all the time.

It didn't take long before the pair left the confines of the farm and headed for a series of trails in the woods adjoining their property. Annie still had over two hours of daylight, and she planned to use it all.

At dusk, hoping she hadn't left Eugene with too much to handle, Annie pulled off her boots inside the entryway to the kitchen and rounded the corner. The sight that confronted her caused her to stop dead in her tracks. Will and her husband were standing in the middle of the kitchen, both of them with legs spread wide, both of them with hands on their hips, *both* of them in just their shirts and underwear.

Annie practically did a double take. This wasn't exactly what she had expected to come home to.

"Momma, we're big boys," Will said in his little two-year-old voice.

"Yep," Eugene confirmed. "You're lookin' at two big boys."

"So I see," Annie confirmed, smiling at Eugene and raising her eyebrows.

"Go wook, Momma." Will pointed down the hall for Annie to go check out the bathroom.

"Well, I think I will." Annie swatted Eugene on the bottom as she passed him on her way out of the kitchen. Moments later she was back, clapping and cheering, telling Will what a fine job he'd done. Will cheered too and started jumping up and down with glee. Annie swooped her son into her arms and danced around the kitchen praising her *big boy* all the while.

Eugene spoke up, "Will says he's going to be a big boy again tomorrow. Isn't that right, buddy?"

"Uh huh. Big boy!"

Annie gave him a great big kiss and told him how proud she was. Then she put him back on the floor and said, "Now you two go put on your *big boy* pants."

Eugene just grinned, and when Annie came back from Jake's bedtime feeding, to her amusement, both of her boys were still in their underwear.

***

By the time October rolled around, Jake was a big healthy nine-month-old. He had learned to sit up on his own two months before and, right after that, figured out a new way to get around. He hadn't quite mastered the art of crawling, but he quickly learned how to get where he wanted to go by scooting around on his bottom. Eugene loved coming in for supper just to watch him scoot across the kitchen floor.

"Whew, buddy, you're gettin' fast." Eugene reached down and scooped Jake up in his arms and kissed him. Will came running into the kitchen and threw his arms around his daddy's right leg. Eugene grabbed him around the waist and lifted him into his other arm.

Looking around for Annie, Eugene noticed all the windows and doors were wide open in the house. "Where's your momma?"

Will pointed out to the backyard.

"What's she doing out there?"

His son's little shoulders drew up in the air and he answered, "I dunno."

Eugene headed over to the kitchen window to look out back. He caught a glimpse of Annie underneath the persimmon tree, hard at work on something. He decided to go check it out.

As he approached, he could feel the tension in the air around her. "Hey, sweetheart, what's goin' on?"

Annie whirled around and met him with heat in her eyes. He didn't know whether to ask what was wrong or turn around and go back into the house.

She held up a cooking pot and nearly screamed, "Look!"

Eugene inched a little closer and peered inside the pot. "What is it?" As soon as the words came out of his mouth, he wished he could take them back.

Annie let out an exasperated groan and threw the pot on the ground at his feet before turning and stomping all the way back into the kitchen.

Eugene squatted down and examined the cooking pot a little closer. Whatever it had been was now unidentifiable—charred beyond recognition.

Putting Will down on the ground, Eugene stood up and rearranged Jake in his arms. He stared at the kitchen window for a while wondering what to do. Go back in the house or stay outside—which would be safer? Will didn't seem to be struggling with that dilemma as he headed right back into the house. Eugene decided if Will could do it, he could too.

Stepping inside the kitchen, Eugene cringed when he heard Will say, "Momma, I'm hungry. Eat now?"

Annie looked at her son through puffy eyes and retorted, "Your supper's out there in that pot."

Before Eugene could say anything, Annie's chair scraped the floor, and she headed into the bedroom, closing the door behind her.

Eugene looked at little Jake in his arms, contentedly sucking his thumb. "Well, buddy, at least she didn't slam it."

Twenty minutes later, Eugene lightly tapped on the bedroom door and opened it slowly. Annie was lying on her stomach on the bed and didn't bother to look up. He quickly changed his clothes, then sat down on the bed and put his hand in the middle of her back.

"Annie?"

"What?"

"Come 'ere."

Slowly, Annie sat up and allowed Eugene to wrap his arms around her. He softly said, "I'm really sorry, sweetheart."

"No, Eugene. I'm the one that's sorry." Annie pulled away from her husband and swept the hair out of her face. "I worked all afternoon to surprise you with a roast and carrots and potatoes, and you saw how it turned out." She shook her head. "I'm a failure when it comes to cooking."

"Well, I happen to be glad about that."

Annie looked at her husband as if he were crazy.

He brought his hand up to cradle her cheek and said cheerfully, "'Cause if you could cook, then you'd be perfect, and that would make you awfully hard to live with."

"Eugene." She said his name with chagrin, shaking her head.

He took her left hand and held it to his lips for a long moment while looking into her eyes. He could feel the tension leaving her body. "Come on, I wanna show you something."

Still holding Annie's hand, he pulled her up off the bed and walked her into the front room. Will and Jake were sitting on the rug in the living room playing with their wooden train cars—dressed neatly, hair combed.

For the first time, Annie looked at Eugene and noticed he'd changed out of his work clothes. "What's going on here?" she asked.

"The boys wanted to take you out to eat tonight, so I told them I'd like to come along too. That is, if it's okay with you." Eugene stood grinning at his wife, hoping she'd take the bait. He could tell he had caught her off guard and was thoroughly enjoying the moment.

A slow smile worked its way across Annie's face. Eugene could visibly see her frustration start to dissolve and he gave his boys the *ok* sign when she headed for the bedroom to change clothes. Within the hour, they were all seated at a restaurant in downtown Louisville with a view of the Ohio River. Eugene hoped he hadn't insulted his wife by bringing her here considering the name of the eating establishment was *Burning Embers Steakhouse.*

The following week, one of Nathan's farmhands drove onto the property with a newfangled contraption used for transporting livestock. Eugene studied the way it was hitched to the back of the truck and ran his hands down the steel rails along the side. Nathan had called it a trailer, and Eugene didn't know if he'd like using this thing or not. He was used to loading his horses onto the bed of a farm truck with tall wooden sides. Eugene still preferred riding his range horse and driving cattle to the market in Louisville. But if he was going to take a horse to auction in Lexington, transporting it by truck was the way to go.

As he considered the trailer, he knew he would need to put blinders on his thoroughbred to keep him from being frightened. However, one thing was certain; it appeared that loading animals onto a trailer would be much easier since it was considerably lower to the ground.

"Thanks for bringing it over, Mike." Eugene stuck his hand out to the man he had formerly worked with on the Harrison's farm. "And thanks for taking care of things around here while I'm gone."

"Not a problem." Mike removed his hat and scratched the top of his head. "I suggest you drive her around a bit before headin' out on the road. She's kinda wobbly at times." He shoved the hat back on top of his head. "Just takes a little gettin' used to, is all."

"I'll do that."

Glancing up at the house, Mike told him, "Mr. Harrison said he'd be out round noon to pick up Annie and the boys."

It was comforting to know that his family would be staying at the Harrison's and Mike would be overseeing his farm while he was gone. Eugene was heading to the Lexington Horse Auction for the next five days. He didn't actually need that long for the sale, but there was something he wanted to take care of in Winchester—something he didn't want his wife to know about.

Mike threw him the key to the truck. "How 'bout you drive it down to the barn and I'll help you load up yer horse."

Eugene did more than drive it to the barn. He decided to take it for a short jaunt on the highway before actually putting one of his horse's lives at risk. When the two men returned, they found Annie with the boys down at the barn.

"Eugene, do you have time for me to take him out one last time?" Annie held Jake in her arms while she rubbed her hand along Hero's muzzle.

His heart went out to his wife. She'd been working with Hero for the past four months; the two had developed quite a rapport. Reaching for Jake, he quietly said, "Take all the time you need."

An hour later, Annie watched as Mike and Eugene loaded Conquering Hero onto the new trailer. Mike disappeared into the barn when Eugene moved close to his family to say good-bye. First, he squatted down and gave Will a firm hug, instructing him to be good for his momma. He kissed Jake in Annie's arms, then turned his attention to his girl. "Do you have any idea how much I love you?" He took hold of the back of her neck and kissed her tenderly.

When he released his hold, Annie said, "Mmm, I think I do." She laid her left hand on his chest, and he held it there for a moment. "Why do you have to be gone so long?" she asked.

Eugene brought her hand to his lips then said, "It won't be that long. It's just 'til the end of the week."

After one more kiss, Annie watched him stride to the truck. "Be careful, Eugene."

"Don't worry, Annie. I'll be back before you know it."

Eugene threw his arm out the truck window as he pulled away, and Will yelled, "Bye-bye, Daddy!" Annie helped Jake wave good-bye and silently breathed a prayer for her husband.

That night, Annie and the boys sat at the table with her folks, enjoying spare ribs that were so tender they practically fell off the bone. Every time Annie took a bite, she shook her head. *How did her mother do it?* Not only did she have a wonderful meal on the dining room table, she was also feeding three farmhands in the kitchen.

"Poor Mike," Nathan commented. "He's missing out on some good chow tonight."

Claudia laughed. "Don't count on it. I loaded him down with food before he left this morning."

"Well, that's good to hear." Nathan turned to Will, noticing the trouble he was having with his corn on the cob. "Hey bud, how about letting Gramps cut that corn off for you."

Will looked up with butter all over his face, and replied, "Okay."

As Nathan sliced down the cobb with his knife, he told the women that he would be exercising his right to have Will all to himself this evening. "You ladies will just have to find something else to do. We boys have our own plans."

When supper was over, Nathan told Annie not to even worry about bedtime. He had that covered too. Annie watched the pair walk out of the dining room hand in hand. She smiled when she heard her daddy ask, "Hey Willie, what time is bedtime anyway?"

Will shrugged his shoulders, and answered, "I dunno, Gramps."

"Good! Me either."

Annie just shook her head when Nathan looked back at her and winked.

"Mother, how do you do it?" Claudia had joined her daughter in the swing on the front porch. Jake was down for the night, and the October sky had already turned to dusk. Light was filtering onto the porch from the lamp in the front room.

"How do I do what?" Claudia asked, as she threw a light quilt over their legs to ward off the early autumn chill.

"Cook like that. I just can't get it right. I don't understand how you can plan everything so it's all ready at the same time."

Smiling, Claudia looked at her daughter. "I've had years of experience. Just give it time."

"Time is not going to help; I've had plenty of time. It's so frustrating. I'm letting Eugene down."

"Has he told you that, honey?"

"You know Eugene," Annie let out a soft laugh. "He never complains. But he deserves better than what I'm able to give him."

Claudia gazed out into the autumn twilight. She let the swing rock gently back and forth for a moment while she chose her words. Finally, she turned back to her daughter and said, "I'm sorry, Annie. I'm afraid it's all my fault."

"Why would you say that, Mother?"

"Because I allowed you to be with your father and the horses all the time. I never took the time with you I should have when you were younger." Claudia had a pained look on her face that was troubling to Annie.

"Mother, it's not your fault; trust me. Even if you'd tried when I was younger, you wouldn't have been able to keep me in the kitchen long enough to teach me anything."

At that moment, the sound of laughter from inside the house reached their ears. Both of the women smiled at the spirited ruckus going on in the living room. Annie thought it would be a miracle if her father could get Will to settle down enough to go to sleep tonight. She looked over at her mother, surprised that her smile had faded so quickly.

"What are you thinking, Mother?"

"I don't know—hearing your father in there with little Will." She let out a deep breath. "It just reminds me of the little boy we lost."

Tears instantly sprang to Annie's eyes. In all the years she'd known her mother, not once had she ever really talked about the baby that was lost. Annie sat quietly, hoping that her mother would talk to her about the big brother she never knew. But Claudia remained silent, staring out into the night.

Annie didn't want to prod her mother into talking if she didn't feel like it, but she didn't think she could take one more minute of silence. "Mother, tell me about him." She reached over and gently covered her mother's hand. "Please."

Claudia looked at her daughter for a long moment, then slowly nodded her head. "I don't know if you know this or not—my first pregnancy ended with a miscarriage at nine weeks. But within six months, I was pregnant again and this one made it to full term."

She went on to tell Annie how difficult her labor had been. "Sarah Slater was the midwife. That's back when the Slaters owned the farm to the west of us. When I went into labor, your daddy rode over and got her. She stayed up with me all night long, but I just couldn't seem to deliver the baby." The midwife had been concerned about Claudia's narrow hips and was afraid the baby was struggling to enter the birth canal.

Claudia's voice became subdued when she said, "Nate decided to ride into town for the doctor the next morning. When the doctor arrived, he gave me some sort of drug that was supposed to help the baby deliver quicker. Right after that, I went into a more stressful labor." She laid her hands across her abdomen as if she were experiencing the feeling again. "I don't know if that drug was the cause, but an hour later the baby was stillborn."

"Oh Mother, I'm so sorry." Annie could only imagine what her mother must have gone through waiting for her baby boy to take a breath.

"The doctor was as distraught as your father and I were. He said never again would he give that drug to another woman."

There was a short silence, and Claudia looked away. "You know what I regret the most? I never got to hold my son. They took him away without laying him in my arms." She now looked into her daughter's eyes. "I'd give anything if I could've held him—just for a moment."

Annie had no idea how her mother could sit there without crying. She, on the other hand, was a basket case. Claudia reached over and took her daughter into her arms.

"It's all right, honey, it really is. Eventually, I *will* get to hold him."

Annie felt so grateful for her mother's deep, abiding faith. Even though she had spent more time with her father growing up, her mother was the one who had molded her spiritual heart. Annie only hoped that she could meet the storms of life with the same unshakable spirit.

"I guess that's why I let you spend so much time with your father." Claudia gave her daughter a fond squeeze and released her. "I felt like I had somehow deprived him of a son, so I wasn't about to deprive him of you."

"Mother, I can't believe you never told me any of this before."

"Honey, a lot has changed since you got married. You're no longer just my daughter." She reached over and cupped Annie's face in her hands. "You're also my friend."

Annie's hands reached up to cover her mother's. Her heart was so full. Quietly she breathed, "I love you so much."

Claudia looked at her daughter with an affectionate smile, and the two friends held each other for a very long time.

The house had been quiet for a while, and the women wondered what was going on when they entered the living room. Pillows from the couch and chairs were strewn all over the floor.

"My goodness, it looks like a cyclone came through our house," Claudia remarked, as she righted a straight back chair that was supposed to be sitting in the corner of the room.

"Mother, it's almost too quiet."

"Do you think they're still inside?"

Annie put the pillows back on the couch and headed for the stairs. "I'm going up to see what's going on."

When Annie finally came back to the living room, Claudia had it fairly well back to normal except for the window curtain that was stuck on top of the lampshade.

"Did you find them, honey?"

Annie laughed. "I found them all right. They must have worn each other out. Both of them are asleep on your bed."

Claudia smiled and shook her head as she headed into the kitchen. "Why don't we have a nice cup of tea while we wait for your daddy to come around."

As Claudia put the kettle of water on the stove, she innocently asked, "Why is Eugene staying in Lexington all week?"

"What do you mean? He's at the horse auction."

"Yes, but the auction is tomorrow, isn't it? I was just wondering why he's not coming home until Friday."

Annie felt a little embarrassed that Eugene hadn't told her about the auction being on Tuesday. That wasn't like him to keep anything from her.

Claudia must have noticed the color rising to Annie's cheeks, and said, "Honey, it's none of my business. I shouldn't have brought it up." She turned back to the stove to check the flame under the kettle, then reached for the cups in the cabinet.

Annie's mind instantly started racing. Why would Eugene not tell her about staying in Lexington three days longer than necessary? Maybe he had mentioned it and she just hadn't heard him. No, that was absolutely not the case; she would've remembered if he had discussed plans other than the horse auction with her. Throughout their years together, she had never been given a reason to distrust Eugene, and she had no intention of starting now. She just wished she could somehow eliminate that little tinge of suspicion that had edged up to her heart and opened the door.

Chapter 7

The next morning, everyone in the Harrison household climbed out of bed with the sun. Sounds of bacon frying and the hint of maple syrup wafting in the air made it impossible for anyone to avoid the kitchen. Farmhands and family members alike knew to pick up their plates on the counter and fill them at the stove. Breakfast was always eaten around the long oak table in the kitchen. Annie walked in with little Jake in her arms and asked her mother if she had seen Will this morning.

"Oh, your daddy and Will have already eaten and headed down to the barn to see the horses." Claudia reached into her apron pocket and took out two yellowed letters. "When you're done eating, you may be interested in reading these letters from your grandmother."

Annie gave Jake a kiss on the cheek and worked his chubby legs into the wooden high chair by the table. Nathan's wrangler, Charlie, reached over and lightly poked his belly, making a funny face at him. Jake rewarded him with an adorable giggle.

Noticing the date on the first letter, Annie asked her mother, "Does this have something to do with what we talked about last night?"

"Yes, honey it does. And since you don't remember your granny very well, I thought you'd like to read her letters."

Annie felt like her mother had just handed her a treasure. She vaguely remembered her granny. There were times a certain smell could bring back memories of sitting at her kitchen table or the feel of her arms while sitting in her lap. But her grandmother had died when Annie was only five. Her father's mother was still living, but sadly, Nathan had not been in contact with her in over twenty-five years. She knew her mother was praying that her daddy and Grandma Harrison would be able to repair their relationship before it was too late. Regrettably, Annie had never even met her paternal grandmother.

There was no time for Annie to read the letters. She was immediately reminded of how hard her mother worked every day to ensure that the men on this farm, including her father, were well taken care of. As soon as the breakfast table was cleared and dishes washed, the women were only able to get a few household chores done before preparations for the noon meal began.

Annie felt ashamed for having rarely helped her mother in the house the way she should have. Growing up, she had spent nearly every waking hour with the horses on their farm. Her father had taught her how to take care of a foal from the time of its birth. She had been comfortable on a horse since she was three years old. She could ride English and Western and could compete in dressage as easily as rope a calf. Annie actually had a fondness for wrangling and had spent her afternoons after school rounding up the cattle with Nathan's two full-time wranglers. She was far more comfortable mucking a stall than following a recipe.

But today, she was determined to help her mother as much as possible. Maybe she could pick up some good cooking tips that would help her feel better about the food she set in front of her husband every day. Even though Will had been brought back to the house by mid-morning, Annie still managed to get some time in the kitchen with her mother. Not nearly as much time as she could have if Will hadn't been in such a fussy mood.

"I think your father must have kept him up too late last night," Claudia commented, as she observed Annie struggling to calm him down from a fit. Will was determined to keep his boots on in the house, despite the fact that the rule of the house was that boots had to be left at the back door. "Oh honey," Claudia went on, "just let him wear his boots."

"Mother, he is not going to wear his boots in the house. He needs to learn to mind."

Before it was all said and done, Will's boots were forcibly removed by Annie despite his howling protests. As soon as the boots were placed by the back door, Annie swept her son up in her arms and whisked him right up the stairs. She would have spanked him if he hadn't been so tired. She knew last night's roughhousing with Gramps was certainly the culprit. He had gone to bed later than usual and gotten up early—a sure formula for disaster. It took several long minutes for Will to totally wear himself out of his raging tantrum, and when he did, Annie was there to take him into her arms. She rocked her son lovingly as the tears dried on his cheeks and his warm body melted into hers.

The old rocker had been in Annie's family for three generations. It made a familiar creaking sound as she gently pushed it back and forth on the wooden floor. Will turned his face toward hers, and she kissed him lightly on the cheek, then on the nose.

"I love you so much, sweetheart." Will's sleepy blue eyes looked into hers for just a moment, then he slowly closed them and snuggled his face into her neck.

Lord, You know everything about this little boy; You knit him together in my womb. I confess I don't know what to do with him at times. Please help me to do the right thing. I give him utterly and completely to you. Please use me, and Eugene, to bring him up for You, O Lord.

Softly Annie began to sing a song that her granny had sung to her when she was a young child.

Cast your cares on the Savior,
He careth for you.
Give him all of your burdens,

He will see you through.
Once He was a young babe,
In His mother's arms.
Now abideth in heaven,
Keeping you from harm.

Annie allowed the rocking chair to fall silent—testing if her son was truly asleep. He was. She laid him in the baby bed that had once belonged to her. Nathan had pulled it out of the attic when Will was born in their home nearly three years ago. She left the door ajar and headed back downstairs to join her mother in the kitchen.

"Annie, would you like to take the lunch out to the men today? I think it would do you good to get some fresh air."

What would she do without her mother—she was a saint. Annie glanced over at her youngest son in his playpen. "What about Jake?"

"Look at him. He's been like that all morning."

She had to laugh. Her little Jake was lying on his back, sucking on his big toe at the moment. He had been perfectly content since breakfast to play with his stuffed bear and watch his grandmother work in the kitchen.

"He should be about ready for his bottle. Are you sure you don't need me to stay?"

Claudia moved to the playpen and pulled Jake up into her arms. "You go on, honey. The men will be hungry."

Annie knew that Leroy always came to the house at noon to pick up lunch for all the men. It was fifteen minutes early today. No doubt her mother had timed it so she would have a chance to get outside for a while. "Bless you, Mother."

Claudia smiled and watched her daughter put on her jacket and boots then disappear through the kitchen door with the lunch satchel slung across her shoulder. *No wonder Annie never learned to cook,* Claudia thought, it didn't seem fitting to keep her free-spirited daughter cooped up in the kitchen. Claudia realized for the first time that she had some apologizing to do when Eugene came home at the end of the week.

Annie practically felt like skipping all the way to the barn on this beautiful October day. She told herself she wouldn't be gone long—long enough to say hello to her daddy and see a couple of her favorite horses. She met Leroy as she stepped inside the stables.

"Oh, hey there, Missy. I was just about to head up to the house to pick up the chow."

"I saved you the trouble," Annie replied with a cheery smile. "Have you seen Daddy around?"

"Yes, ma'am. I just left him in the office."

Annie handed the satchel of food over to Leroy and headed down the long row of stalls to the open door near the end. Nathan did most of his horse-trading business in his office in the stables. It had rustic furnishings—leather chairs with carved wooden armrests and a hand-carved desk with a swivel chair. A picture of the famous racehorse, Man o' War hung behind his desk, and several other pictures of horses from his own stables hung around the walls. Annie felt as much at home in this office as she did in the house.

Nathan's smile demonstrated how much he adored his daughter. He rose from his chair and came around the desk, kissing her cheek. "What brings you down here? I was about to head up to the house for lunch."

"Mother asked me to bring the lunch down to Leroy, so I thought I'd drop in to see what you're up to."

"I'm just about finished. Give me a minute and I'll walk back up with you."

Plopping into the nearest chair, Annie watched her father as he sat back down at his desk and continued working in his ledger. In his late forties, her father was still a very handsome man. She had gotten her coloring from him—his thick brown hair had once been a lighter color like hers, but his distinguishing features were his eyes. Annie had never seen anyone with blue eyes like his. They were almost a midnight blue framed by long, brown eyelashes that any woman would envy. As he worked, Annie began to contemplate what could've happened between him and his mother to justify having no relationship whatsoever. Maybe that was a question she would reserve for her mother.

"Okay, honey," Nathan said, closing his ledger. "Let's head up to the house and see what's for lunch."

Walking arm in arm through the stables, Nathan stopped at one of the large stalls so Annie could see Lady Gwenevere.

"Daddy, you know I can't stop here or I'll have to take her out."

A broad grin crossed Nathan's face. "So, what's stopping you?"

"Well, for one thing, I've got two little boys up at the house. One will be going down for a nap soon and the other will be waking up." Still Annie couldn't resist stopping to rub Lady G's muzzle. When she turned back around, she had to laugh. Her father was standing with his arm outstretched, holding a bridle in his hand.

"Daddy, I can't—"

"I insist."

"What about the boys?"

"You think your mother and I can't handle a couple of varmints for an hour or so?"

Annie gave her father a knowing smile. "Yeah, but this morning, I took the brunt of last night's escapades."

Nathan's eyes filled with remorse. "Sorry about that, honey. I just couldn't help myself last night. I promise I'll behave the rest of the week." He laid the bridle in her hand. "I wouldn't offer if I didn't mean it."

A proposition like this was too good to refuse. Annie opened the gate and kissed Lady G's forehead. "Tell Mother I'll be back to help her with supper."

She didn't know whether to be amused or upset when she heard her father's laughter fill the stables as he headed for the door.

The Harrison farm was one of the largest on the west side of Louisville. There was plenty of room to wander without ever leaving the confines of the fence. Annie spent the first half hour putting Lady G through a prescribed set of movements that showed off the thoroughbred's athletic abilities, then she headed for the pasture. A long stretch of smooth, open land was just where Annie was leading her.

As soon as Lady G recognized the direction they were going, she began to release an energy that sent her rider's heart to racing. Annie could feel the power of the mare's muscles beneath her, and both horse and rider equally anticipated the exhilaration to come.

The very second Annie bent low over her neck and released the pressure of the reigns, Lady G bounded forward with incredible force. Annie clasped the horse's reddish mane in her right hand to keep from being thrown off in the first few powerful strides. After that, it was nothing but pure joy as the pair covered the next mile and a half at break-neck speed. Just the sound of Lady's hooves pummeling the earth was enough to fill Annie with sheer delight. She didn't want to pull up, knowing this mare would eagerly go farther, but they had been running hard and Annie didn't want to injure her girl. A little pressure on the reins brought the mare back to a nice easy gallop and soon they were down to a spirited walk.

The pair entered a small wooded area at the far end of the pasture. At that moment, Annie remembered the letters her mother had given to her at breakfast. She couldn't believe she'd forgotten all about them in the pocket of her sweater.

She dismounted by a small stream that meandered across the property and allowed the mare to drink from the cool water. Sitting down with her back to a tree, Annie dropped Lady G's reins to the ground. The mare had been trained to stand perfectly still when the reins were dangling in front of her.

"You're such a good girl, my lady." Annie reached up and rubbed her muzzle before opening the letter in her lap.

My dear, dear children,

It's so hard to write and tell you how sorry I am to hear of the loss of your dear little one. My heart aches so for you, but I hope and pray that you get along all right. It is so hard to say God's will be done sometimes, but we know that He knows best, and when those little ones leave us, it will only make us strive harder to go meet them someday.

We will see to it that everything is done that can be done for your little one. My dear Claudia, I won't write anymore for now, but please write when you feel you can. Have Nathan drop us a card to let us know how you are getting along.

With much sympathy,

Your loving mother

Annie let her hands drop to her lap as she leaned her head back against the tree. She could only imagine how devastated her mother must have been losing her child—a little boy. And what about her father? How on earth had he made it through the loss of a son? Surely he must have been crushed to think he would never be able to see his boy grow to be a man.

Replacing the letter in the fragile envelope, Annie opened the second letter from her maternal grandmother in Tennessee.

My dear children,

I will try and write you this evening and tell you the best I can of how we cared for your little darling. Your loving father went over to the depot at 8:00 and got the little body. We had planned to have the funeral at 3:30 over at the cemetery, but some thought it would be too hot there, so we just had it at the house. Brother Leon said a few words and offered prayer, and we sang two songs, "Safe in the Arms of Jesus," which we know he was, and "When He Cometh to Make Up His Jewel," because we know he was one of them. Then we laid the little body to rest.

He sure was a big baby, Claudia, and I believe he would have looked a lot like Nathan if he could've lived. But Brother Leon prayed in his prayer that God would bind up your wounded hearts and help you to bear your sorrow.

I know it was hard for you, Nathan, to put that little baby on the train alone to send him here to us, but we are glad to do what we could to help you and, of course, you couldn't leave our dear Claudia. We sure hope she is getting along fine. I am sending you a few of the flowers and the ribbon off of them in a little package soon.

I hope Nathan can write us a card every day or two to let us know how you are getting along.
Will close now hoping you are feeling better.
Worlds and worlds of love.

From, Mother

Tears slid down Annie's cheeks as she thought about the heartache her parents had endured. But something in the first letter kept tugging at her heart. She opened it and reread the words that meant so much to her. *It is so hard to say God's will be done sometimes, but we know that He knows best, and when those little ones leave us, it will only make us strive harder to go meet them someday.* That was her heritage of faith. A strong abiding faith passed down from her grandmother to her mother—and now to her. How amazing that God worked so profoundly to draw people to His heart, even in the midst of tragedy. She was beginning to realize that a deep relationship with the heavenly Father might only be achieved through the pain and suffering of this life. After all, God had suffered the loss of His own son.

Annie sat quietly under the leaves of the autumn tree, breathing deeply of her surroundings. All conscious thoughts and words were lost as her soul communed with the Lord. These moments didn't come often, but she felt incredibly blessed to spend this time with her Creator. It was an eternal moment that would shore up her spirit and give her the strength she needed to live a life of grace in the midst of struggles. Before leaving her haven, Annie was convicted deep within her soul that this was the heritage she would pass on to her children, and to their children, for as long as she lived on this earth.

That night after the boys were in bed, Annie joined her parents in the front room of the house. Nathan checked his pocket watch when his daughter entered the room. "Oh, so this is when bedtime is."

"Very funny, Daddy."

"I hope all is forgiven," he said with a tender smile.

Teasingly, Annie replied, "I think Lady G helped me find it in my heart to forgive you."

Nathan laughed. "I guess I owe her a little treat tomorrow."

Before sitting down on the sofa, Annie handed her mother the two letters she had read that afternoon. Claudia searched deeply into Annie's eyes, wondering what effect the words of her mother had had on her daughter.

When it appeared that Annie was struggling for words, Claudia quietly asked, "Is there anything you want to know, honey?" She gave her daughter a warm smile. "It's all right. You can ask us anything."

Annie pulled her legs up underneath her on the sofa and relaxed into the soft cushions. "I do have one question. I was wondering why Daddy got to hold the baby and you didn't."

Nathan seemed to be taken off guard and moved uncomfortably in his chair.

Instantly Annie said, "I'm sorry, Da—"

"No, no, no. It's okay, really. I just wasn't expecting that one." Nathan looked over at his wife in the easy chair next to his. Her sweet spirit had always had such a calming effect on him. Claudia reached for his hand and nodded for Nathan to answer his daughter's question.

Clearing his throat, Nathan turned his attention back to Annie. "I don't know, honey, it all seemed to happen so fast. The doctor and the midwife were nearly overcome with panic when they couldn't get the baby to breathe. I guess they felt like it was best not to let your mother see him in such a way. They probably thought they were protecting her."

That made sense to Annie. It seemed perfectly natural that the doctor would want to protect his patient and not put her into further distress.

"Besides, your mother needed to get to the hospital," Nathan continued. "The doctor took care of the baby, and I hitched up the buggy to take Claudia into town." He gave his wife's hand a firm squeeze before releasing it. "I wasn't about to lose your mother too."

"So the baby is buried in Tennessee?" Annie asked curiously.

Claudia spoke up then. "That's where all of our family lived. Your daddy and I both grew up in Carthage. You may remember traveling there when you were very young. We hadn't lived in Kentucky long, so we sent our sweet baby home. My parents are buried next to our baby boy."

Claudia was afraid her daughter might bring up the question of Nathan's parents. She knew this was not the time to delve into her husband's past. But thankfully Annie's last question was one they could both handle.

"What would you have named him?"

Letting out a soft laugh, Claudia replied, "I don't think you'd believe me if I told you."

"What, Mother?"

"If it was a boy, we had already decided to name him William."

***

At the end of the week, Eugene finally came home. Annie didn't think she could've lasted one more day without him. He had made it to the Harrison's farm just in time for supper Friday evening. Afterward, Nathan loaded up the entire family and drove them back to their house.

Annie enjoyed watching Eugene with their boys at bedtime. He couldn't seem to get enough kisses from them. She stood by patiently waiting for her turn with him.

A few hours later, she lay in bed in her husband's arms, resting her head on his shoulder and keeping her left hand on his chest. The strong, steady rhythm of his heart gave her a peaceful reassurance that all was well—still.

"Eugene," Annie breathed. "Why didn't you come home after the sale on Tuesday?"

He didn't answer. She raised her head slightly to see if his eyes were open. They weren't. He must be asleep. Annie wondered how she would be able to sleep with that nagging question on her mind. After several long minutes, she lifted her hand from his chest and started to roll over on her side of the bed. Immediately, his grip tightened on her shoulder and he pulled her back to his chest.

"Do you trust me, Annie?"

She rose up on her elbow, and this time, his eyes met hers in the darkened room. "With all my heart, I trust you."

"Then let it go," he whispered.

Trust had never really been an issue with Annie but curiosity had. However, as the busy days flew by, she soon forgot about Eugene's longer-than-necessary stay in Lexington. He had been pleased with the auction price for Conquering Hero and was thankful to pay down much of the debt on their property. A few more sales like that, and he would own his farm outright. They were barely breaking even with the cattle, considering the cost of feed and hay and the veterinary bills. But it wouldn't be much longer before he would be making a profit even there.

During the following year of 1925, Eugene didn't have a horse ready for auction, but he made some private sales and trades in Louisville that helped the farm. The year after that was a different story. Once again, he made the trip to

Lexington in October and stayed an entire week. Before he left, Annie asked him straight out what day the auction was, and he didn't bat an eye when he told her it was early in the week. Annie gave her husband a more passionate than usual good-bye kiss, and she made sure the last words he heard were, "I trust you completely."

Eugene had pulled her in close saying, "That's my girl." But his next words had left Annie perplexed for quite some time. "And great shall be thy reward."

PART TWO

Hope itself is like a star—not to be seen
in the sunshine of prosperity, and only to be discovered
in the night of adversity.

~Charles Spurgeon

When you reach the end of your rope,
tie a knot in it and hang on.

~Franklin Delano Roosevelt

Chapter 8

July 1930

Rachel couldn't remember the last time she had been so anxious. She had never wanted to be a burden to anyone, particularly to Eugene and his family. But she simply saw no other way. Her son would have to know the truth; she had put it off far too long. At the sound of the car pulling up in her driveway, Rachel knew she would be reduced to begging in a matter of minutes.

There was a light knock at the door, and Eugene entered before she even rose from her chair at the kitchen table. Rachel had no idea how she could face her son and daughter-in-law, but she prayed that God would give her the strength to do so.

As soon as Eugene entered the kitchen and made eye contact with his mama, he turned to the boys and told them to head down to the neighborhood park for a while.

"Will, take care of your brother," Eugene instructed. "Don't run off and leave him."

Will gave his younger brother a friendly shove and told him, "Come on, let's see if there's a stickball game we can get in on."

Without hesitation, six-year-old Jake headed for the door—he would follow his brother anywhere. Will was only two years older but acted like he knew everything and could do anything. Jake spent most of his time just trying to keep up.

Rachel rose to her feet and accepted a warm embrace from her son, then gave her daughter-in-law a kiss. "Do you mind if we sit around the table?" Rachel asked. "I have a few papers I need to show you."

"Not at all, Mama." The deep furrow in Eugene's brow conveyed his unease. "Are you all right?"

A nervous feeling rushed through Rachel like a howling wind, and she wished with all her heart she didn't need to have this conversation. But she had no choice. The entire country was hurting, and she was no exception. Trouble was, she knew Eugene was hurting too. With that thought, Rachel almost decided to back out of her conversation. But then what would she do?

Taking in a deep breath, she silently prayed for the courage to ask for help. "I'm really sorry about this." Rachel shook her head, trying to form the right words. "I never wanted to weigh you down with more responsibilities than you already have. But I just don't see any other way." An aggravating tear slid down her cheek. She had told herself that was not going to happen.

"Mama, whatever it is, we're here for you. Just tell us what's happened." The compassion in Eugene's voice was so comforting and unnerving all at the same time. And bless Annie's heart, her eyes were already moist and she didn't even know what was going on.

"You remember how I sold your papa's five horses to George Collins in Lexington back in '19?"

Eugene nodded.

"At that point, I was set for life—or so I thought. There was enough money to buy this house, and the rest was invested for me to live on. Obviously, I've lost quite a bit of my investment in the last nine months."

Rachel was referring to the crash of the New York Stock Exchange last October that had put the banking industry into a tailspin. Many other countries were also in a financial crisis as a direct result of the market failure in the United States.

When Rachel hesitated, Eugene said, "Mama, I know it's been rough for you, but I assumed you would tell me if you were struggling."

With a quiet laugh Rachel said, "I guess that's what I'm trying to do now. When Kentucky First National closed its doors, a lot of other banks were affected. As you know, my money has always been with Citizens Mutual Savings & Trust. They informed their investors last month that they were going into liquidation." Rachel handed Eugene a letter she had received from her bank stating that during liquidation, the bank's creditors were being paid off in order of preference, and the rest would be distributed back to the stockholders.

"Son," Rachel swallowed hard. "I only received 6 percent of my investment back." She showed him another letter dated two weeks ago informing her of the catastrophic loss to her investment. She knew some people who had gotten back nearly the entire amount of their investments at other banks, but she was not so fortunate.

"If I sell the house . . ." Rachel's words hung in the air, as she was unable to finish the sentence.

Immediately, Annie took hold of her mother-in-law's hand. "Yes, sell the house and move in with us!"

A bit taken aback by her daughter-in-law's enthusiasm, Rachel glanced at Eugene. After all, this would be a huge decision for his family. But her son was grinning from ear to ear, nodding his head.

"Mama, Annie's right. You should sell this house and move in with us. I've been worried about you anyway, living here in the city all by yourself. Maybe this was a blessing in disguise."

"Do you know what you're asking? That's another person in your household that you would be responsible for. I know how hard you all are working to keep your farm going as it is."

"Actually, Mama, this would be perfect timing for us. I can't afford to hire a full-time farmhand, but this would free up Annie to be able to take over some other responsibilities."

"Oh, darlin'," Rachel said to Annie. "I'm so sorry about this. I didn't mean for it to become a burden for you."

Annie laughed, almost gleefully. "Are you kidding? That's what I live for."

"She's right," Eugene agreed. "And Mama, if you don't mind, you could do the cooking!" Annie looked sharply over at Eugene, and Rachel noticed the sheepish expression on his face.

He almost stuttered when he added, "You know, so Annie would be able to help me tend to farm business."

"Go ahead and say it, Eugene." Annie sat back in her chair and folded her arms across her chest. "Tell her what you're really thinking."

A light shade of red worked its way across Eugene's face. "Annie, I wasn't implying . . ."

"No, it's okay—really," Annie retorted. "Just try to contain your excitement though." It appeared she was trying to make Eugene suffer a bit for his obvious enthusiasm about Rachel taking over the cooking duties.

Eugene's mouth was open, but no words were coming out. Finally, Annie turned to Rachel and said, "Mama, I know it looks like our family is being well-fed, and we truly are blessed to have food on our table these days. But my cooking is . . . shall we say, nothing to brag about."

When Eugene made a small choking sound, Annie pointed her finger at him. "Don't you say a word!"

Eugene couldn't contain himself any longer and burst out laughing. He reached over for Annie, and she slapped his hand away. He reached again and grabbed her by the wrist, pulling her out of her chair and onto his lap.

"Sorry about this, Mama," Eugene said, as he wrapped his arms tightly around his wife and kissed her neck.

Rachel shook her head and laughed as she got up from the table and moved over to the counter. Looking outside the kitchen window, she felt like an overwhelming burden had just been lifted from her shoulders. She would love to spend every day cooking for her family and helping with the household chores. The truth was, she had been a bit lonely living in this house all by herself.

When she turned back around, Rachel felt the warmth rise to her cheeks. She teasingly put her hands on her hips and cleared her throat. "That's enough of that in my kitchen."

Eugene released the hold on his wife and allowed her to get up. Annie jabbed her finger into his side and laughed when he nearly twitched out of his chair. As he stood up, Eugene said to Rachel, "So it's settled, right? You're moving in with us."

"If you'll have me."

Annie moved around the table to give Rachel a loving hug. "No, if you'll have *us*. And thank you."

"Yes, thank—"

"I mean it, Eugene," Annie scolded. "Not another word!"

***

Eugene and Annie's three-bedroom farmhouse needed a little work before Rachel could move in during the first week of August. Eugene built a bunk bed for his boys, and Jake's belongings were moved into his big brother's room. Will had protested at first, but when he found out the top bunk was his, he settled into the idea fairly quickly. Annie had already taken over the care of the horses, which gave her husband time to finish important business in town with his mama.

Rachel insisted that the remainder of her investments should be put into Eugene's bank account, and as soon as the house sold, that money would be applied there too. That was a lifesaver as far as Eugene was concerned. He and his family had been living hand-to-mouth for the last few months. But the extra income was exactly what he needed to help him turn a corner.

Long before the sun came up, Rachel rose from her bed and spent time in prayer with her heavenly Father. Not one day had gone by that she hadn't thanked Him for putting Eugene in her life. And now her heart was full. Eugene had been blessed with a beautiful wife whom Rachel considered as her own daughter, and together they had given her two wonderful grandsons. No amount of money could compare to the treasure she had been given through this family.

It was Rachel's first morning on the farm, and before she started breakfast, she felt like walking outside for a moment. Quietly she left the house in the grayish light and walked slowly down the road leading to the barn. The lowing of the cattle in the field was like a melody to her spirit. She had missed life on the farm in Winchester with Franklin and Eugene.

Rachel's feet stilled when she heard the sound of a faint whistle drifting through the morning air. It brought a chill up her spine, and she moved toward the horse pasture to see where it was coming from. Tears instantly sprang to her eyes as she watched the poignant scene unfold. Eugene was standing in the middle of the pasture. The early morning mist swirled around him as all of the horses gathered to his side, forming an almost perfect circle around the man who had trained them. As long as she lived, Rachel would never fail to be in awe of such a sacred gathering. How many times had she watched Franklin draw his horses to him in such a manner? Her heart quickened at the thought of her beloved husband.

Eugene began to gradually move among the herd, speaking to each horse, using his hands to draw their heart to his. Even at a distance, it was obvious how much love was flowing between Eugene and these magnificent animals. Rachel was instantly reminded of the little boy who had wandered onto their farm so many years ago. She closed her eyes, grieving over the memory of his body, so badly beaten. Before she even knew who he was or where he had come from, the boy had become as much a part of Rachel's heart as if he were her own flesh and blood. Growing up, Eugene had always thought that Franklin and Rachel had saved him, but truth be told, *he* had saved her.

That night at supper, the family looked a little weary, but everyone had enjoyed a good day. During the summer, Will and Jake had specific chores they were required to complete before they were allowed to play. If they didn't piddle, they were usually done by lunchtime. After that, they got to ride their horses, go fishing in the pond, or just wander around the farm.

"So how's the fort coming along?" Eugene asked his boys over a fried chicken dinner that brought a smile to his face.

Jake answered first. "It's awesome, Dad! We're gonna make it so you can't get in unless you climb the tree and go through a trap door on the top."

"Well, I guess that leaves me out," Rachel declared.

"We can help you up in the tree, Gramma." Jake sincerely believed with a little help his grandmother would be able to enter their fort.

Will shook his head. "I dunno about that. Maybe we can make a secret door or somethin' on the side."

Rachel had seen the contraption they were trying to build. She would be afraid to enter it, even from ground level. "That's okay, boys. I saw what it looked like inside before you got it done. I don't want you to have to put in a secret door just for me."

When the meal was over, Eugene asked everyone to stay around the table. "How would you all like to take a little vacation this summer?"

Will and Jake nearly bounced out of their chairs with excitement.

"Eugene?" Annie had the most surprised look on her face. "What are you talking about?"

Grinning, he said, "I thought it would be fun to get away for a week before school starts. Jake's starting first grade and Will's going into the third grade, and we've never really had a chance to get away from the farm."

"Where are we goin', Dad?" Will asked eagerly.

"I know about this great little hunting and fishing lodge," Eugene responded. "It's kind of rustic, and we'd have to bring in our own food. But if you two are good at huntin' and fishin'," he nodded toward his boys across the table, "we should have plenty to eat. So what do you say?"

By this time, Will and Jake were on their feet jumping around the kitchen. Annie was pretty excited about it herself, but Eugene could tell by the look on her face that she would have some questions for him in private.

"What about Gramma?" Jake asked.

"Oh, especially Gramma!" Eugene exclaimed. He was enjoying the astonished look on his mama's face.

"When are we going on this little adventure?" Rachel asked.

"School starts September first, so I'm thinking we ought to leave in about a week."

That brought more enthusiastic whoops from the boys and even a cheer from Annie.

Later that night as they were getting ready for bed, Annie asked Eugene how they were going to pull off this vacation. "Who's going to take care of the farm while we're gone?"

Eugene took off his shirt and threw it across the chair. "I've got everything taken care of with Mike and your dad."

"Can we afford to pay Mike?"

"No worries, Annie." He slipped under the bed sheet and folded his arms behind his head. "I've been planning this for a long time."

Annie gave her husband an exasperated look. "A long time? How could you keep something like this from me?"

"Trust me, it wasn't easy."

"I do trust you, remember?"

"Oh yeah, I forgot about that," Eugene teased, then he reached up and pulled his wife into bed.

***

The family automobile was about as loaded down as it could get. Eugene wasn't sure there would even be enough room for all of the family members. He reached through the car window and honked the horn a couple of times. "Come on, gang, daylights a wastin'."

"Hold your horses, Eugene. We don't want to leave anything." Annie had an armload of provisions, and he had no idea where she was going to put them. Right behind her, the boys came flying out of the house, laughing and shoving each other all over the place.

"Okay, fellas, take it easy. We've got a long ways to go and you all need to settle down."

"Dad, how far is it?" Jake asked as he slipped into the backseat.

"Just under a hundred miles. We'll be there in less than three hours."

Annie climbed into the backseat with the boys so Rachel could have the front. For the first hour, the boys were fine. During the second hour, Annie was sitting between them. But for the last hour, Will was stationed in the front seat between Eugene and Rachel, madder than a hornet.

"I didn't start it!" he yelled.

"Will, don't say another word. Do you understand me?" Eugene reprimanded.

Will crossed his arms across his chest and let out a groan. But thankfully nothing more came out of his mouth. Eugene knew his anger would melt away when they arrived at their destination.

As soon as they skirted around Lexington, Rachel looked over at Eugene. "Where is this hunting and fishing lodge located, Son?"

Eugene glanced her way and read the look in her eyes. "Oh, I think you already know, Mama."

It wasn't long before Eugene stopped the car on the side of the road and hopped out. "Come on, Will. Help me move this log." Eugene could've moved the log by himself, but he wanted Will to feel good about helping out. He looked up the trail and was glad to see it was still clear enough for the car to make it up the steep grade. He thought about the backbreaking work he'd done to make sure it would be passable.

When Eugene pulled the car up to the old Winchester farmhouse, the women sat stunned. It didn't take the boys long to wiggle out of the car, but the women simply sat and stared. Finally, Eugene came around to Rachel's door and opened it wide.

"Come on you two. Don't just sit there gawking. Get out and let me give you the grand tour."

As soon as the women were out of the car, Will jumped off the porch yelling, "Look, Momma! Look at the sign above the door!"

Annie looked up and read the sign: *Will & Jake's Hunting & Fishing Lodge*. She looped her arm through her husband's and said, "Eugene, you never cease to amaze me."

He kissed the top of her head, then turned to Rachel. "So what do you think, Mama?"

"Son," Rachel gasped. "How on earth did all of this get done?"

The old farmhouse had been miraculously transformed. Where holes once existed in the side of the house, boards had been nailed. The railing of the porch had been repaired, and a lock was on the door leading into the kitchen.

"Every time I came to the horse auction in Lexington, I stayed a few days longer so I could work on this place. It still needs more repairs, but I think you'll like what I've done on the inside too."

Annie gave her husband a playful shove. "So this is what you were up to." She shook her head. "You could've told me, you know."

"What? And miss this reaction? Not on your life."

Eugene took the key out of his pocket and opened the door for everyone to go in. The first thing they noticed were the chairs around the kitchen table.

"You mean it's furnished too?" Rachel asked.

"Somewhat. I picked up a few things here and there—and built all the beds"

Will and Jake started running from room to room. They came flying out of the first room yelling, "There's only one bed in there." Then Jake peeked out of Eugene's old room and yelled, "Hey, look everybody, there's bunk beds in here!"

Eugene said, "Mama, you'll have your old room, and the rest of us will sleep back here in the bunk beds."

"Oh no, I can sleep back there with the boys. You and Annie need to have the front room."

"No, Mama. I'm sorry. At Will & Jake's Hunting & Fishing Lodge, the young folks get the bunk beds."

Rachel laughed and realized this was an argument she wouldn't be able to win.

"Okay everybody," Eugene called. "Let's get the car unloaded and our gear put away, so we can go exploring." He particularly looked at the boys. "There's a little secret about this house that I think you're going to want to see!"

Chapter 9

Eugene and Rachel relaxed into the chairs on the front porch, enjoying each other's company. Annie was inside the house helping the boys get cleaned up and ready for bed. The first day at the hunting and fishing lodge had been a wild success. The family spent the entire day exploring the farm and listening to Eugene tell stories of growing up here. Will and Jake particularly loved the cave underneath the house and even asked if they could sleep down below. Eugene had laughed just thinking about how scared they'd probably be after the first five minutes.

Seeing the enthusiasm of his boys when he showed them the cave had caused Eugene to remember how awestruck he had been the first time he saw it. The large cavern underneath the house had been a refuge during the winter from the cold, breezy house above. There was even a long passageway that led to a room where the farm animals could seek shelter.

"This place brings back so many memories," Rachel commented.

Eugene noticed the contemplative look on her face. "What are you thinking about, Mama?"

"Actually, I've had something on my mind all day—I think it's being back on the farm after so many years." She glanced at her son sitting beside her, then said, "I want you to know that a few years ago I was able to forgive those men from Winchester." The very day she spilled her heart to Annie and Claudia at the Oak Hill Church, she had forgiven the men for their horrible acts of brutality.

Eugene was thankful that she had been able to find closure after such a terrible, life-altering experience. But he was a bit taken back by the question she now posed to him.

"Have you forgiven Louis for what he did to you?"

Eugene leaned forward in his chair and rested his elbows on his knees. Scenes of brutal beatings flashed through his mind—some beatings so savage he had lost consciousness. After a moment, he sat back and said, "I haven't really considered it forgiveness, but I've gotten over what happened. I don't harbor any ill feelings because I choose not to think about it anymore. So I guess in a way, you can call it forgiveness."

"I haven't." Rachel had a fire in her eyes that Eugene had rarely seen. It surprised him.

"You haven't what?"

"I haven't forgiven your stepfather for what he did to you. So many memories have come back to me since being here on the farm again. For some reason, I can't get Louis off my mind. I think God is telling me it's time to forgive him."

Eugene leaned forward in his chair again and stared nervously out over the pasture. The frogs were beginning to sing their evening melody while swallows swooped low over the pasture searching for their final meal before sundown. Surely, she wasn't suggesting they should meet with Louis face to face. It was troubling enough just to talk about him, much less see him again. While Eugene had never wished his stepfather harm, he most certainly had never wished anything good for the man. For the first time in his life, he realized how much Louis needed God. Something gripped his heart that had never been there before—maybe it was pity.

"Mama, what are you saying?"

"I think I'm saying that I need to make it right with God. It's a sin for me to have an unforgiving heart where that man is concerned." Rachel had fiercely protected Eugene when he had first wandered onto their farm at the age of eleven. She was now realizing after nearly twenty years that she was still holding a grudge.

Eugene now leaned back in his chair and looked Rachel directly in the eyes. He could tell she was close to tears, and his heart went out to her. "How can I help you, Mama?"

"Would you pray with me?" Rachel's eyes were pleading with him to help her find relief.

At that moment, Annie and the boys started laughing in the house—maybe one of Annie's funny bedtime stories again. Eugene took Rachel's hand and said, "Let's walk out to the oak."

After the boys finally settled down for the night, Annie came out onto the porch hoping to join in the conversation with her husband and mother-in-law. To her surprise, the porch was empty. Scanning the pasture, she eventually spotted Eugene and Rachel sitting on a log underneath Franklin's oak tree. Their heads were bowed, and Eugene's arm was around Rachel's shoulders. Even from this distance, she could tell Rachel was crying.

The next morning, Rachel smiled as she flipped the sizzling bacon in her frying pan. There was a commotion of epic proportions going on in the next room. Between growls and shrieks, Rachel enjoyed the delightful sounds of laughter. At times, she feared the bunk beds might overturn. She glanced behind her just in time to see the door whisk open and two boys come flying out of the room with the *bear* in hot pursuit.

"Save me, Gramma!" Jake grabbed hold of her skirt and tried to hide behind her.

"Careful, darlin'. I don't want you to get burned." Rachel moved away from the stove and pretended to save Jake from the vicious, growling bear by waving her spatula in the air.

Will was still on the move, trying to elude his daddy as he was chased around the table. Annie emerged from the bedroom laughing and joined in the pursuit, helping Eugene trap their eldest son in the corner. When they finally caught him, Eugene flung him up over his shoulder and paraded him around the kitchen. Annie grabbed Jake around the waist and pulled him into her lap in one of the kitchen chairs, kissing his neck and making him giggle.

Rachel moved back to the stove to make sure the bacon wasn't getting too crisp. "If the bear family doesn't settle down, there will be no breakfast for any of them this morning!"

Instantly, all four put a halt to their shenanigans. "But Gramma, I'm hungry." Jake had such an innocent look on his face—as if she really would withhold his breakfast.

"I'm hungry too, Gramma!" Will wanted to make sure he too would get fed this morning. "If I'm gonna catch the biggest fish, I need to eat a big breakfast."

"Well, let me tell you, there's a monstrous catfish living out there in the pond . . . that is, if he's still around. Your daddy tried many times to catch him."

"He's a sly one, Goliath is." Eugene ruffed up Will's hair. "But with all four of the Wyatts coming after him, he doesn't stand a chance."

"I wanna be the one to get him," Will said with determination.

Rachel knew that Will would be disappointed if another member of the family actually hooked Goliath. Annie must have been thinking the same thing as she said, "Honey, if any of us catch Goliath, it'll be a miracle. And even if one of us does, it'll be a victory for the whole family."

Annie smiled at her son as she got up to help Rachel finish getting the breakfast on the table. The sun would be up soon, and they planned to start their fishing excursion as early as possible. Rachel was looking forward to working on some projects around the old house while the rest of the family was away.

As soon as the morning meal was over and everyone was dressed, the *bear* family headed out the door to pick up their fishing poles on the porch. Eugene had rigged each of the cane poles with fishing line and a hook, which was securely fastened to a cork bobber so no one would get poked before they made it to the pond. He had also added a tiny weight to each line to keep the bait from floating to the surface.

The family marched out with poles resting on their shoulders, picking their way across the pasture, hardly noticing the wet dew soaking their feet. When Eugene caught a glimpse of the old pond, his heart was gripped with a longing to be with his papa again. He knew Franklin would've been so proud of his two little boys. He longed to possess his papa's wisdom when it came to raising these two rascals. What he wouldn't give right now to fish the morning away with the man who had so profoundly influenced his life.

"Dad, where do you think the best spot is?" Will was clearly hoping to get an advantage over the rest of the family.

"Well, you see those tree limbs sticking out of the water over there?" Eugene pointed to a beech tree that had fallen into the pond. "I'll bet there are some cats hanging out around those branches. You'll wanna keep your bait on the bottom of the pond, but also keep your line tight—that way you can feel if a fish takes hold of it."

Annie took the lid off the bucket of bait and filled a tin can with dough balls for Will. Rachel had helped them roll the balls of cornmeal the night before and had kept them moist by clamping a tight lid on the bucket.

Eugene continued his instructions. "Now remember, you have to be patient fishing for catfish. They can't see very well, so we gotta hope they like the smell of Gramma's cornmeal." He gave Annie's side a little pinch. He knew she never sat still for long, so this might be a tough morning for her. She swatted his hand away and headed to the other side of the pond.

One by one, each member of the family found a spot on the bank and began throwing his or her line into the water. Annie didn't have much of a chance to get bored, as she was the first to pull a catfish out of the pond. Jake and Eugene cheered when she held up the tiny catfish—much too small to keep.

"Look here, boys, this is how it's done," Annie teased.

Eugene noticed Will's reaction and knew that he was upset that he hadn't caught the first fish. *Lord, I know this is a small thing, but could you please send a fish Will's way?*

The rest of the morning went by slowly with an occasional nibble here and there. Each of them caught at least one catfish worth keeping for dinner though.

Eugene quickly put his pole aside when he noticed Jake start pulling in a decent-sized fish. "Daddy, help me get him!" Jake was grinning ear to ear as he fought with the foot-long fish.

Just as Eugene started helping Jake pull in his fish, they were all startled by a loud yelp from the other side of the pond. Will had hooked a massive catfish and was fighting with all his might to hang onto his pole. Eugene knew he couldn't leave Jake and quickly looked for Annie. Thankfully, she wasn't too far from Will's position, and he saw her toss her pole on the bank and take off running.

Eugene watched eagerly to see if his wife and son would be able to drag the fish to shore. Will's pole was bent nearly in half, and he worried that it might just snap in two. He could hear their excited voices carrying across the pond.

"It's Goliath, I know it is!" Will's tongue protruded from his mouth, and he was biting down hard on it.

Nearing her son, Annie yelled, "Hang on tight!" She reached out to grab the line, praying that it wouldn't break before they could get the fish up on shore. The cat swam furiously back and forth, breaking the surface, then diving below, fighting with all its might to break free.

Will slowly inched backward, pulling the massive fish ever closer to shore. When they finally hauled him up on land, Annie was nearly terrified to touch it.

"Mom, it's him, it's really Goliath!"

"You got him, all right!" Annie cried. Then she yelled across the pond, "Will caught Goliath!"

Jake and Eugene let out a loud whoop and almost forgot they had a fish of their own to contend with.

Will kept the line tight, but there were moments when he thought the fish would drag him into the pond. "Momma, get him!" He was getting aggravated that his mother couldn't seem to figure out how to get a hold on the fish.

Annie finally clamped her hand down on the back of his enormous head, but she needed help and all Will could do was grip the pole. She had already learned the hard way about the sharp barbs on a catfish's fins. She wished she had a pair of leather gloves on so she could just reach around the body of the fish and throw him up higher on the bank.

"Keep pulling him, Will!" Annie's heart was about to beat out of her chest, as she feared they would lose Goliath. She couldn't hold him down; he was proving to be as fierce as the name her husband had given him.

Suddenly, without warning, the line snapped and Will was sent hurdling to the ground. He landed with a thud on his back, legs sprawled clear above his head. In desperation, Annie grabbed the fish with both hands. The pain was excruciating as the barbs dug into her palms and her first reaction was to let go. Goliath needed only a second to realize the hold on his life had been broken, and she watched in horror as he took a flying leap back into the pond.

Annie instantly dropped to her knees in the mud at the edge of the water. Tears clouded her vision as she watched Goliath break the water at the surface one last time before diving into the deep recesses of the pond. With palms turned upward, she noticed they were both cut sharply by Goliath's fins—blood was already dripping to the ground.

There had not been a sound from Will since the fish had regained his freedom. Disheartened, Annie turned around to face her son. He was now on his feet, and his face was a dark shade of red, eyes burning with anger.

"Oh honey, I'm so sorry—"

"You let Goliath go!"

Annie rose to her feet. "I didn't *let* him go . . . he got away."

"All you had to do was hold him, Momma. That was the only fish I wanted to catch and you let him go!"

Annie moved toward her son, but Will stepped out of her reach. He didn't seem to notice or care that her hands were wounded and bleeding.

"Will, I couldn't hang onto him; he was just too big. I didn't mean to let him—"

"I hate you!" he yelled. Hot tears stung his eyes.

"William Wyatt, you will not speak to me—"

"I don't care, it's true."

Will turned away from his mother and took off running in the opposite direction of the house. Annie called for him to come back, but he ignored her. She watched in frustration as he disappeared into the woods at the other end of the pasture.

"Momma, you're bleeding."

Annie turned around just as Eugene and Jake reached her side. "I can't win with him; nothing I do is ever right."

"You're bleeding, Momma," Jake said again. His compassion was so touching.

"I know, sweetheart, I know," she said quietly.

Eugene's heart hurt for Annie. He knew how hard she tried to have a good relationship with Will. She was such a good mother, but Will was living up to his name. No doubt about it, he had a *stubborn will* along with a fiery temper. He and Annie were a lot alike; they both had the same passion for life, but Will hadn't learned how to control that passion, especially when something made him angry.

"Annie, I'm really sorry. I'll get you and Jake back to the house and go find him. He'll be punished for the way he talked to you." Eugene reached out and held the back of Annie's hands looking at her palms. "Mama, will take care of these hands for you." Then he added with a slight grin, "You put up a good fight against Goliath."

"Yeah, and I've got the scars to prove it." Annie took a deep breath and leaned her forehead into her husband's chest. He kissed the top of her head and said, "Jake, do you think you can carry all of our poles?"

"Yep, I'll get 'em." Jake ran around the pond gathering up the fishing poles. He even set the hooks in the cork bobbers, all except for the pole that was missing its hook. Somewhere beneath the murky water was a monstrous catfish sporting a hook in his lip.

Eugene still hadn't come home, and everyone was beginning to get a little worried. Rachel had already fried the catfish for supper, and it was sitting on the table along with fried squash and cornbread, but there was still no sign of her son and grandson. Finally, she stepped out onto the porch and told Annie and Jake it was time to eat.

"They'll be along any time now, you'll see." She was hoping to reassure her daughter-in-law, but one look at Annie's face wedged a lump of fear deep inside her chest.

Annie nudged Jake ahead of her into the house but turned back to Rachel before entering. "I don't have a good feeling about this, Mama."

Rachel felt her heart quicken; she didn't either. But she wasn't about to say so to Annie. Instead, she gripped her shoulders and said with conviction, "God knows where they are. He'll bring them home."

As the three of them sat down at the table, Rachel asked a blessing over the food and prayed that the Lord would indeed take care of Will and Eugene, wherever they might be.

Jake was the only one who seemed to enjoy the meal. He ate plenty of fish for the three of them, and he didn't seem to notice that his mother and grandmother were only picking at the food on their plates. Finally, Rachel left the table and started covering the rest of the food. "I'll try to keep it warm in the oven for when they come in."

Annie helped her clean up the kitchen in silence, then went back out on the porch. She leaned her shoulder against the post on the top step and looked down at her bandaged hands in the fading light. How had they gone from the *bear* family this morning to *barely* a family at all tonight? Raising her head, she caught a glimpse of Eugene as he emerged from the woods at the far end of the pasture. Leaping down from the porch, she took off at a run to meet him.

"Where's Will?" Her voice sounded frantic.

Eugene was shaking his head. "Did he not come home?"

"No, Eugene. No!"

"Calm down, Annie. You know he didn't go far. As a matter of fact, he's probably hiding out in the cave. Did you all think to look below the house?"

Suddenly, Annie felt a wave of relief wash over her as Eugene took hold of her arm and started walking her back toward the house. Before they reached the corral, Eugene left her and said he'd start through the passageway. "You go through the house, and I'll meet you in the cave." She couldn't help but notice how tired her husband looked.

Annie was standing in the cave with Rachel and Jake when Eugene appeared through the passageway. Everyone but Jake was holding a lantern.

"Eugene?" Annie beseeched her husband as if her pleading would somehow produce their son.

"He's not in the cave?" Eugene asked in surprise.

Tears spilled out of Annie's eyes. "No," she breathed softly. "What do we do now?"

Eugene let out a deep sigh. "I'll go back out to look for him."

Rachel stepped forward then. "Eugene, come upstairs and let me give you some supper. You need to eat and rest a while."

He nodded his head wearily and followed the rest of the family upstairs.

Eating was as difficult for Eugene as it had been for the women. He took a few small bites but couldn't seem to force himself to consume the food Rachel had put in front of him. All he could think about was finding his son.

Jake was sitting in Annie's lap at the table, and his eyelids were growing heavy. He leaned his head back against his mother's breast and soon was fast asleep. Eugene's eyes held Annie's without wavering. He had no words to offer, but he committed all the love that he had for her with his steady gaze.

Rachel went into her room to turn down the bed. She would let Jake sleep with her tonight—not that sleep would come easily. Eugene stood and came around the table to take his youngest son into his arms.

"Hey, Jakie." He spoke softly into his son's ear. "Buddy, we gotta go to the outhouse before you get in the bed." Jake came around in his daddy's arms, giving him a sleepy smile. Eugene disappeared through the door with Jake's arms wrapped around his neck.

After tucking her little fella safely into Rachel's bed, Annie stepped out onto the dark porch with her husband. He instantly wrapped her in his arms and held her close. "The Lord's given us a hunter's moon tonight."

"Let me go with you," she pleaded.

"Annie, you need to stay with Mama and Jake. I know this area like the back of my hand. I used to hunt these woods and hills at night when I was growing up."

Annie's body started shaking. "I can't stand the thought of Will being out there alone. I don't know what I'll do if anything happens to him."

Eugene held Annie away from him and looked deeply into her eyes. "He's okay, I know he is—and I'll find him." Taking her left hand, he brought it to his lips, bandage and all, and Annie watched as he disappeared into the shadowy night.

Chapter 10

"Mama?" Eugene stuck his head in the door of Rachel's bedroom in the early morning gloom. He noticed Jake asleep under the covers, but the two women were lying on top of the bed still dressed in the clothes they'd been wearing the night before. Annie didn't stir.

Moving into the reading room, Eugene dropped wearily onto the couch. Rachel lit the lantern and sat down beside her son regarding him with deep concern.

"Did you find any sign of our boy?"

"Nothing, Mama. I trained as a scout in the war, but I couldn't even find the slightest trace of him."

With elbows on his knees, Eugene slumped forward and put his head in his hands. Rachel moved close to her son and settled her arm around his shoulders. He was reminded of his childhood as she moved her hand through his dark hair and rubbed the tightness out of his neck. He fought a tremendous desire to fall apart in her arms, but he simply couldn't afford himself that luxury.

Slowly, Eugene sat up and held his mama's gaze. "I'm going for the sheriff at sunup."

Rachel dropped her hand from his shoulder and stiffened her back. "What if it's still Sheriff Boyd?"

"Then it's still Sheriff Boyd," he replied soberly. "At this point, we need all the help we can get. I'm going to insist they bring the dogs."

Rachel nodded as a tear slipped down her cheek. "Eugene, there's nothing you can do until daylight. Why don't you take off your boots and lie down a while?"

Dog-tired and feeling defeated, Eugene rose to his feet and went into the other room. Moments later, he emerged, barefooted, wearing a clean set of clothes. He needed to be with his wife at least for a little while.

Annie lay on her side facing Jake, who was sleeping soundly on his back in the middle of the bed. Eugene pressed up close behind her and wrapped his arm around her waist. Annie's first reaction was to press her body closer to his, until she abruptly awoke and started to sit up. Eugene pulled her tighter and forced her to lie still.

"Eugene, please tell me you have him," she pleaded.

A deep breath escaped Eugene's mouth. "Not yet, sweetheart."

The mournful cry that emanated from his wife was almost more than Eugene could bear. Her shoulders started shaking with one sob after another.

Eugene turned Annie toward him and pulled her into his chest. Neither of them spoke for a very long time. Finally, Jake turned to his mother and nestled up close behind her as Eugene included him in his embrace.

Later on that morning, Annie felt Jake pull away from her; she turned her head slightly to watch Rachel leading him from the room. Faint light was edging through the window, giving her a clearer picture of her sleeping husband. She stared at him as he breathed deeply, his features at long last devoid of all tension. Eugene was so exhausted she hated to wake him. Something in the look on his face took her back in time to their very first meeting at the horse auction in Lexington. A smile caressed her lips as she remembered how awkward he had been at trying to make conversation. But when he had shared the story of how he saved his beautiful stallion's life at birth, Annie was not only taken with the horse, but she was taken with Eugene as well. They had only been sixteen at the time.

A dreadful anxiety clutched at her very core as Annie's thoughts were drawn back to their precious son. "Eugene," she whispered. He didn't move. A little louder this time, she said his name and nudged his chest with her bandaged hand.

Blinking through the haze, Eugene finally raised his head and fully opened his eyes. The worried look returned to his face and he sat straight up on the bed.

"What time is it?"

Annie sat up too, as she answered, "I don't know, but the sun is just coming up."

Dropping his feet to the floor, Eugene quickly told Annie of his plans to go into town and report Will's disappearance to the sheriff.

"I'm going with you. I have to do *something, anything* to find Will."

There was no argument from Eugene. "I want you with me. I can't do this alone anymore."

After a brief time of prayer with Rachel, Annie and Eugene kissed Jake and told him not to worry. All four stepped outside and called Will's name loudly, then strained their ears in hopes of hearing his voice. Only the high-pitched *purdy, purdy, purdy* of the cardinals in a nearby bush answered their call.

Rachel hugged her son and daughter-in-law and reassured them that they would be covered in prayer. "Hopefully, you'll come home to a tired and repentant little boy." She watched them drive away with a lingering knot in her throat.

***

"How may I help you?" The clerk behind the desk at the Clark County Courthouse had just put down her steaming hot cup of coffee and smiled broadly at the young couple standing in front of her. Her bobbed, gray hair and precise movements gave her an air of efficiency.

Eugene answered first. "We need to report our son missing."

"He's only eight years old," Annie added frantically.

With prompting from the clerk, Eugene began to tell the story of Will's disappearance into the woods on their farm. "We haven't seen him since eleven o'clock yesterday morning."

The clerk took notes and asked several more pertinent questions, then instructed Annie and Eugene to have a seat on the wooden bench by the wall. She disappeared into the sheriff's office carrying her notes and her coffee. After what seemed like an eternity, the clerk came through the door and told them Sheriff Boyd would now see them.

The mention of the name *Boyd* sent a charge through Eugene's chest, but he resolutely clinched his jaw and hurried into the office, Annie close on his heels. Eugene was surprised to see an older, gray-haired man sitting behind the desk, head down, reading the clerk's notes.

"Have a seat." The sheriff had yet to look up, so Eugene and Annie took the two chairs facing his desk.

Still with his eyes on the paperwork the sheriff asked, "Do you think your son is at a friend's house, maybe decided to sleep over and didn't tell ya?"

"No sir, he doesn't have any friends in the area."

The sheriff then read the name on the top of the paper out loud—very slowly, eyes narrowed. "Eugene Wyatt." He looked up and stared straight into Eugene's eyes. "That name sounds familiar. Do I know you?"

Eugene's first impulse was to lie to the man he now recognized from his youth. But he had no time for that. "Sheriff, you may remember me as Louis Tillman's stepson."

A slow smile played on the sheriff's lips. He leaned back in his swivel chair, nodding his head. "Now I remember you. Did you ever make it to Camp Travis?"

"Sir, I made it all the way to France."

Annie had heard enough and rose to her feet in front of the sheriff's desk. "He risked his life for your freedom and for mine. Now we're asking you to help *us*, Sheriff!"

Eugene was surprised by his wife's outburst, but even more surprised to watch the sheriff's expression change to one of concern.

"Carl, get in here," the sheriff yelled over his shoulder. As soon as the young man entered the office, Sheriff Boyd introduced Annie and Eugene to his deputy, Carl Walker then said, "We're gonna take a ride out to the Wyatt's farm and look for their son."

Eugene immediately stood up. "We need dogs. I was a scout in France, and I've searched everywhere without finding a trace."

Deputy Walker looked at the sheriff for his permission, then left the office to call for Ernest Taggert and his bloodhounds. Eugene and Annie were kept anxiously waiting another half hour until everyone was assembled and the dogs had arrived.

Once on the farm, Annie ran into the house to get one of Will's recently worn shirts. As soon as Mr. Taggert's bloodhounds got a good scent, they began to strain and pull at their leather leashes.

Sheriff Boyd barked, "Turn 'em loose, Ernest."

The hounds took off across the pasture like a shot out of a cannon, barking and sniffing. Instantly, they picked up Will's scent at the pond and headed for the woods at the other end of the pasture.

Eugene and Annie joined the sheriff, along with three deputies and Ernest Taggert. As they entered the woods, they followed the sounds of the dogs down to the stream. The hounds had already picked up Will's scent again and were heading down a trail along the water's edge.

Eugene was surprised at how far his son had wandered. The search party had already been walking for half an hour on the meandering trail next to the stream.

Mr. Taggert was no young man. He reached into his overalls, pulling out a bandana to wipe the sweat from his brow. Suddenly, he threw his hand into the air and waved the bandana for everyone to halt.

"Ya hear that? The girls are on ta somethin'."

It was an eerie sound, almost like a melodious whine echoing through the trees.

"How far away, Ernest?" Sheriff Boyd was also wiping sweat from his forehead with the sleeve of his shirt.

"Not more'n a quarter mile, I reckon."

Eugene took off running with Annie close behind. Two of the sheriff's deputies stayed with them while the older men walked briskly behind. Coming out into a clearing, Eugene noticed the two hounds standing close to the edge of the river. This was the spot where the stream emptied into the Kentucky River.

No one spoke until Mr. Taggert came onto the scene.

"This'd be where he went in." The statement was made with such insensitivity Eugene reached for Annie to steady her.

Impossible! The scene before them was horrifying. The river was a choppy, brown monster. No one could survive going into that savage brew.

Annie's eyes were wild with fright. "What do you mean this is where he went in? Will did *not* go into that river!"

"Ma'am," Mr. Taggert must have realized how he'd sounded before, and softly said, "I'm sorry, but the trail ends right here. He didn't go nowhere else but the river."

Annie wiggled away from Eugene and steadied herself on a nearby tree— wounded hands gripping the trunk, forehead against the rough bark. "Oh God, please, no. Please don't let it be true—please!" Tears of anguish gushed down her cheeks as she pictured Will trying to survive in that raging beast.

Eugene stood by helpless, on all accounts. If he could jump in that river and somehow rescue his son, he would do it right now. And he would give anything to be able to bring an ounce of comfort to his wife. But as it was, he could barely keep from crumpling into a heap right there on the bank and start bawling. He felt like his life was falling completely apart. Eugene was well acquainted with pain and loss, but never before had he felt the unbearable agony of losing a son.

One of the sheriff's deputies informed the gathering about the water being released from the dam yesterday. "The river's been really low the past couple of weeks. They just opened the floodgates yesterday at noon."

Eugene calculated the time it would've taken Will to make his way down to the river. It would've been raging by the time he got to this point.

The exhausted search party made their way back to the farmhouse, and Mr. Taggert caged the bloodhounds in the back of his truck. Rachel had been trying to keep Jake occupied on the porch for the last couple of hours, hoping to catch a glimpse of her *entire* family walking together across the pasture. She now descended the steps of the porch looking for signs of hope on their faces. There were none. One look at her daughter-in-law's expression communicated everything she had been dreading. Without hesitation, Rachel enveloped her sweet Annie into a loving embrace and held her tightly. Annie began to sob uncontrollably, clinging to Rachel as if she were her only lifeline. Rachel's heart burst into a thousand tiny pieces, and tears flooded her cheeks as Annie's anguish became her own.

Eugene stepped to the porch and lifted Jake into his arms.

"Daddy, where's Will?"

"Jakie, we don't know yet. But don't you worry, God knows where he is, and that's all that matters right now." Eugene set his son down and looked him in the eyes. "Momma will be okay; she just needs to cry with Gramma right now. I'm going with the sheriff for a little while, and I'll be back as soon as I can."

Despite the tears in Jake's eyes, he bravely replied, "Okay, Daddy."

Eugene kissed him, then turned to his wife and mother. "I'll be back soon. I love you both."

Annie reached up and grabbed the front of his shirt, pulling him to her and Rachel. He wrapped his arms around them both for only a moment then gently broke free of her grasp. Neither of the women thought to ask where he was going or why.

Chapter 11

Time meant nothing to Annie as she sat against Franklin's giant oak tree with her knees drawn to her chest. She was exhausted from all of her crying and had wandered outside to be alone. Eugene had been gone a long time, long enough for her to fear the sheriff had taken him away again. What would they do then?

"Oh sovereign Lord . . ." she breathed the words out loud, but nothing else came to mind. What could she possibly say? She had already beseeched Him for hours on behalf of Will—and had lost him anyway to a raging torrent. She knew her faith would never waver, but she wondered how God would ever be able to relieve her of such immense pain.

Memories of Will began to flood her mind—holding him in her arms at birth, hearing him say "momma" for the first time, cheering as he took his first steps, teaching him to ride a horse. And *fishing* with him. "Oh God, how could losing a fish have caused our family so much grief?" Annie listened intently for an ethereal answer, but all she received was a gut-wrenching feeling of despair.

Still deep in her own thoughts, Annie didn't hear the car door slam on the other side of the pasture, nor did she hear the commotion playing out near the house. She was oblivious to the shouts of her mother-in-law and youngest son. She didn't even hear her husband calling her name. But one voice began to drift into her consciousness—unearthly at first, until it grew louder and closer. The voice was calling "Momma! Momma!" A cruel joke she thought, until she finally broke free from her pensive bonds.

In a flash, Annie jumped to her feet, squinting her eyes in disbelief. Someone was running across the field toward her, and she instantly broke into an all-out sprint to meet him. When their two bodies collided, Annie thought she would die from sheer exuberance.

"Momma, I'm sorry . . . I didn't really mean it . . ." Will's arms came up around Annie's neck, and she picked him up off the ground nearly crushing his ribs. "I love you, Momma . . . I really *do* love you!"

"And I love you with all my heart, William Wyatt!"

Soon Eugene, Rachel, and Jake joined the two in the middle of the pasture, laughing and celebrating, sharing hugs, and letting out an occasional whoop. Uninhibited tears of joy adorned each face, flowing freely out of gratitude to the One who had brought Will home.

Annie eventually reached for her husband and kissed him hard on the mouth. "Where on earth did you find him?"

"I talked the sheriff into letting the dogs search the opposite bank. We crossed the bridge two miles downriver and came back up the other side."

In amazement, she turned to Will and asked, "How could you possibly have crossed that water?"

"Momma, when I crossed the river it was only up to my knees. But right after I got to the other side the water came up so fast I had to climb the rocks. I couldn't get back across."

Will moved in between his parents and held both of their hands as they all started walking back toward the house.

"Daddy told me when we go hunting, that if I ever get separated from him to just stay put. He said he'd find me no matter what . . . so that's what I did."

"Oh sweetheart," Annie responded, "I'm sorry it took us so long to find you. Were you scared?"

Will looked up at his daddy, almost as if he were asking permission to admit to being frightened out of his wits. Eugene grinned at his son and nodded his approval.

"I was *so* scared, Momma. I thought I was gonna die."

Annie didn't dare tell him that she thought he already had.

When they made it back to the house, Sheriff Boyd was the only person still left on the property. He had been sitting on the edge of the porch watching the joyous scene unfold. Eugene couldn't quite read the look on his face and began to feel a bit uneasy. As Annie and Rachel approached, they offered their thanks for helping bring Will home. Sheriff Boyd tipped his hat and murmured, "My pleasure."

Will told his momma and gramma that he was nearly starving to death, so they took him inside to feed him, Jake trailing in their wake. The sheriff, however, didn't move from his position on the porch. Eugene stepped forward and offered him a hand of thanks but felt awkward when the sheriff didn't move to take it.

"Eugene, I've been trying to put two and two together. Maybe you can help me out here."

Eugene let his hand drop and moved to the side of the sheriff so he could lean against the porch. He had a feeling this was not going to be a good conversation.

"What is that older woman in there to you?"

Suddenly, the memory of sitting in the dark, hiding from this man nearly twenty years ago came rushing over Eugene. Worse yet was his recollection of trying to protect his folks' identity when he had been forced into the army by the sheriff and his stepfather. Eugene's senses now were on heightened alert. He would still do anything in his power to protect Rachel.

"Sheriff Boyd, I don't mean to be disrespectful, but why do you want to know?"

The sheriff removed his hat and twirled it in his hands absentmindedly. "I came out here to this farm a long time ago, and that woman in there was living with a darkie. Said they'd been married for a long time." Sheriff Boyd cast a sinister eye toward Eugene. "Come to think of it, I was lookin' for *you* at the time."

Eugene's heart pounded wildly in his chest, but he didn't respond to the sheriff's statement. He just looked out at the pasture and waited to see where this was going.

"So why all of a sudden do I come out here and see this house fixed up a bit and you and your family livin' with *her*?"

Lord, please give me the right words. Eugene swallowed the lump in his throat, then made the decision to tell the sheriff about Louis Tillman's abuse and the night he ran away. He even told the sheriff about his adoption into Franklin and Rachel's family.

Sheriff Boyd's face remained devoid of all emotion as Eugene finished his explanation. He twirled his hat a couple of more times, then plopped it back on top of his head. His next words sent a shiver up Eugene's spine.

"Louis Tillman got hit by a car last year in town. Stepped off a curb and never saw it comin'. Killed him instantly." Rising to his feet, the sheriff looked squarely at Eugene. "Just thought you oughtta know."

Slowly the sheriff turned and made his way out to his car. He opened the door and rested his arm on top of the doorframe. Unexpectedly, his weathered features softened and Eugene thought he was about to receive an apology for the past. Instead, Sheriff Boyd stared out into the pasture for a long moment, then looked back at Eugene one last time. "I'm glad we found yer boy," he said quietly.

Eugene released a deep breath and let his shoulders relax a bit. "Thank you, sir. And thank you for telling me about . . ." His voice trailed off, unable to speak his stepfather's name.

The old man nodded unobtrusively, then climbed into his automobile and drove away.

That night, Eugene sat on the top step of the porch with his back against the post, one leg bent at the knee, the other settled on the next step. Looking up at the full moon he felt a deep sense of satisfaction knowing his eldest son had been found unharmed. He owed the Lord a great debt of gratitude. It was purely by God's grace that Will had not been swept up in the violent waters.

Earlier that evening, he had helped Annie bathe both of their rascals and get them into bed. Will had been so tuckered out he was nearly asleep before his head hit the pillow. All four family members had prayed out loud together, praising God in their own way for Will's safe return. Watching him put his arms around Annie's neck and ask for her forgiveness was a very emotional moment. Eugene suspected his wife and son's relationship would change a bit after such a traumatic episode. The Lord always had a way of bringing good out of even the worst of circumstances.

A soft light flooded the porch as Annie opened the door and stepped outside. Without hesitation, she sat down between her husband's legs and leaned back into his chest. He kissed the side of her neck and wrapped his arms around her.

"Am I intruding?" Rachel asked, as she followed Annie outside.

Eugene grinned and said, "Not at all, Mama. As a matter of fact, I have something to tell both of you."

Rachel eased into a nearby chair on the porch and waited for him to say what was on his mind.

"The sheriff told me something about Louis this afternoon." Eugene didn't quite know how to say it without sounding relieved or insensitive. When he hesitated, Annie turned in his arms and gave him a curious look. He didn't want to be looking at either of them when he said what he had to say, so he gently pulled her back up against his chest.

"Sheriff Boyd said Louis was hit by a car last year in Winchester." Rachel let out a muffled gasp before Eugene added, "He was killed instantly."

The two women were silent for a very long time. Neither seemed to want to be the first to speak. Finally, Rachel broke into their thoughts. "I guess we can truly put the past behind us now."

Eugene nodded and quietly said, "It's finally over."

Annie and Rachel visibly relaxed after taking in his last words. Eugene knew he should relax too, as far as his past with Louis was concerned, but there was still something gnawing at his gut. He had told Sheriff Boyd the truth about his past, and somehow that just wasn't sitting well. He took in a slow, deep breath, determined to push it aside for now and focus on the blessing of recovering his eldest son.

A pale, orange moon slid higher in the sky, and Eugene leaned his head back against the rough porch railing. He felt relieved to finally leave the horrible deeds of his boyhood behind—for good. He grinned, enjoying the delightful chatter of his wife and mother as they observed the gorgeous moon. And when it was time to turn in for the night, Eugene followed the women inside, totally underestimating the size of the hole in his heart bored out by a malicious stepfather.

The next morning, Rachel silently opened the door to the bedroom next to hers. The sun had come up hours ago, and still there were no sounds of her family stirring. She couldn't help but stand motionless for several long minutes and survey the scene before her. All of the mattresses had been drug from their frames into the middle of the floor and pushed together to form one giant bed. The boys were both asleep between their parents—Will wrapped in his mother's arms. It was a poignant image that Rachel would carry with her the rest of her life.

"Thank you, Father," she breathed, then quietly closed the door.

***

During the course of their three remaining days on the farm, Will's plan of punishment was made crystal clear. Two full hours of each morning would be spent chopping wood, his afternoons would be filled with chores around the house, and worse yet, he would not be allowed to go hunting with his dad and brother. That was the hardest one of all to swallow. He loved hunting with his daddy—it gnawed at him the morning he watched the two head out on their expedition without him. But he would never let anyone know how much it bothered him. Deep down, Will knew he deserved his punishment. He had a good heart, but he also possessed a healthy dose of pride that he would struggle with for a long time to come.

***

The smells radiating from the kitchen were heavenly. It was the family's last night at the lodge, and Rachel decided they should celebrate with her legendary chicken and dumplings. She and Annie had gone into town early that morning to buy all of the necessary ingredients. Will set the table as part of his household chores for the day while Annie mashed the potatoes. Eugene and Jake wandered in off the porch with mouths watering.

"Eugene, when supper is over, there's something I want to show you." Rachel had turned from the stove holding the large pot of dumplings.

"Mama, do you need help with that?" Eugene came to her side to see if he could take it from her, but she told him she had it situated just right and would be able to get it to the table.

After the blessing, everyone started digging in to the meal, and Eugene finally asked, "What do you want to show me, Mama?"

"It's down in the cave. There's something in the cedar chest we need to find."

Instantly Will spoke up, "Can I go down there with you, Gramma?"

"Yeah, me too!" Jake chimed in.

"Not tonight boys. Your daddy and I have something we need to discuss. Maybe tomorrow we can go back down and make sure everything's all right before we leave." Rachel smiled at both of her grandsons, hoping that would hold them off for tonight.

Eugene was curious about the conversation to come and yearned for just a hint. However, he could tell that his mama wanted to have a private talk with him, so he reluctantly let it go.

When everyone had eaten their fill, Annie rose from the table. "Mama, I've got cleanup duty tonight. The boys and I will take care of everything." She reached over and gave Rachel's shoulder a squeeze. "Go on down with Eugene and have your talk."

Rachel covered Annie's hand lovingly. "Thank you, darlin'. I believe I'll take you up on that offer."

Grinning at his wife, Eugene said, "Have fun!"

The musty odor of cedar escaped into the air as soon as Eugene lifted the lid on the old chest. There were still a few pieces of furniture left in the cave that would probably always remain—the weathered, brown chest was one of them. Growing up, Eugene had known better than to mess with the contents of the cedar chest. But a few times he had peeked in just to see all the money inside. After every horse auction, Franklin would stash the money away to be used when needed. But now, all that remained were a few old papers.

"Mama, is there a particular paper you're looking for?"

Rachel had set her lantern on the table and joined her son at the chest. "Let's put them all out on the table. That way we can go through them together. There's one in particular I need to give you."

Eugene couldn't imagine what she wanted him to have, but he was quite eager to find out. He held his lantern over the chest and gathered the few yellowed papers at the bottom, then carried them over to the table. Both lanterns provided just enough light to read the fragile documents.

Rachel smiled when she saw the paper on top. It was a certificate of freedom given to Franklin at the age of thirteen, signed by her father, the plantation owner, Samuel Hawkins of Lexington. Another certificate of freedom for Franklin's father, Isaiah, lay underneath. The next paper caused an unexpected catch in her throat, and Rachel smoothed her hand across the document before holding it up to the light.

"Eugene, this is the paper your papa and I were given after we were married on the plantation." Rachel's eyes grew misty as she thought about the man she had loved so deeply. She wondered if she would ever get over the heartache of losing him.

Eugene strained to read the faded words and remembered the day his folks had shared their story with him. It had been a beautiful morning of listening to Franklin and Rachel reminisce over their past—a morning he would never forget.

The next document was the one that Rachel had been looking for. "This is it, Eugene. This is the paper Samuel Hawkins gave Franklin's father—it's the deed to this property." She held it out to him. "I want you to have this."

"Mama, I appreciate the gesture, but I think you need to hang on to all of these important papers. I can't believe we left them down here all these years."

"I know. I should've taken them with me when I moved away. But I want you to have them now. I have a reason for giving them to you, especially now."

Eugene cocked his head curiously, but waited for Rachel to explain her purpose.

"Times are hard, Son. I don't want you to feel like you have to hold on to this farm. If you think you need to sell it, then please don't let me hold you back. I'm giving all of it to you now . . ." She hesitated for just a moment, then added, "while I'm still alive."

"Mama, is there something you're not telling me?" Eugene's face was creased with worry. "You're not sick or something, are you?"

Rachel let out a soft laugh, then reached for Eugene's hand. "Darlin', I'm not sick—at least not that I'm aware of. But I fear if something happens to me, you'll lose this farm. We have no papers proving your adoption into our family, and legally, your last name is Wyatt." She let go of his hand and added, "When we get back to Louisville I want to transfer the deed into your name while I can still prove ownership of the farm."

Rachel carefully gathered the documents together and went on to say, "You need to keep all of these papers, Eugene. And someday, we'll know when the time is right to do something about this place."

Eugene leaned over and kissed his mama on the cheek then held her in a sweet embrace. Rachel wrapped her arms around her son, grateful as always, to have him in her life.

When Rachel and Eugene returned from the cave, they noticed the dishes had been washed and the table cleaned, but saw no sign of Annie and the boys. Soon they heard laughter coming from outside, so they stepped onto the porch just in time to witness the melee going on around the pump.

"Catch her, Will!"

Jake was chasing his momma with a bowl full of water, but he couldn't quite get close enough to throw it on her. It wouldn't make much difference; she was soaking wet from head to toe—all three of them were. Annie was holding them at bay with a wet kitchen towel that she snapped menacingly if either of the boys came near.

Finally, Will got her trapped next to the pump and was able to get a hold around her waist so Jake could get in close. Right when he launched the water from the bowl, Annie grabbed Will by the shoulders and turned him into the downpour. Will took the brunt of it, but Annie got a face full. After sputtering water from her mouth, she looked at Will who was holding his arms away from his body, letting the water roll off his chest. The same thought crossed their minds simultaneously, and both of them yelled in unison, "Get him!"

It didn't take long for them to catch Jake and carry him to the pump. Annie held him under the spout while Will worked the handle up and down. Jake shrieked and laughed as cold water poured over him *and* his momma.

Eugene yanked his shirt over his head and joined in the fray. He whisked Will into his arms and held him under the spout while Annie and Jake pumped the handle enthusiastically. Rachel stood on the porch cheering them on until Jake filled his bowl again and headed her way.

"Jakie, no!" Eugene tried to cut him off at the pass, but it was too late. Rachel got hit with the deluge right at her midriff.

Everyone froze—no one dared to even breathe.

Rachel put her hands on her hips and exclaimed, "Young man, you're in a heap of trouble." She descended the steps, snatched the bowl right out of Jake's hand, and headed for the pump. Looking at the rest of the family she announced, "If you'll catch him, I'll soak him!"

The chase was on. And by the time the sun started to disappear behind the trees, Rachel was thoroughly drenched, exactly like the rest of her family.

Chapter 12

Winter 1932

Times were hard. Many families in the city of Louisville were barely able to feed their families, but for those who could work, there were enough factories in the city to keep most of the population from going under. Newspapers were calling it the Great Depression—it was hard to find anyone who hadn't been affected in some way.

While Eugene didn't raise his cattle for slaughter, he had already butchered two steer from his herd this year to help feed his family. He felt blessed for being able to care for his wife and sons and mother, but there were people in the Oak Hill congregation going hungry. On top of that, this winter season was colder than normal, and many of the brethren couldn't even afford to heat their own households.

Max Lawson owned one of the local butcher shops and also happened to be a member of the Oak Hill Church. After worship on Sunday, he made a special trip to his shop to open up for only one customer. That's when Eugene came by to pick up the packaged meat to distribute it to people in need, particularly those in their church who were nearly starving. Only a small portion from this steer would go toward his own family; there were too many brothers and sisters who needed it more.

Stopping the car in front of the Bascombe house, Eugene turned around to face his boys in the backseat. "Sometimes it's hard for people to accept a handout," he said. "But that's not what this is. The Lord wants us to share what we have with those in need."

"Kinda like Christmas?" Jake interjected eagerly.

"In a way, yes. The whole reason for giving at Christmas is to celebrate the best gift of all—God's only Son. And that's the reason why we're doing this now. It's not because we have to; it's because we want to and because we love the Bascombes."

Everyone in the car now turned his attention toward the house. The porch roof had caved through in the middle, and the floorboards were sagging. It was more of a shack than a house among a long row of shacks. Eugene wished he had enough to give to everyone living on the Bascombe's street.

As soon as they knocked on the flimsy door, Earl opened it a bit at first, then threw it wide open to welcome Eugene and his family inside. They all kept their coats on, just like the Bascombe family. It was nearly as cold inside as it was outside.

"God bless ya, Eugene. This'll go a long ways to feedin' my young'uns." Earl had accepted the large package of meat and laid it on the table in the kitchen.

Eugene put his hand firmly on Earl's shoulder. He could feel the bones sticking out, even through the man's coat. "Earl, someday maybe my family and I will be in need, and you'll be able to help us."

Earl had lined up his children in the house, all six of them, and asked them to thank Mr. Wyatt for his generosity. One by one, with big brown eyes, each one of Earl's children respectfully thanked Eugene for the meat he had provided. As soon as that was taken care of, Will and Jake asked the two oldest boys to play outside with them despite the chilling wind.

In the back room, Annie and Rachel helped Earl's wife, Janet, lay out a simple quilt on the bed. "Oh my, it's beautiful." Janet's thin fingers gently swept over the quilt. She looked up at Rachel with tears in her eyes. "My three babies sleep in this bed. They need this cover bad." She reached out for Rachel's hand, but Rachel took Janet into her arms and held her close.

"You and your family are in our prayers," Rachel breathed softly. "God will provide all your needs."

Janet stepped back and looked first at Rachel then to Annie. "Well, I'd say you'ns are God's servants, and I thank ya from the bottom of my heart."

Annie put her arm around Janet's shoulders as they walked out of the room and joined the men.

"We need to be on our way," Eugene said as the women came in. "Earl, if you and Janet need anything, you let us know."

"And same goes for you," Earl said with a smile, as he extended his cold hand to Eugene, thanking him again for the kindness shown to his family.

The rest of the afternoon, the Wyatt family drove from house to house sharing God's blessings with those who had fallen on hard times—white and black folks alike.

That night after eating Rachel's delicious potato soup, the entire family cleared the table so they could play a game of Wahoo. Eugene had seen the game the last time he was in Lexington. Instead of buying it, he had made his own Wahoo board and used some of Will and Jake's marbles for game pieces. The only thing he had to purchase was a set of dice.

Annie screamed when Jake overtook one of her marbles on the board. He laughed as he put it back in its starting position.

"Atta boy," Eugene said, grinning at his son. "She's been mean to me all night."

"Someone better watch out for Will," Rachel declared. "He's about to get his last marble home."

"Shh, Gramma. No one's paying attention to me."

Rachel giggled and winked at her grandson.

It was Eugene's turn, and he had a chance to knock Will's marble off the board but just missed. The whole family groaned. Will kept trying to roll just the right number so he could get his last marble into the safety zone and win the game, but he just couldn't seem to roll a three. Finally, Annie came around the board and got within striking distance. The longer Will rolled, the more frustrated he became. Annie rolled a six, which not only gave her an extra turn, but it also put her within two spaces of Will's marble. He held his breath as he watched his mother roll, then let out an angry yell when the die landed on two.

"Will," Eugene cautioned. "Calm down, it's just a game."

Annie half grinned at her son. "Sorry about that, buddy. You still have a shot at winning." She could see by his red face that all the fun had gone out of the game. And by the time Annie got all of her marbles home first, Will was fit to be tied. He picked up the die and threw it all the way across the kitchen, then knocked the marbles off the board, sending them rolling all over the table and floor.

Eugene immediately got out of his chair and came around to his son. "Pick up all the marbles right now. You are not going to act like this over a game." Will bowed up to his dad. He crossed his arms over his chest and refused to move.

"I mean it, Will. You have to the count of three to start picking up those marbles."

"I'll get 'em, Daddy." Jake had such a concerned look on his face, willing to do anything to keep his older brother out of trouble.

"No, Jake. This is not your responsibility." Eugene turned to Will. "One . . . two . . . three."

Will stubbornly held his ground.

Eugene reached underneath his arm and pulled him up from the chair. "Let's go," he said. Then he turned back to the rest of the family. "Leave everything where it is. Will's going to clean it up after we have a little talk."

Annie watched Eugene and Will leave the kitchen and, moments later, heard the bedroom door shut. "He needs to be spanked," she said.

Rachel looked like she was about to say something to Annie but remained silent. Instead, she rose from the table and started putting away the supper dishes that had been previously washed and dried.

"Jake," Annie said. "Go get cleaned up. You've got school in the morning, and we need to get you into bed."

"Okay, Momma."

Annie watched her younger son head down the hall to the bathroom. He was so much like her husband, not only in looks, but in demeanor as well. Jake shared his father's dark hair and handsome features, but with one difference; he had his grandfather Nathan's deep blue eyes. Jake had his moments, but for the most part, he had an even-keel temperament, combined with a positive outlook on life. He could melt Annie's heart with just a smile.

Rachel came back to the table and sat down across from her daughter-in-law. Annie let out a deep sigh. "What are we going to do with him, Mama?"

"Annie, darlin', just keep putting him before the Lord. He'll give you all the wisdom you need." Rachel paused for a moment then added quietly, "Eugene will never be able to spank him. You know that, don't you?"

Annie nodded her head. "I know. But I fear that's what Will needs the most."

"If you could've seen the shape Eugene was in when he made it to our farm. He was only a year older than Will is right now. I just can't imagine what he must have endured at the hands of his stepfather. God saved Eugene; He'll save Will too . . . just in a different way."

At that moment, the women heard the bedroom door open, and Will came plodding into the kitchen. Without a word, he picked up the die and put it in the jar, then started picking up the marbles that had scattered all over the floor. Without making eye contact with his mother or grandmother, he plopped the jar down on the table and headed back down the hall to get ready for bed.

Annie got up to go help Eugene tuck in the boys. Rachel's gentle words caused her to pause momentarily in the doorway.

"He has a good heart, you know. I can see it."

Without turning around, Annie urged her mother-in-law, "Please keep reminding me of that." Then she headed down the hall.

Later, lying in bed beside her husband, Annie thought about her son. No, she *worried* about her son. At least Will had allowed her to kiss him before he had gotten into bed tonight, but she could still feel his resentment toward her. How could a ten-year-old have that much anger inside of him? A tear slid from her eye onto the pillow. She hadn't meant to, but before Annie could stop herself, she was crying.

When she started sniffling, Eugene rose up on one elbow and looked at his wife who was facing away from him. "Are you okay?" he asked quietly.

The only answer he received was the sound of another sniffle.

Eugene reached out and tenderly caressed her shoulder and arm. He leaned in and kissed her neck, then wrapped his arm around her, holding her close. Annie intertwined her hand with his and brought it tightly to her chest. "I love you, Eugene."

"I love you, too, sweetheart," he whispered.

***

Claudia pulled her wool scarf a little tighter, burying her chin and mouth inside. The wind whistled mercilessly along the Louisville streets, sending a chill through every citizen braving the cold weather. Snow and ice still covered the roads and Nathan had cautioned Claudia about the dangerous conditions before she had left the farm to come into town. She had two reasons for driving into the city on this blustery December day. First of all, it was Miss Ruby's sixtieth birthday, and Claudia had baked her a pumpkin pie, and secondly, she needed to pick up some extra supplies at the grocer for her upcoming family Christmas dinner.

Driving onto Miss Ruby's street had proven to be impossible. The ice was so thick that Claudia had to leave her car a few blocks away and walk the distance to her friend's house. Now on her way back to the car, struggling against the wind, she wished she had thought to wear her boots. Even though she walked with her head down to ward off the biting chill, Claudia noticed a movement out of the corner of her eye. She watched briefly as a young black woman entered an old abandoned house across the street. The door was hanging off its hinges, and the woman had to step around it to get inside the house. Something in the back of Claudia's mind was troubled by what she saw, but the frigid wind compelled her to persevere toward her destination.

All the while, as Claudia shopped, she couldn't seem to escape the feeling that something wasn't right. She kept thinking about the old house with boarded-up windows and no heat. What kind of circumstances must that young woman be in to have entered such a house? Claudia simply couldn't let it go. After paying the bill, she loaded the trunk of her car with groceries, then headed back to Miss Ruby's neighborhood on foot.

The old house seemed a bit ominous as Claudia stood on the sidewalk observing how dark it looked inside. A nervous feeling took hold as she walked up to the front porch.

"Hello. Is anybody home?" Her voice shook a little, and not just because she was so cold.

Not sure if the porch would actually hold her, Claudia took one tentative step up, and then another. "Hello?" No answer. The sound of her voice echoed through the empty house.

Now standing firmly on the porch, Claudia leaned her head to the side trying to see past the broken down door. It was no use. The boarded-up windows left nothing but dark shadows inside.

"Is anyone in there? I'd like to talk to—"

A soft voice called out from behind the door. "What you want?"

Now that she thought about it, Claudia wasn't sure what she wanted. All she knew was that she had felt compelled to come back to this house and check on this woman. She timidly answered, "I just wanted to see if you're all right." There was a short silence, so Claudia continued. "It's awfully cold. Is this where you live?"

"Yes'm." Claudia detected a hint of fear in the young woman's voice. Her heart went out to her.

"May I come in?" Again, no answer came from behind the door, so she crept a little closer and said, "My name is Claudia. What's your name?"

Claudia heard a shuffling sound behind the door, and finally the young woman moved into view, but just barely. "My name's Mattie, ma'am."

"Mattie, are you here alone?"

"Yes'm."

"May I come in?" Claudia asked. "Just to get out of the wind?"

Mattie stepped back away from the door and gestured for Claudia to enter. Once inside, it took a few moments for her eyes to get used to the dim light. When they finally did, she noticed nothing but a couple of blankets piled in one corner of the room.

"Have you had anything to eat today, Mattie?"

"No, ma'am, not today." Mattie bowed her head as if she was embarrassed about her situation.

"What about yesterday? Did you eat then?"

Mattie's head stayed low as she shook it back and forth.

"You poor girl." Claudia looked around the room. "Where's your family, Mattie?"

"Ain't got no more family, Miss Claudia. My mama died givin' birth to me, and my papa succumb to scarlet fever back in October."

"I'm so sorry, Mattie. Is this where you and your papa were living?"

"No, ma'am. Our house was over on Sycamore Street. When papa passed away, some man just come along with his whole family and made me leave. This is where I been ever since." Mattie shook her head again. "Can't find no job. I been lookin' every day."

Claudia thought her heart was about to break into pieces. This young woman was starving. There was not a doubt in her mind that she couldn't just walk away and leave her here alone.

Convicted deeply by the Spirit, Claudia reached out and gently took hold of Mattie's arm. "Come with me, child. I know where you can get a job."

"Where's that, Miss Claudia?"

"At my house," she said firmly.

***

Later in the afternoon, Claudia tapped lightly on the bathroom door. "Is everything all right in there, Mattie?"

"Oh, yes'm. I'm so sorry, Miss Claudia. This water feel so warm, I just can't seem to get myself outta the tub."

Claudia laughed. "Take all the time you need, honey. I've laid some clothes out on the bed for you. I think they'll fit you just fine." Claudia knew they would hang on her a bit. The poor girl was nothing but skin and bones.

Several minutes passed before Claudia welcomed Mattie into her kitchen. "Come on in, honey. How do you feel?"

"Oh, Miss Claudia, I feel so warm and blessed!" Mattie's enthusiastic response brought a feeling of pure joy into Claudia's heart.

"What can I do to help ya, ma'am?"

"There's nothing to do right away. I've had a beef and vegetable soup simmering all day." Claudia gestured toward the table. "Why don't we sit down and get to know each other better."

Mattie took a seat at the table. She gratefully accepted a cup of hot tea and a warm biscuit from her new employer. "Thank ya, kindly. Do ya mind if I eat this now?"

"Please do," Claudia said, as she took a seat across the table. "How old are you, Mattie?"

"Twenty. And my real name is Matilda—Matilda Davis. But I never know'd my papa to call me anything but Mattie."

One thing was certain—Mattie wasn't shy. For the next half hour, Claudia had to ask very few questions; Mattie was ready to share her life freely. She had been living alone in that abandoned house for two months, scared to death that someone would discover her.

"'Cept I'm so thankful you was the one to find me." Mattie's smile was genuine and beautiful. "You is an angel, Miss Claudia, an angel from heaven above."

"Well," Claudia said as she reached across the table and squeezed Mattie's hand, "I was just thinking the same thing about you."

Much to Mattie's surprise, she was invited to eat in the dining room that night as a guest.

"Oh, no ma'am, I could never do such a thing as that. I can take my supper in the kitchen with Mr. Nathan's hired help."

Claudia thought for a moment, then said, "Well in that case, Mr. Nathan and I will join you in the kitchen tonight. We'll all get to know each other better."

And that's just what they did. It was a wonderful dinner party around the old oak table—Nathan and Claudia along with Mattie, Mike, Leroy, Charlie, and Devlin—wranglers, farmhands, and a housemaid, laughing and sharing stories as if they all belonged to the same family. The north wind howled outside, but light and warmth and love flooded the Harrison's kitchen throughout the evening.

Later as the two women washed and dried the dishes together, Mattie glanced over at Claudia through misty eyes. "Ain't it amazin' how God works to bring folks together?"

"Truly it is," Claudia replied. She contemplated how miserably cold and hungry Mattie must have been, living in that abandoned house. Mattie herself was an abandoned soul. It occurred to Claudia for the first time that this dear girl had never known what it was like to be held by her mother. Just the thought of it grieved her and brought a feeling of tenderness to her heart. Claudia took the dish from Mattie's hand and laid it on the counter. Then she reached out, took the young woman into her arms, and held her close to her breast.

Even though it seemed that God had rescued Mattie from her dire circumstances, His true plan was yet to be revealed. Neither woman had any way of knowing that God had brought an angel of mercy into Claudia's life at just the right time.

Chapter 13

Christmas 1932

The Wyatt family loved traditions. One of their all-time favorites was spending Christmas Eve with the entire family in the Harrisons' rambling farmhouse. There was plenty of room for everyone to sleep, and the meals were beyond compare. Anytime Claudia and Rachel combined their efforts in the same kitchen, the results were nothing short of spectacular.

Christmas Eve fell on a Saturday this year. Annie and Rachel drove over early that morning to help Claudia deliver food to some of the needy families in their church. From the time Annie was big enough to walk, she could remember carrying jars of preserved green beans, corn, and squash while following Claudia on her mission of love. This year, Mattie had spent nearly the entire week baking turkeys then packing them in ice to preserve them until Saturday morning.

"Mother, where's your list?" Annie had just put the last box of vegetable jars in the trunk of the car and came back into the kitchen to see if the other women were ready to leave.

Claudia looked panicked for a moment until she remembered she had left it in the pocket of her apron, which now hung on a wall peg by the stove. "It wouldn't do to lose that, would it?" She pulled it out and handed it to her daughter. "See what you think."

Annie recognized most of the names on the list, but there was one in particular she wasn't familiar with. "I'm not sure I know who the Butler family is," she said, glancing up from the list.

A knowing look transpired between Claudia and Mattie. After a brief pause, Claudia said, "Mattie, would you like to tell her about the Butlers?"

Mattie didn't hesitate to dive right in. "Miss Annie, that'd be the family that done drove me outta my own house. I figure they musta been awful desperate to take away somethin' that didn't belong to 'em. That man had a passel o' chil'uns to feed. Won't hurt me none to show 'em some Christmas kindness." She gave Claudia a broad smile. "'Specially since the Lord seen fit to give me somethin' even better."

Annie loved this girl. Her honest outlook on life was refreshing, and it was obvious how much Mattie meant to her mother. She had to laugh inwardly. It appeared that Claudia had finally found someone to keep her company in the kitchen.

That night, Will and Jake were in their pajamas, and everyone was enjoying the warmth of the roaring fire in the front room of the house.

"E-6," Eugene called out with confidence.

"Ha, you missed!" Nathan declared.

Will ran over to look at his grandfather's paper. Nathan grabbed him around the waist and pulled him onto his lap, even though Will's legs were so long, his feet were still on the floor. "I think I've got your daddy right where I want him." When Will started to say something, Nathan gave him a little squeeze. "Shh, we can't let him know where my submarine is hiding."

Nathan and Eugene often enjoyed a friendly game of Battleship, drawing out grids with a pencil, and hiding their five ships on a piece of paper. Each of the men had already sunk four ships. Now the race was on to discover where the last one was hidden.

"As soon as your game is finished, we need to hang our stockings," Claudia announced.

"It won't be long, Nana," Will declared. "Gramps just found Daddy's biggest ship."

"Don't rub it in," Eugene said, good-naturedly. After a few more minutes, he conceded the defeat to his father-in-law, and everyone joined Claudia at the fireplace.

Rachel had made a stocking for Eugene when he was growing up and had enjoyed making two more for Will and Jake when they were born. Annie and her parents had stockings too, and each member of the family took a turn hanging them in the designated order along the mantel.

"Okay, boys," Annie announced. "It's time for bed."

"Aw, Momma. Can't we stay up a little longer?" Will begged.

"Yeah, just a little longer . . . please?" Jake chimed in.

Nathan picked Jake up off the floor and kissed him on the cheek. "You'd better mind your momma. You don't want to find a lump of coal in your stocking tomorrow."

Jake threw his arms around his grandfather's neck for a brief moment, then wiggled out of his arms. "In that case, I'm goin' to bed right now!"

Everyone laughed and then thoroughly enjoyed the next few moments as Will and Jake gave their grandparents a goodnight hug and kiss.

Annie finally put her hands on their backs and nudged them toward the stairs. Eugene picked up the Bible and followed them to the room where the boys slept. Eugene and Annie always enjoyed this particular Christmas Eve tradition with their sons.

"Okay guys, hop in," Annie said, as she held the quilt back. Will hopped in first and settled the pillow behind his back against the headboard, then Jake followed, mirroring his brother's every move. The boys shared the same bed at Gramps and Nana's house. As soon as Will and Jake were settled under the quilt,

Annie sat down by Will, and Eugene sat down beside Jake. All four family members would be taking turns reading a portion of the story of Jesus' birth.

Jake asked his daddy, "Can I read first this year?"

Eugene looked over at Will. "Is that okay with you?"

Will nodded his head. "Uh huh, I'd like to read last this time."

Opening the Bible to Luke, chapter two, Eugene handed it to his youngest son and pointed to the passage. "You can start reading here and end right here."

Jake cleared his throat and scooted up a little higher in the bed. *"And it came to pass in those days that a decree went out from Caesar Augustus that all the world should be registered . . ."*[7]

A rich peace settled over the family as each one earnestly read the passage of scripture allotted to them. And when it finally got to Will, he read his portion with such passion that Annie was deeply moved.

". . . So it was, when the angels had gone away from them into heaven, that the shepherds said to one another, 'Let us now go to Bethlehem and see this thing that has come to pass, which the Lord has made known to us.' And they came with haste and found Mary and Joseph, and the Babe lying in a manger."[8]

When Will fell silent, he gently closed the black, leather Bible in his lap, and Annie wiped tears from her eyes. Eugene reached across the bed for her hand, then took hold of Jake's. Annie laced her fingers with Will's, and the two boys clasped hands, completing the circle. Following in the tradition that Papa Franklin had started twenty years ago, Eugene bowed his head and expressed thanks to God for sending His only Son as a little baby all those years ago.

***

Will's feet felt like chunks of ice as he tiptoed back into the dark room. He slipped back into bed underneath the warm quilts.

"What did you see?" Jake asked enthusiastically.

"Shut up, Jake. We don't want anyone to know I went down there."

It was four o'clock in the morning, and both boys were as wide-awake as if it were four o'clock in the afternoon.

"Well?" Jake whispered this time. "Was there coal in my stocking or not?"

"I couldn't see inside, but it sure felt like it."

Jake plopped his head back on the pillow in frustration. "But I thought I was a good boy." He sounded like he was close to tears.

That's when Will started laughing. "I'm just kiddin', goober. I didn't even touch 'em. But I could tell they were full."

Jake excitedly kicked his legs around under the covers and started giggling. That is, until he got punched hard in the upper arm by his brother.

---

[7] Luke 2:1, NKJV.
[8] Luke 2:15–16, NKJV.

"I mean it, Jakie. Shut up!"

Jake instantly got still and quiet but started rubbing his arm to get the sting out.

Finally at five o'clock, Will spoke up again. "Hey Jake?"

"Yeah?"

"Go down the hall and ask Dad if we can get up now."

"*I'm* not doin' it," Jake replied.

"Yes you are."

"Why me?"

"Because I said so. You don't wanna get punched again, do ya?"

Will knew he could get Jake to do just about anything. All he had to do was threaten him every now and then to keep him in line. Jake's temperament was such that he wanted to please his big brother at all costs, so he slid out from under the covers and headed down the hall.

"Daddy?" Jake whispered.

No answer.

Jake edged his way around the bed and put his face only inches away from Eugene's.

"Hey, Dad?"

Eugene's eyes opened slowly, then he rose up with a start, nearly bumping heads with his son.

"Jakie? What are you doing?"

"Can we get up now?"

"What time is it?" Eugene asked quietly.

"I heard five bongs on Nana's clock."

Annie lifted her head off the pillow. "Five o'clock?"

"Yeah, Momma." Jake flew around to her side of the bed. "Can we get up now?"

"Well, it looks like you already are," she laughed.

"But can we go downstairs yet?" he begged.

"Not yet, sweetheart. We need to wait for Gramps and Nana to get up. Here, get in with us." Annie held the covers back, and Jake immediately squirmed his way in between his parents.

"Whoa, keep your feet to yourself, buddy. They're freezing," Eugene teased.

Jake giggled, and all three settled back down under the covers for a while.

Several minutes passed before Will came wandering into the room. As soon as he saw Jake in between his parents, he got angry. Jake not only hadn't gained permission to go downstairs, but he had crawled into bed with Mom and Dad. Somehow it made him mad that his little brother was getting all of their attention. He let out a frustrated groan and turned to leave.

Annie opened her eyes and noticed Will leaving the room. "Hey, Will. Merry Christmas! Come 'ere."

She scooted over toward Jake and held the cover open for Will to join them. When he hesitated, Annie asked, "What is it? Are you too big for us now?"

"Maybe," Will said, irritated with the whole situation.

"Let's take a vote." She rose up on her elbows and looked at Jake and Eugene. "How many of you guys think Will *isn't* too big to join us."

Eugene and Jake both raised a hand up out of the covers. Annie smiled and put her hand in the air too. "Well, it's unanimous." She held the cover open again and said, "In you go!"

Will couldn't seem to get past his stubborn irritation.

"No thanks," he mumbled and started out the door.

In a flash, Eugene was out of bed. He grabbed Will around the waist, hoisting him off the floor. "Oh no you don't—we voted!" he said, laughing.

Will didn't resist as he was carried to the bed and thrown down beside his brother. Pretty soon, there was an all-out tickle war going on that had Annie screaming and all four of them fighting for covers. Lights went on all over the house and, within a few short minutes, the boy's original mission was thoroughly accomplished.

Finally, Jake and Will were the center of attention as they dumped out their stockings in the middle of the living room floor to see what was inside. Walnuts and fruit came tumbling onto the floor, as did ten pennies, two nickels, and a shiny tin box. Neither boy could get his box opened fast enough. Through hoots and hollers, they began to compare the little tin cars that came rolling out. Each one had a different set of colorful cars with wheels. One of them could even be wound up to roll across the floor without being pushed. Will and Jake were both so excited with their gifts that they didn't notice the one sitting on the table by the sofa.

"Hey look, guys. There's something else. This one's for the whole family." Eugene was pointing to a Philco model radio inside a handsome wood cabinet.

Jake's eyes grew the size of his two nickels. "Is that for us? Really!"

"Yes, sir." Eugene replied. "Now we can listen to radio shows after dinner in the evenings."

After a beautiful Christmas service at church and a delicious afternoon meal, Eugene worked with his boys to gather up their belongings while the women finished in the kitchen.

Rachel helped Claudia cover a portion of the ham, as well as some of the potatoes, corn, and green beans. "Thank you, Claudia. These leftovers will go a long way this week." Rachel noticed her dear friend seemed a bit tired and hoped everything was fine.

Claudia smiled, but there was very little color in her cheeks. "You're quite welcome. This has been a wonderful Christmas."

Reaching out to embrace her, Rachel asked, "Are you feeling all right?"

Claudia gave Rachel a firm squeeze then stepped back, smoothing her hand through her dark hair.

"I'm just feeling a little tired, that's all. I guess I haven't gotten as much sleep as I needed this week." She gave Rachel another warm smile. "I'm fine, just fine."

Annie and Mattie came back from the large pantry at the back of the kitchen. They were talking and laughing, obviously enjoying each other's company.

Turning toward Claudia, Annie said, "Mother, thank you again for a wonderful Christmas." She didn't hesitate to be drawn into her mother's loving arms.

After a long moment, Annie started to step back, but Claudia held her fast, not letting go. She quietly asked her daughter, "Do you know how much I love you?" Then she kissed her cheek and released her.

Annie smiled, and replied, "Almost as much as I love you."

Briefly, she looked into her mother's eyes. "Are you okay, Mother?"

"Of course," Claudia laughed. "I just wanted you to know how much you mean to me." She turned from her daughter and began to gather up the leftovers that would be going home with their family.

Rachel watched the exchange between mother and daughter with a fluttering sensation in the pit of her stomach. She couldn't quite put her finger on it but chalked it up to the lack of sleep, and Christmas sentimentality. Hopefully, Claudia would take a long nap after the house was quiet.

When Eugene pulled up in front of their own farmhouse half an hour later, the doors of the automobile flew open, and the chorus of "Jingle Bells" continued as the family tromped into the house carrying their gifts and leftovers.

"Hey Will," Eugene said, as he closed the front door. "I was thinking about something today." Will turned to see his dad setting the radio on the table beside the couch.

"I was wondering if you'd like to help me add an extra room onto the back of the house?"

Will's eyes instantly lit up. "A room for what?"

Eugene's grin widened. "A room for a boy who'll be turning eleven in just a few weeks."

Rachel heard the conversation and joined in. "You know your daddy came to live with me and your grandpa Franklin when he was eleven." She wasn't really looking at Will; her warm eyes were tenderly locked on Eugene.

Will didn't seem to notice the sentimental exchange between his father and grandmother. All he could think about was finally getting a room of his own. Jake was always messing with his stuff and underfoot every time he turned around. Most of the time he didn't mind his brother tagging along, but there were times Jake could be downright annoying.

"So when can we start, Dad? Can we start today?"

Chuckling over Will's excitement, Eugene said, "We can't start building today, but I thought you and I could go out back and take a look at the porch. I think we can cover in a portion to make a good-sized room and actually cut a door beside the pantry for the entryway."

Will jumped straight up in the air and pumped his fist.

"Come on, champ." Eugene put his hand in the middle of his son's back and gave him a little shove. "Let's go out and have a look, then we can sit down at the kitchen table and make a list of the supplies we'll need."

Jake excitedly fell in behind his older brother but wisely stayed inside the house after receiving a well-placed elbow to his breadbasket.

The following Sunday after church, Will shared with his gramps the progress he and his daddy were making on the new room.

"We're still working on the framing. It's gonna take us a while to get it done since I have to go back to school this week."

"What's your time frame for completion?" Nathan asked his grandson.

"Dad thinks if we can work all day on Saturdays, we can be done by March."

"How about I join in the work on Saturdays and maybe we can get that thing done by the time your birthday rolls around in February?"

Will's smile spread across his face. "Could you?"

"Sure, I think I can lend a hand to such an important family project." Nathan ruffled the top of Will's blonde head, then put his arm around his shoulders. "Come on; let's see what's taking Nana so long. My stomach's growling."

"Mine too!"

Nathan and Will scanned the thinning crowd of the congregation and spotted Claudia speaking with Mattie and another black woman in the back corner of the lobby. As they approached, Nathan noticed the young woman was crying, so he steered Will toward the door.

"Looks like Nana has an important conversation going on. What do you say we find your folks instead?"

Claudia barely noticed her husband and grandson; she was so intent on hearing what this young mother was telling her. Mattie kept a protective arm around her new friend's shoulders as Roberta Bradshaw shared her burden with the two concerned women.

"I finally got me a real payin' job as a domestic, but they say I gots to live with 'em and can't bring my two young'uns. What am I gonna do?" Roberta choked back a sob. "I can't be turnin' down such a fine job, but I got no family to take care o' my Wallace and Lillie."

Mattie rubbed solicitous circles around Roberta's back as she locked eyes with her employer. Claudia instinctively knew what Mattie was thinking, and her stomach did a flip-flop. Here she was living in a four-bedroom farmhouse, and only two of those bedrooms were being used. She had no excuse for telling Roberta that she would be praying for her and God would provide. She might as well say "be warm and filled" and just walk away. But what would Nate say if she told him they were taking in two young children? Well, he would simply have to deal with it. Without a doubt, this was the right thing to do.

Claudia's shoulders straightened, and with a confident resolve, she told Roberta, "Don't you worry for one more minute about Wallace and Lillie. They're coming to live with me."

***

Mattie couldn't stop smiling as she listened to the conversation around the Harrison's Sunday dinner table. The boys were overly excited about Eugene's chocolate birthday cake sitting on the counter in the kitchen. The whole time they were eating, Annie kept telling them to slow down. "The cake isn't going anywhere," she chided.

Mattie had just put fresh rolls on the table near Jake and nodded her head to Claudia, thinking now might be a good time to share the news with the family. Claudia gave her a sheepish grin and raised her brow, making a slightly funny face. The girl had to hold back a giggle and quickly scampered back into the kitchen.

Claudia ceremoniously cleared her throat and waited until all conversation ceased. "Well, everyone," she began, "I have some interesting news to share."

Chapter 14

Claudia opened the door to Lillie's room to make sure she was sleeping comfortably. She let out a sigh and smiled. The sheets and blankets were rumpled, but the bed was empty. Seven-year-old Lillie had resolutely declared that she would be sleeping in her own bed every night this week, but so far, she hadn't been able to stick to her guns.

Lillie and Wallace had grown up all their lives sleeping in the same bed, and only being a year apart in age, they both found a great deal of comfort sleeping together at night. Claudia didn't mind; she knew life had dealt them a tough blow having to be separated from their mother.

Heading down the hall, she quietly opened the door to Wallace's room. The two siblings were sleeping tight up against one another, back to back. Claudia laid a light kiss on Lillie's forehead and gently pulled the blanket around their shoulders. Two more days, and they'd be able to spend a full day with their mother.

Roberta's employers had thankfully given her Sundays off. She met up with the family at church, then rode home with the Harrisons for dinner and spent the rest of the day with her children. So far, they had been together for three straight Sundays. The arrangement seemed to be working out well. Roberta was saving every dime of her money and continued searching for a job that would bring her family back together under one roof. But in the meantime, Claudia was enjoying these two sweet children.

Even Nathan, after the initial shock, had warmed to the idea of taking in Wallace and Lillie. Their mother had done a fine job raising them to be respectful and polite. They were even beginning to join in on chores around the farm. Nathan was particularly pleased to see that Wallace had a way with horses.

The next morning, Mattie walked the pair out to the truck where Leroy was waiting to take them to school. Some days Nathan would take them in the car if he had other business in the city, but for the past few weeks, Leroy had been designated to drive them to school.

"Now you two better behave today and learn all you can." Mattie said the same thing every morning as she loaded them into the truck beside Nathan's most trusted farmhand.

"Yes'm, Mattie. We will." Lillie gave the young maid a toothy grin as she accepted a hand up into the truck.

Mattie reached across Lillie and tapped on Wallace's knee. "What about you, little man? You hear me?"

"Yes'm, Mattie. I hear ya."

"All right then. Leroy, you watch 'em till they get inside."

With a finger to his hat and a smile on his lips, Leroy replied, "I always do."

Before closing the door, Mattie added, "If any of your schoolmates is hungry at lunch, I put an extra biscuit in your pails. Don't you be keepin' that for yourself."

Both children replied, "Yes'm" in unison. Satisfied that all was well, she firmly shut the door and waved to the trio.

Mattie pulled her sweater a little tighter as she stood and watched the truck make its way down the long drive to the highway. She wished she'd been able to stay in school past the sixth grade. Maybe then she'd be qualified for a secretary's job or something important like that. She had been forced to drop out of school and work odd jobs in order to help her papa keep food on the table and a roof over their heads. Nothing had ever come easy for the two of them, but she had always admired and respected the good man who had raised her. He had refused to be dragged down by the difficult hand life had dealt him.

"Oh, Papa." Mattie's breath came out as a smoky trail into the chilly morning air. "I miss ya so much." She turned and walked slowly onto the front porch. "You and Mama rest in peace."

For the next hour, Mattie followed her usual morning routine of making beds and cleaning the two indoor bathrooms. Washing her hands, she joined Claudia in the kitchen to help her finish cleaning up the breakfast dishes and start on lunch preparation for the men.

Claudia was standing by the sink drying the bacon platter with a preoccupied look on her face. "There you are. I thought you were going to stay in bed all day."

Puzzled by her statement, Mattie replied, "Miss Claudia, I done already helped you cook breakfast and get the young'un's off to school this mornin'."

Color rose into Claudia's cheeks as she turned back to the sink. "Oh, I guess you did."

Mattie watched Miss Claudia closely. She seemed to be moving stiffly. Something wasn't quite right. Walking over to her side, she said, "Here, let me take that and finish dryin' these dishes. Why don't you sit down and drink a nice cup o' tea? Just take a little break." Mattie winked at her. "I won't tell nobody."

"Sounds like a good idea. I've got plenty of flour in the cupboard," Claudia replied.

"Miss Claudia?" Mattie was worried now and took her by the arm. "You come right over here and have you a seat."

Claudia allowed herself to be led to a kitchen chair and sat down slowly.

Mattie knelt down in front of her and clasped her cool hand. "I'm gonna make you a nice, hot cup o' tea with honey. You just need a bit o' rest."

Nodding her head slowly, Claudia agreed that she might need to take a little time before starting on lunch.

Heading into the pantry, Mattie wondered if she should go get Mr. Nathan down at the barn. The distant look in Miss Claudia's eyes was a bit disconcerting.

Before she could retrieve the tin of tea from the pantry shelf, Mattie heard the most awful groan resonate from the kitchen. She turned and ran around the corner just in time to see Claudia grab the back of her head and start to fall out of the chair. Mattie was at her side in a flash and threw her arms around Claudia's waist, saving her from a fall onto the floor. Mattie was barely able to get her back into the chair.

"My head!" Claudia screamed as she doubled over at the waist.

The young maid continued to hold her firmly, but Claudia slid from the chair onto her hands and knees. Mattie went with her, keeping her arm around Claudia's waist and grasping her shoulder to steady her. Suddenly, Claudia began to throw up on the floor and Mattie held her burning forehead while keeping her arm securely around her heaving midsection.

"Oh, Miss Claudia, you hang on. I gotcha. I'm so sorry."

Without warning, Mattie's employer went completely limp in her arms, and the girl struggled to keep her from falling into the pool of vomit. Mattie rolled to her side, pulling Claudia on top of her. She scooted her feet along the floor, dragging her as far away from the mess as possible. Quickly she wrestled herself out from under Claudia and took hold of her ashen face with both hands.

"Miss Claudia! Miss Claudia! Speak to me!"

There was no response. Instinctively, Mattie dropped her head onto Claudia's chest, listening for a heartbeat. Thank the Lord it was still there, and she could feel the slight rise and fall of her chest. Maybe a cool, damp cloth would revive her. But even after cleaning up Claudia's face, there was still no response.

Frantically, Mattie ran to grab a pillow and afghan from the couch in the front room. She raised Claudia's head onto the pillow and swiftly covered her body.

Laying her cheek right next to Claudia's she said, "Don't you leave me, Miss Claudia—you hear me? Don't you leave me!"

Without even putting on her coat, Mattie tore out the back door of the kitchen, screaming Mr. Nathan's name as loud as her lungs would allow. She hiked up her skirt, and the girl's long, athletic legs carried her like a gazelle for the half mile down to the barn.

"Mr. Nathan! Mr. Nathan! Come quick! You gotta come quick!"

Nathan hurriedly came from his office at the other end of the stables and covered the short distance to Mattie in only a few strides. He grabbed the girl by the shoulders to stop her from crashing into his chest.

He was nearly panic-stricken himself after hearing Mattie's screams. "What is it, Mattie? What's happened?"

Mattie gulped in the cold, winter air, trying to get her lungs to fill enough to tell Mr. Harrison what had happened to his wife. "It's . . . Miss Claudia. She's . . . passed out . . . on the . . . kitchen . . . floor."

Nathan didn't wait to hear another word. He pulled the keys from his pocket and ran to the car, dragging Mattie by the hand.

Mattie sat shivering in the car, thinking she could run back to the house faster than they could drive there. She glanced over at Mr. Harrison, worried to death. He wouldn't stop muttering, "Not like her mother. Oh please, God, not like her mother."

Inside the kitchen, Claudia lay so still Mattie feared she had already died. She dropped to her knees behind the woman's head and took her beautiful face in both hands, watching as Mr. Harrison felt his wife's throat for any sign of life.

"She still has a pulse," he breathed with minimal relief.

Mattie dropped her lips briefly to Claudia's forehead.

"Come on, you've got to help me get her to the car. We've got to take her to the hospital right now." Nathan reached under the afghan to scoop his wife into his arms while Mattie helped him lift her up from the floor.

Running ahead, Mattie opened the kitchen door and then the backdoor of the car. She slid in first and Nathan laid his wife into her waiting arms.

Leroy came riding up on his horse as Nathan ran around to the driver's side of the car. "What happened, Boss?" he yelled.

"Claudia passed out, and we can't revive her. We're taking her to the hospital," Nathan frantically replied.

Dismounting quickly, Leroy asked, "What can I do to help?"

"Go get Annie."

"Right away, sir. What should I tell her?"

Before closing his door Nathan said, "Try not to worry her—just get her to the hospital as fast as you can."

***

Annie's face perspired as she mucked the sixth and final stall of the morning. Even though she could see her breath, her winter jacket hung across the stall door. Annie's dungarees were covered in mud, and she used her flannel shirtsleeve to wipe the dampness from her forehead. Eugene entered the barn whistling an unknown tune and plopped a bale of alfalfa in the stack next to the wall. He reached up for his tool belt hanging on a peg and made his way over to Annie, who was just emerging from the stall.

Pulling off one of his leather gloves, he reached out and brushed a stray lock of hair from Annie's eyes. "You've been working hard this morning." Admiration for his wife was evident.

Annie jabbed her pitchfork into a nearby pile of hay. "I wanted to get all the stalls cleaned this morning so I could train with Josie this afternoon." Josiah's Reign was a young gelding that Annie worked with as often as possible. He had all the makings of a fine show horse.

Flicking the tool belt on Eugene's shoulder, she asked, "What are you up to?"

"I found a gap in the fence this morning near the southwest corner. I need to repair the wire before the herd discovers it."

"Yeah, we don't need another escapee this week."

Eugene bent his head and kissed Annie on the mouth and then laughed as she slapped his thigh. Walking backward toward the barn door, he said, "I may want some more of that later."

"Oh, go fix your old fence," she retorted, with a playful smile.

Just then, a truck pulled up on the other side of the barn, and Leroy came bursting through the door. One look at his face sent a shock of alarm through Annie's heart. She instantly threw her work gloves on the bench and moved quickly in his direction.

Eugene strode toward Leroy and caught up with Annie. "Leroy, what's happened?" he asked quickly.

"Missy." Leroy's look was full of sympathy and concern. "It's your mother."

Annie's hand shot up to Leroy's arm, "What is it? Is she okay?"

"Your daddy and Mattie have taken her to the hospital after she passed out this morning. He asked me to carry you over there as soon as possible."

Annie didn't wait for any more information. She took off for the house calling over her shoulder, "I'm going to change clothes. Pick me up by the porch."

A few minutes later, Rachel stepped out on the porch with Annie and gave her a quick hug. "Please call me from the hospital as soon as you know what's going on."

"I will, Mama."

Eugene stood at the open door of the truck. "We'll wait for your call. I'll get the boys from school and come up there if you think we should."

Annie kissed her husband, then hopped in the truck telling Leroy to hurry.

***

One look at Mattie's moist, red eyes and the anxious look on her father's face told Annie that this was not a good situation. She and Leroy entered the quiet waiting room less than an hour after Claudia had been brought in.

"Daddy?" Annie choked out his name as she flew into his arms. "What's happened to Mother? Is she okay?"

For a moment, Nathan had a hard time forming the words. They were words he had hoped never to say to his daughter. He had already seen Claudia lose her own mother for this very reason. He tried to shove the thought away that Annie might have to go through the exact same thing.

"Sweetheart, she has a brain aneurysm. The doctors have her in the operating room right now."

Annie's confusion was understandable. She pulled out of Nathan's arms and looked into his troubled eyes. "How could this have happened? What caused it?"

"It was probably hereditary. Your grandmother had the same thing happen to her." He took Annie's arm and led her over to the corner where she could sit on the wooden bench between him and Mattie.

Mattie instantly took hold of Annie's hand and, with a sweet gesture, brought it to her lips. She had no words to say. It was obvious she was feeling the terrible angst that now gripped Annie and her father.

Annie gratefully squeezed Mattie's hand, then turned her attention back to Nathan. "Daddy, how old was Granny when she died?"

He didn't answer her right away. It somehow seemed easier to pretend he didn't know. But Annie wasn't going to let it go.

"I was five when she died. Did she die of the aneurysm?"

Nathan took in a deep breath and closed his eyes. *Lord, I can't make it without her. Please don't take my Claudia away.*

"Daddy?"

Finally releasing his breath, he conceded to his daughter's questioning. "Yes, she died of the brain aneurysm," he said softly. "She was fifty-four."

Annie was distraught. "But that's Mother's age!" she cried.

Mattie instantly covered her face with her hands while Leroy started pacing the waiting room floor. Nathan merely reached around his only child and held her close while she wept.

***

At four o'clock in the afternoon, Eugene searched the waiting room for his family. He finally saw Annie and her father sitting silently, side by side in the back corner. Leroy had taken Mattie to pick up Wallace and Lillie at school and drove them back to the Harrison's. Mattie wanted to keep their routine as consistent as possible although it was driving her crazy not to be there when Miss Claudia came out of surgery.

Eugene had picked up Will and Jake after school and had taken them home to be with Rachel. He had changed clothes and rushed into the city to be with Annie and Nathan for whatever news was about to confront them.

Slowly, Annie rose to her feet and melted into Eugene's open arms. He wrapped her securely against his chest and told her quietly how sorry he was. "But your mother's strong—if anyone can make it through this, she can," he reassured her.

Annie looked into her husband's sympathetic eyes. "Surely God knows how much we need her."

Eugene nodded and kissed Annie's forehead. "He knows."

Nathan took Eugene's outstretched hand and pulled him into a brief embrace. Eugene let him know that Rachel was keeping Claudia covered in prayer.

A comforted look passed across Nathan's features. "No doubt your mama is on her knees as we speak."

The three sat down in silence and waited another hour. Finally a young nurse, dressed in white with a pointed white cap, emerged from the hallway.

"Mr. Harrison? Is Mr. Harrison in the waiting room?"

Nathan leapt from the bench with Annie and Eugene right behind him. "How is she?" he asked impatiently.

"Please come with me," the nurse quietly said, lightly touching Mr. Harrison's arm. "Your wife made it through the surgery about an hour ago, and Dr. Gardner will give you all the particulars." She turned to walk down the long hallway, motioning for Annie and Eugene to follow as well.

Dr. Gardner was studying a chart at the Senior Nurses' desk near the end of the hall. He was of medium build with jet-black eyebrows and a matching pencil-thin mustache, which contrasted starkly with his thick, white hair.

"Mrs. Harrison's family is here to see you, Dr. Gardner," the nurse announced.

The doctor paused for one moment, then looked up from Claudia's chart, extending his arm for the family to pass in front of him. "Let's all step inside where we can have a little more privacy."

Nathan stepped back, allowing Annie to enter the small, private waiting room first. There were six cushioned chairs lining the small room, but for the moment, no one sat down.

"Please folks, have a seat. There's a lot I need to discuss with you."

Annie's heart immediately jumped into her throat. Something about the doctor's manner had her on edge. Instinct told her the information she was about to hear was going to be difficult to endure. Eugene sat down beside her and reached for her hand.

"Mr. Harrison, I have to tell you that by sharing the information about your mother-in-law's aneurysm with us when you brought your wife in most likely saved her life. That, coupled with the description your maid gave us of Mrs. Harrison's symptoms, allowed us to zero in on the diagnosis in a timely manner."

Annie looked at her father and noticed his eyes brimming with unshed tears. Nathan nodded his head to the doctor, which released a stream from both eyes.

"At the time Mrs. Harrison was brought in, I believe there was a rupture of a cerebral aneurysm that was causing a hemorrhagic stroke. Fortunately, it wasn't quite so severe."

Dr. Gardner went on to explain that an aneurysm is caused by the weakening of an arterial wall; in this case, it was at the base of Claudia's brain. "This explains her sudden, thunderclap headache and vomiting. When you brought Mrs. Harrison in, her heart was under a substantial amount of stress, and her lungs had already begun to accumulate fluid." He briefly glanced at Claudia's chart and added, "We had to stabilize her blood pressure and intubate her before we could get her into surgery."

Annie didn't think she could listen to one more detail about her mother's medical condition. "I'm sorry, Doctor," she interrupted, "but is my mother going to be all right?"

For the first time, Dr. Gardner let a brief, sympathetic expression pass across his face. "For now, your mother has been stabilized, but we won't know the extent of damage done to her brain until she wakes up." The doctor hesitated for a moment, and then added, "I think it's important that I tell you about the procedure we used today. Do you think you're up to it?"

Eugene covered Annie's hand with both of his, infusing her with greater strength and patience. She realized how rude she must have sounded and apologized for her interruption.

"No need to apologize. I know this has taken a great toll on you and your family today."

After clearing his throat, Dr. Gardner began to explain a new procedure developed in the last couple of years by a Dr. Harvey Cushing in Edinburgh, Scotland. "The procedure involves wrapping the aneurysm with muslin to promote scarring around the aneurysm wall and thereby decrease the risk of bleeding. The most excellent news we received during Mrs. Harrison's surgery was that the aneurysm had not completely ruptured."

A collective sigh of relief hung in the air between the doctor and the family.

"However," Dr. Gardner continued, "some blood had leaked into the brain by the time we located the exact spot of her aneurysm. Unfortunately, any amount of blood discharged into the brain will cause some sort of damage. We'll just have to wait and see to what extent."

"When do you think she'll be waking up?" Nathan asked.

"It's hard to say, Mr. Harrison. Your wife appears to be in excellent shape and of strong constitution. It could be anywhere from a couple of hours to a couple of days. We really have no way of gauging it."

Annie leaned forward in her chair. "Can we see her now?"

Dr. Gardner closed the chart inside its shiny, stainless-steel case. "We can allow you to go into the room for a short while, but no visitors are permitted overnight." He rose from his chair and invited them to follow him to Claudia's room.

Down the hall, Dr. Gardner led the trio into a sterile, dimly lit room. Annie thought her mother looked surprisingly peaceful compared to the trauma she had endured today. The top of Claudia's head was completely covered with smooth, white bandages, and she noticed the dark circles underneath her eyes. But she appeared to be breathing easily. A middle-aged nurse stepped away from the side of the bed when Annie and her father approached.

"I need to touch her." Annie looked up at the doctor, pleading for his permission. Dr. Gardner didn't speak but nodded his head in assent.

Annie took hold of her mother's hand and leaned closer to bring it to her cheek. "I love you so much, Mother." She kissed her hand and laid it back at Claudia's side, but continued to hold it gently. "I love you," she whispered again.

Nathan stood with his hand on Annie's shoulder, stroking his precious wife's arm.

Dr. Gardner cleared his throat then asked Nathan to join him in the hall.

"Mr. Harrison," he began, "I'll allow you to sit in Mrs. Harrison's room until eight o'clock this evening, but after that, you'll need to go home and get some rest. We're doing everything in our power to take care of your wife, and we'll call you if there's any kind of drastic change in her situation."

Nathan nodded his head and asked, "May we come back in the morning?"

"Yes, at eight o'clock you can come back to sit with your wife if you so desire. Just check in at the Senior Nurses' desk."

Nathan reached for the doctor's hand and thanked him profusely for saving Claudia's life.

"You're welcome, Mr. Harrison. She may have a long road of recovery ahead of her, but for now, we can be thankful for a small miracle."

Dr. Gardner dipped his head and took his leave. Nathan started to go back into the room but stopped briefly and leaned up against the cold wall.

Lord, if this truly was a small miracle, I thank You from the bottom of my heart.

Chapter 15

Nathan entered his wife's hospital room with a cup of coffee in both hands. He and Annie had been waiting beside Claudia's bed for the better part of the day, watching for any indication that she would soon wake up. So far, she had been sleeping peacefully which, according to Nurse Renfro, was a good sign. There had been no change since her emergency surgery the day before, and her vital signs remained strong.

"I'll be back to check on Mrs. Harrison in an hour." Nurse Renfro smiled at the pair as she straightened Claudia's blanket and exited the room.

Nathan handed his daughter a cup of coffee, but he set his cup on a table next to Claudia's bed and started pacing the small room. He wasn't the kind of man who could sit around for very long. Annie was exactly like him and had already worn a path from her mother's bed to the door. If Claudia were awake, she would have laughed at both of them.

"Daddy, why don't you come sit down and enjoy your coffee?"

"Honey, I feel like a caged animal. I don't think I can do this again tomorrow."

Waiting around seemed so unproductive. He was used to getting things done, making things happen, taking care of business. This was downright frustrating. There wasn't one thing he could do to help Claudia wake up, and it was starting to drive him crazy.

"Please sit down for a minute. I have a question for you."

Nathan picked up his coffee cup and sat down in the chair next to his beautiful daughter. "What's on your mind?"

Annie looked at her father curiously. "What happened between you and your mother?"

Nathan bristled at the question, but Annie didn't seem to notice.

When he didn't answer right away, she continued. "I've been wondering why you haven't spoken to your mother in over thirty years. I can't imagine what could've happened to keep you all apart."

"Annie," he sounded impatient, "some things are better left alone." Nathan could tell by the look on his daughter's face that she would not be satisfied with that answer. Frankly, he wasn't satisfied with it either, but there was no going back to change the past, and he sure wasn't going to dredge it all up now.

"Daddy, do you know how old I am? I'm thirty-two. Thirty-two! I think I deserve to know why I've never been allowed to meet my grandmother."

Annie's voice was raised slightly, and he raised his own in response. "Honey, I know how old you are; you don't have to remind me." He stubbornly said nothing else.

"Well?" she countered.

"Well, what?"

"Why won't you tell me what happened? Is it some kind of secret or—"

"Just drop it," Nathan interrupted. "Please." He felt his nerves on edge from being cooped up in this room all day and worrying about his wife. The last thing he wanted to do was get into an argument with his daughter.

"I'll be glad to drop it if you'll just tell me why!"

"What . . . are you two . . . arguing . . . about?" Claudia's words were slurred, but her eyes were open and her right hand had moved up to her head.

Nathan and Annie both set their coffee cups on the floor and took opposite sides of the bed. Each one took hold of one of Claudia's hands, and Nathan put his other hand on his wife's shoulder.

"What . . ." there was a short pause while Claudia slowly licked her lips, "happened?"

"Sweetheart, you had surgery yesterday." Nathan was unsure whether he should tell her what kind of surgery it was.

She let go of his hand and raised it gingerly to her head again. Her brow was deeply furrowed. "Was it . . . my head?"

"Yes. It was an aneurysm. But the doctor was able to repair it. You're going to be fine."

"Where . . . did Annie . . . go?"

Nathan looked across the bed where his daughter was still holding Claudia's hand and stroking her arm. A stab of fear eked into his chest. She couldn't feel Annie's touch or see her.

"Mother, I'm right here."

Claudia slowly turned her head and a half smile crossed her lips. "Oh . . . there you are."

Annie bent down and kissed her mother's cheek. "How do you feel?"

"My . . . head is . . . pounding." She licked her lips again. "Could . . . I have . . . water?"

"I'll go get Nurse Renfro," Nathan said quickly. "I'll be right back."

Annie, too, had realized that Claudia couldn't feel her touch, so she moved around the bed and held onto her mother's right hand.

"You . . . look worried." Claudia faintly squeezed Annie's hand. "Honey . . . don't worry . . . about me."

How typical of Claudia to begin comforting her daughter as she lay helpless in her own hospital bed.

Before Annie could answer, Nurse Renfro swished into the room and took hold of Claudia's wrist to check her pulse. "Well, hello, Sleeping Princess."

Annie immediately voiced her concern. "She's asking for water. Can we give her some?"

"I'll bring in a cup of crushed ice and let her start working on that," the nurse said as she thrust a thermometer into Claudia's mouth.

"What can we expect now that my wife has awakened?" Nathan asked anxiously.

"Oh, I'm not at liberty to discuss the prognosis of any patient. You'll have to wait for Dr. Gardner to examine her. He's the only one who can discuss Mrs. Harrison's case with you."

"When can the doctor see her?" Annie asked.

The nurse continued to hold the thermometer in place, checking her watch.

"He's just down the hall and will be here shortly. Try not to worry; he'll answer all of your questions."

Within minutes, Dr. Gardner entered the room and reached for Claudia's hand. "Mrs. Harrison, it's a privilege to meet you. I'm glad to see you're awake. I'm Dr. Gardner." He lowered her hand to the bed and took out his stethoscope to listen to her chest.

When he was done, he said, "Nurse Renfro, please help me sit her up so I can listen to her lungs."

Together they gradually raised Claudia to a sitting position and the nurse held her steady. "Can you take a deep breath for me, Mrs. Harrison?"

Claudia opened her mouth and took in as much air as she could. "That's good. Again, please."

Finally, they lowered her back to a lying position, and the doctor declared that her lungs sounded clear. "That's a very good sign. Now, please squeeze my hand."

Claudia took hold of Dr. Gardner's hand and applied as much pressure as possible. Then he took hold of her left hand. "Squeeze my hand again, please."

Silence permeated the room while Nathan and Annie anxiously waited to see what would happen.

"Mrs. Harrison, can you feel my hand?"

A light pink color splashed across her worried features. She turned her head to look at their hands—clearly touching one another—then began to shake her head.

Dr. Gardner gently laid her hand back at her side and took a fountain pen from the pocket of his white coat. Running the cap end of the pen up her right foot drew a marked response from Claudia, but her left foot had no feeling at all. Finally, he took out his pocket torch to look into her eyes. After careful examination, he turned to Nathan and asked if he might step out into the hall for a moment.

As they had done the night before, both men walked outside the room to talk about Claudia's condition.

"Mr. Harrison, it's not uncommon for patients to experience some sort of numbness or paralysis, even the loss of sight after this type of brain trauma. Your wife has lost sight in her left eye and is experiencing numbness and paralysis on her left side. I'll do a more thorough examination in a few minutes, but I wanted you to know that it's not necessarily permanent."

Nathan took in a deep breath, listening intently to what the doctor was saying.

"Many patients who survive a brain aneurysm regain their sight very quickly, but if she is to regain use of her left side, she'll have to go through several weeks of physical therapy. Even then, there are no guarantees."

"So are you telling me she may never be able to walk normally again?" For the first time, Nathan allowed himself to think about the possibility that Claudia's life was about to radically change.

Dr. Gardner looked at Nathan sympathetically. "It's a very real possibility. But right now, that's the least of our concerns. We need to keep her under close surveillance for the next forty-eight hours. You have to understand how lucky she is just to be alive."

"I understand, Doctor." Suddenly, Nathan felt extremely tired and defeated. Why would God allow something like this to happen to such an amazing, vibrant woman?

"You'll need to excuse me, Mr. Harrison. I need to start my examination immediately."

"Of course."

Nathan and Annie kissed Claudia and told her how much they loved her. Then they headed down the hall to wait for the examination to be completed.

Later that night at home, Annie joined Rachel and Eugene in the living room after the boys were tucked into bed. Rachel instantly stood and drew Annie into her arms, kissing her cheek tenderly. "I know how you must be feeling right now, darlin'. But God has our dear Claudia in the palm of His hand."

Annie savored her mother-in-law's embrace for a long moment and then sat down in Eugene's arms on the couch. Somehow she felt like all of the joy in her life had packed up and walked right out the door.

"I don't know what'll become of my daddy if something happens to Mother," she sighed.

"Your father is stronger than you think," Eugene said with concern. "He'll manage under the circumstances."

"Yes, but my mother holds his heart entirely. He can't make it without her."

Suddenly, Annie thought about the conversation she had started with her father earlier in the day. She sat up from Eugene's arms and looked at Rachel. "Has my mother ever told you anything about my Grandmother Harrison?"

Rachel looked surprised by the abrupt turn in conversation. "Well, she did tell me once that they hadn't spoken since Nathan was a young man. Maybe you should ask him about it sometime."

"That's just it," Annie replied. "I brought up the subject with him this afternoon, and we practically got into an argument about it."

"Then maybe you should let it go. Some things are better left alone," Eugene remarked from experience.

Annie shook her head and let out a soft groan. "That's exactly what *he* said. You sound just like him," she complained.

"Hey, all I know is he must have his reasons," Eugene replied carefully. "It may be too painful for him to talk about right now."

Rachel chimed in, "Darlin', today might not have been the best time to ask your father about his past. I'm sure when he's not so worried about Claudia, he'll be more likely to talk."

Annie thought about that for a moment, then leaned back into Eugene. She realized she must be overreacting. She was worried sick about her mother and hadn't slept all night. She needed to give her father the benefit of the doubt and let it go for now. But she knew when the time was right, she would definitely broach the subject again—and then she wouldn't take no for an answer.

***

Claudia spent the next six weeks in the hospital, successfully fighting off an infection and working to regain her health. Thankfully, the vision in her left eye cleared within three days of the surgery, but her left arm and leg remained useless. She had recovered feeling in her limbs but would have to relearn how to use them.

Mattie came to the hospital during the last week to be trained in the ways of physical therapy. She and Claudia together had decided that nothing would get in the way of a complete recovery. Dr. Gardner told her it would take an incredible amount of work each day, but her tissue and muscles were receiving a good amount of blood flow. He didn't rule out the possibility that Claudia would be able to walk again and use her left arm and hand.

The Harrison's house was full of well-wishers on the Saturday that Claudia was released from the hospital. Nathan and Eugene carried her in her wheelchair up the porch steps and wheeled her into the house to the sounds of clapping and cheering. One by one, family members, church folks, and farmhands hugged and kissed the woman they adored and made her feel like a queen for the day. Claudia drank it all in, enjoying the luxury of being home, knowing that this was the only day she could afford to sit in her wheelchair and be waited on hand and foot. She and Mattie had already planned their strategy, and it would take every ounce of willpower she had to pull off their plan.

When the church members and neighbors left for home, and the farmhands went back to work, Nathan carried his wife upstairs to take a quiet nap. Mattie asked Annie if she wouldn't mind joining her outside on the porch. Both women put on their sweaters as a protection from the cool March wind.

"Miss Annie, I got a proposition for ya. I'm sorry to spring this on ya sudden like, but me and your momma didn't come to this conclusion till this morning when we was on our way home from the hospital."

Curious, Annie motioned for Mattie to sit down on the swing with her. "What kind of proposition are you talking about?" she asked.

"We was wonderin' if you might be able to take our Wallace and Lillie in for a while. Your momma and I have a plan to help her get better, but it's gonna take all the free time I have to work with Miss Claudia and take care of Mr. Nathan and his farmhands too." She smiled and elbowed Annie playfully. "I'll take care of your mother if you'll take care of my Wallace and Lillie."

Annie took in a deep breath and looked out over the pasture. She knew it was the right thing to do even if Mattie wasn't working to help her mother get well. This young woman simply couldn't be expected to keep the entire household running by herself and take care of her mother too. But why was she hesitating so?

All of a sudden, it hit her like a ton of bricks. If they took in Wallace and Lillie, Will would have to give up his new room. Either that, or Jake would have to move in with him again. Just thinking about it made her inwardly cringe.

Noticing Annie's hesitation, Mattie said, "I know how hard you work, Miss Annie, to keep your farm goin' and all. We don't want this to become a burden to ya."

Annie said, "No, no, it's not that. I was simply thinking about the sleeping arrangements in the house, that's all." Determined to make it work, she looked Mattie squarely in the eyes and stuck out her hand. "You've got a deal."

Both women shook on it and sealed it with a firm hug. Now all she had to do was sell her eleven-year-old son on the idea.

Chapter 16

"Where are you goin', Son?" Eugene called out.

Almost before the car came to a halt, Will jumped out and started running for the barn. The boy's face was red and his fists clenched as he sprinted at top speed in the opposite direction of his family. He didn't bother to answer or even slow his pace.

"Eugene, he's got to come back and face the consequences for his behavior." Annie was about as angry as her son at this point but not for the same reason. She couldn't get over how rude he had been to the family on the way home from her mother's *welcome home* party.

"He can't just run away every time something doesn't go his way," she said in frustration. "I'm going after him."

Eugene laid his hand on her arm before she could even turn toward the barn. "Let him go, Annie. He's got to blow off some steam before we can even begin to talk to him."

Annie shrugged off her husband's hand, irritated by his seeming composure. She opened her mouth to say something but realized she was about to take her anger out on the wrong person. Anything she said to her husband in exasperation would simply make things worse. But how was she supposed to deal with the problem of her son's behavior if he wasn't even around to be held accountable?

"Eugene, he's only eleven! Can you imagine what he's going to be like when he's sixteen?"

Rachel made her way around to Annie's side of the car. "Darlin', I know this is hard, but we can't go borrowing trouble five years down the road. Today is all that matters—trust God for the future." She reached out and put a loving arm around Annie's shoulders. "Let's just take each moment as it comes."

Annie felt her initial anger begin to melt away even though a profound sense of anxiety lay underneath. "Are we doing the wrong thing by bringing Wallace and Lillie here tomorrow?"

"No," Eugene said immediately. "That is absolutely the right thing to do. Those two kids and your mother need us right now. Don't give that decision another thought, Annie."

Suddenly, Annie was filled with a deep sense of gratitude for her husband. "I'm relieved to hear you say that," she replied humbly. It would've been so easy for Eugene to say no to the idea, but he had agreed to Annie and Mattie's deal as soon as they presented it to him only a couple of hours ago.

"Let's go in," Eugene said, turning his wife toward the house. "If he doesn't come home before supper, I'll head out to the barn."

***

Will had his bay stallion, Comanche, saddled in record time. He yanked the bit into his mouth so forcefully that it caused the horse to throw his head in the air and take a step backward.

"Whoa, now boy. I'm sorry . . . come on now."

Will calmed himself enough to woo the powerful beast into lowering his head again. Even though he felt like slamming the bridle up against the wall, he controlled himself enough to get it positioned correctly into Comanche's mouth. He checked the leather cinch on the saddle one more time to make sure it was tight enough then led his horse outside the barn. Will quickly put his left foot into the stirrup and swung himself up with ease into the saddle.

"Hup!"

He dug his heals into the stallion's side, and they were at top speed within four strides. The back gate of the property came into view, and Will pulled back hard on the reins causing Comanche to come to a rough stop. The animal seemed to be feeding off his rider's emotions and began throwing his head. Irritation swirled through Will's veins. Thoughtlessly, he slapped Comanche's head back down with his hand. If his daddy had seen him do that, he would've been reprimanded.

Will jumped to the ground and led his horse over to the barbed-wire gate. He had to squeeze the top of the gate close enough to the wooden fence post in order to unlatch it at the top, then he lifted it out of the bottom loop of wire. The gate landed with a thud on the ground. For a second, Will toyed with leaving it there, but he wisely picked it up and set it back into place.

"Yaw!"

Comanche and Will took off through the trail in the woods at a reckless pace, dodging tree limbs, cutting around sharp turns, and leaping over fallen branches. Once, when the horse stumbled on a large rock in the path, Will pictured, with sadistic pleasure, his parents finding his dead body along the trail. *That would show 'em!* But the athletic thoroughbred pulled out of the stumble and continued his dangerous trek down the hillside.

At the bottom of the hill lay a level, tree-lined dirt road that ran between his family's property and that of Wendall and Marcella Crowley. Mr. Crowley was a spindly, gray-haired man that Will had nicknamed Mr. Scare-Crowley. Jake always laughed when he heard it, but his momma had told him that Mr. and Mrs. Crowley were good people, and she didn't want them being made fun of.

Will didn't slow Comanche when he hit the open road. Instead, he urged him on at a punishing speed. Flying around a blind curve in the road, he suddenly yanked back on the reigns, forcing Comanche hard to the left. Horse and rider narrowly escaped a head-on collision with Mr. Crowley's truck.

Wendall Crowley stomped hard on his brakes, and the back end of his truck fishtailed toward the opposite side of the road. A few tense seconds later, it came to a halt in a cloud of dust.

"Will!" Mr. Crowley yelled as he opened the door of his truck. "What in tarnation is goin' on? I coulda killed you and your horse both!"

Will's heart slammed hard inside his chest, and the anger that had driven him down this road evaporated into the cool, afternoon air. Still, he had to restrain himself from slapping Comanche's head back down. The horse was in an agitated state, pawing the ground, throwing his head wildly, and snorting out a thick liquid from his nostrils.

Mr. Crowley strode over to the pair and reached for the horse's bridle, pulling his head back down into submission.

"Whoa there, buddy. Calm down." With his other hand, he wiped a handful of white lather from Comanche's neck and held it up for Will's observation. "What'r you trying to do, kill your horse? Or maybe you were hoping I would do it for ya."

Will knew Mr. Crowley was awfully irritated with him. He didn't blame him; his devil-may-care attitude could've killed them all. "I'm sorry, Mr. Crowley," he said remorsefully.

"Is that all you have to say for yourself? You 'bout gave me a heart attack, Son."

"I really am sorry . . . I just . . ." Will's voice trailed off.

He just what? He just thought he'd take his horse for a little ride? He just thought he'd come by for a visit? Honestly, *he just* had no excuse for his careless behavior. None whatsoever. But he didn't know what else he could say to his neighbor.

"Get down."

Mr. Crowley's command was gruff. "I can't let you take your horse back to your daddy lookin' like that." Wendall headed over to his truck. "Walk him down to my barn and we'll cool him off proper."

Mr. Crowley turned his truck around in the road and slowly drove the quarter of a mile back to his barn while Will walked shamefacedly behind.

The Crowley's had a much bigger spread than his parents' farm, and all Mr. Crowley raised was thoroughbreds. He had at least thirty head on his property and a large, white barn and stables. But Wendall Crowley wasn't one of those uppity, rich horse breeders like some of the others who lived farther down the road. He and his wife had worked hard to keep their horse farm going throughout their forty-five years of marriage. Even though his herd had dwindled down by half in the last few years, Mr. Crowley raised some of the finer horses in the region.

"My trainers are off for the day, so you and I are gonna have to cool him down ourselves."

Will's neighbor held the gate open for him to bring Comanche into the large, airy barn.

"Keep walkin' him for another five minutes or so until he catches his breath."

Comanche was still taking in rapid puffs of air, so Will obediently did as he was told. In the meantime, Mr. Crowley hooked up a hose in the barn and tested the temperature of the water. It was too cold to spray directly onto the horse. They would have to spray it on his legs in order to cool down the blood that would eventually circulate throughout the rest of his body.

As Will led Comanche, Mr. Crowley spouted horse talk. "You know the horse is a symbol of strength and speed and beauty. I don't suppose there's a more majestic animal on God's green earth than the one you're leadin' right now." He motioned for Will to keep walking. "In a herd, they all know their place—kinda like a pecking order of sorts. But in a horse hierarchy, even the one at the bottom has a sense of belonging. He knows his place in the herd, so to speak."

Will noticed Mr. Crowley was watching him intently, and he wondered if this was more than just horse talk.

"Okay, bring him on over and get his tack off."

Will worked quickly, removing Comanche's saddle and blanket while Wendall removed the bridle and slipped a halter over his head. He then attached a lead rope and looped it over a post.

"You start scraping while I spray his legs down."

Mr. Crowley handed Will a curved steel blade with a handle, used to scrape sweat from a horse. "If you don't get all that lather off of him, his coat'll dry up and might even bleach out his color."

The horse stomped his hooves impatiently on the barn floor as the cold water was sprayed up and down his legs. Will had a hard time staying dry because the spray from the hose kept hitting him. He was curious if Mr. Crowley was doing it on purpose.

Finally, the old man turned off the water and fetched some drying towels from the tack room. Together, the pair rubbed every inch of Comanche's coat, making it shine even in the dimly lit barn.

"Will?" Mr. Crowley turned to the boy with a slightly more benevolent look on his weathered face. "I don't know what you were up to out there, but you're lucky you and your horse are still alive."

Will sheepishly nodded his head, and Wendall continued.

"I'm not gonna tell your daddy . . . although I probably should." He reached up and stroked Comanche's beautiful neck. "But if I ever see you mistreat another animal again, you and I are gonna have a serious talk, and your daddy will be there. Do you understand me?"

"Yes, sir, Mr. Crowley. You won't ever have to have that talk . . . I promise."

The two neighbors worked to get Comanche saddled again. Mr. Crowley didn't like putting the wet saddle blanket back on him, but he told Will it would be all right until he got him back home.

"And you need to cover him up tonight. The weather's still chilly, and you don't want him gettin' sick or sore muscles."

"Yes, sir."

The sun was about to set when Will led Comanche out of the barn. He knew he'd better get home in a hurry or he'd miss supper.

Mr. Crowley had an uncanny way about him. "Now don't you go gettin' in a hurry just 'cause it's growin' dark. Your momma will save your supper. Just walk him home, you hear me?"

"I will, Mr. Crowley. Don't worry."

Will quickly mounted his horse, thanked his neighbor for the kindness he'd shown, then turned Comanche toward home. Even though the horse still had a little spirit in him, Will wisely held him to a steady walk.

With every step toward home, Will wrestled with his stubborn pride. He pictured himself standing up to his folks and not backing down under any circumstances. Then half a minute later, he pictured throwing himself into his mother's arms and asking for forgiveness. He knew the second option was the right thing to do, but it made him feel so powerless. Whatever was about to happen, the darker the sky grew, the more nervous he became of the consequences he'd no doubt be facing when he got home.

Will entered the darkened barn, and his heart jumped clear up into his throat when he realized his daddy was sitting on a bale of hay beside Comanche's stall. It looked as though he'd taken a piece of hickory and fashioned it into a paddle of sorts. It was sitting on the bale by his side.

Pulling the string to the lightbulb hanging over Comanche's stall, Will began to remove the horse's tack. He couldn't bear to look at his dad; the disappointment on his face unnerved him. Neither one spoke during the entire time it took Will to put away the saddle and cover Comanche with his blanket. He stayed in the stall stroking the horse's neck simply because he didn't know what to do next.

"Come on out, Son," Eugene said in a low voice.

Slowly, Will walked out of the stall and latched the gate.

"The way you acted today was wrong. You were mean to your brother and disrespectful to me, your mother, and your grandmother."

Will's head dropped; he couldn't even make eye contact with his dad.

"We've raised you better than that. I've talked and talked and talked to you—until I can't talk anymore. It's time you took some licks."

Will's head jerked up when he heard his father's voice crack.

Eugene cleared his throat, took hold of Will by the arm, and pulled him over his knee. Three swift, hard licks brought tears to Will's eyes, and then it was over.

Eugene let Will up then stood, looking down at his son.

"You'll be a man soon, and you need to start thinking about what kind of man you want to be. When you're old enough to move away and live on your own, I guess you can live the way you want. But while you're living under our roof, you'll treat all of us, including your brother, with respect." Eugene narrowed his eyes at his son. "Have I made myself clear?"

"Yes, sir."

Will tried to brush away the tears with the back of his hand but more kept coming.

"Tonight, you'll have supper in your room, and tomorrow after church, you'll move out of it and back in with your brother."

Will let out a muffled gasp and started to protest.

Eugene's hand went up in the air to stop him.

"Maybe if you had discussed this situation with us in the right way this afternoon, we might have come up with a different solution. But as it stands, you're going to make a sacrifice for two children who have no papa and only get to see their mama on Sundays. Do you understand?"

Will nodded his head in deep regret. He loved his new room and the freedom he had felt in it.

"And . . . if you *ever* talk to your mother again like you talked to her today, I won't hesitate one second to bring you back down to the barn and use this." He slapped the paddle down on the nearby workbench, causing Comanche to throw his head and let out a startled whinny.

Will had never seen his father like this in his whole life, and to be honest, he never wanted to see this side of him again. One thing was certain—he'd do whatever it took to keep from taking any more licks.

***

Rachel tapped on the door of her grandson's room and waited for a quiet voice to call, "Come in."

"Darlin', I was wondering if you're done with your supper dishes."

Will turned from the window. "I'm done, Gramma."

Instead of taking the tray immediately, she sat down in the chair next to his bed and remarked, "Kind of a rough day, huh?"

"You can say that again." Will sat down on the bed cross-legged and rested his elbows on his knees.

"I wish you could've known your grandpa Franklin. He was the most patient, kind-hearted man I've ever known." She let out a quiet laugh. "Now don't get me wrong; he could get riled up every now and then, but that was usually if someone was mistreating the ones he loved."

A quiet settled between them as Rachel delighted in the precious memory of her dear Franklin. Finally, she took in a slow breath and looked into Will's blue eyes.

"Do you need to talk about anything?"

Will couldn't hold her gaze and uncrossed his legs, letting them dangle from the side of his bed. Rachel was comfortable with the silence, determined that Will would have to be the one to break it.

Finally, he cleared his throat and said, "It's not fair."

"What's not fair, darlin'?"

"I built this room . . . well, Dad and I built this room . . . for *me*. Nobody cares about that."

"That's not true, Will. Not one person in this family wanted you to have to give up your room. Besides that, it may not be for long. But one thing is certain; by giving up this room, you're helping your nana get better. You understand that, don't you?"

Will nodded and stood up, rubbing his hands up and down on his behind.

Rachel noticed the gesture, wondering what that was all about. She stood too and reached out to take her grandson into her arms. He allowed her to hold him for a brief moment.

Letting him go, she picked up the tray from his bedside table and walked to the door. Before she opened it, Rachel turned back to look at him. She was reminded once again just how much he looked like his mother—if only he had her temperament.

"Don't forget, Will," she said softly, "you always reap what you sow . . . always."

***

Annie pulled the top quilt off the bed and slid her feet into her slippers. Quietly, she made her way through the dark house and onto the front porch. At least this time, Eugene had thought to pull on a t-shirt. He seemed to be breathing normally—*he must have been out here for a while.*

"Eugene?" She said his name softly as she pulled the door closed behind her.

"Hey," he responded in his usual voice.

She draped the quilt around his shoulders then climbed underneath it beside him. "Are you okay? It's two o'clock in the morning."

Eugene wrapped his arms around his wife and pulled her up close to his side. For a while, the two sat in complete silence, sharing each other's warmth. Only the sound of the early spring crickets and the rustling of the tall grass in the breeze kept them company.

Finally, he said, "I spanked him tonight."

Annie sat up a little straighter and looked into her husband's face. "You did?"

He clenched his jaw and nodded his head.

She waited for him to go on, but it was clear she was going to have to prod him a little. "How did he take it?"

"He cried. I know it hurt him."

Eugene fell silent again.

"But it hurt you too, didn't it?" she inquired softly.

His jaw clenched tight again, and he nodded ever so slightly.

"Eugene, it was the right thing to—"

"Annie, don't go there. I know I should've spanked him a long time ago."

"I wasn't making a judgment, sweetheart. You're a wonderful father; you're raising two amazing boys." She brought her hand up to his chest. "Will's as headstrong as they come. He needs a patient father like you to guide him through life."

Eugene grasped her hand and held it in place. She could feel the steady rhythm of his heart.

"Why tonight?" she asked.

For the first time, Eugene looked over at Annie with an intensity that threw her off guard. "I couldn't stand the way he talked to you today. That was *my wife* he was being rude to. I don't know—it was like all of a sudden I pictured him treating his own wife like that someday, and it scared me. I knew talking to him wasn't going to do any good."

Annie was suddenly overwhelmed by a deep appreciation for her husband. She reached up and pulled his head down to hers, kissing him in a way that conveyed all of the love and passion she possessed for him.

He turned and pulled her as tight against him as he possibly could, then without a word, scooped her up in his arms and carried her back to bed.

Chapter 17

Agonizing tears gushed down Claudia's cheeks as she practically yelled, "No, keep going!"

Mattie was bawling her eyes out but did exactly as she was told. It seemed Miss Claudia's will was stronger than her own. She reached down and took hold of her employer's left hand and placed it on top of her wrist, compressing Claudia's fingers and thumb around its circumference.

"Again!" Claudia sobbed.

Mattie slowly moved backward away from Claudia's chair, forcing the woman to grip her wrist and pull herself up from the chair. Claudia had instructed Mattie to tie her good arm down to her waist, thereby keeping her from being tempted to use it. As a matter of fact, she had refused to use her good arm for the most part of the last three days.

Just as Claudia was about to stand to her full height, her hand slipped from Mattie's wrist and she fell backward with a hard thud into the wheelchair.

"Miss Claudia," Mattie choked out her name. "You has worked long past the two hours we planned. Please!" she begged. "Please take a rest. I can't stand to see ya fall even one more time." She dropped to her knees, threw her arms around Claudia's legs, and laid her head on her lap.

Claudia slowly began to catch her breath as she allowed her limbs to relax. *Poor girl, she must think I'm a hard-hearted woman.* Claudia narrowed her eyes and concentrated with all of her might on her left arm and hand. Slowly and painfully she watched it lift from her lap, and regrettably, plop rather roughly on top of Mattie's head. Little by little, she moved her hand back and forth across the girl's head, but it was taking everything she had just to continue that small motion.

"Mattie?" she said tenderly.

"Yes'm?"

"I'm sorry for the toll this is taking on you. I understand if you want me to let you out of our agreement."

Mattie's head shot up, and Claudia's hand landed in her lap with a thump. "I can do this, Miss Claudia, I can," she fervently appealed. "I promise." She clutched both arms of the wheelchair and drew herself up onto her knees, looking right into Claudia's face. "I'm sorry I'm so weak, truly I am."

"Mattie, honey?"

"Yes'm?"

"Untie my right arm, please," she said gently.

Mattie worked to loosen the cloth belt she had tied around her waist. The very moment Claudia's arm was free, she reached for the girl and pulled her into an impassioned embrace. Holding her dear Mattie, she released fresh tears and prayed that God would give her the courage to be more patient.

The doctor had told her it could take weeks to retrain her muscles and remind them how to work again. He believed intense therapy would in essence rewire her brain to return to normal. But she was pushing too hard. There was no way the two of them would be able to keep up this pace and survive.

Claudia released her hold on the girl and leaned back in the chair. Mattie remained on her knees, exhausted.

"I'm sorry, Mattie." She reached out and cradled the side of the girl's sweet face in her one good hand. "I shouldn't have pushed you like that. You've been working so hard around here . . . I didn't have the right to require so much." She felt ashamed of the demands she had placed on this young woman.

"No ma'am, Miss Claudia, don't you go apologizin' for nothin'. That's exactly what's gonna get you well. That extra determination is just what it's gonna take for you to walk again."

"Well, from now on, we'll only work for an hour, three times a day. There are certain things I can do on my own." She took hold of the cloth belt and handed it to Mattie. "As a matter of fact, I should've been helping you in the kitchen instead of focusing on myself so much. Even with one hand and sitting in a wheelchair, I can still help out around here."

Just then, Nathan came striding through the back door. Both women began wiping their faces and smoothing their hair.

He stopped abruptly in the doorway to the front room. "Is everything all right?"

For the first time this morning, a smile played on their lips. Claudia breathed deeply and responded, "We're fine, honey."

"Good. You had me worried there for a second." He returned his wife's smile and moved to her side. "I came up to help you get in the tub. You ready?"

"I'm ready," she said, and reached up to loop her right arm around her husband's neck. Remarkably, her left arm reached up at the same time.

Mattie's eyes grew wide. "Did you see that, Miss Claudia? Your left arm done jumped right up there!"

"I know!" she said excitedly. "I didn't even tell it to!"

A squeal rose from Mattie's throat, and she jumped up and down, clapping her hands.

Even though Claudia was unable to continue holding her left arm around his neck, she giggled all the way up the stairs in Nathan's arms while Mattie followed close behind. They worked together to get Claudia into the tub, then Nathan stepped out so Mattie could help her wash. When the task was complete, Mattie called him back in to lift his wife from the tub and help wrap her in a warm robe.

He carried her into the bedroom and sat her in a wooden chair beside the bed where Mattie could help her dry off and get dressed.

"I'll be downstairs in my study. Just let me know when you're ready to be carried down." He leaned over and kissed Claudia on the mouth and told her he was proud of her progress. "Keep it up," he teased. "I plan to take my girl dancing soon."

He tweaked her chin playfully and breezed out of the room.

Mattie reached for a towel and turned back toward Miss Claudia, but Claudia pushed her hand away.

"Quick," she cried with excitement, "go get my calendar!"

"Miss Claudia, you is soakin' wet. There's time for lookin' at your—"

"I need to see it now," she interrupted. "Please, Mattie . . . just humor me."

"Okay, but don't go blamin' me if you catch yourself a cold or somethin' like—"

"Mattie, please."

"Yes'm, I'm goin', I'm goin'."

Mattie held out the towel to her. "Here—use that left hand of yours to start dryin' off."

The girl winked at her and headed down to the kitchen where Claudia kept her calendar hanging by the telephone. That's where she wrote all of her important dates—birthdays, anniversaries, church functions.

Before Mattie could make it up the stairs, she heard Claudia yell, "And don't forget my pencil."

Mattie let out a good-natured sigh and turned back around to retrieve the pencil. When she got back to the bedroom, Claudia was no drier than when she left her.

"Miss Claudia, what did I tell ya? Is you up here daydreamin' or somethin'?"

"Just hand me the calendar, please," she responded, with a sparkle in her eyes.

Mattie held it out to her employer and practically had it snatched right out of her hand. "What has gotten into you, Miss Claudia? I ain't never seen you like—"

"Shhh, I'm counting." Claudia was bent over the calendar counting the days as if her life depended on it.

Mattie decided she better not say *diddly-squat* lest she get shushed again. But it truly was driving her crazy that Miss Claudia was still dripping bath water onto the floor.

"Sixty-five!" Claudia exclaimed.

"Okay, Miss Claudia, I'll play along. Sixty-five what?"

"Just sixty-five days until June 1." Claudia dropped her finger smack dab on top of the date. "Hand me the pencil please."

Mattie put the pencil in Claudia's right hand and watched her write something on the calendar, then she flipped it back to the month of March.

"Do I get to know what all the fuss is about, Miss Claudia, or did I just run up and down them stairs for nothin'?"

"First, help me dry off and get dressed. I'm freezing."

Mattie shook her head and clucked her tongue. "Miss Claudia, what am I gonna do with you? What am I gonna do?"

Claudia realized her behavior today had been more than a little out of character. She wasn't normally prone to such mood swings. But six weeks in the hospital had taken more of a toll on her nerves than she had expected. One thing was certain—she was going to have to be more careful with Mattie. The poor dear was already sleep deprived in the four short days since she'd come home.

Mattie was so gentle with Claudia, making sure she kept her dignity, even though it was intensely humiliating having to depend on someone else to keep her clean and dressed. She finally watched the girl's hands move quickly to get her blouse buttoned, and it dawned on her for the first time that Mattie was not only her maid; she had already become a dear friend and confidante, and this was no way to treat a friend.

When the task was done, Claudia sat dry and dressed on the bed. Mattie plopped down beside her and let out a deep breath. She was nearly worn out, and it was still morning.

"Can you share that secret with me now, Miss Claudia?" she asked quietly.

"Yes, honey. I'm sorry—I'm not trying to keep a secret from you." She looked at her with that gleam in her eye again. "But I am trying to keep a secret from my husband. Can I trust you?"

"Ab—so—lutely. Your secret goes right into this vault." Mattie threw her hand up to her heart. "And I'll throw away the key."

Claudia laughed, then excitedly told the girl what she had planned in sixty-five days.

***

That afternoon, Annie drove over to check on her mother. During the six weeks Claudia was in the hospital, Annie had been by her side every day. Now it troubled her that she couldn't be a part of her mother's ongoing recovery. While she knew it was best for Mattie to focus on helping Claudia get well, Annie couldn't help but somehow feel left out. She was doing her best to repress such feelings, but as soon as she walked in the front door, a possessive emotion took her in its grip.

"Oh, Miss Claudia, you is doing so good," Mattie praised.

Annie observed Mattie on the floor helping Claudia raise and lower her left leg. When Claudia noticed her daughter walk in the room, she beamed with joy.

"Look how much progress we're making."

Instantly, Annie moved to her mother's side and kissed her cheek. "That's wonderful." Then she turned to Mattie. "I'll be glad to take over for a while, Mattie. I don't need to pick the kids up from school for a couple of hours."

"Oh no, no, Miss Annie. Me and your mama has us a little routine now." Mattie kept her hold on Claudia's ankle and looked up into her employer's face. "We come to a good understandin' this mornin', didn't we now, Miss Claudia?"

Annie noticed the loving exchange between the two women.

"Yes, we did indeed," Claudia responded. Then, looking up at Annie, she asked, "What brings you out here this afternoon?"

Annie couldn't help feeling hurt by her mother's innocent question. All of a sudden, it seemed like she was an outsider here. She was on the verge of heading back to the farm; after all, she had left Eugene with an extra workload, even though he was more than happy to bear it so she could be with her mother.

"Well, I just thought I'd check on you and see if you needed anything." She gave her mother a thin smile. "But I see you have everything you need."

Claudia looked bewildered. "Honey, you don't need to rush off so soon, unless of course you have work to do. We'll be done here in fifteen minutes, then you and I can have a nice chat."

"No, Mother, but thanks. I really should be getting back to help Eugene." She leaned down and brushed Claudia's cheek with her lips. "I'll call you tomorrow."

"Bye-bye," Mattie called to Annie as she made her way to the door.

"Honey, it was good to see you," Claudia added.

Annie waved to the women, then stepped outside closing the door behind her. For a long moment, she stood in the middle of the porch wrestling with an emotion she had seldom, if ever, dealt with. Is this what jealousy felt like? If so, she didn't want any part of it. It seemed like something eating away at her sensibility; even her chest felt tight.

Walking to the end of the porch, Annie stood at the railing that overlooked the horse pasture. She was acting like a spoiled child who wanted her way and hadn't gotten it. How ridiculous. She and Mattie had come up with this plan to help Claudia recover, and now that the plan was working perfectly, she was making it all about herself instead of her mother.

Annie knew if she left now, these feelings would only fester. She couldn't live with herself thinking she might damage their relationship because of her own self-centeredness. There was nothing left to do but go back inside and confess her feelings, as hard as it would be. Still, she lingered on the porch for another minute or two until she got up the nerve to follow through with it.

Knocking softly, Annie opened the door and stuck her head in. "I've decided to stay after all," she said quietly.

Claudia's face lit up again. "I'm so pleased. Come sit down beside me; we're almost finished."

Annie sat down in the armchair next to her mother's wheelchair and watched as Mattie gently and skillfully helped Claudia through her routine of exercises. She was amazed at how well the two worked together. Even so, Annie had yet to rid herself of the tinge of jealousy clawing for attention in her heart.

"Well, that about does it, Miss Claudia."

"Thank you, honey . . . for everything."

Mattie rose to her feet and gave her employer a broad smile. "You is more than welcome. Can I help you down for your nap?"

"No, but thank you. Maybe later," Claudia said. Then she added, "Why don't you lie down and rest a while. You've worked so hard today."

"Oh no, Miss Claudia. I'm as fine as fine can be. Can I get the two of you anything?"

"No Mattie," Annie quickly responded. "If we need anything else, I'll take care of it." She noticed the puzzled look on Mattie's face and gently added, "But thank you."

Mattie took her leave and headed into the kitchen to start preparations for supper.

When Annie turned her attention back to her mother, Claudia was lightly biting on her lower lip. She looked as if she might say something but remained aggravatingly silent. Annie could feel the heat rising to her cheeks.

"Mother, I'm sorry about earlier."

Claudia raised her brow. "For what?"

Annie knew deep down that her mother had read her like a book. Still, this was going to be harder than she thought. "I guess I . . ." Her voice trailed off, not sure how to put her feelings into words.

Claudia reached over and laid her good hand on Annie's arm. "It's okay, honey. You can say anything to me."

Annie took in a few quick breaths then lowered her voice so Mattie wouldn't overhear. "Mother, when I walked in and saw you and Mattie working together, I wanted to be a part of that, but you all didn't need me. I know it sounds selfish, but I got my feelings hurt."

When Annie paused, Claudia calmly prodded her. "Go on."

It was beyond her how her mother knew there was more. But she was right— there was, so Annie made the decision to hold nothing back. "I was by your side through six long weeks in the hospital, Mother, and now I'm back home working like crazy on the farm and taking care of two more children, all the while worrying about you and wanting to be with you. But the two of *you*," she gestured toward the kitchen, "seem to have everything under control. You don't need me anymore."

Claudia's features suddenly took on a forlorn appearance. Knowing she was the cause of it crushed Annie's heart. Maybe she should've kept the last part to herself.

"That's not true," her mother responded vehemently. Tears sprang into Claudia's eyes, and her hand gripped Annie's arm with surprising strength. But Claudia's voice was now shaky and weak, not at all what it had been moments ago.

"Annie, my darling, the truth is I need you more than anyone right now. I've felt so depressed after coming home from the hospital. You're the one who gave me the willpower to go on, day after day—sometimes hour by hour in the hospital. And now . . . now I miss you every minute of every day."

Painful tears filled Annie's eyes. "I didn't know," she breathed. "I'm so sorry for what I said."

"Annie?"

"Yes?"

"I just need you to hold me . . . please."

"Oh, Mother."

Immediately, Annie knelt in front of her mother's chair and pulled her into her arms. Claudia laid her head on her shoulder and wept while Annie drew her ever closer.

A shuddering sob wracked Claudia's body. "I don't want to go through this anymore."

"Shh, Mother, I know. But I'm with you now. We can make it through this together."

Annie gently caressed her mother's hair and rubbed her back, trying to soothe her deep despair.

After several minutes, Claudia leaned back in her chair, still holding on to Annie with her right hand. "I can't do this without you, but I know you already have too much on your plate right now."

Annie shook her head. "We'll find a way, Mother. And it won't be too much on me, I promise. As a matter of fact, I already have an idea."

The corner of Claudia's lips turned up slightly.

Annie sat back down in her chair and excitedly laid out her plan.

***

Friday morning, the front door to the Harrison's house burst open without a knock. What looked like a small herd traipsed through the kitchen. This was one of Annie's ideas—to bring the children over for hugs every day before school. Claudia had no idea such a simple activity could bring so much joy and anticipation, but every hug seemed to energize her soul for the day.

She threw her right arm open for the first hug. It came from her sweet Jake who kissed her right on the mouth. "I've missed you, Nana."

"Oh, Jakie—it's only been since yesterday." She pinched his cheek lightly with her right hand. "But I missed you more."

Next came Will who was a little more reserved. Claudia got a firm hug from her oldest grandson, but she knew how stingy he was with his kisses. Surprisingly, he gave her a quick peck on the cheek.

But the hug parade didn't stop there. Little Lillie was next in line, and she crawled clear up into Claudia's lap and threw her arms around her neck, wiggling her small body back and forth as if she couldn't seem to get close enough.

"Easy now girl—you don't wanna go breakin' Miss Claudia's neck." Mattie gave Lillie's arm a squeeze, and the girl loosened her grip.

"Miss Claudia." Wallace stood in front of her wheelchair. He had said her name with such reverence, it brought a sudden rush of emotion.

As soon as Lillie peeled herself away, Wallace slowly wrapped his arms around Claudia's neck while maintaining eye contact the entire time. She knew this boy ran deep—it felt like his eyes could penetrate down to her soul. She folded him into her arms and felt the peace emanating from him. Releasing the boy from his heartfelt embrace, she wondered what special gift God had given him.

Rachel was next—a truer friend could never be found. Claudia had missed her dearly; visits in the hospital were simply not enough. It felt so wonderful to be enfolded in Rachel's loving arms. What would she do without her?

And finally, the hug she'd been longing for, not that the others hadn't held deep and special meaning. She loved them all immensely but none as deeply as her sweet daughter. Annie dropped down to her knees and wrapped her arms around her mother tenderly.

When Annie slowly pulled away, she took hold of her mother's left hand. "I think I felt your arm squeeze me a little, Mother. How was your session with Mattie yesterday?"

Claudia glanced briefly at Mattie with a glint of sympathy in her eyes. "Well, she hasn't left me yet—"

"Now Miss Claudia, don't you go talkin' like that. We's makin' it just fine . . . just fine."

Annie leaned in to give her mother a kiss, then rose to her feet. "I've got to get this crew off to school. We'll see you this afternoon. I hope this doesn't wear you out."

"No," Claudia replied, with enthusiasm. "I'm looking forward to Fridays now, more than ever."

Getting Rachel and Claudia together on Fridays had been another part of Annie's plan. She would drop her off at the Harrisons before taking the kids to school, so Rachel could spend a good bit of the day keeping Claudia in high spirits as well as help Mattie with a few household chores. Rachel also had plans to prepare a big family dinner for the evening.

A conspiring look passed across Claudia's face, and she reached up with her good hand to clasp Annie's arm.

"Is there any way you can drop back by after the kids are in school? Mattie and I have something we want to share with you and Rachel."

Annie's brow rose in curiosity. "This sounds like fun. I'll definitely swing back by on my way home. How about a little hint."

"Oh no, honey—that will have to wait. We'll see you when you get back."

Annie laughed as she started herding the kids out to the car, and within half an hour, she was back, finding the three women in the kitchen cleaning up the breakfast mess.

"So what's going on around here, Mother?"

Claudia wheeled her chair over to the kitchen table and motioned for everyone to join her. As soon as the women were seated at the table, Claudia said, "I need you all to be praying about something."

Annie instantly reached over and covered her mother's hand on the arm of her wheelchair.

"I know all of you are already praying for me every day—believe me, I can feel those prayers. That's the only way I'm making it."

All of the women nodded, and Claudia acknowledged openly that the power sitting around this table was enormous—not their own power, but the power of their heavenly Father.

The conspiratorial expression reappeared when Claudia glanced over at Mattie. The girl gave her the most encouraging smile that brought a special joy to her heart. She had felt so little joy in the last few weeks. To be honest, there had been times when she just felt like giving up. Those were the times these women must have been interceding for her in prayer because God had never failed to pull her out of the pit.

"I've done something," Claudia went on, "that involves all of you." She decided the best way to tell them was to plunge right in. "I've made reservations for our whole family on the *Idlewild* for June 1."

The *Idlewild* was a famous steamboat on the Ohio River that had arrived at the Louisville Wharf only the year before. She was a beautiful boat with powerful engines and boilers, boasting a large, wooden dance floor on one deck and elegant dining on another. The *Idlewild* provided night cruises three times a week from downtown Louisville to Rose Island, fourteen miles upriver.

"June 1 is your anniversary, Mother."

"I'm quite aware of that, honey. And that's why I want us all on the *Idlewild* that night. That's the night I plan to dance with your father."

A slow smile crept across all of the women's faces, and Rachel pressed a hand to her heart, feeling the emotion around the table. "Does Nathan know about this?" she asked enthusiastically.

"No, he doesn't have a clue. I want this to be a complete surprise for our anniversary." She searched the women's faces. "Are you all in?"

"I'm in!" Annie cried with excitement.

Rachel raised her hand in the air, as if making a pledge. "I'm in!"

"You know I'm in!" Mattie declared.

Every one of them searched out another one's hand, as if doing so sealed their solidarity. Claudia knew she would have to be relentless in pursuit of her goal. She would have to make some sort of progress every day if she was going to be able to dance in her husband's arms. She was determined to do everything in her power to make it happen, but she would trust God above all else for the outcome—no matter what.

"We need to pray!" Annie exclaimed, as she had done on so many other occasions.

Each of their hands tightened on the others while Annie began to pour her heart out to God. And as she fell silent, one by one each of the women boldly petitioned the Lord of mercy, who held Claudia's future in His hands.

From that day forward, Annie continued bringing the children by the house every morning for hugs, and then she would return to pray with her mother.

Annie's plan had been exactly what Claudia needed. There were still days when she felt dispirited and weak, but with Annie's continual motivation and encouraging prayers, she gradually began to feel vitality returning to her body and spirit alike.

Chapter 18

“Giddyup, Gracie! Giddyup!”

Lillie squealed with delight every time the horse picked up her pace.

Annie didn't know when she had enjoyed a trail ride more than this one. It was a beautiful April Saturday morning—signs of spring were everywhere along the trail, and the sun brought a warmth that hadn't been felt in months. Lillie sat in the saddle while Annie rode behind her on Gracie's haunches. She kept a protective arm around the girl, especially since her feet didn't quite reach the stirrups.

Not having a daughter of her own had caused Annie a bit of anxiety when they first decided to take in the children. So many questions begged to be answered. Would she know how to relate to a little girl? Would she be able to protect her from all the boys in the house? Would she know how to fix her hair? For some reason, that one had troubled her more than any of the other concerns. She knew plenty about pretty dresses and such—her mother had made sure that she was taught the proper ways of a young lady. But to actually do her hair? The thought of it was nothing short of intimidating.

All of those worries, however, flew right out the window the very minute Lillie stepped foot inside their house. What a joy this little ebony child had turned out to be.

“Pull back on Gracie's reins, sweetheart.” Annie had given Lillie the reins, knowing the mare would follow obediently behind the other horses on the trail.

“Whoa, Gracie,” Lillie said in her sweet, little voice. She pulled back on the reins, lifting them high above her head, which caused Annie to laugh.

“Good girl,” Annie said, as she jumped to the ground and reached up to help Lillie out of the saddle. “You're a fine cowgirl!”

Lillie was small for her age, making it difficult for her to reach Gracie's head while standing on the ground, so she pressed her hand onto the horse's shoulder and rubbed up and down. “You're a good girl, Gracie. Thanks for the ride!”

Annie tethered the mare beside the other horses and joined the family around the fire pit. The boys were busy building a structure with the firewood they had gathered around the site while Eugene placed the kindling in strategic places.

“Come on, Lillie. You can help me get the food out of the saddle bags.”

Together, the two females took out all of the food Rachel had prepared for their special picnic in the woods. Jake had begged Rachel to join them on the trail, but she graciously declined, saying it had been far too long since she'd sat on top of a horse. "You can ride with me, Gramma," he had begged. But as tempting as that offer had been, she decided this adventure would need to be for the younger members of the family.

Eugene reached into his shirt pocket and pulled out a book of matches. "Here you go, Will. What do you say we get this fire goin'?"

Will struck a match and held it up to the kindling until it burned clear down to his fingers, then he dropped it quickly into the dry sticks. Nothing seemed to be happening, so he struck one more and tried a different spot. As soon as he dropped the match, he leaned down and blew on the orange glow of the twigs. Within seconds, a small blaze came to life.

"All right everybody, if you wanna eat a hotdog, you've gotta find your own stick to roast it on. And let me give you a hint," he added with a wry smile, "the longer the better!"

One by one, sticks began to appear at Eugene's side, waiting for him to strip the bark and sharpen the end with his knife. Annie stood by ready to stick the wiener on each roasting stick. She enjoyed the giggles and good-natured jostling for the best spot around the fire. Lillie had gone to the other side of the fire pit away from the boys but soon realized her mistake. She waved her free arm through the air and made exaggerated coughing noises, then nudged her brother toward Jake so she could move out of the choking smoke.

Hotdogs and pickles with Rachel's potato salad and sweet lemonade assuaged the hungry crew. When all had had their fill and helped clean up the lunch fixings, Will went back to his saddle bag and pulled out a rubber ball and the homemade paddle his daddy had used on him a couple of weeks ago.

"I've got a game we can all play."

Jake's eyes grew in diameter. "Is that the one?" he asked his older brother.

Will sheepishly cut his eyes toward his father, then turned back to Jake. "Yep, that's the one."

Annie thought his chest puffed out a notch, almost as if he was proud of surviving an encounter with the paddle. "What's your game called?" she asked.

"Tree ball. And we're gonna play it in the clearing."

They all excitedly followed Will down the path and out into a small meadow surrounded by budding trees. Standing at the base of a large Kentucky coffee tree, Will proceeded to go over the rules.

"We'll have two teams, and this is the tree your team wants to protect." He pressed his hand against the wide trunk, then shaded his eyes searching for the closest tree at the edge of the meadow.

"And that tree," he pointed out, "is the tree you have to run to after you hit the ball."

Eugene walked over to a red maple about twenty yards away. "This the tree?" he called out.

"Yep, that's the one," Will answered.

"After you hit the ball pitched, you have to run and touch the maple tree, then run back and protect the coffee tree. If the other team can get the ball to their pitcher, and the pitcher hits the coffee tree, you get out, and the next person bats."

Jake asked, "How close can the pitcher stand?"

Will took ten large steps away from the tree and laid down a stick. "This is as close as the pitcher can get to the batter and the tree." He strode back over to the family. "And, if you make it back to the coffee tree before the ball hits it, you keep batting until the pitcher finally hits the tree. If you think you can run to the maple tree more than once on your hit, you can do that too."

Annie laughed. "Will, how did you come up with this game?"

"I don't know, Momma," he shrugged. "It just came to me before we started out this morning."

"Clever boy," she said, giving his shoulder a nudge. She couldn't get over how tall he was getting. She was five foot seven, and he wasn't but an inch shorter than she was.

Eugene chimed in, "How about me, Jake, and Lillie take on you three?"

Will pressed his lips together looking at the family. Finally, he agreed, "That sounds fair."

After a lively rock-paper-scissors competition between Will and Jake, Eugene's team headed out into the field to play defense.

Will decided the batting order for his team, so Wallace took the paddle and stepped in front of the tree. Eugene tossed the ball in, and Wallace gave it a good whack. He didn't bother to drop the paddle, using it to reach out and touch the maple tree while Jake and Lillie chased down the ball. By the time Wallace returned to the coffee tree, Eugene was just catching Jake's throw.

"One run!" Will yelled out, while Annie cheered. Wallace was breathing hard and gave his teammates a big grin, then readied himself for the next pitch.

As the afternoon wore on, the tree shadows lengthened, shifting positions across the meadow, while spirited whoops and hollers reverberated through the woods. Everyone had peeled off their jackets long ago, as sweat trickled down their faces and backs.

"Come on guys; we have to get her out this time," Eugene called to Lillie and Jake, just before pitching the ball.

Annie hit the ball as hard as she could, sending it whizzing past Eugene's head and into the woods. Throwing the paddle to the ground, she sprinted to the maple and back.

"Go again, Momma! They can't find the ball."

"Yeah, go again, Miss Annie!" Wallace yelled.

Laughing, Annie took off for the maple again, but just as she touched the tree and turned around, she was met head on by her husband. He grasped a hold around her waist and carefully pinned her back to the tree.

"Hurry up, guys," he called over his shoulder, "find that ball!"

Lillie cried out, "We're trying, Mr. Eugene!" She and Jake were running frantically through the woods, slapping weeds and bushes out of their way.

"Eugene Wyatt, you let me go," Annie declared, throwing her hands up to his shoulders. She pushed against her mischievous husband, but he wouldn't budge. As a matter of fact, he moved in closer, pressing her tighter against the tree.

"Eugene," she whispered, through the struggle. "Your shin is going to be hurting any second now if you don't let me go."

"You wouldn't dare," he chuckled, as he snuck a kiss on her neck.

"Ooh, Dad. Stop it!" Will yelled from the coffee tree.

"Yeah, you heard your son," Annie protested, teasingly.

Eugene's laughter grew louder while Annie twisted to free herself from his grasp.

"Hey!" she exclaimed, peering over his shoulder. "They found the ball!"

Eugene loosened his hold as he turned to look, and that was just the opening Annie had been waiting for. She bent her knees, scooting down the trunk, and wiggled free of his grasp, taking off for the coffee tree.

"Fifty-two!" the boys yelled as Annie slapped her hand against the rough bark.

"Go again, Momma!"

Annie watched as Eugene joined his teammates in the woods searching for the ball.

"No, I don't think that would be fair. Maybe we should go over and help them out."

Ten minutes later, Eugene finally declared the ball lost for good.

"I guess we win," Annie squealed, playfully pinching her husband's side.

He looked as if he might pin her to another tree but restrained himself when Annie's finger twittered back and forth in front of his face. He tilted his head, raising his brow—a signal to his wife that she was going to be in trouble when they got home. Annie felt the pink rush to her cheeks, and an impish smile flitted across her face. The entire exchange was lost on the kids.

"You know we didn't get our fair ups," Jake countered.

"That's right," Eugene cut in. "We might have beat you all with our last at bat."

"Not a chance," Will laughed. "You all were down by thirteen."

Jake shrugged, clearly not wishing to get into a dispute. "You never know," he said sportingly.

"Yep, we'll never know." Eugene threw his arms around Jake and Lillie and congratulated them on a fine effort.

On the way home, Annie listened to Will and Wallace's lively conversation. They were reminiscing about certain plays they had made in the Tree Ball game. Watching them ride together on Comanche filled her with such a feeling of hopefulness where her eldest son was concerned. Wallace had ridden with Eugene that morning, but now he was mounted behind Will, holding on to the back of his saddle. It had been her son's idea for Wallace to ride with him. Annie was grateful that his initial reaction to the children living with them had developed into a tolerant acceptance of Wallace and his sister—even though the siblings were now sleeping in his room. Her mind wandered briefly to the wooden paddle in Will's saddlebag. Hopefully, he had learned a valuable lesson after experiencing its rigid discipline.

The hour was later than Eugene had hoped upon their arrival back home. By the time everyone had brushed down their horses and given them oats and water, the sky had turned to a dark, orange hue. Rachel met her family on the porch, and straightaway Eugene felt a twinge of guilt when he saw her face. He was sure she had supper waiting for them and must have been worried.

"Mama, I'm sorry we didn't get back earlier." He took the porch steps two at a time.

At first, she didn't respond, letting his words drift past her. He thought she was going to tell him something but must have decided against it when she firmly pressed her lips together.

"Are you okay?" Eugene asked, and then his eyes rested on the letter in her hands.

"Eugene, darlin', why don't we go in and get everyone fed. I've got supper prepared and warming in the oven."

A knot seemed to twist its way into his stomach, and Eugene wasn't sure he would be able to eat. He knew his mama all too well. Something had happened, and he knew that letter held the key. He watched her tuck it into the pocket of her apron as they walked into the house.

When supper was over, Annie filled the tub and started the Saturday night bath ritual. Eugene and Rachel stayed at the kitchen table to talk.

"Son, we received a letter today from Oklahoma."

When she paused, Eugene quietly asked, "Was it bad news?"

"I'm afraid so." Rachel's words were soft and her eyes held compassion. She pulled the letter from her apron pocket and fingered the edges of the envelope. "It's from Susan Gano. She said that Ralph passed away last week."

Eugene closed his eyes briefly and took in a deep breath. Letting it out slowly he asked, "What happened?"

"All she said was that he had some sort of heart condition. The doctor seemed to think he had a heart attack."

Eugene closed his eyes again, feeling the hot tears well up behind his lids. Will Gano's face came to memory as clearly as if he were sitting here with him in the kitchen. Eugene was reminded of a time after the war when he wished Will had made it home instead of him. He would've gladly traded places. Will had a dear family and fiancé waiting for his return, and at the time, Eugene had felt so lost without a family of his own. He respected Will's parents for not being bitter about their son's death after the war. Mr. and Mrs. Gano had treated him just like a son, and had even offered their home to him if he needed a place to live.

Rachel's hand reached across the table and covered her son's. "I feel so deeply for Susan's loss."

"As do I, Mama." A tear slid down his face, and he reached to brush it away. All he could think about was the fact that Ralph Gano was now reunited with the son who had sacrificed his life for their freedom.

"Would you like to read the letter?"

Eugene nodded his head, and Rachel laid the letter in his hands. He read every word Susan had written, feeling her pain and loss. Finishing the letter, he looked up and noticed his eldest son standing awkwardly in the doorway of the kitchen. For a moment neither one spoke, but Eugene noticed the lines of worry on Will's face.

"Come 'ere, Son."

Eugene pushed away from the table and held out his arm. Will hesitated for only a second, then came slowly to his father and sat down on his leg. Eugene wrapped his arms around him, and Will leaned back into his daddy's chest, keeping his feet on the floor.

"I know I've told you this many times, Will, but your namesake was an amazing man. He was only twenty-three when he died in the war, but he taught me so much . . . and his character was above reproach. I hope you'll grow up to be like him."

Sounds of splashing bath water could be heard down the hall, but the kitchen held a solemn silence connecting the three generations.

Finally, Eugene broke the quiet. "One afternoon during the war, Will and I left our post and started heading back to our lines when we came upon a young man sitting up against a tree. As soon as we saw him, he raised his rifle and aimed it at us, and we did the same thing to him. None of us said anything; we just stood there pointing our weapons at each other."

Will rose up a bit and looked anxiously at his daddy. "Was it a German?"

"Yes, he was a German, and he had a badly broken leg. So when Will noticed how twisted the soldier's leg was, he lowered his rifle and laid it on the ground, then he nodded for me to do the same thing. So I did."

"What did *he* do?" Will inquired.

"He lowered his rifle too. In fact, he turned it around backwards with the muzzle facing away from us and put it on the ground. The man was in a lot of pain; I thought he was about to pass out."

Eugene glanced over at Rachel. She was sitting forward in her chair, hanging on his every word. He realized he had told her very little about the war, and she was probably relishing this rare moment.

"We bent down to look at his leg, and Sergeant Gano decided that the only way to move him was to put some sort of splint on it. The soldier asked us if we spoke German and I said no, so I asked him if he spoke English, and he said *nein*. But then he said, 'Parlez-vous Français?' And I said, 'Oui.' So after that, he and I spoke only in French, and I translated for Will. We even introduced ourselves; his name was Wolfgang Schneiman."

"Eugene, that's amazing," Rachel breathed.

"Oh, it gets better." Eugene smiled for the first time since he'd come home this evening. "After we got his leg secured in a splint, we had to decide what to do with him. I guess the smart thing to do would've been to take him prisoner, but Will thought by the shape his leg was in, he'd probably get a free ticket back home to Germany. I wasn't so sure what we should do. That's when Will asked, 'What if this was you, and the Huns found you with a broken leg?'"

Will interjected enthusiastically, "You'd want them to take you back to the US lines!"

"Exactly! So we hoisted Wolfgang up between us and headed for the German lines. Just before we got there, Will took out a white lace handkerchief that belonged to Mary, his fiancé, and put it in Wolfgang's hand over my shoulder so they would know we were coming in peace. We had left all of our rifles back at the tree."

Will nervously squirmed in his daddy's lap.

"The closer we got to the trenches, the more rifles we could see pointed at us. It seemed like a hundred or more must have been aimed in our direction. All of a sudden, Wolfgang yelled something really loud in German, and I remember closing my eyes tight. I didn't know if he was telling them to shoot us or not."

"But they didn't . . . right?"

"Right. Slowly, the rifles all disappeared down into the trenches." Eugene could feel Will's breathing slow down from its rapid pace. Rachel, however, had her hand pressed to her mouth, still taking quick, shallow breaths.

"Two German soldiers climbed up the ladder of their trench and met us a few yards out. They came alongside of us and took Wolfgang's arms and looped them over their shoulders." Eugene narrowed his eyes remembering the French words the young German had said to them before being carried away by his comrades. He recited them for his mother and son. "Que Dieu vous bénisse pour votre gentillesse. Il peut vous voir à travers toutes les batailles."

Rachel dropped her hand to her lap and repeated quietly, "God bless you for your kindness. May He see you through every battle."

Nodding his head, Eugene continued with his story. "We watched as they lowered Wolfgang down into the trenches. He cried out a few times as they tried to get him lowered without hurting him worse than he already was. Of course, Will and I felt pretty vulnerable standing out in the open like that. When we turned around to leave, I imagined a big red target painted on our backs. I was in favor of backing away, but Will started calmly walking across no man's land like he was walking across his own wheat field."

"They didn't try to shoot you all, did they?"

In response to his son's question, Eugene said, "I thought they were going to. We heard a booming German voice yell something that made us stop dead in our tracks." Eugene let out a muffled laugh. "I couldn't turn around. I was pretty sure all of those rifles would be pointed at us again. But we heard someone running to catch up with us, and when I looked, I saw one of their soldiers reach out to hand Will his handkerchief. Will thanked him in English and put it back in his pocket. That's when I noticed there was not one rifle in sight. We walked all the way back to the place where we'd found Wolfgang and picked up the rifles, then headed back to our lines."

"That's awesome, Dad!"

"Eugene," Rachel said, shaking her head, "that's an incredible story, but you could've been shot."

Eugene's arms tightened around his son, and he dropped his face close to Will's. "I'd like to think Wolfgang is at home, sitting by the fireplace with his son on his lap, telling him the same tale."

No one spoke for a while as the enormity of the story Eugene had just related sunk in. Finally, Annie called Will's name and told him it was his turn for the bath.

Before releasing his hold on Will, Eugene breathed quietly, "I hope you never have to go to war, Son."

Rachel watched her grandson head down the hall to take his Saturday night bath, then turned her attention back to Eugene. "Surely there will never again be such a war as that."

Softly, his words filled the air between them. "Let's pray you're right."

Chapter 19

June 1933

Eugene couldn't keep his eyes off his wife. She was standing in the Harrison's living room holding Lillie's hand, wearing a new dress that set her figure off perfectly. He was used to seeing her in muddy jeans throughout the week and a skirt on Sundays and Wednesday night prayer meetings but nothing like what she was wearing now. He couldn't wait to get out on the dance floor with her—even though he didn't know how to dance.

The women had all decided to dress upstairs at the Harrison's before their big night on the *Idlewild*. Eugene had put on his nicest suit at home before driving the family over. When Rachel appeared on the top landing, he thought his heart wouldn't be able to take anymore. Stunning was the only word he could think of at the moment. He rushed to the bottom of the stairs and offered her his elbow as she took the last two steps.

"If Claudia looks anything like the two of you, I don't think my heart can take it," he announced. Both women blushed with the attention.

Just then, the boys came out of the kitchen with a cookie in their hands.

"We're going to be having dinner on the *Idlewild*," Annie chastised. "You boys don't need to be eating cookies."

"I'm so sorry, Miss Annie. I thought it'd be all right for the young'uns to have a little snack before they leave," Mattie apologized as she followed them out of the kitchen. "I just couldn't resist such handsome fellas." Her big smile took in Will and Jake in their pressed slacks, white dress shirts, and ties.

Nathan cleared his throat at the top of the stairs, and everyone moved their gaze upward.

"Nana." Jake said her name with great admiration.

Annie moved to take Eugene's arm, beaming up at her mother.

"Wow," was all he could think of to say.

Locking eyes with his son-in-law, Nathan commented, "We're going to have to keep our eyes on the womenfolk tonight. We don't want anyone to steal them away from us."

"No problem there, sir." Eugene grinned and put his arm around Annie's waist, drawing her close to his side.

Claudia was wearing a full-length, cream-colored evening gown with matching elbow-length gloves. Her dark hair was swept into a lovely swirl, held by mother-of-pearl combs. Nathan looked handsome in his black, long-tailed tuxedo and shiny black boots. He reached down to sweep Claudia into his arms and carry her downstairs. She was still a bit unsteady when it came to navigating the stairs. Her cane leaned against the wall near the bottom step, and she reached for it as her husband placed her back on her feet.

"Wallace and Lillie, y'all come on in the kitchen for supper." Mattie turned toward Annie again. "Don't you worry none about the young'uns. I'll put 'em to bed upstairs and keep 'em for the night."

"Thank you, Mattie."

"And Miss Claudia," she beamed, "you is gonna have a glorious time tonight!"

Claudia opened her arms to the girl and hugged her warmly. "This night would not be possible without you."

"Oh no ma'am, it weren't me; it's all Him." Mattie pointed upward, deflecting the praise toward God.

"Yes, but He used you to do His work. Thank you." Claudia gave her hand a squeeze and turned back toward her husband.

Nathan pulled the car keys from his pocket and stuck his elbow out for Claudia. "Shall we?"

The sun dipped toward the river but still provided much of the lighting for dinner on the lower deck. The *Idlewild* was more beautiful than Claudia had imagined. They were seated at a long table covered with an Italian lace tablecloth, napkins monogrammed with an *I*, china plates, and crystal glasses. She looked at the tin ceiling and marveled at the intricate, picturesque designs.

Lowering her gaze, Claudia noticed her husband staring at her. "It's lovely, isn't it?"

"Very," he said.

She felt the warmth rising from her throat at his passionate response, knowing it had nothing to do with their opulent surroundings.

Claudia's eyes danced with delight. Nathan had no idea what was about to happen tonight. He thought they would only be having dinner and a stroll along the upper deck. The weather had cooperated perfectly, and no doubt they would end the evening on deck, walking arm in arm in the moonlight. But for the past sixty-five days, she had worked, cried, sweated, and prayed to get to this evening, and now, God had seen fit to answer those prayers.

A black waiter filled their goblets with champagne, then poured lemonade for the boys. Even though none of them drank, Eugene raised his glass and proposed a toast for Nathan and Claudia's thirty-four years of marriage.

"And may God bless the next thirty-four," he concluded. The tinkling of crystal filled the air and each one took a sip, then left them for the remainder of the evening.

Nathan rose to his feet and stood behind his wife's chair, hand extended. "Would you like to join me at the buffet?"

In her most stylish voice, she responded, "Why certainly."

The rest of the family followed suit as they made their way to the seafood buffet. Claudia enjoyed watching Will and Jake try to figure out what kind of creatures were being served onto their plates. She felt certain they would have a hard time with the raw oysters. But what a grand, once-in-a-lifetime experience they were having. She planned to savor the evening—every moment of it.

By the time dinner and dessert were over, the women excused themselves to the ladies' room. When they returned, the men couldn't help but notice they were up to something. This time, Claudia stood behind her husband's chair and held out her hand. "Shall we?"

Mimicking his wife's earlier response, they headed for the stairs. Nathan reached down and took his wife into his arms, carrying her to what he thought would be the upper deck. But when they reached the landing for the dance floor, she whispered, "Put me down."

Nathan hesitated, "But don't you want to go for a stroll on deck?"

Claudia looked at him with all the love she had, and something else—there was a slightly mischievous appeal in her eyes and manner.

"Nate," she said a little more forcefully, "please put me down."

A slow smile moved across his face, and Nathan obeyed his wife's command.

An orchestra was already playing on the far end of the dance floor. Gaslights illuminated the shiny wood surface where several couples glided to the music in each other's arms.

Nathan watched as Annie stepped forward and kissed her mother affectionately. Rachel followed suit, then turned her gaze to Nathan. "Try not to let her wear you out."

He laughed and looked down at his beautiful wife. "I guess I'm the last one to know what's going on here."

Claudia handed Rachel her cane and took her husband by the hand. "Nate, I was wondering if you would like to dance with me?"

For just a moment, Claudia noticed Nathan struggle with his emotions. He took in a shuddered breath and cleared his throat, the moment passing quickly. He grinned his most handsome grin, and said, "I thought you'd never ask."

The family watched as Nathan circled his arm around Claudia's waist and swept her onto the dance floor. Their steps were tentative at first, but soon they whirled among the other couples, flowing with the music, eyes only for each other.

"You want to give it a try?" Eugene held out his hand to Annie.

She wiped an emotional tear from her cheek and gave her husband a nervous laugh. "This should be interesting."

"No doubt," he responded with a grin.

Rachel and the boys stood at the edge of the dance floor enjoying the scene. Whenever their parents or grandparents came into view, Will or Jake would point them out and sometimes laugh at the awkwardness of their dad.

Rachel noticed she was receiving the attention of an older gentleman across the way, and quickly turned to her grandsons. "Why don't we leave the adults to their dancing and go walk on the upper deck."

She was relieved when both boys responded with enthusiasm. "Could we?" Jake asked.

The gentleman was on his way over as Rachel grabbed each of their hands and led them to the staircase. She had to admit an interesting feeling had tickled her insides, but her heart would never hold another man the way it had Franklin. Never.

The steamboat paddle churned with ease as the *Idlewild* glided back down the river toward Louisville. Stars covered the heavens while a fingernail moon smiled from above. Nathan took off his jacket and put it around Claudia's shoulders as they stood at the railing watching the banks of the Ohio River slip by. She turned to face him, and he didn't hesitate to take her in his arms.

"Thank you for being so patient with me these last few months." Claudia drew back and looked into her husband's eyes, knowing how hard the situation had been for him. Her recovery was still ongoing, and she feared it would never be complete. "I know this hasn't been easy for you."

Nathan's smile was more contemplative than joyous. "Sweetheart, please don't apologize for the past months." He let out a long, slow breath and cradled her face in his right hand. "I thought I was going to lose you. I'll go through whatever it takes to keep you with me; I hope you know that."

He leaned down and kissed his wife, long and slow. Claudia reveled in the moment—there had been so few of them since her illness. Nathan had been treating her as if she were made of glass. She hoped that dancing with him tonight had given him a glimpse into her vigor and strength.

Pulling back from the kiss, Nathan turned his wife toward the railing and surrounded her with possessive arms. She leaned her head back onto his chest, feeling the steady cadence of his heart.

"Thank you for tonight, Claudia. I never dreamed we would be dancing on our anniversary."

Claudia let the evening play through her mind again—the expression on her husband's face when he realized she intended to dance with him, the ability God had given her to move her feet to the rhythm of the music, the river breeze blowing across the dance floor, the passion in Nathan's eyes as they moved in unison. It truly was like a dream, a beautiful dream she would never forget.

This time, she turned in his arms and kissed *him*.

"And the evening isn't over yet," she breathed softly against his mouth.

***

Summer was Will's favorite time of the year. No school for three months. Even though learning came easy for him, he simply didn't like having to put so much effort into something he would never use. At least that was his way of thinking. His teachers were always telling him how smart he was and then in the same breath asking why his grades didn't show it. Will found it sickening how much Jake enjoyed school. His younger brother always did his homework and studied for tests. It didn't bother him though; if Jake wanted to waste his time on the books, that was his problem.

The sun hadn't even made an appearance, and Will was already on the move. "Are you comin' or not?" He shook his younger brother in the bottom bunk.

Jake rolled over and started wiping the sleep from his eyes. "What time is it?"

"Almost six o'clock. O-Mok-See starts at eight." He yanked the sheet back and threw a pair of jeans at his brother, trying to get him to move. "The flag race is first and that's my best event. Let's go."

"Okay, okay . . . I'm up."

Will headed into the kitchen for breakfast. It was nearly impossible to beat his grandmother out of bed. Rachel already had scrambled eggs and bacon on the stove.

"Where's Jakie?" she asked, then spotted him shuffling barefoot down the hall. She let out a giggle, seeing his dark hair standing straight up, no shirt on, and his jeans still unbuttoned. But what a sweet smile he gave her when he entered the kitchen. An expression like that from Jake could melt her heart no matter how early it was in the morning.

Rachel filled a plate for both boys, then joined them for a morning blessing at the table. The brothers dug into their meal in a hurry. "So where's the O-Mok-See today?" she asked.

Will answered his gramma with a mouthful of eggs. "It's at the Cutter place. We gotta get goin'—it starts at eight."

"I guess you do. That's a good ways down the road."

Eugene entered the kitchen looking much like his younger son—dark hair standing straight up and barefoot. At least he had thrown on a t-shirt and buttoned his jeans. Kissing both sons on the top of their heads, he commented, "Big day, huh boys?"

"Uh, huh," Jake responded.

Eugene laid a hand on Rachel's shoulder, giving it an affectionate squeeze, then fixed himself a plate.

"Will," he said to his oldest son, "you need to take care of your brother, you hear me?"

"I hear ya."

"Even though it's a little faster to cross the stream near Yancey's farm, I want you to go on down to the bridge. It's a lot safer. You'll get there in plenty of time." Normally, Eugene would've gone with the boys to their O-Mok-See. The rodeo games for kids were a lot of fun to watch and the competition could be fierce. But today he had a lot to do, and he felt like it was time to give them a little freedom.

As soon as their plates were clean, Will nudged his brother and told him to meet him down at the barn as fast as he could.

Jake wiped his mouth with his hand. "That was good, Gramma. I'll see you this afternoon." He took off like a shot out of the kitchen and ran smack into Annie as she rounded the corner.

Startled, Annie muffled a shriek and grabbed Jake by the shoulders. "Whoa, Jakie. Watch what you're doing."

"Sorry, Momma. I'm kinda in a hurry."

"So I see."

"Will's already headin' down to the barn, and I gotta catch up."

She instantly turned toward the bedroom to help him finish getting dressed. When Jake finally tugged on his boots, Annie put her hand in the middle of his back and ushered him out the front door.

"And wear your hat all day," she called to him. "You don't want to get your neck blistered like last time."

Jake yelled over his shoulder, "I will, Momma," running as fast as his legs would carry him down to the barn.

Forty-five minutes later, Will brought Comanche to a halt and allowed Jake to catch up. Jake's bay mare, Sage, was a smaller thoroughbred than Comanche. She stood fifteen-and-a-half hands high and had the perfect temperament for her nine-year-old rider.

"We're goin' this way, Jake." The brothers had just reached the Yancey place, and Will pulled Comanche's reins to the left.

"Uh, uh, Will. Daddy told us to take the bridge."

"Yeah, but we're gonna be late, and this way's a lot faster."

"Yeah, but Daddy said—"

"But Dad didn't know we were gonna be late. Besides, I didn't promise him not to go this way."

Jake's conscience agonized over the decision he now had to make. Finally, he said, "Will, I'm not goin' that way; I'm takin' the bridge."

"Suit yourself. I'll see you at the Cutters'."

Jake's heart raced as he watched Comanche gallop away with his brother. Maybe he should follow; after all, his daddy didn't want him to be separated from Will. But Will was disobeying.

Clods of dirt flew into the air behind Comanche's powerful hindquarters. Will kept his eyes trained on the barrel at the far end of the arena. Comanche obeyed his rider's every command, slowing enough for Will to grab the red flag sitting on top. Swiftly changing directions, the horse raced to the second barrel across the arena, and Will jabbed the flag down as hard as he could into the bucket of dirt on top. The speed with which horse and rider crossed the finish line caused cheers to rise up from the dozens of spectators sitting along the arena fence. Comanche came to an aggressive halt, and Will held tight to the saddle horn to keep from being thrown over his head.

Mr. Cutter opened the gate of the arena for Will and Comanche to exit. He reached up and slapped the horse on the neck. "That was a fine ride, Will. You have the fastest time so far."

Will beamed with excitement. After that, he anxiously watched the last two riders, then waited to hear the winner's name called.

"With a time of 10.8 seconds, first place goes to William Wyatt."

The gate to the arena opened again. Will cantered in on Comanche to pick up his blue ribbon from Mr. Cutter. More cheers arose from the friends and neighbors who had come out to watch the O-Mok-See competition.

Will and Comanche competed in the next event, which was a horse and rider obstacle course. At certain times, the rider was required to dismount and crawl through a barrel or pick up a bandana from the ground. Good-natured laughter rang out as many horses took off across the arena while their rider was still inside the barrel.

The third race of the morning was a rescue race. It was his brother's favorite. Jake would stand on top of a barrel at the far end of the arena. As Will rounded the barrel with Comanche, Jake hopped on the back and held on for dear life as they raced for the finish line. A couple of times, Jake had jumped too late and landed in the dirt. The brothers had finally come up with a plan for Will to reach out and let Jake grab his arm as he jumped onto Comanche's haunches. The last two times they had used that method, the blue ribbon was theirs.

Will felt certain they could win the rescue race today, but so far he hadn't seen his brother. His eyes searched the crowd. There was no sign of Jake or Sage. A guilty feeling lodged inside his chest. He had been so caught up in getting to the competition on time, he hadn't taken care of his brother like he should have.

Weaving in and out of the other horses and riders, he inquired if anyone had seen Jake. No one seemed to have seen him all morning. Maybe he just decided to turn around and go back home. Will certainly hoped that wasn't the case; he'd be in big trouble if Jake went home without him. But still, he worried about his brother's conspicuous absence.

Chapter 20

Sage skidded to a halt, nearly slamming into the wooden gate on the Wyatts' farm. She skittered wildly back and forth, desperately trying to get down to the barn. If she could throw her head she would, but Jake had attached a tie-down under her bridle before leaving that morning. Her reigns whipped violently into the air, then down toward her front hooves, threatening to trip her.

With an uncharacteristic wildness in her eyes, Sage turned from the gate and galloped helter-skelter down the farm road toward the highway . . . without a rider.

Annie pushed Gracie to her top speed. She had been riding in the lower pasture when she noticed Sage's frenzied arrival. Dust and wind stung her eyes as she begged the Lord for Jake's safety—and Sage's too. She set her sights on the mare running out of control down the road, stumbling on the reins that dangled in front of her. Annie knew she had to stop the mare's panicked flight before she reached the highway or hurt herself.

At the sound of Annie's shrill whistle, Sage jerked her head around, meeting resistance from the tie-down, but the poor girl was spooked; running was her natural instinct. Gracie knew exactly what her job was; it was innate. She had wrangled hundreds of stray cows and horses in her twenty-four years. Annie rarely pushed her this hard, but she knew Gracie could do it.

The pinto mare charged up alongside of Sage. Annie let go of her reins and held tight to the saddle horn as she leaned out toward the fleeing animal to grab her reins. Sage flipped her head away violently and cut to the right. Gracie cut with her—Annie shifted her weight perfectly with the cut.

Forty yards to the highway . . . thirty . . . twenty . . .

It's not that the highway into the city was a busy one, but plenty of trucks and automobiles made their way along this stretch throughout the day. And the ditches on either side were steep and treacherous for any horse.

Gracie knew as well as Annie that they had to stop Sage's progress before the farm road ended. Annie gave Gracie her head, and she bolted with a powerful surge past the wild mare. Knowing what was coming, she tightened her thighs for the aggressive turnabout, which caused Sage to slam her back haunches to the ground to keep from colliding with Gracie.

Annie felt sorry for her. If she hadn't been wearing a tie-down, Sage could've thrown her head high enough to balance herself. But as it was, she fell on her side and slid toward Gracie. Gracie held her ground.

"Whoa, girl, whoa now." Annie had already dismounted and grabbed Sage's reins as she struggled back to her feet.

"It's all right . . . you're okay, girl." Annie's calming hands moved over Sage, and she brought the mare's head into her chest. Sage's nostrils flared and puffed quick breaths of air. Annie quickly released the tie-down from Sage's breast collar, and the horse felt her freedom. She raised her head, letting out a whinny that set Annie's hair on end.

"Where's Jake?" she pleaded emotionally.

Wasting no time, Annie held tightly to Sage's reins and hopped back onto Gracie. They trotted urgently toward the house. That's when she noticed Rachel running toward her, hand pressed tightly to her breast.

"Annie, I saw what happened. Where's Jake?" Her words came with such intensity Annie had to push back the panic that was threatening her sanity.

"I don't know . . . Sage came home without him."

She handed her mother-in-law the mare's reins and noticed Wallace running up from the barn.

"You and Wallace take care of Sage; I'm going to the Cutters'. When Eugene gets home, tell him to drive there with the truck."

Wallace had heard Annie's flurry of instructions as he came alongside her horse. He reached up and laid his hand on her lower leg, looking deeply into her eyes. Strangely, a peace came over Annie that couldn't be explained. The boy's words, however, set her heart racing just as quickly as his touch had calmed it.

"You'll find him, Miss Annie. He's waiting for you."

Wallace's hand fell to his side as Gracie bolted forward at Annie's urgent command.

It took only twenty minutes for Annie and Gracie to make it to the Yancey's place. The dirt road forked to the right leading to the bridge, but the left fork led to the Yancey's large, sprawling farmhouse. She knew there was a shortcut to the Cutters' about a quarter of a mile down the road toward the house. A trail led through the trees lining the road and eventually to a stream that separated the Cutter and Yancey property. The stream could be quite dangerous during the spring rains. It flowed from the Ohio River and would occasionally take over the road, leaving the Yanceys stranded on their own farm.

For a moment, Annie agonized whether to follow the road the boys had taken to the bridge or get to the Cutters' as fast as she could. Her head told her to go right; her instinct told her to go left. Instinct won the battle.

Gracie covered the quarter of a mile swiftly, and Annie brought her back to a trot as they entered the trail through the trees. Noticing the stream was a narrow, summer flow, she made the decision to jump Gracie across, and that's when she saw the body. Not just *any* body, the body of her youngest son.

"JAKE!"

She screamed his name as Gracie took the stream in one fluid motion. Annie was out of the saddle before the horse came to a complete stop. That's when

Jake's head raised up from where he lay on his back in the rocks beside the stream. His face and lips were an unnatural, pasty tint—even the color of his dark blue eyes seemed to have faded.

Annie dropped to her knees by his side and brought her face close to his. She felt the coolness of his skin. Swiftly, she worked her hands over his upper body.

"Where are you hurt, sweetheart?"

His words came out raw and scratchy, indicating dehydration, not to mention a possible serious injury. "My leg . . . I think."

Annie moved her hands along his left leg until she reached his boot. "This leg?"

"No, ma'am."

Oh, sweet boy . . . how long have you lain here all by yourself?

Slowly and methodically, she began working her hands down his right leg. It seemed straight and fine until her hands touched the top of his boot. The cry of pain was intense, and his face seemed to find a new shade of pale.

"It must be your ankle," she breathed, moving back to cradle his face in her hands. "We have to leave your boot on to keep it secure." But how on earth was she going to be able to move him? She feared he would go into shock at any moment. He needed to be wrapped in a blanket and rushed to the hospital.

"Sweetheart, I'll be right back."

Annie kissed his forehead, grabbed Gracie's reins, and sprinted up the hill toward the road that led to the Cutter farm. Across the road, she tied the horse's reins to the fence post, then sprinted back to her son. If Eugene, or anyone else for that matter, came down the road, they would see Gracie and know where Annie was.

"Jakie," she said softly.

His eyes fluttered open.

"I'm going to help you sit up a little bit."

"Momma, please don't move me." The rims of his eyes turned red in sharp contrast to his face.

"I'm not going to let your legs move at all; I just need to get in behind you."

Jake's eyes batted, and she noticed the set of his jaw. He was bracing for whatever pain he was about to experience.

As gently as she knew how, Annie raised his head, then neck, then back, as slowly as possible. Scooting along the rocks, she straddled her legs around him and carefully lowered him onto her chest. The slope of the bank gave her back just enough support. She wanted to give him as much bodily warmth as she could to prevent him from going into shock. She also knew she needed to keep him talking.

"Did you and Sage try to jump the stream, sweetheart?"

Jake choked out, "I'm sorry, Momma. I—"

Annie's arms took in more of her son, and she knew this was a subject best saved for later.

"It's okay, Jakie. Sage made it home just fine." In as cheery a voice as she could muster, she said, "As a matter of fact, she came to get me. Daddy's coming, too; he'll be here any minute." *Come on Eugene. Come on.*

Deciding on a different tack in conversation, Annie asked, "What would you like for your birthday?" This was the ploy she always used when trying to get him back to sleep after a bad dream. She'd rub his back soothingly and take his mind as far away from the nightmare as possible—only this wasn't a dream, however much she wished it to be so.

"It's not till January," he softly chided.

"I know, but surely you can think of something you'd like."

There was a long silence between them, but Annie could tell he was thinking hard on the subject. Finally, he said, "I want a puppy."

"Ooh, me too! What kind?"

"A German shepherd."

"Girl or boy?"

"Boy."

"What would you name him?"

"Hmm." Jake thought a while on that one. Then he turned his head to the side, trying to see his momma's face. "Scout."

"I like that. Why Scout?"

"Because Daddy was a scout in the war and—"

"Eugene!" Annie yelled his name as loud as she could, startling Jake. "I'm sorry, sweetheart. Do you hear a truck?"

"Yes," he breathed.

"Eugene! Down here!" She could hear the truck idling on the road. "Help . . . please!"

The engine cut off and the sound of a door opening, then slamming shut, seemed like a glorious melody to Annie's ears.

"Annie?"

Eugene's voice seemed even more glorious as he came flying down the path toward the stream. He slid to his knees beside the pair, taking hold of Annie's arm and laying a light hand on Jake's chest.

"Is he okay?"

The corners of Jake's mouth turned up slightly. "Hi, Daddy."

Annie thought she could eat him up with a spoon.

"It's his right ankle, Eugene. We can't move him unless it's immobilized somehow."

Eugene straddled one leg over his son and looked him in the eyes. "I'm going to get something from the truck. You and Momma hang on for a few more minutes, and we'll get you to the doctor."

Annie pleaded with her eyes for Eugene to hurry. When he came back a couple of minutes later, he was carrying a panel he had ripped from a wooden crate and a burlap sack. Working quickly with his pocketknife he started a tear in

the opening of the bag then ripped it all the way down its seam. Annie watched him position himself beside Jake's right ankle.

"Jakie," he spoke reassuringly, "I'm going to slide this wood underneath your lower leg and tie it down with the burlap."

Eugene gave Annie a look that said *hold him tight*.

The groan that rose up from Jake's throat just about did her in. But Eugene had his son's leg on the board and tied down in less than a minute's time. Quickly, he reached between Jake and Annie so she could move out from under him.

"I'm gonna pick him up, but you need to hold his leg steady and straight on that board."

Without a word, Annie moved in position for them to work in unison. Slowly, the two carried their son to the road, and Eugene led them to the back of the truck.

"Annie, if you want to drive, I'll ride in the back with him."

"No, I'm fine in the back."

She noticed he had dumped out one of the feedbags all over the bed of the truck—obviously the bag he had used for the splint. He had even separated the other bags to provide a protective boundary around whoever rode with Jake. Fortunately, the scattered horse feed made it easier for them to slide into position.

The truck engine came to life and Eugene forced it into gear, turning it around in the road as quickly as possible. As soon as they started moving away from the Cutters' farm, Annie spotted Will and Comanche riding over the ridge.

"Eugene, stop! It's Will."

Eugene brought their forward progress to a smooth halt. The truck idled almost impatiently as he set the break and ran to meet his son. Annie could barely hear the conversation but was thankful when she saw her husband hand him Gracie's reins.

She studied Will's demeanor as he stood motionless in the middle of the road. His eyes remained unswervingly on his brother until the truck disappeared around the curve. She hadn't quite been able to read the expression on his face but was certain it had to be one of two possibilities—either a deep concern for his brother or shame.

It was nearly dark when Eugene pulled the truck up to the front porch that evening. Jake sat between his parents, wrapped in his mother's arm. He sported a white cast on his right leg clear up to his knee. Annie couldn't get over how much time they had spent at the hospital today.

When they had finally been able to see the orthopedic doctor after waiting over an hour, it took another painstaking half hour simply to remove Jake's boot. His ankle and leg had swollen so badly, the boot had to be removed with a saw. Icing had not brought the swelling down sufficiently for a cast, so after another hour had passed the decision was made to drain the blood. Annie thought she was going to pass out as they stuck a syringe into his swollen ankle and drew out blood, over and over again. Finally, they deemed it possible to put on the plaster cast. Poor fella, he was completely worn out. They all just needed to crawl into bed.

Eugene came around the truck and opened Annie's door. He reached in and took Jake out of her arms, carrying him gently into the house. Rachel met them inside the door. She immediately cradled Jake's face in her hands and kissed his forehead.

"I'm so sorry about your fall, Jake."

He looked at Rachel through heavy eyelids. "It's all right, Gramma." A slight grin stretched across his face. "I got a cast."

"I see that, darlin'. Would you like something to eat?"

Jake was too tired to even answer. He just shook his head.

Eugene carried him to the bathroom, then into the boy's bedroom and laid him on the bottom bunk. Together, he and Annie got him undressed and into his pajamas. Eugene said a prayer over their son, then he and Annie kissed him but remained on the side of his bed for a while.

Will stood in the doorway to the bedroom, watching his parents with Jake. He knew he was mostly responsible for his brother's condition. Seeing Jake hurt like that truly bothered him, but saying the words *I'm sorry* would make him entirely responsible. Something inside of him would not allow it. As much as he cared about Jake, his pride, in some twisted way, came first. He was determined to do everything he could to make it up to his brother; he just wasn't sure how he was going to do it.

When his parents rose from Jake's bed, Will's mouth suddenly went dry. He wondered if his father would deem it necessary to take him down to the barn for an encounter with the hickory paddle. He still wasn't even sure how Jake broke his ankle.

Surprisingly, Annie reached out to him and pulled him to her. Will wrapped his arms around her and let his momma hold him for a long moment. All he could feel was her unconditional love, so he reveled in the moment, not sure of what would happen next. Releasing him, she said quietly, "Let's go talk."

All three headed into the living room where Rachel sat underneath the lamp reading her Bible. She laid it on the table when Will sat down on the couch. Eugene and Annie took a seat on either side of him.

"Can you tell me what happened this morning, Will?" His dad's face looked weary. Will knew he had missed a whole day's work because of Jake's injury. There were still feedbags in the truck that needed to be unloaded.

Nodding his head, he began with how he and Jake had reached the fork in the road at the Yancey's farm earlier this morning.

"We were running late, and I knew the flag race was first. If I didn't take the shortcut over the stream, I was gonna miss it." There appeared to be no look of condemnation on his parents' faces—so far, so good.

"Jake said he didn't want to take the shortcut, and I told him that was fine. The last time I saw him he was heading down the road to the bridge. I knew he'd make it to the Cutters' about fifteen minutes after me by goin' that way."

"Is that it?" Eugene asked.

Will turned his palms up and shrugged his shoulders. "I don't know what happened after we separated. He must've changed his mind and decided to follow me . . . but I didn't know."

Annie drew his attention then. "Didn't you miss him at the Cutters'?"

"Momma, I just thought he was around somewhere. It wasn't until the rescue race that I started lookin' for him and couldn't find him."

No one said anything. The steady *tic tic tic* of the mantle clock filled the silence in the living room. Will felt certain his parents were trying to come to some sort of decision, but he had no clue what that would be.

Finally, his dad brought up the conversation they had had at the breakfast table. "Do you remember the two things I told you?"

Will clinched his jaw; he didn't want to repeat the instructions. "Yes, sir."

"What did I say?"

"You told us to take the bridge."

"What else?"

Will sat stubbornly silent.

"What else?" Eugene repeated.

He let out the breath he'd been holding. "You told me to take care of my brother."

Tic tic tic . . .

It seemed like a long time before his dad finally broke the silence again. "That was your last O-Mok-See for the summer."

Will's head dropped low.

"And your brother's going to be in a cast for the next six or eight weeks. That means your work just got doubled around here. As a matter of fact, it starts tonight. I've got a whole truckload of feed that you're going to stack down at the barn before you go to bed."

Will nodded his head.

"Don't you have anything to say?" his mother asked.

He knew she was fishing for an apology, but they could sit here all night waiting for that. The only thing he could think of to say was, "It won't happen again."

He rose to his feet and told his daddy he was ready to unload the truck. His gramma, however, had the last word.

"Will?"

"Yes, ma'am?"

"People are always more important than the games they play."

He let that sink in for a minute, then headed out the door.

***

"Hey, sleepyhead, wake up." Will gently shook his brother's shoulder until Jake's eyes peeled open. "I brought you some breakfast."

Jake naturally awoke with a pleasantness that irritated his older brother most days of the week, but not today. Today, he planned to start making amends for yesterday's mishap.

"Do you need some help getting to the bathroom?"

"I got crutches," Jake said, almost with an air of excitement.

Will fingered the crutches leaning up against the bunk bed. "Yeah, I see that. You know how to use 'em?"

"Naw, I haven't had time."

Will pulled back the cover and reached underneath Jake's arms. "Come on. I'll get you to the bathroom, and you can practice on your crutches after breakfast."

After the brothers returned to their room, Will propped up pillows behind Jake's back and positioned the breakfast tray on his lap.

"Have you already eaten?" Jake asked.

"Not yet. I'll eat after you're done." But that didn't stop Will from pilfering a piece of bacon from Jake's plate. Sticking it in his mouth, he scooted back against the wall at the foot of his brother's bed. "Does it hurt?"

Jake let a mouthful of grits slide down his throat. "A little. It kinda throbs."

Will was curious about the accident and decided to ask what happened. He was secretly hoping that something Jake might say would let his conscience off the hook.

"How'd you fall off Sage?"

Jake looked up from his plate and scrunched his mouth over to one side. He seemed to be pondering exactly how that must've happened. "I guess I wasn't ready for Sage to jump the creek. I thought we were just gonna walk through it, but at the last second she jumped." He shrugged his shoulders. "I hung on till we got across, but my right foot got twisted in the stirrup when I was falling, and then I landed on it really hard."

A long silence fell between the brothers while Jake finished his breakfast. Will wasn't exactly sure what else to say. Eventually, he hopped off the bed and opened his dresser drawer. When he turned back around, he held out the blue ribbon he had won yesterday in the flag race. It wasn't just any blue ribbon—it had a round shiny circle at the top, surrounded by ruffles, and the picture of a horse's profile in the middle of it.

"I want you to have this." The thrilled look on Jake's face made the gesture completely worthwhile.

"Are you sure? You earned that."

"Yeah, you take it. I shoulda been back there at the creek with you."

Will exchanged the ribbon for the breakfast tray in Jake's lap. He guessed that was about as close to an apology as he could possibly get. Besides, his little brother never held a grudge.

As soon as Will left the room with the tray, Eugene popped his head around the door. "You ready to get dressed and try out those crutches?"

Jake's earlier cheerfulness faded a bit at the sight of his daddy. He knew he deserved to be punished for not taking the bridge yesterday. He didn't feel worthy of his dad's gentleness, helping him pull his pajama bottoms off over the big, white cast. Before they could figure out how to put a pair of pants over the awkward object at the end of his leg, Jake couldn't hold back his emotions any longer. He threw his arms around Eugene's neck.

"I'm sorry I disobeyed you yesterday," he said in a most penitent voice.

He felt his father's arms surround him for a moment, then his dad moved to sit down beside him on the bed. "You know Jake, there are consequences for every choice you make. Unfortunately, your consequence for not taking the bridge is a painful one. Plus, you won't be able to ride for the rest of the summer."

Jake mournfully nodded his head.

"Will has consequences too," Eugene continued, "because he took the shortcut and didn't take care of you like I asked him to. So both of you have your own punishment to deal with."

Eugene lightly clasped his hand around the back of Jake's neck. "I'm disappointed in the choice you made, but I love you and I forgive you."

A sheen of tears covered Jake's eyes. "I love you too, Daddy."

Eugene ruffed up Jake's hair, then kissed the top of his head. "Now what are we gonna do about getting some pants on you today?" The nurse at the hospital had already cut the leg of the jeans he was wearing yesterday all the way up to his thigh. "I guess its shorts for you."

Eugene pulled a pair of shorts from the dresser. He helped Jake finish getting dressed and supervised a few laps around the room with his crutches until Jake decided he was ready to show off in the kitchen.

***

It didn't take long for the novelty of crutches to wear off. By the time August rolled around seven weeks later, Jake had long since done away with the annoying wooden contraptions. His momma wouldn't let him ride with a cast on his leg, even though he knew he could. Jake was well aware it was all part of his punishment, and he would be obedient even if it killed him. Besides, the worst consequence of all was how much his leg itched inside that cast. His dad cut him a piece of thin plywood about the size of a ruler so he could fit it down inside the smelly plaster for scratching purposes. He just kept reminding himself that he would be free in just a matter of days.

By the third week of August, preparations were being made for all of the children to return to school. Annie and Rachel had enjoyed a trip into town to buy two new dresses for Lillie who had grown a little since she first came in January. Her squeal of delight over getting a new pair of shoes was something neither of the women would forget for a long time. The boys had also been taken to town separately for their shopping, which had taken less than an hour before they were ready to go home.

Just four days before school was to begin, the whole family enjoyed a lazy evening outside after supper. The adults sat on the front porch trying to catch a summer breeze while the boys tossed a ball around in the yard. Music from the radio meandered through the open windows of the living room.

Lillie perched on one end of the porch swing while Annie gently pushed it back and forth.

"Lillie, do you want to join the boys in the yard?" Annie asked her.

"No ma'am, I'd rather be right here with you."

The most precious smile covered Lillie's face as she scooted in closer. She raised her face toward Annie's, lips puckered. Annie brushed her lips on the sweet child's and pulled her up into her lap. Even though it was a warm evening, she enjoyed being able to give Lillie some extra loving.

"Are you excited about third grade?"

"Not much."

"Not much?" Annie laughed. "Why not?"

"'Cause of Rufus Washington."

"Who's Rufus Washington?"

"Only the meanest boy in school. He's in the fifth grade."

"Has he ever hurt you, Lillie?" Annie asked with concern.

"No ma'am. But he's hurt some of my friends, and I don't like it."

Annie rubbed a consoling hand up and down Lillie's arm. "Well, we'll just have to pray for Rufus tonight, won't we?"

Lillie seemed to ponder that for a while, then she looked up into Annie's face. "I'm thinkin' you'll have to say that prayer."

She tried not to laugh, but Annie couldn't help it after Lillie had made her statement with such conviction.

Just then, the telephone rang and Eugene hurried inside to answer it. He was gone for quite some time before returning to the porch.

"Who was it?" Annie asked her husband.

Eugene casually sat back down in his chair.

"I'll tell you later."

He acted as if it was nothing important, but Annie had already noticed the way he avoided her eyes. And that wasn't all; there was something about those tiny lines forming between his eyebrows that sent a stab of concern straight to her heart.

Chapter 21

Eugene and Annie stood outside the redbrick Victorian mansion on Kentucky Street, holding firmly to Wallace and Lillie's hands. Even in the shade of the expansive porch, the sweltering August heat left them all perspiring through their clothes. Eugene shifted the suitcase in his hand and opened the door, then waited until everyone else stepped inside the darkened hallway. He found himself hoping that the apartment they were seeking would be on the first floor. When he realized there were four apartments on each floor, it became evident that number nine would unfortunately be on the third floor, just under the attic—the heat would be unbearable.

He smiled at Wallace, who looked up at him with large, brown eyes, sweat running in a stream down the side of his face. For a second, he thought Wallace could read his mind, especially when the boy squeezed his hand reassuringly. It was true—Eugene did have reservations about Wallace and Lillie living in the middle of the city, cooped up in an apartment, on the third floor no less. For the past eight months, they had been free to roam dozens of acres. They had learned how to ride, care for farm animals, and tend a garden. He knew the children needed to be with their mother above all else, but he couldn't help but feel sorry for their present circumstances.

The stairs creaked as the foursome climbed to the third floor. The carpet was well worn and the banister a bit wobbly, but the rich paneled wood spoke of an elegant, beautiful house in its earlier days.

Wallace pointed out apartment number nine at the top of the staircase. For a moment, no one made a move to knock on the door—the mood was somber, not what Eugene had expected in reuniting the children with their mother.

He cleared his throat and raised his hand toward the door, but Wallace unexpectedly pulled his arm back just before his knuckles made contact with the wooden surface.

"Mr. Eugene, I just wanted you to know that I'll never forget what you did for me and my sister." He looked solemnly into Eugene's eyes. "It's been the best part of our lives."

Eugene knew why Wallace had stopped him from knocking on that door. The boy didn't want his mama to hear such a declaration. He had an overwhelming urge to scoop these two children up and take them right back to the farm. But Eugene was remembering the unexpected phone conversation with

Roberta only two nights ago. She could barely contain her excitement over a new job as a hotel maid and a place for her and the children to live together again. It would be selfish to keep Wallace and Lillie separated from their mother even one more day.

Squatting down to Wallace's level, Eugene straightened the boy's collar, trying to hold back an unexpected wave of emotion. "It was our pleasure." He took Wallace by the shoulders, and said, "You and Lillie are family now. We'll have you out to the farm as often as we can."

Eugene stood up and made the mistake of glancing over at Annie. Her eyes glistened with tears, and Lillie stood by her side crying unashamedly. He quickly turned his attention back to Wallace. "Are you ready?"

Wallace slowly nodded his head. "Yes, sir."

At the sound of his knock, rapid footsteps echoed on the other side of the door, and suddenly both children were being smothered in their mama's loving arms. Eugene hoped Roberta perceived their tears as tears of joy.

He took notice of their surroundings as Roberta continued loving on her children. They stood in a small living room, which contained a threadbare Victorian sofa, possibly a leftover from the previous owners of the mansion, and a straight-back chair. The other three matching chairs stood around a small kitchen table indicating where the living room ended and the tiny kitchen began. There was only one window at the end of the living room, but it was a large one letting in a decent breeze, albeit a scorching one. A tall lamp stood next to the sofa with a tattered shade, and a small tan rug covered the middle section of the floor. Only two other open doors were visible from where he stood—a small bedroom that he assumed all three would share and a bathroom directly off of the kitchen.

When Roberta was through hugging and kissing her children, she invited Eugene and Annie to stay for homemade cookies and lemonade.

"I don't know how I can ever thank you and your parents, Annie, for takin' in my sweet young'uns during these hard times. They's told me so many things about your kindness."

Annie reached for her hand and told her what a pleasure it had been for their family.

As they sat around the table, Roberta excitedly told them of her new job as a maid at the prestigious Brown Hotel only three blocks away. She would have to leave in the morning before the children went to school, but she got off work at three o'clock every day and would be here when they came home.

"Wallace and Lillie's school's just a short walk 'round the corner. Findin' this apartment was a godsend."

The children stood beside the table barely touching their cookies and lemonade.

When it was finally time for them to leave, Eugene and Annie tried to keep the mood light. "We'll get to see you every Sunday at church," Annie said enthusiastically. "And I want to hear all about your first week of school." She winked at Lillie. "I'll be praying about Rufus Washington." That seemed to bring a smile to Lillie's lips.

Annie opened her arms to the precious girl, and Lillie hugged her neck tightly.

"I love you, Miss Annie."

Annie pulled back and looked into Lillie's big, brown eyes. "I love you too, sweetheart." They kissed, then Annie turned to Wallace while Lillie went into Eugene's extended arms.

Finally back at the car, Annie let her pent-up emotions loose. She wept for the better part of the trip back to the farm. Eugene tried to think of something to say that would ease her pain, but he had to admit this had been harder than he'd ever imagined. Wallace and Lillie had become an important part of their lives. Taking them back to their mother had left a gaping hole.

The next few days took some getting used to. Annie missed helping Lillie with her hair or having a quiet conversation with Wallace. Rachel went back to cooking for a family of five instead of seven while Eugene missed the joy of teaching Wallace and Lillie something new about life on the farm. Will moved into his room again on the back of the house. And while Jake complained of feeling lonesome in his own room, Will rejoiced in being alone in his.

Even though the new school year was off to a fine start, the whole family seemed to be trapped inside the doldrums. That's when Mr. Crowley's phone call changed everything.

Annie had just come in from taking the boys to school. She slipped off her shoes and headed for the back door to pull on her boots when the telephone rang. Rachel was already working outside in the garden trying to beat the heat of the day, so Annie ran down the hallway and lifted the receiver.

"Hello?"

"Mrs. Wyatt?"

"Yes?"

"This is Mr. Crowley." His formality never ceased to amaze her.

"Good morning, Mr. Crowley. How are you today?"

"Never better, and you?"

"I can't complain."

Mr. Crowley proceeded with the reason for his early morning phone call. After much discussion, Annie agreed to have Will ride over to his place as soon as he got home from school. Hanging up the receiver, Annie hoped she had done the right thing by agreeing to Wendall Crowley's proposition, especially since she hadn't bothered to check with Eugene.

Later that afternoon, Will saddled Comanche and headed over to the Crowley's farm. He had no idea what to expect when he got there. In fact, he had been a bit nervous when his mother told him that Mr. Crowley had asked him to come by. The last time they had been together wasn't exactly the most pleasant experience for either one of them.

Will made sure Comanche walked the entire distance to the Crowley's barn, so he wouldn't be sweating or breathing hard when he got there. It didn't seem to matter. The first thing *Mr. Scare-Crowley* asked him was how he was treating his horse. Will dismounted at the gate to the barn and told him he was taking care of Comanche very well. With a minor inspection, Will's neighbor gave a nod of approval and opened the gate.

"I'm glad to see you're treating this fine horse with respect. I think it's important that we learn to take care of the animals that the good Lord has put in our care." Mr. Crowley led Comanche to a water bucket, then continued to lecture Will on the finer points of horse care.

When the older man settled down on a bench, Will feared he was in for a long afternoon. He tried to listen as respectfully as possible and wondered if this was the only purpose for his visit.

Finally, Mr. Crowley turned to his young visitor and said, "Do you understand what I've been saying?"

Will nodded, "Yes, sir."

"Then come with me, Son. I've got somethin' to show ya."

Mr. Crowley rose from the bench and stretched his long frame before walking across the barn to the tack room. He opened the door and stepped back for Will to go in first. Will walked inside, then stopped dead in his tracks at the sight before him.

He felt Mr. Crowley's spindly fingers nudge his shoulder.

"Well, go on. Get in there."

An hour later, Will walked through the kitchen door holding a burlap sack. Rachel nearly had supper ready for the family and called out for everyone to get washed up. She glanced over her shoulder and noticed Will's bundle.

"What have you got there?"

"You'll see, Gramma."

Rachel knew it must have been something special because she hadn't seen an expression on Will's face like that since last Christmas.

One by one, the family filed into the kitchen. Rachel noticed the look on Annie's face was nearly identical to Will's.

"Hey, what's in the bag?" Jake asked.

Will carefully laid his bundle down. "Come take a look."

He opened the sack letting the contents spill out onto the floor.

Jake instantly dropped to his knees squealing with delight as two little puppies untangled themselves and started moving around the kitchen floor on wobbly legs.

Rachel found herself thoroughly enjoying the excitement of the moment. The delight on her grandsons' faces warmed her heart. She had half a mind to get down there in the floor with them—until she became aware of Annie's expression and realized something was amiss. The enthusiasm she had noticed on her daughter-in-law's face the moment before had now turned into a look of consternation.

"Will, what have you done?" Annie demanded.

Will stood up and faced his mother. Rachel thought there was going to be an argument, but thankfully the confrontational, dark cloud that could so easily appear, remained at bay.

"Momma, I know you thought I was only bringing home one puppy, but I wanted Jake to have one too. I owe him for what happened this summer."

Annie looked toward Eugene, but apparently he wasn't going to be a bit of help. He already had one of the puppies snuggled in his arms. Even worse, he had just planted a kiss on top of its head.

"Eugene!" She said his name in exasperation.

With his typical good-natured grin, Eugene thrust the puppy into her arms, then reached down and scooped up the other one. "One for you and one for me." He kissed the top of the other puppy's head, then leaned over to kiss Annie.

"Not on your life, Eugene! You just kissed a dog, for goodness sake."

"Momma, please let us keep both of 'em," Jake begged.

"Yeah, please Mom," Will chimed in. "Besides, now they can keep each other company. Mr. Crowley said the puppies have bonded with each other. He said they were the only two puppies to survive out of a litter of four."

Rachel laughed when Annie looked her way. "I can't help you, darlin'. I think you're outnumbered." She reached over and stroked the furry creature in Annie's arms. "They are awfully cute, aren't they?"

Annie seemed to notice the puppy in her arms for the first time, and a slow smile crept across her face. Without giving in quite yet, she asked, "What kind of puppies are they?"

"Boys!"

"I didn't mean that, Will. What breed are they?"

"Mr. Crowley only knows that they're half German shepherd because his dog, Sadie, had the puppies. But he thinks the other half may be yellow Labrador retriever 'cause he caught the Moultries' Lab on his property a few times."

All three of the Wyatt males wore the same silly grin, waiting for Annie's response.

"Oh, all right," she said, letting out a groan of surrender. "It looks like we have two more mouths to feed around here."

The kitchen was filled with whoops of victory, and Annie rolled her eyes at Eugene who kissed her right on the mouth before she could turn away.

Rachel asked Will, "Which dog belongs to you and which one is Jake's?"

"Dad's holdin' mine, and I've already named him Ranger."

"Then this must be Scout." Annie and Jake said his name at the very same time. Everyone looked between the two of them in surprise.

Annie smiled and held the puppy out to Jake. "That's our little secret."

Jake took Scout from his mother and wrinkled up his nose. "Uh, sorry about that, Momma." He nodded his head toward her blouse.

Eugene started laughing until he handed Ranger to Will.

"Well," Rachel said, trying to suppress her laughter, "I guess we'll hold supper until the two of you change your clothes."

The next few weeks of puppy training were filled with moments of both sheer delight and extreme aggravation. Will and Jake had taken full responsibility for the training of their own dog inside the house as well as outside around the cattle and horses.

The two puppies were easy to tell apart. Ranger had the yellow coloring of the Labrador retriever, but that wasn't all. He seemed to take on Will's temperament and personality. In the house, he became known as the sock bandit. Countless ruined socks were found in the pantry where Ranger liked to hide out and chew to his heart's content. When the household wised up to his sock escapades, he started in on their shoes. Eugene finally bound up a piece of leather with a belt that served as a chew toy for Ranger.

Scout, on the other hand, had the coloring of his German shepherd mother. He loved to cuddle and slept every night in Jake's bunk. Will tried to get Ranger to sleep with him, but the dog was far too independent and preferred curling up on the floor rug. While Scout followed Jake's every move, Ranger was partial to roaming the property with or without Will. Both dogs were suited perfectly for their young owners.

Eugene was proud of the way his boys took care of their dogs. He had always wanted a dog of his own growing up, but his papa had much preferred horses over dogs. Franklin had never seen much of a reason to have a four-legged mutt hanging around their farm. Nevertheless, Eugene believed his boys were learning good qualities such as dependability and a sense of duty that they might not have otherwise learned. But he worried about his eldest son. While Ranger seemed to take an edge off his temper for the time being, Will began to acquire a more defiant independence that often pitted him against the very people who loved him the most.

As the next few years quickly passed, Jake made the decision to give his heart to the Lord. The entire Oak Hill congregation gathered at the pond behind the building to witness Eugene immersing his son into Christ. It was a glorious celebration as Jake came up from the watery grave. Eugene was reminded of the night he gave his heart to the Lord. He remembered the guilt he had felt as a boy concerning his mother's death. Even though that guilt had been forced upon him by a malicious stepfather, it had been so freeing to lay it all at the feet of Jesus. Jake's young life had been nothing like his own, but his youngest son's heart was so pliable and supple in the hands of the Almighty—a true blessing to their family.

Will, however, was rebellious in ways of the heart. He had stood at Jake's baptism on the edge of the crowd with a dispassionate countenance. Something was holding him back. Eugene prayed earnestly that whatever that *something* was

God would take it and melt it away. In order to be shaped into a useful tool for God's kingdom, he feared that Will would need to undergo an extraordinary amount of time on the anvil. Eugene was all too familiar with the heat of the fire and the pain of the blacksmith's mallet. He only hoped that his eldest son would listen and turn before it was too late.

Chapter 22

January 1937

"Rain, rain, go away!" Annie hung her rain slicker on a peg in the back entryway, then pulled off her sodden boots. She noticed her muddy trousers and decided she couldn't walk through the house with them on. All of the men were still down at the barn, so she stepped out of her pants and left them on the floor. She would have to soak them in the metal tub on the back porch to get all the mud stains out.

"Sorry about this, Mama."

Rachel turned just in time to see her daughter-in-law run through the kitchen half dressed. She let out a giggle. "I'm hoping you were wearing pants when you left the barn."

With a laugh, Annie called out from the bedroom, "Yes! I left them by the back door."

"I'll go put them in the soak."

"Oh Mama, you don't have to do that. I'll be right out to take care of it."

"I've got it, darlin'." Rachel stepped to the back door and held up Annie's pants. "If the boys' trousers look anything like yours, we may have to soak them overnight," she called out.

Annie scurried back into the kitchen, dressed and pulling her hair back in a short ponytail. "I'm afraid theirs will be even worse. We just can't keep the barn floor dry. I'm worried about the horses' hooves staying wet for so long."

She knew that if their hooves stayed wet for an extended period of time, they would become weak. The weight of the horse could cause the bottom of the hoof wall to flare outward, which might lead to any number of problems.

"How's our Lucy coming along?" Rachel was referring to Lucky Lucy, the sorrel brood mare who was very heavily pregnant.

"She's the one I'm most concerned about. She could foal any day now. We actually built a platform in her stall today to keep her higher off the ground. She'll need a nice dry place when she's ready."

Rachel stepped out onto the screened-in porch and dipped Annie's trousers into the tub. "I want to be there when she foals."

Annie smiled as she stood in the doorway. "Don't worry, Mama, we won't let you miss it. I just hope this rain lets up before our little foal makes its appearance."

Rachel shook her head. "Nineteen straight days of rain. This has to be a record."

Both women returned to the kitchen, trying to escape the cold, damp air. Rachel dipped her hands in the washbasin and scrubbed them with soap. After drying them, she lifted the lid on a big pot of chili. It had been simmering on the stove all afternoon.

Annie breathed in the mouth-watering aroma. "That smells delicious. I'm so hungry."

Rachel took a spoon from the drawer and dipped it into the chili, then waved it up and down in the air to cool it off a bit. She held it out to Annie, keeping her hand underneath as she slipped it into her daughter-in-law's mouth.

"Mm. That tastes as good as it smells. Thank you."

Rachel smiled, obviously pleased with Annie's response. "It's nearly dark. Did Eugene say when they were coming in?"

Just then, the back door burst open. Eugene and the boys had already removed their boots on the back porch. They jostled each other in the entryway as they peeled off their soaked rain slickers and hung them up on a peg.

Annie threw her hands up as they headed into the kitchen. "Hold it right there, guys. Trousers go in the soaking tub first."

Rachel immediately turned her back. Even at ages thirteen and fourteen, the boys had no qualms about dropping their jeans to the floor. Eugene took his off on the back porch and made sure his mama's back was still turned before he traipsed through the kitchen.

Rainy weather dominated the supper conversation along with talk of President Roosevelt's inauguration the next day. Will and Jake were excited to have the day off from school. This was the first time that a president was going to be inaugurated on January 20 due to a change in the 20th Amendment to the Constitution.

"I thought we'd listen to the inauguration on the radio at noon tomorrow, then take a drive over to the Ohio River," Eugene announced to the family over dessert.

With a mouthful of cherry cobbler, Will said, "I heard at school today that it's nearly up to flood stage. Mr. West told us that the normal river level is twenty-eight feet and flood stage is fifty-five. This morning it was measured at fifty-two feet."

Rachel looked worried. "Fifty-two feet already? Do you think it's safe to drive into the city tomorrow?"

"It'll be fine, Mama. If the river starts to overflow, we'll come back home."

The next day promised little change in the weather, ushering in more of the dark, persistent clouds. Rain continued pelting the soggy landscape, and Eugene began to worry about his cattle, which had endured twenty straight days of precipitation.

At noon, the family gathered around their radio, warm and dry, to listen to President Roosevelt's inauguration speech for a second term in office. The boys tussled with their dogs while they waited. The weather in Washington was much like the weather in Kentucky—rain and sleet fell on the crowd in front of the capitol building.

"Shh, it's starting," Annie said, as the president's strong voice resonated through the crackling radio reception.

When four years ago we met to inaugurate a president, the Republic, single-minded in anxiety, stood in spirit here. We dedicated ourselves to the fulfillment of a vision—to speed the time when there would be for all the people that security and peace essential to the pursuit of happiness. We of the Republic pledged ourselves to drive from the temple of our ancient faith those who had profaned it; to end by action, tireless and unafraid, the stagnation and despair of that day. We did those first things first.

Eugene marveled at the progress this president had brought to the country in his first four years of office. He had inspired a nation to hope again and brought it out of complete despair. But President Roosevelt went on to say that millions of Americans were still living in poverty. He warned against complacency among those who had enough, likening it to immoral behavior.

The test of our progress is not whether we add more to the abundance of those who have much; it is whether we provide enough for those who have too little.

Feeling blessed, Eugene knew their family could do more for those in need. Maybe it was even time to hire a farmhand and give someone a job who needed one.

In taking again the oath of office as President of the United States, I assume the solemn obligation of leading the American people forward along the road over which they have chosen to advance.

While this duty rests upon me, I shall do my utmost to speak their purpose and to do their will, seeking Divine guidance to help us each and every one to give light to them that sit in darkness and to guide our feet into the way of peace.

Eugene turned the radio up a notch as Chief Justice Charles Evans Hughes administered the oath of office. When it was concluded, Rachel and Annie headed into the kitchen to prepare a lunch of sandwiches and leftover chili.

Holding hands around the kitchen table a few minutes later, Eugene led his family in a blessing over the food as well as for their nation and president. Everyone seemed to hurry through the meal, excited about a trip into the city to see the rising river. Even though Rachel still had qualms about the adventure, she quickly pulled on her boots and raincoat as Eugene brought the car up close to the porch.

The six-mile trip into the city of Louisville was through hilly country. They noticed several ponds overflowing, and the ditches on either side of the highway looked like swift-running streams.

"Do you think the water might overtake the road, Eugene?" Rachel sat in the front seat, obviously worried about the rushing water beside the road.

Eugene was suddenly reminded of the story she had told him once about his papa Franklin's mother and sister. Their carriage had been caught in a flashflood near Lexington and swept into the river. The Hawkins plantation owner had lost his wife and daughter along with three slaves that day, Franklin's mother and sister among them.

He reached over and covered his mother's hand in her lap. "We'll be fine, Mama. Don't worry; I won't drive through any water standing on the road."

She gave his hand a quick squeeze, then pulled it away. "You just keep both hands on the wheel, please."

Eugene laughed and did just as he was told.

Main Street was still a bustle of activity with a few citizens running for cover from the rain while dozens of black umbrellas bobbed up and down along the sidewalks. Eugene parked near the 4th Street Wharf, and everyone pulled up their hoods as they stepped out of the car into the rain.

"Whoa!" Jake exclaimed, as he ran along the wharf toward the yellowish torrent.

The sound alone was deafening and certainly produced terror for anyone living or working along the Ohio River banks. Eugene and his family were in awe of the sheer power passing within a few feet from where they stood.

Alarmed by the creaking timbers of the wharf, Rachel raised her voice over the roar. "Eugene, get the boys back. I don't think it's safe."

Without hesitation, he whistled loudly and motioned for the boys to join them on the pavement. For just a moment, Will looked as if he might disobey the command, but Jake grabbed his sleeve and pulled him away. The boys joined their family and several dozen spectators who had braved the weather to watch the rising menace.

After several minutes, Eugene directed his family away from the river. "Why don't we head over to Rosie's and get some ice cream?"

That brought an enthusiastic response from the boys, so they all walked back up Main Street.

A little bell jangled over the door of Rosie Corners Cafe. Only a handful of people were inside. A bald man in a white apron appeared from a back room. "Have a seat folks. I'll be right with ya."

Eugene was the last to hang his raincoat on a rack by the door before joining his family at a table in the middle of the room. Even from where they sat, the roar of the river was still quite distinct. At that moment, a policeman stepped in out of the rain and removed his drenched cap.

"Mr. Rose?"

"Yes, sir?" the bald man responded.

"We're asking for voluntary evacuation of all of the businesses along Main Street. The river's still rising, and we don't know when it will crest."

Mr. Rose looked a little leery. "Is everyone else closing up shop?" he asked.

"Like I said, it's voluntary. We're just trying to get the word out."

"Thanks all the same. I think I'll wait it out," Mr. Rose said with confidence.

"Suit yourself. But if I were you, I'd be packing up as much as I could and moving into the hills."

He turned his attention to the few customers sitting about the spacious room. His voice echoed off the wooden floor and brick walls. "Any of you folks live in the city?"

A few customers nodded their heads.

"Folks, I don't have to tell you that we're in danger if we get much more rain. Our city sits low in the Ohio River Valley, and the river's rising two feet per day. I'm sure you know what that means in the next couple of days—unless the good Lord sees fit to intervene."

The officer turned toward the door, pulling the soggy cap back down on his head. He paused with his hand on the knob, then turned back to the people in the diner. "God be with you folks," he said in a low voice.

A shiver worked its way up Eugene's spine. All of a sudden, he felt like he was standing on the deck of a sinking ship. Apparently, the rest of the family felt the same way. When Rachel suggested they go home and make a batch of sugar cookies, no one protested—not even Will or Jake, who under normal circumstances would've begged to stay for ice cream.

"Dad, if the river overflows, will it reach our farm?" Jake asked on the way home.

Eugene concentrated on the wet city streets. "Not likely, Son. But we'll need to keep an eye on the stream that runs by the Yancey place. I heard the Yanceys have already moved their livestock to higher ground and have left their house temporarily."

On Friday morning, Annie turned on the radio before breakfast. The news she heard left her heartsick. Main Street was already flooding. She wondered if Mr. Rose had heeded the policeman's advice after all. Schools were closed in the city, which was outstanding news to the boys, especially to Will.

By that afternoon, Eugene had altogether changed his mind about the answer he had given his son in the car on Wednesday. There had only been a short break in the rain on Thursday morning, and now sleet and snow were predicted for tonight and Saturday. Nathan and Claudia drove over after lunch to talk about the situation.

"Rachel, why don't you come home with us in case the water makes it this far?" Claudia pleaded. The Harrison's farm was five miles to the east and higher up in the Kentucky hills.

Sitting in the comfort of their living room, Rachel contemplated the offer. "Our Lucy is just about to foal. I really don't want to miss it."

"Mama, it might not be such a bad idea," Eugene spoke up. "If the roads get icy tomorrow, we may all be stuck here."

She took in a deep breath, apparently wrestling with the decision. "I just can't imagine this farm getting flooded."

"I would hope your house is on high enough ground," Nathan said to Eugene, "but I'm not so sure about your lower pasture and barn. Claudia and I drove as far as we could to the Yanceys' place before we came here. The water is as wide as a lake and running as fast as the Ohio."

He turned his attention back to Rachel. "You're welcome to come with us."

Rachel still hesitated. "I appreciate the offer, but you all picked up Roberta and the kids yesterday in the city. You already have a houseful."

"If you change your mind before we leave," Claudia interjected, "I'll help you pack up some of your belongings.

"Thank you," she said with a timorous smile.

Around four o'clock it started sleeting. The Harrisons decided to head home before the roads got too slick. As Nathan hugged Annie, he told her he hoped they would be blessed with a healthy new foal soon.

Claudia kissed the boys and Annie before turning to Rachel one last time. "Are you sure you won't come with us?"

Rachel nodded with slightly more conviction. "I'm sure." She gave Claudia a tight hug. "Be sure and give Roberta and the children our love."

Eugene stepped out onto the porch to help Claudia into the car as Nathan pulled it up close to the steps. Nathan leaned across his wife to speak quickly to his son-in-law. "Why don't I come out with the trailer tomorrow and pick up some of your horses? You don't want to get caught off guard."

"Not a bad idea. Let's see what condition the roads are in tomorrow. Give me a call in the morning," he said as he closed the car door.

That night, the banks of the Ohio River surrendered to the advancing army of water. The city of Louisville began to flood in earnest. Already, the river was fifteen feet above flood stage and still continued its terrible ascent, hour after hour.

When Eugene and his family awoke on Saturday, January 23, they did so without electricity. There was no way to hear news of the flood on the radio and worse yet, telephone wires were down. The landscape was covered in a light snow and ice, leaving them stranded on their farm with no way of knowing that the roiling monster was headed their way.

Chapter 23

Saturday, January 23

Annie was glad to have Rachel's company down at the barn. Eugene and the boys had left on horseback earlier in the afternoon to check on the progress of the floodwaters near the Yancey place. With the ground covered by snow and sleet, she prayed that their horses would be sure-footed today.

Lucy paced the floor of her stall, obviously in discomfort. Both women knew she was getting ready to foal.

Rachel wrapped her wool scarf tighter around her neck. With the electricity out, three of the barn's windows gaped open, letting in light. She was dressed like a farmhand today, wearing trousers and boots with a heavy wool coat. She moved close to her daughter-in-law's side.

"Do you ever marvel at the miracle of birth?"

"Mm," Annie responded, nodding her head. "Every time."

"As do I."

Something in Rachel's voice caused Annie to glance at her mother-in-law. She seemed pensive—almost sad. It was rare to see Rachel in such a somber mood.

Annie slipped her arm through Rachel's. "Mama, is everything okay?"

Rachel let out a quiet sigh, her breath leaving a wispy white trail in the air. "I feel closer to God every time I witness the miracle." She looked at her daughter-in-law briefly, then turned her gaze back to the mare. "But there was a time when it left me bitter and heartbroken."

The two women moved to the bench beside Lucy's stall and huddled together to stay warm. Annie and Rachel bore no secrets between them. They had always been able to discuss whatever was on their hearts. For that reason, Annie felt no reservations in asking Rachel, "Was it because you were unable to have a child of your own?"

Rachel nodded her head slowly. "I felt like Hannah in the Bible, praying earnestly for God to open her womb. Believe it or not, I once prayed that same prayer from the first chapter of Samuel. I didn't know how I was going to do it, but I told God I would dedicate my child to Him if He would just let me have one."

A wry smile unexpectedly tipped the corner of Rachel's lips. "It took me a good thirty-five years or so to finally drive out the last bitter remnant."

Annie wondered what it must have been like for her to watch the birth of so many foals over the years, knowing that she would never be able to share in the same experience. She had a hard time picturing Rachel as a bitter woman.

"What made you change?"

"Oh, I think you know the answer to that. Eugene. He changed everything."

Annie laid her head on Rachel's shoulder. "I guess that's about as much of a miracle as anything I can think of."

"No doubt," Rachel replied, kissing the top of Annie's head.

The two sat in peaceful silence until Lucy let out a mournful nickering sound, propelling both women to their feet. They watched as she turned several circles in the stall, then plopped down into the fresh hay and lay on her side. Occasionally, her head popped up as she tried to nip at her belly.

A gurgling sound on the other side of the barn caused Annie to turn sharply. She rushed to see what was happening. The sight she encountered caused a feeling of panic to rise up in her chest.

"Mama, water is coming in through the side of the barn."

She ran to the door and stepped outside to see what was causing so much water to seep in. Panic turned to terror in a matter of seconds. The highway in front of the house had become a river, eating its way across their lower pasture.

Just then, she felt Rachel grasp her arm tightly. "The barn's going to flood."

Annie willed her body into action. "Help me get the horses into the upper pasture!"

Together, the two women led each of the six thoroughbreds out of the barn and turned them loose among the cattle on slightly higher ground. Even then, Annie feared they wouldn't be able to escape the trespassing waters. But for now, that was the least of her worries. Lucy couldn't be moved into the icy pasture in her condition.

When Annie ran back to the barn, she found Rachel on her knees inside the mare's stall. Her lips moved in silent prayer as she gently stroked Lucy's neck. Annie stopped in the doorway, adding her prayer to that of her mother-in-law's.

Rachel looked up with tears in her eyes. "I'll hold her head steady; you need to check on her progress."

Annie moved to the other end and knelt in the hay, running her hand down the slope of the mare's thigh. Lucy raised her head slightly, letting out a low nicker when Annie bound up her tail. "It's all right, girl. It's all right," she said softly.

After a few moments of observation, Annie shook her head. "The foal has turned into position, but nothing seems to be happening. Let's see if we can get her up and walking. Maybe her water will break and get the process going."

Lucy didn't seem to want to get up, but Annie coaxed her with an apple until she finally heaved her body off the ground. With a firm hold on the halter, she took her from the stall and walked her the length of the barn. When they reached the other end, Lucy was rewarded with a bite from the apple before she was forced to walk again. At one point, Annie had to fight off the mare as Lucy tried to take a bite out of her arm instead of the apple. Annie didn't like messing with a mare ready to foal, but she clearly had no choice.

Rachel remained at the barn door watching for Eugene and the boys. It was getting close to three o'clock; they'd been gone for more than two hours.

Finally after twenty minutes of walking, Lucy's water broke. Annie led the mare back into her elevated stall onto the fresh hay.

"Come on, girl. Let's get on with it." She knew it could still take hours for the mare to foal—hours they simply didn't have. Annie prayed fervently for God to speed the birth along. The rising water had already overtaken a large portion of the western side of the barn.

Rachel turned from the doorway; her face was washed in relief. "They're coming!"

"Oh, thank you, Lord," Annie breathed. She joined Rachel at the barn door and noticed how slowly their progress was on horseback. She was sure the terrain was treacherous from the light sleet that was still pelting the landscape. Ranger and Scout trotted beside the horses, having no problem keeping their footing.

Eugene's jaw was tight, and his eyes narrowed. Annie thought he looked like a man on a mission. He dismounted inside the barn and immediately started giving orders. It was comforting to finally have someone making decisions, but it was also disconcerting to hear the urgency of his commands.

He turned to the boys first. "Take care of our mounts with food and water, then head up to the house and pack some of your clothes. You can put one item in your saddlebag that means something to you, but that's all. You have ten minutes."

Will and Jake started on their task without hesitation. Eugene then turned to the women. "We're driving the cattle and horses to Nathan's tonight. We'll have to go up and over the ridge to the Crowleys', then take the back roads. It'll take us all night, so put on as many layers of clothes under your coat as you can. We'll wear rain slickers over our coats."

He had an anxious look on his face when he turned to Rachel. "Mama, do you think you can ride?"

"Son, I know it's been a while, but I've done a lot harder things than this." She raised her chin in confidence. "I can ride."

Eugene gave her arm a quick squeeze, but there was no smile for his mother. "Good, you'll ride Gracie. She's as steady as they come."

His gaze now moved to Annie. "I'm taking the truck up to the house if the road's not too slick. I'm praying we don't lose the house, but we're going to lose the barn. While I'm doing that, you go up and get Gracie and whichever mount you want, then—"

"Eugene," Annie interrupted, "what about Lucy? She's just about to foal."

"Leave her." His words came out with no emotion . . . heartless even.

Annie felt like he had taken a knife and opened a gaping wound in her chest. She took a step back toward Lucy's stall. "I can't leave her—look at her."

He didn't move.

"Look at her, Eugene!"

"No Annie, look at this!" He pointed toward the dark, spreading liquid now overtaking a third of the barn floor.

She turned toward Lucy's stall, but Eugene took hold of her arm firmly.

"Let go of me, Eugene. I need to check—"

"Annie!" He spoke her name with such harshness she turned to him in surprise. "Do you want to save this horse or your family, because right now, that's what it's coming down to?"

For a second, she looked at each family member, standing motionless, holding one collective breath. Jake's eyes were wide with apprehension—he was close to tears. Will stood stiffly beside his brother—stoic. Rachel held unreserved compassion in her eyes for the impossible situation they now found themselves in. Annie knew, of course, she would save her family above all else. She simply hadn't expected it to come down to a choice—either the family or Lucy.

Hot tears stung her eyes. "I'm sorry. I'll go get the horses from the pasture."

Eugene didn't give her another glance but quickly turned to his sons. "Take Gramma up to the house so she can pack her things. Don't let her fall on the ice."

Immediately, the boys flanked Rachel's side, and they quickly left the barn.

In less than thirty minutes, the family had made all of their preparations. Five horses stood in the barn, saddled and loaded with supplies. Murky, gray clouds hovered in the late afternoon sky ushering in an earlier-than-normal dusk.

Eugene rapidly briefed the family concerning their jobs on the trail. "I'll take the lead and keep us on the right path. Mama, you and Jake will ride in the middle of the pack. Try to stay on the outside of the cattle and keep funneling them toward me. Annie and Will, you take up the rear. You shouldn't have a problem with strays once we get out on the road. All we have to do is keep them between the fences. It's the trail down to Crowley's road I'm worried about."

Will assured his dad that he'd take care of the strays.

Eugene finished with one last piece of advice. "No one get in a hurry. The trail and road will be slippery." He looked with concern at Rachel. "Mama, if you have any trouble at all, drop back with Annie. Gracie can handle both of you, if need be."

Finally, Eugene turned his gaze toward Annie. "If you need to say good-bye, now's the time."

Annie couldn't speak; she was only grateful for the chance to be with her Lucy one last time. She stepped inside the stall and fell to her knees. Steam was rising off the mare's neck; she could foal at any moment.

A sob escaped Annie's throat as she looked into the mare's shiny, brown eyes. She laid her face next to Lucy's. "I'm so sorry, sweet girl. I'm sorry for you and your little one."

Annie moved her hand gently along the mare's protruding belly, feeling the foal's body enfolded there. Fresh tears poured from her eyes.

"Annie." Eugene called her name, more patiently this time.

"I'm coming," she choked out, kissing Lucy's soft muzzle.

When she stood to leave, Annie was surprised to see Will standing in the doorway to the stall. He held her gaze for a moment then softly said, "Let's go, Mom."

Eugene handed her Josiah's reins, and she led him from the barn into the stinging sleet. The pasture was wet and slippery, making Annie and Will's job the hardest until they got the herd onto the trail.

By the time the cattle and the other horses had all made it safely down the hill to the Crowleys' road, the sky had turned dark. The layer of snow had made the trail less treacherous and was now giving off a white reflection that partially illuminated their way.

Will pulled up beside his mother as they came down onto the road. "I spotted a stray about twenty yards up the trail. I'll go back and get him."

"Okay, be careful."

"I will." He tugged on the reins and whirled Comanche about.

In a few minutes, he was back with the stray and moved to the other side of the herd. Annie didn't seem to notice when he returned; she was so lost in thought. She was trying so hard not to picture Lucy being engulfed in the icy floodwaters. But the unwelcome images hovered over her mind like the heavy clouds above. Even worse was the thought of Lucy giving birth and trying to save her foal. Such dark thoughts threatened to drive her crazy, so she tried to concentrate on the task at hand.

"Hup. Hup, cattle."

Annie could hear Jake's voice above the drone of the cattle. Ranger and Scout stayed at the rear, barking out their commands. The herd wasn't too terribly large, but it was sixty strong. She knew Eugene would not want to lose even one.

Suddenly, Annie's thoughts were drawn to her husband and the way he had treated her this afternoon. She had been shocked by his manner. Even more surprising was hearing him raise his voice toward her. In all of the years she had known him, Eugene had never once yelled at her—or the boys for that matter.

Oh Lord, calm his heart.

The stress of the situation had sent him into some sort of survival mode she had never seen before. Most likely this was the mode that had gotten him through the war. She tried not to take it personally, but it hurt to think of how uncaring he had been about Lucy. Her eyes stung afresh with tears as she prayed for God to make the end as quick and painless as possible for the mare and her foal.

Finally, after four hours on the trail, the sleet and rain let up. Annie couldn't imagine what the city of Louisville must be going through at this very moment. Where would everyone go to escape the icy waters?

Eugene spent much of his time looking over his shoulder. He was trying to catch a glimpse of Rachel to make sure she was all right. It was hard to believe that she was seventy-eight and driving cattle in the middle of the night—in a winter storm no less! Her resiliency was incredible. Thankfully, the break in the weather made the going a little easier, but the biting wind made it feel a lot colder than it really was.

By his estimation, they were about halfway to the Harrison's farm. The family was going to be totally exhausted by the time they covered the next two-and-a-half miles.

Eugene wished he could see how Annie and Will were getting along at the rear. He worried about how Annie was taking the loss of Lucy and her foal. Eugene was heartsick over it. He had purposely kept from saying the mare's name to try to emotionally detach himself from the situation. If he had even glimpsed at Lucy in her helpless condition, he would've broken down and cried. He couldn't wait to get this drive over with so he could take Annie in his arms and grieve with her. He owed her an apology for the way he had treated her. It was an apology he intended to give in front of Will and Jake.

An hour later, Eugene came upon the Harrisons' farm truck in the ditch. Nathan must have tried to get to them somehow. Having no means of communication had added that much more to the day's frustrations. And now he worried what Annie would think when she saw her father's truck on the side of the road. *Just stay focused*, he kept telling himself. *The Lord is with us.*

At half past two, Eugene spotted the stone gateway leading to the Harrison's farm. He turned the herd toward the gates, then blocked the road so none would escape. What a surprise it was going to be for Nathan to find sixty head of cattle and a few thoroughbreds milling around in his yard in the middle of the night.

Relief surged through him as Jake and Rachel passed by wearily. If they felt anything like he did, they were beyond frozen. Soon, Ranger and Scout followed the last cow through the gate with Annie trailing just behind.

"Is Will chasing a stray?" he asked as she came alongside his mount.

For a second Annie looked stunned. "What do you mean?"

"He didn't come through the gate. Did he go after a stray?" he repeated.

Shaking her head in confusion she said, "Not that I'm aware of."

"When did you see him last?"

The crease between her eyebrows deepened. "Eugene, I really haven't noticed him since we started out on the Crowleys' road. He brought in a stray from the trail and settled in on the opposite side of the herd."

Eugene let out a frazzled sigh. "I'll go back a ways and see if I can find him."

"I'll go with you."

"No, Annie, you need to get up to the house and take care of everything with your parents. I'm sure he's not far."

Thank goodness she was too worn out to argue with him. She nodded her head and apologized for losing track of Will. He watched her stiffly dismount and close the gate, then he turned his horse back toward home, praying that nothing had happened to his son along the way.

Chapter 24

Rachel and Jake had already entered the Harrisons' farmhouse when Annie dragged through the front door. They had removed their coats and boots and were stoking the embers in the fireplace. Jake threw another log onto the grate and a hundred tiny sparks danced upward toward the chimney flue.

"Jake, sweetie, you've got to take care of the dogs. They can't come in until you dry them off."

"Gotcha," he responded and ran to the linen closet down the hall. Moments later, he returned with one of Nana's old towels and headed out onto the porch where Ranger had already started howling.

Rachel shook her head. "Where does that boy get his energy?"

"I don't know," Annie responded. "But I could use a little of it right now."

Just then, Nathan came rushing down the stairs to see what all the commotion was. He had already gotten dressed and was carrying a lantern that he promptly set down on a table beside the couch.

"What's going on, honey?" He threw his arms around Annie and kissed her icy cheek.

"Our farm is flooding," she answered, her voice quavering. "We drove our herd here tonight."

Nathan sprang into action. "I'll go out and help Eugene get the cattle into the barn. We'll pack them into the arena for warmth and get them some hay and water," he said.

"Daddy, Eugene's gone back to look for Will. He didn't come in with us."

Rachel let out a muffled gasp.

"It's all right, Mama," Annie said with an assurance she didn't really feel. "We think he must have gone back for a stray. They'll be here any minute. I'm sure of it."

Thoroughly exhausted, she turned back to her father. "I'll help you get the cattle to the barn and take care of our horses."

Nathan was already shaking his head. "Not a chance. I'll go wake up the boys in the bunkhouse and make 'em earn their pay."

Just then, Claudia carefully descended the staircase while tying the sash of her robe. "Oh my goodness, how did you all get here?"

One look at her mother, and Annie felt herself falling apart. She closed her eyes, begging the tears not to come, but as soon as she felt her mother's arms draw her in tightly, one sob after another wracked her body.

Claudia began removing Annie's coat as if she were her little girl again. She led her to the couch and bent to pull the boots from her frozen feet.

"Everything's going to be fine, honey. Just relax." Claudia sat down on the couch and held her, letting Annie spend the emotions that had been repressed throughout the night.

While tenderly caressing her daughter, Claudia asked Rachel, "Are you all right? This must have been a terrible night for you."

Rachel continued warming her hands by the fire. "I'll be fine, but I think I should lie down in a little while."

All of a sudden, Annie felt so thoughtless. She should've been taking care of Rachel's needs above her own. She sat up and brushed the tears from her cheeks, looking at Claudia with deep gratitude. "Mother, thank you for that. I'm fine . . . truly I am. It's just been a long night."

Claudia cradled Annie's face in her warm hands and kissed her lovingly. "It's okay, honey. You've all been through a lot, I'm sure."

Annie decided not to tell her mother about Lucy—at least not now. It was far too painful to even broach the subject at this time of night. Besides, her concern for Will far outweighed the loss of her mare, even though the wound penetrated deep into her soul.

She noticed Rachel sitting in a chair by the fire massaging her legs. She had to be bone-tired and aching from so many hours on horseback.

"Mother, do you mind if I make something warm for all of us to drink, then maybe Jake and Rachel can get to bed?"

"Let me make us all some herbal tea," Claudia said.

At that moment, Jake opened the front door and let the dogs in. Scout went right to Rachel beside the fire while Ranger wandered into the kitchen. Jake pulled off his boots and gave Claudia a hug.

"Hi, Nana."

"Hi, Jake. How would you like something to eat?"

His eyes lit up. "I'm starving!"

Annie stood to join her mother in the kitchen, but Claudia told her to sit with Jake and Rachel by the fire.

"All three of you need to thaw out and rest." She took the lantern with her, leaving the three in the glowing light of the fire.

Rachel leaned her head back on the comfortable chair and closed her eyes while Annie sat down on the rug beside Jake.

"Momma, are you okay?" he asked.

She ruffled his dark hair, then let her hand slide down his back. "I will be, as soon as your daddy and Will get here."

After hot tea and a biscuit with honey, none of the three could seem to keep their eyes open. Claudia told them they would make new sleeping arrangements tomorrow, but for now, Rachel was going to bed with her.

"Roberta and the children are taking up two bedrooms and Mattie's in the other one," she explained.

"What if Nathan comes back in?" Rachel asked.

Claudia laughed. "Oh, he can just go out to the bunkhouse for the rest of the night." She turned to Annie then. "Do you want to stretch out on the couch, and we can make a pallet for Jake by the fire?"

"That sounds perfect," Annie said. "I want to be down here when Eugene and Will get back."

Rachel extended her arms toward Jake. "How about helping an old lady out of her chair?"

He immediately hopped to his feet and took hold of Rachel's hands. "You're not old, Gramma," he said, pulling her slowly to her feet.

"Thank you, darlin'."

Rachel stood by the fire for a long moment stretching out her back. She gave her grandson a warm hug and told him how proud she was of him. "I watched you on the trail, so I'd know just what to do. You're one of the best cowhands I've ever seen."

Jake beamed at his grandmother's praise.

Rachel then stepped over to Annie and hugged her fiercely. "I'm so sorry about everything," she whispered. "I love you, darlin'. Please let me know when our boys are back."

"I will, Mama. I love you too." Annie held on to Rachel for a moment longer. "I'm so amazed by you."

Rachel pulled away, letting out a weary laugh. "It'll be *amazing* if I can get out of bed tomorrow."

After Claudia took Rachel upstairs, Jake settled in with Scout by the fire, and Annie lay down on the couch under a blanket. She didn't bother to get undressed, hoping Eugene and Will would be here soon.

Lord, please bring them home safely. Give them strength to make it back.

"Momma?" Jake's voice drifted across the room.

"Uh, huh?"

"Where do you think they are?"

Annie shuddered at the question. Was it possible that something had gone horribly wrong? They really should've been back by now. Taking in a deep breath, she turned over on her side to face Jake. He was lying on his back, gazing up at the shadows dancing across the ceiling from the firelight. "Sweetheart, they'll be back anytime now. Try not to worry."

After a short silence he asked, "Do you think Will had an accident?"

That question sent an alarm through her entire being. "Jake, look at me."

He turned over on his side, staring at her through troubled eyes.

"Right now, we have to trust that God is taking care of your daddy and Will. Just keep praying that He'll give them the strength to make it home."

Her words didn't seem to bring Jake the comfort she hoped they would. Taking the blanket with her, she scurried across the room and sat down beside him.

"Turn toward the fire, and I'll scratch your back."

Jake had never been able to resist a good back scratching. After a few minutes, she could feel him relax, and when she started working her fingers through his dark hair it wasn't long before he was sound asleep.

Annie gave Scout a pat on the head, then leaned over and kissed Jake's warm cheek before tiptoeing quietly across the room. She pulled the curtain back from the front window and stared out into the dreary night. It was hard to ignore the turmoil going on inside of her. How could she stay in this warm house while Eugene and Will were still out there somewhere?

As she pressed her hand to the cold window, she thought about how faithful the Lord had been to bring Will home when he was a child of eight. Maybe it was because of the lateness of the hour or extreme fatigue, but she suddenly wondered how many times God would continue to answer that prayer. Would there ever come a time when He'd grow impatient with her son and turn His back on their pleas for him?

Annie shook her head trying to dislodge the very thought of it. She knew God was patient and longsuffering, not wanting any to be lost. But still she prayed, *Lord, no matter how far he strays, or how often, please keep bringing Will home.*

After several agonizing minutes, Annie finally decided to rest her weary body on the couch. She had no intention of going to sleep—she just needed to get warm for a while under the blanket. Snuggling down deep into the cushions, it wasn't long before the tension began to seep out of her muscles. She pulled the blanket up a little higher and closed her eyes just for a moment . . .

***

Somewhere in the deep recesses of her mind, Annie could hear someone calling her name. Fighting desperately through the darkness, she battled to keep her head above the water. Plunging beneath the waves, her body screamed for air, but none could be found. She thought her lungs would burst like a swollen balloon—the pain was unbearable. Something underneath the surface brushed past her, struggling as *she* was, to rise to the top. When she realized it was Lucy, she grabbed hold of her rust-colored mane, hoping the mare would carry her upwards. But both of them sank deeper and deeper into blackness.

"Annie. Annie wake up."

Her eyelids felt like they were glued shut; she couldn't seem to get them open.

Nathan finally took hold of his daughter's shoulders and shook her with a little more force. When her eyes opened with a start, he sat down on the edge of the couch and gently brushed the hair from her face.

"Annie, honey, it's me. Everything's okay."

For a moment, Annie had no idea where she was or how she'd gotten there. There was only faint, gray light filling the room—*it must be dawn.* She stared at her father, trying to work everything out, but her mind was so muddled. The chill in the air compelled her to draw the blanket up around her neck.

Finally, Nathan took hold of Annie's hands and pulled her into a sitting position. "Annie, you've got to come with me now. There's something you need to see."

All of a sudden, everything came back to her in much too vivid detail. Her chest felt heavy with grief. She didn't want to get up; she just wanted to pull the blanket over her head and forget yesterday ever happened. But something in her father's expression kept her from going back underneath the black waters.

"Okay, Daddy, I'm coming."

He already had her boots waiting beside the couch and held her heavy wool coat open.

"Hurry," he instructed, as if she were a soldier under his command.

Annie wasn't even given a chance to button her coat before Nathan had his hand on her back, pushing her toward the front door. Feeling the sting of the early morning chill on her face made her want to run back inside and huddle with Jake by the fire. How could he be so uncaring to bring her outside on a morning like this? She pulled the coat tightly around her midsection and buried her face inside the wool collar.

Nathan said nothing as the scene unfolded before them.

Gradually, Annie's mind began to clear, and she raised her chin from the warmth of her coat, watching the shadowy figures straggle along the road toward the farmhouse. All of a sudden, her emotions turned into a tangled mess—she wasn't sure whether to laugh or cry.

When Annie glanced at her father, his eyes were shining. "Go to them."

She bound from the porch into the snow, no longer caring about the bitter cold or the fact that her coat flapped open as she ran down the road.

Eugene dismounted and caught her around the waist, reaching inside her coat to pull her up against him. She didn't stay in his arms long but pulled away quickly turning toward Will and the little foal, stretched across his lap, wrapped warmly in a blanket.

"Oh, Will—" Annie couldn't finish her sentence; the words somehow wedged inside her throat. Will held Comanche steady as she took hold of the foal's soft muzzle and raised its head from his arms. She rubbed affectionate hands over the foal's soft face and floppy ears.

"Mom, it's a filly," he said, smiling through extreme fatigue. "And Lucy's here. She's fine."

Annie laid one hand on Will's leg, then rose up on her tiptoes, pulling him down toward her. He didn't resist. He leaned over in the saddle, allowing her to kiss him right on the mouth—something he hadn't done in years.

"What an amazing gift from God," she said breathlessly.

She moved over to Lucy and rubbed her face and neck lovingly. "Oh girl, I thought I'd lost you."

Annie looked back over her shoulder at Will. "I want to hear all about it, but I think we'd better get our girls down to the stable and warm them up first."

Eugene mounted his horse, then reached down for Annie's arm and swung her up behind him. She wrapped her arms around his waist and leaned into his back, still watching her son with the little filly. *What must he have gone through to save Lucy and her precious little foal?*

Once the filly was released from the warm blanket, she lay in the fresh hay, taking in her new surroundings. Lucy remained nearby in their roomy stall, ready to accept her offspring when she was hungry.

"We stopped along the way to let her feed," Eugene told Annie. "She hadn't been given enough time to figure out how to stand, so Will held her up to Lucy so she could get some nourishment."

Will sat down inside the stall and leaned back against the wall. He stretched out his long legs in the hay, watching Lucy and her foal with satisfaction. Annie sat down beside him, relinquishing the feelings of despair that had burdened her throughout the night.

Softly she said, "Tell me everything, sweetheart. How did you save them from the flood?"

Will turned to look at her, still leaning his head on the wall. Even though his body was completely drained, his eyes held an excitement that thrilled her heart.

"Her name is Bébé de l'eau—French for water baby. Dad and I named her." He turned his gaze up toward Eugene who was leaning over the gate.

Poor Eugene, his eyes bore dark circles underneath. He looked like he could pass out at any moment. Annie patted the hay beside her, and without hesitation, he hung the lantern on a hook and joined his wife and son. She laid her left hand on his thigh, and he covered it with his own then brought it to his lips. The bristly stubble on his unshaven face almost tickled. She wanted to lean over and kiss him but knew Will would probably give her an earful at such a display of affection.

"Okay," she said, turning her attention back to her son. "I want to hear everything—but before you get started, tell me what made you go back."

Will looked away, almost as if that was the one question he didn't want to answer.

When the silence grew, Eugene tried to prod him a little. "Tell her what you told me."

Annie watched her son take in a couple of deep breaths while keeping his attention on the filly who, at this point, was trying to figure out how to get up. Finally, he said quietly, "I couldn't stand to see you so upset." He turned and looked at her again. "I did it for you."

The tears came before she could stop them.

"Mom!" He said her name in exasperation.

"I'm sorry, honey. I've been having trouble controlling my emotions lately."

He grinned at her, and she let out a quiet laugh, despite the stream of tears running down her cheeks.

"After I brought in the stray," Will began, "I just gradually fell behind. You didn't even notice when I turned around and headed back toward the barn. It was pretty bad when I got back. The water was all the way up to Lucy's stall. If we hadn't built that platform, it would've already been flooded."

Annie shuddered just thinking about it.

"I got the lantern lit and hung it up right when the filly's feet started coming out. I was pretty scared about the water, so I took hold of her feet and pulled every time Lucy had a contraction. Then when her head and neck slid out, I broke the sac and cleared her nose as fast as I could. When the rest of her came out she splashed into water." Will shook his head. "That's how fast the floodwaters were rising."

As if she knew they were talking about her, Bébé de l'eau looked directly at them and rose up on awkward, spindly legs. Will and his parents watched in delight as she took her first clumsy steps. Then without warning, she crashed to the hay, snorting dust from her nostrils. Undeterred, the precious filly gave it another shot, this time taking several more uncoordinated steps before a nosedive at Lucy's feet. The mare lowered her muzzle and gently nudged her foal back into action. If Bébé was going to be able to eat, she'd have to figure out how to stay on all fours.

Annie elbowed her son, impatient to hear the rest of the story.

Will pulled his knees up to his chest, resting his elbows on top. "I grabbed the filly in my arms and stepped down into the water. It was already up to my knees, and it was freezing. I just prayed Lucy would follow me—thank goodness she did. I don't think she wanted to let her foal out of her sight.

"I took her up to the house and laid her on the back porch." A sheepish expression covered his face. "I hope you don't mind, Momma, but I pulled the quilt off my bed and wrapped her up in it."

Annie glanced at her son, an unwelcome sadness filling her thoughts. "It's okay, Will. There may not be anything left by the time we go back."

He raked his hands through his blonde hair, nodding soberly.

"What about the placenta?" she asked.

"She delivered it beside the porch. It looked fine. I'm sorry I couldn't save it for the vet."

"It's all right, sweetheart. You did an amazing job under the circumstances."

"Anyway, I changed clothes and gave Lucy and Comanche some water, then headed here. It was unbelievable, Bébé didn't struggle in my arms at all."

"When did you find them, Eug—"

Annie stopped in midsentence when she noticed her husband was lying prone in the hay, snoring softly. She wished she had a blanket to cover him.

Will and Annie shared a rare smile together. "Where did he find you?" she asked in a hushed voice.

"We'd just turned off of Scare-Crowley's road when I saw him coming."

"Will!" This time she said her son's name with chagrin.

His eyes twinkled—he had said Mr. Crowley's nickname just to get a reaction out of her.

"Dad made sure Lucy was okay to keep going. About an hour after that, we stopped to let Bébé feed. She knew exactly what to do when I held her up."

Annie enjoyed the wonder in his voice. He had participated in a sacred experience last night that she hoped would make a profound difference in his life.

Eventually, the two watched as Bébé supported herself on semi-steady legs and found her mother's milk again, this time completely unaided.

***

Annie slowly raised her head at the sound of the steady rain on the stable roof. Falling asleep against the wall had left her neck both stiff and throbbing. Someone had laid a blanket across her legs without waking her. Will's head was in her lap, and her arm was draped over his shoulder. He, too, was covered in a blanket, as was Eugene, who hadn't moved from the position she last remembered seeing him in. Even Lucy had been covered in a horse blanket and was now sleeping peacefully beside her little Bébé de l'eau.

She reveled in the peaceful moment. How long had it been since she last held her son? Far too long, by her reckoning. Will was turning fifteen in a week's time, and he had long ago made it clear that physical displays of affection were no longer welcome. The only ones who could seem to sneak a hug in these days were his grandparents.

Annie longed to work her hands through his hair the same way she had with Jake. But for now, she didn't want to wake him; she just wanted to be still and watch him sleep.

Oh Lord, forgive me for not thanking You earlier for bringing Will home. You've heard my prayer once again and answered. Thank You for Your faithfulness.

As Will drew long, slow breaths, she prayed that last night would be a breakthrough in their relationship. So many times lately, they found themselves at odds with one another. Rachel kept reminding her of the good heart beneath his tough exterior. All too often, however, his words and actions made it difficult to even catch a glimpse of that heart. But the sacrifice Will had made by going back to save Lucy and her foal was a monumental one. It was the kind of experience that could change a person's perspective on life and faith.

After several more minutes, Annie became restless and knew she needed to get up. She decided it was the perfect opportunity to shower Will with all the affection she could before he woke up. She started gently rubbing his back and arms, and by the time his eyes fully opened, she'd already run her hands through his sandy blonde hair—more than once.

Will started rubbing his eyes, but lingered in Annie's lap, letting her massage his head. Finally, she leaned forward and kissed his cheek, then told him she needed to get up.

He sat up slowly. "What time is it?"

"I wish I knew. I can't even fathom a guess."

Eugene's eyes opened slowly, but he didn't move. "Listen to that rain," he said in a scratchy voice. He cleared his throat and stretched his arms above his head. "That can't be good for the people in the city."

Annie shook her head. "I've been praying about that while you and Will were sleeping." She laid her hand on his chest and said, "I'm sorry about the barn, Eugene."

He wrinkled his brow and covered her hand with both of his. "Annie, I'm the one who's sorry about last night." He pushed himself up into a sitting position to face her. "The way I talked to you was wrong, and I need you to forgive me."

The sincerity of Eugene's apology drew her heart to his. "I forgive you," she said softly.

"I was so worried about getting our family out of there. You should've seen the Yanceys' farm."

Will spoke up. "Yeah, Mom, we watched their house get completely destroyed. It was scary."

"When I saw what the flood did to their farmhouse," Eugene continued, "I couldn't get to you and Mama fast enough. All I could think about was getting all of us out of there as soon as possible." He reached over and brushed her cheek with the back of his knuckles. "I know how much it hurt you to leave Lucy in her condition. It hurt me too—I just couldn't show it."

"I know," she said. "It was just a shock. I'd never seen you like that before."

"Dad, do you think our house will still be there?"

Eugene let out a deep sigh as he rose to his feet, pulling Annie with him. "We can only hope, Son."

Will got up and turned his attention to Lucy who was now awake, keeping watch over Bébé. He adjusted her blanket and checked the water and feed buckets.

Annie took the opportunity to slip her arms around Eugene and give him a quick kiss while their son was occupied with the mare.

"Eugene Wyatt?" she whispered.

"Yes, ma'am?" he said, pulling her up against him.

"I think I love you." She reached up and brushed the hay from his dark hair.

He kissed her again, and said, "I think I love you back."

"Oh, come on," Will complained loudly.

Eugene and Annie laughed, then proceeded to completely ignore their son.

When the three made their way back to the house, it was close to two o'clock in the afternoon. The entire household was sitting around Nathan's battery-powered radio while a fire blazed in the fireplace. Had it not been for the devastating news concerning the flooding of Louisville, it might have been a cozy scene. Fully half of the city was already engulfed in water according to the announcer. The Ohio River now raged at seventy-one feet above normal flow and was rising two feet per hour. Eugene's hopes of saving his farm seemed to sink the moment he walked through the door. But that concern was hastily pushed to the back of his mind as his eyes scanned the room, and it dawned on him that one member of the household was noticeably missing.

Chapter 25

Sunday, January 24

For the second time, Eugene's gaze swept the room, but his mama was the only one who appeared to be absent from the gathering.

Claudia instinctively knew who he was looking for. She immediately came to his side as he stood by the door and laid a gentle hand on his arm. "Your mama's still upstairs. I thought it best for her to stay in bed. She took some lunch about an hour ago and is sleeping again."

"Is she okay?" he asked anxiously.

"She'll be fine. I think she just needs to rest for a couple of days."

Eugene felt horrible for placing such demanding expectations on her. What must he have been thinking yesterday? Surely, he could've come up with some other alternative for her.

"Come in the kitchen and let me feed you," Claudia said, including Annie and Will in her invitation. "I'll take you up to Rachel after you eat." She gave Eugene's arm a reassuring squeeze.

Mattie jumped to her feet and gave Annie a hug. "Y'all must be plumb starved to death."

While they ate, Lillie sat at the table talking Annie's ears off. She was now a young lady of twelve and was quite the social butterfly. Eugene watched in amusement as the two of them talked and teased one another as if they were best friends.

Eventually, the conversation traversed a more serious path as Lillie asked about the farm.

"Oh, sweetie, we don't know what to expect. The water's already flooded the barn."

Claudia brought the pitcher of milk to the table and refilled the glass Will had drained in one gigantic gulp. When she took a seat across the table, she addressed her grandson directly. "Gramps told me you came riding in this morning with the little foal in your arms."

Will nodded his head proudly, and swallowed the bite of cornbread he had just dunked in his fresh glass of milk. "You should see her, Nana, it's a filly!"

Claudia beamed with joy. "I've seen her; she is beautiful! Gramps and I are the ones who covered all of you up while you slept in the stables. You must've been completely tuckered out."

There was no prompting Will this time as he gladly recounted the story of Bébé's birth. Eugene listened intently, amazed once again by the miracle rescue. He had to admit this was one time Will's rebellious nature had paid off, but it scared him to think about what could've happened if the water had destroyed the barn with his son still inside. Images of the Yanceys' sprawling farmhouse breaking into pieces and being sucked away by the muddy onslaught still plagued his memory. Just the sound of the splintering wood had sent an overwhelming anxiety pulsing through his veins.

Tomorrow he planned to return to his farm to see what was left. But for now, Eugene did his best to focus on the positive. All of his family was safe and warm under one roof, none of his livestock had been lost, and there was a new little filly out in the stable celebrating a victory over the flood.

Do not worry about tomorrow, for tomorrow will worry about itself. Eugene took considerable comfort contemplating the words of Jesus.

Eventually, Mattie began clearing the table, and Claudia turned her attention toward Eugene. "I'm sure Rachel would be awfully proud to hear Will's story. Would you like for me to go upstairs and see if she's awake?"

"Could you, please?" He shook his head letting out a low sigh. "I hope I haven't hurt her or made her ill."

Annie rose from the table to join her mother. "I'll go up with you." She gave her husband a tender smile, then rested her hand on his shoulder. "We had no other choice, sweetheart. It wasn't your fault."

Eugene reached up and squeezed her hand, then watched her leave the kitchen with Claudia.

Moments later, his mother-in-law returned with a broad smile. "She's awake and wants to see you both."

"How is she?" Eugene asked, uneasily.

Claudia laughed. "I had to stop her from coming downstairs if that tells you anything. You'd better hurry and get up there before she decides to do it."

Eugene took the stairs two-at-a-time with Will right on his heels. When he rounded the corner of the room, Annie kissed Rachel and rose from the side of the bed.

"Thank you, darlin'. I'm feeling much more rested now." Rachel gave Annie a warm smile. The pillows had been arranged behind her back as she sat up in bed covered with blankets.

Eugene moved to take Annie's vacated spot on the bed. He had the most apologetic look on his face, causing Rachel to sit up a little straighter.

"I'm not an invalid, you know. I'm just resting." She gave his hand a little pat. "I've been dreaming about being on horseback all day."

Still holding back a smile, Eugene needed to get his concern for her welfare off his chest. "Mama, be honest with me, how are you feeling?"

"Eugene, I'm fine—really. A sore backside, yes, but other than that, I'm actually proud of what we accomplished last night." Her deep brown eyes flickered with a hint of enthusiasm.

"You're not sick or anything?" he persisted.

Rachel glanced at her daughter-in-law standing at the foot of the bed. "Annie, would you please tell your husband I'm fine and that I'd like to become one of his wranglers when we get back home."

Annie burst out laughing and turned toward the door. "You heard her, Eugene," she called over her shoulder. "I don't think you have anything to worry about with your new wrangler. I'll leave you two to tell her about the latest addition to our family."

Annie paused in the doorway long enough to hear Will dive into the story for the third time as he took a seat on the other side of his grandmother's bed.

When Annie returned to the front room, she was staggered by the horrific news pouring from the radio. Many of Louisville's citizens had unfortunately discounted the seriousness of the rain and snow and had remained in their houses up until the bitter end. By the time the whistles and sirens began blowing throughout the city last night at midnight, their worst fears had already been realized. Thousands had been forced to flee for their lives. Hundreds were stranded in subfreezing temperatures without a coat, trying to escape the floodwaters—some even running barefoot through the snow.

Soon after Annie had taken a seat by the fireplace, Governor Chandler began issuing a statement to all Kentuckians.

The worst catastrophe in the history of Kentucky has fallen upon our people in the valleys of the rivers and streams of Kentucky and the Ohio River.

The governor's voice sounded grave, not at all what Annie had remembered when she heard him speak at the State Fair in Frankfort last summer. His nickname was "Happy" Chandler, but today there was no trace of the characteristic joviality in his voice.

Thousands upon thousands of families have been driven from their homes without food or clothing. Many thousands of these people have lost all their personal belongings. Today they are exposed to the terrific weather without food or the proper housing. All state departments of government have devoted their entire time toward an attempt to relieve these stricken people. The federal government is giving its aid, the Red Cross is giving highly helpful service, and many other organizations and individuals are working faithfully to try to relieve this horrible situation. Let me call upon the citizens of Kentucky to get in touch with the Red Cross units or other organizations in the stricken communities at once and offer what they have in the way of food, clothing, bedding, and money for these thousands of stricken homeless people.

What no one knew at the time of the governor's statement was how horrific it truly was. There were already 230,000 homeless Louisville citizens desperately seeking assistance, many barely clinging to life. Some had already drowned, but the greatest threat to those who were left homeless was the frigid weather and inability to find shelter.

Claudia sprang to her feet spouting a barrage of instructions, jolting the rest of the household out of their stunned silence. Mattie and Wallace were sent to the pantry for supplies, Nathan was directed to the cellar for jars of preserved fruits and vegetables, and Jake was instructed to help his grandfather carry them. Roberta, Lillie, and Annie were ordered to follow Claudia into the storage closet beneath the stairs.

Within half an hour, the dining room had been piled high with linens, blankets, clothing, shoes, and food. As soon as Eugene and Will's feet hit the bottom stair, they too were pressed into service carrying supplies to Nathan's truck, which had been rescued from the ditch earlier in the day.

"Nate, it'll be dark in two hours. We've got to get these supplies to the Red Cross as soon as possible."

Eugene put his hands on his mother-in-law's shoulders, feeling her energy pulse through his arms. "Claudia, I'll go with Nathan. There's no need for you to get out in all of this."

For a second, he thought she was going to argue with him until Nathan stepped in. "Honey, you've done your part. Now let me and Eugene take care of the rest."

"Do you even know where to go?" she asked, still having trouble relinquishing her duties.

"If we can make it to the National Guard Armory, I'm sure they know where the supplies will be most needed."

"Then go—we don't need to be standing around talking." Claudia nearly shoved the two men out the door. "But please be careful. If it gets dark and you can't get to the armory, come back and we'll try again in the morning."

"Don't worry about us. We'll be back as soon as we can."

The second Nathan closed the door of the loaded truck, he glanced over at Eugene. "I hope you know I don't plan to come home until we get these supplies to someone in need."

"I'm with ya, Nathan. Let's do this."

The roads were a little less treacherous as they had turned to slush during the afternoon. Still, it was slow going, and Nathan worried that they might not be able to see the flooded areas after dark. He tried to hurry along as fast as possible without losing control of the truck. Luckily, Nathan knew which roads would keep them on high ground. He felt so fortunate that his farm was situated higher up in the Kentucky hills than most; there would be no chance of the floodwaters ever making it to their home.

Eugene kept his eyes focused on the frigid landscape. He could already see where the water had crept into the lower-lying countryside.

Nathan noticed his son-in-law suddenly move forward in his seat, bracing his hands on the dashboard.

"What is it?"

"Look down below."

The truck slowed to a crawl as Nathan's eyes followed the direction that Eugene was pointing.

"I don't see anything."

"Stop the truck!"

Nathan brought the truck to an abrupt halt.

"Look across the water at the tree line. Do you see people down there?"

It took a few seconds before Nathan finally picked up a slight movement underneath a stand of trees. He looked at Eugene with a sense of urgency in his eyes. "They're trapped by the water."

"Move the truck forward. They may not be completely surrounded."

Sure enough, as they moved up the road a bit, Eugene noticed a narrow strip of land. It would be their only chance of escape.

"We've got to see if we can help them, Nathan."

Nathan pulled the vehicle a little farther up the road, parking it as far over to the side as he could. Both men leapt from the truck, climbed a wooden fence, and headed across a mushy pasture toward the small peninsula of land Eugene had spotted. It turned out to be more of a marsh than either had expected, but thankfully the mud wasn't more than ankle deep on their boots—for now anyway.

After trekking a little over half a mile, they spotted what appeared to be a family, huddled together against the trunk of a large oak tree. Something about the scene caused the hair on the back of Eugene's neck to stand on end. It was eerily quiet. The damp freezing air seemed as heavy as the steel gray sky above. The ominous lapping of water all around them was the only sound that could be heard, other than their mucky footfalls.

Nathan called to them from a few yards out. "Hello there. Can we help you folks?"

A young man raised his head from where he squatted against the tree—his arms were wrapped around a young woman who held a baby close to her breast. Neither the man nor woman was wearing a coat; in fact, they wore nothing but their nightclothes. At least they had thought to pull on a pair of shoes.

Both Nathan and Eugene ripped off their coats as the man rose slowly to his feet. Eugene noticed a bluish tint to his lips and knew they were all suffering from hypothermia.

Nathan threaded the young man's arms into his wool coat while Eugene moved to help the woman to her feet. As he reached underneath her arm to help her stand, he noticed something on the other side of the tree. It was only a glimpse, but it caused the chill to move back up his spine. Someone was laid out straight on the other side of the oak.

Eugene turned his attention back to the woman and asked her name as he pulled the warm coat around her shoulders. All he received in return was an empty, blank stare.

"May I?" he asked, reaching for the infant in her arms.

At first, the young woman held her baby tighter, and Eugene feared it might be dead until he heard the tiniest of whimpers. Immediately, he pulled the thick sweater over his head and unbuttoned his flannel shirt. He reached out for the baby, and this time, the mother didn't resist. She allowed Eugene to wrap the little girl in his sweater, and he tucked her inside his shirt, pressing her face to his warm abdomen.

"Come on," Nathan said, "we've got to get you all to shelter."

"Ca, ca, can you take care of m, m, my wife's mother?" the man shivered through his heartfelt appeal.

Nathan looked at Eugene, puzzled by the request. Eugene nodded his head toward the other side of the tree, so Nathan quickly stepped around the trunk. After a long moment, he returned, laying his hand on the young man's shoulder. "I'm sorry," he breathed quietly.

The young man nodded his head gravely. "The na, name's Charles, and this is my wife Em, Emily."

Nathan put his arms around the couple and began guiding them through the sludge. "What about your baby?"

"Oh, that's our little C, Claire," Charles replied. "She's six m, months tomorrow."

Eugene held the sweet baby girl closer to his heart. *Oh God, please save this little one*, he pleaded silently.

When they got to the truck, Emily and Charles were ushered inside the cab with Nathan. As soon as they were settled, Eugene placed little Claire in her mother's arms, then pulled a blanket from underneath the canvass tarp in the back and covered the despondent young family. He closed the door and jumped into the back, buttoning his shirt and searching desperately for another blanket as they sped down the road.

Chapter 26

Eugene passed an army sergeant inside the Louisville National Guard Armory and threw him a salute, then wondered where on earth that had come from. He hadn't saluted another person since Will Gano's funeral in 1922.

"Are you army?" the sergeant asked, causing Eugene to stop in the crowded hallway leading to the armory offices.

"Not anymore, sir."

"Served in the Great War, did you?"

"Yes sir—357th Infantry out of Camp Travis in Texas."

"Ahh, the TO unit. Fine reputation."

"Thank you, sir."

"You're not in the National Guard then?"

"No sir, my father-in-law, Nathan Harrison, and I were bringing in some supplies for the Red Cross but happened to find a family out in the cold on our way here."

"They bein' looked after?" the sergeant asked.

"Yes, sir. Nathan is with them right now making sure they get everything they need. I was on my way to the office to try to help them with another matter."

"Maybe I can help. What do they need?"

Eugene let out a deep breath and proceeded to tell the sergeant about the body of Emily's mother lying underneath the oak tree.

"That's a shame. You have no idea how many people have already died from exposure. We just can't get everybody into shelters fast enough." The sergeant pointed back toward the gymnasium facility. "We've already got over three hundred people crammed into the armory just for tonight. Most of them need medical assistance."

Eugene shook his head, knowing the supplies they had brought in were only a drop in the bucket.

"It's getting dark," the sergeant said, "but do you think you can help us locate the body tonight?"

Before Eugene could answer his question, the sergeant grabbed a young man by the arm as he walked by. "Hey, Dunnaway, you're with me. We've got a body to pick up."

Suddenly, Eugene's stomach turned queasy; it felt like he was back in the war.

"Give us a minute to get a stretcher, and we'll follow you to the site," the sergeant said.

"Sir, I've got to find my father-in-law to let him know what's going on."

"Sure, we'll meet you out front in ten minutes."

Eugene hurried off to find Nathan. He scanned the large gymnasium and was a bit taken back by the hush in the room. Row after row of families and individuals were sitting on blankets on the hardwood floor. The look of utter shock and devastation was imprinted on every face. How could a tragedy of such magnificent proportions have taken place in their city?

He turned abruptly as Nathan's hand clamped down on his shoulder. "Are you ready to go?" Nathan handed him his sweater and coat.

"Yeah, but we need to lead a couple of men from the National Guard back to Emily's mother if you don't mind."

Nathan nodded and led Eugene through the crowd back outside to his truck. A couple of minutes later, the sergeant drove up in an army vehicle and said they would follow Nathan.

Dusk had left the landscape covered in a dismal gloom. Once again, the men tromped through the slush until they made it to the oak where the poor woman had succumbed to the harsh elements. The sergeant switched on his hand-held flashlight, illuminating the woman in her wet, flannel gown. Ice had formed in her hair and on her eyelashes; Eugene averted his eyes. Memories of France suddenly slammed up against his chest. He thought he was going to be sick.

"Nathan," he said in a low voice, "I think we can go now. I'm sure everyone back home is worried about us."

Nathan agreed and thanked the sergeant for the duty he was performing.

The thirty-minute ride back home was wrapped in total silence. Eugene was thankful for the descent of darkness. He had an overwhelming fear of happening upon another dead body. He noticed his palms were sweaty; he felt edgy. Suddenly, he had to quell an urge to rip off his coat and jump out of the truck. He knew his father-in-law had no idea what he was going through right now.

Eugene closed his eyes and clenched down hard on his jaw. *Breathe, just breathe.* He took in several deep breaths through his nose, letting each one out as soundlessly as possible.

When the truck came to a halt in front of the house, Eugene reached for the door handle. Before he could exit the vehicle, Nathan said, "I'm going to let you out here and drive on down to the barn for a while. Tell Claudia I'll be up in about an hour."

"Okay," Eugene said in a strained voice, then shut the door to the truck sharply.

He stood for a moment watching the truck roll away and then stared at the front door of the house. He knew he needed to give Claudia the message and let everyone know they were back, but there was no way he was going to be able to enter that house and act normal. He needed to run or do some sort of intense physical labor to rid himself of the panicked feeling in his gut.

Taking in an enormous deep breath, he strode onto the porch and quickly opened the door to the house. Looking at no one in particular, Eugene offered, "We're back and heading down to the barn for a while. See you in about an hour."

He purposely blocked out the questions the women hurled his way and closed the door. Then without hesitation, he leapt from the porch and took off running down the road. When Eugene reached the highway, he ripped off his coat and threw it next to the gate. Turning toward his farm, he lengthened his stride and gulped in heaps of frigid air. He had no recollection of time passing, just the easing of tension, slowly untangling the knotted mass inside his belly.

By the time he reached the Crowleys' road, he noticed his sweater was missing too. Still, Eugene ran all the way up the trail until he reached the top of the ridge that overlooked his farm. He stood motionless, sweat pouring down his back, chest rising and falling in a steady rhythm as his lungs dragged in the necessary oxygen.

It was dark, but there were sparkling glimmers of light reflecting off the water. Gazing upward, Eugene saw the stars for the first time in twenty-four days. The whirring sound of the dark liquid was mesmerizing, and the vast array of stars in the inky sky began to restore his spirit. Even more exhilarating was the sight of his house, firmly planted on solid ground, standing guard over the river!

Breaking into a jog, Eugene headed down to his house intoxicated by a sense of salvation—not just for the house but for himself as well. He stopped at the farm truck parked behind the back porch and laid his hand on the pile of equipment that he'd been able to salvage from the barn. He didn't want to even think about the difficulty he would face rebuilding his barn and fences.

Heading inside the house, Eugene rummaged through a drawer in the dark kitchen and found a flashlight they used whenever the electricity went out. The light played across the floor of the living room as Eugene made his way to the front door and out onto the porch. The water ran within five feet of his house. Silly, how he had an urge to drag out a fishing pole and fish from the front porch steps. He chuckled out loud at the thought, then turned back inside.

Shining the light on the mantel clock brought Eugene back to a more pressing reality. While it was only seven thirty, he knew it would take over an hour for him to make his way back to his family. What if Nathan had already come back from the barn? The last thing he wanted to do was put Annie through another night of worry.

He knew precious seconds were ticking off as he stood in the darkened room. Finally, he made his way to the bedroom and pulled his flannel shirt over his head, not bothering with the buttons. Grabbing a clean shirt from the drawer, he threw it on and pulled out a wool sweater. Hopefully, he'd find his other one somewhere along the road.

Just as Eugene turned from the dresser, his eye caught the glimmer of Annie's favorite necklace, hanging on the mirror. It was a beautiful silver cross that she loved to wear to church on Sundays. He gently reached for it, buttoning it inside his shirt pocket underneath his sweater.

As badly as he needed water, Eugene knew the cistern had been compromised by the viral floodwaters. Rachel's orange juice, however, hit the spot as he polished off the entire pitcher. Wiping his mouth on the back of his hand, he headed out the kitchen door and jogged back to the top of the ridge, hesitating only long enough to turn back toward his farm and breathe, "Thank you, Lord."

A few minutes before nine, Eugene quietly opened the door to the Harrisons' farmhouse. Relieved to hear everyone talking in the kitchen, he hung his coat on the rack by the door and pulled off his soaked work boots. The front room flickered in shadow from the low-burning fire. Just as he started for the kitchen, a movement near the fireplace caught his attention.

"Eugene."

Annie rose from her chair. She had been sitting alone in the front room, obviously waiting for him to come home.

He went to her immediately, enclosing her in needy arms. Surprisingly, she didn't ask where he had been; she just allowed him to hold her tenderly by the warmth of the fire.

Eugene was amazed by his wife's intuition. He didn't even know what had really happened to him this afternoon, much less been able to explain it to anyone. Obviously the distressing situation with the flood, coupled with the family they had found freezing to death, and the worry over losing his farm had sent him into a dark place—a place he hadn't journeyed in a very long time. He appreciated Annie's gracious silence more than she knew.

Eugene pulled away from his wife just enough to reach underneath his sweater and into his shirt pocket. He enjoyed the look of bewilderment on her face as the silver necklace dangled from his fingers, glinting in the light of the fire. Even more enjoyable was watching the slow smile play across those gorgeous lips.

Annie suddenly squealed like a schoolgirl, then grabbed Eugene around the neck and kissed him. He wasn't about to let it be a quick smack on the lips and drew her in closer for a slow and satisfying diversion.

When he lifted his head, he noticed his mother-in-law standing in the doorway, grinning unashamedly. Eugene pulled Annie down into the chair with him and chuckled when he heard Claudia barring anyone from coming into the front room.

"Yes, Eugene is back," she informed the family, "but he and Annie need to talk a while. Why don't we give them some privacy?"

Eugene reached up and clasped the silver chain around Annie's neck as she sat in his lap.

She lifted her hand to cover the cross resting on her chest. "Eugene, thank you for this, but please don't keep me in suspense any longer. Tell me about the farm."

Eugene surprisingly found himself telling Annie about his panicked run. She kept her hand on his chest as he told her about the stars sparkling above their farmhouse and the peace God had brought to him on top of the ridge.

Twenty minutes later, the whole family came pouring out of the kitchen. Eugene gladly reported about finding the farmhouse untouched by the flood, but purposely withheld the reason that had propelled him there.

"Tomorrow, I'll ride over with the boys and pick up some more supplies from our house." He grinned mischievously at Will and Jake. "There's something else I want to do while we're there."

Both boys asked, "What?" at the same time.

"You'll see; it'll be a surprise." He couldn't wait to take them fishing on the front porch. "And Wallace," he added, "I want you to saddle up, too, if you'd like to come along."

"Yes sir, Mr. Eugene. I'd like that," Wallace replied.

"Well," Claudia said as she rose to her feet, "we've had a long night and day. I think it's time for all of us to get to bed. But before we do, Eugene, would you be willing to ask the Lord's blessings over those in distress tonight?"

Eugene stood and reached for Annie's hand. The beautiful patchwork of a family gathered around, joining hands while Eugene poured his heart out to God on behalf of their city. Thousands would be spending another harrowing night out in the cold, clinging to a slender thread of hope.

"Oh Lord, please rescue them all," Eugene pleaded.

When the prayer was concluded, Claudia began lighting candles and directing traffic. Mattie stayed with her, making sure everyone had enough covers for the night. Mattie would be sleeping in the kitchen on a cot Nathan had pulled from the attic. She had insisted on giving up her room, so Rachel would have a place to rest and recuperate.

Roberta put her arms around her two sweet children and led them up to her room. Lillie would be sleeping in the bed with her mother while Wallace was taking the other cot Nathan had found in the bunkhouse.

Eugene and Annie kissed their boys, making sure they were settled in with blankets and pillows by the fire. Then hand-in-hand, they climbed the stairs to the room Lillie and Wallace had vacated.

Finally satisfied that all was well, Claudia tiptoed into her bedroom where Nathan had already turned in for the night. A candle was still burning on the bedside table, so she could see to change into her gown.

"Nate?" She spoke his name hoping he wasn't already asleep.

One eye opened. "Uh, huh?"

"I can't get that poor couple off my mind—Charles and Emily."

Both eyes opened as Nathan agreed with his wife. "I know what you mean. They wouldn't have made it if Eugene hadn't spotted them."

"Tomorrow, I want you to go get them."

Nathan rolled over on his side and rose up on one elbow.

"What do you mean?" he asked in surprise.

Claudia slipped under the covers but left the candle burning, as she wanted her husband to see how serious she was concerning this matter.

"Just what I said, I want you to bring them—"

"Now wait a minute," he interrupted. "In case you haven't noticed, honey, we already have a full house."

"Nate." Claudia sat straight up in bed. "I wouldn't ask this if I didn't think it was the right thing to do."

Nathan threw out another excuse. "We don't even know their last name."

Claudia laughed, but not out of amusement. "How hard will it be to find them at the armory? You know their first names and the name of their baby, plus, you would recognize them."

"Why on earth do you want them here so much? They'll be taken care of at the armory. Besides, the army medics are there to help them. They were all suffering from hypothermia."

Shaking her head, Claudia refused to let it go. "I'm sorry, I know this is hard for you to understand, but poor Emily just lost her mother—even worse, she watched her freeze to death. Who's there in that armory holding her and comforting her through such a tragic loss?"

Nathan opened his mouth but then closed it.

"Who, Nate?"

Letting out a long, slow breath, Nathan laid his head back down on the pillow and stared at the ceiling. Finally, after a long silence, he turned to her and said softly, "Honey, we can't save everyone—there are too many."

"No," she said as she snuffed out the candle, "but we can save *them*."

Chapter 27

The next morning while Eugene fished with the boys from his front porch, Nathan made his way into the crowded armory office. As he waited, he worried about the toll all of this would take on his wife. Even though she had gotten a good report at her yearly check up with the doctor, he had specifically told her to stay away from stressful situations. If a house full of people in the middle of a flood wasn't a stressful situation, Nathan didn't know what was. Claudia had never fully recovered grip strength in her left hand, but most people would never notice. Every other function on her left side had returned to normal long ago.

Nathan realized it was going to take a long time simply to get the attention of someone who could help. He had no patience for waiting, so he headed down the hall to the gymnasium. Perhaps he could spot Charles and Emily in the crowd. Who knows, maybe they would even prefer to stay here.

One look inside the gymnasium caused his heart to skip a beat. It was the most pitiful situation he had ever laid eyes on. Children were crying—some with no adult to comfort them. Men and women wearing hand-me-down clothes sat staring at nothing in particular. After a few moments, Nathan purposely stopped making eye contact with anyone. The hopelessness he saw in their eyes left him disconsolate.

Slowly, he walked through the depressing rows of humanity and realized Claudia was right. There was no way on earth he would leave Charles and Emily here with their baby girl, not as long as they were well enough to come home with him.

"Sir?"

Someone from behind Nathan touched his elbow. When he turned around, he found himself face to face with Charles who was wearing a pair of worn-out, baggy trousers and a button-down shirt at least two sizes too big.

Nathan couldn't help himself; he grabbed Charles by the shoulders and embraced him. "How's your wife and daughter?"

Charles pointed toward the corner. "They're over there," he said but gave no hint to their condition.

"Do you have anywhere else to go besides staying here? Maybe family living away from the River Valley?" Nathan probed.

Charles dropped his gaze and shook his head.

A long pause followed while Nathan looked toward the corner. Finally, he said, "My wife was wondering—" He wrinkled his brow and started over. "I mean, my wife and I were wondering if you'd like a place to stay. Our house is a little crowded right now, but we have room for the three of you if you'd like."

Charles smiled for the first time since Nathan had met him, sporting dimples on his smooth, boyish features. By the looks of him, this was not a man who worked outdoors or in one of Louisville's many factories. Even though he wore ill-fitting clothes, Charles had taken the time to comb his neatly trimmed, brown hair and had tucked in his shirt.

"Sir, I'd do anything to get my wife and baby out of here."

Nathan realized he hadn't properly introduced himself. "By the way, I'm Nathan Harrison."

"Charles Bannan," he said, reaching for Nathan's hand.

***

Just before ten o'clock, Nathan led the Bannan family up the steps of his porch and into the house. Emily had said nothing on the ride from the armory, and he could tell that Charles was worried sick about her. Little Claire had been given a clean bill of health by one of the medics on site, but she had yet to cry or eat since the family had been rescued. She and her mother both seemed to be in a state of shock and despondency.

All of the women, including Rachel, rushed from various parts of the house to greet their new guests. They each took turns introducing themselves, welcoming them into the Harrisons' home.

Nathan turned to Charles. "What do you say I take you down to the barn and show you around. I may even put you to work if you feel up to it."

Smiling, Charles nodded his head. "I'd like that, but I'm not so sure I can be much help on a farm."

"What's your occupation?" Nathan queried.

"Teacher. I'm a history professor at the University of Louisville. I'm in my second year."

It was Nathan's turn to smile. "Good. Maybe you can answer some of my most pressing history questions."

"Like what, sir?"

"Oh, I don't know," Nathan said as he put his hand on the door knob. "I'm sure I'll think of some."

The young man hesitated for a moment beside his wife, causing Nathan to take a step closer. "She's in the finest hands in Louisville, Son. There's not a problem these five women haven't been known to solve." He inclined his head toward the door. "It'll be fine, I promise."

Charles put his arm around Emily's shoulders, then leaned forward and kissed little Claire. "We're safe now," he whispered. "Everything's going to be fine." He kissed his wife's dark, auburn hair that hung loosely around her shoulders.

Emily looked at her husband through troubled, emerald eyes and gently nodded her head.

As soon as the men stepped out the door, Annie glanced in her mother's direction, waiting to see how they should proceed. There were tears glistening in Claudia's eyes. Amazing how Claudia rarely shed tears for herself, but she was already shedding them for this young woman who had lost her mother.

Annie reached for baby Claire, and Emily slowly relinquished her. Immediately, Claudia moved forward and tenderly wrapped her arms around the young woman.

At first, Emily remained as she was, arms stiffly by her sides. But when Claudia whispered, "I'm so sorry about your mother. I'm here for you," Emily reached her arms around Claudia and sank into her sympathetic embrace.

Claudia held Emily as long as it took for her heart-rending sobs to subside. The rest of the women went about their duties in the house, knowing that Claudia would be able to bring much healing to Emily's heartache.

Eventually, she led Emily to the couch where Annie and Lillie sat cuddling with sweet baby Claire. Annie had enjoyed showing the precious little girl some much-needed affection. She noticed the child had her mother's auburn hair and button nose.

Emily pushed her thick hair back behind her ears and sat down close to Annie's side.

"How long since she's eaten?" Annie asked.

Shaking her head in bewilderment, Emily answered, "I'm not sure. I know that sounds bad, but I don't think I've fed her since we . . . since we . . ." She looked into Annie's eyes, showing deep remorse.

Annie reached for Emily's hand and gave it a gentle squeeze. "You've been through so much. Sometimes babies pick up on the stress of their parents in traumatic situations."

"I'm sure that's it. I can't believe she hasn't even cried. Do you think she's all right?"

Annie nodded reassuringly. "She seems fine. Do you want to try to feed her now?"

Emily quietly replied, "Yes."

Lillie released her gentle hold on Claire's tiny hand and headed into the kitchen to help with lunch preparations.

Annie led Emily to a chair near the fireplace and laid Claire in her arms. "I'll give you some privacy."

Immediately, Emily looked distressed. "No. Please."

Annie noticed her quick, shallow breaths. The poor girl was terrified of being left alone. She knelt down in front of her and laid a calming hand on Emily's arm. "I'm not going anywhere. Try to stay relaxed; it'll help Claire relax too."

Emily took in a deeper breath as Annie settled into the comfortable chair across from hers. For the next few minutes, she purposefully rambled on about how she and Eugene had first met. Finally, she noticed the corner of Emily's mouth tip upward.

"Success?"

Emily simply nodded her head.

Annie watched for a moment, then laid her head back in the chair and stared into the fire. Where had the time gone since she had held her boys like that? They were practically men now. She stole another glance at mother and child. *Hang on tight, Emily. Before you know it, Claire will be all grown up.*

At mid-afternoon, Eugene and the boys returned from their trip to the Wyatt farmhouse. They entered rambunctiously through the back door of the kitchen carrying supplies to the pantry. Eugene had wisely taken a mule wagon while the boys rode their mounts. He had to park the wagon on the Crowleys' road since there was no way to take it up the trail over the ridge.

Mr. Crowley had come to check on them, worried sick about his neighbor. He was lucky; only his lowest pasture had flooded—the ridge had saved his farm. Wendall vowed to Eugene that he would help him rebuild his barn and fences as soon as the waters receded.

Rachel glanced up from the potato she was peeling. "Looks like the raiding party is back."

Eugene smiled at her with a sack of cornmeal over his shoulder. "Good to see you up and about, Mama. How do you feel?"

"Don't start that again, Eugene. I would've ridden over to the farm with you this morning if it hadn't been a boys-only affair," she teased.

"Gramma!" Jake called, excitedly. "Wait till you see what we brought home."

"What is it?"

"Come look!"

Rachel couldn't resist. She wiped her hands on her apron and headed for the back porch. There, lined out across the floorboards, were at least a dozen fish of various types.

"Where on earth did these come from?"

"Gramma, we got to fish right off our front porch!" Jake said enthusiastically. "Nearly every time we caught a fish, it was something different."

"Well," Rachel said admiringly, "that's going to make for an interesting supper."

Jake pointed out the different species. "Look, we've got bass, bluegill, perch, and even a trout and catfish. We figured they were all confused about where they were supposed to be with the flood and all."

If the fish were confused, the people of Louisville were even more so. The city continued to flounder in mass chaos and confusion. Governor Chandler had declared Martial Law that morning, and later that evening, as the ever-growing Harrison family gathered around the radio, they learned that the Ohio River was churning at eighty-two feet above flood stage. It was predicted to crest at eighty-five feet sometime during the following day.

The radio announcer boasted of their ability to keep broadcasting from the fifteenth floor of the Brown Hotel. "Folks," he blared, "the first floor is completely flooded, but we vow to stay with you and keep you up to date on the latest news concerning Black Sunday." He even bragged about catching a two-pound fish in the hotel lobby.

When reports of the latest death toll began to air, Nathan switched off the radio, making the excuse that he wanted to save the battery. The truth was, he preferred to spare Emily any further heartbreak. Leaning forward in his chair, he glanced at his wife and daughter, then surveyed the living room full of people. "We've been blessed," he declared. "I propose that all of the men of our household offer our services to the National Guard tomorrow. They'll need all the help they can get."

He turned toward Charles. "You can stay here; your wife and baby need you right now. Don't feel obligated to get out in all of this too soon."

Charles nodded his head and drew Emily closer to his side.

A few minutes later, after Wallace led the household in prayer, Nathan asked all of the men to join him in the study. He looked specifically at his grandsons and Wallace. "You three are a part of this too. You can work as hard as anyone else."

All three smiled and practically ran into the small room at the back of the house.

Nathan's take-charge personality zipped into action as he laid out his plan. "First thing in the morning, we'll all go to the armory, and Charles, you and I will make arrangements for the burial of your mother-in-law."

Charles thanked him somberly.

"Eugene, you'll need to find out where you and the boys can be put to work. We'll take two vehicles, so I can bring Charles back to the house, and I'll head back out. We'll carry a lunch with us." All of them stood nodding their assent. Then Nathan added, "Make sure you take water and work gloves and be back at the house by five o'clock. No exceptions. We're not going to worry the women."

Later as the family members settled down for the night, Eugene stood by the kitchen door hugging his wife. Nathan had already headed out to the bunkhouse, which was where Eugene had also been relegated for the time being. Annie would be sleeping with her mother since the Bannans were given the bedroom she and Eugene had shared the night before.

Annie pulled back slightly from her husband's embrace, surprising him with her proclamation. "I'm going with you tomorrow."

Eugene tried to catch the look in her eyes to gauge if she was by any chance teasing with him. Only a small candle flickered on the kitchen counter, leaving her face bathed in shadow.

Before he could give her an answer, Annie continued. "There are plenty of women around here to take care of this household. It would drive me crazy not to be out there helping in the relief effort."

Eugene slowly shook his head. "Sweetheart, I don't think your father would allow it."

"Eugene, that's not my father's decision to make; it's ours. I know I could be as much help out there as the rest of you."

"I have no doubt of that," Eugene said with a grin. "But I don't have any idea what we're about to encounter."

"Please don't fight me on this; I feel very strongly about it."

"I know, and I agree—"

"You do?" she broke in, with a hint of excitement.

"I do. But I want to make a deal with you first."

Annie remained silent as she waited for her husband to proffer the deal.

"Let me go out tomorrow and see how it is—kind of get a feel for the situation—then I'll be able to let you know what it's like, and you can decide whether you want to go with us or not."

"You mean it? It'll be my decision?"

"Well, let me put it this way, it'll be *our* decision. Remember?"

Annie nodded compliantly. "Thank you, Eugene."

"For what?" he asked, pulling her in tight.

"For being you," she whispered up close to his lips.

He gave her a quick kiss, then pulled away knowing he'd have a hard time heading out to the bunkhouse if he didn't get away from his wife forthwith.

The following night, supper was served for everyone in the dining room. Claudia and Mattie had added every leaf available to the table, making enough room for thirteen people to eat comfortably. Tales of the flood's devastation were being told, one right after the other—some at the same time. The men were spent and weary, but what they had done that day had made a difference in someone else's life.

"Honey, were you able to get to the church building?" Claudia asked Nathan, who sat at the opposite end of the table.

"No, not yet. That's the first place I tried to go after I brought Charles home, but there's no way to get to it. Besides, I didn't even recognize where I was once I got to the outskirts of the city."

"Mm," Eugene interjected, as he finished a swig of tea. "I heard from a Red Cross worker that Oak Hill Church is being used as a shelter."

"Oh, thank the Lord it was saved," Rachel cried.

Throughout the dinner conversation, Annie kept trying to get her husband's attention, but every time he looked her way, it was with a dopey grin. He was taunting her; she could feel it.

After the table had been cleared and the kitchen cleaned, Nathan ushered Claudia and the Bannans into his study and closed the door. They needed to talk to Emily about the arrangements for her mother's funeral. Roberta and Lillie played with Claire on the couch.

When Annie came into the living room, she noticed Eugene sitting cross-legged on the floor playing a game of spades with the boys.

"Who's winning?" she asked.

"We are," Will declared, pointing across to his partner, Wallace.

Between hands, Eugene asked, "Hey guys, do you think your momma could handle going out with us tomorrow?"

All three boys nodded their heads—Jake even threw in a confident, "Sure!"

"Then it's settled. You wanna tag along tomorrow?" Eugene asked, winking at his wife.

Annie flung him a half smile. "I thought you'd never ask."

***

Over a month passed before the family was able to make it to the Oak Hill Church building and reconnect with their brothers and sisters. Their first worship service since the flood took place on February 28. In the meantime, Eugene had moved his family back home after a week at the Harrisons and the electricity and phone lines had been fully restored thanks to the hard work of the National Guard. They watched day by day as the water gradually disappeared from their farm, leaving a layer of mud so thick they couldn't get a vehicle down their road to the highway until mid-March.

Will's fifteenth birthday on February 4 had been celebrated with one of Claudia's famous Mississippi Mud chocolate cakes, which the boys promptly renamed Louisville Mud. The Bannans moved into a small house only a block from the Louisville University campus after living with the Harrisons for three and a half weeks. They had lost everything in the flood, but thanks to Nathan and Claudia, they were on their feet once again. The young couple had been so moved by the loving hospitality they had received, they began attending Oak Hill Church on a weekly basis. To show their gratitude, Charles and Emily threw a family picnic in their backyard on a warm Saturday in April, which also included Roberta and her kids, along with Mattie.

It took over five months for the Brown Hotel to reopen, but when it did, Roberta's job was waiting for her. Until that time, she and her children stayed on with Nathan and Claudia much to everyone's delight. Nathan's fears concerning Claudia's health never came to fruition. She declared that she had never felt better in her life and continued to reach out to friends and strangers alike who were still in need of assistance due to the flood.

Not a soul from the Oak Hill congregation lost his life, but many were added to their number from those who had spent weeks taking shelter in their building. Overall, the city of Louisville lost ninety of its citizens, some to drowning, but the majority to exposure. Had it not been for the tireless efforts of city mayor Neville Miller and Governor "Happy" Chandler, the city may have lain in ruins permanently. But a beautiful, new Louisville gradually arose from the mud, thanks to their tireless efforts and unflagging loyalty to the citizens who had suffered through such an immense tragedy. Under their leadership, a floodwall twenty-nine miles long was built by the Works Progress Administration to prevent further catastrophes from occurring in the Ohio River Valley.

The Kentucky National Guard, over eleven hundred in number, had sacrificed much to help the people of Louisville and Frankfort. By the end of March, they returned to their homes as distinguished heroes.

Schools were closed for several weeks, which Will had declared was the best birthday gift he had ever received. His birthday, henceforth, marked a memorial of sorts for their family, commemorating the thousand-year flood of 1937. But by the time his seventeenth birthday rolled around, Will himself had taken monumental strides. Unfortunately, for the sake of his loving parents and grandparents, they were strides being taken in the wrong direction.

PART THREE

He who troubles his own house shall inherit the wind.

~Solomon (Proverbs 11:29, NKJV)

Oft hope is born when all is forlorn.

~J. R. R. Tolkien

Chapter 28

Summer 1939

"**S**on, while we're gone, I want you to take care of your mother and grandmother."

Will snatched up another bale of hay and flung it on top of the stack in the barn. Dust and straw clung to his sweaty, muscular arms, and he turned toward his father, waving a giant horsefly away from his face.

When he didn't verbally respond, Eugene repeated his instructions. "I mean it, Will. Jake and I will be gone for four days and that leaves you the man in charge around here. You need to look after your mother and grandmother."

Pulling off his leather gloves, Will reached into his back pocket and yanked out a blue bandana. He roughly wiped the sweat off his forehead and around his dirt-streaked neck. Averting his eyes from Eugene's, he said, "I hear ya."

Eugene moved in close and clasped his hand on top of Will's shoulder. "I know you hear me, but I'm asking you to do it."

"I got it, Dad," Will muttered and moved out from under his father's grasp.

Before heading to his truck, Eugene said, "I love you, Son."

Just as he expected there was no response, but he was determined that Will would know he was loved unconditionally, no matter how much he acted like he didn't care.

Eugene checked the trailer one last time and made sure the hitch was secure before getting into his truck. It was slow-going up the road toward the house pulling the trailer loaded with four steer and two heifers for auction in Lexington. Eugene and Jake planned to spend a couple of days at the farm in Winchester, too, maybe even do a little hunting.

Jake jumped off the porch with his bag and threw it in the back of the truck before it came to a complete stop.

"Where's your mom and gramma?" Eugene asked as he set the brake on the truck.

"They're comin'—I've already told 'em good-bye."

Eugene stepped out of the truck and grabbed two bricks from the bed, jamming them into place in front and behind the rear tire.

"Be careful, you two." Rachel came down the steps of the porch and gave Eugene a loving hug. "And if you get a chance, check underneath the porch on the farm in Winchester."

"I will, Mama." Eugene let out a good-natured chuckle. Rachel had told him recently that she remembered Franklin burying a jar of money underneath the steps. The trouble was, she wasn't quite sure if she'd dreamed it or not. He thought it would be worth a shot and had thrown a shovel in the bed of the truck just in case.

Rachel walked around to the other side of the truck to tell Jake good-bye one more time as Annie hurried off the porch and threw her arms around her husband's neck. "Be careful, Eugene." She kissed him passionately, then laid her hand on his chest, smiling playfully. "You'd better come back to me."

Eugene pressed her hand to his heart then to his lips, gazing into her blue eyes. "How could I resist?" Then more seriously he added, "Annie, I want this to be a good week for you and Will."

She nodded her head and glanced down the hill toward the barn. "It will be; don't worry about a thing." She gave him one more quick kiss, then released him.

Eugene hopped into the truck beside his son and shoved it into gear. The engine revved, but the truck wouldn't budge.

Annie started laughing and yelled, "Hold on a minute—the bricks!"

As soon as Eugene pressed his foot firmly on the brake, she kicked the bricks out of place and tossed them into the bed of the truck. Eugene reached his arm out the window and gave her a pat on the backside. "What would I do without you?"

"Obviously you'd never get off the farm!" she called as the truck rolled toward the highway.

Later that evening, Annie knocked lightly on the door to Will's room and waited until he said, "Yeah?" before she opened it.

"Goodnight, sweetheart. I'm heading to bed."

Will was lying on the bed with his baseball glove, tossing a ball repeatedly in the air. He didn't look at her when he said, "G'night."

Watching Will toss the ball reminded her of springtime. Last school year was the first time both of her boys had been able to play on the high-school baseball team together. Will was a speedy centerfielder, and Jake played first when he wasn't pitching. Annie looked forward to Will's senior season. He had a chance to play in college if he could keep his temper in check. The coach had sat him on the bench during an important regional game last spring because of his blow-up after a loss to their cross-town rivals. Will left no doubt in anyone's minds that he hated to lose. She just hoped he would be able to get his emotions under control for his senior year.

"Don't forget worship service in the morning. I love you."

Will's only response was to nod his head, so Annie closed the door and headed for bed.

When Will didn't join the women for breakfast the next morning, Rachel said she'd go get the rascal out of bed.

A moment later she quietly called, "Annie, darlin', can you come back here?" Her voice carried a hint of bewilderment that caused a flutter in Annie's stomach.

Immediately, she rose from the table and joined her mother-in-law in the doorway. Even though Will's bed was neatly made, Annie knew that it hadn't been slept in—the baseball glove and ball were lying on top of the quilt.

Annie could feel her heart racing with confusion and fear. Where could he have gone last night? Even though she was dressed for worship, she took off down to the barn, hoping and praying he had slept there for the night.

"Will!" she called loudly, stepping inside a ways.

There was no answer, and at that moment, she knew without a doubt that her son was not on the farm. Comanche's head shot up over his stall, making it clear he hadn't left on horseback.

Rachel stood on the back porch waiting for Annie's return.

"Mama, what should we do? He's not down at the barn."

"Oh Annie, I'm so sorry. Maybe you should call one of his friends."

A trace of relief coursed through Annie's mind, but it was short-lived. His best friend Jimmy was home in bed sleeping soundly. As she talked to his mother, Corrine, Annie learned that she was just about to rouse Jimmy for church. If Will had been out all night, there was no doubt in her mind that he would've been with Jimmy.

"What do we do now?" she asked, anger beginning to replace the earlier fear.

Taking Annie confidently by the shoulders, Rachel declared, "We go to church. Either he'll show up there or be here when we get home—I'm sure of it."

Annie drew in a deep breath and nodded her head. "I'm sure you're right, but I'm going to have an awfully hard time concentrating this morning."

"Me too, darlin'. Me too."

Will, however, didn't show up for worship service, nor did he appear for Sunday lunch at the Harrisons'. Annie was trying hard not to worry her parents, but she could see the concern on their faces.

"Honey, I'm in charge of a committee meeting at church this afternoon," Nathan said, "but I'm going to make some phone calls and then I'll be right out. It won't take long."

Annie welcomed her father's company this afternoon. He would know just what to do if Will was still missing.

Claudia kissed her daughter and hugged her firmly. "Call me when you get home; let me know if he's there."

"We will, Mother."

Twenty minutes later as Annie parked the car beside the house, Rachel exclaimed, "He's back! Look at the barn door—it's open."

"Oh, thank the Lord."

Annie practically ran into the house, changing out of her dress as fast as she could, then sprinting to the back door to pull on her boots. Rachel sat silently in the kitchen watching her whirlwind of a daughter-in-law.

"Mama, please say a prayer for us. I need wisdom to deal with him."

"Darlin', I haven't stopped praying since we walked into this house."

"Thank you," she said earnestly. "Please keep 'em comin'."

Even though she felt like breaking into a run, Annie walked to the barn with purposeful strides. She needed a little time to convince herself not to overreact to anything Will was about to tell her.

Stay calm—don't get angry. Reaching the barn, she paused briefly in the doorway, *Oh God, give me wisdom.*

As she walked down the row of stalls, the horses began stomping their impatience. They threw their heads restlessly hoping to be let out to pasture or fed their oats.

"I know, I know," Annie said out loud. "You guys are going to have to wait."

At the end of the row, she saw Will's hat hanging on the gatepost of Bébé's stall. When she looked over the gate, there he was, lying in a fresh pile of hay in the corner. He was so soundly asleep that he didn't even move when she opened the gate and stepped inside.

Something about Bébé drew Annie's attention before she attempted to wake her son. The two-year-old filly kept her head low; her neck drooped down unnaturally. Annie ran her hand along her sleek neck down to her shoulder, then she squatted in front of her, massaging the filly's left foreleg with both hands. Bébé lifted her left foot off the floor in obvious pain. She didn't welcome even the slightest touch. Annie's heart flipped over in dismay as it dawned on her that their beloved girl was lame.

"William!" She said her son's name much more forcefully than she'd planned.

His arms and legs gave a violent jerk as he was jolted awake by her voice.

"Get up right now!"

Will sat up in the hay, rubbing his hands groggily across his face.

"Where have you been and what has happened to Bébé?"

Will ran nervous hands through his hair. Finally, he pushed himself up off the ground like a slow-moving freight train.

Annie felt hot tears already stinging her eyes. Oh, how she wished Eugene were here to help her through this situation. She sensed her emotions were already careening out of control.

Will's eyes focused on everything except his mother, then dropped to his feet. Annie kept her jaw clenched tight, waiting for him to explain himself. She knew he was clever with words. No matter what she said, he was always able to turn it somehow—make her sound like she didn't know what she was talking about. It frustrated her to no end. She knew when this conversation was over, she'd probably think of a thousand things she should've said.

But for now, he shifted his weight from one foot to the other. He seemed to be searching for what to say. Annie knew if he answered her while looking down it would be a boldface lie. Surprisingly, he raised his head and looked her directly in the eyes.

"I entered the night race at River Park."

"You what? How did you get there?"

"Jimmy brought his trailer and I met him down the road."

All of a sudden, Will threw caution to the wind, as he must have done last night, and started boasting. "She can fly, Mom. She won! Bébé won the midnight race! You know how much money that is?"

"Will," Annie seethed, "how could you? You think winning the race makes everything all right?"

Suddenly, her temper flared; she barely felt in control of the words she was about to say. "She hasn't been training, and you're too heavy. Look at her! You've crippled her!"

She continued to rake her son over the coals, letting him know how much it would cost for an emergency veterinarian visit, not to mention the fact that Bébé may never recover from the injury. How could he be so uncaring about the filly he had bravely brought into this world?

Will's jaw set stubbornly, and his eyes narrowed. Whatever patience he might have possessed seeped away into the straw at his feet. He suddenly let out an angry stream of words, including an expletive directed toward his mother. Before she could stop herself, Annie's open hand struck his face so hard he staggered back a step.

Instantly, she regretted her actions; she had shocked even herself. But before Annie could apologize, Will covered his cheek with one hand and kicked the gate open to the stall.

"I'm sorry, Will, I didn't mean to slap you," she cried as he walked out the gate.

"Whatever, Mom." He dug down deep into the front pocket of his jeans and pulled out a wadded roll of bills, slamming it down on the workbench.

"Here!" he yelled. "Use this to pay your stupid vet."

As Will walked away, Annie felt herself shaking. "Will, don't you walk away from me until this is settled!" she yelled.

Another cussword rolled off his tongue, and he yelled back, "I'm done!" He turned to face her while walking backward toward the open door. "You care more about your precious horses than you care about me anyway!"

The door slammed so hard behind him that every horse in the barn was startled.

Annie put her head in her hands, then dropped down on her knees into the hay. "Anne Marie Wyatt, you're an idiot!" she cried aloud. She took in several deep breaths, pushing each one forcefully out of her lungs. She was so angry with herself for letting this whole thing get out of control.

Suddenly, Rachel's words, spoken five short years ago, seared her memory. "Don't go borrowing trouble five years down the road." *Well, it's five years down the road, and trouble is still with us.* Scorching tears of anguish—the only kind that someone you love more than yourself can cause—poured from her eyes, and a hopeless feeling settled over her like a heavy quilt.

"I don't know who he is, Lord . . . I don't have a clue." Her hands turned upward as her supplication filled every corner of the barn. "But You do. You know everything about him . . . You knit him together in my womb." The words that came next, she had uttered a thousand times. "I give him to You—totally and completely. I lay his life—his very soul— in Your hands. Take him and work a miracle in his heart, O Lord."

She moved from her knees to a sitting position, pulling her knees up to her chest, releasing her distress in sobs. *Oh God, I'm so weak.*

After a while, she felt completely drained and lay down on her back in the hay where her son had slept earlier. Annie tried not to feel sorry for herself—especially after praying such a prayer to her heavenly Father—but fresh tears trickled down her cheeks for the lost love between a mother and son.

She let out a long and languid sigh. "Forgive us both, Lord."

***

Nathan stood by his car near the house and studied his grandson as he walked up the road from the barn. Will looked completely disheveled—his shirttail was hanging out in the front and his hair was wild, much like the look in his eyes.

"Get in," Nathan demanded quietly and opened the passenger side of his car.

Will stopped dead in his tracks.

"I won't say it again."

Nathan remained by the door until Will obediently slipped inside. After closing it, Nathan looked up at Rachel standing on the porch. "Would you call Claudia please, and tell her I'll be home later this evening?" Moving around to the driver's side he added, "We'll be back here for supper."

Rachel nodded and watched until the car turned onto the highway. Annie had yet to emerge from the barn, and Rachel wondered what she should do. It had been impossible not to hear Will's final words to his mother as he stormed out of the barn.

Knowing Annie the way she did, it would probably be better to let her have some time alone. When she was ready to come up from the barn, Rachel would be waiting with open arms and a sympathetic ear. She said a little prayer for her sweet Annie, then went back inside to call Claudia.

Nathan didn't speak to his grandson until they reached their destination. He hadn't been out to the old railroad bridge since the boys were young and, for some reason, this seemed like the best place to talk. It was a majestic iron bridge built in the 1850s, standing tall over a rambling fork of the Ohio River.

This particular rail spur had been closed for nearly two decades, making it a great destination for exploring or fishing. Today, however, the bridge would be used for neither. It was time to have a serious conversation with his grandson, and

Nathan wanted to be far enough from the farm that Will would have no chance to walk away.

"You remember coming out here with me when you were little?" Nathan was careful to watch his step as they walked out onto the bridge. He peered through the railroad slats at the river running far below.

"I remember," Will said with a grin. "I also remember fishing over there in the middle of the bridge and almost being pulled into the river by a gar."

Nathan laughed. "Yeah, if it hadn't been for your overalls, I would've been fishing you out of the river that day." He remembered vividly grabbing Will's straps as he was about to be yanked off the bridge.

"Why don't we go sit down in our old fishing spot and have a little talk?"

Will silently made his way to the middle of the bridge and sat down beside his grandfather in the shade of a giant iron beam. A long minute passed before he finally asked, "What did you wanna talk about, Gramps?"

"Well, for starters, where were you last night? I take it you already told your momma and it didn't go so well."

Will breathed out something between a laugh and a sigh. It took him a while to get started, but finally he told Nathan about sneaking out with Bébé and taking her to the midnight race at River Park. "Gramps, she was the fastest filly there— even with me riding her!"

Nathan had been training thoroughbreds for the better part of forty years now. His heart went out to Bébé, knowing how much damage Will might have done to her. When his grandson finished his story, Nathan asked, "Do you think that was a wise decision you made last night, Son?"

"Gramps," he said dolefully, "I know it wasn't the right thing to do."

"Then why'd you do it?" Nathan had a hard time keeping the condemnation out of his voice.

"I don't know."

Nathan laughed out loud. "Oh yes you do—come on, let me hear it."

A long moment passed while Nathan wisely waited for a response from his grandson.

Finally, Will answered quietly, "I wanted the money."

"The money? Whatever for?"

"Ah, Gramps, I've never had a job. I have to do all my work on the farm, and there's no pay in that," he said sarcastically.

"That didn't answer my question. What do you want the money for?"

Will leaned forward, bracing his hands on the wooden slats of the bridge. "I got plans."

"What sort of plans?"

Shaking his head, Will acted as if he misspoke. "I mean, I just wanna go out and have some fun every now and then. That's all."

Nathan pondered that for a while, trying to remember again what it was like to be seventeen and decided to let it go and move on to the real reason for their talk. "Can you tell me what's going on between you and your mother?"

When Will started to get up, Nathan took hold of his arm and forced him back down. By the set of his jaw and look in his eyes, he conveyed a strong message to his grandson: *you're not going anywhere until we talk about this.* "I know your relationship isn't going very well right now. I want to know why."

"Well, for one thing, I don't wanna go to college. Mom keeps nagging me about my grades and baseball," Will complained.

"What do you want to do with your life?"

"I don't know," Will said, as if the question had rubbed him the wrong way. "I'll figure it out."

"Well, I hope it doesn't take you as long as it took me."

Surprised by his grandfather's declaration, Will asked, "What do you mean?"

Somewhere in the back of his mind, Nathan had figured he was going to open up the past with his grandson today, but he hadn't consciously prepared for it to happen. Pride beckoned him to shove the ugly memories back inside the corroded box that he'd supposedly buried decades ago.

Nathan now fought his own urge to get up, but he knew that the best thing he could do for his grandson today was speak from the heart.

"Will," he began, "I had a pretty rough upbringing. I had a father who came home drunk every night of the week, no exceptions. Believe it or not, he never laid a hand on me, but I think I might've been able to handle it better if he had. He just made sure that I knew day after day that I was a worthless, no-good son. I knew as soon as I was old enough that I'd do just what my older brother and sister had done—run off the first chance I got."

Nathan now struggled with how much to tell his grandson. Would revealing his terrible mistakes of the past help him or harm him? Something from deep within his soul urged him to release what he had never spoken of before, not even with his wife. Claudia was well aware of his rough family life, but the day he had married was the day he started his life over again. It was like being given a major do-over, and he wasn't about to mess it up. Repressing his former life hadn't been so difficult in the beginning, but the closer his heart was drawn to God's, the harder it was to let it rest. Maybe today would bring a healing of sorts to both him and his grandson.

"When I got to be around twelve or so, I started stealing. I stole from neighbors when they were out working their land—trinkets, money—whatever I could get my hands on. I'd trade stuff with other boys at school who were doing the same thing. It wasn't long before we were stealing liquor. I couldn't steal it from my papa; he would've noticed, but I knew places in town I could get my hands on it. The guys and I would hide out behind the livery stable and drink ourselves into oblivion sometimes. I couldn't see that I was going down the same road as my father, coming home drunk every day—it just made me not care anymore about the names he called me."

Nathan went on to tell Will how gambling had taken a hold on his life around the age of fifteen. "I was hanging out at the track every day while my mama thought I was in school. Any coin I could steal I was betting on the horses. And that was a whole different kind of life down at the tracks. These weren't the kind of race tracks we have around here; they were seedy, filthy places with a lot of bad characters hanging around." Nathan sighed deeply. "I became just like them."

He looked out over the river, then turned and made eye contact with his grandson. In a cold voice he said, "I wasn't a good man, Will." His throat tightened, and Nathan feared the deep emotions forcing their way through his chest would cause him to break down. He took in several deep breaths to counter those emotions while concentrating on the tranquil flow of the water below.

It was so long before Nathan spoke again, Will eventually asked, "Why are you telling me all of this, Gramps?"

Nathan tried to rub the tightness out of his neck and continued to stare out over the water. "Because I don't want you to treat your mother the way I treated mine."

For the next several minutes, Nathan told Will about the anger he harbored toward his mother. Not one time had she ever protected him from his father's verbal abuse. Nathan had longed for her to stand up for him or at the very least tell him that none of those awful things were true.

"I can remember my mama telling me that she loved me, but it was meaningless if she wasn't going to stand up to my papa. I never believed her. If she really loved me, she would've never let him say all of those things to me. So when I was about your age, I pretty much gave her a piece of my mind and left home for good. I vowed to her that I'd never speak to her again."

Will's expression had turned to one of dismay. "You really mean it? You never spoke to her again?"

Nathan honestly and solemnly answered the question, then he admitted how terrible he felt keeping Annie away from her grandmother all these years. "My stubborn pride wouldn't let her be a part of my life or my family's life. Annie knows nothing about her grandmother. She's begged me, I don't know how many times, to tell her, but I can't bring myself to do it."

Nathan went on. "I can't stand to hear you talk to your mother the way you did today. For one thing, that's my little girl. I don't want to see her go through the same thing I put my mother through all those years ago."

He laid a hand on Will's shoulder. "You need to swallow your pride and apologize to your mother."

Will responded passionately. "So do you, Gramps!"

"What do you mean?"

"You owe my momma an apology too. You still haven't told her about her grandma—talk about pride."

Out of exasperation, Nathan let out a muffled laugh. How dare his grandson turn the tables on him? But how dare he not—he deserved it. He was sitting out here on this old bridge telling his grandson to take the splinter out of his eye when he had one about the size of the beam he was leaning against in his own. Touché!

"All right," Nathan agreed, "I accept that challenge. I'll tell her everything she wants to know if you apologize for last night and the way you talked to her today."

Will slowly nodded his head. "When?"

"Right after supper. As a matter of fact, I'll go first," Nathan declared, sticking out his hand.

Nathan's hand accepted Will's, and he held it firmly, along with his gaze. "I fear you're too much like me, Will."

"If that's the case, Gramps," Will said as he pulled Nathan to his feet, "then I guess there's hope for me yet."

Chapter 29

Clarence Simmons, the local veterinarian, gave a friendly wave to Nathan and Will as they passed on the road to the house. Will's stomach twisted like a wet dishrag. He hadn't once entertained the thought that what he was doing last night might've crippled his filly. He wondered if going down to the barn would be a wise decision. He wanted to know what the vet had told his momma, but not if she was in the same mood he had left her in. As the car came to a halt, he saw her come out of the barn, heading for the house.

Will stepped out of the car and watched Annie walk toward them. Her head was down, and she walked slowly up the road. His stomach twisted even tighter; there was no way she had good news. He looked to his grandfather, hoping he would be the one to ask about Bébé, but Nathan promptly shut the car door and walked straight into the house.

Doggone it, Gramps—help me out here.

Will cleared his throat, fearing his mother would walk right past without noticing him. She lifted her gaze and stopped a few feet away. He couldn't explain the sudden feeling of compassion that overwhelmed him. The look in her eyes was almost more than he could handle.

"How's Bébé?" he asked quietly.

"Thank God, she'll recover. She'll never race again, but she won't be permanently crippled."

Surprisingly, that's all his momma said. She looked weary, almost as if she'd been the one to stay up all night instead of him. Without another word, she gave him the faintest of smiles and headed into the house.

Will stood with his mouth half open, watching his mother disappear inside. He hadn't known how to respond to her. It would've almost been easier if she was still mad at him—after all, he deserved it. But to see her looking utterly defeated truly bothered him. It dawned on him that he knew full well how to argue with her, but he had no clue how to reach out to her as a loving son—none whatsoever.

Supper turned out to be the most awkward meal Will had ever been a part of. Gramma did her best to cast out a few conversation starters, but no one took the bait. His momma only ate a few bites, then spent the rest of the meal fumbling with her food. Gramps was wound as tight as a drum, and Will knew it was because he had to swallow his big ego and confess some hard things to his daughter tonight. He was well aware that his time was coming as soon as Gramps left for home. Trouble was, he didn't know how on earth he was going to do it. He could hear his dad saying, "It's time to step up and be a man, Son."

Eventually, Nathan pushed away from the table, and cleared his throat. "Um, Annie, I was wondering if you'd take a little walk with me as soon as you're done eating?"

Annie looked up from her plate for the first time since the meal began. "Sure, as soon as I get the kitchen cleaned up." She stood and carried her plate to the counter.

"Oh no, darlin', you go on out with your daddy." Rachel glanced at her grandson and winked. "I've got all the help I need tonight."

Annie nodded, and Nathan said, "Thank you, Rachel, for a fine meal. I'm sorry we weren't much company this evening."

"You're welcome, Nathan. You two run along and have a good talk."

Annie leaned down and laid her cheek affectionately next to Rachel's, giving her shoulder a light squeeze, then followed Nathan out the back door.

Father and daughter walked up the hill behind the house to the top of the ridge overlooking the farm. The sun dropped slowly toward the horizon, leaving the pasture and cattle bathed in a warm, evening glow. Nathan reached for Annie's hand and walked with her as he had when she was young. This evening she found herself missing those *little girl* days. Things seemed so much easier back then. She hoped her father would be able to give her some much-needed insight into her son's behavior, but Nathan's tack in conversation surprised her.

"Honey, it's time for me to tell you about your grandmother," he said as they settled down on an outcropping of rocks.

"Your mother?"

Nathan nodded and turned his face toward the dying sun in the west. "Before I tell you about her, I need to tell you what my life was like growing up. I've never hidden the fact that your mother saved me from a life of . . ." He paused for a moment. "Well, a life of who knows what. I'd probably be dead or in prison right now if it wasn't for her. She represented everything that was good and pure. I knew without her I was lost—I've always known that."

None of this was new to Annie, but she sensed there was much more to be told. She sat silently as Nathan recounted what his life had been like with an alcoholic father and a weak-willed mother that he had never fully trusted.

When he confessed the vow he had made never to speak to his mother again, Annie looked at her father with tears burning in her eyes. It literally made her sick to her stomach to think that he could treat his mother so thoughtlessly.

Nathan refused to return her gaze. "When I met Claudia, I completely changed who I was. I wanted to abandon that terrible person I had become. The only way to do that was to completely bury the past, and in my mind, that meant everyone I'd ever known was dead to me."

While Annie admired what her father had done with his life, she still couldn't understand how he could've harbored such ill will toward his mother after so many years. How could he have been so stubborn, especially in keeping her away from her own granddaughter?

She couldn't be quiet any longer. "Daddy, you have to make it right with her before it's too late. I'm sorry, but that's wrong for you to keep that vow."

"I know honey; I've known that for a very long time."

Nathan now turned to face his daughter. "I've already done something about it."

"You have?" Annie exclaimed. "When?"

"A few years ago, when Will was younger, I recognized myself in him. It bothered me—even hurt me—every time I saw the two of you argue. The reason it hurt me so much was because I saw what it did to you." He breathed a deep sigh. "I finally realized how devastated my mother must've been when I turned my back on her."

Annie drew both hands up to her chest. Her heart felt so heavy for the woman she had yet to meet.

"I took a trip down to Carthage the year before your mother had the aneurysm."

"Did you find her?"

"Yes."

"Did you apologize to her?"

"Yes."

"What did she say?" Annie begged earnestly.

Nathan shook his head remorsefully. "Annie, I begged for forgiveness at the foot of her grave."

It took a moment for Nathan's words to sink in, but when they did, Annie felt like she had just lost her own mother. A tear spilled down her cheek, glistening in the waning sun as she turned away. She wanted to choose her next words carefully. While she felt a deep sadness for her father's situation, she also found herself angry at his stubbornness and pride.

"Daddy," she said softly, "I don't know what to say." Then her eyes flashed, "Why didn't you tell me about this years ago? You've known she was gone for what, seven years now?"

"And that's why I owe you more than one apology. I just couldn't bring myself to tell you."

"Why ever not?" she asked, incredulously.

Nathan shook his head. "Because I have too much pride." He looked out over the pasture and added softly, "I didn't want to admit I'd failed, and even worse, I didn't want to look like a failure in your eyes."

To hear Nathan's solemn declaration hurt Annie far deeper than he probably realized. She had never thought that her father had any weaknesses whatsoever. But he had hidden them well—disguised them behind a self-assured bravado that said he had the world wrapped around his little finger, when in reality, he carried some deep, grievous wounds.

Annie stood and paced slowly along the top of the ridge, trying to get her thoughts together. It had already been a long day that had left her emotionally drained. And now, she not only had a disobedient son to deal with, but her father's revelation had left her reeling. She regarded him sardonically from a distance—so he was human after all.

Finally, Annie made her way back to Nathan's side and sat down. "You know what hurts me more than anything? Not that *you* kept all of this from me, but the fact that Mother did. All the times I asked her about my grandmother, she acted like she didn't know."

A dark shade of red worked its way across Nathan's face. He looked like he was about to break down. Annie didn't know if she could handle that or not, and then it suddenly hit her out of the blue. "She doesn't know, does she?"

Nathan's silence said everything. Even though a few inches separated the two, Annie felt like her father was now on the other side of a chasm that couldn't be breeched. She hated the way she felt, but still a sense of bewilderment lingered. Why did she feel so strongly about his admission?

He looked intently into her eyes and put into words what her mind had been unable to surmise. "I know what you're thinking; you've always trusted me, and now you don't know if you can."

Annie's eyes remained fastened on her father's. A hundred different emotions coursed through her body and welled up inside of her all at once.

In a gravelly voice, Nathan's words poured out. "Please forgive me, Annie. I couldn't live with myself if I thought that look in your eyes was meant for me."

Instantly, her expression softened as a wave of compassion filled her heart. It almost seemed like their roles had been momentarily reversed. "Oh Daddy," she choked out, "I'm sorry—I forgive you." She leaned toward him, and he lovingly enveloped her in his arms, drawing her gently into his chest and kissing the top of her head.

After several minutes, Nathan released his hold but continued to keep a protective arm around Annie's shoulders. "Thank you for your forgiveness, honey; I know I don't deserve it, but you have no idea how much it means to me."

Annie leaned up and kissed him on the cheek, then settled her head against his shoulder again. It would probably take a long time to process everything her father had just confessed, but no matter what he had done, her love for him would never waver.

"I guess we should talk about your son for a bit," Nathan said at length.

"If you don't mind, I'd rather not have that conversation right now. I'm too worn out to talk anymore." She stood and brushed herself off. "Besides, I think you need to go home and talk to Mother. She needs to know everything you told me."

Nathan stood up beside his daughter. "Are you sure?" he asked. "I don't mind staying a little longer if you need to talk about Will." He reached for her hand again as they began walking along the ridge.

"I'm positive."

They fell into a comfortable silence until Nathan reached his car. "I love you, honey. I'm really sorry about everything."

"I know. I love you too, Daddy." Annie melted into his arms and thanked him for being here today, as hard as it had been.

"I'll call you in the morning," he said. "Sleep well tonight."

Annie raised her brow and let out a weary laugh. "I'll try."

She watched as he started the car and headed down the road toward the highway, then she walked up the steps into the house.

It was quiet in the front room. Rachel sat in her chair under the lamp mending socks, but her son was nowhere in sight.

"Where's Will?" Annie asked, as she plopped down on the couch.

"He's back in his room. Are you okay, darlin'?"

Annie let a deep breath escape before answering. "I will be in the morning. I just need to go to bed."

Before she could move from the couch, she heard her father's automobile returning up the drive. "What's he doing back?" she mused aloud and went to the front door.

Just when she thought her day couldn't get any worse, Annie was suddenly dealt another punishing blow. A car pulled up in front of the porch and made a wide turn so it now faced toward the road to the highway. Will's best friend, Jimmy, was at the wheel and Annie noticed another boy and three young ladies inside. Her mouth dropped wide as her son came running around from behind the house and headed for the backseat of the car.

"Will! What are you doing?"

Will stopped briefly with his hand resting on the door handle, then suddenly opened it and slid inside.

Annie immediately walked down the porch steps to the car. "Jimmy, what's going on? Will isn't going anywhere tonight."

A light shade of pink spread across Jimmy's broad features, and he turned around to Will in the backseat. She couldn't hear their exchange of words, but when Jimmy turned back around, his flushed face wore a rueful expression.

He shrugged his shoulders. "I'm sorry, Mrs. Wyatt." And with that, he put his foot on the accelerator, leaving her in a cloud of dust. The laughter that streamed from the open car windows hurled extra darts into her chest.

Annie didn't move from her position in front of the house for the next few minutes. She felt like Lot's wife and wondered what Eugene would do if he came home four days later to discover his wife had turned into a pillar of salt on this very spot. If she had enough energy to be angry, that would've been her choice, but for the time being, her emotional storehouse had been depleted.

The sky let go of its last remnant of light as Rachel came to Annie's side. She drew her into a compassionate embrace, breaking the spell with her words of encouragement. Annie leaned up against the older woman, thankful that she didn't have to endure this alone. After a long moment, Rachel released her hold but kept her arm around Annie's waist as she led her up the porch steps into the house.

"Have a seat on the couch, darlin'. I'll bring you a glass of iced tea."

"Thank you," she said softly.

When Rachel returned, she sat down next to her daughter-in-law. "I'm so sorry about all of this, Annie. What can I do to help you?"

Annie shook her head despondently. "Nothing, Mama, but thank you."

"Would you like to talk about it?"

"I don't know what there is to talk about," Annie admitted. "Right now I feel like a total failure as a mother. Of all times for Eugene to be gone," she sighed.

Rachel scooted in closer and turned her palms upward. With a great sense of relief, Annie put her glass on the table beside the couch, then laid her hands inside Rachel's. She couldn't think of anyone she'd rather pray with right now than this woman of God. Almost immediately, Annie began to feel the tension leave her body, and before long, a profound peace settled over both women as they relinquished their worrisome load at the foot of the cross.

When it was over, Rachel leaned in and kissed Annie's forehead. "This too shall pass, darlin'." Then she moved across the room to her chair and picked up the Bible.

Annie leaned her head back as she listened to Rachel's melodious voice. Her eyes closed peacefully as verse after verse of Philippians drifted through her consciousness: *"For to me to live is Christ, and to die is gain . . . let this mind be in you which was also in Christ Jesus . . . that at the name of Jesus every knee should bow . . . work out your own salvation with fear and trembling . . . I press toward the goal for the prize of the upward call of God in Christ Jesus . . . Rejoice in the Lord always: Again I will say,. . ."*[9]

Rachel's voice suddenly hushed. When Annie opened her eyes, she was taken aback by another presence in the room. Will stood motionless in the doorway leading from the kitchen.

"I have something I need to say."

Instantly, Rachel rose to her feet. "I'll just go on—"

Will didn't let her finish. "No, Gramma, you need to stay." He moved across the room and took the chair opposite from hers.

As much as Annie wanted to ask why he'd come back, she decided it would be better to hold her tongue and let Will say his peace. She wasn't about to mess things up the way she had this afternoon down at the barn. Thankfully, she didn't have to wait long for an explanation concerning this evening.

"Momma, I'm sorry about tonight; I didn't mean for that to happen." He stared down at his shoes for a moment. "I forgot that Jimmy told me he was coming to pick me up tonight."

"Then why did you get in the car?" she asked calmly.

"I just had to handle it my own way."

---

[9] Philippians 1:21, 2:5, 2:10, 2:12, 3:14, 4:4, NKJV.

Annie nodded and remained silent.

Will leaned back in his chair and rubbed the back of his hand across his mouth, his right heel tapped a nervous rhythm on the hardwood floor. Annie noticed Rachel had leaned forward in her chair, no doubt praying earnestly for her grandson.

After a long, slow breath, Will looked straight at his momma and said, "I'm not a very good son."

Annie's heart shattered into pieces, right there on the spot. If she had any intentions of keeping her emotions in check, they all just flew out the open window behind her.

"Will—" she said, overwhelmed by her deep maternal love.

"No, it's true, and I hope to make it up to you someday. But I just want you to know that I'm committed to trying."

Annie made a move to get up, but Will threw his hand in the air. "Uh, uh. I have more I need to say."

She scooted back on the couch but leaned forward with her elbows on top of her legs.

"I'm really sorry about Bébé. Jimmy knew he had to get home and be in bed before his mother woke him up for church, so he dropped us off a couple of miles up the highway."

Will shook his head, then stuck his thumb and index finger into the corner of his eyes. With a quavering voice, he said, "I cried all the way home. If I could've carried her on my back, I would've."

There was no restraint left in the room now. All three wept openly over the scene Will had just described.

It took a moment of sniffling and wiping his eyes before Will could finish what he had to say. Finally, he looked at Annie again through red-rimmed eyes. "I'm sorry for what I said to you down at the barn, Momma. I didn't mean it; I promise I didn't."

Annie didn't care what he thought now; she was not going to let Will stop her from holding him. Thankfully, she didn't have to force the issue. As soon as she moved across the room, he stood up and opened his arms to her.

Stepping into his embrace, Annie drew her son in close. He lowered his head over her shoulder, apologizing again through his tears.

"Oh, Will, I'm so sorry I slapped you."

"No, Momma," he said, releasing his hold, "I deserved that."

Annie reached up and laid her hand gently on the side of his face then kissed the cheek she had struck. "I hope you know how much I love you. No matter what you do, I will always love you."

He lowered his eyes and pressed his lips together. Then he said softly, "I love you, too."

Annie sensed his awkwardness, so she looked toward Rachel who had been waiting patiently beside her chair. Will stepped around her and encircled his grandmother in a loving embrace.

"I'm sorry for all the trouble I've caused, Gramma."

"You've got a good heart, Will, I can see it." Rachel gave him a firm squeeze then added, "I love you, darlin'."

"I love you too, Gramma."

Annie knew Will must be completely exhausted after a sleepless night—they all were. With nothing more to discuss, they told each other good night and headed to their separate rooms.

The next morning, Will couldn't seem to make himself roll out of bed. There was a lot of work to be done on the farm, especially with Jake and his dad gone, but his head still felt so groggy. Even the tempting smells of breakfast couldn't manage to get him moving. He lay on his stomach, letting the morning breeze drift over him from the open window.

The tap on his door wasn't unexpected. He knew it had to be past seven already.

"Uh, huh?"

Annie cracked the door a bit without looking in. "May I come in?"

"Yeah," he said, turning his face toward the door.

"I wanted to bring you something."

She made her way across the room and sat down on the side of his bed. When he recognized what she laid on his bedside table, Will raised up on his elbows shaking his head.

"No, Momma, you need to take that back."

"Will, I thought about this for a long time last night. I've already paid the bill for the vet and set aside a good amount for your college education, but I'm going to let you have the rest."

Mentioning his college education irritated Will to no end, but he was determined not to let it show.

"It's not a lot, but we've never been able to give you much in the way of money. I realized you may want to take a girl out on occasion, and this would help."

Will gathered the pillow up underneath his bare chest and dropped back down on it.

"Thanks," he muttered.

When she didn't say anything else, he lifted his chin and looked up at her. There was a resolve in her blue eyes that he had seen many times before. He was certain something more important than money was about to be discussed. Deep down, he feared what it was, but she had him trapped. There would be no escaping the conversation.

"Sweetheart, have you given much thought to giving your heart over to the Lord?"

Will sighed. "Momma, I don't wanna talk about that right now." When he realized how harsh that sounded, he calmly added, "If you don't mind."

She rested her hand briefly on the middle of his back, then bent down and kissed his hair, lingering for a moment while she whispered, "He loves you so much, and He's waiting for you to come to Him."

Will couldn't explain the tears that sprung to his eyes, but he quickly turned away so she wouldn't see them.

Squeezing his shoulder lightly, she stood up. "I'll see you down at the barn."

When the door closed quietly, he turned over on his side to face it. Even though she wouldn't know it, his mother's words had affected him deeply. His life felt so messy at times. Why was it such a struggle to do the right thing day after day? He didn't understand how Jake didn't even have to try—he got up every morning a good man, just like his dad. Will knew in his heart that he wasn't a very good son, but he had no clue how to change that fact, or even what it meant to give his heart to the Lord. None of it made sense.

Annoyed, he flung the sheets off and sat up on the edge of the bed. His eyes wandered to the money on the bedside table, and suddenly a feeling of euphoria took over. He picked it up and thumbed through it, counting the bills twice. A wry smile crossed his lips—no way would he be wasting that money on a girl.

Quickly crossing to the chest of drawers, he pulled the bottom one completely out of its slot and laid it on the floor. The secret envelope lying underneath didn't have much in it, but he was excited to add the money his mother had given him. Feeling its thickness and anticipating the future, he calculated how much more it would take for him and Jimmy to set their plan into motion.

Chapter 30

Will dismounted outside the paddock and looped Comanche's reins over the fence. The calf he was bringing in had given him a spirited challenge out in the pasture. The little guy didn't want to be separated from his mother.

"Hey, you got him!" Annie exclaimed as she came around the backside of the barn.

"This one has a little mischief in him. We may have to name him." Will led him toward the gate Annie had just opened.

"Maybe we should name him William," she said with a gleam in her eye.

"Ha, ha. Very funny, Mom."

"Hang onto him and let me run in and get the salve."

Annie headed back inside the barn while Will inspected the open wound on the calf's rear left flank. He had had a run-in with the barbed wire fence. Apparently, he was way too spunky for his own good.

After a moment, Annie returned from the barn. "Got it," she said, stepping inside the paddock with a tin of salve, a pan of water, and a clean rag. "Do you think you can hold him still?"

"I can try," Will said, tightening his hold on the rope and reaching for the calf's tail.

As soon as Will grabbed his tail, however, the calf kicked up his heels, giving him quite a fight.

Annie stepped back. "Looks like you're going to have to wrestle him."

If this little fella thought he could stand up to Will, he had another thing coming to him. Will had him on his side and wrapped up tight before he knew what had happened to him.

Moving quickly, Annie cleaned the wound, patted it dry, and applied a thick layer of salve. As soon as she was done, Will loosened the rope and let him up, careful not to get in the way of his hind legs. The little guy had not appreciated the tender loving care—not one bit.

Hearing the sound of a truck, Will looked up to see his dad and Jake coming in from their trip to Lexington and Winchester. An odd flutter darted through his stomach. He wasn't looking forward to facing his daddy with the news of last Saturday night's race.

"They're home," he said, in a matter-of-fact voice.

Excitedly, Annie turned to look. Eugene had by-passed the house and was steering the truck toward the barn.

"Uh, Mom, how are you gonna tell him about Bébé?" He was trying not to let his anxiety show, but he knew she probably heard it in his voice.

For a moment, Annie's eyes narrowed, then her expression softened a bit. "I don't plan to tell him anything." She laid the tin in his hand and slapped the rag over his shoulder. "That's your job."

With that declaration, she smiled and ran out the paddock gate to greet the men.

Eugene pulled the truck to a halt in front of the barn and waved to his wife as she walked briskly from the paddock. Even dressed in her work clothes and boots, Annie was the most beautiful sight he'd ever seen. As much as he had enjoyed his excursion with Jake, he always missed Annie tremendously when they were apart.

As he got out of the truck, Eugene almost did a double take. Right on Annie's heels was their eldest son with, of all things, a grin on his face. While Eugene was expecting a warm welcome from Annie, he hadn't anticipated any kind of greeting whatsoever from Will. But there he was, throwing Jake into a headlock and rubbing his knuckles playfully on the top of his head. Scout came flying down the hill from the house and pounced on both boys, sending them into a rowdy free-for-all.

Annie's arms came up around Eugene's neck, and he picked her clear up off the ground, giving her a sweet kiss.

"You miss me?" he asked, lowering her to the ground.

The dimple in her cheek appeared, and Eugene couldn't resist taking hold of her chin and covering it with his thumb.

"More than you know," she said with an expression that left him speculating.

Before he could ask her about it, Will sauntered over. "Hey, Dad."

Eugene did his best not to look surprised, especially when Will opened his arms and allowed him a brief hug. Wow! Here he'd been worried every day about what was going on back home, when apparently his anxiety had been totally unfounded. He couldn't wait to have some time alone with Annie to find out what had caused such a drastic change in their son.

"You need help with the trailer?" Will asked.

"As a matter of fact, I do. Thanks."

"Come on, Jake," Annie said. "Why don't you walk with me up to the house and tell me all about your trip."

Eugene knew at that moment something was up; otherwise, Annie would've hung around just to be near him. He watched her walk up the road with their youngest son. Jake draped his arm around Annie's shoulders and was already entertaining her with tales from their hunting expedition. Eugene felt so blessed listening to their laughter as they made their way up to the house.

Will had already pulled the pin from the hitch and was waiting for his dad's help. As they rolled the trailer back from the truck, Eugene stole a glance at his son. While he seemed concerned about something, there was a calmness about him that hadn't been there last Saturday. He seemed to have grown up in the few days Eugene had been away.

When the trailer was secured in its place beside the barn, Will said, "Dad, can you come inside the barn? I need to show you something."

"Sure. What is it?"

Will took a deep breath then repeated, "I just need to show you something."

Eugene followed him inside the barn and down the row of stalls. Having been gone for the week, he enjoyed walking in to the smell of new wood. Even though the barn was two years old, having been rebuilt after the flood, it still had a hint of the fresh wood smell that Eugene was partial to.

Opening the gate to Bébé's stall, Will stepped back and allowed his dad to enter. When Eugene caught a glimpse of the white bandage running all the way up the filly's left front leg, he immediately asked, "What happened?"

Will removed his hat and pretended to study the red bandana tied around its crown. Without looking up he said, "I did something I shouldn't have done last Saturday."

There was a long pause, long enough that Eugene finally said, "Go on, Son."

"I snuck out with Bébé and took her to the midnight race at River Park."

"Please tell me you weren't the one riding her."

"Dad, I know it was stupid—I just wasn't thinking."

Eugene squatted down in front of the filly and ran his hand lightly down her leg. Without looking over his shoulder, he asked in a quiet voice, "Is she crippled?"

"No, the vet said she'll recover."

Eugene let his head drop down, and the breath he'd been holding escaped in relief. Slowly, he stood and moved in until his chest was against her, wrapping a gentle arm around the filly's neck. Bébé lowered her head over Eugene's shoulder then nudged his head lovingly with her own. He had been her sole trainer since the day she was born. An unusually strong bond had been established between the two. Eugene had felt so remorseful about leaving her to die during the flood that he spent an extraordinary amount of time with the filly. Bébé not only responded to his gentle training, but her heart formed an intense loyalty to his. Annie sometimes teased him about having a mistress down at the barn.

After a long moment, Eugene stepped out of the stall to face his son. "How did it happen?"

Will swallowed hard. "I'm not really sure; it didn't happen until the race was over. We were running middle of the pack until the last turn, and I got her to the outside. Dad, you should've seen her. She kicked into another gear and left the rest of the pack in the dust. She won by four lengths!"

Eugene made it clear he wasn't sharing his son's enthusiasm.

"When I pulled up after the finish line, she started hobbling," Will quietly added.

"Sit down, Son. We need to talk." Eugene walked over to a bench by the wall and waited for Will to join him.

For the next half hour, father and son spoke intently about the situation and what had happened between him and his mother afterward. It seemed to Eugene that Will was keeping a lot of pertinent information to himself. Even after their long talk, Eugene was still puzzled over the drastic change in his son's attitude. He knew Annie would have to fill him in on all the details that Will was obviously leaving out.

Eventually, Will gave his dad a heartfelt apology about the harm he'd done to Bébé. "I never dreamed she might come up lame."

"That's just it, Will, you're a man now. You've gotta start acting *and* thinking like one."

Eugene noticed a look of irritation flash across his son's face. "What is it? Did I say something to make you mad?"

Will ran his hands through his hair then stood up and paced a few steps. When he turned back around he said, "I feel like a man, but I get treated like a boy around here. I don't know if I can handle this much longer."

Surprised, Eugene asked, "What are you thinking about? Moving out?"

"No!" Will exclaimed quickly, almost too quickly.

If Eugene didn't know better, he'd think that Will was hiding something. "What's going on, Son?"

"Nothin' Dad. Nothin's going on."

Eugene looked at Will closely. "Do you know where I was at your age? I was completely on my own. I was in a filthy trench in France trying not to get killed. You don't know how good you've got it around here. You just need to concentrate on graduating from high school and then you can make a decision about what you want to do with your life."

Will looked away, and Eugene sensed his son's edgy demeanor returning. Somehow he had tripped upon a sensitive subject with him. Deep in his heart, he knew what his son needed the most—he needed the Lord in his life. Without the Spirit guiding him, he would always be lost. Every time he tried to broach the subject though, Will always found a way to shut him down. Eugene worried about what it would ultimately take for him to see the light.

"Hey look," Eugene said, as he stood, "your mom and I want what's best for you, we always have. You just need to be patient. We're not trying to stop you from making your own way in life, but—"

"It sure seems like it," Will rudely interrupted. "You said it yourself; you were out on your own by the time you were my age."

Eugene could feel every muscle in his body tightening. It almost felt like he'd been punched in the gut. The tone of his voice was sharp enough to let Will know that he had walked out onto thin ice. "You have no idea what I went through—none whatsoever. I would've given anything to be back on the farm with my folks instead of overseas fighting a war. Trust me; it wasn't my choice to be out on my own."

Will's face instantly turned red, and he looked down at his feet. "Sorry, Dad. I don't know why I said that."

For some unexplained reason, Eugene was reminded of the crescent-shaped scar on the back of his left shoulder, and he reached up to massage it. On Christmas day when he was eleven, a pregnant mare had attacked him on their farm in Winchester. Rachel had stitched him up and made sure the wound had healed without infection. He only wished the emotional wound he carried from the war had healed as neatly. Sometimes, the mere thought of what he had faced at Will's age still seemed like a raw sore that refused to scar over.

Eugene looked at his son with tenderness, then reached out and drew him briefly to his side. "It's all right, Son, let's just forget about it. What do you say we get out of here and see what's for supper?"

Visibly relaxing, Will nodded his consent. As they headed out of the barn, he changed the subject altogether. "Hey, what about the jar of money Gramma was talking about? Did you find it?"

"No," Eugene responded with a chuckle. "We struck out on that one. I dug around as much as I could, but I was either digging in the wrong place or Gramma was mistaken."

"Too good to be true, huh?" Will responded with amusement.

Grinning, Eugene reached out to his son again. "Sure seems like it."

Amazingly, Will didn't move away from his embrace all the way up to the house. Even so, Eugene contemplated his son's last statement, *too good to be true*, and wondered if that applied to his change in demeanor as well.

Later that evening after supper, Eugene took Annie's hand and led her out to the swing on the front porch. "I need a little time with my girl," he said, putting his arm around her and letting the swing rock gently back and forth.

Annie rested her head on his shoulder and took in her husband's earthy scent. "I missed you so much this time."

"How so?"

"I just needed your wisdom and cool head more than anything else. Last Sunday was pretty rough."

"So I've gathered." Eugene sifted his hand through Annie's hair, then let it drop to her shoulder. "Why don't you tell me your version of it? I'm not so sure I got the full story from Will."

Annie sat up and faced him; there was so much to tell. Eugene listened patiently to every detail beginning with the terrible argument at the barn, moving on to Nathan's surprise confession, and finally ending with Will's penitence. When she was finished, Annie felt nearly as worn out as she had last Sunday night.

"What I regret more than anything is slapping him. I let myself get out of control," she confessed.

Eugene nodded thoughtfully. "I can see how that could happen considering his temper and language."

"I'm so worried about him, Eugene." Annie drew her hand to her heart and spoke with deep emotion. "Even though his attitude has been so much better these last few days, I feel some kind of dread hanging over me."

"What do you mean?" Eugene asked, wrinkling his brow.

"I don't know—it's hard to explain. I think I feel an urgency where his faith is concerned. I don't have any idea what's holding him back."

"I feel the same way," Eugene said. "We'll just have to double our prayers for him," he added, sounding more and more like Rachel.

At that moment, Jake came flying around from the back of the house and yelled, "I'm ready!" All of a sudden, he ran hard to his left and caught a baseball in his glove.

"Here it comes!" he shouted and heaved the ball up and over the house.

From the backyard, Will yelled, "Ha, I caught it!"

Eugene and Annie watched in amusement as Jake caught nearly every ball on the fly, even making a spectacular diving catch in the front yard grass. They clapped and cheered, enjoying the diversion.

"Harder, Will," Jake called loudly. He briefly glanced at his parents. "Watch this!"

"Hey," Eugene yelled, "watch out for Gramma's apple trees."

At that very moment, the ball sailed through one of the trees, knocking a small branch to the ground.

"What's this I hear?" Rachel asked curiously, opening the screen door to the porch.

Eugene and Annie exclaimed in unison, "Nothing, Mama!"

Jake kicked the branch behind the tree trunk and looked innocently toward the porch. "What do ya mean, Gramma?"

"Just for that!" Rachel exclaimed, and marched straight across the porch wiggling her way in between her son and daughter-in-law on the swing. Her legs pushed vigorously to get it moving, all the while ignoring the amused laughter on either side of her.

"Just for that!" Eugene retorted, and he leaned forward pulling Annie toward him, kissing her passionately right in front of his mama.

Rachel put her hands firmly on both of their shoulders and said, "Okay, okay, I'm getting up."

Annie's face was a bright shade of pink when she looked at Rachel. "Mama, I'm sorry about your son," she teased. "He's clearly out of control."

Rachel moved to a rocking chair. "Clearly."

Eventually, Will showed up in the front yard, wondering why the ball had failed to make its way back over the roof. The two boys remained out front throwing each other pop flies and picking up grounders until it got so dark they couldn't see the ball anymore.

Annie cherished every moment of that evening. It felt like a precious gift from their Eternal Father. For the first time in a very long while, she felt a beautiful peace come to rest on their family, and she silently thanked the One who had so kindly provided it. Much later in her life, she would remember it all in vivid detail, as if this particular evening had symbolized the proverbial calm before the storm.

Chapter 31

September 1, 1939

The evening news echoed through the kitchen as Rachel prepared supper. She yanked the boiling pot of potatoes off the stove and quickly drained the water. In her haste, steam burned her hands, but she ignored the pain. She wanted to get into the front room and join the rest of the family around the radio.

Eugene's eyes immediately snapped up to meet hers. Rachel detected a hint of anxiety replacing his normally tranquil demeanor. The words that had sent her into such a tizzy still looped through her mind with astounding resonance—*Germany has invaded Poland.* She dropped to her chair in disbelief.

German air raids had begun at six o'clock that very morning in Europe, bombing several Polish cities as well as immobilizing a massive ground invasion. Britain and France had already called for a general mobilization of their own militaries. The news on this Friday evening broadcast was delivered with measured calmness, yet it left Rachel and her family, if she was reading their expressions correctly, deeply disturbed.

A well-known voice suddenly penetrated the tense atmosphere in their living room, bearing with it a minute sliver of hope.

This nation will remain a neutral nation. But I cannot ask that every American remain neutral in thought as well. Even a neutral has a right to take account of things. Even a neutral cannot be asked to close his mind or close his conscience.

Rachel turned her gaze back toward Eugene, noticing his shoulders visibly relax. He stared intently at the radio as if President Roosevelt himself were sitting in their living room.

I have said not once, but many times, that I have seen war and that I hate war. I say that again and again. I hope the United States will keep out of this war. I believe that it will. And I give you assurance and reassurance, that every effort of your government will be directed toward that end.

The president's speech lasted only a minute, but he had spoken sufficient encouragement to Rachel's heart, at least for the time being. A troubling thought, however, arose unbidden. If the United States were to go to war again in Europe, Will would be old enough for a draft in less than six months, Jake only twenty-three months after that. She looked down at her red hands, noticing the steam burns for the first time. No physical pain could even begin to compare with the pain of watching her grandsons go off to war. She had seen firsthand what war had done to Eugene—she would not wish that on anyone else, especially her grandsons.

Several minutes later as the family sat around the supper table, the usual talk of a new school year, which was to begin on Monday, was replaced with Germany's invasion of Poland. It had come without warning or declaration of war, and now Britain and France were preparing to fulfill their promise to support Poland.

"It almost seems as if the Great War never ended," Rachel stated matter-of-factly.

Eugene responded to her statement. "Germany's been unsettled ever since the war ended. Now the Socialist party has risen to power, and they're ignoring the terms of the Treaty of Versailles."

"What were the terms, Dad?" Jake asked curiously.

"I don't know that much about it," Eugene told him, wiping a napkin across his mouth. "Mostly, it forced Germany to take responsibility for starting the war, plus they had to disarm their military."

"It doesn't sound like they disarmed," Jake mused.

"No, apparently under Adolf Hitler's leadership, they've been rebuilding their army."

Annie looked worried. "Do you think President Roosevelt can keep us out of the war?"

Pushing his empty plate away, Eugene propped his elbows up on the table. "You heard what he said. I think he'll do everything within his means to keep us from going to war again."

With a sigh, Rachel added, "Let's hope and pray he can do it."

Not long after the supper table was cleared, the Evans family dropped by for an evening of conversation. Their son Sam was Jake's best friend from school and their daughter Charlotte was two years younger than the boys. Stan and Abigail had an older son and daughter who were already out of school and on their own.

The Evans had made it a habit of dropping by once or twice a week during the summer, even though they lived in town. Stan worked as a foreman in the Louisville Electrical Factory but had come to enjoy peaceful evenings out in the country. Many times, he and Eugene would walk down to the barn to be around the horses, which would help take Stan's mind off the stress of the factory. Jake and Sam usually played catch in the front yard or occasionally took an evening trail ride when Charlotte could talk them into it.

This evening, Jimmy Jackson had also driven out to the farm to see Will. For the first half hour, everyone hung out in the shade of the front porch with nothing but the subject of war dominating the conversation.

Eugene glanced at his elder son now and then. Even though Will and Jimmy were sitting on the porch steps taking in the discussion, he noticed a look pass between the two friends more than once. He couldn't put his finger on it, but he had the distinct impression that they were just biding their time.

After a while, Will rose to his feet and said he and Jimmy were heading down to the barn.

"Are you going for a ride?" Annie asked.

"Maybe."

"Can we go too?" Charlotte asked, glancing at Jake and Sam.

Will immediately looked defensive. "Uh, we're probably not going riding. I think we'll just hang out at the barn and talk a while."

Clearly, the two boys were eager to be alone. Jake spoke up then. "Get your glove, Sam. Let's throw the ball around."

Charlotte put on her best pouty face, but to no avail. None of the boys wanted a girl hanging around, no matter how cute she was.

Just after dark, Stan and Abigail gathered the children and said their good-byes. Everyone waved as the Evans' car headed down the drive.

"I've got to get myself to bed," Rachel declared. "All of this talk of war has left me worn out."

Eugene went to his mother's side and kissed her on the cheek. "Goodnight, Mama. I hope you sleep well."

She offered him a faint smile. "After a little time on my knees, I'm sure I will. Goodnight, everyone."

"Goodnight, Mama." Annie gave her a sweet hug, then turned to Eugene. "You don't think Will and Jimmy went riding, do you? It's awfully late."

Looking toward the barn, Eugene could see light seeping through the door. "No, I'm sure they're still down at the barn. I think I'll go check on them. You and Jake go on in. I'll be back up in a few minutes."

As his wife and son entered the house, Eugene walked down the road to the barn. It was a humid night, with no breeze, and a half moon to light his way along the road. When he entered through the barn door, there was only a single light illuminating the entryway. Other than that, the rest of the barn was shrouded in darkness.

"Will?"

No answer.

Walking down the row of stalls, Eugene noticed none of the horses had been taken out. He reached into the drawer of his workbench and took out a flashlight. Since the boys weren't in the barn, maybe they were somewhere close by. As he strode around the side of the barn, Eugene thought he heard laughter coming from out back.

"Will?"

The immediate silence drew his senses to full alert. *What are they up to?*

He heard a shuffling sound around the backside of the barn just as he turned the corner. Jimmy was on the ground and threw his hand up to block the beam of light. Will was already on his feet backing away. Eugene immediately trained the flashlight on his son.

"What's going on back here?" he asked, more brusquely than he had intended.

"Nothing, Dad."

Without warning, Eugene's stomach lurched. Just the smell of the alcohol caused an overwhelming nauseous response. He had to deliberately swallow in order to keep everything down—something about the humidity, and the darkness, and the smell. A backhand across the face, a kick to the ribs, a broom handle cracking on top of his head. Sweat mingled with sour breath, angry cusswords . . . the flashes of brutality were happening here and now . . . or so his mind believed.

"Dad?"

Vaguely, Eugene heard the voice of his son just before his head hit the side of the barn. The tinkling sound of a bottle hitting the ground reverberated in a far off place.

"Daaad!"

He was inside a box or a coffin—his ears felt full of water. Why couldn't he see anything?

"Dad, what's . . . wrong?"

Eugene's eyelids batted uncontrollably before they gradually opened. It took a long moment before he realized he was lying flat on his back in the dirt. Someone's hands were on his shoulders shaking him lightly. It was Will. The smell of alcohol somehow brought him back to his senses, and he sat up unsteadily.

Eugene grabbed the back of his head and moaned. His hair was sticky, his hand moist and dark when he pulled it away.

"Dad, you're bleeding." Every word was slurred.

An anger rose up in Eugene that threatened to take complete control. He was not only angry with his son, but he was angry that the memory of his stepfather Louis had encroached on his sanity. He knew he would have to curb his emotions in order to deal with this repulsive situation. To make matters worse, Jimmy started crying.

"Yer not gonna tell my parents, are you?" he begged. And then, as if someone had flipped a switch, he asked, "Did you . . . hurt yer head?"

Eugene knew reasoning with these two in their state of drunkenness would do no good. But it didn't stop him from reaming them out for the decision they'd made and letting them know how disappointed he was with their behavior. Before it was all said and done, both boys were sobbing and practically groveling at his feet.

He stood slowly, letting the dizzy feeling pass, then he reached down for the bottles lying in the dirt. Each one had nearly polished off an entire half pint of whiskey. He threw them angrily back on the ground and grabbed Will by the collar. Eugene pulled him roughly to his feet. "How long has this been going on?"

Will shook his head and staggered sideways. Eugene steadied him while still hanging on to his shirt. "How long?"

"Only . . . only . . ."

"A few times," Jimmy stammered from his position on the ground.

"Get up, Jimmy!" Eugene reached for his collar, too, and pulled him to a semi-standing position. "We're going up to the house and calling your daddy."

"Oh . . . no! Oh no, oh no, oh no . . ."

"Shut . . . up, Jimmy!" Will's eyes were suddenly blazing, and Eugene worried that he might not be able to control these two. He noticed he was getting blood all over their shirts, but that was the least of his worries. He had a splitting headache and not just from hitting his head on the side of the barn. How was he going to present this miserable situation to the rest of the family? It pained him to think of how it was going to break their hearts. It was breaking his as it was.

It took several long minutes of shuffling the boys along the road before he slammed them both down on their rear ends on the back porch.

"Don't you dare move from this spot, do you hear me?"

"Yes . . . sir," they mumbled in unison.

Eugene stepped inside the kitchen trying not to get blood everywhere. He could hear Annie and Jake having a conversation in the front room. How could he get their attention without—

"What on earth happened?" Annie's eyes were wide with fright as she rounded the corner and saw Eugene. She was at his side in a flash. "Your hands are bleeding."

"It's not my hands, Annie. I'm okay. Calm down." Her hands were all over him, trying to figure out where the blood was coming from.

"Oh my goodness! It's your head." He could see the fear in her eyes but couldn't seem to figure out how to tell her what had happened.

"Where's Will?" she asked frantically.

"He's on the back porch with Jimmy."

"Are they okay?"

Jake came around the corner to see what the commotion was all about. "Dad, what happened?"

"Listen, both of you. I'm gonna be okay, I hit my head on the side of the barn. I'll explain what happened later. I'm just sorry about what I have to tell you."

Annie drew her hand to her mouth. "Eugene, you're scaring me."

Eugene wanted to reach out to his wife and calm her, but he couldn't do it with so much blood on his hands. "Will and Jimmy decided to go drinking behind our barn tonight."

"They what?" Annie cried in disbelief.

"They've done it before apparently. I caught them red-handed."

"Are they the ones that hurt you?" she asked, her voice quavering.

"No. Like I said, I'll explain my injury later. Just help me get cleaned up, so I can call Jimmy's folks to come get him."

Annie forced him into a kitchen chair before filling a basin with water and grabbing a clean washcloth.

"Jake, can you do me a favor?" Eugene asked as he pulled his shirt off. "I need you to step out on the back porch and make sure the boys are still sitting there."

Jake hurried across the kitchen and out the back door. Moments later, he returned. "They're both laid out on the porch."

"Keep checking on them until I get cleaned up."

Annie gently parted the hair on the back of Eugene's head. "We may need to get you into town, sweetheart. You must've hit a nail or something. I'm afraid you're going to need stitches."

"Just clean it and wrap it tight with a bandage. It should be fine for tonight."

Annie did her best to care for the wound. "It's not just a cut; you have a nasty knot back here." Her voice broke, and Eugene looked back at his wife.

"I know how you're feeling right now. It literally made me sick when I saw what they were up to."

"Eugene," Annie said quietly. "We're losing him, aren't we?" Her eyes were filled with helpless tears.

He felt it too, and it was killing him. How had they failed as parents? The only thing he was sure of was that they couldn't give up on him, no matter what he'd done.

"We're not going to lose him, Annie. You hear me? We're not." Eugene spoke with confidence, hoping to convince his wife, if not himself.

A tear slid down her cheek as she continued working on Eugene's head. Jake checked on the boys again and reported that Jimmy was sobbing.

"Good," Annie declared. "I hope both of them are."

Jimmy's father, Russell Jackson, showed up several minutes later in a foul mood. He and his son shared a strong resemblance. Russell was a bull of a man with broad shoulders and square jaw. He'd been the center for the University of Kentucky football team back in the early twenties. He and Eugene talked for a while to make sure their boys' punishments would be the same. Both men agreed it was high time these two young men took more responsibility for their behavior. For the next two months, the only place Will and Jimmy were allowed to see each other was at school. Period. If they wanted to be treated like men, they were going to have to start acting like men.

Eugene kept Will awake until the wee hours of the morning, worried about the effects of the alcohol on his system. Annie was willing to stay up, too, but Eugene had insisted she go on to bed. Jake headed to bed at the same time as Annie without so much as a word. A long talk tomorrow with his youngest son was definitely in order. Eugene could tell how troubling all of this had been to him.

It was half past three when he finally slipped into bed. He had to lie on his side to protect the injury to the back of his head. Eugene faced the window and noticed the curtains rested motionless on the sill. Where was a night breeze when you needed one?

"Eugene?" Annie's voice was barely audible. "When did you come to bed?"

"Just now."

"What about Will?"

"He's asleep. We'll have to let him sleep this off tomorrow."

A long silence passed between them before Annie ran her hand along his arm. "Are you okay?"

"Yes," he said simply. "We'll talk about it in the morning."

She rose up and kissed his shoulder, then lay back down on her side of the bed. "I love you, Eugene."

What would he do without this woman? Life would be so meaningless without her. "I love you too," he said, then closed his eyes for a few hours of much-needed sleep.

***

Eugene rolled over on his back to escape the morning sunlight. A deep moan escaped his throat before he realized he had made the sound. He turned toward Annie's side of the bed to ease the pain and opened his eyes. She had already gotten up, obviously letting him sleep in.

He sat up on the edge of the bed for a long moment until the throbbing in his head subsided, then he dressed and headed into the kitchen. Rachel was the only one present. When she saw Eugene, she simply told him to sit down at the table.

"Annie told me you might need stitches. As soon as you're done eating, I'll take a look."

She went to the stove and uncovered a plate of scrambled eggs and bacon. Then she poured him a steaming cup of coffee and a glass of orange juice. Satisfied that he was taken care of, Rachel turned back to the counter and busied herself with cleaning.

Eugene knew what she was doing—biding her time until he was finished eating. If they started talking about last night, he would be in danger of not eating his breakfast. A half smile crossed his lips as he took in a mouthful of eggs.

"I guess Annie told you what happened," he ventured, after his plate was clean.

"As a matter of fact, I heard it from Jake. He was already sitting in the kitchen when I came in this morning." Rachel cleared the breakfast plate from the table, then took a seat across from her son.

"He's about as upset as Annie is," she added.

"Yeah, I know." Eugene rubbed the back of his neck before reaching for his coffee. "I plan to spend some time with him this afternoon."

There was no hiding the anguished look on Rachel's face. Eugene wished he had words of comfort for her, but truth be told, he needed those words himself.

"I miss Papa." The remark came out of his mouth before he realized the thought was even in his head. Instantly, he regretted saying it when he noticed the deep emotion it evoked in Rachel.

"I miss him every day, Eugene." Tears spilled from her eyes, and she added softly, "Every day."

"I'm sorry, Mama. I didn't mean to make this harder than it already is."

"Oh no, darlin'. You have no idea how much I love hearing you say that. I don't ever want your papa to be forgotten." She wiped the moisture from her cheeks. "I think we should talk about him more often, so the boys will come to know their grandfather."

Eugene nodded his head as he contemplated Franklin's practical wisdom.

"Annie and Jake couldn't seem to tell me what happened to your head." Rachel leaned forward, begging Eugene with her eyes to tell her everything.

He placed his coffee cup on the table and sat back in the chair. This could be a difficult conversation. Rachel was already worried enough about Will, and he had no intention of giving her more reason to fret. But he knew the rest of the family was speculating about his injury, and he needed to clear up the mystery. He didn't want them blaming Will for his own debility. Or mental defect—or whatever it was.

"It's kind of embarrassing actually."

Eugene looked away, preferring not to talk about it at all. He searched for a way to tell her what had happened without opening a terrible emotional wound that she obviously thought had been healed. He had literally gone for years without so much as a thought of his stepfather, then out of the blue, one putrid whiff of alcohol had caused an intense reaction that had carried him back twenty-seven years. It had seemed so real last night, and that fact alone scared him.

He suddenly came to the conclusion that he couldn't tell her exactly what he had experienced. Chances are, it would never happen again. Just the thought of talking about it made his head pound like a drum.

"I think I just got overheated. It was so humid last night and the shock of seeing Will and Jimmy drinking—"

Rachel's brow creased deeply. "Are you telling me you fainted?"

"I know, it sounds crazy doesn't it? But the next thing I knew, I was lying flat on my back in the dirt."

Looking agitated, Rachel came to her feet. "Son, is it possible one of the boys did this to—"

"No," Eugene interrupted, rising to his feet as well. "They were not anywhere near me. I was just hot, and the smell of sweat and alcohol . . ." his voice trailed off.

A knowing look gradually spread across Rachel's features. The rise and fall of her chest quickened. "Oh, Eugene," she whispered. "I'm so sorry." She moved around the table, ready to take him into her arms, but he held her off by reaching up for the bandage around his head and unwrapping it. He was afraid to give in to her embrace for fear of losing control of his emotions. Maybe later—just not now.

Eugene turned toward the chair and straddled it backward before Rachel could get close enough. "See what you think, Mama." Looking back at her with a feeble grin, he added, "If you don't mind."

She laid a hand on his shoulder, letting it gently linger there before parting the hair on the back of his head. "Darlin', it's a wonder Annie got the bleeding stopped. This is quite a gash." She continued her inspection. "You should've put ice on this last night. There's still a lump."

"Do you think I need stitches?"

Rachel squinted her eyes and made a closer inspection. "It wouldn't hurt to have three or four near the base of the gash. It looks like the top part is closing up."

He let out a long, slow breath. "If you think the rest of it will close up, then let's just wrap it tight again."

Rachel dropped her hands to his shoulders. "Eugene, I'm not sure that's such a good idea."

"Is it bleeding?"

"No."

"Then just clean it and wrap it tight."

Her hands didn't move from his shoulders.

"Please, Mama. I need to be here for Jake and Annie, and I don't want to be away when Will wakes up."

Rachel let out a sigh, then agreed to his instructions. "But if it doesn't close up on its own in the next couple of days," she chided, "you're going to the doctor for stitches."

"Deal."

***

Will was still sleeping even after lunch had been cleared away. Eugene took the opportunity to walk with Jake down to the pond. They sat in the shade and tossed rocks into the water, watching the ripples make their way to shore.

Eugene had noticed how quiet his son had been during lunch and was hoping he'd let him in on what he was thinking. Jake had always been his talkative child, easy-going and intuitive. He also had a sensitive side to him that unfortunately seemed to be missing in Will.

"You okay, Jake?"

"Yeah," he responded softly.

"You've been pretty quiet since last night." Eugene tossed another rock into the pond. "You wanna tell me about it?" Bewildered by Jake's silence, he finally nudged him lightly with his elbow. "Come on, you can talk to me, buddy."

"Not much to talk about."

What would it take to get his son to open up? Eugene decided to use a more direct approach. "How'd that make you feel last night seeing your brother in that condition?"

"Dad, I've seen some of the other guys at school in that condition before. I figured it was a matter of time before Will tried it."

Eugene raised his brow, surprised by Jake's matter-of-fact attitude. If his son wasn't troubled by seeing Will and Jimmy in a drunken stupor, then what was eating at him?

Jake glanced over at his dad. "Don't get me wrong; I was pretty mad at him for doing it. I've always looked up to Will. But seeing him all messed up like that made me realize how stupid he can be sometimes."

They both chuckled and threw another rock in the pond at the same time.

"Ha, mine went further," Eugene bragged, keeping the mood light.

Just to show him up, Jake uncorked a throw that landed on the opposite bank. He was a pitcher, after all.

"Ouch," Eugene commented, letting the next rock he had planned to throw drop from his hand.

Jake pressed his lips tight and narrowed his eyes, staring out over the pond. A long silence lingered between father and son. Eugene finally came to the conclusion that if Jake wasn't ready to talk, he wouldn't press him any longer.

After a few minutes, he clapped his son on the back and rose to his feet, but Jake's statement compelled him to sit back down.

"If Will hurt you, Dad . . ." Jake's voice trembled as he left the words hanging in the air.

So that's what was troubling his youngest son. Jake thought Will had been the one who injured him. While he *was* responsible in an indirect way, Eugene realized he needed to clear up the situation with Jake.

"Son, neither Will nor Jimmy did this to my head."

Jake's eyes bolted around to meet his dad's. "Then why won't you tell us what happened?"

Eugene let out a nervous laugh. "'Cause it's kind of embarrassing . . . I fainted."

Jake stared, wide-eyed for a second, then suddenly laughed, breaking the tension. "You what?"

"I know, I know. I can't believe it either."

"You fainted?"

"Dead as a doornail."

"Whoa." Jake looked away momentarily. "You fainted," he repeated, shaking his head. "Why?"

"It's complicated."

"Try me."

Eugene stared at his fifteen-year-old son, wondering how little he could tell him. Obviously, Jake wasn't going to be satisfied with a pat answer.

"Remember how I told you my stepfather was mean to me after my mother died?"

"Yeah."

"The reason why he was so mean was because he started drinking to take the pain away. Alcohol had a really bad effect on him; it made him *more* than angry—it made him downright cruel. Unfortunately, at the time, I was the only one around." Eugene cleared his throat. "He took most of his anger out on me for a little more than a year."

Jake's eyes softened as he took in his dad's words.

"The only thing I can figure is that the smell of alcohol last night somehow took me back to that awful year. It just laid me out flat on the ground."

"I'm sorry, Dad."

"Yeah, me too," Eugene said as the two came to their feet. "But it's all in the past."

They stood beside the pond in the shade for just a moment longer.

"Thanks for being such a good dad," Jake said quietly.

Eugene felt a strong emotion rising up inside. He knew if he didn't move quickly he might just lose control. He reached out and grabbed his son, holding him tight up against his chest.

"Thanks for being such a good son," he said in a hoarse voice.

As the two walked over to the barn, Eugene knew he needed to have a similar conversation with Annie. It would be a lot easier now that he'd made it past Rachel and Jake. In fact, he looked forward to spending time with her alone. They had a lot to discuss considering the choice their eldest son had made last night. And with that thought, Eugene's stomach once again turned sour. He was not looking forward to a confrontation with Will.

Chapter 32

A light shade of green was the best way to describe Will's face. He sat at the supper table looking miserable. No one paid a bit of attention to the fact that he refused to even glance at the food in front of him.

Eugene had forced him out of bed around four o'clock in the afternoon, and he'd barely made it to the bathroom before throwing up. Just one look at him now, and it was easy to see that he was sick as a dog. *Good,* Eugene thought. *Maybe this will be a huge deterrent next time he thinks about drinking.*

All four of the other family members kept a light-hearted conversation going throughout the entire meal. It almost seemed as if they'd conspired together beforehand, but they hadn't. They knew Will was paying the price for his foolish decision, and they were happy to let him pay in full.

At seven o'clock, Jake turned on the radio for one of their favorite Saturday evening programs, and everyone made themselves comfortable in the living room.

The makers of Ex-Lax presents, Strange as it Seems.

The beginning commercial message went on for the next few minutes. When the announcer declared, "Ex-Lax tastes like smooth velvety chocolate . . ." Will pressed his hand to his mouth and took off for the bathroom. No one asked if he was okay, but Rachel whispered, "God bless him," while Eugene chuckled. By the time he returned, the show had just begun.

Tonight's episode was about a small village in Austria who, *strange at it seems,* consume arsenic every day for good health. When it was concluded, Eugene turned off the radio and noticed Will was looking less ill, which was amazing considering the subject of the program. Returning to the sofa, Eugene insisted it was now time for a family talk.

"Will," he began, "I want everyone to tell you how last night affected them." Eugene looked around the room at each member of the family. "I know none of you knew we were going to do this, but I thought about it all afternoon. We're a family—the world's a hard enough place to live in, so we need to stick together. When one of us makes a decision for good or bad, it will always affect everyone else. Always. Last night is no exception."

Eugene leaned back on the sofa and appeared to relax. "So who wants to go first?"

For a moment, the room was filled with an awkward silence. Will was unable to make eye contact with anyone as he fidgeted in his chair. Eugene waited patiently for someone to speak up. He was determined to go last.

"I look up to you, Will," Jake told him unequivocally. "I always have since we were little. I've spent my whole life trying to keep up with you, trying to make you like me." He paused for a moment, collecting his thoughts. "Last night when I saw you lyin' on the porch drunk, I wasn't so much shocked as I was disappointed. I kept going out there checking on you and Jimmy and, I don't know, it was like for the first time in my life I didn't want to be like you."

Will's head snapped up and a genuinely hurt expression twisted his features.

"I didn't like feeling that way," Jake added, as color rushed into his cheeks. "I don't ever want to feel that way again."

Wow! Eugene thought, *if that didn't get to him, nothing will.*

Rachel didn't allow a silence to fall before she expressed concern for her grandson's welfare. She told him how much she loved him but wasn't sure her heart could handle any more of his shenanigans. Will simply hung his head in shame.

Annie teetered on the edge of the sofa, most likely wrestling fervidly between her deep maternal love and her obvious disappointment. Eugene worried that an argument might break out, depending on which way she leaned. He prayed silently for the Spirit to give her the right words.

Everyone but Will watched her take in and let out two very deep breaths before proceeding. "Will," she said softly, "you were born in Gramps and Nana's house seventeen and a half years ago at just past eleven o'clock at night. When you were put in my arms, I thought I would simply die of joy." She turned and gazed fully into Eugene's eyes. "Your daddy knelt down beside my bed, put his hand over your tiny chest, and dedicated you to the Lord when you were just minutes old."

Eugene held her gaze unwaveringly, remembering the scene vividly.

She turned her attention back to Will, who surprisingly, was now looking up. "I think you need to know what I prayed before you were even conceived. I prayed that God would not allow me to have a child if that child wasn't going to be saved." She paused for a long moment, letting that statement sink in.

"Obviously when you make a choice like the one you made last night, it causes me to doubt. Today, I've had to keep reminding myself over and over again that God answered my prayer the day you were born."

There was such an extended silence that Eugene wasn't sure if he should begin. But just as he was about to speak, Annie whispered, "I would give my life for you, Will, if it meant we would all spend eternity together."

Rachel let out a quiet sob and Annie went to her. She knelt beside Rachel's chair and wrapped her arms around her. After a moment, she gave her a loving squeeze and kissed her cheek before returning to the sofa. She let Eugene know through her tears that she was done talking.

Clearing his throat, Eugene now wished he had gone first. He didn't expect to be affected so deeply by his wife and mother's emotional state. He decided to turn a deaf ear to their sniffling and proceed with what he had planned to say. "William Franklin Wyatt," he pronounced slowly. "You were named after two great men. They weren't great on their own. They were great because they were men of God. Your grandpa Franklin was a simple man, but his wisdom ran deep. I learned honesty, patience, and integrity from him. He taught me to love and respect other people no matter what color their skin was, or how much money they had. He simply loved everyone the best he could and left the rest up to the Lord. I wish you could've known him."

Fortunately, the women seemed to have stopped crying for the time being, which made it much easier to continue.

"William Gano was also a man of honesty and integrity. I watched him resist so many evils during army training and during our short time together in France. He stayed true to himself, and to the Lord, through a time that tempted every one of us to throw our morals right out the window. He taught me how to remain faithful and strong in the worst of circumstances."

Eugene swallowed the lump that had been forming in his throat and leaned forward on the sofa. "Last night brought up some pretty bad memories for me, Son. But it also made me remember how I was led to your grandpa Franklin and Gramma's farm when I was only eleven.

"I was standing on the porch of my stepfather's house one night and noticed a light way off in the distance, and for some unexplained reason, I was drawn to it. I'm convinced now that God showed me that light in a dream earlier in the day just so I wouldn't mistake it when I saw it."

All eyes in the room were now riveted on Eugene. Annie had never once heard her husband speak of such a light.

"That light led me to safety. As a matter of fact, I had just received the worst beating of my life." Eugene glanced at Rachel when she let out an anguished sigh, but he continued in a steady voice. "God's light has been leading me ever since. Will, God works miracles every day in people's lives—all He asks is that we give our life over to His Son. He won't work in someone who's full of himself; it just doesn't happen that way. You have to empty yourself out and let *Him* fill you up."

Eugene took in a long, slow breath, then finished what he had to say. "I wish you could've known the two men you were named after, but I guess in some ways you do. I am who I am today because of them. But last night, I realized that I've failed to instill in you what those two men instilled in me. So I humbly ask you to forgive me, Son."

It was obvious Will was fighting to hold back his emotions. His leg shook uncontrollably, and his fists were balled up tight on the arms of the easy chair. He kept his eyes trained on the wall between his brother and grandmother.

Eugene stood and walked over to him. He extended his hand and asked once again, "Do you forgive me?"

Will finally blinked, releasing a stream of tears. He wasn't ready to take his daddy's hand just yet, not until he told him how he felt.

"Dad, you didn't fail me. There's nothing to forgive." He now locked eyes with Eugene and spoke with conviction, despite his quavering voice. "All of those things are in me, I promise. I've just been stubborn, so I'm the one asking—"

He stopped for a minute, realizing he was about to step over a massive barrier. It was a wall of pride he'd unconsciously built, brick by brick, for nearly all of his life. It had pitted him against every member of this family at some time or other—particularly his mother. All of a sudden, he caught a glimpse of who he needed to be. He was so tired of being the outsider in this family.

"I'm asking *you* to forgive *me*," he pleaded, rising to his feet.

Eugene took his hand and held his gaze for a prolonged moment, then he grabbed him and pulled him into a tight embrace. Will felt vulnerable in his daddy's arms, just like a child again, while Eugene kissed his head and expressed his forgiveness and love.

When his dad released him, he willingly went into his mother's arms for the second time this summer. But something was different this time. Will knew now what he needed to do, and there was no way to do it without God's help. He allowed her to hold him as long as she wanted, and when she finally let go, he surprised her with a kiss.

Gramma followed with her one-of-a-kind hug before he and Jake exchanged a brotherly embrace. "I'm sorry, little brother. I won't let you down again."

He gave Jake a playful shove, then turned back to his mother. "Call Gramps and Nana. I think they'll wanna be here."

A slow smile crept across Annie's face, and she kissed him before hurrying out of the room to call her parents.

Several minutes later, before the sun dipped below the skyline, Eugene pulled his eldest son up from the pond into a new life with Christ. No one remained dry as they each took Will into their arms again on the shore.

As the family circled in close, Eugene reached for Rachel's hand. "Mama, would you be willing to lead us in prayer?"

Beaming with joy, Rachel pulled Will and Eugene a little closer to her side and poured out her heart with praise and thanks for uniting their family in the Lord. ". . . and may Will understand, along with the rest of us, the breadth, and length, and depth, and height of the love of Christ, through whose name we pray." And the whole family said, "Amen."

***

Annie had not known such peace since Will was a baby. She had thought it would take years, perhaps decades, before she would ever be able to have a close relationship with her eldest son. But day by day, the eggshells she'd been treading turned into solid stones. It wasn't long before a trust built up between the two that she had longed for all of Will's life. She didn't neglect to thank the Lord for their newly formed bond every day.

A peaceful household helped make at least some of the world's worries a little easier to bear. But every day, the situation in Europe grew dire. Since Germany's invasion of Poland, they had gone on to crush six other countries in three short months. Denmark, Norway, Belgium, Luxembourg, The Netherlands, and France. By Christmas, they had conquered Yugoslavia and Greece.

Canada had almost immediately declared war on Germany, and now, the United States shifted its policy from neutrality to preparedness. The armed forces were expanding, and some of the Louisville factories were converted into defense plants. President Roosevelt called upon the United States to be "the great arsenal of democracy." He committed immeasurable amounts of aid to the allies, stopping just short of entering the war.

Will was having one of his finest school years ever. Even though his focus on studying was not up to par with Jake's, he was at least making an unprecedented effort. He had turned eighteen in February, and now the spring baseball season was underway. He still had his quick-tempered moments on the field, but it was obvious, even to his coach, that there was something different about East Louisville High School's fleet-footed centerfielder.

Annie had always loved the month of April. March was usually windy and cold, but April brought the promise of warmth and spring, along with one of her favorite pastimes—cheering for her son's baseball team.

On this particular Saturday evening, the stands were full as the East Louisville Wildcats took on their cross-town rivals, Jefferson County High. The contest was living up to its yearly billing—"The Hottest Game in Town."

Going into the eighth, the score was tied at three. East Louisville's star pitcher, Ben Abernathy, had pitched a jewel, but with two outs in the top of the inning, he had given up two straight walks.

Coach Grimes motioned to his sophomore first baseman to take the mound. Jake's eyes sparkled as he trotted to the coach's side and accepted the ball. Ben slapped him on the back and said, "You got this, Wyatt," before trotting into the dugout amidst a rousing ovation.

It only took two pitches for Jake to force a groundout to second and the inning was over. Will's best friend, Jimmy, pulled off his catcher's mask and sprinted into the dugout, ready to do damage with his bat. But the Jefferson County pitcher had other ideas, and the stocky catcher went down on strikes in the bottom of the eighth. He slunk back into the dugout after overanxiously swinging at a ball outside the strike zone.

Joining Jake at the end of the bench, Jimmy started strapping on his catcher's gear. "Hey, kid," he said, as he pulled his sweaty chest protector over his head. "Just throw strikes. Let your defense do the work."

Jake continued watching the game and nodded his head confidently. He knew how badly these seniors wanted to beat Jefferson County. In all four years they'd been playing, they had yet to defeat them. Jake had personally seen the raging disappointment each of those games had produced in his brother. Every year they'd come so close, but something bizarre had happened in each game to snatch victory right out of their hands. Such was the game of baseball. Jake relished the opportunity to close on the mound for an East Louisville victory.

The Wildcats, however, went down one, two, three in the bottom of the eighth. Jake grabbed his glove and jogged toward the mound.

"Just strikes, Wyatt. Just strikes," his coach called out.

Jake tipped his cap and toed the rubber for his warm-up pitches.

"Comin' down," Jimmy yelled.

After Jake's final warm-up pitch, he stepped off the mound and watched Jimmy throw a bullet to the shortstop covering the bag. All of the infielders excitedly came together at the mound as the shortstop deposited the ball in Jake's glove. Every one of the players gave Jake a pat on the back or a swat on the bottom.

"We're behind you, kid."

Jimmy pushed his finger into Jake's chest. "Just throw strikes." Then he took a hop step and jogged back to the plate.

Jake started the top of the ninth with a fastball strike on the inside corner. The crowd cheered, and Jimmy pointed at Jake, nodding his head encouragingly just before throwing the ball back. When the dust finally cleared on the inning, Jake had pitched a fly ball out to left field, a called third strike, and an unassisted groundout to the first baseman. The sophomore closer leapt from the mound with a fist pump, which was about as much emotion as Jake usually displayed. The air in the dugout, however, was electric. Will had worked his teammates into a frenzy.

The East Louisville fans were on their feet chanting, "Let's go, Wildcats!" while Coach Grimes checked his lineup. The bottom of the order was due up. Jake heard him murmur, "This could go extra innings."

A few minutes later, Coach Grimes gritted his teeth and yanked off his cap after the first two batters of the inning struck out. He looked as if he could rip someone's head off. All the players in the dugout wisely kept their distance. But a glimmer of hope arose when the number nine batter coaxed a stingy walk from the Jefferson ace. The Wildcats were back to the top of their order now.

Will excitedly made his way to the plate. He went through his usual warm-up swing, a tap of the plate with his bat, and one twirl of the bat in his right hand, before crouching into his stance.

First pitch—ball one. Second pitch—a bit wild, squibbing away from the catcher, and sending the base runner down to second. Will stepped back to the plate looking for an 0–2 fastball. When he saw it, he put the sweet part of the bat right on the ball, sending it back up the middle, just inches from the pitcher's head, into centerfield. Rounding first, he looked back toward the plate and watched his teammate slide in under the catcher's tag. The umpire yelled, "Safe!" and the stands erupted.

The entire East Louisville baseball team slammed together in a massive heap of exuberance at home plate. Will sprinted across the infield and landed on top of the melee. Jake was somewhere near the bottom trying to protect his face from fists and cleats. Eventually, he felt someone pulling him out of the pile by his jersey. It was Will, wrapping him in such a tight bear hug, Jake thought he wouldn't be able to breathe.

"Way to pitch, little brother!"

When Will put him down, Jake congratulated him on his game-winning hit, then fans began pouring out onto the field.

An hour later, Eugene walked through the infield gate and whistled for Will to come to the car. His son was sitting in the dugout with Jimmy. They appeared to be deep in conversation.

"Let's go, Will," Eugene called. "Everyone's ready to go home."

Will held up his index finger, indicating he'd join the family in just a minute.

Eugene watched the two from a distance and wondered what they could possibly be talking about so intently.

On the way home, he discussed the finer points of the game with his excited sons while Annie and Rachel kept heaping on compliments and praise.

After the boys had bathed, Rachel treated her grandsons to chocolate cake and ice cream. While baking the cake that morning, she had hoped it would be eaten in celebration instead of consolation. She watched in satisfaction as they gobbled it down ravenously, still jabbering on about their historic victory.

Later that night, Eugene awoke with a start. He thought he had heard a noise, but when he looked over at Annie, she was still sound asleep. He laid his head back down on the pillow with an uneasy feeling. Something wasn't right.

Slipping out of bed, he reached for his jeans from the chair and pulled a t-shirt over his head. Silently, he walked barefooted into the living room and stood motionless for a few seconds. He thought he heard a thud outside and went to the front window, drawing back the curtains. Sure enough, he caught a movement beside the porch and noticed the light-colored hair. It was Will. Eugene's heart slowed a bit as he quietly opened the front door.

Will jumped back into the shadows when Eugene stepped out onto the porch, but it was too late to hide.

"What are you doing, Son?" Eugene whispered.

A very long, awkward pause hung between them. Will remained stock-still in the shadows. Eugene descended the stairs and walked around to the side of the porch. To his shock, Will was standing beside the house, fully dressed, with a duffle bag hanging over his shoulder.

"What's this all about?" he asked quietly.

Will let out a deep breath in the form of a sigh. "Dad, you weren't supposed to see me."

"Obviously. But that doesn't answer my question."

"I left you all a note."

"Where were you going?"

"You mean, where *am* I going?"

Eugene noticed Will's anxious glances, so he turned to look out toward the highway. When Eugene turned back to his son, he asked, "Are you waiting for someone?"

"Dad, please just let me go for tonight. The note explains everything." Will moved around his dad and started heading toward the driveway.

"Hold on a minute," Eugene said, grabbing his son's arm. "I'm not waiting until you're gone to read some note. You're going to tell me right here and now what you're doing."

Will dropped his head, obviously aggravated, while his dad added, "Come sit down on the porch with me. I'm not letting you leave here without an explanation."

Both men took a seat on the porch steps, and Will laid his duffle bag on the ground between his feet. Eugene could tell he wasn't eager to share the least bit of information. He was going to have to pull it out of him somehow.

"I need to know right now, Will. Where are you going?"

"California."

He had said it so quietly, Eugene wasn't sure he'd heard it correctly. "Did you say California?"

Will nodded.

"What for?" Eugene asked, grasping at anything that would help make sense of what he had just heard.

"Jimmy and I are joining the Army Air Corps," he said matter-of-factly.

Eugene couldn't sit there any longer; he thought his chest was about to explode. He stood up and took a few paces away from the porch, running his hands over his face. When he turned back toward his son, Will was on his feet and had thrown the duffle back over his shoulder.

"No, sit back down," Eugene demanded. He tried to calm his emotions and sat down beside his son again.

"How long have you been planning this?"

"Jimmy and I have been planning this since we were sixteen. We were just waiting until he turned eighteen. We've saved enough money between us to get to California and enlist."

Eugene recognized a fire burning in his son's eyes that he had seen many times before. He remembered heading to Texas with a trainload of boys just like Will. They all had some kind of romantic notion in their heads about the war. Sadly, many of those boys never returned home, and the ones who did were never the same. He knew that all too well.

"Will," Eugene said as calmly as he could. "I'm afraid our country is heading into the war in Europe—"

"I know, Dad," Will interrupted. "Jimmy and I are gonna be ready for it."

Just then, a set of headlights appeared on the highway, and Will leapt to his feet hauling the duffle bag over his shoulder.

Eugene jumped up and grabbed the front of Will's shirt, holding him back. "I can't let you do this—"

Will looked him fully in the face. "You have no choice, Dad. I'm eighteen now, and this is what I want to do with my life."

"But why like this? Why sneak off in the night without telling anyone good-bye?"

"Because of what you're doing right now. All of you would try to find a way to keep me here, make me graduate from high school—"

"That's the best way, though," Eugene pleaded.

Will reached up and peeled his dad's hand off his shirt, shaking his head. "You can't stop me from doing this, Dad." Then before Eugene could say another word, he took off at a sprint down the road.

"Will, wait!" Eugene yelled.

Surprisingly, Will slowed down and turned back to face his daddy. Eugene closed the distance between them, and Will dropped his duffle to the ground, accepting his father's passionate embrace.

"I love you, Son."

"I love you too, Dad."

"What about your mother? You can't leave without telling her good-bye."

Will pulled out of Eugene's arms shaking his head. "I have to!"

"Why?"

"You don't understand."

"Son, you have no idea how much this is going to hurt her. Why can't we go wake her up?"

Will suddenly reached up to block a tear that had already escaped his eye, then grabbed his duffle bag off the ground. Eugene was stunned by his son's answer.

"Because she's the only one who could make me change my mind."

And with that, he turned on his heels and ran toward the waiting car.

Chapter 33

"Bad dream or too excited about the game to sleep?"

Annie sat down on the porch step beside her husband, working her arm through his. She leaned her head on his shoulder, waiting for an answer. When he didn't even attempt one, she rose up and looked into his face. Something was definitely wrong. It must have been a nightmare. *Bless his heart. Will he be destined to carry this burden the rest of his life?*

She reached up to run her fingers through his hair, but he caught her hand before she even touched him.

"Eugene? What's the matter?"

Suddenly, she noticed a piece of paper in his other hand.

"What is that?"

Eugene pulled her hand to his chest, just as he'd done so many times before. They locked eyes for a brief moment, then he looked away. She knew as soon as she saw his eyes that her husband had tough news to share. She felt her heart flip-flop in her chest.

"This is a note from Will. He left tonight to enlist in the Army Air Corps."

Annie shook her head vehemently. "Wait a minute—just hold on a minute. What are you talking about?"

"Not so loud, Annie. We don't want to wake everyone else up."

"Sorry." She took her voice down a notch. "Did you know about this?"

"No, sweetheart, it was just as much a shock to me as it is to you. I caught him just before he left. Jimmy picked him up down at the highway."

"Is it too late to go after him? We can't just let him run off now. What about graduation? What about baseball?"

"I know," he agreed, "I tried to reason with him, but he had his mind made up. He and Jimmy have been planning this for two years. Apparently, they were waiting for Jimmy to turn eighteen, which he did last week."

"Where do they go to sign up for the air corps? Maybe we can find him in the morning and talk him out of it."

Eugene let go of her hand and pulled his wife into his arms. "Sweetheart, they left for California. I imagine they're already on a train heading west."

With those words, Annie suddenly felt overcome with sadness. "Did he not have enough decency to even say good-bye?" She sat up straight, but Eugene kept his arm around her waist. "Have these last few months been a complete farce? Was he playing us?"

"No, Annie, absolutely not! Don't judge his motives. I know these last few months were genuine—he truly turned his life around. Please don't let this make you think otherwise."

Annie closed her eyes, feeling so ashamed for even suggesting it.

"Did you get to hug him?" she whispered.

Eugene simply nodded his head.

"Why didn't you wake me?" she begged through her tears.

"I asked him the same thing. I knew how hard this was going to be for you. But I think you need to know something." Eugene turned and looked fully into her face. "He said you were the only one who could cause him to change his mind and stay."

Annie drew her hand to her mouth, choking on a sob. "You should've—" She could say no more.

Eugene gathered her in his arms again and held her while she quietly wept.

After a long time had passed, Annie turned in Eugene's embrace, leaning back against his chest so he could encircle her with his arms. That's the position Rachel found them in just at the break of dawn.

Most Sunday mornings, Rachel spent time on the front porch—long before anyone else stirred in their beds—enjoying a cup of coffee and talking with the Lord. However, this morning, to her surprise, the porch was already occupied when she stepped outside.

There was just enough light to see Eugene looking at her, but it was obvious Annie was asleep against his chest. Rachel tilted her head slightly, giving her son an inquisitive look. He in turn nodded his head toward a folded piece of paper lying on the porch beside his leg.

She put her coffee cup on the railing and reached for the note. It was a bit dark on the porch, so she quietly descended the steps and walked out into the yard. Unfolding the paper, she read:

Dear All,

I know this will come as quite a surprise, but Jimmy and I have decided to join the air corps. We've been planning and saving our money for two years, so we could go out to California and enlist. I knew if I told you our plans that you would all try to talk us out of it, but our minds have been made up for a long time. We want to join up and help defend our country, if that's what it comes down to.

Please don't be sad or disappointed in me. I want to make you proud, I always have. Lately I've been praying about it a lot, and I still feel like it's the right thing to do.

I'll send word when we get there to let you know I'm okay. Thank you for everything you've done for me. I couldn't ask for a better family.

Your loving son,
Will

Rachel looked back toward Eugene with such a weight on her chest she didn't think she could bear it. These last few months had been so incredible with Will. The good heart she had seen all along had finally emerged. So why would he leave now?

Walking back to the porch, she sat down beside her daughter-in-law. Rachel's heart broke for her, and she couldn't help but reach out to cover her hand.

Annie stirred in Eugene's arms and slowly opened her eyes. When she realized Rachel was holding her hand, she sat up and leaned into her mother-in-law's tender embrace. No tears were shed; they simply found a reassuring solace in each other's arms.

***

Claudia asked Mattie to add two extra plates for Sunday lunch. "We've invited Mr. and Mrs. Jackson to join us. They worship in the city, and their service gets out a little later than ours. They'll be here in a few minutes."

Mattie reached for the extra plates in the cupboard, still eyeing her employer protectively. "Miss Claudia, is you gonna be all right?"

"Oh Mattie, dear, I'll be fine. I didn't expect our boys to stay babies forever, you know." Claudia opened the silver chest for two more place settings. "It's just that I didn't expect Will to leave so suddenly—without even a good-bye."

"Oh, you know Will, Miss Claudia. That boy done gone his own way all his life. Ain't never known him to do things like the rest of you."

"No truer words were spoken," Claudia agreed. "But lately, things have been different. This was so unexpected. Nathan is simply heartsick over it."

Mattie reached for the silverware in Claudia's hands, so she could finish setting the table. "I couldn't help but notice our Annie seems a bit down in the dumps," she remarked. "You reckon she's gonna be all right?"

Claudia glanced through the door leading to the kitchen and noticed her daughter standing motionless at the counter, staring out the window. She couldn't imagine the shock it had been for Annie to wake in the middle of the night and discover that her eldest son had left without a word.

"Our Annie is a strong one," Claudia whispered. "Let's just hope and pray she'll be all right."

Not long after Jimmy's parents arrived, they all gathered at the table while Nathan led a blessing for the food. Before concluding the prayer, however, he asked the Lord to guard and guide their two young men, as well as protect them from evil.

When Annie raised her head after the prayer, she found herself staring directly into the eyes of Corrine Jackson, who happened to be seated across the table from her. They held each other's gaze for a long moment before Jimmy's mother reached for her napkin to wipe a tear from her eye. Annie hadn't shed any more tears since her time with Eugene in the middle of the night. Right now, she simply felt flat and emotionless. Everything around her seemed so dull.

She impassively listened as Russell told Nathan about his Buick dealership in the city. While he owned the dealership, he also raised thoroughbred racehorses on their farm outside the Louisville city limits. "It keeps me pretty busy," Russell noted, "but I've always loved cars and horses."

"Now I heard something interesting about Buick adding turn signals to their automobiles," Nathan mused.

"That's correct, Mr. Harrison. The Ford Company has been toying with them for a while, but in January, Buick made them standard on all of our latest models."

"You mean you won't have to stick your arm out the window anymore?" Jake asked curiously.

"That's right, Son," Mr. Jackson said proudly. "You just move a lever on the steering column, and a tail light flashes on the left side or the right side, depending on which way you want to turn. Our sales have really picked up lately."

Throughout dinner, Annie and Corrine shared brief glances, but neither one joined in the conversation. Eventually, the subject that they had all so carefully tiptoed around made its way to the surface.

"When do you think we'll hear from the boys?" Claudia ventured.

For a moment, no one seemed to want to speculate about the boys' journey to California. Finally, Russell spoke up. "I expect we'll hear something in the next couple of days." He then addressed Eugene. "Did Will say anything in his note about where exactly they were headed?"

"No," Eugene responded. "All he said was they were enlisting in the Army Air Corps in California."

Russell told everyone that they had picked up the car at the train station before church this morning. "Jimmy told us in his note where to find it. I went in to check the train schedules, and the best I can tell, they hopped a 2:00 a.m. to Kansas City."

Annie noticed the color flooding into Corrine's cheeks. She seemed to be on the verge of breaking down. Immediately, Annie stood up and placed her napkin on the table. She walked around to Corrine's side and softly asked, "Would you like to join me on the porch for a while?" Then she looked at Claudia. "Thank you for a wonderful lunch, Mother."

"Yes, thank you so much, Mrs. Harrison," Corrine added. "It was lovely."

Corrine quickly took her leave and followed Annie outside. The two women had known each other for many years, ever since Will and Jimmy became best friends in grade school. Annie and Corrine had never socialized much; the Jacksons tended to run in an altogether different social circle than the Wyatts. Nevertheless, they had spoken many times over the years and were fond of each other's sons. Jimmy was an only child, which most likely made this situation even more difficult for Corrine to bear.

Annie put her arm through Corrine's and led her to a park-style bench out in the yard underneath a giant oak. She had climbed this tree many times in her youth, sometimes hiding out near the top just to keep from setting the table at dinnertime.

For a while, the two women sat side by side in silence, lost in their own thoughts. Finally, Annie turned to Corrine. "I'm sorry if this was Will's doing."

Corrine shook her head and turned her troubled eyes toward Annie. "This wasn't Will; I know for sure it was Jimmy. I should be apologizing to you."

Surprised by Corrine's certainty, Annie asked, "How do you know that?"

"Because Jimmy and his father have talked about flying all of his life. Russell keeps talking about buying an airplane someday. All of that talk of flying scares me to death."

Annie could only imagine what it was like to live with Russell and Jimmy. Their giant personalities must have overshadowed this soft-spoken woman sitting next to her.

Corrine was rather striking, with porcelain features and silky, brown hair cut in the latest style. She had always dressed quite fashionably—today being no exception. But she had never made Annie feel inferior. Corrine had always made her feel genuinely welcome in their lovely home, and the two had often sat together at the boys' baseball games.

"And now they're going into the air corps," Annie said with little emotion.

"I'm sorry, Annie. I truly am." Tears glistened in Corrine's eyes.

Annie, for the time being, was fresh out of tears. She reached over and covered Corrine's hand. "It's not your fault. Those two boys have always felt so invincible together." She breathed deeply, drawing the spring breeze into her lungs. "Maybe they'll change their minds when they see how difficult life in the military can be."

"Oh, do you think so?" Corrine asked, grasping for the lifeline Annie had tossed out.

"We can always hope," Annie offered, with a confidence she didn't really feel.

***

It was three days later when a young man on a motorcycle traversed the driveway of the Wyatt farm. Rachel looked up from her chair on the porch where she had been sitting for the last hour snapping beans. She snapped one more green bean, then dumped her apron-load into the pan at her feet and watched the young man dismount.

"Good afternoon, ma'am. I'm from the Western Union office. I have a telegram for Mr. Eugene Wyatt. Is he home to sign for it?"

Rachel came to the top of the porch steps. "I'm afraid not. He's at our neighbor's place at the moment. But I'm his mother. May I do the signing?" She felt certain it was a telegram from Will, and Rachel wasn't about to let this young man get back on his motorcycle without delivering it.

His hand temporarily hesitated inside the satchel across his shoulder. "Ma'am, it was specifically sent to Mr. Eugene Wyatt. I'm not allowed to deliver it to anyone but him."

"And what did you say your name is?"

"I didn't, ma'am, but it's Luther."

"Have you been working at the Western Union office long?"

"No, ma'am. Less than a month."

"Well, Luther, it's a pleasure to meet you. I can see you're doing a fine job delivering telegrams, but I happen to know that the Yanceys, just over to the south of us, have had telegrams delivered right to their mailbox. How can that be?"

"Uh, ma'am," Luther nervously shifted his weight, "if no one's home, we're allowed to leave it in the mailbox . . . provided there is one."

Rachel stood for a moment mulling over Luther's declaration. "Then how about you just head on down to our mailbox and deposit it there?"

"Well, ma'am, I can't do that."

"Why ever not?"

Luther's face turned a bright shade of pink. "Because, ma'am, someone's home."

Rachel let out a deep breath in exasperation. "All right then," she said, descending the porch steps, "I have work to do in the garden. And Luther, when I'm in the garden, I can't hear anyone knocking on the door. So when you knock, which you will in a moment, no one will be home." She stepped a little closer to Luther, making sure he understood exactly what she was getting at. "When no one answers the door, you can get right back on that motorcycle and put the telegram in Mr. Wyatt's mailbox. Are we clear?" she asked in her most authoritative voice.

Luther gulped. "Perfectly, ma'am."

Rachel then gave the young man her sweetest smile. "Would you care for a cookie or a glass of lemonade before you go?"

"No thank you, ma'am, that's very kind of you, but I'll just be going."

"Don't forget to knock," Rachel instructed one last time, then turned on her heels and headed for the garden in the back.

A few minutes later, after the sound of the motorcycle had died away, Rachel emerged from the garden and headed straight down the road to the mailbox. To her delight, Luther had followed her instructions to a T, although she wasn't so sure he had actually knocked on the door. But that didn't really matter now; the only thing she cared about was reading a telegram from her grandson, if that's what this was.

As she walked slowly up the road, she unfolded the crisp paper and began to read:

Safely at March Field Riverside County California stop
Enlisted in US Army Air Corps stop
Begin training next week all is well stop
Your son Will

Rachel immediately quickened her step as she turned toward the barn to find Annie. Eugene wouldn't be home from the Crowleys' until supper. Wendall's loft had partially collapsed due to a rotten beam, and Eugene was always willing to help his neighbor at the drop of a hat. Wendall and Marcella had been so good to their family over the years, especially after the flood.

Drawing closer to the barn, Rachel caught a glimpse of Annie as she longed one of their thoroughbreds in the arena out back. Her daughter-in-law momentarily faced the other direction, so Rachel stopped at the fence to watch.

With a kissing sound from Annie, the horse continued her graceful canter at the end of the longe line. As Annie turned with the mare, she noticed Rachel and gave her a warm smile.

"It's good to see you down here, Mama." Annie clicked her tongue when the mare slowed her gait.

"Thank you, darlin'." Rachel didn't think she could wait any longer to tell Annie the news. "We've heard from Will!" she called excitedly, holding the message above the railing.

Annie's face lit up. "We have? Whoa, girl. Whoa, now."

Annie worked her hands quickly along the rope, drawing the mare to her side. She gave her a quick pat on the neck as she released her from the tether. Running to the fence, Annie breathlessly reached for the telegram. Rachel watched her read it, then look up briefly before reading it again.

"It's not much to go on, is it?"

"For now, it's something, darlin'."

"Yes," Annie breathed, pressing the telegram to her chest. "At least we know he made it safely." Then she read it again—twice.

Over the next few months, Will wrote several letters, much to the delight of his family. None of his posts were more than five or six lines, but Annie kept each one in a special box, in the order in which they arrived. They now had an address and were able to write to him as well. Between his mother and two grandmothers, Will seldom went more than three days without a bit of news from home.

The news coming out of Europe, however, grew worse by the day. President Roosevelt's fireside chats strongly encouraged the American people to do their part to help millions of ordinary citizens across the European continent, who were now running from their homes to escape machine gun fire and bombs. He urged every American to give as much as their means would allow to the American Red Cross. Women and children and old men were destitute and starving, and the American people had the ability to do something about it. With the sound of a crackling fire in the background, FDR urged his people to open their eyes.

"Day and night I pray for the restoration of peace . . . I know you are praying with me . . ." he declared.

***

Eight long months had passed since Will and Jimmy had left for the air corps. For Annie, Christmas Eve had always been such a joyous occasion in the past, but without Will, it seemed less so.

"Who wants to hang Will's stocking?" Claudia asked as the family gathered around the fireplace.

"If no one objects," Nathan spoke up, "I'd like to do the honors."

There were no objections, so Claudia held it out to her husband. "Nate, the honor is all yours."

He grinned and lovingly hung it next to Annie's. Jake then stepped forward and hung his last, in keeping with tradition.

Mattie brought in a tray of hot apple cider and waited until everyone was comfortable before she made her way around the room.

"Mattie, dear, why don't you join us?" Claudia asked, as she took a steaming mug from the tray.

"Oh, no ma'am, but thank you kindly."

Claudia held the young woman's gaze. "Honey, I insist. It's Christmas Eve. You need to spend it with your family."

Mattie leaned in and whispered, "Is you sure, Miss Claudia? I don't wanna intrude none."

Annie moved closer to Eugene on the couch. "Mattie, I'm saving you a place. Go get a mug of cider and come sit with me."

A sparkling smile spread across Mattie's sweet face. "All right then, I be right back," she said as she scurried into the kitchen.

Mattie went to the cabinet to get herself a mug, but it was nearly too far back for her to grasp. She leaned against the counter and stood as tall as she could on her tiptoes, but it was just out of her reach.

"Here, let me get that for you," a voice whispered behind her.

When she turned around, a scream rose up in her throat, but a large hand was placed against her mouth, mostly muffling the sound.

"Mattie?" Claudia called out. "Is everything okay in there?"

"Oh yes'm," she said breathlessly. "Everythin's just fine. Don't you worry yerself none. I'll be right in."

All of a sudden, Mattie was swept up into a pair of strong arms, and she had to fight for all she was worth to hold back a squeal.

"Oh my Lord, Mr. Will. You is a sight for sore eyes!" she whispered excitedly.

He put his finger to his lips, then gestured for her to go back into the front room. She knew better than to take a drink with her, for fear of spilling it all over the house out of excitement.

"I thought you were getting a mug of cider," Annie commented, as Mattie took a seat beside her on the couch.

"Miss Annie, if you don't mind, I think I'll just take yours."

Annie looked at her in surprise. "Whatever for?"

"Seein' as how I don't want you to spill it or nothin'." There was a short pause in which Mattie reached for the mug and took it right out of her hands.

"Mattie, what on earth . . ."

"Momma!"

Annie's hand jumped straight to her heart as tears of joy sprang into her eyes. She was across the room in an instant. Before she knew it, her feet were off the ground and she was enfolded in the arms of her *prodigal* son. His laughter filled the deepest corner of her soul.

When Will put her down, she held him at arm's length. "Let me look at you!"

He stood tall and handsome in his air corps uniform. She rose up and kissed him, then stepped aside, beaming with delight, while the rest of the family took their turns.

As the evening continued, Will was bombarded with a hundred questions, which he patiently answered. At first, they were questions about his journey home, his health, his living conditions, and anything that pertained to his training. But it wasn't long before the conversation turned to the war in Europe.

"If you don't mind," Will said, "I'd prefer talking about that in a couple of days. I'd rather enjoy Christmas without thinking about that right now."

"Of course, you would," Claudia spoke up. "We'll not mention it again until you're ready." She leveled her gaze at everyone in the room, reiterating his request.

"When do you have to go back, Son?" Eugene asked.

"I have a week. We have to go back after New Year's."

Will pulled off his boots and stretched his legs out in front of him. He sat between his parents on the couch, and neither one could seem to keep their hands off him. Finally, Annie intertwined her arm through his and kept it there for the rest of the evening. He didn't seem to mind.

Late into the evening, eyelids began to grow heavy, so Eugene went to the bookshelf and took down the Bible. Before he sat back down, Jake asked, "What'll it be, big brother, first or last?"

"I'll let you pick it, kid."

Jake grinned and reached for the Bible in his daddy's hand. "I like it when you read last."

Will nodded, and the family, momentarily unencumbered by the world's hostilities, listened to the story of their Savior's birth, as read by two sons whose lives would never again be the same.

Chapter 34

December 1941

Eugene pulled his truck up to the loading dock behind Hammond's Feed Store, then got out and hopped onto the platform. Oscar Hammond and one of his sons began tossing bags of oats into the back. Eugene joined in.

"What do ya hear from your boy these days, Eugene?"

Eugene heaved a fifty-pound bag into the truck. "Got a letter from him yesterday. He's coming home for Christmas again this year."

"I reckon the missus is glad about that," Oscar said, a little out of breath.

"We all are," Eugene responded.

Oscar took a breather while Eugene and Milt Hammond continued working. "Is he a full-fledged pilot now?"

"No, nothing like that. Although he's already logged a lot of time in the air." Eugene stepped down into the bed of the truck to rearrange some of the feedbags. "They're training Will to be a tailgunner."

"You don't say." Oscar sat down on a stool he kept on the loading dock specifically for times like these. He could catch up on all the latest gossip while watching his son do most of the work.

"Say, what about that Jimmy fella he ran off with? How's he makin' out in the air corps?"

"He's doing really well in pilot training. As a matter of fact, they just sent him over to Hawaii. I think Will was a little disappointed to have to stay in California. They do a lot of their ground training in the desert. It can be pretty rough sometimes."

Oscar chuckled. "I guess Jimmy got the better end of the stick on that one."

"Yeah, Will was a little jealous."

"What about yer other boy? Has he registered for the selective service yet?"

Eugene stepped back up on the dock, satisfied that his load was secure. "Not yet. He's still too young."

Oscar slapped his hands on top of his legs, then stood up to take Eugene inside to settle the bill. "All four o' my sons have registered. I don't wanna see us get into that war or all my help'll be gone around here." He let out a cynical laugh. "The more I hear the president talk, the more it sounds like he's gonna get us into this war."

Eugene followed behind Mr. Hammond to the front counter, listening to him rail on the president all the while. "If you ask me, what's goin' on in Europe is none of our business. There's plenty o' salt water between us to keep our country out of it."

Eugene did his best to ignore the expletives Mr. Hammond had thrown in to make his point.

Oscar finished writing out the bill of sale and pushed it across the counter for a signature. "How do you feel about all this buildup of the military?"

It was a tough call as far as Eugene was concerned. He prayed every day that the war would end swiftly. But without a strong defense, what would keep the Axis powers—Germany, Japan, and Italy—from turning their sights on the United States. For Eugene and his family, the stakes were high. He had two sons poised on the brink, awaiting the dreaded words from their president: *we are at war.*

"Oscar, I'm not in favor of war and never will be. But if it comes to that, all I can say is, we'd better be prepared."

It took another fifteen minutes before Eugene could politely walk away from Mr. Hammond's ranting. He knew Oscar was frightened of losing his sons as well as his business if war should come.

Eugene spent the entire trip home in prayer. Thankfully, by the time he pulled the truck up to the barn, the knot in his stomach had mostly dissolved. Even so, he felt a heavier-than-normal burden on his heart the rest of the morning.

The following day a terrifying word spread among the Oak Hill brethren as the congregation fellowshipped after the morning worship. Eugene gathered his family quickly and headed for the car. Annie's face was as white as the gloves on her hands. Eugene took her by the arm and helped her into the backseat beside Jake before assisting his mama into the front. As soon as the car roared to life, he switched on the radio.

In a few short seconds, the announcer blared, "President Roosevelt confirmed that the Japanese have attacked Pearl Harbor from the air. I repeat, the Japanese have attacked Pearl Harbor in Hawaii, from the air." Details would be forthcoming as it was still too early to assess the damage. But for now, it appeared as though Japan was bringing the war to the United States—ready or not.

Annie closed her eyes and softly breathed the name, "Jimmy."

"Thank God our Will is in California," Rachel murmured. "Oh Lord of mercy, put your hand on Jimmy."

The days to follow brought with them horrific news out of Hawaii. Hundreds, if not thousands, of American servicemen had lost their lives in the attack. Nearly a third of the docked naval fleet had been destroyed. On Monday, President Roosevelt and the joint sessions of Congress declared war on Japan. And by Thursday, four days after the attack on Pearl Harbor, Germany and Italy declared war on the United States. Without hesitation, President Roosevelt reciprocated.

Friday afternoon, five days after the Japanese attack, the early tides of war suddenly broke over Louisville. Two of her sons had been killed at Pearl Harbor.

The phone rang at noon as Eugene sat down for lunch with his wife and mother. "I'll get it," Annie said quickly. "Go ahead without me."

As Annie answered the phone, she was greeted by a deep, raspy voice on the other end. "Annie, this is Russell Jackson." He cleared his throat then slowly continued. "We've had terrible news."

Annie could hear a choking sound on the other end of the line. Her eyes immediately filled with tears. "Oh no, Russell. Please tell me it's not Jimmy!" she pleaded.

"I'm afraid so. He was . . ."

Annie sank to the floor in the hallway, still holding the receiver in her hand. She could hear Russell quietly sobbing on the other end. "We lost him, Annie. We . . . lost Jimmy."

Annie wept uncontrollably, trying to choke out her condolences when Eugene gently took the phone from her hand. "Russell, this is Eugene. I'm so sorry. We'll be right over."

He hung up the phone and sat down in the floor with Annie, letting her weep in his arms. Rachel remained at the kitchen table, softly crying and praying. Eventually, the three changed clothes and made their way to the Jacksons' farm, leaving a vague note for Jake, who was still at school.

Half a dozen cars already lined the driveway to the Jackson's home. Reverend Bloomfield from the Methodist Church opened the front door to greet them respectfully. Immediately, Russell rose from a chair in the front room and enveloped Annie in a despondent embrace. Eugene and Rachel followed before Annie asked after Corrine.

"She's upstairs," Russell informed her through red-rimmed eyes. "She's been waiting to see you. I'll take you up."

Annie's heart quickened with an extra layer of anguish. The house was eerily quiet as she followed Russell to the top of the stairs and down the hall. Just before opening the door he said, "Jenny Bloomfield, our reverend's wife, is sitting with her."

Annie laid a sympathetic hand on his arm before entering the spacious bedroom. Corrine was sitting on the edge of the bed with her back to the door, staring out the window. Mrs. Bloomfield rose from her chair nearby to introduce herself to Annie while Russell gently put his hand on his wife's shoulder.

"Annie is here," he said quietly.

Annie moved forward and realized Corrine was hugging a picture of Jimmy to her breast. But it was obvious she'd been waiting for her. Corrine immediately laid the picture aside and rushed into Annie's open arms. Annie held her while wave after wave of sobs wracked her body. She wished she had the words that would make it all better, but there were none. All she could do was surrender herself to Corrine's grief and let their tears flow together.

Eventually, Corrine began to calm, and Annie led her to the settee across the room.

"Oh, the picture!" Corrine exclaimed.

Mrs. Bloomfield jumped to her feet. "I'll get it."

Corrine took the frame from Jenny and held it out for Annie to see. "Look at Jimmy in his uniform."

Fresh tears sprang to Annie's eyes. "Oh Corrine, he's so handsome." Looking at Jimmy's youthful, vibrant face, it was difficult to imagine that he was already gone.

Corrine cradled it lovingly to her chest again while Annie put a compassionate arm around her shoulders. For the next half hour, the two women shared sweet memories of Jimmy, and Annie listened as Corrine reminisced about his childhood.

When they started talking about Jimmy's friendship with Will, Corrine turned to Annie with a horrified look on her face. "Oh dear, what about Will? Do you think he knows?"

Annie suddenly felt grief-stricken at the very thought of it. Who would tell him? She fought the urge to leave Corrine's side to find Eugene. She couldn't imagine what Will was going through right now if he already knew.

There was a light knock on the door, and Russell stepped back into the room. "Your brother Ralph is here with his family, darling. Do you think you can come down for a while?"

Corrine took a deep cleansing breath and closed her eyes. Annie could see the tears forming in the corners and knew how gut-wrenching it was going to be to face her family.

"I can," she said bravely.

Annie took both of Corrine's hands in hers, trying to infuse as much courage into her friend as possible. "I'll be here for you day or night if you need me, Corrine. I mean that. You call me anytime, and I'll be here."

Corrine nodded her head. "I know, and thank you. I just can't believe this is really happening. I keep thinking Jimmy's going to come storming through the back door, filling our house with noise and laughter . . ." Her voice trailed away, and she closed her eyes again trying to gain composure.

When the two women stood, Corrine reached for Annie again and clung to her for a long moment. Annie kissed her cheek, then walked downstairs, leaving her with Russell and Jenny.

In the car, Annie discussed Will with Rachel and Eugene. "Do you think there's any way that he already knows about Jimmy?" she asked with deep concern.

"Possibly," Eugene responded. "The military tends to make lists of casualties for the enlisted men to read. I'm surprised the Jacksons found out so quickly."

"We need to contact him somehow, Eugene. Losing Jimmy will be like losing a brother."

"I know. I've already thought about that. As soon as I drop you and Mama at home, I'm heading to the Selective Service office at the courthouse. Hopefully, they can tell me how to contact him by phone."

But that evening Eugene returned with bad news. "There's no way to contact Will right now. In fact, if we write to him in California, the letters will have to be forwarded to his new location."

"And where is that?" Annie asked.

"They made some phone calls and found out he's been on a ship for the last four days."

"And?"

Eugene paused, not wanting to share the news. "He'll be at Pearl Harbor tomorrow."

***

Will had already jogged eight laps around the upper deck of the cruiser. His back and chest were burned in the Pacific sun, his hair bleached to a lighter shade of blonde. He had a lot of pent-up energy on this fourth day at sea and didn't think he could spend one more second below deck. Tomorrow, he would be reunited with Jimmy. Just thinking about it caused him to pick up his pace.

Every day, the men on the ship were briefed about the conditions they would be sailing into at Pearl Harbor. The officers had told them to prepare for the worst. Despite the number of casualties, Will knew beyond a shadow of a doubt that Jimmy would be there to greet him with a hundred crazy stories to tell. Jimmy wasn't stationed on any of the ships in the harbor; he was living in the barracks near the hangars at Hickam Field. Although Will had heard that the hangars were destroyed, he had also heard that the barracks had been spared. What a reunion they were about to have!

The next morning, Will lined up on deck in his dress uniform. All of the men were in perfect formation as the cruiser slipped into the mouth of the harbor. Will's chest suddenly tightened—the devastation was indescribable. He felt a deep emotional response, particularly when the men were called to attention on deck. His commanding officer remained stock-still as a giant tear slid down his cheek. Will blinked several times to keep his own tears at bay. Many other men wept openly until the ship came into dock.

Will had several duties to perform aboard the ship before he could disembark. He did them swiftly and efficiently, then was granted liberty with his bunkmate, Mac Harris. Mac had also known Jimmy in California and was almost as eager to see him as Will. They soon learned that getting any kind of information on specific soldiers was nearly impossible.

"Come on, let's hop a ride to Hickam Field," Will said.

The two corpsmen soon found a small convoy heading to the airfield and jumped into the back of a truck just as it was leaving. They were dropped off near the field and walked the last half mile.

From the looks of it, the barracks had received only minor damage, but Will could see the twisted pile of charred remains near the airstrip. The barracks were quiet since most of the enlisted men were working, but Will and Mac stepped inside to take a look around. A list hanging on the bulletin board caught Mac's eye.

"Hey, take a look at this. They have a list of known deceased. We should check it to see if there's anyone we know from March Field."

"You can check it if you want to. I just wanna find someone who knows where Jimmy's working." Will headed for the door ready to leave. Maybe if they walked over to the airfield, they might at least find someone who could lead them in the right direction.

Mac had his finger on the list working his way through the names. Will opened the door and stepped outside into the bright sun, but just before the door closed, he heard Mac call out, "What was Jimmy's middle name?"

Will caught the door, and said, "Allen—James Allen Jackson."

"Hey, man," Mac said softly. "You need to get back in here."

Will tried to ignore the queasy feeling that suddenly took hold of his stomach. Mac may have found a Jackson on the list, but there was no way on earth it was Jimmy. He stepped back inside and read the name above Mac's finger— James Allen Jackson, Louisville, KY.

He must have read it six or seven times before the terrible truth sunk in. When it finally did, it felt like a sledgehammer had just hit his chest. Will slammed his fist into the wall, then leaned his forehead onto the list of casualties.

"No, no, no!" he yelled.

Mac put his hand on Will's shoulder, but he was inconsolable. He turned his back to the wall and slid to the floor, drawing his knees up to his chest. Will ran his hands roughly through his hair, then grabbed a handful of hair as if he would tear it out. A low, guttural moan penetrated the room. Nearly every breath he took was a moan or a groan.

Mac sat down beside Will on the floor, ready to stay by his side all night if he had to. Eventually, Will looked up at Mac with a red face and bloodshot eyes. "I hate the Japs!" he seethed. Then he yelled out a curse on the ones who had killed his best friend, fervently vowing revenge.

***

Every member of the family including Jake wrote a letter to Will expressing his love and concern over Jimmy's death. It was a particularly troubling task for Eugene, as it brought back so many memories of the Great War. They wondered how long it would take for their letters to catch up with him considering he was probably already flying military missions over the Pacific.

Immediately after the attack on Pearl Harbor, President Roosevelt implemented the draft for ages eighteen to forty-five, but all men from eighteen to sixty-five were required to register. At the age of forty, Eugene worried about Annie and his mama if they should call him into service. Even Nathan, at the age of sixty-three, had gone to the courthouse to do his duty.

Christmas had come and gone with only one letter from Will. In it, he thanked them for their letters of condolence and wished them all a Merry Christmas, sorry that he couldn't be with them this year. They all prayed for him daily, not just for his physical safety, but that he would be strong in the Lord, as well.

Jake's eighteenth birthday had also come and gone the following month. For the family, it was a day of mixed emotions. While they were immensely proud of their youngest son and excited for his special day, it had also caused them no small amount of anxiety as he had registered for the draft that very morning. Now there was a constant prayer on their lips for both of their sons.

By May, only three other letters had arrived from Will, one in February and two in April. There was no mention of his military missions, but his February letter had been quite disconcerting. Will had made his hatred of the Japanese very clear. However, the two letters in April made no mention of his loathing for the enemy—he simply told them how busy he was and how much he missed them. The family continued to write often, hoping that their letters were getting through. As far as they knew, he was still stationed at Pearl Harbor.

Amazingly, it appeared as though Jake would make it to graduation. While some of the senior boys had already been called into service, Jake was thankfully still at home. He speculated that it was because his last name started with a W, and the government hadn't made it that far yet. However, his best friend, Sam, was still around, and his last name began with an E, so that pretty much blew his theory out of the water.

Saturday morning, two weeks before graduation, Annie made her way up toward the house after seeing the mail truck on the highway. Rachel sat on a low stool in the garden with her hands in the dirt.

"Mail's here, Mama."

"You go on, darlin', Jake and Eugene are back from town. They're already inside. I told them to let me know if there's a letter from Will."

"Okay, don't work too hard."

"I won't. I'm just trying to take advantage of the morning hours before it gets too hot. I'll start lunch in an hour or so."

"No rush, Mama. I'll stay up here and help with lunch."

Annie let the screen door slam behind her as she pulled off her riding boots and left them in the entryway leading to the kitchen. Seeing Jake and Eugene at the table, she started in on her many frustrations with Sweet Tooth, her not-so-sweet, one-year-old filly.

"I wish I had your patience when it comes to—" Annie stopped in mid-sentence when she noticed both of her men clutching papers in their hands.

She tilted her head back and closed her eyes. "Oh God, please—not *both* of them." Her legs suddenly refused to bear weight, and she leaned back against the kitchen counter.

Eugene instantly pushed his chair away from the table and reached for his wife, but Annie threw her arms out and held him off.

"No!" Her voice was shaky, but firm.

When he stepped closer, she locked her elbows tighter, as if by holding him off, she would somehow be able to change the course of events. "Not both of you," she breathed. "I've already given them one man, I can't give them *two* more." Her last words came out as a sob, and Eugene reached up to break her grasp on his shirt.

He held her hands securely in his. "Annie, we have no choice. You know I wouldn't leave you if I didn't have to."

All resolve to hold him off left her, and she melted into his arms, pressing her face into his chest. Eugene held his wife tenderly, caressing her thick hair and wiping tears from her cheek.

Hearing Jake's chair scrape the floor, Eugene released his wife and allowed her to step into her son's arms.

"We'll be all right, Momma. We need to help win this war," Jake said with conviction.

Annie pulled back and looked into her son's normally tranquil, blue eyes. But this time, she saw something different—something that gave them a steely gray appearance. He *wanted* to go, and that thought scared her to death. Her heart was reminded of Will who had left for the service out of defiance.

As if he had read her mind, Jake said, "Momma, I'll write you every week. You'll know where I am and what I'm doing all the time."

Annie cupped his face in her hands and kissed him lightly on the mouth. "Do you know how much I'm going to miss you?"

"Not as much as I'm gonna miss you," he said with a wide grin.

"I gotta go tell Sam I've been drafted. Can I take the car, Dad?"

"That's fine but don't be gone long. We've got a lot of things to take care of before we report for duty."

Jake whisked his papers off the table and ran out the back, letting the screen door slam as hard as his mother had moments earlier.

"Come 'ere, you." Annie grabbed Eugene by the collar of his shirt and pulled him in close. She looked into his deep brown eyes for just a moment, then lifted her lips to his, kissing him hard. How could she possibly let this man go? There were so many emotions pulsing through her body—she knew she couldn't put any of them into words right now without sounding angry. She just needed to physically be with him.

Eugene wrapped his arms around Annie's waist, pulling her tight up against him. It was all she could do not to burst into tears again, but Eugene quickly brushed that notion away as he reached down and swept her up into his arms.

"How long do we have before you go?" she asked.

Tightening his hold and smiling, he said, "Long enough."

When Rachel came in from the garden an hour later, she was surprised to see Annie and Eugene side by side preparing lunch.

"Well, this is a nice treat, but you do know it's not my birthday, don't you?" She laughed as she hung her sunbonnet on the hook by the door.

Eugene wiped his hands on a towel at the counter and walked over to the kitchen table. "Mama," he said, holding a chair out for her, "come sit down for a minute. I need to tell you something."

For a moment, she stood completely still, her features taking on a worried look. "It's Jake, isn't it? He's been called."

Eugene nodded his head, then asked her again to have a seat. As soon as she complied with his request, Eugene pulled out a chair and sat down in front of her, almost knee to knee.

"That's not all, Mama. I've been called too."

Instantly, Rachel's hand flew to her throat then she reached out and took hold of Eugene's arm in disbelief. "You don't mean it!"

"I'm afraid so."

Rachel felt as if she had fallen into a pit that she'd never be able to climb out of. "But you've already been to war. Can't they leave you out of this one?"

"Mama, they're going to need every able-bodied man to fight this one. It's already bigger than the last war."

"Surely they won't make you go into combat," she speculated.

"I'm not as worried about me as I am Will and Jake. I'm sure at my age I'll be safely behind the lines." He covered her hand on his arm, then leaned over and kissed her cheek before rising.

"After we eat," he added, "we'll all sit down and talk. There's a lot we need to take care of before I leave."

"For instance?" Annie asked her husband.

"Well for one thing, it's time to hire a farmhand."

Rachel remained seated, contemplating her daughter-in-law as she continued with the meal preparations. How were the two of them going to be able to manage to keep this place going without Eugene or the boys? Just the thought of hiring a farmhand caused a great deal of concern. However, Rachel's anxiety over the farm was no match for her distress over the fact that now, her son and *both* grandsons would be dragged into this terrible war.

Chapter 35

May 1942

"Mama, come walk with me."

Rachel gladly reached for Eugene's arm. Mother and son descended the front porch steps on this beautiful May evening. She glanced up at the branches of her apple trees as they walked underneath. Who would harvest her apples this season? Will and Jake had always climbed the trees and picked her apples. Oh, how things had changed.

Eugene led her slowly down the road toward the barn, stopping for a while to watch the horses in the upper pasture. Their newest foal was putting on quite a show, running at top speed then suddenly kicking his hind legs into the air. All of the other horses ignored his antics, but he produced a momentary distraction for Rachel and Eugene.

Rachel wondered how many times her son's mind would wander back to this farm over the course of the war. She couldn't imagine the dread he must be feeling on the eve of his departure. He had been called back to his former regiment, the 357th Infantry of the 90th Division. Surprisingly, Jake had been called to the same division. They would both be leaving for Camp Barkeley in Abiline, Texas, in the morning.

"Promise me that you won't worry about me while I'm gone, Mama."

Rachel didn't know how to answer her son. What he was asking her to do would be an impossible task. The first time he had gone to war, she hadn't known where he was. While the *not knowing* had nearly driven her crazy, how much harder would it be now, knowing that he was heading back into harm's way.

She looked up into his thoughtful eyes. "Darlin', I can't make that kind of promise. You're just going to have to come to terms with the fact that I'll worry about you until the day you come home."

Eugene gave her a half grin while he contemplated his next words. "There's something I want to tell you before I go," he said, looking away toward the pasture. "Before I came to live with you and Papa, I was worse off than you ever knew. I don't know how to describe it, except to say I didn't think my life was worth much. I still remember what it felt like—I actually thought about asking God to just let me die."

Rachel felt her heart constrict, and she stared at the side of his face, wondering why he had chosen this moment to tell her such a thing. She knew all too well how battered Eugene had been by his stepfather, but she had never heard him talk about it like this.

"When I came to you and Papa, the two of you showed me there was a life worth living. You gave me a reason to go on."

At that moment, a fleeting thought sprung unbidden into Rachel's mind—she wondered if this would be the last time she'd see her son on this side of glory. A visible shiver pulsed through her body.

"Are you okay?" he asked, looking over at her.

She forced a nod, trying to convince herself that the terrible thought had never infiltrated her mind. Still holding his arm, she moved in closer to his side, but said nothing.

Now he turned his full attention to her, holding her eyes with his steady gaze. "I'm not sure I ever properly thanked you for what you did for me, but I feel compelled to thank you now."

Warm tears flooded Rachel's eyes as Eugene turned and opened his arms to her. She stepped into his affectionate embrace, wishing wholeheartedly that tomorrow would never come.

"Thank you, Mama," he whispered.

Even though this was the first time he had expressed his thanks outright for rescuing him from his stepfather, Rachel had felt his thanks in a thousand other ways over the years. She buried her face deeper into his chest, trying to regain her composure. *Oh Lord, please don't let tomorrow be the last time . . .*

"It's all right, Mama. I didn't mean to upset you like this. I just wanted to make sure you knew beyond a shadow of a doubt how much I appreciate what you've done for me."

She lifted her head and looked into his eyes, unprepared for what she saw. There was a twinkle in his eye.

"What is it?" she asked.

"You remember the time I had that run-in with a skunk?"

Rachel let out a sigh, appreciating very much what Eugene was trying to do to break the tension of the moment. She pressed her hand to his chest, backing slightly out of his arms.

"I thought I was going to have to take a switch to your backside for traipsing into my kitchen with that awful stink on you!"

Eugene chuckled. "You were pretty mad. I remember Papa marching me outside and making me strip my clothes off while he poured kerosene on them and burned them right there in front of the house."

"Yes," Rachel laughed. "And then he filled the wash tub at the pump and scrubbed you down with the tomato paste I made. Do you remember that?"

"How could I ever forget?

"I thought we'd never get that smell out of your hair."

Eugene smiled, gently pulling Rachel to his side, and the two stood with their arms around each other. The little foal had finally tuckered himself out and lay in a heap at his mother's feet.

Rachel eventually spoke up after a long silence.

"Eugene?"

"Uh, huh?"

"You have permission to come bursting into my kitchen any time—I don't care how bad you smell."

Eugene looked down at his mama with a grin that had melted her heart for the past thirty years. "I plan to take you up on that."

The next morning, Eugene and Jake stood on the platform of the train station, saying their final good-byes. Nathan kept a protective arm around Claudia as she cried while Claudia reached out to hold Rachel's hand. Even Sam Evans and his family had come to the station to see them off.

Both Eugene and Jake had purposely left Annie for their final farewell. Even though the family had shared a more personal good-bye the night before, this was still going to be a difficult parting.

Jake went to his mother, and she held him tightly, begging him all the while to be careful. She vowed a constant barrage of prayers on his behalf.

When Annie released her hold, he gave her a wide smile and told her he loved her.

"I love you, too, sweetheart." She kissed him affectionately and watched him walk over to the Evans family to say good-bye. The only security Annie felt in letting her son go was knowing that Eugene would be with him, at least for a while.

But oh, the heavy price her heart was paying in order to let Eugene get on that train. At that moment, he moved in front of her and took her left hand, bringing it to his lips. Then he held it to his heart and said, "You'll be on my mind and in my heart night and day. I'll be home before you know it."

"Eugene . . ." Her eyes filled with tears, and she didn't think she could say another word.

He surrounded her with strong arms and held her for a long moment. Finally, she gained enough composure to pull out of his arms and look him in the eyes.

"You'd better come back to me," she said fervently.

"You mean you'll wait for me?"

Annie laughed and slapped him on the arm but immediately turned serious again. "I mean it, Eugene, you'd better come back to me."

"That's the plan," he said with confidence.

She rose up and kissed him passionately, not caring who might be watching. When she was done, he cradled her face in his hands and said, "Annie, I love you so much."

"I love you with all my heart, Eugene Wyatt."

He kissed her forehead, then reached down for his suitcase and headed toward the train with Jake trailing behind.

Right at that moment, a girl's voice called Jake's name from the crowd. When he turned around, Sam's sister, Charlotte, threw herself into his arms and gave him a long, passionate kiss. When she pulled away, Annie noticed the tears streaking the girl's cheeks as she pled with Jake to come home safely. Even though Jake's face was a bright shade of red, Annie noticed the genuine smile he held for Charlotte. To her amazement, he dropped his suitcase and took her in his arms, kissing her again. Then he quickly released her and reached for his bag, running for the train.

Charlotte turned toward Annie and must have noticed the look of surprise on her face. Blushing brightly, she said, "I'm sorry about that, Mrs. Wyatt."

Annie blinked and shook her head slightly. "No Charlotte, no need to apologize. I guess I didn't realize you and Jake were . . . seeing each other."

"Oh we weren't. I just wanted him to know how I felt about him before he left."

"Well," Annie said, raising her brow, "I think he knows now."

Annie walked over to her parents and Rachel. Together, they waved and blew kisses to their men as the train pulled slowly out of the station. When it was completely out of sight, Annie took in a long, slow breath. She already felt worn out, and the day had barely begun.

Nathan reached for his daughter and gave her a loving hug. "I'll be out in a little while with Leroy. He's all packed up and ready to move to your place."

"Daddy, thank you for letting him work at our farm. I feel bad taking him away from you."

"Oh no, you shouldn't feel bad about that. When Leroy heard you were needing a farmhand, he came to me without wasting any time. He said he wouldn't allow anyone else to help you but him."

Annie smiled, thankful for Leroy's years of loyalty. He had come to the Harrisons' farm at the age of nineteen. Annie was a child of four, but Leroy had let her tag along with him from the beginning. Over the last three decades, he had protected her as if she were his own daughter. Nathan had told Eugene not to worry about Leroy's salary—it had already been taken care of. Eugene had protested, but Nathan was insistent. If all of the Wyatt men were going to be fighting for their country, the least he could do was take care of what they were leaving behind.

Before departing the train station, Claudia kissed Annie affectionately. "Honey, why don't you and Rachel come stay with us for a few days—just until things have settled down a bit."

"Thank you, Mother, but we'll be fine. Besides, I want to help Leroy as much as possible while he gets settled in."

Claudia squeezed her daughter's hand. "Well, if you get lonely or need anything at all, you can always come home."

An hour later, the house seemed unnaturally quiet as Annie and Rachel walked inside. Suddenly going from a vibrant family of five down to a quiet household of two seemed incredibly lonesome. Annie stood in the middle of the living room, feeling desolate.

"What is it, darlin'?" Rachel asked, moving to her side.

Annie exhaled deeply and turned to face her. "I don't know, I just feel so melancholy." Her eyes misted. "I feel like crawling into bed and staying there the rest of the day."

Rachel laid a tender hand on her arm. "Tempting, isn't it?"

"Very," she said with a sigh. But Annie knew it would be of no use to wallow in self-pity. Instead, she straightened her shoulders and attempted a smile. "I just need some fresh air. I think I'll change and head down to the barn. When Leroy gets here, you can tell him where I am."

"Good idea, darlin'. We both just need to stay busy for now. I'll make sure Will's room is ready for Leroy."

"Thank you, Mama." Annie reached for Rachel and gave her a firm hug, then headed to the bedroom to change.

That evening at supper, Leroy sat at the table with Rachel and Annie. Already he was suggesting changes for the farm. "If we separate the calves from their mama's earlier, we won't have to spend so much on feed," he suggested.

"You mean take them to auction at a younger age?"

"That's right. We've got nine right now that I could take down to the stockyard next week. They'd ship out west and save us the extra feed money."

Annie contemplated Leroy's proposition for a moment. She and Eugene had talked about doing that very thing a couple of years ago, but it hadn't turned out to be cost-effective.

"Have you put pencil to paper on it, Leroy?" she asked. "If we're taking them to auction earlier, we won't get as good a price."

Leroy nodded in agreement as he slathered butter onto his last bite of Rachel's cornbread. "And you'd be right about that if it was still 1939. But now with all the meat rationing, you'll actually make more money doing it this way—at least until the war's over anyway."

Annie glanced at Rachel, wondering if she should make such a decision. After all, Eugene had always kept the books on the farm and made nearly every decision on how it was run. She had worked hard to learn what she could in the week before he left, but this was a big decision. She wished she could call him. Eugene had told her to trust Leroy in these types of matters, and she did, but still she hesitated.

Noticing Annie's uncertainty, Leroy threw out an idea. "I tell you what, Missy, why don't we run it by your daddy in the morning and see what he thinks. Would that make you feel a little better about changing the cattle plan around here?"

Annie breathed a sigh of relief. "Yes, it would, Leroy. It's not that I doubt your plan or anything; it's just a big decision to make without Eugene."

Leroy chuckled and stuffed the rest of the cornbread in his mouth, then finished off a large glass of milk. "Miss Rachel, that was a fine meal. I can see right now I may be gaining some extra weight livin' over here."

That seemed to please Rachel as she got up to clear the table. "Well, I doubt that will be the case since I know what kind of meals Claudia makes. But we'll do our best not to let you go hungry."

Leroy gave her a big grin, causing his thick, gray mustache to turn up at the corners. "If you ladies don't need anything else, I think I'll have another look at the calves."

"When we get the kitchen cleaned up, we'll be out on the porch if you'd like to join us," Rachel offered.

"Thank you kindly, but I plan on reading tonight. The boys in the bunkhouse always make fun of me for readin' so much." Leroy was an avid reader of Western dime novels. He devoured them by the dozens. "I can't wait to have some peace and quiet."

Both women laughed and said they'd try not to disturb him.

Later in the evening, Rachel asked Annie to join her on the porch. "Why don't we sit in the swing and talk a while."

"I'd like that," Annie responded, thankful not to be alone tonight.

For a while, they chatted about Leroy's reading obsession, and Annie shared a few stories about him from her childhood. But eventually the conversation changed to Eugene and the boys. They wondered how each one was getting along.

Rachel then turned to Annie with a look of concern. "Darlin', are you going to be all right? I know how hard this must be for you."

Annie pondered her mother-in-law's question. She wasn't sure at this point if she would ever be all right again, especially if one of her men didn't come home.

A shiver coursed through her very soul. She couldn't afford to think like that. Not ever. "I'll be fine, Mama. It's just going to take a while getting used to this new way of life."

Rachel wrung her hands nervously in her lap. "Annie, I have something to propose, and I want you to consider it seriously before you give me an answer."

Annie nodded her head, even though Rachel's demeanor caused her to worry.

"I think you should take your mother up on her offer. You need to go home and live for a while."

"No, Mama . . ."

"Darlin', I asked you to give it serious thought. I mean what I'm saying. I'll be fine taking care of the house and garden, and Leroy's here to see after the livestock. You can come out and work with the horses any time you want, but you'd be living at home with your folks. Why would you want to be anywhere else under the circumstances?"

When Rachel fell silent, Annie complied with her mother-in-law's request. Slowly, she rose from the swing and walked across the porch to the railing. Her heart was hurting like never before. Two sons were gone and her bed would be empty tonight. She felt an immense pain penetrate to the very core of her being.

She had to admit Rachel's offer sounded tempting, even if just for a while. But how could she be sure it was the right thing to do? Annie felt burdened as she walked down the steps and out into the yard. *Lord, what would You have me do?*

She made her way out to one of Rachel's apple trees and laid her hand on the sturdy trunk. It was at that very moment that the answer came to her. It rang out clear and strong through her mind and heart, leaving no doubt what her answer would be. Immediately, she made her way back to Rachel, who sat patiently waiting for her response.

"Mama." Annie spoke her name with love and tenderness, dropping to her knees in front of the swing. "I could never leave you." She reached for Rachel's hands. "Please don't ask me to. If we have to bear this burden, then I want us to bear it together. I love you dearly."

She laid her head in her mother-in-law's lap, and Rachel gently caressed her hair.

"And I love you with all my heart," Rachel replied, tears welling up in her eyes. "My beloved daughter."

That night before bed, Rachel sat in her chair under the lamp and read the book of Ruth to Annie from start to finish. When she looked up, she noticed a lovely smile spreading across her daughter-in-law's face.

"Entreat me not to leave thee," Annie remarked delightfully.

Rachel softly laughed. "I never shall again."

"Mama, what about you? Are *you* going to be all right?"

"Mm," she said with a nod. "Remember, I've been through this before."

"Yes, but to send your son off to war for the second time must be awfully difficult."

"Of course it is, but this time is different."

"How so?" Annie asked in surprise.

"Well, darlin', this time I have *you*."

Chapter 36

August 1942

"**S**on!"

Jake turned sharply from where he stood in the aisle of one of Camp Barkeley's four movie theaters. He hadn't seen his dad in nearly a month, and his heart quickened at just the sound of his voice.

Eugene was hastily climbing over a row of officers who had come to watch the latest Gary Cooper movie, *The Pride of the Yankees*. When he finally freed himself from the mass of knees and toes, he grabbed Jake and pulled him into a tight hug.

"It's good to see you, Son."

"You too, Dad!"

"I thought you might be here tonight considering it's a baseball movie."

Jake laughed. "You know, I was just thinking the same thing about you. Do you wanna sit together?"

Eugene hesitated. "Are you sure? It looks like you're here with your buddies."

"Who, these guys?" Jake smirked, shoving one of his pals. "I have to live with these cronies. Come on, let's find seats together."

One of the men on the end of the row Eugene had just vacated moved down a seat and waved them over. As soon as they were seated, the soldier leaned toward Eugene. "Wyatt, you gonna introduce me to this young fella?"

"Sure. Sergeant Hudson, this is my son, Jake."

Jake leaned forward in his seat and took the outstretched hand. "Pleasure to meet you, sir."

"Pleasure to meet you, Jake. You look just like your old man," the sergeant said, elbowing Eugene in the side.

Jake smiled. "I'll take that as a compliment, sir."

"How's training going for you, Son?" the sergeant asked.

"Pretty well, sir. We have our first fifteen-mile march in full gear on Monday."

Sergeant Hudson snorted out a laugh. "That'll be a pleasant experience in August!"

"Yes, sir, I can't wait," Jake responded with his usual good nature.

As soon as the sergeant started talking to the officer on his left, Jake turned his full attention to Eugene. "How's training going for you, Dad?"

"I'm not sure they push us older guys like they do you youngsters. But believe it or not, I'm training harder than I did twenty-five years ago at Camp Travis."

"I bet you're tearing it up on the range, aren't you?"

Eugene grinned. "Got my first Sharp Shooter medal last week."

Jake let out a whoop. "That's awesome, Dad! How do you like the M-1?"

"It's a pretty amazing rifle. Nothing like we had in the Great War."

Just then, Sergeant Hudson butted into their conversation. "Say, Jake, did your old man tell you he's gettin' a promotion next week?"

Jake got excited. "You're kidding? Why didn't you tell me?"

"'Cause Corporal Wyatt here just lets his shootin' do the talkin'." The sergeant snorted again. "But he better watch out or they'll put him on the front line for sure."

"Dad, that's great news. So are you moving up to sergeant?"

"Yep, one more stripe," Eugene said modestly. "So you better not forget to salute, or I might get my feelings hurt."

Jake felt overwhelmingly proud of his dad. *Sergeant Wyatt*—he liked the sound of that. He hoped his dad would never hit the front lines, not at his age, but it sounded like he was working his way up through the ranks at a fairly quick pace. "So what'll you be in charge of?" Jake asked.

"Besides training my squad, I'm also in charge of ammunition, small arms, and rifles. I'll be responsible for keeping a company fully supplied."

"Wouldn't that be somethin' if you were assigned to my company?"

"Slim chance of that, Son, but yeah, that *would* be somethin'."

"Hey Dad?"

"Yeah?"

"Are you missin' Mom?" Jake knew the answer as soon as he saw the look in his dad's eyes. He almost wished he hadn't brought it up, especially when he heard his reply.

"Every day."

The words just hung in the air between them for a while. More than a couple of hundred men talked and shouted all around them, but neither one seemed to hear any of it.

Jake pressed his lips together, thinking he should change the subject, but Eugene beat him to the punch. "You are writing home, aren't you?"

"Every week, sometimes twice!"

"Atta, boy," Eugene said. "You don't wanna be in hot water when we go home on leave."

"Don't I know it."

At that moment, the lights dimmed and a newsreel lit up the screen. A hush instantly spread through the packed house.

On screen, an angry-looking eagle hovered above the words EVERYBODY JOINS THE WAR EFFORT, and dozens of movie stars were shown boarding the war-bonds train across America. They were stopping in three hundred cities trying to sell one billion dollars' worth of war bonds in one month.

"Yes, in America," the announcer bragged, "everyone is doing his bit. There goes Jimmy Stewart on his way to enlist."

Boxer Joe Lewis was also shown enlisting in the army, along with actor Tyrone Power being sworn in to the marines, and the king of Hollywood, Clarke Gable, enlisting in the US Army Air Force at the age of forty-one.

Jake nudged his dad. "Hey, he's your age. I bet you're in better shape."

Eugene chuckled.

The second half of the newsreel showed production plants in the Midwest cranking out hundreds of anti-aircraft guns per week. The announcer declared, "America's 130 million citizens are in the war!"

And finally, American-built bombers appeared in an actual raid across the English Channel into Germany-occupied France. Jake was instantly reminded of his brother, who was now a tail-gunner on a B-17 Bomber in the Pacific.

"I wonder how Will's gettin' along," he whispered to Eugene. But surprisingly, his dad didn't respond. He just kept his eyes trained on the screen. Jake's intuition told him there was a reason. After the picture show, he intended to find out what it was.

An hour and a half later, Jake followed Eugene outside the theater. Dusk was settling over the camp.

One of the enlisted men strode up to Jake's side and clasped down on the back of his neck. "Hey, Wyatt, you headin' over to the club?"

"Dad," Jake said, "I want you to meet my good buddy, David McAllister. David, this is my dad."

"Pleased to meet you, sir." The tall, sporty-looking soldier took Eugene's hand. "You can call me Mercy."

"Yeah, Dad, everyone calls him Mercy 'cause he was studyin' to be a preacher before he got called in the draft."

"Well, Mercy, it's nice to meet you. Where are you from?"

"Wichita, Kansas, sir."

Eugene smiled, then turned his attention to Jake. "I really enjoyed watching the picture with you tonight. I'm sure you guys have plans—the night's still young."

"Dad, I was hopin' we could go talk somewhere—maybe catch up on everything."

Eugene's face brightened. "I'd like that, but I don't want to keep you fellas from having some Saturday night fun. You haven't had much downtime since we got here."

"Go on with your pop," Mercy said. "I'm not gonna hang out at the club long. Maybe one game of billiards and call it a night. I'm preachin' tomorrow and need to do some studyin'."

"Which chapel?" Eugene asked.

"Chapel twelve over on the south side." Mercy gave the pair a big smile. "Nine o'clock. You should join us, sir."

"I think I will," Eugene said, offering his hand once again to Private McAllister. "It was nice to meet you. Lookin' forward to hearing you preach tomorrow."

"Thank you, sir. See ya later, Jake."

"See ya, Mercy," Jake called as he watched his pal catch up with some of the men from their unit.

"Did you walk over here, Dad?"

"No, I hitched in with a couple of guys."

Camp Barkeley was huge, housing sixty thousand men. It was twice the population of Abilene and sported a hospital with over two thousand beds, two cold storage plants, a bakery, two service clubs for the enlisted men, fifteen chapels, and thirty-five postal buildings. Most of the enlisted men lived in hutments while four thousand others lived in barracks.

"I'll walk back with you to your hut," Eugene offered.

"Yeah, but you'll have a long way back across camp."

"I don't mind, Son. Sometimes I just need a long walk all to myself."

Father and son turned down the walkway, which had mostly cleared since the moviegoers were heading to various sections of camp. Eugene glanced over at his son as they walked. He had seemed like just a boy when they left Louisville, but now, almost three months later, he was walking beside a well-built, confident young man. Eugene couldn't help but smile.

"What, Dad?"

"I'm proud of you, Jake. I just can't get over how much you've grown up."

Jake gave his dad an appreciative grin.

"Has it been hard being here, away from home?" Eugene asked.

"At first it was. Just being thrown in with a bunch of guys I didn't know was rough. But then the training started, and it wasn't long before we all got really close. You realize pretty quick how much you're gonna have to rely on these guys to survive."

Eugene knew exactly what his son was talking about. He thought about the Texas-Oklahoma unit and the camaraderie they had shared during the first war. He had trusted those men with his life every single day. And now, Jake was learning what it meant to sacrifice unconditionally for a group of men who would be doing the same for him. No one could fully understand the brotherhood of soldiers without experiencing it firsthand.

For the next few minutes, Jake told his dad about Mercy and the other guys in his unit. Nearly every one of them was a God-fearing believer, and those who weren't were open to the message. It caused an even stronger bond to form between the men he lived with twenty-four hours a day.

Just before making it to the hutment city, Jake asked his dad the question that had been on his mind for the last couple of hours. "Has anyone heard from Will lately?"

Eugene felt his chest tighten. He spent most of his days worried about his eldest son, but he certainly didn't want Jake to know that.

"The last letter I got from your mom said they'd heard from him. He's flying B-17 bomber missions against Japanese shipping and air fields."

"I'm worried about him, Dad. I heard something the other day that really bothered me."

"What'd you hear?"

"I heard our air force is losing over a hundred aircraft a day in the war. A hundred!"

Eugene had heard worse. He had heard the number was over 150 per day.

"Yeah, but most of those losses are over France and Germany. It's not quite as bad in the Pacific." He knew the only reason for that was because they didn't have as many aircraft committed in the Pacific theater. But still, a lot of good men were being lost every single day in the air.

Eugene put his hand on Jake's shoulder as they continued walking. "Son, I'm just as concerned about Will as you are, but there's nothing we can do except keep him covered in prayer. God will keep a watch over him for us."

Jake solemnly nodded his head and the two walked in silence until they reached the first row of living quarters.

"I guess I'll leave you here," Eugene said. "It was so good to be with you tonight."

"You too, Dad. You are coming to the service tomorrow, aren't you?"

"Sure thing. I'm looking forward to it."

"Chapel twelve."

"I'll be there."

The two stood face to face for a long moment, neither one really wanting to part company. Finally, Eugene reached over and took his son by the back of the neck and drew him in close, kissing his forehead.

"You take care of yourself, Son."

Jake gave him a tight smile. "I will, Dad. You too."

Just then, some of the guys from Jake's unit passed by, laughing and talking. He got caught up in their wake as one of them shoved him into a buddy who hooked an arm around Jake's neck and dragged him along. Eugene stood smiling as he watched them engulf his son in their joviality.

But Jake wrenched himself free and turned back to face his dad. Eugene wanted to tell his son how much he loved him, but didn't want to embarrass him in front of the guys. Instead, he made a fist and pounded it to his heart. This time, Jake gave his dad a vibrant smile, drawing his fist to his chest briefly before one of his pals yanked him back into the pack.

***

It was the wee hours of the morning over the Pacific Ocean, and the crew of The Gray Lady was running short on time and hope. Navigation had been knocked out on their raid over a Japanese convoy heading to the Philippines. The

Lady's bombs had been deadly accurate, mainly because Captain Lance Craig had taken the B-17 to a lower-than-normal altitude. Even though they were safer at a high altitude, it was much harder for the bombers to hit their targets. Captain Craig had run it by his crew before making the fateful decision. Every last man had agreed to the mission.

Will sat in his gunner's perch at the tail of the plane, all alone, listening to the crew on the interphone. During the raid, he had managed to fight off a couple of Japanese Zeroes dogging their tail, but not before they dealt The Gray Lady a punishing blow. They had knocked out her navigation and radio communication systems. When The Gray Lady flew into an active storm cell, the crew managed to lose the enemy fighters, but they also lost all sense of direction. The weary crew had now been flying aimlessly for hours over an infinite expanse of dark water.

They were down to their last liters of fuel, and one by one, the engines began to fail. The calm voice of Captain Lance Craig resonated loud and clear in Will's headphones.

"It's been the greatest honor of my life to serve with you gentlemen. There could never be a more courageous or dedicated crew to the cause of human liberty. May God bless us all with His grace and mercy." His voice quavered as he concluded. "You have my sincerest thanks and admiration. God be with you."

Will knew the pilots were doing everything within their power to keep the nose from pointing toward the ocean, but he now felt his position at the rear of the bomber tilting upward. His chest began to heave as he awaited the inevitable. All he could think about was the fact that he was devastatingly alone. This is not how he thought the end would come.

Scene after scene of a life spent with his loving family rushed through Will's mind. He longed for their embrace and ached for his mother's touch. The deafening roar of the crippled bomber was but a distant murmur as Will's life came into sharp focus. He had allowed his spirit to be consumed with hatred, but that was not the way at all. His family had shown him *the way* over the course of his whole life. The entirety of his existence was now narrowed down to one clear, precise, truth—love. He could read it on the tiny head of a pin, but it engulfed his universe. Love. Everything that was meaningful and good and worthwhile was enveloped within its folds. LOVE!

"Oh Jesus!" he cried out, "I've been so wrong. Forgive me . . . forgive me . . . forgive me . . ."

***

Tuesday morning, the basement of Oak Hill Church buzzed with conversation as the ladies tore sheets and rolled bandages for the Red Cross. Several other women put together food packages and blankets that would be sent to prisoners of war. Annie finished rolling another bandage, then turned to her mother who was trying to tear a strip from one of the clean, white sheets. She noticed the look of concentration on Claudia's face. Her left hand simply didn't have enough grip strength for the task.

"Mother, why don't you switch jobs with Miss Ruby. She's organizing the bandages in boxes. I'm sure she wouldn't mind ripping sheets for a while."

Claudia took in a deep breath and appeared to focus all of her energy on finishing what she'd started, but very little progress was being made. Annie reached across the table and took hold of her mother's hands and the sheet. The two women completed the undertaking together.

"Thank you, honey. This is so aggravating sometimes."

Annie continued holding her mother's hands lovingly. "I know, but I'm just thankful you're still here with me."

Claudia smiled warmly at her daughter. "I'm sorry, honey. I don't have a right to complain considering what's going on in the world."

"You weren't," Annie said matter-of-factly. "I'm sure it can be frustrating at times." She picked up the strip they had torn and began rolling another bandage.

Miss Ruby waddled over and reached for the one Annie had just finished. "You done with this one, child?"

"Yes, ma'am. And Miss Ruby, would you mind tearing a few sheets for a while and let Mother organize the boxes?"

A knowing look passed between the two women, and Ruby put on her most pleasant smile. "Why, I thought you'd never ask."

Miss Ruby took a seat and picked up a clean sheet from the pile. She measured the width before cutting it with the scissors and ripped the full length with her plump fingers in no time. But tearing sheets was not Miss Ruby's main task. She was full of stories and lived for such days as this when she had a captive audience at her fingertips, so to speak.

"I guess you ladies haven't heard what happened to me the other night."

All the women gathered in a little closer to hear another one of Ruby's tales.

"I declare, it liked to taken ten years off my life, it done scared me so bad." She licked her lips and shook her head.

"You all know how hobos sometimes come right off the train to my back door for a bit o' food? Well, I'll feed anybody who needs a handout, but oh my, my . . . I don't know whether I ought to tell this or not."

Rachel looked up from her task of sewing. "Now Miss Ruby, you can't lead us on like this and not tell us what happened."

The room echoed with assent.

"You'ns have got to promise not to go tellin' this around town."

"Oh we promise, Miss Ruby."

"Please, tell us, Ruby."

"Don't leave us hangin'."

Ruby looked around, beaming at her expectant audience. "Well, it was a bit after midnight and I had to get outta bed to go to the bathroom. I don't like to turn on no lights 'cause it just keeps me from goin' back to sleep. So I went to the toilet in the dark, and started to lift my gown, and low and behold a deep voice says, 'I'm already on here.'"

All the ladies in the room gasped while Miss Ruby's voice rose another octave.

"Why I jumped and screamed like a stuck pig! It's a wonder I didn't wet all over that poor man."

Shrieks of laughter rang out through the basement, Ruby being the loudest of all. Then she continued with the wild tale of how she turned on the lights and realized it was one of the hobos she had fed last month. He had made himself right at home, knowing Miss Ruby never locked her door.

As all the women laughed and talked, a queasy feeling came over Annie. She felt light-headed and the voices around her faded into the background. A dull ache gripped her heart, but it wasn't physical. It almost felt like her spirit was being drawn out of her body.

With the entire basement engulfed in chatter and mirth, no one really noticed when Annie stood up and headed for the stairs. In a few short moments, she found herself outside on the front steps of the building, needing to fill her lungs with fresh air in the worst way. She breathed deeply through her nostrils and pulled in as much as possible.

The most uncomfortable feeling hung over her like a cloud—almost otherworldly. Strangely, Annie took account of *herself*. She was still breathing, still moving, but she felt unsettled and restless.

Heading slowly down the steps onto the sidewalk, she walked across the road for no particular reason. She'd been on this property many times, but not since the old church had burned down. The burnt timbers had been removed years ago, but the old foundation remained—grass and weeds pushed through the cracks.

Almost as suddenly as the sensation had come upon her, it left her. She now took stock of her surroundings and wondered what had lured her here. As hard as she tried to process what had just happened, there seemed to be no logical explanation.

A low, stone wall still stood guard over the old foundation. Annie dusted her hand across the rough stones and sat down under the shade of a spreading mimosa tree. Will and Jake had played here many Sundays after worship service, waiting for Eugene to whistle them to the car.

Oh Sovereign Lord, my heart is so heavy. Hold Eugene and Will and Jake in Your mighty hands. She let out a deep sigh. *If one of them is in trouble, please surround them with Your protection and love.*

Annie continued to pour out her heart to God on behalf of the men she loved. Then she sat silently, letting the warm August breeze wash over her face. A delicate, pink mimosa bloom floated lightly down from the tree's branches, landing on the wall not far from where she sat. She paid it little attention until two more floated gracefully to the very same spot.

Absently, she moved down the wall and picked up the wispy blossoms. They smelled sweet and light—soothing her soul. Annie opened her palm and blew them out into the breeze, but one landed back on top of the wall. Instead of picking it up again, she studied it pensively, and that's when she noticed something carved on top of the stone.

Annie brushed the blossom to the ground and stared at the worn markings. They had been hewn roughly with another stone, over and over again. The letters had faded from years of rain and snow, yet the impressions still remained legible.

With deep emotion, she ran her finger unhurriedly over every letter—tracing the pattern of each character until her hand lingered at the end . . . *Will.* She spoke his name aloud with a depth of affection that only a mother could feel.

Tenderly, she covered his name with the palm of her hand, feeling the warmth of the stone. Moist tears covered her cheeks, then dripped to the stone as she knelt and brushed her lips on top of his name.

Oh thank You, Lord, for bringing me here. Thank You.

Annie pulled herself from her knees and sat down again on the wall, never letting her hand stray from Will's name. She had not felt so close to him since the war had begun. This would be her sanctuary—her haven—until he came home . . . until they *all* came home.

Eventually Annie stood, and as she walked across the highway, Claudia came outside through the front door of the building.

"Honey, is everything all right?" she called out.

"I'm fine," Annie responded. "I just needed some fresh air."

Annie noticed her mother's thoughtful glances and wondered if it would be possible to mask her emotions. While part of her wanted to share the beautiful treasure she'd found with her mother, an overwhelming portion of her soul needed to keep it just between her and God.

"Something's different," Claudia said as Annie ascended the steps.

"What do you mean, Mother?" Annie felt the catch in her throat and hoped she could keep her emotions under control.

Claudia reached up with her right hand and cradled the side of Annie's face, looking deeply into her eyes. "This is the first time I've seen joy in your eyes in the last three months." While Claudia didn't ask outright what had transpired during the last half hour, she gave her daughter a quizzical look.

Annie wasn't sure joy was the right word, but maybe a hint of delight still lingered from the tangible pleasure she had experienced of touching Will's name.

"I just needed some time to myself to pray. I feel much better now." She reached for her mother and shared the remnant of delight in a loving embrace—a hopeful remnant that would soon be shattered.

Chapter 37

Annie watched in amazement as Leroy led the seven little calves right into his clever trap. He had built a small holding pen near the pasture gate for such an undertaking as this. It had been far too difficult trying to wrangle the first group of nine away from their mamas for auction back in May.

"I got 'em good and primed last evening with this batch of sweet feed. Now they know just how good it is, don't ya little'uns?"

Annie giggled, watching the tiny herd follow behind Leroy as if he were the Pied Piper. They gobbled up the feed as fast as he could spread it on the ground. As soon as they were all inside the pen, Leroy closed the gate and looked at Annie leaning over the fence.

"It sure is good to hear you laugh, Missy."

Annie felt the warmth rise to her cheeks. "Has it really been that long?"

Leroy removed his hat and wiped a bandana over his balding head. "It's been a while," he said thoughtfully. "But I don't blame you none. Hasn't been much to laugh about lately, has there?"

"No," she said quietly, "I'm afraid not."

Leroy moved among the calves in the herd, giving each one a gentle slap on the rump or the neck. "Well, I guess it's time to see if they'll follow the feed right up into the trailer."

Sure enough, five minutes later, every one of the little calves huddled together in the front of the trailer. Leroy checked the latch on the back, then opened the door to the truck.

"I think we'll get a fairly good price for these young'uns. It'll take a few months to see the profit, but it'll come. Don't you worry about it."

"I'm not worried, Leroy. I believe we're doing the right thing, and so does Eugene."

Leroy closed the door of the truck and leaned his elbow out the window. "You wanna come along?"

Annie gave his arm an affectionate pat. "Sounds fun, but not today. Maybe next time."

"Alrighty then, Missy. I'll see you this afternoon."

Annie stood watching the little calves press into a tight cluster as they bumped along the farm road. She caught herself smiling, and it felt good. Since her men had left for the army, she had found little joy in life. Truthfully, it was hard just getting out of bed every morning. She despised the anxious feeling that had taken up residence, but as hard as she tried, there seemed to be no way to get rid of it.

Leroy was right though; it had been far too long since she'd laughed out loud. She would have to make a more concerted effort to be cheerful, no matter the circumstances.

No sooner than Leroy and the calves were out of sight, but another vehicle turned up the drive. Annie remained still, watching the car make its way slowly toward the house. As soon as it came to a halt, a man stepped out in military dress, holding an officer's cap. Her heart jumped clear into her throat.

Rachel immediately stepped out onto the porch while the man approached the steps. Annie pictured herself running in the opposite direction as fast as she could. She realized what a ridiculous notion that was. But whatever this man had come to say, she didn't want to hear it. When Rachel pointed toward her on the road, the officer laid the cap against his chest and nodded respectfully her way.

Annie didn't want this man to see her in her work clothes. If he came bearing bad news, she should at least be dressed decently for a visitor. Heart pounding wildly, she walked around to the back of the house and snuck into her bedroom as Rachel brought the officer inside.

Almost in a daze, Annie began to change clothes. Her fingers shook uncontrollably as she buttoned her blouse and pulled on her skirt. She looked in the mirror over the dresser and tried to smooth out her hair, then sat down on the edge of the bed to put on her shoes. But when the task was done, she couldn't move.

What if it's Will? Annie felt like a knife was ripping through her heart. *Oh Lord, what if it's not.* She couldn't bear to think about what news this man was bringing.

A soft knock sounded on the bedroom door, and Rachel quietly came to her side. Annie couldn't look at her. She knew if she gazed into those deep, tender eyes, she would lose her tenuous composure.

Rachel simply reached down and took her hand gently. "He's waiting for you, darlin'."

"Mama, I don't know if I can bear it."

Rachel sat down on the bed beside her, and the two women clung to each other. "We'll bear it together, darlin'."

After a brief moment Rachel said, "Annie, look at me."

Annie slowly turned her face toward Rachel's and held her gaze steadily. Though she perceived a deep sadness in her mother-in-law's eyes, there was also something so calming and so reassuring, she couldn't help but be strengthened.

"God has promised not to put more on us than we can bear," Rachel declared fervently. "We need to claim that promise right now. You and I, right here . . . we claim that promise."

While just the moment before Annie had felt like running and hiding, she now felt her spirit being shored up by this remarkable woman. How hard would this news be for Rachel to bear as well? After all, this was about one of her grandsons, or God forbid, her only son.

The officer stood as the women came into the front room. The moment seemed so surreal. *This can't be happening,* Annie thought.

"Mrs. Wyatt?"

"Yes," she whispered.

"My name is Lieutenant Stiles." He had such a kind face—surely he wasn't bearing bad news.

"Ma'am, I'm very sorry to inform you that your son, Corporal William Franklin Wyatt, has been reported as missing in action."

Annie let out the breath she'd been holding with a languid sigh. "What do you mean missing? Does that mean he's still alive?" she pleaded.

Lieutenant Stiles appeared to be extremely uncomfortable. He opened a folded piece of paper, and Annie asked, "Does that say what happened?"

"Yes, ma'am."

Rachel put her arm around Annie's waist and led her to the couch. She nodded for the lieutenant to have a seat as well.

Annie sat on the edge of the sofa and stared at the paper in his hand. "Please . . . I need to know."

The lieutenant cleared his throat. "I'm afraid it's rather vague," he said. "It's sometimes very difficult to know the circumstances in such cases."

He cleared his throat once again then read, "Corporal William F. Wyatt, of the United States Army Air Corps, along with his crew, failed to return from their mission of 24 August 1942 somewhere over the Pacific. A seven-day search and rescue mission was completed on 31 August 1942 with no remains of the aircraft or its crew recovered. If other details or information become available, you will be promptly notified."

Lieutenant Stiles carefully folded the piece of paper and looked at the two women. "The United States Army Air Corps expresses its condolences to you both." Then a compassionate expression spread across his features. "I'm very sorry to bear such bad news to you, Mrs. Wyatt, and ma'am."

"But surely they can't give up, not until they've found evidence," Annie said incredulously. Where at first she had felt herself falling apart, now she felt outrage that the search was over.

"Ma'am, I understand this is distressing news, but seven days is actually a longer-than-normal search period. Captain Lance Craig and the men of The Gray Lady were a beloved crew according to the reports we were given. They went well beyond the regular three-day search."

Through her tears, Rachel asked, "Is there any way we can find out more? There has to be someone we can write to or speak with that has more information about Will."

"Within the next few days, you should receive a letter from your son's commanding officer with more information," Lieutenant Stiles offered. "But I'm sorry, that's all I can tell you at this point."

When he came to his feet, the women did the same. Rachel offered the officer her hand and thanked him for coming.

"My condolences, ma'am," he said respectfully. Then he turned to Annie and handed her the paper. "Mrs. Wyatt, I'm very sorry to give you this news about your son, but the United States government wishes to express their profound gratitude for Corporal Wyatt's service to his country in a time of war."

Annie accepted the paper, unwilling to give in to the fact that Will's fate had already been sealed. "Thank you," she murmured softly.

"I'll show myself out, ma'am."

Rachel considerately followed the lieutenant onto the porch, but Annie opened the paper and read it again. "Oh, Father," she breathed aloud. "You alone know where he is." She didn't know if she dared hope that her son would still be alive, but somewhere in the deepest portion of her heart, he always would be.

Before the noontime hour, Annie and Rachel found themselves with a house full of visitors. Annie's parents had naturally been the first to arrive as soon as they received their daughter's phone call. Claudia took it upon herself to greet every caller and fill them in on the news, so Annie and Rachel wouldn't have to continually hash through it.

Annie knew her mother was at her best when circumstances were at their worst—it was a gift God had given her. But she was also conscious of how deeply Claudia must be grieving over the terrible news of her grandson.

Nathan, on the other hand, displayed his grief without reservation. Will had always had a special place in his heart as the first grandchild, born right in his own house. Something about Will's personality and demeanor had given the two a special kinship from the very start. Watching her father pace through the house now put Annie's nerves on end.

When the phone rang late in the afternoon, Annie's neighbor Marcella Crowley and Miss Ruby from church were the only two visitors remaining. Claudia rose to answer the phone as she had done throughout the day.

"Oh Eugene, I'm so thankful you were able to call!" Claudia cried.

When Annie heard her mother's declaration, she hastily ran down the hall.

"Eugene, I'm praying for you and Jake, especially now," Claudia said. "I love you, honey. Here's Annie."

Annie tried not to rip the phone out of her mother's hand, but Eugene was the only one she wanted right now. She longed for his loving arms around her; she ached for her husband's touch. But for now, his voice alone would have to suffice.

"Eugene!"

"Annie, sweetheart, I'm so sorry about the terrible news. If I could be there with you right now, I would."

"Oh Eugene, is there any way you can come home . . . just for a few days?"

There was a short pause before Eugene spoke again. "Sweetheart, I've been trying all day to get leave, but I was denied this afternoon."

Annie's hopes deflated right there on the spot, and she sank to the chair beside the phone. "Why would they do that? Don't they know you need to be with your family right now?"

"Yes, they know. But for now they're only granting leave for the men whose family members have actually . . ."

When Eugene hesitated, Annie completed his sentence. "Been killed?" As soon as she said the words out loud, she felt herself topple over the brink. All day she had been balancing on the edge of an abyss, tiptoeing carefully along the rim, trying not to look into the terrible darkness. But now, she was falling headfirst into its clutches.

"Annie, I'm so sorry. I know it doesn't seem right," he offered. "I love you so much, sweetheart."

Annie's shoulders began to shake uncontrollably. "Eugene, I love you and miss you so much," she sobbed.

His voice was filled with strength and comfort.

Why can't he be here to hold me?

"Sweetheart?" Eugene said. "Jake's standing here with me. He wants to talk to you."

Without hesitation, Jake's voice rang through the phone loud and clear. "Mom!"

Annie put her hand over her mouth, trying to hold back the next sob.

"I wish we could be with you right now."

"Oh sweetheart," she managed to say, "I wish you could too."

"Are you gonna be okay, Mom?"

Annie squeezed her eyes shut, willing her turbulent emotions into submission. "I'll be fine, honey." She wiped her nose on the handkerchief Nathan had given her earlier in the day. "The rest of the family is here . . . we'll get through this together. What about you, Jake? Are you okay?"

"I'm trying, Momma. It's just hard to believe he's . . . "

Jake was so much like his father, always thoughtful of her feelings in every situation. She knew he would be wondering how much to say to her now. His voice sounded raspy; it was obvious he'd been crying.

"I know it's hard to believe the news," she picked up. "But I'm so thankful you and your dad are together right now." She realized how much more difficult this would've been if Eugene and Jake weren't together.

"Uh, Mom, we're going to have to hang up."

"Oh no, no, don't hang up, please."

"I'm gonna let you talk to Dad one more time."

"Jake, it was so good to hear your voice. You're in my prayers every second of the day."

"You're in mine too, Momma. I love you."

"I love you more, Jake. Be safe."

"Annie," Eugene spoke her name with a great deal of emotion. Even a thousand miles away, she could feel his tenderness toward her. "God's will above all else. Trust Him completely."

"I do, and I will, Eugene. I love you more than you know."

"And I love you."

Immediately the connection was broken, and Annie heard a droning buzz through the receiver. Still, she spoke once more before hanging up. "Come back to me Eugene . . . please come back to me."

Late that night, Annie lay on her side in bed staring at Eugene's empty place. She had refused to go home with her parents, needing to be in this house where she had raised her sons and loved their father. She knew beyond a shadow of doubt that sleep would not come to her tonight, but she didn't care. This night was not meant for sleep, it was meant for suffering. She suffered through every thought, every memory, and every supplication.

Finally, after midnight, Annie got up to get a drink of water. Returning to her bedroom, she noticed a light under Rachel's door. For a moment, she hesitated outside her mother-in-law's room, not wanting to wake her if she'd fallen asleep with the light on. But all of a sudden, Annie didn't want to be alone. Asleep or not, she needed Rachel desperately.

Without knocking, she opened the door quietly. Rachel was sitting in bed and looked up from the Bible in her lap when Annie peeked in. For a moment, neither woman spoke, they simply stared at each other—no words seemed to fit the situation.

Rachel gently threw back the sheet on the other side of her bed. Annie gratefully walked around and slipped in, laying her head on the pillow.

"Your timing is perfect, darlin'. I have something to read to you."

Annie rolled over on her side, gathering the pillow underneath her head.

"And not only that," Rachel began in the fifth chapter of Romans, *"but we also glory in tribulations, knowing that tribulation produces perseverance; and perseverance, character; and character, hope. Now hope does not disappoint, because the love of God has been poured out in our hearts by the Holy Spirit who was given to us."*[10]

Rachel fell silent for a moment, letting the words wash over them. Then she looked intently into Annie's eyes. "Thank God for hope, darlin'."

"Amen," Annie breathed softly.

Rachel closed the Bible in her lap, lightly rubbing her hand over the soft, leather cover.

"Mama?"

"Yes, darlin'?"

"Do we dare hope for Will?" Annie's voice quavered over her son's name.

Rachel reached over and tenderly brushed her hand across Annie's hair. "The Good Book says that we glory in tribulation because it produces perseverance and character, which leads to hope. We shouldn't give up hope."

---

[10] Romans 5:2–6, NKJV.

"But I'm finding it hard to glory in this tribulation."

"Darlin', life is just plain hard; that's all there is to it." Rachel continued caressing Annie's hair as she spoke. "If we persevere through these hard times with character and keep our focus on the Lord, He'll make everything right in the end. That's where our hope lies."

Annie's eyes grew moist wondering if she could keep her focus on what's to come instead of what's happening at this very moment. Her heart and soul were crying out for relief, but nothing seemed to help. How many times today had she heard that *time heals all wounds*? That may very well be the case, but when each second was ticking by agonizingly slowly, statements like that seemed of no use to her.

Rachel set her Bible on the bedside table, then declared with amazing conviction, "Annie, darlin', until they tell us otherwise, I think we should hope for Will's return. We should pray to that end with all our hearts." She flipped back the sheets and got out of bed. "Come on."

Annie got up and knelt beside the bed with Rachel. Together, they lavished their deepest concerns on the Father and cried out for Will's return. Only the Lord understood this mystery of life, and they vowed to trust Him unwaveringly to bring Will home, whether it be now or in the life to come.

Chapter 38

Eugene didn't care how late it was or how tired he felt at the end of the day, he was determined to write Annie a note every single night before he went to sleep. At the end of each week, he mailed all seven notes in one envelope. It had been over five months since Will had been declared missing, and Eugene's heart seemed to ache twenty-four hours a day, seven days a week. Writing to Annie each night gave him a sense of peace he couldn't seem to find during the day.

"Tell her I love her!"

Eugene jabbed his foot against the bedsprings above his head, almost sending Staff Sergeant Winston Porter over the edge. Winston peered over the side of the bunk bed, holding tight to the metal rail.

"Watch it now, Wyatt. I'd never try to steal your girl away." Winston lay back on his bed, locking his hands behind his head. "But Annie sure is a looker."

With that comment, he took another swift kick through the mattress.

"Winston, that's *my* wife you're goin' on about," Eugene said sportingly. "You'll show some respect by calling her Mrs. Wyatt."

Winston Porter had quite a sense of humor and loved to joke around as often as he had an audience. Sometimes it was hard for Eugene to get his note written to Annie because of his jovial bunkmate.

Eugene held his pen still for a moment, trying to regain his previous thought. Just as he presumed it was safe to continue, Winston's head appeared over the side of the bed.

"I just had a great thought. Why don't you send Ann . . . I mean, *Mrs. Wyatt* a picture of me? That way, if anything happens to you in the war, she'll be used to looking at my mug." He flashed Eugene a wily smile. "Come to think of it, as soon as she sees my picture, she'll probably leave you on the spot."

This time, Eugene used both of his feet and sent the staff sergeant flying out of his bunk. Winston was a few years younger than Eugene—small and wiry with cat-quick reflexes. He grabbed the railing of the bunk bed as he was going over, averting a painful fall onto the wooden floor.

Eugene reached out to break the fall, not wishing any harm.

"If you two don't pipe down over there, you're both gonna spend the night in the cold." Master Sergeant Kyle Jarvis was the highest-ranking member of Eugene's twelve-man hutment. He too had a great sense of humor and normally joined in their light-hearted banter, but not tonight. None of the men was looking forward to tomorrow or the next few months for that matter.

"Sorry, Kyle. I think we're squared away now." Eugene turned his sights on his comrade. "Right, Squirrel?"

The staff sergeant stood beside Eugene's bed, grinning from ear to ear and gave his friend a mock salute. "If you say so." Then Winston did his signature move that had earned him his nickname. Standing flat-footed, he leapt from the floor clear up into the top bunk, grabbing the railing on the way over. His leaping ability had earned him fame throughout the regiment, along with his beloved moniker—the Squirrel.

But before Eugene could get back to his note, Winston kidded, "I'm not too young for her you know."

"I mean it, Squirrel," the master sergeant bellowed. "Put a sock in it!"

Eugene chuckled and turned his attention back to Annie's note.

I'm afraid this will be my last letter for quite some time. Tomorrow we start living in the hills and woods around Camp Barkeley. For the next few months, we'll be outdoors most of the time. We're not even allowed fires. My men are in top physical condition now—nearly all of us have gained an extra ten pounds or more. I'm guessing that's mostly muscle since we work out all the time.

Even though I can't write for a bit, I want you to know how much I love you. At night when I look up at the stars, I'll be thinking of you.

Happy New Year, Annie!
Eugene

By the first of April, the men of the 357th Infantry had been living and training primarily outdoors. Eugene and his company of men could cover twenty-five miles in less than eight hours in full army gear, carrying the maximum load of field equipment. Eugene had never dreamed that he would be in such top physical condition at this time in his life. He was proud of his men for the three months of harsh conditions they had endured. Finally, they were allowed back into camp for a reprieve.

Dinner, their first night back in Camp Barkeley, was a grand occasion. Every last man from private to general was fed a juicy steak, a hearty baked potato, and a plateful of brown beans. Eugene savored every bite, not wanting this dinner to end.

"I heard we've got a fifteen-day furlough coming," Squirrel announced over dinner. "Is that right, Jarvis?" he asked.

Master Sergeant Kyle Jarvis stuffed a huge piece of steak in his mouth and nodded his head. As soon as he was able to swallow, he followed up on the Squirrel's comment. "That's right, fellas. We're headin' home in a couple of weeks."

That was the best news Eugene could've imagined. He'd been away for eleven long months and craved a taste of home more than he craved the steak in front of him.

Winston elbowed Eugene in the side. "What do ya say I go home with you, Wyatt? I can't think of a better way to spend my fifteen days."

Eugene laughed. "Not on your life, Squirrel. You're not coming anywhere near Louisville . . . or my wife for that matter." He jabbed his fork into the baked potato and took a long swig of lemonade, then looked over at Winston. "Where *will* you go?"

Squirrel had never married and had no immediate family left. He'd been a bit of a rolling stone, working odd jobs most of his life. But when the army came calling, he immediately found his niche. He had worked hard to move up in the ranks. At the pace he was going, he would probably be a first grade sergeant before summer's end.

"I've got a great-aunt and uncle in Toledo who kind of think of me as a son. I'll probably head up there for some R&R," he said.

All the men around the table excitedly discussed their furlough plans. Each one knew in his heart it would be the last time they'd see home for quite some time unless, by some miracle, the war came to an end. News coming out of Europe and the Pacific made that seem like nothing but wishful thinking. By the time their training was complete, these men would be thrown into the thick of battle. Unlike the first war, there were no friendly shores to land on. No matter where they disembarked, they had to be prepared to do battle on the spot. It was a prospect that Eugene didn't even want to think about.

That night when he crawled into his bunk, Eugene immediately pulled out his writing tablet and pen. He had already spent the evening reading letters from home and couldn't wait to give Annie the news of his furlough. This was a letter he intended to mail first thing in the morning. Mindful that Jake would be on furlough, too, made it almost seem like Christmas in May.

My Sweetest Annie,

I hope everything is going well at home. I received all of your letters, along with Mama's and Claudia's. Even though it was old news, it was new to me. It made for great reading this evening now that we're out of the woods and back in camp. All those letters sure made me homesick, but not for long. I found out tonight that we're getting a fifteen-day furlough starting May 10. Jake and I will both be home all the way through the 24th! I can't tell you how much

I'm looking forward to being with you. I've missed you more than you can imagine. It'll feel so good to be home for a while.

Well, I guess that's about all I can write tonight—I can barely keep my eyes open. They fed us a steak dinner this evening, and it feels awfully good lying on this old mattress for a change.

I love you, sweetheart, and I'll see you soon! You better be waiting!

Your loving husband,
Eugene

***

With every passing window, Annie searched frantically for Eugene and Jake. The train from Texas was packed with servicemen, and the station platform was just as crowded. As soon as the train came to a halt, Annie called out to her parents and Rachel, "Let me know if you see them!"

She stood on her tiptoes, anxiously peering over the crowd. Scene after joyous scene unfolded in front of her, causing a jealous feeling to rise up within. Why couldn't she catch a glimpse—

"Annie!"

She turned sharply and felt her breath catch in her throat. Her gorgeous husband was pushing his way through the thick crowd, waving his cap and smiling. Joyous tears streamed down her cheeks as she squeezed through an opening in the throng, and in a few short seconds, she felt her feet being lifted off the ground. Eugene kissed her longingly, refusing to put her down. Annie tightened her arms around his neck, drowning in his embrace.

When he finally lowered her to the ground, he kissed her again, then opened his arms to Rachel. "Mama, I've missed you so much."

Rachel kissed his cheek, then burst into tears. Eugene smiled compassionately and pulled her into his chest. After a long moment, he released her and was immediately engulfed in Claudia's embrace and then Nathan's.

Annie clung to his arm. "Where's our Jake?"

"I'm not sure; he was four cars behind mine. I only saw him once on the trip."

"Let's go look for him!" Annie exclaimed.

Eugene put a possessive arm around her waist. "No, I think it's better for all of us to wait in one place." He bent and kissed her again. "He'll find us."

As they waited for Jake's appearance, Annie looked up at her husband. His eyes were focused only on her. "You're supposed to be looking for our son, remember?"

"Uh huh," he said, raising his brow and gazing at her more intently.

Annie felt the warmth flooding her cheeks.

"You waited for me," he said playfully.

"Was there any doubt?" she asked with a wry smile.

At that moment, Nathan called Jake's name loudly and started waving.

"Oh, there he is!" Claudia cried, pointing through the crowd.

Jake made his way through the crush of people and straight to his mother. Annie couldn't believe the difference in the boy she now held in her arms. Her son had become a man while he was away. She kissed him as fresh tears flooded her eyes.

"Jake, I can't believe you're really home. I missed you so much."

"You look beautiful, Momma."

Annie laughed through her tears and kissed him again. "Thank you, sweetheart."

Jake spent time with each of his grandparents, so thoughtful and loving toward each one. Annie couldn't get over how much more like Eugene he had become. Just watching him with the family filled her heart with a sorrowful regret that Will could not be here too.

When she looked at Eugene, she knew he had read her mind. His eyes grew moist and he pulled her back into his arms. "I miss him too," he said in a hoarse voice.

"Dinner is waiting at home," Claudia announced. "I hope our two heroes are hungry."

Jake declared that he was starving and put his arm around Claudia's shoulder. She beamed with delight, then asked where his duffle bag was.

"It's right outside the car I was on." He gave her a quick peck on the cheek, then ran back to get it. Eugene went to find his as well.

Annie felt like she was on a wild carnival ride. One minute, her emotions were as high as they could get, and the next, she felt dejected and heartbroken. She realized this reunion was going to be harder than she thought. As much as Annie had looked forward to Eugene's return, all she felt like doing was sobbing in his arms for the son who hadn't come home.

Claudia moved to her daughter's side and held her hand lovingly. "Try to enjoy dinner, honey. I know this is bittersweet."

Annie squeezed her mother's hand but didn't dare look at her. A giant tear slid down her cheek as she took in a long, slow breath. Finally, she managed to say, "I will, Mother. Thank you. Thank you for understanding."

That evening at dinner, Mattie hung around the dining room so she could hear the men tell their stories. Claudia invited her to have a seat, but she merely stood nearby listening attentively.

As much as Eugene was enjoying dinner and family, he couldn't wait to be alone with Annie. He could tell she was having a difficult time with Will's absence, and truth be told, so was he. They just needed time alone to sort through their grief and emotions.

Finally, Nathan wiped his mouth and laid the napkin beside his plate. He looked over at Eugene and Annie sitting side by side. "We have a little surprise for you two. We've made reservations for you at the Brown Hotel for next Friday night. You can take in a movie at the Palace Theater and go out to dinner. You all deserve some time away together."

"Sorry, Jake," Claudia added with a wink. "This is just for your parents."

"No problem," Jake said with a grin.

Annie blushed. "Daddy, thank you so much. That will be nice, won't it, Eugene?"

"Yes, it will. Thank you, Nathan."

"You're quite welcome."

Claudia then spoke up in her usual gracious manner. "As much as I'd love to keep you all here the rest of the night, I'm sure you're anxious to get home." She turned to her husband. "Nate, why don't you take them home now, and we'll see you all at church tomorrow."

That was a blessed thought to Eugene. Home. How many times a day had he thought about being there over the last year?

As the women left the dining room talking and hugging, Nathan came up beside Eugene and lowered his voice. "Is there a timetable for being shipped overseas?"

"Not a definite one," Eugene responded in a hushed voice. "The High Command doesn't want to send our US troops into battle too soon."

"So you'll go back for more training?"

Eugene nodded. "Soon we'll head out to California for desert training and maneuvers."

"I heard they try to simulate battle conditions in training," Nathan commented.

Jake couldn't resist joining in the conversation. "Gramps, we've already been trained with live artillery shot over our heads."

Nathan laid his arm across his grandson's shoulder. "What'd you think about that?"

For a moment, Jake didn't answer. Eugene tried to read his son's expression, curious about what he would say to the terrifying week they'd spent on live maneuvers at Camp Bowie, Texas, back in December.

"It was tough—even knowing the artillery wasn't aimed at us. It was nerve wracking."

"I guess they want to see how you perform under stressful conditions," Nathan commented.

"Yeah, and it was stressful all right," Jake admitted.

Just then, Annie called out from the front room. "Are you all coming?"

Nathan pulled Jake up close to his side and answered his daughter. "We're coming, honey."

"You two go home and relax," he said to Jake and Eugene. "I'm proud of you both."

"Thanks, Gramps." Jake gave his grandfather an appreciative hug, then walked into the front room.

Nathan put his hand out to Eugene and held his gaze unwaveringly. "I just wanted you to know that I'm here for you, Son. If you need to talk about anything, and I mean anything, I'm here."

Eugene felt his throat tighten as he held firmly to his father-in-law's hand. "I appreciate that, Nathan. More than you know."

Nathan grabbed Eugene and pulled him into a tight embrace then let him go. "All right then," he said, clearing his throat and slapping Eugene on the shoulder. "I'll take you out to the farm and see you tomorrow. It's good to have you home."

"It's good to be home," Eugene responded gratefully.

Being back on his farm after such a long absence was like a little taste of heaven as far as Eugene was concerned. The whole family meandered down to the barn together, so Eugene could see the horses. His heart literally flipped over in his chest when he saw Bébé's reaction to the sound of his voice. She threw her head over the stall door, stamping her feet and nickering loudly.

"Yeah, it's me, girl." Eugene reached up to stroke her muzzle, but she threw her head excitedly, demanding that he come into the stall. When Eugene opened the gate, everyone drew close to watch the animated reunion.

Bébé barely let her trainer step inside before she began nudging Eugene's face and chest. And there was nothing gentle about her greeting. Eugene had to brace himself to keep from losing his footing. He couldn't help but laugh as she practically mauled him.

"Settle down, girl, settle down." He reached his arms around her neck then rubbed his hands along her sleek body. "Yeah, I missed you too, Bébé."

Leroy came strolling into the barn and approached the stall to watch Eugene and his mare. "You told me those two were close," he said to Annie, "but I didn't realize how attached she really is."

"Leroy! It's good to see you." Eugene walked out of the stall and took Leroy's hand with gratitude. "Annie's told me what a fine job you've done with the farm."

"It's been my pleasure, Eugene. It's good to have you home for a while."

"Thank you. I'd like to sit down with you sometime tomorrow after church to go over the books, if you don't mind."

"Sounds good," Leroy responded. "I think you'll be pleased with how the cattle plan is working."

Jake came out of Sage's stall and greeted Leroy before they all headed back up to the house. With a little daylight left, they decided to sit out on the porch and talk. Leroy excused himself to his room to start on the latest novel that had arrived in the mail this afternoon.

Eugene took Annie's hand and pulled her into the swing while Rachel and Jake sat down in the rocking chairs. Over the next hour, both men told stories of their adventures living in hills around Camp Barkeley. Eugene was interested to hear some of the clever exploits Jake and his company had pulled off. While he was proud of his son's prowess, it also troubled him. As a sergeant, those were just the kind of achievements Eugene looked for in his men. Such deeds would get a man noticed by the high-level command as an elite soldier. He didn't even want to consider the fact that Jake was about to be shoved into harm's way.

As the sky grew dark, Rachel declared it was past her bedtime. She rose from her chair and walked over to the swing. Eugene got up and gave her a tender hug.

"I'm so glad you're home, Eugene. Even if it's for a short time."

"Thank you, Mama," he said, then kissed her cheek.

Jake got up too and gave his gramma a hug then kissed Annie. "I'm heading to bed too," he said. "I didn't sleep a wink on the train."

Eugene laughed. "I can see why. Your car was so rowdy; I could barely walk through it. I wasn't about to stay back there with that crew."

"I know. I should've come up to your car," he admitted. "Goodnight, everyone."

"Goodnight, sweetheart. I love you," Annie said.

"I love you too, Momma."

He headed across the porch, and just before opening the door, he turned around to face Eugene. Both men pounded their fist on their heart at the same time before Jake disappeared inside.

"What was that all about?" Annie asked, pressing closer to her husband's side.

"That's how two soldiers say *I love you.*"

Eugene put his arm around Annie, and she laid her head on his shoulder. He reached for her other hand, lacing his fingers through hers. For a while, they sat in silence as he gently rocked the swing back and forth. He'd waited so long to have her all to himself, and she felt so good. But all evening they had tiptoed around their mutual heartache. Down deep, he realized this was probably going to be a very long night.

Finally, he made the decision to break through the silence. "Annie—"

"Wait, Eugene," she interrupted. "I think I need to tell you the advice my mother gave me before I left tonight."

Annie let go of his hand and sat up a little straighter. "She told me to save our talking for tomorrow."

"But, sweetheart, if you need—"

Annie put her hand over his lips. "Hush, Eugene," she demanded impishly. "My mother is a wise woman."

Eugene looked into his wife's eyes and wondered how he could love a woman more deeply than he loved Annie right now. A slow smile played across his lips as she released her hand from his mouth. He traced the outline of her jaw with his thumb then found the dimple in her cheek that he could so seldom resist.

"Remind me to thank your mother tomorrow at church."

Annie laughed and pulled him to his feet. "Not on your life, Eugene. Not on your life!"

***

After the Sunday worship service, Eugene felt like he'd had ten pounds hugged right off of him. Nearly every member wanted to show appreciation to the two men on furlough from the 357th. Miss Ruby's embrace was an experience all to itself. She wrapped him in a tight cocoon that made him thankful for his freedom when she finally let go. One thing was certain, if Miss Ruby loved you, she did so with every fiber of her being.

When the whole family came together in the churchyard, Annie told her mother that she and Eugene would be late coming out to the house for lunch.

"If you don't mind, Mother, there's somewhere I want to go with Eugene first."

"Honey, we'll hold lunch until you arrive. That won't be a problem."

Annie glanced briefly at Eugene, then back to Claudia. "If we're not there in thirty minutes, go on without us. We'll be there as soon as we can. Mama and Jake will need to ride out to the house with you."

Eugene's curiosity was piqued, and he started to ask her where they were going. But when he saw Annie's expression, he decided to wait patiently for her to explain. She didn't seem to be in a hurry to leave; as a matter of fact, they were the last ones still in the churchyard when Annie took his hand.

"Walk with me."

Eugene smiled. "I thought you'd never ask."

She led him across the highway onto the old church property. He was fully aware that this wasn't just a Sunday stroll; there was intent in every stride. Annie led him onto the old foundation to a low wall of stones underneath a spreading mimosa tree. Something about this place was soothing.

Annie sat down on the wall and gently pulled him down beside her. "Close your eyes," she said softly.

He didn't hesitate to do her bidding. She reached across him and pressed his right hand to the wall, then said, "You can open them."

Eugene's eyes opened, and at first, he gazed only at Annie. Her eyes glistened with tears when she told him to lift his hand. Slowly he raised his hand from the stone and felt a sudden warmth pulse through his entire body.

"Will," he breathed.

Annie reached across him, and together they laid their hands over their son's name. That one act was his undoing. He had held back his emotions far too long. When the tears finally came, they came in torrents. He reached for Annie and pulled her roughly into his arms, and together they released their worst dread—their deepest fear—in agonizing sobs.

"I'm sorry, Annie," he cried. "I'm so sorry."

The pain of losing his eldest son was almost unbearable. He felt cursed by the very God he loved. His life would never again be free of pain or sorrow.

At long last, Eugene let out a sigh in the form of a groan. He wanted desperately to be strong for Annie but feared he had only caused her further grief with his breakdown. Slowly he loosened his hold to reach into his back pocket for a handkerchief. Despite the fact that he needed it, he offered it to Annie.

"Thank you," she muttered. "I miss him so much, Eugene."

Looking down at Will's name etched in stone brought fresh tears to his eyes. Eugene quickly looked away in order to gain some semblance of composure. He wiped his hands across his wet face. "I miss him too . . . all the time."

"Do you think there's still a chance?" Annie looked deeply into his eyes. He knew she was still hanging on to hope. But he had spent years in the army—and not just in the army, but in actual war. He was surprised they still had his son listed as missing in action when it was relatively certain that that was no longer his status.

Eugene didn't know whether to share such information with Annie or not. If he told her to accept the fact that Will wasn't coming home, she would be devastatingly crushed. But as long as she held on to that hope, she would never be able to move on. He searched his soul for the right response.

"Annie, I . . ." he hesitated, realizing he was about to tell her the harsh reality. Instead, he cradled her face in his hands and simply said, "I don't know."

He drew her forehead to his lips for a long moment, not wishing to look into her eyes. He felt certain that those beautiful, blue eyes would be able to read the truth in his.

Annie and Eugene ended up missing lunch at the Harrisons' altogether. They spent the afternoon reminiscing over Will's life, taking turns telling story after story. Some of them brought joyous laughter while others brought them back to tears. They walked the property and talked but never strayed far from the etched stone. At one point, they sat in the grass beneath the mimosa tree, holding hands and praying.

Finally Annie said, "I can go now."

"Are you sure? I'll stay until dark if you want to."

She gave him an affectionate smile, then brushed a gentle kiss on his lips. "I'm afraid our mothers would have the police out looking for us by then. I can go if you're ready."

Eugene nodded and pulled her to her feet. Before leaving, they walked over to the stone one more time. Once again, they laid a hand over Will's name, each one covering half—one hand of finality the other of hope. Then they turned and walked away, hand in hand.

Chapter 39

September 1943

Autumn had always been Annie's favorite time of year. The air somehow seemed cleaner—the beautiful vistas of red and gold felt redemptive. Josiah took the trail over the ridge with an agility that she had long admired. Ever since her sweet Gracie had gone blind at the ripe old age of thirty-three, Josiah had been her mount of choice. As much as she loved him, no horse would ever again take Gracie's place in her heart. Annie dreaded the day when Gracie's stall would stand empty.

Arriving at the Crowleys' farm, Annie took Josiah into the stables, waving to Wendall's trainers. She tethered her horse beside a bucket of water and untied the pouch from her saddle, holding it up to her nose. The smell of Rachel's raisin bread, fresh out of the oven, was heavenly. She hoped it would bring good cheer to Mrs. Crowley who had fallen last month, breaking her hip. Marcella had only been home from the hospital for two days and was completely bedridden.

"Mrs. Wyatt, please come in." Mr. Crowley held the door wide for Annie to enter their sprawling ranch-style home. Before closing the door, he took a step outside. "So you rode down today?"

"I couldn't stand the thought of driving the car on a gorgeous day like this."

Mr. Crowley gave her an approving smile.

"How is Mrs. Crowley today?" she asked with concern.

"I'm afraid she's still in a lot of pain. Of course they gave her some pills for that sort of thing, but do you think she would take them?" His exasperation was apparent.

Annie reached out and gave his arm a sympathetic pat. "I'm sorry, Mr. Crowley. Do you want me to see what I can do?" Annie had known her neighbor for more than twenty years. Marcella was a wonderful lady, but often headstrong, much to Wendall's chagrin.

"You're welcome to give it a go. I suppose it wouldn't hurt."

He led the way through their rich, paneled living room and down a long hall past Mr. Crowley's study. "We've got her set up in our guest room since it's the easiest room to get to."

The door was open, and Wendall stepped back for Annie to enter. "Marcella, you have a visitor," he announced.

A bright smile spread across her weathered features, but Annie glimpsed the pain in her neighbor's eyes. "What a pleasant surprise," Marcella said. "Can you believe this awful situation I got myself into?"

"I'm so sorry about your accident. I know how frustrating this must be for you."

Marcella gave her husband a deprecating glance, then looked back at Annie. "Mr. Crowley thinks I should never ride again. But we'll see about that."

Wendall seemed put out with such talk and told the women that he would be in his study if they should need him.

Annie almost forgot about the bread in her hand. "Oh, Mr. Crowley, this is for you and Mrs. Crowley. It's a loaf of Rachel's raisin bread. You may want to cut a slice now while it's still warm."

He gratefully accepted the bread as if it was the only thing that had given him pleasure in quite some time. "I think I will. Was Miss Rachel not able to join you today?"

"I'll bring her by tomorrow. She and my mother were visiting another lady from our church who's quite ill."

Wendall tilted his long neck toward her, then thoughtfully asked his wife if she would care for a slice of bread.

"Not right now," she said. "I'll let you know."

Wendall bowed his head again in submission and left the room.

Annie took a seat by Mrs. Crowley's bed and covered her hand. "Are you in much pain?"

With a loud exhale, Marcella admitted that the pain was terrible.

"Did the doctors give you something for it?" Annie prodded.

"Well yes, but it makes me drowsy. If I took it I'd be sleeping my life away."

"Marcella, I'm no doctor, but I think if you'd take the medicine, at least at night, you'd be able to sleep without pain and get well sooner. Besides, it looked like your husband had dark circles under his eyes."

Marcella laughed. "He always looks like that, my dear."

Annie smiled inwardly. "I tell you what, why don't we make a deal? If you'll agree to take your pain medication at night, I'll talk to Mr. Crowley about letting you ride again once your hip is healed."

A sly look came into Marcella's gray eyes. She laid her index finger over her mouth and tapped her lips. "You'd really do that for me, dear?"

"Absolutely. But you have to keep your end of the bargain."

Marcella thought about it for a moment and slowly nodded her head. "Then I'll do it."

"That's the spirit," Annie said exuberantly. "I'll bring Rachel back out tomorrow afternoon to check on you."

Annie rose from her chair and planted a light kiss on Marcella's forehead. "If you need anything, don't hesitate to call." She noticed the phone beside her neighbor's bed and hoped she knew how serious she was about the offer. The

Crowleys had always been such good neighbors, and Annie wanted to return the favor in their time of need.

"Thank you for dropping by, dear. And Annie?"

Annie hesitated at the foot of Marcella's bed. "Yes?"

"Tell Wendall on your way out that I'll do it for *you*."

"Now, Mrs. Crowley," Annie chided, "you'd better tell Wendall you're doing it for *him*. We're trying to get him to let you ride again, remember?"

Marcella's eyes narrowed as if she was part of a major conspiracy. "Right you are."

Annie giggled and blew her a kiss, then headed down the hall. Mr. Crowley wasn't in his study, so she decided to try the kitchen. Sure enough, Wendall was sitting at the kitchen table enjoying a rather large chunk of raisin bread.

"Come join me, young lady." He stood and held out a chair. "Would you like a piece of your mother-in-law's delicious bread?"

"Oh, no thank you. You and Mrs. Crowley enjoy that loaf. There's plenty more where that came from."

Mr. Crowley smiled graciously, then asked what news there was from Eugene and Jake.

"They're heading out to California in a couple of weeks for desert training. Eugene said they'll be living in tents out there for about a month."

"I admire your husband greatly," Wendall told her. "Mrs. Crowley and I are praying every day for him and your youngest."

Annie felt a melancholy befall her spirit. She sat up a little straighter, willing it into submission. She needed to focus on the beautiful fall day the Lord had provided.

"Thank you, Mr. Crowley. That means so much to all of us."

"I'm glad they were able to come home back in May. Any chance they'll get furlough for Christmas?"

"Not likely. It's possible they'll go overseas after they leave California." Suddenly, Annie felt herself losing composure. She needed to change the subject before she embarrassed herself.

Forcing a smile, she declared, "Mrs. Crowley may be ready to take her pain medication tonight."

Wendall raised his brow. "You don't say?"

"Yes, and I think you should take her a slice of raisin bread. That should lift her spirits a bit."

Mr. Crowley gave her a knowing smile and cut off a generous slice for his wife.

Annie rose to her feet, needing to get back outside and breathe in the fresh autumn air. Something was stirring deep within her soul—something troubling. Even though it was a spacious kitchen, the walls seemed to be closing in on her.

"Mr. Crowley, it was good to see you," she managed to utter. "I'll bring Rachel out tomorrow afternoon if that's okay."

She barely waited for Wendall's response before heading to the front door. He had to quicken his stride to catch up and hold the door for her.

"Please thank her for the bread," he said. "Have a nice ride."

"Thank you," she called, heading across the yard to the stables as fast as she dared without appearing to be rude.

***

"Claudia, thank you so much for picking me up," Rachel told her dear friend. "Why don't you come in for a while?"

"I'd love to." Claudia parked the car in front of the house. "I wonder if Annie is in?"

"Highly doubtful. That girl only comes inside when she has to."

Claudia laughed as she came around the car and took Rachel's arm. "Some things never change."

As the women entered the house, they realized immediately that they were not alone. Claudia definitely thought she heard a noise at the back of the house and commented on it to Rachel. "Do you think Leroy is in his room?"

"Not at this time of day, but maybe we should check."

Leroy's door was standing open at the back of the kitchen, and Claudia's heart sank as she recognized the sound of her daughter crying. As soon as she and Rachel stepped into the back room, Annie came up off the bed and threw herself into her mother's arms. Claudia pulled her to her breast and took Annie's anguish upon herself without question.

Rachel quietly sat down on the edge of the bed and picked up the telegram Annie had dropped—a telegram that read:

> THE AIR FORCE DEPARTMENT DEEPLY REGRETS TO INFORM YOU THAT THE STATUS OF YOUR SON CORPORAL WILLIAM FRANKLIN WYATT PREVIOUSLY LISTED AS MIA HAS BEEN CHANGED TO KILLED IN ACTION IN THE PERFORMANCE OF HIS DUTY AND IN THE SERVICE OF HIS COUNTRY ON 24 AUGUST 1942. THE DEPARTMENT EXTENDS TO YOU ITS SINCEREST SYMPATHY IN YOUR GREAT LOSS. ON ACCOUNT OF EXISTING CONDITIONS THE BODY IF RECOVERED CANNOT BE RETURNED AT PRESENT. IF FURTHER DETAILS ARE RECEIVED YOU WILL BE INFORMED. TO PREVENT POSSIBLE AID TO OUR ENEMIES PLEASE DO NOT DIVULGE THE NAME OF HIS AIRCRAFT OR STATION.

Claudia noticed Rachel begin to weep as she read the telegram. She squeezed her eyes shut, unable to watch. It was more than she could bear, and she still had no idea what it said. Annie was so distraught; she was unable to even communicate. But her daughter had been sitting in Will's old room—there was a baseball on the bed. *Oh God,* she cried inwardly, *help us. They must have found our boy.*

At that thought, a violent sob shuddered through her body. Rachel came to their side and gently led them to the bed. Claudia was thankful; her knees suddenly felt so weak.

After a long moment, Rachel gained her composure. "Annie, darlin', I'm so sorry."

Annie sat up out of her mother's arms and went into Rachel's. "No, I'm sorry I fell apart like that. I thought I could work through this alone before I had to share it with anyone."

Claudia swept Annie's hair from her face and kissed her. "And then you saw *me*."

Annie breathed deeply reaching for her mother's hand. "And then I saw *you*."

"Rachel, may I see the telegram?" Claudia asked. A new batch of tears formed in her eyes as she read the words on the light yellow paper. *Killed in action in the performance of duty* . . . those were devastating words.

She looked up from the telegram and let out a languid sigh. "How will we ever tell your father?"

That evening after a light supper, no one wanted to turn on the radio and listen to the latest news of the war. It was too depressing. Claudia and Rachel sat together on the porch while Nathan took his daughter up on the ridge to talk.

Deep in thought, Claudia sipped her iced tea then set the glass on a small table between her chair and Rachel's. "I never dreamed life would be this hard, did you?"

Rachel looked earnestly into her eyes. "Claudia," she said softly, "I've known life was hard since I was a child. I was born a slave."

Claudia felt a wave of shame pulse through her veins. "Oh my sweet friend, I'm so sorry I said that. Of course you've known hardships I could never imagine."

Rachel gave her a sympathetic smile. "It's all right, I don't want you to feel bad about what you said. I don't think of it often; it was such a long time ago. But I still remember how it felt as if it were yesterday." She straightened in her chair a bit, and her eyes crinkled at the corners. "Sometimes I witness acts today that make me feel like it hasn't yet ended."

Claudia didn't know what to say. Her heart felt heavy for the hatred and ignorance that permeated the society in which they lived.

After a short pause, Rachel said, "That's why I've never felt comfortable in this world. This is not my home."

What an amazing woman, her dearest friend. Born into slavery, motherless, rejected by her true father, brutally attacked because of her marriage, widowed, and now enduring the loss of a grandson.

"Rachel," Claudia said her name with deep admiration. "I'm so thankful for you."

"And I, you."

Both women sipped their tea in silence for quite some time until Rachel expressed her concern for Annie. "I'm worried about her. She's always relied so heavily on Eugene, and now he's not here to help her through this."

"Oh Rachel, I pray fervently night and day for this war to end, so he can come home. I think right now we *all* need closure," Claudia admitted. "We've been in limbo for so long with our dear Will. I just can't believe it's final."

Rachel brushed away a tear that had strayed down her cheek. "A memorial service will help."

Claudia agreed. The only way Annie or any of them could move ahead would be to have a memorial service for Will. The Oak Hill congregation had already been through one such memorial this year for a fallen serviceman. But that was different. There had been a body.

Just then, Claudia noticed Nathan and Annie walking hand in hand through the yard. She hoped their time alone had brought healing. She herself already felt stronger from spending this time with Rachel.

Father and daughter ascended the porch steps and sat down together on the swing. Nathan put his arm on the back of the swing, and Annie laid her head on his shoulder.

Claudia was overwhelmed by the intensity of her love for these two. Yes, life was hard, but God had given her a faithful husband and an amazing daughter to walk by her side. Together, with the help of their heavenly Father, they would find a way to deal with Will's tragic death.

"Honey," Claudia said, addressing Annie. "Rachel and I have been talking. We think there needs to be a memorial service for Will soon."

She was fairly taken aback by her daughter's reaction. Annie sat straight up and shook her head. "That would make it final."

"Well, yes, honey. We need to celebrate Will's life and find closure."

Annie looked at her father. "Do you agree with that?"

Nathan didn't speak; he simply nodded his head.

"Mama?" she inquired of Rachel.

"Yes, darlin'. I agree."

Annie's agitation was palpable. Claudia searched her heart for what to say that could help her daughter. But Annie didn't give her the chance. She got up from the swing and briskly walked into the house. A moment later she returned, clutching the yellow telegram. All three of them watched her descend the porch steps and stride out into the yard.

Claudia rose to her feet but Nathan spoke a word of admonishment. "No, Claudia, let her go. She's trying to work this out in her mind."

He held out his hand, inviting her to join him. While she desperately wanted to be with her daughter, Claudia conceded to her husband's request. He was right. Annie's independent spirit was now taking control. It was the only way she could function without Eugene in the picture.

Taking Nate's hand, she sat down at his side, praying silently for the Spirit to take control of Annie's thoughts. It was obvious by looking at her that there was a terrible battle going on inside of her. Annie disappeared around the back of the house for quite some time. It was all Claudia could do to stay where she was.

Nathan must have sensed her dilemma as he put his arm around her shoulder and held her close.

At long last, Annie came back around the house and joined them on the porch. Sitting down in the chair Claudia had vacated, she drew in a long breath. "You're right, we need to have a service for Will," she said matter-of-factly.

Nathan let go of Claudia and leaned forward putting his elbows on his knees. "Annie, I'll pay for a marker. There's space near Franklin."

Annie looked incredulous. "No. No marker. We'll have the service, but there will be no marker."

Claudia felt a stab of pain in her chest. "Honey, we want to have a marker to honor Will's memory. Please let us do that for you . . . for all of us."

Annie got up again and paced the length of the porch, then slowly made her way back to the chair. Her tone was firm but respectful. "I need all of you to hear what I'm saying, and I don't want to hurt your feelings. I can do the memorial service to help you find closure, but I simply cannot have a marker put up. I don't know how to say it any other way."

Claudia had no idea what was going on in Annie's head. Clearly, she was wrestling with her emotions. Who could blame her—she'd just been told that her son had been killed in action. Claudia's heart went out to her precious child. "Honey, of course. We'll do whatever is best for you in this situation. I'm just so sorry we have to make plans like this in the first place."

Annie seemed to visibly relax, especially when her father and Rachel agreed to her terms. They spent the next several minutes sharing memories of Will and making plans for his service. Although Claudia didn't understand Annie's reluctance to put up a marker, she felt certain that, in time, she would change her mind. She wondered if she should take the telegram home with her. Perhaps having it out of sight and out of reach would be of help.

No longer able to restrain herself, Claudia got up and went to her daughter. Annie stood and released the telegram on the table as she went into her mother's arms.

"I love you so much," Claudia spoke softly. "And I—"

Claudia's next thought came to an abrupt halt as she caught sight of the telegram on the table. If there was any doubt about what her daughter had been thinking earlier, there certainly was none now. While Annie had walked alone in the yard, she had torn the thin yellow paper to shreds. No wonder she didn't want a marker—she still believed her son was coming home.

The next afternoon, Annie walked along the row of stalls in Mr. Crowley's stable and admired some of his fine horses. She had brought Rachel to see Marcella but didn't have the heart to go inside. For some reason, Annie felt she needed a few minutes to herself before checking on Mrs. Crowley.

After greeting one of Wendall's trainers, Annie wandered outside and sat down on a bench in the shade underneath the eaves of the stable. Her neighbor owned such a beautiful farm. Colorful maples stood guard around the house while pristine, white fences ran with the ebb and flow of the Kentucky hills. Annie felt so torn inside. Half of her wanted to praise God for the sight before her while the other half floundered in immense anguish.

As soon as she made the decision to join the others, Mr. Crowley walked outside and waved to her. Annie waved back and watched him saunter across the yard in her direction.

"Hello, young lady," he said as he sat down beside her and stretched out his lanky legs. "I see you're taking in the fresh air this afternoon."

"Good afternoon, Mr. Crowley." She gave him a somber smile. "I was just about to come inside to see how your wife's getting along."

Wendall displayed a wily expression. "I don't know about *her*, but I got a full night's sleep last night."

That made Annie laugh. "Well, congratulations. She must have taken her pain medication."

"Indeed she did," he remarked cheerfully.

For a moment, Mr. Crowley grew quiet, and his demeanor changed to one of concern. He pulled his legs in and placed his creased hands on his knees. "Miss Rachel told my wife about the telegram you received yesterday. I wanted to tell you how sorry I am and that I feel your loss as well."

Annie felt warm tears fill her eyes. Mr. Crowley's expression of sympathy was so touching. "Thank you," she said quietly. "It came unexpectedly, but then again . . ." She looked away, "I guess I should've been expecting it."

The two neighbors lingered through a long silence for which Annie was grateful. She hadn't anticipated getting so emotional with Mr. Crowley. But sitting here next to him, she could literally feel his compassion.

"You know," he said, "your Will was something else. I imagine he never told you about the time I almost ran over him on the road, did he?"

Annie noticed the twinkle in Mr. Crowley's moist eyes.

"No," she said in surprise.

"Goodness, it was probably ten years ago. He came flying around the bend on our road, riding Comanche like he was being chased by wild Indians. He looked like he was madder than a hornet. He's lucky I didn't hit him with my truck."

"What on earth was he doing?" she asked.

"Come to think of it, I never asked him. But he came with me down to the barn to get Comanche cooled off. He'd worked him into a terrible lather."

Annie knew it had to be one of Will's angry moods. "I'm sorry about that," she offered.

"Oh no, I didn't tell you that to get an apology. I wanted to tell you because I saw what a good and respectful young man he was. Why, I lectured that boy up and down for over half an hour on proper horse care—even sprayed him with cold water—and he didn't do anything except listen politely and say 'yes, sir.' He even thanked me when I sent him on his way."

That brought a smile to Annie's face.

"Mrs. Wyatt." He looked earnestly into her eyes. "You raised a mighty fine son. He had a genuine heart, and that's what matters most."

Annie took in a shuddering breath. "Oh Mr. Crowley, you have no idea how much that means to me."

Wendall pressed his lips together, then looked away. Annie noticed him reach up to wipe a tear from his cheek.

"Well now," he said standing up, "would you like to go in and see our model patient?"

Annie breathed deeply and stood up beside her neighbor. "I'd love to."

Mr. Crowley surprisingly offered her his arm, and Annie took it, enjoying the leisurely pace across the yard with her kind neighbor. Something was stirring within her spirit, and she wasn't quite sure what it was. But for now, she would be thankful for her neighbor's affirmation of Will's genuine heart.

Chapter 40

The memorial service for Corporal William Franklin Wyatt packed Oak Hill Church beyond its limit. There was an overflow crowd standing in the lobby. Not only had the church members come out in numbers, but many community friends had also come to show their respect for the Wyatts and the Harrisons and Rachel Hawkins. Annie was amazed and overwhelmed by their demonstration of love and support.

Throughout the service, she had caught her mother's watchful eye on her. Annie felt certain Claudia was looking for signs of grief, but for some unexplained reason, grief was not what was filling her soul. While her heart *was* heavy, there was still a small flame burning somewhere deep within her—a flicker of hope that couldn't be extinguished. In Annie's mind, it didn't make sense why she couldn't accept what everyone else around her had. But this was not a matter of the mind—it was a matter of the heart.

At the end of the memorial service, two officers from the Great War came to the front and slowly unfurled the American flag while two other soldiers stood at attention. When the flag was on full display, the soldiers brought their hands slowly into a salute then gradually lowered their arms back to their sides. The flag was then methodically folded back into a triangle and handed to Annie with deep reverence. That gallant gesture had caused her momentarily to lose composure. Nathan put a protective arm around her shoulders and held her tightly against his side.

Afterwards, the family walked outside and received each person with warmth and thanks. Annie's gaze frequently wandered to the old property across the highway. It was all she could do not to make a mad dash over to Will's stone. What immense comfort she would find there. If only Eugene were at her side . . .

Suddenly, Annie's attention was drawn back into sharp focus as her dear friend, Deborah Garrett, lavished words of sympathy upon her. She and Deborah had grown up in this church together, sharing the same love of horses and adventure. Her friend now lived in New York working for *Outdoor Life* magazine. Every time the two were together, it seemed like they had never been apart, even though their paths in life had taken them in two very different directions.

"What was that you were saying?" Annie asked.

"I was wondering if you'd like to accompany me to Abilene? I'm going down to spend time with my younger sister and maybe you could see Eugene and Jake before they ship out to California."

Annie's heart quickened. "When are you going? Eugene told me they leave on October 21."

"I'm leaving this Friday, the fifteenth. If you don't mind a couple of stops along the way for my editor, we can be down there on Monday. That would give you time to see your men before they go."

Annie glanced over at her family and wondered what they would think of her taking off across the country for more than a week. But if it gave her one more chance to see Eugene and Jake before they left the country, it would be worth it. Still she hesitated.

"I don't know. There's so much to do on the farm with everyone gone."

"Annie, my love, it's time for you to get away." Deborah took hold of her shoulders and looked her square in the eyes. "I would love nothing more than to have you by my side on this road trip. It would be just like old times."

Smiling soberly, Annie mulled it over in her mind. It truly would feel good to get away for a while. It seemed like she'd been melancholy for so long.

"Let me think about it and talk it over with my family first. Are you staying at your mother's?"

"Uh huh, you can reach me there."

"When's the latest I can let you know?"

Deborah grinned and raised her brow. "I'll give you two more minutes."

"You're afraid I'll talk myself out of it?"

"Annie, dearest, Eugene and Jake are waiting for you. What's to think about?"

Feeling an overwhelming need to get away, Annie came to a quick decision. "You're right. I need to see them both . . . I'll do it!"

Deborah gave her an encouraging embrace. "That's the spirit. I'll pick you up Friday morning at seven. Oh, and before I forget, you'd better wear trousers the first couple of days. We're going to have an adventure in Tennessee and Arkansas!"

Annie closed her eyes and laughed softly. "Thank you for this, Deb."

A slow smile crept across her friend's sweet face. "My pleasure, Annie." And then she added sympathetically, "I'm really sorry about Will. My heart is breaking for you and your family."

"Thank you, Deborah. That means so much."

Friday morning came sooner than Annie had anticipated, and she was still running around the house trying to make sure everything was done.

"Darlin', calm down. We can take care of this place without you for a while." Rachel was getting tired just watching her.

"I know, I know. It's just that I don't want to leave you with so much to do."

Rachel reached out and grabbed Annie's arm as she whizzed by her in the kitchen for the third time. "Is your suitcase packed?"

"Yes," Annie answered breathlessly.

"Did you remember the blue dress that Eugene likes so much?"

"Yes."

"Then stop your rushing about. I guarantee everything is going to be fine around here. Your father has promised to come out every day to check on things."

"Speaking of my father," Annie said, finally standing still for a change. "He wasn't too keen on the idea of me going on this trip."

A horn sounded in front of the house, and Annie's nervous energy sprang back to life. Rachel headed out onto the porch and waved to Deborah, who was lifting the trunk of her blue Plymouth.

"I hope you girls have a safe journey," she called.

"Thank you, Mrs. Hawkins." Deborah climbed the porch steps in her neat brown trousers, white blouse, and sporty boots. "I'm so excited Annie is going with me. I wasn't looking forward to such a long, boring drive by myself."

Annie looked flustered as she came out onto the porch with her suitcase. Compared to Deborah's calm demeanor, the two were quite a contrast.

Deborah laughed and reached for the suitcase. "You look like you've never been on a trip before."

"It's been a long time," Annie admitted.

While Deborah stored the suitcase in her trunk, Rachel reached out to her daughter-in-law with a warm embrace. "Annie, darlin'?"

"Yes?" Annie said as she pulled away.

"I need you to do me a favor."

"Anything, Mama. What is it?"

"Please give Eugene and Jake a hug and kiss for me, and tell them how much I love them."

"I will," Annie promised.

"And one other thing," Rachel said with a gleam in her eye. "Have fun!"

Annie grinned, displaying the dimple in her cheek.

"I mean it, darlin'. Let this be a time of renewal for you. Don't worry about anything at home. I promise, we'll all be fine."

Annie leaned in and kissed her cheek affectionately. "Thank you, Mama. I love you."

"I love you too, darlin'."

Rachel stood on the porch, watching and waving until the blue Plymouth drove out of sight. She would pray Annie and Deborah all the way to Texas and back. Even though Nathan had voiced reservations about two women *traipsing* across the country alone, Rachel felt certain this was just the experience Annie needed to bolster her spirits. For goodness sakes, if she were twenty years younger herself, she might just go with them.

Rachel turned and walked into the house with a little spring in her step. Annie had always been so full of life and joy, but not lately. It had been difficult to watch her daughter-in-law slip into a state of sadness and despair. She hoped and prayed that a change of scenery and the chance to see Eugene and Jake would lift her dear girl out of the dark pit she had fallen into.

***

It was mid-afternoon when Deborah and Annie made it to their first destination just outside of Memphis, Tennessee. Deborah's editor had asked her to check in with a man who owned an alligator farm in a swamp near the Mississippi River. It was an unlikely location for such a farm so far north, but the transplanted Louisiana native had brought his first pair of gators up from his home state nearly twenty years ago. At present, he tended over one hundred of the gnarly-looking reptiles on his farm.

Lester Timmons gave the two women a quick tour of his place. Annie was none too thrilled about crossing a narrow footbridge over the swamp with dozens of creepy eyes peering out of the water. They spent an hour with Timmons, listening to tales of alligator escapes and daring rescues. Then, the two spent a night in a motel, just outside of Memphis.

The next morning after breakfast, Deborah warned Annie about their second stop. "We're heading up into the Ozark mountains near Harrison, Arkansas. I have a story to do about the hog-hunting women of Boone County."

"What in the world!" Annie exclaimed.

Deborah rolled her window down, letting the autumn air whip through the car. She swept her dark hair out of her face while keeping one hand on the wheel. "I don't know what we're getting into. Somehow my editor found out about these women up in the mountains whose men were all called into the army, so they decided to take care of their families by hunting wild hogs."

"And you plan to interview these women?"

"Well," Deborah looked over with a sheepish grin, "it may be more than an interview."

"You mean we're going hunting with them?" Annie asked in surprise, then noticed her friend's mischievous expression. "We are, aren't we?"

Deborah laughed gleefully. "Yes, we are! And I haven't told you the best part yet—they hunt for hogs at night."

Annie's eyes grew wide. "You mean to tell me we'll be running around in the dark woods with a bunch of women carrying shotguns?"

"Don't forget about the wild hogs!"

Annie screamed, sending Deborah into a fit of laughter.

"You never dreamed it would be this much fun, did you?"

"Oh Deb," Annie let out a satisfying sigh, "it's been such a long time since I've felt so carefree." She turned to her dear friend with gratitude in her heart. "Thank you for bringing me along. I needed this."

"You're welcome," Deborah said with a quick glance, but then she added, "I hope you're still thanking me after tonight."

Annie laughed and rolled her window down too. The breeze in her face felt invigorating, the cares of the world seemed so far away.

A few miles ticked by before Annie picked up the conversation. "Deb, do you ever regret not getting married?"

Deborah pressed her lips together for a moment, then answered, "Not really. Don't get me wrong; there was a time when I came close, which you know about, of course. But when I think about it now, I'm really thankful I didn't marry. Any man in my life now I would've lost to this terrible war."

Annie felt a painful twinge rush through her heart.

"Oh, Annie love, I am so sorry I said that." Deborah reached over and grabbed Annie's hand. "Please forgive me for that. My quick tongue gets me into more trouble."

"For which your mother was always chastising you." Annie gave Deb's hand a reassuring squeeze. "It's all right. You were just saying what you feel."

"Still, it was insensitive of me."

Deborah put both hands on the steering wheel and stared intently at the winding Arkansas highway. "I admire you so much, you know."

Annie turned in the seat to face her dear friend. "For what?"

"For the decision you made to marry Eugene. Benjamin would've taken you all over the world, given you a fancy house and cars. But you had the guts to turn it all down and follow your heart." Deborah briefly looked at Annie through misty eyes. "I wasn't brave enough to do it. When I told you I don't regret being single, that's not completely true. There are times I feel desperately lonely and wish my life had turned out differently."

Annie's heart went out to her friend. "It's not too late, you know."

Deb took in a deep breath and let it out slowly. "I know. But it's too late for Ted."

"Oh," Annie said softly. "So he still holds your heart?"

"Pretty much. So you see, girlfriend, I haven't really given myself a chance with any other man since I left college."

Annie contemplated Deborah's exciting life in New York with a magazine job that had her traveling all over the country. Her friend's life had always seemed like such an adventure. She never dreamed that behind that self-assured exterior dwelt a lonesome spirit, full of regret.

"You know I saw him a couple of years ago. We ran into each other when I was home visiting Mom."

"What was he like?" Annie asked curiously.

"Same old Ted—handsome as ever. But I knew when I looked in his eyes . . . the love was gone."

This time, Annie laid a gentle hand on Deb's arm. But she shrugged her shoulders and put on a lighthearted bravado. "It's okay. I made my bed a long time ago." She let out a soft laugh. "I just wish I'd made it with Ted."

After a while, the two got off on the subject of their high-school adventures, and the time flew by along with the miles. Ironically, they stopped for a late lunch at the Hog Call Café just outside of Harrison. The owner of the diner drew a map for Deborah on a napkin, detailing the twisting back roads through the Ozarks. He knew exactly who Cornelia Baggett and her hog-hunting companions were.

"They're practically legendary 'round these parts," he said. "As a matter of fact, Cornelia and her bunch keep me in pork year round."

Deborah smiled enthusiastically. "We're supposed to go hunting with them tonight."

"Oh dear," was all the man said before heading back into the kitchen.

Annie and Deborah briefly looked at each other in shock, then burst out laughing.

"I think you're definitely going to get a story out of this," Annie told her friend.

Cornelia Baggett was nothing like Annie or Deborah had pictured. The five foot two bundle of energy swept out of her house with a toddler on her hip and a young child hanging onto her skirt. One more child stood in the doorway to their small log house, which was butted right up next to the mountain.

Deborah approached the feisty woman with her hand outstretched. "Mrs. Baggett?"

"In the flesh." Cornelia's backwoods accent easily turned the word flesh into two-syllables.

"I'm Deborah Garrett, reporter for *Outdoor Life*. It's so nice of you to allow me to do a story on you and your . . . uh, colleagues."

"Well, we never had us a reporter come all the way from New York to do no story before. That's fer sure." Cornelia flipped her long, auburn braid off her shoulder and adjusted the child on her hip. "And who'd ya bring with ya?"

"Oh, this is my friend, Annie Wyatt, from Louisville. She'll be going along with us if that's okay."

"The more the merrier, I say. Please to meet ya, Annie."

Annie offered her hand to Cornelia, who took it quickly, then let go and slapped the head of the little girl who had completely disappeared underneath her skirt.

"Get yerself outta there, Agnes, 'fore I take a switch to yer backside."

Agnes dropped to her knees and crawled out from under Cornelia's skirt.

"That's more like it. Now," she said, turning her attention back to Deborah and Annie, "would you care to come inside?"

"Thank you," Deborah said graciously. "We'd love to."

Deborah looked over her shoulder and winked at Annie as they followed their hostess inside. While the house smelled of a strange odor and was sparsely furnished, at least it appeared to be neat and orderly. A second-story loft ran the length of the interior.

Annie turned her attention toward little Agnes, with her big, brown eyes and dirty bare feet. "Do you sleep up there?" she asked softly.

Agnes gave Annie a frightened look and scrambled up the ladder to the loft. Her older sister was already there, peering through the railing.

"Oh, don't pay no mind to my ragamuffins," Cornelia said. "They'll come 'round after a while."

Annie gave the girls a friendly smile, hoping to coax them back down the ladder, but the gesture only caused the two faces to disappear completely.

"We'll be goin' to Ermaline's this evenin' for vittles. That's when you'll meet all the rest," Cornelia told them. She put the toddler down on a woven rug in the middle of the floor, then blurted out, "Goodness me, will ya look at my manners? Please have yerself a seat."

Annie and Deborah looked around the room. There was a bench along the back wall, one straight back chair near the fireplace, and wooden stumps around the table. Annie raised one eyebrow, causing Deborah to bite back a smile.

"You know," Deborah said, pulling a notebook from her satchel, "I think I'll sit at the table. I'd like to interview you, Mrs. Baggett, if you don't mind."

Cornelia's face turned two shades of red as she sat down across the table from Deborah. "I ain't never been interviewed in my whole life," she said in a soft voice. "This is somethin' special." Then, without warning, she looked up toward the loft and bellowed out, "You hear that girls? I'm a gettin' interviewed!"

Annie heard the girls giggling in the loft and wanted desperately to climb the ladder to play with them. But instead, she decided to start with the little boy sitting in the middle of the floor chewing on a wooden spoon.

The next couple of hours passed by quickly as Annie played with all three of Cornelia's children in the loft and listened to her sad story. Cornelia had already lost her husband over a year ago while he trained at Fort Bragg, North Carolina. Other women in the area had lost a husband or a son as well.

"It's not like we had bunches o' money to begin with, even havin' our men around," Cornelia told Deborah. "We're nothin' but poor folks anyway. But us women knew we had to do somethin' right quick-like to survive with our young'uns." She went on to describe the particulars of their successful wild hog co-op.

As the shadow of the mountain began to crawl over the little house, a young girl, who looked to be twelve or thirteen, came bursting through the front door.

"Oh my!" Cornelia cried. "Would ya look at the time?" She jumped up from the table and ran into a small bedroom at the back of the house.

"Billie Jean!" she yelled. "Don't just stand there starin' at these fine ladies. Introduce yerself while I change clothes."

"Hi y'all," Billie Jean said as Annie climbed down the ladder. Deborah stood and introduced herself and Annie.

"Do you belong to Cornelia?" Deborah asked.

"Oh, no'm. I stay with the young'uns while our mamas kill razorbacks."

"Razorbacks?" Annie cried.

"Yes'm. Meanest pigs on earth," she said matter-of-factly.

Annie nervously looked around for the bathroom, then realized there wasn't one in the house. "Um, Billie Jean, where might I find the facilities?"

Billie Jean wrinkled her brow and looked at Annie as if she were speaking a foreign language.

"Is there an outhouse?" Deborah corrected.

"Oh. Toilet's out back."

Annie rolled her eyes at Deb and quickly made her way to the back door. When she returned, only Billie Jean and the children were in the house.

"They're out front waitin' fer ya."

"Thank you, Billie Jean. Have a nice night."

"Uh, Miss?" Billie Jean said as Annie reached for the doorknob.

"Yes?"

"Don't get yerself in front o' Cornelia while she's huntin'."

A chill ran all the way up Annie's spine. She turned to Billie Jean with a slightly wild look in her eyes. "Trust me, honey. I don't plan to."

That evening, Annie and Deborah followed a party of twelve hog-hunting women along a series of beautiful Ozark Mountain trails. Though the canopy of autumn leaves cast an early shadow of darkness over the landscape, their eyes adjusted quickly. Cornelia had told them that once their eyes got used to the dark, they'd be able to see as well as any owl or rabbit at night.

After a long hike, the women came into a large clearing. Cornelia walked out into the middle and let the bag of corn she was carrying drop to the ground. She immediately addressed the other women in the group. "Wait on my call, tonight. Bertha, don't you go to shootin' so early this time."

Bertha's round, ruddy face took on a penitent expression. "I ain't gonna let that happen again, Cornelia. I got all worked up on account of—"

"I know, I know." Cornelia interrupted. "The biggest hog you ever laid eyes on. Well, I don't care how big they is, you wait fer my signal."

"I will," Bertha promised.

The women split up into groups of four and headed for two other locations. While Cornelia spread the corn all over the clearing, Annie noticed that only one other woman in their group had a shotgun. The other two were young girls of fourteen or fifteen named Betsy and Augustine.

"Do you not hunt?" Annie asked the girls.

"Oh no'm. Me and Betsy is the runners."

Cornelia finished her task and came to their side. "That's right. Them two girls is the fastest runners in Boone County."

Augustine's freckled face beamed with pride while Betsy gazed shyly at her feet.

"Now, let's git," Cornelia prodded the group to the edge of the clearing for cover.

While Cornelia and her fellow hunter, Dervine, took their places behind a large mossy log, the two girls sat down and relaxed behind an outcropping of rocks. As soon as the two hunters were settled, Cornelia motioned for their two guests to join them. Deborah crouched beside Cornelia while Annie took her place beside Dervine.

It wasn't long before the entire forest was engulfed in an eerie darkness until the moon began to rise in the sky. Cornelia had told Deborah that the women only hunt on the full moon for two precise reasons: it's easier to see the hogs when they come into the clearing, and the full moon seems to increase the activity of the wild animals in the forest.

Dervine jabbed Annie with her elbow, indicating the first hog strutting into the clearing. Annie's eyes were now fully adjusted to the dark, and she had already picked out three other hogs following the first. These were no ordinary hogs. They had long snouts adorned with short tusks on either side. The sound of their grunting as they began rooting around in the corn made Annie wish she had a shotgun in her hands. Cornelia had earlier pointed out a boulder to scramble onto for safety, just in case one decided to come after them.

As soon as half a dozen or so hogs were in the clearing, Betsy and Augustine quietly took off in two different directions to check on the other hunting posts. It took no more than ten minutes for the girls to reappear, but Cornelia was visibly upset. When they finally returned, she let them have it, albeit in a low whisper. "What in the name of Moses took you two so long?"

Augustine whispered softly that Todie's clearing had only two hogs and they had to wait a couple of minutes.

"So's we're ready?"

"Yes'm."

Annie nearly jumped out of her hiding place when Cornelia let out a high-pitched, shriek, and the shooting commenced. When it was over in a matter of seconds, Deborah and Annie took their hands from their ears and surveyed the clearing. Five hogs lay dead, spilling their blood on the scattered corn. A whoop rose up from all three hunting posts, indicating success.

"Now's the fun part!" Cornelia exclaimed, leaning her shotgun against the log and pulling out a long knife. The blade glinted in the light of the moon—even from where Annie stood, she could tell it was razor sharp. She and Dervine stepped over the log and headed toward their kill.

Deborah and Annie stayed where they were, not sure if they should follow until Cornelia turned back around. "Don'cha wanna see?"

"Sure," Deborah said sportingly, and she grabbed Annie's arm, dragging her into the clearing.

"First thing we gotta do is make sure we got 'em dead."

Dervine giggled devilishly, causing Annie's hair to stand on end.

All of a sudden, one of the hogs let out a loud snort and kicked its legs wildly, rolling over onto its back. Before Annie and Deborah could even jump back, Cornelia had slit its hairy throat from ear to ear. Blood spattered all over her, but Cornelia didn't even flinch.

"The rest are goners," Dervine declared.

Cornelia waved Deborah to her side. "Watch me gut this'n, so you and Annie can do that'n there." She pointed to a sizable hog in the middle of the clearing. Annie felt her insides churning and hoped she could keep her vittles where they belonged.

She watched the robust Ozark women drag the first hog to nearby trees where ropes had already been tied. Augustine and Betsy had each lit a torch and stood over the hog, providing necessary light for the task. Cornelia quickly had a rope tied to each of the hog's legs and stretched it out for the undertaking.

Long into the night, the fifth hog was finally gutted, and it was time to carry them out of the forest. Each one was cleverly tied to a long pole to be carried between two people. Deborah and Annie hoisted a hog pole onto their shoulders, then stared in amazement as Dervine and Cornelia lifted a pole onto each shoulder, and the girls did the same with the two smaller hogs.

It was rough getting along the winding trails in the dark mountains. Several times Annie and Deborah nearly lost their footing on rocks or tree roots, but not the others. They were as sure-footed as if they were walking along a smooth path.

By the time they reached their trucks at the base of the mountain, the sky was showing its first hint of dawn. Annie and Deborah heaved the hog carcass into the back of Cornelia's truck and collapsed on the ground out of sheer exhaustion.

"Glad you two was with us or we'd o' had ta make us a second trip."

"Our pleasure," Deborah uttered as she sucked in another breath.

Cornelia checked with all the other women and did a headcount. When that was complete, she walked over to her two weary guests. "Git yer other clothes outta the truck. It's time to git cleaned up."

Annie stood and pulled Deborah to her feet. Both of them were covered in hog blood from head to toe. She felt fairly certain that this was one set of clothes that would have to be burned.

As they followed the satisfied hunters back through the forest, Cornelia spoke to Deborah and Annie over her shoulder. "Yer in fer a treat today. Full moon was on a Saturday this time. Soon as we wash, there'll be a worship service near the river."

Morning fog hovered over the slow-moving Buffalo River as the huntresses made their way to the water's edge. Annie watched as the women stepped into the river, clothes and all. Several of them squealed as they waded deeper into the frigid water.

"Come on, you two. Don't bother to take nothin' off but yer boots. This is how we git clean," Cornelia said, plowing into the water.

"Here goes," Annie said, tossing her boots and socks on shore.

Deborah reached out and grabbed her hand, and the two friends pulled each other into the current.

Annie's teeth chattered uncontrollably, but she didn't care. The flow of the river over her tired and achy muscles felt invigorating. She plunged beneath the surface, washing the blood from her face and feeling the water glide through her thick hair. Coming up for a quick breath, she immersed herself once more in the dark, crystal waters. Encountering the soundless realm below and the rush of the chilly river somehow reanimated her spirit, washing away the veil of despondency that had clung so long to her heart. When she came back up the second time, Annie couldn't help but smile. Something was different in the core of her being.

The women played in groups all around her, sometimes splashing each other or joking about the night's adventure. Annie realized this was probably one of the few opportunities they had to relax from the endless toils of life.

After scrubbing their clothes in the cold water, the sun began to filter through the dense forest. Annie looked toward the opposite bank of the river and was awestruck by the view. Magnificent bluffs lined the other shore like a giant fortress standing guard over its territory. The spectacle was overwhelming. Annie tangibly felt her long-lost serenity being restored and praised God for the sight before her.

Deborah broke into her thoughts. "How majestic."

"Amen," Annie breathed in awe.

Cornelia made her way over and turned her gaze toward the bluffs as well. "This'd be where I feel most at home."

Her long hair had been loosed from its auburn braid and drifted freely in the current. She drew it back with her hands, then told them, "If yer clean, it's time ta git dressed fer worship."

All of the women scattered to various places along the shore and dried off the best they could before changing. In groups, they headed down the rocky bank to a large clearing. Much to Annie and Deb's delight, a huge bonfire had been built and was already roaring to life. Drying racks made from branches stood around the fire and the women laid their wet clothes out to dry.

Annie and Deb crowded in with their new friends, feeling a kindred spirit and taking in the warmth from the flames, until an old woman's scratchy voice cried loudly, "Our *God* is a consumin' fire. But He is righteous and just."

One by one, the women sat down on logs at the feet of a bent and wrinkled woman known as Mama Mabel. She sat upon a smooth boulder with a wooden cane at her side and a well-worn Bible in her hand.

"Just as you washed them stains from yer clothes in the river, our Lord hath washed the stains from yer very life with His t'rrible sacrifice. Yer no longer covered in blood and guilt," she thundered. Then in a quavering voice, she whispered, "Yer *whiter* than snow."

For nearly an hour, the old woman preached the Word, never once opening her Bible. Then the small gathering began to sing hymns, ministering deeply to Annie's much-wounded heart.

Be still, my soul: the Lord is on thy side.
Bear patiently the cross of grief or pain.

Tears quickly flooded her eyes as the words and melody conversed with her soul.

Leave to thy God to order and provide;
In every change, He faithful will remain.

The breath caught in her throat, making it almost impossible to continue singing. Cornelia grabbed her hand and held it tightly, singing all the louder. Annie felt a bond between them that only the Spirit could create.

Be still, my soul: thy best, thy heavenly Friend,
Through thorny ways leads to a joyful end.

When the hymn was over, Cornelia gave Annie's hand a squeeze, then stood to pray, not forgetting to thank the Lord for bringing them a bountiful harvest of hogs.

Before the little assembly dispersed, Deborah took pictures of the hog-hunting women of Boone County along with a few shots of the night's conquests. Finally, after a breakfast of sausage and grits at Cornelia's, Deborah and Annie said their good-byes.

Cornelia clung to them tightly with tears in her eyes. "You brung me great pleasure by comin' here," she declared.

"The pleasure has been all ours," Deborah insisted.

"Yer gonna send me that article, ain't ya?" Cornelia called from the front porch as the two made their way to the car.

"Of course," Deborah called back. "And who knows, I may even deliver it myself."

"Aw, I'd love that! Annie, you come back too."

Annie smiled brightly. "I'd love that as well."

"Annie, dearest," Deb said, closing the trunk lid, "do you think you could drive? I can't wait to start writing about the hunt."

As fatigued as Annie felt, she knew driving would not be a problem, at least for now. Something had happened to her in the river that had given her a new perspective on her present troubles. It was something she hadn't had time to think through yet, but she hoped to figure it out along the winding Ozark highway.

Just before getting into the car, Cornelia yelled out once more. "You're in fer a real treat!"

Annie glanced back toward the porch. "What do you mean?" she called curiously.

Cornelia's face glowed with enthusiasm. "Just you wait 'n' see." She clapped her hands together in front of her chest. "Just keep that car o' yers on the road!"

Chapter 41

It didn't take long for Annie to fully comprehend Cornelia's warning. The steep, hairpin turns of the Ozark highway made for some tense moments, particularly since she was struggling to keep her eyes on the road. The vistas of beautiful autumn colors on either side of the highway were astounding. It was more than her mind could take in at one time. Brilliant reds, yellows, and oranges carpeted the mountainsides and nudged up against a cloudless, azure sky.

Deborah no longer had her head buried in her notebook. She sat in the passenger seat, gawking at the dazzling panorama.

Finally, Annie couldn't take it any longer. "I have to pull over."

"I don't blame you one bit," Deb responded.

At the top of the next mountain, Annie eased the car to the side of the road, and both women got out. They stood on top of a towering bluff overlooking the autumn spectacle.

Breathing deeply, Annie sensed God tugging at her heart. It was the same feeling she'd experienced earlier that morning in the river. It caused her to go weak in the knees, and she sat down quickly to prevent a tumble over the edge of the cliff.

Deborah dropped down beside her. "Are you okay?"

"I'm not really sure," Annie replied. At the moment, she was feeling completely overwhelmed by the power of the Creator. How could anyone look at such beauty and not feel His very presence?

Deb turned her attention fully to Annie. "Tell me what you're feeling."

Annie closed her eyes and drew in another long breath. When she opened them, she knew without question that God had used His creation to speak to her innermost being. Words would never be adequate.

"I can't," she whispered, tears forming in her eyes.

Annie felt Deb's arms encircle her. Without hesitation, she leaned into her dear friend's embrace knowing Who had sent it.

After a long moment, Annie felt the need to confess her shameful weakness. She withdrew from Deb's arms and turned to face her. "I've been in a terrible place for such a long time. I feel like my life has been in limbo, hovering somewhere between life and death. And to be honest, closer to death than life." She contemplated how selfish she'd been, thinking only of herself at times—as if she were the only one dealing with loss.

She looked out over the stunning scenery again. "I'm so thankful I came with you on this trip. God has taught me a powerful lesson through Cornelia."

"How so?" Deborah asked.

"Raising those poor little children without a daddy. It breaks my heart. But Cornelia isn't a broken woman. She meets life head-on with such courage. I realized how fortunate I am to have such a wonderful family and church supporting me. But Cornelia has so little."

"And yet she feels so blessed," Deborah remarked.

"Exactly. I know something unexplainable happened to me today." The corners of Annie's mouth tipped up slightly. "I feel like I've finally come up for air."

Deb's rust-colored eyes shimmered in the autumn sun. "That's just what I wanted to hear."

Suddenly, Annie felt incredibly tired. Sitting on the side of the road in the warm sunshine had lulled her into drowsiness. She looked over at Deb and realized there was no way they'd make it to Dallas today.

"What are we going to do? I'm about to fall asleep right here on the spot."

"Me too," Deborah said, rising to her feet. She reached down and grabbed Annie's hand. "Come on. I'll drive if you'll talk without ceasing. Fort Smith is on the other side of these mountains. Let's just get a motel room there and drive to Abilene tomorrow."

By the time the two women made it to the Ouachita Motel, they were beyond exhausted. They dropped their belongings on the floor and fell on top of the beds, sleeping all the way through lunch and into dinnertime. Evening shadows had overtaken the room when they finally woke up.

After showering and eating dinner at a local café, Deborah spent the rest of the evening writing while Annie read through other articles her friend had written. Neither one had difficulty sleeping the rest of the night despite their day of slumber.

By six in the morning, Deb was up and ready to hit the road. Annie had no problem with that, feeling rested and ready to see her husband and son. It took ten hours to make it to the gates of Camp Barkeley, and Annie could feel her heart racing wildly as a guard approached the car.

"May I help you, ma'am?" The young soldier leaned down toward Deborah's open window.

Deborah introduced herself and Annie and told the guard they were here to see Sergeant Eugene Wyatt and Corporal Jacob Wyatt.

The soldier wrote down the names on his clipboard, then disappeared inside the guard shack. Annie could see him on the phone. She knew Eugene had been waiting all day for her arrival and hoped he would be able to see her.

Soon two soldiers opened the wide gates and motioned for Deborah to drive inside. The first guard stepped out of the shack and instructed, "Please park your vehicle over there and wait." He indicated a parking area just inside the gates.

Deborah did as she was told and turned off the engine. Annie didn't know if she had the patience to sit and wait in the car, but on the other hand, what would be the point of getting out?

"Take a deep breath, Annie, love. You look like you're about to hyperventilate."

Annie laughed nervously. "I know, I know." She stuck her head out the window, checking her reflection in the side view mirror. "How do I look?"

"In that blue dress? Eugene may eat you up on the spot."

But Eugene was not the first to arrive. An army jeep screeched to a halt behind Deb's car, and before Annie could get out of the car, Jake was already opening her door. When she got out, he grabbed her and pulled her into a loving hug, burying his face in her neck. They held each other for a long time, then Jake released his hold and kissed her.

Deborah came around the car, smiling delightfully. "Oh my goodness. He looks just like a younger version of Eugene." She offered her hand to Jake. "I don't know if you remember me. It's been several years since I last saw you."

Jake graciously took her hand. "Of course I remember you. How was your trip?" he asked politely.

"Very productive, thank you. I'm so glad your mother was along to keep me company."

Jake turned sympathetic eyes on his mother. His voice shook slightly. "I'm really sorry about Will, Momma. I wish we could've been there for his service."

"I wish you could've been there too," she said quietly. "Are you okay?"

Jake pressed his lips together and shook his head slightly. "I still can't believe he's gone."

Those few words threatened to destroy Annie's composure. But thankfully her attention was drawn to a larger army vehicle approaching. She could see Eugene in the passenger seat. He didn't even wait for it to come to a halt before he was on the ground running toward her. Annie covered the rest of the distance and threw herself wholeheartedly into his arms, expressing her love for him. He kissed her briefly, then put his arm around her waist, walking her over to Jake and Deborah.

"Eugene, it's so good to see you," Deborah said as they embraced.

"It's good to see you too, Deborah. Thank you for bringing Annie all this way."

"My pleasure. It's already been quite an adventure."

"I can't wait to hear about it," Eugene said, taking Annie's hand possessively. "I only have two hours, and Jake has to get back to his unit immediately."

Annie was determined not to be disappointed with any length of time she could spend with Eugene and Jake. She knew they were hard-pressed to be able to see her as it was.

"Well, I'll run into town to see my sister. I'll be back out in a couple of hours to pick you up, Annie." Just before getting into the car, Deborah glanced at Eugene and Jake. "It was so good to see you again. Stay safe, you two."

The men thanked her and waved as Deborah pulled away.

"Momma, I'm sorry, I have to go," Jake said.

"I know, sweetheart. It was so good just to touch you."

"I love you," he said, giving her a wide grin.

"I love you too."

Annie pulled him into her arms one more time. "Will I see you tomorrow?"

"Sorry, Mom," he said. "This was all I could get."

He kissed her sweetly, then looked at his dad and pounded his chest. "I'll write to you from California," he told Annie.

"Oh, wait, you get one more hug and kiss from Gramma."

Jake gladly opened his arms again for Rachel's special delivery.

"Be safe, sweetheart," Annie called as Jake hopped in the jeep.

"No worries!" he yelled, waving as he drove away.

Before Annie turned back to Eugene, she noticed a man standing beside the army vehicle, staring closely at her. It made her wonder if she knew the man, and to be honest, his gaze made her a bit uncomfortable.

"Annie, I can't believe I'm standing here with you."

"I know. I can't either," she admitted.

"Come on," he said, taking her hand in his. "Chow's being served and we have a private room."

"All to ourselves?"

"Not exactly. It's just a smaller room away from the enlisted men. We can eat, then go somewhere else to talk."

Eugene led her to the truck and introduced her to the driver. "Annie, this is Sergeant First Class Winston Porter. Winston, meet my wife, Annie."

Annie was taken aback by the sergeant's greeting. For a second, he just stood staring at her, grinning from ear to ear. Then he took off his cap and offered his hand. "A pleasure to meet you, *Mrs. Wyatt.* I've been waiting a long time for this."

Annie felt the warmth rush to her face. "I'm glad to meet you, Sergeant Porter."

"Please, call me Winston," he begged. Then he ran around the truck and opened the door, offering Annie his hand as she stepped inside. "Or you can call me Squirrel if you like."

Annie almost laughed in his face but thankfully was able to hold it in. She found herself sitting between the two men, receiving almost as much attention from Winston as she was getting from her husband. It made her more than a little uneasy, but Eugene didn't seem to be bothered by it.

Even as they ate in the corner of a small dining room, Annie could feel Winston's eyes on her from several tables away.

She leaned in close and whispered across the table. "Okay, Eugene. What is it with that Squirrel guy? He hasn't taken his eyes off me since I got here."

"Who, Winston?" Eugene looked across the room and nodded to his friend. "He's harmless. I think he's doing that to drive me crazy. I'm trying to ignore him, in case you couldn't tell."

"It's kind of hard to ignore him. He's making his attention quite obvious."

Eugene raised his brow and stated matter-of-factly, "Just like every other man in this room." Then gazing into her eyes he said, "You look beautiful, Annie."

Once again, heat rushed to her cheeks. "Thank you," she said. "But you're the only one I want ogling at me."

"I know. Let's finish up and get outta here."

By the time they left the mess hall, Eugene only had an hour left. He took Annie's hand and led her away from the buildings to a small copse of trees growing around an old stone well. A few benches were scattered among the trees, and he pulled her down onto one of them.

"Come 'ere," he said, drawing her tight against his side and wishing this hour would never end. "I've missed you so much."

Annie laid her head on his shoulder. "I've missed you too."

He cleared his throat and reached for her hand. "I'm sorry I couldn't be with you at Will's service. I know how hard that must've been." He couldn't imagine how Annie was getting through these terrible days.

For a while she didn't say anything, and he wondered if she was crying. But to his amazement, she moved out of his arms and began telling him all about the service. Eugene watched her intently as she went into vivid details and recounted how many people had come to show their respects. The more she talked, the more he realized something was different about her. This was not the same Annie he left five months ago. This was not the woman who lamented for her sons in the letters she wrote.

When she fell silent, Eugene had to ask, "Annie, has something happened?"

"Why do you ask?"

He grinned while rubbing his thumb in circles on top of her hand. "Because you seem different to me." He noticed the crease in her brow and added, "In a good way. Stronger somehow."

Annie got up from the bench and walked over to the well. She laid her hands on the stones and looked over the edge, then turned back to Eugene. He read her stunned expression and laughed.

"You were expecting something deeper?"

She giggled as he made his way to the well and reached in for a handful of sand. "Save your coins," he teased, "this isn't much of a wishing well."

Eugene sat down on the edge of the well, and Annie stood in front of him, laying her hands on top of his shoulders. He put his hands on her waist and pulled her in close. He knew something had happened to her but wondered why she hadn't answered his question about it.

Breaking into his thoughts, she asked, "If you could throw a coin into the well and wish for something, what would it be?"

"That's easy, I'd wish for this war to end, so I could come home to you." He reached up and caressed the side of her face. "What about you? What would you wish for?"

She suddenly grew solemn. "I'd wish for all of us to be together again on the farm near Winchester."

"Yeah, that would be nice, wouldn't it?"

Eugene looked at his watch and knew he didn't have much longer. He decided to probe his wife one more time. "Annie, if you don't want to tell me, it's fine, but I know something's different."

She smiled and moved to his side, sitting down on the edge of the sand-filled well. "Eugene, I kind of avoided your question because I'm not exactly sure myself. I had a remarkable experience coming here that's lifted my spirits beyond anything I could've imagined. I've been in such a terrible place for the past year, but the Lord used His amazing creation and a young Ozark Mountain woman to speak to my heart. He finally pulled me out of the doldrums."

"Can you tell me about it?" he asked curiously.

"I'd like to, but I don't think I have time to tell you everything." She took his hand into her lap. "Maybe tomorrow?"

Just then, a shrill whistle penetrated the air, and Eugene knew exactly where it was coming from. Winston was waiting to take him back across camp. They were due in a meeting within the half hour.

Annie looked passed Eugene for a moment, then commented, "There's that Squirrely guy again. What's with him?"

He immediately stood and drew Annie to her feet. "I've got to go, sweetheart. I can meet you again tomorrow at the same time for a few hours, but unfortunately that'll be all. I can't get any time on Wednesday because we're moving out to California the next day."

Another annoying whistle disturbed the evening calm. "I'm sorry, Annie," he said, bringing her left hand affectionately to his lips. "I wish we could be together longer."

Before she could respond, Eugene's hands sifted into her hair and he kissed her the way he'd wanted to when he first saw her. Putting his arm around her waist, he led her back to the truck. He hated to expose her to Winston's perusal again, but that was the only way he could get her back to the gate. Eugene was determined that tomorrow, he would commandeer a jeep for himself—even if he had to steal one.

The next afternoon, Annie drove out to Camp Barkeley in Deb's car. Eugene was already waiting for her with a jeep and a rascally grin on his face. "Hop in," he said as she emerged from the car.

Annie gladly jumped into the passenger seat—she was so thankful to be in a vehicle without the Squirrel. She was surprised when the gates opened and one of the guards handed Eugene a clipboard. He signed it, then turned the jeep down the road outside of camp.

"I hope you don't mind a picnic," Eugene said, indicating a crate of goodies in the back of the jeep.

Annie gave him a delightful smile, her hair whipping about her face. "This is exciting, Eugene. How'd you manage it?"

"I've been a good boy," he said with a wink.

"Oh, so they let you come out to play?"

"Yep!"

Eugene drove a few miles to the south side of Abilene before turning off on a smooth dirt road. As they drove beneath large elm and cottonwood trees, she noticed a wide stream meandering beside the road. He parked the jeep and pulled the crate from the back, and they walked down toward the stream.

Eugene set the crate down, and Annie started looking through it. "You thought of everything." She pulled a blanket from the top and spread it out on the ground in the shade.

He gave her his most handsome grin. "Only the best for my girl."

Annie then pulled out a warm mess pot with a lid on it and looked inside. "Beans and wieners? That's our dinner?" she exclaimed.

"What did I tell ya? Only the best for my girl."

Eugene took the lid out of her hand and set it back on top of the pot. He sat down on the blanket, pulling Annie down beside him. They spent the next half hour laughing and talking light-heartedly, even eating the army chow as if the world around them didn't exist. And when Eugene asked her to tell him about her adventure in the Ozarks, Annie was eager to fully share her incredible experience with him.

"Thank you for telling me about it, Annie." He ran his hand lightly down her arm as she sat facing him. "It helps me to know that you're in a better place."

Annie nodded while inhaling deeply. "I don't want you to worry about anything while you're away."

Eugene leaned back against the tree and held his arms open to her. She nestled up close to his side, basking in the tenderness of his embrace.

"Sweetheart," he said quietly, "after our desert training in California, they're sending us to Fort Dix, New Jersey." He paused for a brief moment before finishing his thought. "After that, we're heading overseas."

Annie felt the chill bumps cover her arms. Her men had been training for over eighteen months. Somehow she had been lulled into thinking this war would end before Eugene and Jake would have to enter it. But all of a sudden, reality gave her a hard smack across the face, and it stung. She was faced once again with the prospect of either entering that cold, dispassionate existence or trusting in the warm embrace of her heavenly Father. Logically, she knew which way to turn. Still, Annie couldn't keep such a dreadful thought from entering her mind—*I've already given my firstborn. How much more is expected of me?*

To her relief, Eugene began to pray out loud. Every word he uttered became a smooth stone, laying a solid foundation for her reality. This was not about her. This was about being an ambassador of peace in a world turned upside down, about spreading love to her fellow man, about trusting that in the end, God would set things right.

Be still my soul.

When he fell silent, Annie poured out her heart to the Lord while a thousand crickets ushered in the autumn dusk. Eugene continued to hold her close, long after she had finished the prayer.

Annie sensed their time together was drawing to a close. She turned her face into his chest and breathed deeply.

"What're you doing?" he asked light-heartedly.

"I'm smelling you. I want to remember the scent of you while you're gone."

Eugene lifted his opposite arm and pretended to sniff under his armpit. "Maybe this will help you remember longer."

"Ooh, Eugene," she cried, playfully yanking his arm back to his side.

He chuckled, then pulled the crate closer. "You missed something 'while ago." He reached inside the crate with his free hand.

"Dessert?"

"Uh, not exactly."

Annie sat up and watched her husband pull a slender box out of the crate. "I wanted you to have this."

He opened the box slowly, holding it out for her to take its contents.

"Oh, Eugene, this is beautiful," she breathed. Annie looked at the gold, heart-shaped locket filling the palm of her hand. It had a beautiful filigree etching of a horse on the front.

"Open it."

Inside was a picture of Will on the left and Jake on the right. It took her breath away.

"How did you get them so small?"

"I have my sources," he said with a grin. "Look at the back."

Annie closed the locket and read the engraved words over and over again—until they were etched within her soul. Tears of joy and grief mingled together on her cheeks as she threw herself into Eugene's arms for one last time.

Until we all come home ~ Eugene

Chapter 42

November 1943

The entire infantry from Camp Barkeley was now billeted in a massive tent camp in the California desert. It had taken seven full trains to get all sixty thousand men to their destination. Conditions were rough. Combat maneuvers during the day took place beneath a scorching sun while sleeping in tents at night was nothing short of frigid.

For the past three weeks, the 357th had gone up against the skillful opposition of the all-Negro 93rd infantry division out of Arizona. Jake had heard some of the men in his company make disparaging remarks about the soldiers of the 93rd. It saddened him to think about the prejudice and blatant lack of respect some people had toward their fellow human beings just because of the color of their skin. He had been raised to respect all people. After all, his own grandmother was half Negro.

Now on guard duty with his company for the afternoon, Jake walked the perimeter around a group of prisoners who had been captured the night before. He had been a part of the daring operation that brought in the 162 men from the 93rd. At present, the black soldiers sat beneath a desert camouflage awning as it flapped lazily in the arid heat.

"You gettin' sleepy, ain't cha?"

Jake grinned and threw his shoulders back. He rubbed his face with his left hand while keeping his rifle trained on the prisoners. He and Mercy had provided the reconnaissance for last night's surprise attack on the southernmost *enemy* outpost. Right now, they were operating on two hours of sleep. The warm breeze was enticing him into a stupor.

He smiled at the young prisoner who had called out to him. "Don't get your hopes up."

At that moment, Corporal Perry Cunningham from Jake's company yelled for the black soldier to shut up, using profanity along with a racial slur. Jake's reaction to the comment came with such emotional intensity, it caught Corporal Cunningham off guard completely.

"Get off me, you idiot. What're you doing?"

When Jake realized he had taken Cunningham to the ground and now had a knee pressing on his chest, he was a bit unnerved. His anger over the comment had yet to subside, and he pushed down a little harder with his knee.

"You owe that man an apology," Jake breathed.

Cunningham laughed haughtily in his face and let out another stream of racial epithets for all to hear. Then he reached up and grabbed the front of Jake's shirt and yanked him to the ground, connecting a hard blow to his jaw.

Jake had not wanted a fight—he had never had a physical confrontation with anyone in his entire life. Whether it was the heat of the afternoon or the lack of sleep, he wasn't sure, but he knew he had definitely made a bad decision to force Cunningham to the ground.

He wasn't about to lie in the sand and let his face get pummeled, though. Jake blocked the next blow with his palm and grabbed Cunningham's wrist. With a hard twist to the right, he was able to roll his opponent over, pinning Cunningham's arm behind his back. But that was a short-lived victory. The corporal deftly pulled out of Jake's grasp, spun to his knees, and landed another hard punch.

A young black soldier in the middle of the throng of prisoners got up and headed toward the fracas.

"Sit down!" one of the guards yelled. He aimed his rifle at the prisoner, but the man kept coming.

"I mean it; sit down, now!"

A wave of murmurs rose up among the prisoners, and the other guards of the 357th now trained their rifles menacingly upon them. No one in Jake's company was paying any more attention to the scuffle in the sand. They were now intent on keeping the prisoners secure.

The young black man continued his advance without regard to the warning. As he came to the edge of the holding area, the guard raised the butt of his rifle, ready to repel the prisoner with force. But the Negro soldier calmly put his hand on the rifle and said, "That's my brother." Then without further interference, he reached down and took both combatants by the shoulder.

Jake felt an immediate calm flow through his body, and to his amazement, Cunningham let go of his hold and stood up. Blood covered Jake's face and was now dripping onto the sand. He wiped his nose on his shirtsleeve, then noticed the dark, outstretched hand in front of him.

"This isn't the way, Jake."

Already ashamed of his actions, Jake looked up into the face of his dear friend and brother, Wallace Bradshaw. Without delay, he took his hand and allowed himself to be pulled up from the sand into a warmhearted embrace.

"I know," Jake murmured. "I'm sorry about all of this, Wallace."

Complete silence now permeated the company of soldiers, prisoners, and guards alike, as Wallace pulled off his t-shirt and pinched it tight against Jake's nose.

Corporal Cunningham reached down for his rifle and smoothed the sand off the barrel. All of the wind seemed to have gone out of his sails. He stood, silently watching Wallace's ministrations to Jake.

But the worst had yet to come. Within seconds, an army jeep screeched to a halt showering grains of sand on the men close by.

"What in Sam Hill is going on here?" Jake's commanding officer, Major Whatley, slammed the door of his jeep. He made his way over to Jake and pulled Wallace's hand and shirt away from his face. Fresh blood streamed from Jake's nostrils.

The commander grabbed the shirt out of Wallace's hand and shoved it into Jake's. "You can go back and have a seat, Son."

Wallace nodded his head respectfully and made his way back to the middle of the prisoners. Several of the 93rd infantrymen slapped his palm and muttered their admiration as he walked by.

"You two, with me. Now!" the commander yelled.

The two corporals wasted no time climbing into the back of the major's jeep. Jake knew he'd messed up big time and worried about what it would do to his record.

By the time they made it to the major's field tent, the bleeding from his nose had stopped. He reached up to touch it, but his face felt painfully numb. He was going to need ice as soon as possible.

"Corporal Cunningham, sit." The major pointed to a canvas chair outside the tent. Perry sat down obediently in the shade underneath the awning.

"Corporal Wyatt, you're first."

"Yes, sir," Jake said, following his commander into the tent.

Major Whatley took a seat behind a wooden desk and indicated a chair for Jake on the other side. Jake watched as his commander pulled a disciplinary sheet out of his desk drawer and picked up a pen. Licking the end of it, he asked matter-of-factly, "Did you start it?"

Jake thought about it for a moment, then looked his commander in the eye. "Yes, sir."

Major Whatley appeared to be taken aback by his answer. "That surprises me, Corporal Wyatt. You have an exemplary record. Not once have you stepped out of line in the last eighteen months."

The major leaned back in his chair and stuck the pen behind his ear. "You're in a lot worse shape than Corporal Cunningham. Did you pick on the wrong guy?"

"Apparently so, sir."

"What happened?"

Jake searched his mind for what to tell the major without sounding like a schoolboy tattletale. There was no excuse for the way he had handled the situation. "Sir, it should never have happened. I just got upset and handled it in the wrong way."

"Did you throw the first punch?"

"No, sir, but I took him down to the ground," Jake admitted.

Major Whatley pulled the pen from behind his ear and put his elbows on the desk. "Why'd you do it, Son?"

"Because of something Corporal Cunningham said." Jake was hoping the major would leave it at that.

"You know better than to pick a fight because you don't like what someone says. We'd have brawls all over the place if everyone took things so personal." Jake watched as Major Whatley filled in a few lines of his report. After a while, the commander looked up. "What did Corporal Cunningham say?"

"I'd rather not mention it, sir."

Major Whatley slammed his cap down on the top of the desk, clearly perturbed with Jake's answer. "If he said something about your girlfriend or mama, I've heard it all. Spit it out right now, Corporal."

Jake felt his face grow warm. "I'm sorry, sir." He cleared his throat. "Corporal Cunningham made some unkind remarks toward the prisoners, sir."

"About being colored?"

"Yes, sir. I just snapped. I'm really sorry, sir."

Major Whatley looked down and started to write something, but his hand stilled for several seconds. When he looked up, he called loudly for Corporal Cunningham to join them.

Sheepishly the corporal parted the opening of the tent and stepped inside.

"Sit down," the major ordered gruffly.

As soon as the corporal was seated, Major Whatley tore into him. He lectured him up and down about respecting his fellow man, particularly those who are fighting for the same cause.

"We're all on the same side!" he yelled. "That's a distinguished group of young men out there. They've kicked our butts for the last three weeks. Those brave soldiers of the 93rd are making you better every day. You're about to be thrown into hades, Son, and if you survive, you'll have those Negro men to thank for it."

Major Whatley abruptly stood, and the two corporals scrambled to their feet. "If I so much as hear that you've *whispered* another racial comment, I'll have you busted back down to private so fast, your head'll spin. Have I made myself clear, Corporal Cunningham?"

"Perfectly, sir."

"Now get outta my sight, Cunningham. Go back to your tent. You're in isolation until morning. Have one of your tent mates bring you chow."

"Yes, sir," Perry said humbly.

"Dismissed."

Corporal Cunningham saluted then left the tent.

Jake knew he hadn't been dismissed because the paperwork had yet to be finished. The thought of telling his dad that he had a disciplinary mark on his service record was gut wrenching. But he would take it and learn from it. He was determined that any fighting from now on would be saved for the enemy. And despite his heartless comments, Perry Cunningham was not the enemy.

"You really ought to develop a left hook, Wyatt."

"Sir?" Jake asked in surprise.

Major Whatley took his fist and put it up to his own jaw. "One good punch right here, and he wouldn't have known what hit him."

Jake smiled painfully. "I wasn't trying to hurt him, sir."

"You did a good job with that," the major joked. Then to Jake's surprise, he picked up the disciplinary paper and tore it in half.

Jake stood respectfully at attention. "Thank you, sir."

The major pressed his lips together and examined Jake through narrowed eyes. "No Corporal, *thank you.*" Then he nodded thoughtfully, "Dismissed."

Jake saluted his commander, then headed for the tent opening. But before he could pull back the flap, the major offered one more piece of advice. "And Corporal Wyatt?"

"Sir?"

"Go get some ice on that nose."

"Yes, sir," Jake said gratefully.

That evening after chow, the prisoners of the 93rd were to be released back to their company. Jake wasn't scheduled to be a part of the proceedings, but he showed up early to see Wallace once more. He knew some of the guys on guard duty, and they granted him permission to see his friend.

Wallace walked over to the edge of the holding area to meet him.

"I brought you something." Jake held out a clean t-shirt for Wallace to put on. The night air would be pretty chilly before the men of the 93rd Infantry made their way back to their encampment.

"Thank you," Wallace said with a grin. He slipped into the shirt, then pointed to Jake's nose. "Is it broken?"

"I don't think so. I'm just gonna look pretty bad for a while. I hope I don't see my dad anytime soon."

Wallace smiled. "I'd like to see Mr. Eugene. Is he out here?"

"Sure is. He's a staff sergeant now."

"Hmm. Your dad's a mighty fine man, Jake." Wallace got a faraway look in his eyes. "That time Lillie and I lived at your place, Mr. Eugene treated me as if I was one of his own sons. I'll never forget that as long as I live." Wallace paused for a moment, then said, "You probably don't know this, but your momma writes to me all the time. She does my heart good."

At that moment, Colonel Owen Lambert drove up in his jeep. When the vehicle came to a halt, he stood on the seat, holding on to the windshield for stability. He began barking out instructions for the release of the prisoners. When the long-winded speech was concluded, the men of the 93rd Infantry were brought to attention by the highest-ranking officer among them. He instructed his men to fall in.

Wallace turned and laid his hands firmly on top of Jake's shoulders. "We'll not see each other again," he said quietly.

Jake felt his next breath catch in his throat. He wasn't exactly sure what Wallace meant.

"Keep the faith, Jake."

"You too, Wallace . . . you too."

Jake pulled him into a tight embrace, then released him. For a moment, the two young men stood motionless—Wallace's moist eyes held Jake's unswervingly. All of a sudden, Jake was back on the farm, remembering what it was like to be young and carefree. It was an uncanny feeling. Somehow he knew Wallace was thinking the exact same thing.

As the men of the 93rd began to march proudly into the desert, Wallace laid his hand on top of Jake's shoulder one last time. "Thank you, Brother," he said. And then he was gone.

***

On the last day of desert training, the company commanders received a memo from Brigadier General Samuel T. Williams to be read to all of the troops. Eugene stood at attention with his unit listening to the memo. When the general explained that this was their last maneuver, they all knew what he meant. Their training had been long and hard. The troops had been trained in every phase of army life—they lacked nothing except experience in battle. And that would soon be rectified.

The day after Christmas, the men of the 357th Infantry made a four-day journey by train to New Jersey. Until mid-March, they trained on the massive staging grounds at Fort Dix. Finally, on March 22, they were moved to New York where Eugene and Jake boarded the *HMS Dominion Monarch*, a 27,000-ton British ex-luxury liner, which had been given to the Americans. The US Army had turned it into a troop transport ship.

It was a thirteen-day voyage with over forty ships in the convoy. When they docked at Liverpool, England, Eugene's mind instantly flashed back to the Great War. He remembered how young and scared he'd been at every turn, or at least until the first time he had participated in hand-to-hand combat in France. Experiencing trench warfare had cost him much in the way of self-respect. The first war had been brutal, not that war could be any other way, but it had hardened him somehow—changed something in his very core. Eugene knew God had forgiven him for the things he'd done, but he still struggled with forgiving himself.

His constant worry was now focused on Jake. Two years of intense training had taught him much, but nothing could truly prepare a soldier for the fury of battle. It pained him to think that his youngest son would be changed forever.

As he waited to board a troop train to Kinlet Park, Eugene pulled a family photo from his breast pocket. He had to willfully hold back his emotions—so strong was his urge to weep over the loss of his eldest son, not to mention his youngest son's imminent loss of innocence to a violent world. Eugene drew in several deep breaths, trying to calm his nerves. This time, he wasn't scared for his own life; he was terrified for the life of the one son he had left.

Oh God, he cried inwardly, *please send an angel to protect him.*

With that plea on his heart, Eugene pressed forward in the throng of hardened soldiers and boarded the train into *hell.*

Chapter 43

April 1944

Annie placed a finger in the corner of her eye to hold back a tear. When she glanced up from the letter in her hand, she noticed Rachel's empathetic gaze from across the kitchen table.

"Would you like me to read it out loud, Mama?"

"Yes, darlin', please."

A deep, cleansing breath helped Annie focus on the sweet letter Wallace had written to her. He had penned it back in February, but it had taken nearly six weeks to make its way to Kentucky. She wondered why it took his letters so much longer compared to the ones she received from Eugene and Jake.

Dear Miss Annie, she read aloud.

I apologize for being remiss in writing to you for quite some time. Our division has been pushed very hard lately. Mind you, I'm not complaining. The busier I stay, the less likely I am to get homesick. Thank you for your many letters. I look forward to each one with great anticipation.

I have some interesting news that no doubt you have already received from Jake. I'm sure he told you that we were able to see each other during desert training back in December. It was quite by coincidence. He and the men of his unit were able to capture over 160 of our men during maneuvers, of which I was one. That was quite a feat. As I was sitting in the desert sand, lo and behold, I noticed Jake was one of my guards. We didn't have much chance to catch up, but we were able to speak to each other on two separate occasions. Miss Annie, you would be so proud of him. I know beyond any doubt that he is a man of integrity. I could never have a truer brother. You can be proud to know that you raised such a fine son.

Jake told me that Mr. Eugene was also on desert maneuvers, but unfortunately, I was not able to lay eyes on him. I want you to know that I consider the two of you to be my family, along with Miss Rachel, your fine parents, and Jake and Will. Lillie and I owe you a great debt of gratitude for the way you've looked after us since we were young. It pains me to be away from home for so long and not be able to see you. But it meant more than you'll ever know that I was able to be in Jake's embrace for just a moment.

In March, our division will be heading into the war in the Pacific. I don't think I'll be able to write again for a long time, so if you don't mind, I want to tell you one more thing. I want you to know how often I think of Will with love and admiration. I know he was difficult at times, but inside of him was a good heart. This one thing I know, Miss Annie, you will see him again.

Please look after Lillie and my dear mama should anything happen to me in this war.

May God be with you always.

Your loving son,
Wallace

When Annie looked up again, she noticed Rachel wiping her eyes with her apron. New tears immediately sprang up, releasing a steady stream down her cheeks. Everything about Wallace's letter had touched her heart deeply. He had such a gift with words but had used them so sparingly throughout his life. Wallace was an observer. He seemed to be able to read people exceptionally well. Even his touch had a calming effect on people.

"What a special young man," Rachel declared poignantly.

Through her sniffles, Annie agreed wholeheartedly. "I can't imagine him fighting in the war. He was always such a gentle soul."

"And still appears to be one," Rachel said, pointing to his letter.

"I think I'll give Roberta a call to see how she and Lillie are getting along. She seemed a little down at church last Sunday. Maybe news of Wallace will lift her spirits."

Annie headed for the hallway, but Rachel stood and pulled off her apron. "Why don't we do more than call? Would you like to go for a visit?"

Annie turned on her heels. "I'd love to. Give me a few minutes to change clothes and let Leroy know we'll be gone for the afternoon."

In less than an hour, Annie and Rachel had made their way to the Bradshaws' home on Maple Avenue. Roberta had done well in her job and had made enough to put a down payment on a small house not far from the Brown Hotel. It had been an improvement from the stifling, one-bedroom apartment on Kentucky Street.

Roberta was the only one home, having gotten off work at the hotel an hour earlier. She was so pleased to have Rachel and Annie calling at her door for the afternoon.

"Oh my, how thoughtful of ya to come." She smoothed out the dust cover on her sofa and asked the two ladies to have a seat. "What can I get ya to drink . . . tea, lemonade, water?"

"I'm fine," Annie said.

Rachel said she was fine too and wanted Roberta just to join them for a chat. The conversation naturally centered around their loved ones at war. At length, Annie told Roberta about the letter she had received from Wallace.

Roberta's hand flew to her chest. "Please, please tell me everythin' it said. When did he write it?"

Annie knew that Roberta had never been taught to read, so she pulled the letter from her purse. She had felt certain she could make it through another reading without crying, but one look at Roberta's face destroyed that notion.

Wiping her face with the palms of her hands Roberta poured out her concern over Wallace's safety. "Why do he keep sayin' he might not come home? Don't he know how much we need him?"

"Roberta, darlin', he's just concerned about his mother and sister, that's all." Rachel leaned forward on the sofa and reached out to pat Roberta's arm. "He loves you both so much."

"But if he don't—"

Roberta's words were cut off as the front door swung open and Lillie breezed into the room.

"I thought that was your car outside!"

Immediately, Lillie rushed to Annie, who had stood to receive her precious girl's loving hug. Lillie, however, was no longer a girl. She was a vibrant young woman of eighteen. Annie was so proud of who Lillie was becoming. She wasn't afraid to work, and in fact, toiled long hours at the Louisville ball bearing plant. But in her spare time, she was developing into quite a good writer. She often shared her stories and poems with Annie after Sunday lunch at the Harrisons'.

After a few minutes of polite conversation, Lillie took Annie by the hand. "I want you to read my latest poem."

Roberta shook her head and let out a gargling laugh. "Can't keep that girl from writin' ever chance she gets."

"Oh, Momma, you know you love it." She flashed her mother a genuine smile and dragged Annie into her bedroom, closing the door.

Annie sat down on the side of the bed and watched Lillie rummage through a box filled with papers and writing tablets underneath the bedside table.

"You know, I think I'll talk to my daddy about finding you a desk for your room. If you're going to keep up with your writing, I think you need to have a good place to do it."

Lillie's face beamed with joy at the very thought of it. She rose from her knees with a paper in her hand. "Are you serious, Miss Annie? You have no idea how much that would mean to me."

"Very serious, sweetheart. In fact, I'll call him this evening and see if there's a desk around the house or the barn not being used."

Still holding her paper, Lillie sat down on the bed beside Annie. Her face grew solemn—she seemed indecisive. Annie wondered if she was having second thoughts about sharing her latest writing.

"Miss Annie, I don't want you to think wrongly of me. I just . . ." She looked at the words on the paper, then turned her gaze thoughtfully back to Annie. "I just needed to say some things that have been on my heart. Wallace has got me thinking lately and . . . well, here." She thrust the paper into Annie's hands then got up from the bed and went to her chest of drawers. "I'll let you read it while I change clothes."

Annie took in a deep breath and pressed her lips together. She couldn't imagine what Lillie might have written to cause such reluctance. She had always been so free with her writings.

After a few moments, Annie looked up from the page. Lillie was standing on the other side of the room watching her intently.

"Come here, sweetheart." Annie opened her arm and Lillie filled the space beside her on the bed. As Annie drew her in close, Lillie laid her head on her shoulder.

"Some things in this life just aren't very fair, are they?"

"No, ma'am, they aren't," Lillie replied.

Annie held her for a while remembering the innocent little child who had lived with her only a few short years ago. "What do you plan to do with this?"

"I guess that's why I wanted you to read it." Lillie sat up and turned on the bed to face her confidante. "Did I write this for your eyes only, or does God intend it for a bigger purpose?"

Annie was filled with a dread and an enthusiasm all at the same time. It was a bizarre combination that caused her heart to quicken. *Oh Lord, give me wisdom.* She looked down and read the last stanza again:

> *Spilling his blood with a pigmented hand,*
> *Surrendering all for an uncaring land.*
> *If he fights for the masses over the sea,*
> *Then by God's perfect grace—a brother he be.*

Words fraught with truth—words fraught with antagonism.

She wondered what changes in society Lillie's generation would witness in the next twenty or thirty years. But for the moment, Lillie was waiting for her best advice. Whichever way Annie told this young woman to go would be wide of the mark. If she told her it was too dangerous to publish such words, Annie would feel the guilt of her society sitting squarely upon her own shoulders. And if she told Lillie to boldly go forward with her writing, much wrath would be brought down on her head. And not just Lillie's. It would most likely affect Roberta as well as Annie's family and the Oakhill congregation. Annie could feel her face growing warm.

Lillie stood up and paced the room. "I shouldn't have shown it to you."

At that moment, Annie felt a stirring in her heart. "Oh yes, you should have." She stood up and took Lillie by the shoulders. "This is an amazing poem. It honors Wallace and all of the Negro men and women who are putting their lives on the line for our country."

Annie reached for the poem on the bed. "How did you know all of this? I don't understand how you could possibly have written something so poignant."

"That's another reason why I brought you back here. I want you to read one of Wallace's letters."

She opened the top drawer of her dresser and reached for a letter underneath her clothing. "Wallace knows Momma can't read, so he included a letter just for me. I got it a few days ago, and I've kept it all to myself, mainly because he told me to." She shrugged her shoulders. "I guess I just couldn't keep it a secret anymore; I had to tell somebody."

"I feel honored," Annie whispered.

She took the letter from Lillie's hand and was appalled at the abuse Wallace and the other Negro men had been suffering at the hands of the very ones who needed them. The letter was long, and Annie read every painful word.

Now that we're finally in the Pacific, Wallace wrote on the second page, *we're being treated more kindly by the island people. They're truly grateful for our assistance . . .*

On the third page he wrote:

The government doesn't use us much in combat, for which I'm thankful, but they don't mind giving us the backbreaking labor that most other men wouldn't bother to spit at. They don't trust us to do anything that requires us to think—as if we're not smart enough or able enough to make important decisions.

Finally, at the end of the fourth and final page, Wallace apologized to his sister for burdening her with his thoughts. He told her how much he loved her and missed her.

Annie felt drained as she returned the letter to its envelope.

"Miss Annie, Wallace and I have shared everything all our lives. Even our thoughts are the same." Tears welled up in Lillie's beautiful brown eyes. "He doesn't think he's coming back. That's why he wrote this letter. I think he just wanted me to know everything before . . ."

Annie choked back a sob as she reached for Lillie. She kissed her and held her tenderly for a very long time.

Finally, Lillie drew back and pointed toward the poem lying on her bed. "So what do I do with this?"

"You hang on to it for now, sweetheart. I think God had you write this for a reason."

"Do you think so?"

"I do. And because of that, I think He'll let you know when the time is right for you to show it to someone else. You and I will pray about it and trust that His timing will be perfect."

Lillie nodded her head then threw herself into Annie's arms once again, bringing back blessed memories of the innocent child of days gone by.

Chapter 44

June 1944
Off the Coast of Great Britain

Poker was the game of choice for most of the American soldiers as they passed time aboard their ships. They had been floating in dock off the English coast for three straight days. Many of the men were separated from an entire month's pay in a matter of two hours' time.

Jake preferred playing spades rather than gamble with his hard-earned money. He and Mercy made a formidable team, which put a target on their backs every time they were challenged to a game. Soldiers in their company began placing bets on when the duo would finally meet their match. Up to this point, no team seemed to be much of a threat to their cunning strategy.

The men aboard ship were growing more restless by the hour. Jake hadn't expected such boredom after reaching the English shores. While there was an air of anticipation permeating the troops, the waiting became more tedious than he had imagined. They had spent the last three weeks practicing landing exercises in tough battle conditions. But after boarding ship on the second day of June, rain had set in. Nothing seemed to be happening.

After finishing evening chow below deck, Jake and Mercy headed up top to catch some fresh air.

"Uh oh, here comes Spivey and Gordon." Mercy shoved Jake through a passageway leading to the other side of the ship. "I don't wanna face those two rats again."

Jake and Mercy broke into a sprint, doubling back around so they would end up behind the obnoxious pair. They had already played them in spades on two occasions, and it was pretty obvious they were trying to cheat to win both times. It hadn't worked.

Finally reaching the stern of the ship, Jake relaxed a bit. This evening, he didn't want to play cards; he just felt like talking to his best friend.

They leaned their elbows on the railing at the aftmost part of the ship and took in the cooler evening air. They had been forced below deck much of the last three days due to the rainy weather.

"Do you feel it?" Mercy asked, keeping his gaze out over the water.
"Feel what?"

"I think we're done waiting."

Jake took in a shuddered breath unnoticed by his friend. "I guess it's just a matter of time."

"Yeah," Mercy said quietly. "I think our time is up."

After a while, Jake asked, "Are you . . ." He didn't quite know how to ask his friend if he was ready for what was to come.

"Scared?" Mercy turned toward him with a look in his eyes Jake had never seen before.

Scared was not the word Jake had been looking for. But for his friend to bring it up must have meant only one thing. Mercy was afraid to go into battle. He didn't even want to think about that possibility.

Jake swallowed hard. "Are you?"

Mercy looked away. "Not for me . . . for my family. I guess I just don't want to be the cause of a lot of heartache."

"Yeah, me too," Jake agreed.

Mercy straightened to his full height and faced his friend. "But you know what? We've trained too long and hard to shy away now. When the time comes, we'll both be ready."

Jake nodded and fell silent, turning his thoughts toward home. "Hey man, I think I'll go below deck and write a couple of letters tonight. You wanna come down?"

"Naw, I'm gonna stay up here for a little while. Me and The Man need to have a heart to heart."

With a smile, Jake pulled away from the railing and gave Mercy a firm pat on the back. "I'll see you at home," Jake teased.

"Yeah, don't wait up."

Jake spent the rest of the evening in his cramped quarters, which were shared by five other soldiers, writing a letter to his momma, to each of his grandmothers, to his grandfather, and to Charlotte. He would post them in the morning before breakfast.

Sleep was hard to come by that night. He kept waking up every hour or so in anticipation of what was to come. Even though no official orders had been handed down, the break in the weather was a pretty good indication that there would be an all-out offensive soon.

By four o'clock in the morning, Jake was certain he was done with sleep for the night. He sat up in his bunk and leaned against the steel wall of the ship. The thrum of the ship's pulse somehow produced a calming effect on his spirit. For the next hour, he prayed for the men of his unit by name and asked God to protect each one. He prayed for their families as well as his own, believing that after today, if his hunch was correct, many folks back home would be receiving bad news.

When the wake-up call came an hour earlier than usual, Jake was already dressed for morning chow. The men were given a hearty, but sparse breakfast, then told to gear up. At 7:30, their ship slipped out of dock and headed along the coast toward Normandy. The waiting was finally over.

***

Eugene stood on the deck of his ship, deeply distressed over the scene before him. Occasionally planes spiraled into the English Channel while artillery shells exploded among the men on the beach. Wave after wave of American soldiers on landing boats surged toward the death-dealing shore. Jake was on one of those boats—maybe already on the beach.

Eugene breathed as if he himself were under direct fire. Not only was his son out there in the smoke-filled chaos, but many of the young men he had trained were on their way. It would've almost been easier to be on one of those landing boats than to stand by as an observer. His anxiety was so sharp that it felt like a physical pain.

As soon as the Americans could clear the bluffs, the supply unit he commanded would head to shore—and not before. His unit would be spared from the enemy's fire.

Oh Jake, hang on, Son. Hang on.

***

"Go! Go! Go!"

Jake pressed forward with his unit, down the ramp, into the frigid water. It was much deeper than he expected, and his head went under. Someone pressed him from behind, forcing him down even longer. He couldn't get a good footing to move forward; he was going to drown.

All of a sudden, the soldier behind him pushed up with a surge of power, and both men broke the surface. His legs drove forward and up the sand bar as he coughed violently, spewing salty liquid from his mouth and nostrils. His eyes and nose stung painfully, but the pain never registered in his brain. Adrenaline surged through his body, propelling him up onto the beach.

Men were yelling all around him, and after a few strides on the shore, he realized he was one of them. When a mortar shell exploded several yards away, Jake was thrown to the ground, planting his face in the sand. He thought for sure he had been struck deaf. Quickly he was up, covering ten more yards before he began to hear the muffled voices of the men around him again. Another shell exploded nearby, propelling his body back into the sand.

Jake glanced up amid the chaos. Thirty more yards and he would make it to the base of the hill. He had to get there at all cost; he had to get off of this murderous beach.

Machine gun bullets ripped through the men on their feet but crawling on his belly would take too long. He glanced to his right, and to his surprise,

Mercy was lying next to him. He appeared to be counting down time, which seemed odd to Jake.

"Now!" Mercy yelled.

The two men pushed to their feet and ran with all their might, crashing headlong into the side of the hill. Several other men of their unit dove in beside them, including their commanding officer, Captain Jack Bellows.

"Keep moving!" the captain barked loudly, and the men began crawling upward.

***

Eugene brought his field glasses to his eyes, surveying the scene more closely. Hundreds of bodies littered the beach, but many more had made it to the hillside. He watched them inch their way toward the German machine gun nests at the top of the hill. The American troops pressed upward toward well-prepared enemy defense positions. Although the 357th Infantry had been a part of the second wave onto Utah Beach, they were still taking heavy fire.

"Poor devils in the first wave," a voice said.

Eugene lowered his field glasses and looked at the sergeant standing beside him on deck. Jamie Hudson was a supply sergeant, same as him, but there was no way he could begin to understand what Eugene was feeling at this very moment. His son was somewhere out there on that hill, or God forbid, still on the beach. Jamie's son was back in Austin, Texas, out of grade school for the summer. What Eugene wouldn't give to have Will and Jake back in grade school again.

Eugene drew an unsteady breath. "They've made a monumental sacrifice today."

"Heroes one and all," Jamie solemnly agreed. He raised his field glasses and began scouring the scene. "With any luck, we'll be on the beach by early afternoon tomorrow."

Peering through his field glasses again, Eugene could see the steady progress of the Americans. Once they cleared the machine gun nests at the top of the bluff, his unit would hit the beach with supplies of ammunition.

Sergeant Hudson continued with a steady stream of commentary as he watched the battle rage. Eventually, Eugene slipped away to another part of the ship. He didn't want any distractions from his ceaseless prayers on Jake's behalf.

***

Jake squeezed his eyes shut trying to erase the last few seconds from his memory. He could hear Mercy yelling above the roar of battle, "Oh God! Oh God, help us!"

Both men had just watched one of their close friends being torn to shreds in a hail of machine gun bullets. He had tried to throw a grenade into the opening of the enemy's defense position at the top of the bluff. It had fallen short of the mark, and now their comrade was gone. Jake forced himself to swallow the bile that burned his throat.

Captain Bellows turned over on his back, wiping a horrid mixture of dirt and blood from his face. He had given the order for Corporal Stevenson to throw that grenade. Quickly, he turned back over on his stomach. "I gotta have a strike," he yelled gruffly. "Who can throw a strike?"

Jake pressed his face into the side of the hill. His heart galloped like a racehorse for the finish line. *This is it*, he thought, *this is how it all ends.*

"I'm a pitcher, sir," he shouted, turning to face his captain. "I can throw a strike."

The captain stared into Jake's eyes for a long moment, then he yelled for the men to lay down cover fire for Corporal Wyatt on his mark.

Instantly, Jake rolled over on his back and pulled a grenade from his belt. His chest heaved violently as he gulped in bucket loads of air. He looked over at Mercy who was aiming his rifle toward the machine gun nest. Without taking his eyes off the target, he murmured, "You can do this, Jake. You were born for this." Mercy's eyelids batted several times as he tried to stave off his emotions.

Captain Bellows nodded his head, and Jake pulled the pin on the grenade. As soon as the soldiers began firing, Jake sprang to his feet and zeroed in on the window of the machine gun nest. Ignoring the bullets whizzing past his head, he threw a perfect strike, dropped to his stomach, and covered his ears.

Seconds later, the Americans were on their feet, charging to the top of the bluff. The machine guns had been silenced; they had conquered their slice of the hill.

***

By late afternoon on June 7, Utah Beach was no longer under attack. While the brave men of the 357th pushed on toward the Normandy countryside, Eugene and his unit landed on the quiet French shore. He shielded his eyes, looking up toward the bluffs. Deep in his heart, he knew Jake was up there somewhere. His gut told him not to search for his son in the blood-soaked sand.

The remainder of June turned out to be the most difficult days for the 357th. The Normandy countryside had been a gift to the German defenders. It was divided into hundreds of small fields, each surrounded by thick hedges and bordered by drainage ditches. German soldiers dressed in camouflage were nearly impossible to see among the hedgerows. The 357th attacked continually against a fanatical enemy resistance. For days on end, the regiment pressed forward under heavy fire, sometimes only advancing a hundred yards in a day. Their only orders were to attack as long as there was daylight.

During the first days of July, the Germans launched a fierce round of counterattacks. They broke through the American lines, nearly making it through to the rear defenses. Eugene and his men had supplied the mortar platoon of Company M with over six thousand rounds of ammunition in just two days. Still, the Germans attacked relentlessly.

On the morning of July 6, Eugene skipped breakfast altogether. A shipment of mortar shells had been brought in overnight, and he knew they needed to get to the fighting men as soon as sunlight broke on the horizon.

"Let's go, let's go." He pushed his unit nonstop, urging them to speed up their packing operation. It was a matter of life and death for the brave men in the field.

Just as the last crate was loaded onto the lead truck, an army jeep sped into camp, skidding to a halt in front of Captain Rex Stanford's tent. The driver jumped out and followed Colonel Barth, commander of the 357th, into the captain's tent. Moments later, Captain Stanford emerged from the tent with orders in his hand. Eugene noticed the grave look on his face as he commanded everyone into the mess tent.

"Listen up, men!" The kitchen staff froze in place at Captain Stanford's bellowing command. A hush came over the crowded tent. "We've just received orders from Colonel Barth."

Eugene noticed the captain's hand shaking slightly as he looked down at the paper he held. When he looked back up at the men, there was an unmistakable fire in his eyes. His voice roared with authority.

"Your presence is required on the front. Every man that can be spared will form a provisional company to plug up the holes in the line. Cooks, drivers, service personnel . . . we will *all* answer the call of duty today. Understood?"

"Sir. Yes, sir!" The men's voices rang out loud and clear.

One of the company cooks looked like he was about to faint. He put down the pot of water he had been holding and leaned on the table in front of him.

Eugene's heart rate skyrocketed at the thought of going back into battle. When his name was called a few minutes later, he swallowed hard and bravely stepped forward. Because of his training and experience, Eugene, along with nine other officers, was taken into the captain's tent for further preparation.

"Men, I don't have to tell you how grave this situation is. The 357th has sustained over seven hundred casualties in just two days."

Eugene could feel the blood draining from his face. *Jake.*

"Most of the men in this provisional company have never been in battle, but they've trained as hard as everyone else. Give them courage by the way you lead, and hopefully, your service will not be required for long."

Captain Stanford spread a large map across his desk and pointed out their defense positions. After several long minutes of instructions, he looked up with stony eyes. "Repel the enemy at all cost." And then his look softened as he quoted from the book of Joshua. *"Be strong and of good courage; do not be afraid, nor be dismayed, for the Lord your God is with you wherever you go."*[11]

The officers came to attention as the captain dismissed them in haste, and before two hours had passed, Eugene was back on the front lines after twenty-six years.

---

[11] Joshua 1:9, NKJV.

***

"Mercy! Mercy!" Jake screamed his friend's name over and over again in the harrowing melee. Smoke filled his lungs as he clawed at the patch of dirt in front of him, unable to see his own hands. Pain seared through his head as he fought to retain consciousness.

"Mercy!" he yelled again, but no one answered him.

Utter darkness engulfed him, and the pain in his head began to ease. An almost peaceful sensation swept over his body. He was home again; his mother's arms surrounded him.

Momma . . . I love you, Momma.

***

Eugene hadn't slept since he hit the front line two days ago. The Germans were relentless in their attacks, leaving no time to rest. Hand-to-hand combat had ensued at night, but thankfully he had yet to engage the enemy face to face. His fatigue was so great that he almost didn't care what happened to him.

Snap out of it, he told himself, rubbing his bloodshot eyes with filthy fingers. *You have to make it home to Annie. You have to!*

He turned over on his belly and chanced a quick peek over the ditch he was lying in. Dirt stung his face from the sniper's bullet, and he instantly ducked his head for cover.

Eugene and his men had surrounded a French farmhouse full of German soldiers, but the sniper in the attic kept the Americans pinned to the ground. He knew an air attack on the farmhouse would take care of their dilemma, but he much preferred taking prisoners. The soldiers of his 357th Provisional Unit had all agreed on the same course of action. They would choose life over death if at all possible.

Right now, however, Eugene felt like killing this guy.

"What do you think, Sarge, can we take him out?" Captain Stanford's driver, Corporal Rich Sawyer, lay next him in the ditch taking a swig of water from his canteen.

Eugene contemplated their situation. Taking out one sniper only ensured the fact that another would take his place. They had to come up with a plan before noon. He didn't want night to fall before they could take this house.

A murmur among the men began to spread along the ditch. He caught sight of a private he didn't recognize, crawling on his belly. One of Eugene's men pointed right at him and the private moved his way.

"Sergeant Wyatt?" The young man spoke his name in a hushed tone.

"That's me."

The private moved into position between Eugene and Corporal Sawyer. "Private First Class Marvin Corley, sir. I have orders to bring you off the front line." The private rolled over on his back and reached into his breast pocket, producing a crinkled paper.

Eugene turned over on his back and took the paper from the young man's hand. It read:

Order for First Sergeant Eugene L. Wyatt to return to Company M supply camp immediately. Signed—Captain Matthew Rex Stanford II, United States Army, 357th Infantry, 90th Division

"What's this all about, Private?"

"I don't know, sir. I'm just followin' orders."

Eugene hesitated a moment, glancing toward his men. Their eyes were all trained on him. He was proud of these guys—none of them had ever been in combat before. But every last one had bravely performed their duty when they were needed the most. Even the cook, Private Second Class Terry Simmons, had served with honor. As fatigued as he was, Eugene was reticent to leave these men.

"Sir?" the private inquired after Eugene's hesitance.

"Who'll lead my unit?"

"That's all been taken care of, sir. You need to come with me."

"Go on, Sarge." Corporal Sawyer nodded to him with concern in his eyes. "Next time we see each other, I'll tell you all about how many Nazis we captured today."

Eugene reached out to the corporal and gave him a firm pat on his chest. "Keep your head down, Rich."

The corporal grabbed his hand and held it for a brief moment. "I'll see you soon."

"I'm countin' on it," Eugene responded, pressing his hand firmly.

A jeep and driver were waiting at a safe distance from the farmhouse to take Eugene back to the supply camp. A sergeant from his company met him along the road.

"Wyatt, good to see you again."

Eugene extended his hand to First Sergeant Kenneth Baker. "Likewise, Baker."

For the next several minutes, Eugene briefed Baker on the situation he was inheriting. He let him know unequivocally of their plan to take the men in the farmhouse prisoners. Baker was a good man and agreed readily to the task at hand.

"Sir, I was hoping we could get on our way."

Eugene could tell his driver was nervous, waiting so long out in the open. He quickly wished his replacement Godspeed and hopped into the jeep just before it lurched forward and sped away.

PART FOUR

Live, then, and be happy, beloved children of my heart,
and never forget, that until the day God will deign to
reveal the future to man, all human wisdom
is contained in these two words,
"Wait and Hope."

~Alexandre Dumas

Now faith is the assurance of things hoped for,
the conviction of things not seen.

~Anonymous (Hebrews 11:1, NASB)

Chapter 45

July 8, 1944
Louisville

Nathan slammed the ledger shut with a thud and nearly threw it across the room. He was on edge for some unexplained reason. He knew he owed his wrangler, Devlin, a heartfelt apology. He'd about taken his head off earlier this morning over an inconsequential mix up on the rope order.

He ran his hands roughly across his face, then pushed back from his desk and headed out into the barn. Maybe if he did a little manual labor this morning, he could burn off whatever was eating away at him.

It was already developing into a scorching day, so Nathan unbuttoned his shirt and threw it onto a nearby bench. It was rare for anyone to see him in a white cotton undershirt.

He had already mucked two stalls, a job he hadn't touched in years, when he heard footsteps briskly coming along the wide corridor of the barn. He began to formulate an apology for Devlin as he stepped outside the gate.

To his surprise, he saw Claudia heading toward his office.

"Down here," he called with a grin, feeling a little better after his physical undertaking.

Claudia turned to face him, and his grin quickly faded. Something was dreadfully wrong.

Nathan covered the distance to his wife in a few purposeful strides. "Claudia, honey, what is it?" He gently took her by the shoulders and led her to the leather sofa inside his office.

Claudia's eyes were red and filled with tears. She choked on a sob, and Nathan's heart began to break on the spot. *Jake or Eugene . . . Jake or Eugene?* His mind was running rampant with fear.

"It's . . . terrible news." Claudia began crying all the harder, and Nathan pulled her to his chest, forgetting about how dirty he was.

Finally, he whispered, "Is it Eugene?"

Claudia shook her head against his chest.

"Please tell me it's not Jake."

"It's not," she sobbed.

Oh, thank God. Nathan still shuddered inside. *Then who . . .*

"It's Wallace." Claudia pulled out of his arms and looked at him in abject misery. "He was killed yesterday in the Philippines." She let out a mournful cry, rending Nathan's heart in two.

Nathan closed his eyes and drew in several deep breaths, then pulled Claudia back up against him. Tears ran down his cheeks and into her hair. The news was almost too much to bear; he had lost yet another grandson.

***

Eugene reached over and caressed the face of the one he loved—silent pleas spilled unceasingly from his heart. He would stay at Jake's bedside as long as it took, and he would hold on to the hope in his heart, as feeble as it seemed.

He allowed his mind to wander to the war he had fought as a youth. A war he had been dragged into against his will, and yet God had protected him and taught him perseverance. He was reminded of the life he had lived following the war. Like Joseph in the Bible, what others had intended for evil, God had intended for good. The Lord had blessed him with a wife and family far beyond anything he had hoped or dreamed of.

But now, something terrible had wrapped itself around his heart. His chest grew tight as he wrestled with an unexpected darkness. Doubt and fear seeped in through any opening they could find. It felt like even the pores in his skin were clogged with uncertainty.

He reached for his son's immovable hand in the bed and brought it to his lips. A tear spilled onto the once vibrant skin. He laid the hand down on the crisp, white sheet, gently wiping the moisture away.

Eugene sat back and chanced leaning his head on the back of the chair. With no intention of sleeping, he now occupied his mind with the passage of time since the previous war. No doubt about it, he had been blessed. Even though mistakes had been made, love had always triumphed—without fail.

Fresh tears streaked his filthy face as he brought it close to Jake's once more. "Can you hear me, Son? I'm right here—I'm not leaving you." Eugene smoothed his son's brow just below the thick, white bandage. "I love you," he whispered.

Sunlight streamed through the hospital windows, shining a long ray down the row of beds. Eugene blinked incessantly before finally holding his eyes open, albeit at a squint. He had tried so hard to stay awake last night but obviously had failed miserably. He rubbed his eyes, forgetting how grimy his hands were. He hadn't left Jake's bedside since they brought him off the front line last night.

"Sir?"

Eugene looked up into the fresh face of a young doctor standing on the other side of the bed.

"Could I show you where to clean up?"

He just shook his head and sat forward in the chair. "What can you tell me about my son?"

"There's been no change during the night, sir. I'm afraid all we can do is wait."

Eugene sat back in his chair. "Then I'll wait."

"Sergeant Wyatt, I really need you to get cleaned up." The doctor moved around the bed to stand in front of Eugene. "I understand your need to be with your son, but keeping this environment as sterile as possible is important for the well-being of our patients."

The doctor took a step back and held out his arm, indicating the way toward the hall.

Eugene glanced over at Jake, then reluctantly came to his feet. The doctor cleared his throat and pointed to the muddy combat helmet turned upside down on the floor. Eugene picked it up and shoved it underneath his arm as he headed down the long row of beds.

"The staff sergeant will be glad to issue you a fresh set of clothes and show you to the showers." The doctor didn't bother to introduce them and immediately returned to the patient ward.

Washing the filth of combat off of his weary body did Eugene a world of good. He had forgotten what it felt like to be clean. When breakfast was offered, he politely refused and headed back to his son's bedside. Eating held no appeal—not while Jake's life hung in the balance.

A nurse greeted Eugene as she changed an IV bottle of fluids running into Jake's arm. "Are you Corporal Wyatt's father?"

"I am." He stood beside his son, marveling at all the tubes running in and out of Jake's body.

"He's a good-looking young man," she said, taking Jake's wrist and checking his pulse.

He stared at his son's features. Even with the discoloration around his eyes and facial swelling, he still looked amazingly like Eugene. It was so difficult to see him in such a terrible condition.

Lines of worry creased Eugene's brow. *What if he never wakes up? What if Jake doesn't make it home?* Eugene's legs turned to jelly, and he sat down hard in the chair. He felt like bargaining with God but had nothing to bargain with except his own life. *Which would be harder for Annie to bear—losing her husband, or another son?*

Eugene chastised himself for thinking such a dark thought. Still the reality of the situation was grim. The doctor had told him last night that Jake's chances of survival were under 10 percent. The swelling on his brain was too great to be hopeful.

"It's the nature of combat," the doctor had told him. "Though he wasn't struck directly by the mortar shell, he was close enough to have sustained an almost fatal concussion." Jake's doctor had looked as fatigued as Eugene had felt last night and didn't bother to mince his words. "His chances are slim. I'm sorry."

Eugene slumped forward in the chair, resting his head in his hands. *Oh God, are You still there, because right now, I can't feel You.* He was certain the Almighty had abandoned him completely.

The nurse moved on to another patient, and Eugene spent the remainder of the day sitting beside Jake's bed. No one could coax him into even a bite of food or a sip of water.

Eugene awoke in the chair on the third day with someone's hand on his shoulder. It took a long moment for his head to clear, but when it did, he recognized his captain, Rex Stanford. He ignored the captain's use of an expletive describing Eugene's appearance. He knew he looked bad—he hadn't shaved in days and his dark beard was already growing thick.

"It's good to see you, Captain." Eugene pushed himself out of the chair and traded a salute for a handshake.

Captain Stanford didn't readily let go of Eugene's hand. "Wyatt, you need to come with me."

When Eugene hesitated, he said, "That's an order."

Eugene leaned over Jake and kissed his forehead. "I'll be back in a minute, Son. I'm not leaving," he whispered.

Captain Stanford led Eugene to the mess hall where breakfast was being served. "Sit down. You need to eat."

Eugene shook his head, but the captain was insistent. "I'm not letting you go back to your son until you eat this meal and drink an entire glass of juice and water. What good are you doing your son by not keeping up your strength? What kind of nonsense is this?"

"Nonsense of the worst kind."

The captain looked surprised that Sergeant Wyatt had raised his voice.

"I can't make sense of anything anymore, sir." Tears welled up in his eyes, and Eugene could feel his composure start to crumble.

Captain Stanford took Eugene by the shoulders with surprising tenderness. "Look at me, Sergeant."

The concern in his eyes was genuine. Eugene felt like such a fool for displaying his anger toward someone who obviously cared about him.

"You're under a great deal of stress right now. It's understandable. But you've gone far too long without food or drink. The hospital staff is beginning to wonder if they'll need a bed for *you* soon."

Eugene's chin dropped to his chest like a little boy who had just been scolded by his father. He didn't know why he'd refused sustenance for so long. Maybe depriving himself had given him some sort of control over this gut-wrenching situation. Not only had he refused food and drink for the past three days, he had refused spiritual nourishment as well. God had left him. Of that, he was quite certain.

Obediently, he took a seat at the table across from the captain and began to eat. Slowly and meticulously he cleaned his plate and washed it down with juice and water. Truthfully, he felt better after eating and vowed inwardly to continue doing so in order to keep up his strength for the long vigil ahead.

"Sergeant." Captain Stanford paused then spoke to him more as a friend. "Eugene, I'm very sorry for your loss . . ."

"I haven't lost him yet, sir!" Eugene cried vehemently.

The captain's hand came up for Eugene to be quiet and listen. "I wasn't talking about your son, *Jake*. I was talking about the son you lost in the Pacific. You've already paid a heavy price in this war." He drew a folded sheet of paper from inside his jacket and slipped it across the table.

"What's that?"

"It's an honorable discharge from the United States Army."

Eugene's mouth dropped open, but no words came out. He unfolded the paper and read it several times until it finally registered in his brain.

"Sir, I don't know what to say." His voice was shaky—the moment seemed surreal.

"I know this was unexpected, but you need to be able to go home to your family."

He knew what the captain had stopped short of saying. Eugene was about to lose his other son to this war, and the army was willing to send him home as his family's only survivor. *Oh God, where are you?*

"Sergeant Wyatt, thank you for your service. Your country owes you a great debt of gratitude."

Folding up the paper, Eugene nodded his head gravely. "Thank you, sir."

"Come on." The captain got up from the table and motioned for Eugene to join him. "I'll sit with you and Jake for a while."

Eugene was astounded that Captain Stanford pulled up a chair and sat with him for the rest of the morning. At noon, he led him back into the mess hall and ate a sandwich with him before departing.

"Godspeed, Wyatt."

"Godspeed, sir." Eugene saluted his former captain one last time and walked with him to his vehicle. He hadn't been outside in days, and coming out into the fresh air felt strange.

To his surprise, Corporal Rich Sawyer was standing beside the jeep, waiting to drive the captain back to camp.

"Rich!" Eugene enveloped the corporal in a big bear hug.

"Hey there, Sarge! I was hoping to see you."

"Well? Don't leave me hanging. Please tell me you captured those sorry Nazis."

"Every last one of 'em, Sarge."

"So you're back to driving for Captain Stanford, huh?"

"Yes, sir. We plugged up all the holes long enough for reinforcements to come in."

Eugene caught himself smiling, and it felt good for a change. "I'm proud of you, Son."

Rich gave him a broad grin. "Thank you, sir."

"No more *sir* for me. I've just been discharged."

"You lucky devil."

Eugene pressed his lips together and nodded his head.

"I'm sorry, Sarge." Rich's expression grew serious. "I know it's because of your son, and I really am sorry."

"It's okay, Rich. I knew what you meant."

"Let's go, Corporal. This isn't the chit chat club." Captain Stanford yanked his cap down on his head and nodded to Eugene from the passenger seat of the jeep.

"Coming, sir."

Rich hopped into the driver's seat, and the engine roared to life.

"Keep your head down, Rich," Eugene called.

"That's the plan, Sarge. That's the plan."

Eugene watched the jeep until it disappeared into the French countryside. He turned his face toward heaven and purposely drew in a long, slow breath. It would be his last breath of fresh air before returning inside to the distinctive odor of death.

Chapter 46

August 1944
Louisville

Annie had labored tirelessly all day on the farm. Hard work usually held her worries and sorrows at bay during the daylight hours. The night, however, was an entirely different story. If it weren't for Rachel's continuous outpouring of hope and confidence, she knew anxiety would overtake her completely.

Lillie had put in an exhausting day at the ball bearing plant but still made time to be with Annie whenever possible. Nathan had dropped her off earlier for a Friday evening trail ride. She planned to spend the night with Annie and Rachel while her mother stayed at the Harrisons' for the night. It had been three weeks since they had buried their precious Wallace. Annie and her family were doing everything they could to comfort Roberta and Lillie through their grief. All of their hearts were breaking, and they needed each other to navigate the agonizing waters.

The two women rode side by side on the old trail along the ridge. A warm evening breeze rustled the leaves, allowing patterns of light from the waning sun to dance through the trees. They rode along making small talk, which they could so easily do, until coming out into the clearing where Will had taught their family how to play tree ball just ten short years ago.

In dismay, Annie pulled Josiah up, and Lillie halted beside her—the Kentucky coffee tree they had used in their game had been split in two by lightning. Its blackened and shattered trunk brazenly symbolized the searing pain their family now endured.

At the sight of the gnarled tree, Lillie began to cry.

"Oh, sweetheart, I'm so sorry." Annie dismounted and reached for Lillie as she came down from her horse. "I haven't been back to this clearing in so long. I didn't know."

Lillie clung to Annie for a moment, then slowly pulled away and walked across the clearing to the tree. Annie tethered the horses and followed, chastising herself inwardly for coming here this evening. If only she had known.

By the time Annie reached the tree, Lillie had dropped to her knees, resting her hand on the lower section of the trunk. "Do you ever wish, Miss Annie, that you could somehow start life over again?" Lillie turned and sat down on the ground, leaning her back into the tree. Tears still glistened on her smooth, brown cheeks.

Annie dropped down beside her and turned her wet face toward heaven. "I don't think I could take it again." She contemplated the lifeless tree they were leaning against. She was trying hard not to become cynical, but it would be so much easier if Jesus would just come back again and end this madness.

Annie took Lillie's hand and held it in her lap. She needed to be strong for the girl, just the way Rachel was for her. She was finding it to be a most difficult task, seeing that she had received a telegram two weeks ago that Jake had been wounded in battle. He was lying somewhere in France in an army hospital. The fact that there were no other details was maddening. What made the news even more unsettling was the fact that she had yet to hear from Eugene. Where was her husband in all of this? Did he even know about Jake?

Lillie broke into her anxious thoughts. "I feel like half of me is missing. Wallace somehow made me a whole person."

"Oh, sweetheart, I know," she sighed. "The two of you were so close."

Lillie's expression changed, as she seemed to be contemplating her next words.

"What is it?" Annie inquired softly.

"Wallace knew things." The look on Lillie's face was uncanny. Annie felt like she was sitting beside Wallace himself. "He could see things the rest of us couldn't see. You know that, don't you?"

Oh yes, Annie knew it quite well. How many times had Wallace told her things that had come to fruition? She constantly played the words from his last letter over and over again in her mind: *I want you to know how often I think of Will with love and admiration. I know he was difficult at times, but inside of him was a good heart. This one thing I know, Miss Annie, you will see him again.*

What did that mean? Was there any chance at all that she would see Will again in this life?

For the next hour, Annie and Lillie shared one incident after another of Wallace *knowing things*. They actually found themselves smiling as they reminisced about happier days.

When the evening shadows began overtaking the clearing, Annie stood and drew Lillie to her feet. Lillie laid her hand on the disfigured tree one last time. "You know I've always looked back on that day of our picnic as one of the happiest days of my life. There wasn't a care in the world."

"I know what you mean. Times just seemed so much simpler back then. I miss all of my children being home together."

Lillie linked her arm with Annie's, and they turned to walk back across the meadow. "I guess you'll just have to make do with your only daughter," she said quietly.

Annie pulled her tight against her side. "And for that, I am truly blessed."

***

"Sergeant Wyatt?"

"Yes?" Eugene quickly stood up beside Jake's bed to face the army hospital's chief of staff, Dr. Marcus Mayfield. Eugene smoothed his hair into place, realizing he hadn't bothered to comb it this morning. It was beginning to grow out, and he knew a haircut was in order. At least he had shaved his beard a few days ago but hadn't bothered to do that today either.

"We're going to transfer your son to the hospital in Liverpool, England. He'll be able to get better care at their facility."

Eugene cleared his throat. "So you think there's a chance they can help him there? Is he getting better?"

Dr. Mayfield tapped his fingers on Jake's chart without looking at the page. "I'm afraid there's been no change. I'm sorry I can't give you the news you're looking for. The fact is, the longer he remains unconscious, the more likely it is that he won't be waking up."

Eugene thought by now he'd be strong enough to deal with such news, but the doctor's proclamation had felt like a blow to his abdomen. It had knocked every ounce of air out of him. He had to sit back down.

The doctor laid Jake's chart on the end of the bed and took out his pocket light. He looked intently into Jake's eyes, then listened to his heart, checked his breathing, and took his pulse.

"Have you done his movement exercises this morning?"

"Yes—all of them," Eugene responded quietly.

The doctor nodded grimly. "Well, I'll go see to the paperwork. He's due to be transferred later this morning."

Eugene sat back in his chair feeling exhausted. He stared at the army cot tucked away underneath Jake's bed. After the first few nights in the chair, the hospital staff had brought him the cot to sleep on at night. It didn't make much difference—sleeping was nearly impossible.

"Mail, sir?"

"Hmm?" Eugene looked into the face of the private standing at the foot of Jake's bed.

"Do you have any mail you need posted, sir?"

Eugene shook his head. "No. No mail." Just like every other day since he'd been here. It wasn't from the lack of trying, however. He couldn't begin to count the number of letters he had started and torn up after the first few lines. Annie deserved to know about his discharge from the army—about Jake most of all—but he couldn't find the words to tell her that their son's situation was practically hopeless.

He leaned forward, placing his forearms on his knees. How ironic. He had so bravely gone into a raging battle but lacked the courage to write just one letter to his precious wife. *God help me.* Even that thought seemed empty and futile.

By evening, Jake had been moved to a much larger hospital off the coast of England in the city of Liverpool where hundreds of American and British soldiers were being cared for by a large staff of army nurses and physicians.

Eugene immediately conveyed his situation to the hospital chief of staff and was allowed to continue his vigil by Jake's side. But at night, he was directed to stay in a waiting room just off of Jake's wing. He pulled two padded chairs together in the corner and used his pack as a pillow. One of the nurses kindly gave him a blanket.

As time went by, Eugene could feel himself falling into a deep depression. He had ignored his family for so long now that he had become deeply troubled. With each passing day, the guilt threatened to swallow him up. The weather was often rainy and gloomy, pushing him deeper into desolation. If Jake died, he would never be able to face Annie with the news. He had already failed her by allowing Will to run off and join the Army Air Corps . . . and look what happened to him.

On his third day in the British hospital, Eugene walked slowly through the queue of beds after another lousy night's sleep. His only thought was to get through the long row of suffering soldiers until he could reach Jake on the other end.

"How are you this morning, David?"

Eugene ignored the cheerful English nurse as she checked on one of her patients. But the young man's response drew him up short.

"Please . . . call me Mercy."

He turned and stared at the young man. Could it possibly be Jake's closest friend lying in that bed? The face was familiar, but the young man's body had taken a terrible toll. His leg had been hoisted into the air by a pulley system above the bed, and both arms lay by his side in plaster casts. He looked to be in misery, yet he had addressed the nurse in such a pleasant tone.

Eugene waited until all of her ministrations were complete before he approached the bed.

"David McAllister?"

The young man's gaze turned upward. Eugene could see the pain in his eyes.

"Yes, sir."

"I'm Jake's dad; we met at Camp Barkeley."

The expression on Mercy's face told him that if this young man could get out of bed right now, Eugene would be wrapped up in a tight hug. For that, Eugene put his hand on Mercy's chest and leaned his face up next to his. When he pulled away, a tear slid down Mercy's cheek. Poor guy, there was nothing he could do about it with both hands in a cast. That's when Eugene realized in horror that Mercy's left arm was not in a cast at all. It was wrapped tightly with bandages and his hand was missing.

Eugene continued to rest his hand on Mercy's chest, grieving over his terrible condition.

"What about Jake?" Mercy stammered. "Did he make it?"

Eugene nodded grimly. "He's at the end of the corridor."

Mercy raised his head from the pillow, stretching his neck to search the beds.

"David . . . uh, Mercy, Jake's not doing very well. He's been unconscious ever since he was brought in."

Mercy's head hit the pillow with a soft thud. More tears streamed down his face and onto the sheets.

Eugene reached into his pocket and pulled out a handkerchief Rachel had given him years ago. He gently wiped the tears from Mercy's face wishing he had words of encouragement where Jake was concerned. There simply *were* none.

Mercy followed Eugene's gaze. "Sir, you should go be with Jake. It was nice to see you."

Eugene took in a deep breath. "I'll be back in a little while to check on you. I won't leave you here alone."

That brought a faint smile to Mercy's lips. "Thank you," he said softly. "And sir?" Eugene hesitated beside the bed. "Tell him I made it."

This time, Eugene had to hold back a powerful surge of emotions. In a choked voice he said, "I will, Son. I will."

At noon, he returned to Mercy's bed and pulled up a chair. When the nurse came with David's lunch, Eugene told her he would feed him. From that point on, Eugene was the only one who fed Mercy at meal times. Often the young man didn't feel like eating, but Eugene began to find within himself a wealth of encouragement. He had suppressed it beneath a thick layer of self-pity and remorse.

Every afternoon, Mercy asked Eugene to read the Bible to him. It had been so long since he himself had been in the scriptures that every word began to sound fresh and alive again. And in the evenings, Mercy dictated letters for Eugene to write to his family in Kansas. Sometimes it took more than one sitting to finish a letter. Mercy suffered a great deal of pain from his injuries, and the morphine made him drowsy, especially at the end of the day.

After a week of the same routine, Eugene happened to be at Mercy's bedside when the doctor released his leg from elevation, causing him a great deal of back pain.

The doctor looked over at Eugene. "He could probably use a back massage to loosen up the muscles. He's been in the same position for so long it will take a while to stretch the muscles back out."

With a coordinated effort, Eugene and the doctor rolled Mercy onto his stomach as he cried out in pain. Eugene spent the next hour massaging Mercy's back until his hands ached. It had taken several long minutes before he was able to work the knots out of his lower back.

Mercy groaned intensely during the workout. He claimed the massage brought him as much pain as it did comfort.

A nurse passing by helped Eugene turn Mercy over onto his back again. Eugene thanked her and pulled the sheet up around Mercy's chest. He looked utterly exhausted, but that didn't stop him from making his request.

"Sir, now that my leg's outta the sling, do you think you could take me to see Jake?"

Eugene looked down the aisle and wondered if there was enough space to roll his bed through. Mercy wasn't hooked up to an IV; it might be possible. "I'll check with one of the doctors and see if we can do it."

Mercy's left arm came up, and he laid the stub end on Eugene's arm. "No, don't ask. Please," he begged. "What if they say no?"

Nervously, Eugene looked around the room. All was quiet except for a few nurses working with some of the men at the opposite end. He quickly came to a decision and started cranking the bed into a sitting position.

"Does that hurt your back or leg?" he asked.

Mercy shook his head. "I'm fine," he said, gritting his teeth.

The wheels had been locked down, so Eugene released each of the clamps and pulled the bed forward. The soldiers who were able watched as Corporal David McAllister's hospital bed rolled down the aisle to the end of the room. There was just enough space for Mercy's bed to fit between Jake's bed and the wall.

For a long time, all Mercy could do was stare down at the shell of a man in the bed. If it weren't for the shallow rise and fall of his chest, he would've thought Jake was already gone. He needed to touch his friend and pray over him, but when he leaned across the bed to take hold of Jake's hand, he froze. The dreadful reality punched him in the gut once again. His hand was gone. When would he ever get that through his head?

Without a word, Eugene reached across the bed and joined Jake's hand to Mercy's arm. He held their connection together with both of his hands. Mercy gave him a grateful nod then began to pray.

Eugene couldn't recall the last time he had heard a prayer such as this. He was reminded of his mama's deep and sincere petitions. There was no doubt that Mercy shared a rich relationship with the heavenly Father, a relationship that Eugene had once delighted in.

When the prayer was over Eugene sat down in the chair while he and Mercy watched over his son. Neither one spoke, leaving Eugene to his own thoughts. He began to wonder when his own prayers had ceased. He felt certain he hadn't prayed since his first night at Jake's side. How had he fallen so far in such a short time? His chest began to tighten as the shame of his transgression overtook him.

Finally, he couldn't take it anymore. "Mercy, I need to get out of here for a while. Can I take you back now?"

The look on Mercy's face reminded him of a lost little boy. "I don't wanna leave Jake's side. Please just let me stay here."

Eugene looked around. "But what if . . ."

"I don't care if they find me here. I have to be with my buddy. Please."

"Is there anything you need before I go?" He came around to stand behind Mercy's bed. "Do you want to lie back down?"

"No, I'm good. I just want to sit here and pray some more."

Another stab of guilt pierced Eugene's conscience. "Okay, I'll be back later." He immediately turned and headed down the corridor.

Once outside, Eugene looked up at the late afternoon sky. The clouds were dark and heavy. They threatened to turn loose at any moment.

After nearly an hour, he found himself aimlessly walking along the shore. When he stopped to look out over the water, his heart began pounding. Storm clouds were rolling swiftly toward land, and the number of jagged lightning strikes was staggering. As he began to search for shelter along the lonely beach, raindrops started pelting the water and sand. He thought he saw a small opening along the rocky hillside not far down the beach, and he took off at a sprint right when the floodgates opened.

Thankfully, the craggy boulders offered Eugene the much-needed shelter he sought. Charred remains of driftwood inside the small alcove told him this refuge had been used before. A well-worn rock stood guard near the entrance, and Eugene sat down, wiping the water from his face.

As the storm raged outside, Eugene marveled at the power of each bolt of lightning. It seemed so close, so menacing, and yet, somehow he felt like God was using the storm to get his attention.

It was working.

Every time a lightning bolt flashed in the sky, Eugene released a sorrowful lament. "I'm sorry," he cried, into the roaring thunder. He stood and turned his face toward heaven. "I'm truly sorry."

A long roll of thunder reverberated through his very soul and his face suddenly flooded with tears. "I'm so ashamed," he rasped, "Please forgive me." Eugene's spirit was thoroughly broken. He had shoved God as far away as he possibly could, but God was pulling him back.

Now the sluice of his heart opened wide. He paced the small shelter, speaking to the Lord in confession and praise, crying out for the life of his son, begging God to teach him how to trust again.

He sat down once more on the rock, leaning forward with his elbows on his knees. What was it he had read just yesterday in the book of Genesis? Mercy had asked for the story of Joseph, and Eugene had read it straight through. Jacob had not wanted his sons to take Benjamin back to Egypt. He had told them if he lost his youngest son, he would die of grief. But his ten sons convinced him that without Benjamin, they would not be given the food they so desperately needed. Jacob had finally accepted the inevitable and said, "If I be bereaved of my children, I am bereaved."

Eugene slipped to his knees. "Lord, if You want to take Jake home . . ." A sob rose up in his throat. "Then take him home. I will trust Your judgment and not my own."

More tears slid down his cheeks as the storm continued to rage. Eugene remained on his knees, finally accepting God's will, whatever that might be. Outside, the tiny shelter violent waves crashed the shore, but inside, perfect peace prevailed.

It was dark when Eugene finally returned to the hospital. He had rummaged through his pack in the corner of the waiting room and changed into dry clothes.

Now he walked down the long corridor toward Jake, but this time his eyes had been opened. He didn't just see beds that he needed to pass by; he saw the men. These were someone else's sons, husbands, and fathers, wounded and dying far from home. How had he missed that?

Eugene noticed Mercy's bed was back in its original position. But drawing closer, it became evident that the soldier in the bed was not David McAllister. His heart leapt into another gear, fearing the worst. His steps quickened until he could see that Mercy's bed had been exchanged for the young man's who had previously been next to Jake.

Nearly everyone in the ward was asleep, Mercy among them. It was good to see his face relaxed and void of all pain for a change. Eugene kissed Jake and told him he loved him, then without conscious thought, did the same to Mercy and sat down between his boys. He planned to stay with Jake and Mercy tonight as long as the staff would let him.

A tablet of paper and pen sat on a small table between the beds. Eugene picked it up and began writing in the light of a dim lamp.

My sweet, sweet Annie,

I must first and foremost beg your forgiveness for not writing in such a long time. Believe me when I say that it was not from a lack of trying. This is a most difficult letter to write. Our dear Jake is lying wounded in the British Army Hospital in Liverpool, England. I have been by his side night and day, for the past month. I know your prayers have been many on his behalf. Please keep them coming. He has been unconscious all this time due to a severe concussion caused by a mortar shell. Three times a day I exercise his arms and legs to keep his muscles from growing weak. I talk to him constantly just in case he can hear me.

You may be wondering how I have been allowed to be with our son for such a length of time. It is because I was given an honorable discharge from the army! I'm sure you and Mama are relieved to hear at least one bit of good news. Since I am no longer required for duty, I'm able to spend all of my time with Jake.

Jake's best army buddy, David McAllister, is also in this hospital. They have moved his bed right next to Jake's. David has suffered many injuries, including the loss of his left hand. He is in terrible pain but has already been praying over Jake. David's nickname is Mercy because he was studying to be a minister before the war. Please include David in your daily prayers.

I must close for now and try to get some sleep. I miss you more than I could ever possibly write on paper. Be strong when you think of Jake. God's will be done.

I love you with all my heart.
Eugene

Eugene leaned back in his chair, satisfied that he had finally completed the letter. He tried to picture Annie's reaction, but it was far too painful to think about. He sucked in a deep breath and let it out slowly, trying to calm his nerves. He still felt so ashamed of his lack of faith for these past few weeks. Someday he hoped to confess his weakness to Annie, but for now, the letter in his hand would have to suffice.

"Sergeant Wyatt?" One of the night nurses stood before him with an armful of linens. "I'll have to ask you to go back to the waiting room now," she said in a soft voice.

Eugene nodded and slowly came to his feet. "Thank you for moving Corporal McAllister's bed next to Jake's."

The nurse smiled sweetly while looking at Mercy. "He wouldn't have it any other way."

"I'm sure he wouldn't," Eugene agreed.

He moved to Jake's side, taking hold of his hand and bringing it to his lips. "I love you so much, Son." And then in a broken voice, he pleaded, "Come back to me, Jakie. Please come back."

When Eugene had walked down the long row of soldiers, the nurse turned back toward Jake for just a moment, then she went on with her many duties for the night. She didn't think it important to tell Sergeant Wyatt that she had wiped a tear from his son's face.

Chapter 47

"That's it, Mercy, you can do this!" Eugene held out his arm in case Corporal McAllister needed it for support, but Mercy gritted his teeth and ignored him.

Several soldiers sat up in their beds, cheering on the corporal. He was trying to take his first steps after more than five long weeks lying in bed. His leg hadn't been broken—the muscles in his thigh had been torn and repaired in surgery. Now it was time to see if he could bear the weight of walking.

Eugene smiled broadly as Mercy shuffled one step forward, and then another. It took him six shuffles to make it the predetermined distance. A groan came out of his throat with every step. Eugene knew this was causing Mercy a great deal of pain, but he wasn't about to restrain the young man's determination to walk.

Mercy leaned against the foot rail of Jake's bed, letting out a huge breath. "I made it!"

"Yes, you did," Eugene said proudly, patting his back. "How about letting me help you get back to your bed?"

"No, sir," he said, and swallowed hard. "If I was able to get here on my own, I can get back."

Eugene, however, stayed by Mercy's side, ready to give him support. But true to his resolve, the corporal made it all the way back on his own bed. The soldiers who had been watching applauded his effort.

"Thank you very much, one and all," David said with appreciation. He dropped down on the side of his bed with a thud.

Eugene noticed the sweat on Mercy's brow. This effort had taken a lot out of him. He lifted the corporal's leg up onto the bed and helped him slowly lie back down. Without asking, Eugene used a cloth to wipe his forehead, then covered him to the waist with his sheet.

"Can I get you some water?"

Mercy shook his head. "No thanks, but could you help me with something else?"

"Sure, anything." Eugene noticed the anxious look on his face.

"Could you unwrap my arm bandage? I think I wanna see it now."

Eugene's heart skipped a beat. "Mercy, how about we wait until the doctor comes by this afternoon?"

Mercy was already shaking his head. "The doc said he was gonna show me this afternoon, but I don't wanna wait. Please."

Eugene took a few shallow breaths and rubbed the back of his neck. Mercy's eyes were dark and pleading. Without further argument, Eugene pulled up a chair to the bed and reached for Mercy's arm. Very carefully, he began unwrapping the bandage. A pungent odor drifted into the air as he got closer to the skin. He did his best to ignore it.

Mercy wasn't watching. He had laid his head back on the pillow and closed his eyes. After one more loop around, his arm was fully exposed. Eugene held it tenderly, staring at the raw stub where once a strong hand had been.

When Mercy opened his eyes, he stared at the ceiling for a while. Then, working up his nerve, he lifted his arm out of Eugene's hand and brought the end of it in front of his face.

His brow was deeply furrowed. "I can still feel my hand there sometimes. The doc said that's natural." He shook his head and closed his eyes again, laying his arm down on the sheet. "I just had to see it for myself. You can wrap it up again, sir. Thank you," he whispered.

Eugene did his best to wrap it back the way it was. He had watched the doctor check the wound many times, but Mercy had never once looked, not until today. Maybe now that he realized he was going to be able to walk, the young man had finally summoned the courage to look at his arm. Bless his soul—without a left hand and a broken right arm, he had been unable to do anything on his own. It had to be humiliating on so many levels. Eugene was practically his sole caregiver for anything other than medical needs. He tried to give the young man as much dignity as possible.

When the bandage was replaced, Eugene stayed by his bed. "Do you want to talk about it?"

Mercy's eyes opened again; his stare remained upward. Eugene feared showing him his arm had been too much.

Finally, he turned his head toward Eugene. "No, sir. I spend all my time just trying to forget about it. But thank you," he added politely.

Eugene stood and laid his hand on Mercy's shoulder. "You're a brave young man. I'm proud of you."

The faintest of smiles passed across the corporal's lips. "I appreciate it, sir."

Eugene turned away to let Mercy get some rest. He had already performed Jake's morning exercises, so he decided to make his rounds. He was trying to get to know as many of the other soldiers as possible, hoping somehow to give them encouragement. It helped give him something to do other than worry himself sick beside Jake's bed.

But at the end of every day, Eugene could feel the temptation toward despair creeping up on him. It always started with tightness in his gut as the shadows overtook the hospital wing. The darkness continually endeavored to work against him. That's when he prayed most fervently for God's Spirit of peace to take control, and eventually, Eugene began to sleep through the night once again.

As another week passed, Mercy grew stronger by the day. The cast was finally removed from his right arm, and he began feeding himself again. He regained some of his lost dignity by being able to take care of things of a more personal nature. He spent a great deal of time beside Jake's bed, holding his hand and praying.

"You know, Jake, you really ought to open your eyes just once so you can see Nurse McGill. She's a real looker." Mercy rested his hand on Jake's shoulder, trying to make small talk. "She's usually on night shift. I'll let you know when she comes around. It should be any time now."

"Okay," came the faintest whisper.

Mercy's heart flopped over in his chest so hard it hurt. He jumped to his feet, and the chair clattered backward onto the floor. Jake's eyes were closed and nothing about his appearance had changed. Mercy wondered if he had just imagined it?

"Jake, can you hear me, buddy?"

No response. Mercy's heart slowed its pace a bit. He stared for a long time at Jake's face, then turned around to pick up the chair.

"Sorry . . . 'bout . . . your hand."

The chair crashed back to the floor, and Mercy turned to his friend wide eyed. Still there was no sign of movement, so Mercy bent low until his face was only inches from Jake's. "You better not be messin' with me, Jake. Can you hear me?"

Jake's eyelids began to flutter, and Mercy let out a whoop of delight. But when he saw the crease in Jake's brow, Mercy apologized for his outburst. "I'm sorry, man. Come on, you can do it. Open your eyes, Jake," he pleaded.

Frantically, Mercy looked around for Jake's dad, but he was nowhere in sight.

Eugene pushed himself up off the floor in the small chapel, just down the hall from his son's hospital wing. He discovered that no one ever used the sparsely furnished room during the evening hours. It had become his solitary refuge for earnest prayer. The more time he spent there on his knees, the more he trusted the will of the Almighty.

As he left the room feeling refreshed, Eugene turned to make his way down the long row of patients, checking to see who was still awake. There was a slight disturbance at the other end of the room, so he quickened his pace. Mercy was standing beside Jake's bed. The closer he got in the dim light the more certain he was that Mercy was crying. His shoulders were shaking.

Eugene paused from several feet away. *Oh God, help me be strong.* He had often wondered how he would handle Jake's passing—and now the time had apparently come. Everything around him faded into the background as he made his way forward. There was just enough light for Eugene to see the tears glistening on Mercy's cheeks. He couldn't bear to look at his son lying there until he heard one solitary word.

"Dad?"

Eugene's eyes darted to the bed, then back to Mercy. His brain could barely register what was going on.

Mercy laughed out loud as tears continued to pour from his eyes. "He woke up! He just . . . woke up!"

Eugene snapped out of his disbelief when he looked back down at Jake's face. His eyes were open; he could see the intense color of blue!

He couldn't get around the bed fast enough. Eugene cupped his son's face in both of his hands and eagerly kissed him. When he tried to speak, the words came out in a sob. All he could do was gather him up in his arms. Quietly, Jake breathed, "I love you, Dad," and Eugene wept uncontrollably.

***

Brother Edwin Jones stood behind the pulpit after Sunday morning's closing song. His round face beamed with joy. "I have some wonderful news to share. Sister Annie Wyatt informed me before the service that her dear son Jake woke up. Praise Jesus!" He looked down toward Annie and her family. "Our prayers have been answered."

The congregation added their affirmation in the form of "Amen" and "Praise God."

Edwin proceeded with the announcement. "She requests that we continue our prayers on his behalf as he tries to regain his strength. As I lead us in a closing prayer, let's also remember all of our men overseas and pray for our Lord to bring a lasting peace to all nations."

When the service was over, Annie found herself in the embrace of just about everyone in the congregation. She answered as many questions as she could, recalling the details from Eugene's most recent letter.

Later at the Harrisons', as the afternoon meal drew to a close, Mattie came into the dining room to clear away the dishes. "Miss Annie, I's on pins and needles 'til you read me Mr. Eugene's letter 'bout Jake."

Annie giggled at Mattie's enthusiasm. "I knew you'd want to hear it. It's in my purse."

But when Annie rose from her chair, she caught a glimpse of Roberta's face across the table. She hoped her excitement over Jake didn't in some way cause the dear woman more grief over Wallace. Lillie took her mother's hand and held it affectionately.

Annie told Mattie, "Why don't I come into the kitchen and help you clean up. I can read it to you there."

"Sounds wonderful, Miss Annie. But don't you go thinkin' you gotta help me clean up."

"Nonsense, it's the least I can do," Annie responded. She went around the table to Roberta and leaned in close, kissing her cheek. "When I'm done in the kitchen, I'd love to spend some time with you talking about Wallace."

"Oh, child," Roberta nearly melted at her touch, "I would love nothin' more."

Lillie raised her face to Annie just as she had done so often as a little girl. Annie smiled affectionately and kissed her, then cleared their plates from the table.

Mattie ignored the dishes when Annie came into the kitchen holding Eugene's letter. She pulled two chairs away from the table and practically yanked Annie down beside her.

"You ain't gotta read me no romance stuff from yer husband. Just read me the excitin' part about Jake."

Annie couldn't help but laugh. "So you don't think the romance stuff is exciting?"

If Mattie could blush, she would be doing so right now. She lowered her head and looked up at Annie with a coy expression. "Miss Annie, I is quite certain it's excitin' for you, but . . ."

"I'm just kidding, Mattie. I wasn't going to read you that part anyway."

Mattie appeared relieved as Annie began to read Eugene's description of Jake's awakening. He believed it was nothing short of a miracle. Eugene had felt like Jacob in the Bible when he saw his son Joseph alive again after more than twenty years in Egypt.

Unable to resist another reading of the letter, Claudia came into the kitchen. She stood behind Annie, resting her hands on her shoulders.

While Jake is still very weak, Annie read, *the doctor sees no reason why he shouldn't fully recover. His brain function appears to be normal, which has baffled the medical personnel. Dr. Emmett, Jake's attending physician, has already admitted it to be an act of God. I have believed that to be so from the very beginning.*

I continue to exercise Jake several times a day while he lies in bed. It will be quite some time before he will be able to control his muscles and regain their function again. If it were anyone other than Jake, there would be cause for discouragement. But, you know our son; his patience is admirable.

Jake's good friend Mercy, David McAllister, continues to gain strength at a rapid pace. It won't be much longer before they discharge him and send him home to Wichita. While he continually tells me that he owes me a great debt of gratitude, it is truly I who owe him. I look forward to telling you all about it in person.

Annie looked up with a wry smile. "He writes a little romance stuff right here."

Mattie laughed and playfully slapped her hand on the table. "Don't you go readin' that part. Yer momma done standin' right behind ya."

Claudia squeezed her shoulders. "Read her the part about Jake's memories."

Annie turned to the next page and picked back up.

I've been fascinated by some of the memories Jake has had, even though he was asleep for over six weeks. He knows things about the war that we had only read in the newspapers. Mercy and I are baffled as to how he could know such things. Of course, we were constantly talking to him while he was unconscious, and on many occasions, I read the newspaper out loud to Mercy within Jake's earshot. Even though he has no recollection of us talking to him, he has retained nearly everything he's heard. One of the first things he told Mercy, upon waking up, was that he was sorry about the loss of his hand. It's almost scary how much he knows.

"Eugene goes on to say that he and Jake will remain in the Liverpool hospital for a few more months. He won't leave until he can bring Jake home with him," Annie stated.

Mattie squealed with glee. "Won't that be the day when yer two men come walkin' through yer door, Miss Annie?"

Annie got a faraway look in her eyes. "Oh yes, that'll be the day."

Chapter 48

November 1944
Louisville, Kentucky

The family purposely kept Eugene and Jake's arrival time a secret from the Oak Hill congregation, needing to have a private homecoming at the airport. They were still unsure of Jake's weakened condition and didn't want a crowd of people to exhaust him. While the late autumn air was crisp, there was no hint of a wind, leaving Annie and her parents and Rachel comfortable in their winter coats as they waited eagerly near the runway.

"Darlin', how are we going to handle this?"

Annie looked over at Rachel's concerned face. "What do you mean?"

"I know you're anxious to be with Eugene and Jake *both* when they get off the plane. Which one are you going to first?"

Annie hadn't really given it much thought. She was far too excited to even think of such a detail. But she realized Rachel was being considerate, not wanting to go to one or the other first, should one of them hold priority to Annie. That thought almost boggled her mind. Now that she was offered a choice, which one *would* she go to first?

"Mama, I don't really know. Which one would *you* rather greet first?"

Rachel shook her head. "I'm not going to make that decision, darlin'. You tell me who you're going to first and I'll go to the other."

They were still going round and round with their greeting options when the plane from New York landed on the runway. Annie felt her heart jump clear up into her throat and instantly forgot about their conversation. It was all she could do to keep from running out to the plane before it even came to a halt.

The roar of the engines ceased while two men pushed the rolling stairs up to the doorway and locked them into position. When the giant propellers slowed to a crawl the main door opened. Several other passengers disembarked into the waiting arms of their loved ones.

Annie and Rachel moved forward, clinging to one another for support. Nathan and Claudia remained where they were, allowing them to have this rapturous moment all to themselves.

At her first glimpse of Eugene in the doorway, Annie could feel her body shaking uncontrollably. She watched as he wrapped his arms around the young man beside him—it was Jake. He had lost so much weight she almost didn't recognize him. But there he was, her precious son, being helped down the stairway, one slow step at a time.

It seemed like an eternity before their feet finally rested on the tarmac. Annie and Rachel closed the distance between them with unrestrained tears flowing down their faces.

Without hesitation, both men uttered the same word at the very same time—"Mama!"

Annie and Rachel choked back a laugh as each one took her son into her arms.

"Oh, God, thank you," Annie whispered in relief. She couldn't seem to pull Jake close enough. His arms surrounded her with surprising strength as he tucked his face into her neck.

"I love you so much, Momma."

Annie wept tears of joy. "And I love you, Jake. I love you more than you'll ever know. Thank God you're home."

It was several long minutes before Eugene tapped on Jake's shoulder. "It's my turn, Son."

Annie laughed and wiped her tears as Jake pulled out of her arms. Eugene took hold of him and gently turned him toward Rachel. Nathan and Claudia came to their side. "I've got him," Nathan said, nodding to Eugene.

Eugene grinned at his father-in-law, then gathered Annie up into his arms. She was laughing and crying all at the same time. When his mouth took possession of hers, she thought she was going to pass out. He gave her a brief moment to catch her breath then covered her mouth again. His hands were on her lower back, urging her mind to anticipate what was to come.

Finally, he kissed her neck and then her cheek. "I missed you so much!" His voice was hoarse and full of emotion.

Annie cradled his face in her hands. "I love you, Eugene Wyatt. With all my heart, I love you."

She laid a gentle, yet urgent kiss on his lips. "Thank you for coming back to me, and thank you for bringing Jake home."

Eugene's eyes grew moist. "I have so much to tell you."

Annie didn't want to let go of her husband, but she realized her mother was standing beside them, waiting to add her welcome. A wheelchair had been brought out for Jake, and he was sitting in it already looking fatigued. She walked around behind him and laid her hands on his chest, leaning down to kiss his cheek.

"Your room is waiting for you. Gramps took the bunk beds out and moved a bigger bed in."

Jake smiled and held her hands up against him. "I can't wait to get home. There's so much I want to tell you."

Annie laughed. He sounded exactly like his father.

Two cars had been driven to the airport to accommodate the extended family. When they made it back to the Wyatt's farm, Nathan came around to assist

Jake into the house. He helped him remove his coat and put him in an easy chair beside the fireplace before getting the fire going.

Everyone sat in the living room talking for over an hour before Rachel and Claudia busied themselves in the kitchen with supper. Rachel had baked a chocolate cake early this morning that still needed icing. The women chattered endlessly about Eugene and Jake's return.

In the living room, Nathan probed the men about the war. Annie felt Eugene stiffen beside her on the sofa. Neither he nor Jake seemed eager to talk about the subject, so she tried to move the conversation in a different direction.

"Jake, please tell me more about your friend David. I'd like to hear all about him."

That seemed to perk Jake up a bit. He started at the beginning, telling her about meeting Mercy at Camp Barkeley and then about seeing Wallace in desert training.

"Dad, I have a confession to make." Jake looked over at Eugene with a wry smile. "I almost got a disciplinary mark on my service record after we captured the men from the 93rd."

When Eugene laughed, Jake said, "You think I'm kidding, but I'm not. I got into a fistfight with Perry Cunningham."

Annie sat up out of Eugene's arms, but he quickly hauled her back to his side. It didn't stop her from asking, "You did what?"

"Yeah," Jake admitted, "Perry was making some racial comments toward the men of the 93rd, and I just snapped. I never punched him, but he got off some pretty hard shots to my face."

"Sweetheart!" Annie was upset with whoever this Cunningham fellow was.

"It's okay, Mom," Jake chuckled. "I probably should've handled it in a better way. But the good thing is I got to see Wallace. He was very brave to come to my aid."

Annie's eyes instantly filled with tears. "My sweet Wallace," she whispered.

Jake swallowed hard. "He told me . . ." When his voice quavered, he looked over at the fire for a long moment, trying to regain his composure. After clearing his throat, he looked back at his parents. "Wallace told me that we wouldn't see each other again. I didn't know what he meant at the time . . . but I guess I do now."

Annie noticed Eugene's breathing pattern had changed. He was trying to keep his composure. "How are Roberta and Lillie doing?" he asked quietly.

Nathan leaned forward in his chair. "It's not been easy for them. They're going through a terrible time of grief. We're doing everything we can for them, but there's no way to ever replace someone like Wallace. He meant everything to them."

Sadness permeated the room as Annie's heart longed not only for Wallace, but for her dearest Will. She missed her son so very much. Wallace's words continued to haunt her every waking moment—*this one thing I know, Miss Annie, you will see him again.* What was she supposed to do with that? She didn't dare share what she was thinking with anyone else. They simply wouldn't understand.

At that moment, Rachel came into the living room with the chocolate cake in her hand. "This evening we're going to do something special. We're going to start supper with dessert!"

Her proclamation seemed to immediately lighten the mood in the room.

"Our two men have come home . . . so we celebrate!" She lifted the cake victoriously into the air.

Eugene stood and pulled Annie to her feet. "I can't tell you how many times I wanted cake before dinner growing up. It takes an act of war to finally get my wish."

Rachel raised her brow. "Watch it, Son, or I'll revoke the privilege."

Eugene went to her and kissed her cheek. "You wouldn't dare." He gave her his most handsome grin, and Rachel's eyes softened.

"Well, come on then, before I change my mind."

Annie went straight to Jake and helped him to his feet. "As soon as supper is over, you need to get some rest, sweetheart."

Jake put his arm around her shoulders for support. "I like the sound of that," he said wearily. "But for now," he gave his mother the same handsome grin, "we celebrate!"

Later that evening, Eugene helped Jake get settled into his room and finally into the new bed. Annie knocked on the open door. "Can I come in?"

Jake pushed up on his elbow. "Sure."

"Oh no, sweetheart, lay back down. I just wanted to tell you goodnight."

"You can sit down and talk a while if you want."

Eugene was already seated on the side of the bed, and Annie sat down in front of him. She couldn't help but reach out and smooth Jake's dark hair from his forehead. "I feel so blessed to have you both home," she said with a great deal of emotion. She felt Eugene's hand come to rest on her shoulder. Fearing she would break down and cry, Annie told Jake about the new doctor he would be seeing.

"Dr. Lindley came to Louisville from Chicago. His credentials are impressive. I've already met with him and shared your recent medical history."

Jake's interest was piqued. "When's my appointment?"

"Well, I haven't made one yet. I was just waiting for you to get home."

"Could you call tomorrow? I want an appointment as soon as possible."

Annie laid her hand on Jake's chest. "Are you okay? Do we need to get a doctor for you tonight?"

He laughed, setting her mind at ease. "Oh no, it's nothing like that. I just have something in mind I want to talk to the doctor about."

Annie glanced over her shoulder at Eugene. Her husband shrugged and gave her a look that said, "You're guess is as good as mine."

"Well, okay then. I'll call Dr. Lindley's office first thing in the morning."

Jake's eyes were nearly half closed, so Annie bent and kissed him. "We'll let you sleep now. I love you, Jake."

"I love you too, Mom."

After Annie got up, Eugene leaned forward and kissed his son's forehead then pounded his fist on his chest.

Jake raised his fist to his chest and fell asleep right there on the spot.

When Eugene joined Annie in the hall, she took him by the hand and led him to the coat rack by the front door. "Put your coat on. I have a little surprise for you."

The Harrisons had already gone home for the evening, and Rachel sat in her chair by the fire. Eugene looked over at her as he buttoned his coat. "Do you know about this, Mama?"

Rachel's joy shone brightly in her eyes. "I sure do. Now get going, you two."

Annie slipped her hand through the crook of Eugene's arm as they walked out into the cold night air. He covered her hand and looked into her eyes. "Where are we headed?"

"Just walk with me." She drew him close up against her and started leading him toward the barn. When she saw the light seeping through the cracks around the door, she felt satisfied that her father had done his part.

Annie's hand paused on the barn door for just a moment. "Take as long as you want," she said, then pushed it open.

Eugene stepped inside the barn, reveling in the smell of it. He had missed his family desperately, but he had also missed his simple life on the farm. Annie rose up and kissed him on the mouth, then moved to a bench and settled there to watch.

When he pried his eyes away from his beautiful wife, Eugene had to swallow a lump in his throat. All of the horses had been loosed from their stalls and were milling about in the barn. He brought his fist to his mouth, trying to choke back a surge of emotions. After clearing his throat, he moved forward and began to whistle Franklin's old tune.

One by one, each of the horses joined Eugene in the middle of the barn, circling around the man they adored. The length of his absence had done nothing to deter their devotion. Every one of them now touched him affectionately, but Bébé was determined to get his attention first. She nudged her way to the forefront and nearly mauled his face with her muzzle. With a soft laugh, Eugene began to work his magic, starting with the demands of Bébé de l'eau.

It was more than an hour before Eugene led the horses into their stalls one by one. When he closed the last gate, he walked over to Annie and sat down beside her on the bench. He didn't move to touch her, and they sat in silence for a long moment.

"You know Annie, there was a time not too long ago that I lost my faith . . . completely."

"Eugene," she interrupted, "we don't have to do this tonight."

"Oh yes we do," he countered. "I can't take you to bed tonight until I get this off my chest."

Annie's eyes brimmed with tears, but she nodded her head in compliance.

"One of the army doctors told me Jake had less than a 10 percent chance of making it. He said I needed to prepare myself that he would never wake up."

Eugene leaned his head back against the wall and took in a deep breath, letting it out slowly. "I thought that I was going to sit there and watch our other son die, and the guilt I felt was almost unbearable. I didn't know how I could possibly face you with the news." He glanced at Annie, then immediately looked away. She was tearing his heart out with the look of compassion in her eyes.

"So instead of sitting by Jake's bed and praying . . . I don't know . . . it's hard to explain. I just got angry with God and pushed Him away." He leaned forward resting his elbows on the top of his legs. "I didn't care anymore. I thought if Jake was going to die, I wanted to die too."

Annie made a choking sound, and immediately Eugene sat up and pulled her into his arms. "I know you didn't want to hear that, and believe me, this isn't easy for me to say. But you need to know that that's the reason why I quit writing to you. I wasn't talking to anyone, not even God. I couldn't even say anything positive to our son. He needed a word of encouragement from his dad, and I couldn't even give it to him."

"Eugene, I'm so sorry," Annie whispered. "It must have been awful for you."

He nodded his head, but kept his emotions in check. "God has forgiven me, and I plan to tell you all about that tomorrow. But right now, I'm seeking your forgiveness, Annie. I wronged you, and I'm sorry."

Eugene held Annie away from him, maintaining her gaze with his earnest plea. For a moment, Annie didn't respond, and he worried about what she was thinking. She dropped her gaze and said, "You have no idea how hard it was getting the news that Jake had been wounded. But not hearing from you," she locked eyes with him again, "that was torture."

He knew he deserved that. It must have caused her a great deal of anguish. This time, he looked away in shame.

Annie's hands took hold of his face and forced him to look at her again. "But Eugene, I forgive you fully and without condemnation. I can't imagine what you've been through in this terrible war. What happened, happened . . . you can lay it to rest because I forgive you unconditionally."

Eugene let out the breath he'd been holding. "Thank you for that, Annie. I love you so much."

"I love you too," she breathed, and kissed him tenderly, bringing tears to his eyes.

They sat for several minutes, clinging to each other, not saying a word.

Finally, Eugene kissed the top of Annie's head. "What would I do without you?" he asked, drawing her to her feet.

"You'd just have to spend the night with your ole horses, I suppose."

"Hmm, that's not a bad idea," Eugene teased, and took a step back toward the stalls. But when Annie grabbed his arm and flipped the lights out in the barn, he didn't give the horses another thought.

Chapter 49

September 1945

Jake was a bit nervous after being out of school for three years. He had trouble eating Rachel's sizeable breakfast, even with his favorite blueberry muffins sitting right in front of him. Eugene had no problem. He buttered a warm muffin and started in on his eggs and sausage.

"You'd better eat, Son, if you don't want your stomach growling in class." Eugene took a swig of orange juice. "That might be kind of embarrassing on your first day at the university."

Trying to relax, Jake responded to his dad good-naturedly. "A growling stomach is the least of my worries."

"Darlin', you're going to pick right up where you left off in high school," Rachel encouraged. "Just think; this is your first day to becoming a doctor."

Jake let out a quiet moan. "If I can hack it."

Annie couldn't help but put in her two cents worth. "Sweetheart, you have nothing to fear. You told us yourself that you felt called to be a doctor since the day you broke your leg. Goodness, that was when you were nine years old." She laid a gentle hand on his arm. "God's the One who called you. He'll give you everything you need."

Jake could feel himself start to relax. His momma always had a way of talking sense into him when he needed it. For crying out loud, he was twenty-one years old, and he'd just fought on the front lines of a world war—how could starting college be that difficult? Besides, this was a gift he couldn't afford to pass up. He was going to school free on the new G.I. Bill.

He gobbled up a muffin and washed it down with milk. "I should get going," he said, pushing back from the table. "I don't want to be late."

"What are you doing about lunch?" Rachel asked.

The color rose into Jake's cheeks. "Charlotte's meeting me for lunch. She has a break from classes the same time I do."

"Atta boy," Eugene responded.

"You just keep your mind on your school work, Son." Annie's expression chided her husband for his remark. Eugene's wink to Jake didn't go unnoticed, however.

She got up from the table and gave Jake a kiss on the cheek. "You're going to do just fine. Have a great day, sweetheart."

"Thanks, Mom, and thanks for breakfast, Gramma. I'm sure tomorrow I'll have more of an appetite."

As Jake headed out the kitchen door, he playfully called over his shoulder, "I can't wait for lunch!"

Eugene burst out laughing, nearly choking on his muffin. Annie and Rachel just shook their heads.

As the three continued with their breakfast, Rachel picked up the conversation. "I'm so proud of Jake when I think of everything he's been through in the war and the hard work he's put in for the last nine months to gain his strength back. He's such a determined young man."

"Not to mention working in Dr. Lindley's office all summer," Annie interjected.

"He's pretty amazing," Eugene agreed. "Just think; he's the first one in our family to go to college."

Rachel gave Eugene a wistful look. "There was a time I had hopes for you attending the university in Lexington."

Eugene nodded thoughtfully. "But fate had other plans."

For a moment, he contemplated the incredible turn of events he had undergone at age sixteen. Life could be so unpredictable.

After a short silence, Annie broke into his thoughts. "Eugene, do you think Jake is truly all right? He spent weeks on the front line in combat but hasn't spoken a word about it since he came home. Now that the war is over, I thought he might at least talk about it."

Eugene locked eyes with Rachel. He knew his mama understood what it was like to live with a son who had fought in a war. Annie had no idea how hard it was for soldiers to come home and talk about their war experiences. It was better to keep such horrific events buried in some chest in an unmarked grave.

"You know, Jake wasn't the only one on the front lines this time." Eugene shocked himself. He hadn't meant to let that information out. When he saw the stunned look on Annie and Rachel's faces, he could've kicked himself.

"Eugene," Annie breathed. "What do you mean?"

He shook his head while rising from his chair. "I'm sorry, I shouldn't have said that. I don't know why I did."

Annie came to her feet and started toward him, but he put his hand up. "No, it's all right, really." He immediately headed for the back door and pulled on his boots.

Annie's personality was incapable of letting something like this rest. "Eugene, please talk to me . . ."

"I mean it, Annie. Let it go!" Eugene surprised himself again by raising his voice. He suddenly felt claustrophobic. He had to get out of the house before he lost control and said something he'd truly regret. For a split second, he stared into Annie's wounded eyes, then he pushed the screen door open and headed for the barn.

Eugene's strides were long and purposeful. He needed to get as far away from Annie and his mama as possible. He felt like such an idiot. He'd been so proud that the night terrors had gone away, but now it seemed they had just switched over to daylight hours.

"Oh Lord, what is it?" he blurted out loud. "Is it my pride?"

He stopped and ran his hands through his hair, looking up toward the heavens. Great! His hat was still hanging by the door in the kitchen. Well, he'd just have to do without it today. He wasn't about to go back inside now.

It wasn't long before Annie came into the barn and laid his hat on the workbench. She didn't say a word; she didn't even look his way. Her mood was palpable, and he knew better than to say anything. Not that he was capable of doing so anyway.

With a sidelong glance, he watched her enter Gracie's stall. It was always Annie's first task of the day. Not that it was a chore—she loved Gracie dearly. The poor girl was blind and feeble, but she just kept hanging on. Eugene was thankful Annie's horse from childhood had lasted throughout the war. His wife had suffered too many losses to endure the loss of Gracie too.

Eugene quickly saddled his horse and headed outside. The cattle would be his only company today—at least that was the plan.

It was well past noon when he finally came back to the barn. Annie was nowhere in sight, but Rachel was sitting quietly on a bale of hay, catching a breeze near the back door. He unsaddled his horse and brushed him down before acknowledging his mama's presence.

"Pull up a bale," she said with a half smile. "I brought you some lunch."

Eugene grabbed a hay bale, setting it down beside Rachel's. He removed his work gloves but fumbled with them, trying to give his hands something to do. "I'm not really hungry."

"I figured you'd say something like that. I'll just leave it here, and you can make a decision on it later."

"Thanks," he said quietly.

Rachel breathed in the warm September air. Her next words were not unexpected. "Eugene, I remember what it was like the first time you came home from the war. I'm not here to ask you to talk about it."

"That's a relief, Mama, because going through it twice was hard enough. Talking about it is like living through it all over again. I can't do that."

"I know that, darlin'." Rachel paused when her voice quavered. "But your wife doesn't."

Eugene stared outside. He marveled at the peaceful scene his farm afforded while inwardly he was feeling the exact opposite. He hadn't been this tense or angry in a very long time. One thing was certain; talking about it would only make matters worse.

"I'd give anything if your papa were here for you."

She didn't elaborate any further, leaving Eugene to ponder how his papa might have helped him through such deep emotional pangs. Surprisingly, just thinking about Papa eased the tension in his gut a bit. He could still hear Franklin's deep, soothing voice pouring out simple words of wisdom. But thinking about his papa wouldn't help him deal with his wife.

Finally, he said, "Annie used to be so patient with me when we first got married. I can't tell you how many times I woke her up in the middle of the night scared to death, trying to catch my breath." Eugene kept his gaze somewhere outside the barn door. "But no matter how many times it happened, she never asked. She was just there for me."

"And she still is," Rachel said with deep conviction. "Nothing has changed, Eugene. You've been home for nine *long* months. How many times has she asked you to talk about the war?"

Eugene was silent.

"How many?"

Eugene's gaze dropped to his feet. Leave it to his mama to cut to the heart of the matter. But something inside of him kept him from conceding to her. He stubbornly sat in silence.

At long last, Rachel slowly came to her feet. Eugene started to rise to help her back to the house, but she immediately put her hand on his shoulder, pressing him back down onto the hay. Her words were quiet, yet incredibly potent. "Eugene, the Germans surrendered in May . . . the Japanese in August. When will you?"

He opened his mouth but closed it again. What could he say? He wasn't even sure he fully understood what she was getting at. She moved around him and headed back through the barn. Eugene straddled his bale of hay, watching her go. She had thrown her shoulders back, reminding him of her tenacity, her purposefulness. He let out a sigh. Who said his papa was the only one who cornered the market on simple wisdom?

Sunday morning, Eugene sat beside Annie in their usual pew. Between his family and hers, they took up an entire row. Charlotte had also been attending with Jake ever since he got home from Europe. Eugene's shoulder was touching Annie's, which was about the closest he had come to her all week. Every night since Monday, he had purposely gone to bed late after she was already asleep. How long would this go on?

If he was honest with himself, he was acting exactly like Will had acted so many times. Just thinking about his son made his chest ache. He missed him so much but hadn't really been able to share his grief with Annie. He harbored such regret where his eldest son was concerned. So many things were wrong right now.

He noticed from the corner of his eye that Annie had looked up at him. He realized he wasn't singing and picked up in the second verse of "A Wonderful Savior" with the rest of the congregation.

Eugene heard very little of the sermon. His mind kept working on the dilemma he and Annie were in. Someone had to surrender. He was suddenly reminded of Rachel's question from earlier in the week. She wanted to know when *he* was going to surrender. But surrender to what?

The congregation stood to sing, and Eugene hastily rose to his feet. Before they had even gotten to the chorus, his throat began to constrict.

All to Jesus I surrender,
All to Him I freely give:
I will ever love and trust Him,
In His presence daily live.

Eugene closed his eyes, taking in the voices of the saints around him. He was no longer capable of singing. He had done it yet again—taken life's burdens upon his own shoulders without truly giving them to the One who was meant to carry them. He reached up to block a tear from tumbling down his cheek. That's when Annie slipped her hand into his. He was the one who needed to surrender, yet his beloved wife had made the first move.

The final lines he sang with conviction—*All to Thee, my blessed Savior, I surrender all.* His hand tightened around Annie's, and she looked up at him with tears in her eyes. How could he have been such a fool?

After the service, Rachel had planned to visit Franklin and Wallace's graves. Annie told her parents where they were going, so Nathan and Claudia came along, inviting Roberta, Lillie, and Mattie. Jake and Charlotte eventually joined the family as they walked toward the massive oak in the middle of the cemetery.

Eugene had yet to let go of Annie's hand. After a few minutes standing beside his papa's grave, he led her away from the rest of the family, deeper into the cemetery. A stone pathway led to a marble bench, and Eugene asked Annie to sit down.

"What about you?" she asked quietly.

Although Eugene felt more comfortable standing up, he knew he should probably sit beside her. He straddled the bench, so he could look at his wife while he spoke.

"I'm sorry about the way I treated you this week, Annie."

She didn't give him an opportunity to say more. "I want to apologize too, Eugene."

He smiled at her. "It wasn't your fault. I know you were just trying to give me the space you thought I needed. But the truth is, you should've hit me upside the head with a two-by-four and gotten it over with."

She giggled, which was just the response he was looking for. "You know, I have a bad habit of carrying guilt around with me." He took a deep breath and looked out over the cemetery. "I've done it since I was a boy." Eugene reached for her hand, and she held it affectionately in her lap.

Rachel began moving down the hill toward the back of the cemetery where Wallace was buried. Eugene watched Jake move to her side and take her arm.

"Mama's the one who called me out on it . . . again. She asked me when I was going to surrender." Eugene now turned his full attention back to Annie. "I'm sorry it took me so long." He scooted close to her and surrounded her with his arms, thankful for the way God's Spirit had spoken to him this morning in the song.

Annie leaned into him laying her head on his shoulder. "I've missed you so much this week."

Eugene reached for her left hand and brought it to his lips. He had a mischievous look in his eye. "Like I said, a two-by-four would've done the trick."

"I'll remember that next time," she quipped.

He stood and pulled her to her feet. "Yeah, that's what I'm afraid of."

When Eugene and Annie joined the others, it appeared they had been deep in conversation. But Annie noticed it came to an abrupt halt as they approached.

"Is everything all right?" She probed the faces around Wallace's grave, fearing something had happened.

Nathan cleared his throat. "Uh . . . honey, we've decided to get a marker for Will. We want a place to remember him too."

Annie felt hurt that they had come to this decision without her. She could feel the heat rising to her face. Fearing she would respond the wrong way, Annie chose to remain silent.

Her mother's arm encircled her waist. "The war's over, honey. It's time," Claudia said softly.

Annie's jaw tightened. She began to wonder if there was something seriously wrong with herself. Everyone in the family, including Eugene, had accepted Will's death. Why couldn't she? To try to explain that to them, however, seemed absolutely ludicrous.

"Do what you like," she finally said in a thin voice. "But don't expect me to visit it."

Everyone bore the news in stunned silence.

"I'm sorry," she whispered and abruptly turned away. Annie was now on a mission. She couldn't get back up the hill and across the highway fast enough. She could hear someone following her and guessed it was Eugene, but she didn't bother to look back.

Sitting down on the stone wall, she laid her hand over Will's name and her equilibrium was restored. This was a place of peace and hope.

Eugene took a seat beside her on the wall, patiently waiting in silence. She could literally feel his skepticism swirling around them. Part of her wanted to ask him to leave, so she could be alone.

After a while, he grew restless. "Annie, what can I do to help you get past this?"

She didn't want to cry, but tears immediately stung her eyes. "You don't understand. This is not just something I'll get past."

"Why?"

His simple question made her angry. She stood up and faced him. "I don't know why. If I did, I'd tell you."

She turned her back on him and looked across the highway. Everyone had walked back up to the parking lot from the cemetery, and they now stared at her and Eugene. She whirled to face her husband again.

"I think I need to tell you something." Annie's heart beat rapidly as she made a decision to tell Eugene about Wallace's letter. "Do you remember how Wallace seemed to know things that no one else did?"

Eugene looked confused but nodded his head.

"He told me in his last letter that I would see Will again. He said he knew it." Heat filled her body; she thought she was going to pass out.

Eugene stood up and took her by the shoulders. "Sit back down . . . please."

She allowed him to lower her back down to the wall. Eugene knelt in front of her still holding her arms. "Wallace meant you'd see him in heaven, sweetheart. That's when we'll all be together again. That's what I meant by this." He pressed his fingers to her chest covering the gold locket he'd given her before leaving for Europe.

Yes, she fully believed they would all see Jesus together someday, but Annie harbored some kind of blind hope that she would see Will long before that day came. She knew it couldn't be explained, and she was pretty sure everyone must think her crazy.

All of a sudden, a terrible thought popped into her mind. What if it was just wishful thinking on her part? What if she spent the rest of her life pining for Will? There were people who did that sort of thing. *Oh God, please don't let that be me!*

Eugene looked worried, and Annie now wished she had never told him about the letter. She needed to put her husband's mind at ease, and there was only one way to do it.

"I'm sure you're right." She closed her eyes for a moment and breathed deeply. "The war is over now. What else could he have meant?"

Eugene visibly breathed a sigh of relief. He let her linger for a while longer then stood and held his hand out to her. "Are you ready to go now?"

Pressing her lips together, she nodded her head and stood, taking one last look at the name etched in stone. She vowed right then never to come back because every time she looked at Will's name on that wall, it screamed to her of hope.

Chapter 50

Spring 1946

Jake rushed into the living room searching for the car keys. He was dressed in a new navy blue suit; his black shoes shone with a fresh coat of polish.

"Wow!" Annie declared. "I don't think Charlotte stands a chance."

A handsome smile spread across her son's face. "That's the plan." He quickly checked for keys on the hook by the door. "Where are they?"

Before she could answer, Eugene came through the front door tossing him the keys. "Here you go. I wanted to make sure the car was clean for your big date."

Jake let out an anxious breath. "Thanks." He put the keys in his pocket and rubbed sweaty palms together. "Well . . . this is it."

Rachel came out of the kitchen smiling brightly. "You look so handsome, Jake!"

"Thanks, Gramma. I guess I won't see you till in the morning." He turned toward his parents standing together near the door. "I'll probably be late tonight. You all go on to bed."

Annie gave him a look that said *not on your life*, but Eugene answered, "We will." He opened the door for his son and walked out with him.

"Jake, stay relaxed. It's gonna be just fine."

"I know, Dad. I just want everything to be perfect."

Jake opened the car door and slid in. As he cranked up the motor, Eugene leaned his head into the passenger window. "You do have the ring, right?"

"Oh, wow!" Jake put the car in neutral and pulled the emergency brake before racing into the house.

Eugene was still laughing when Jake ran back out. "I guess that would've spoiled things a bit," he joked to his son.

"Thanks, Dad! That would've been disastrous."

Eugene tapped his hand on the top of the car. "Have a great time."

"I will. And Dad?"

"Yeah?"

"Thanks for *everything*."

Eugene nodded, feeling a powerful emotion. "Go on," he said, clearing his throat, "you don't want to keep your girl waiting." He backed away and watched as Jake headed down the drive.

Annie descended the porch steps and put her arm through his. Eugene drew her in close, thinking about his awkward proposal to Annie such a long time ago. He was sure Jake would do a better job of it than he had. He only hoped that Charlotte would make Jake as happy as this woman standing beside him had. When he counted his blessings, Annie was always at the top of his list.

"Do you remember when you proposed to me?" Annie's eyes danced playfully, urging him into nostalgia.

Eugene grinned, shaking his head. "If you can call it that. I'm still a little embarrassed about that."

Annie laughed out loud. "It was unique—I'll give you that."

He turned to face her and pulled her up close. "So you think Jake will be able to do a better job?"

"Well, I don't know about a better job. I just hope she knows what he's talking about when he asks."

Eugene kissed her forehead and turned her toward the house. "Are you saying you didn't know what I meant when I asked, *how about it?*"

"Well, let's put it this way," she teased, "if you hadn't had a ring in your hand, I might've thought you were asking me to go on a trail ride."

He chuckled, then looked down at his wife tenderly. "It's been a great ride."

"Amen to that," she responded quietly. "Thank you."

Before reaching the door to the house, Eugene took his wife by the hand and pulled her up short. When she turned a quizzical eye his direction, he asked, "So, how about it?"

Hearing her giggle was music to his soul. "I assume since you're not offering a ring this time, you're talking about an actual trail ride."

With a lopsided grin, he got down on one knee and took her left hand in both of his. "If you'll have me."

Annie raised one eyebrow and feigned uncertainty. "Hmm, I don't know . . ."

He stood and pulled her hand up to his heart. "If you say no, I'll be a broken man."

"Well, in that case . . ." Annie pulled her hand away and took off running toward the barn. "First one to saddle up gets to choose the trail," she yelled over her shoulder.

For a few seconds, Eugene didn't move, enjoying the sight of his wife sprinting down the road. Then, leaping off the porch, he took off after her, making sure not to pass her. He was appreciating the view from behind far too much.

Sometime after midnight, Annie heard the front door open. She hadn't slept a wink, waiting to talk to Jake as soon as he came in. Quickly, she stepped into her house shoes and pulled on her robe.

Jake was about to reach for the lamp when Annie came into the front room.

"No sweetheart, leave it on. I want to hear all about it."

Her son's wide grin told her the evening had been a success. As soon as Annie sat down on the couch, Jake took the chair across from her.

When he just sat there smiling, Annie said, "Don't leave me hanging. I want to hear everything."

Jake laughed, and said, "There's not much to tell. I asked, and she said yes."

"Jacob Wyatt, you know better than that. I need details."

Before Jake could answer his mother, Eugene plodded sleepily into the room. He had pulled a t-shirt on backward and was tugging at the neckline. He slouched down on the couch next to Annie. "Hey, Son. Was it yes or no?"

"It was yes," Jake answered.

"Good," Eugene said, and started to get up off the couch.

Annie let out an exasperated groan, pulling her husband back down beside her. "You two are gonna drive me crazy. Jake, what was Charlotte wearing? Did you ask her during dinner? Was she surprised? Did you talk to her parents?"

Jake patiently waited for all of her questioning to end, then he started by telling her about their nice dinner. Eventually he described how he had asked Charlotte to marry him as they walked along the boardwalk beside the river.

"Her parents were still up when I took her home, so we went inside and shared the news with them."

Grateful for at least a few details from her son, Annie knew she would be able to glean more information from Charlotte. "I can't wait to see the ring on her hand tomorrow at church," she said enthusiastically. "How did it look?"

Jake laughed again and shook his head. "It looked great, Mom."

Eugene sat up a little straighter and gave Jake a more serious look. "Son, you know this is for life, don't you? No matter what hardships come your way, Charlotte is your one and only."

"I know that, Dad." He took in a long, slow breath. "I don't want to live my life without her."

"That's all I needed to hear," Eugene said with a yawn. Then he turned to Annie. "Can we go back to bed now?"

Before she could answer, Jake interjected, "There's one more thing. I want Mercy to preach our wedding."

"Have you talked to Charlotte about that?" Annie asked. "After all, the bride usually decides who officiates."

"I asked Charlotte first, then talked it over with her parents. They all agreed that it would be special for Mercy to marry us." Jake looked over at his dad. "I can't wait to ask him."

Eugene smiled. "He'll do a great job. He was on his way to becoming a fine preacher." He glanced over at Annie. "I got to hear him preach a sermon at Camp Barkeley."

"I'm looking forward to meeting him," she said earnestly. "He sounds like such a special young man."

Jake reached up and unknotted his tie, then pulled it off in one swift motion. "You may not have to wait long."

Annie sat straight up with wide-eyed excitement. "What do you mean?"

A coy expression played on her son's face. "Charlotte wants to get married in May."

"That's less than two months. Can she pull it off by then?"

"We both want a small wedding—something simple. We just don't want a lot of fuss."

When Jake came to his feet, Annie immediately went to him and kissed his cheek. "I'm so excited for you, sweetheart." She turned back toward Eugene, who was still tugging at the neck of his shirt. "There's so much to think about. Where will they live? What about a honeymoon? What am I going to wear to the wedding?"

Eugene chuckled and put his arm around her shoulders, turning her toward the bedroom. Winking over his shoulder at Jake, he said, "I'm proud of you, Son. We'll talk more tomorrow."

Jake pounded his chest. "Thanks, Dad." Then he smiled when he heard his mother say, "Eugene, stop pulling on your shirt. You're going to ruin the neck."

He watched his dad reach down and yank the shirt over his head and throw it all the way down the hall. "There. Is that better?" he said humorously, ushering her into the bedroom and closing the door.

A few seconds later, the door opened again, and his mother, apparently exasperated, hurried down the hall to retrieve the t-shirt. Folding it neatly as she walked back, she blew Jake a kiss and whispered, "I love you."

"I love you too, Mom."

For a long moment after their door closed, Jake stood in the middle of the living room contemplating his parent's marriage. He prayed that his and Charlotte's would be as solid and steady. He knew the reason for its fortitude— Christ had always been in the center. He vowed then and there that he and Charlotte would follow their example. They had taught him so much by simply loving God and loving each other. He couldn't wait to get started on a new life.

As Jake turned out the light and quietly walked down the hall toward his room, he thought he heard his mother crying. What on earth could have changed her mood from excitement to sadness in such a short amount of time? Then he heard her say Will's name, and an unexpected emotion socked him in the gut. Will should've been here sharing this moment with him. His brother should be standing beside him on his wedding day to hand him Charlotte's ring.

Without thinking, Jake leaned against the wall in the dark hallway and slid down to the floor. Tears ran down his cheeks as he overheard his mother sobbing and his father's soothing words of comfort. Now, for the first time in his life, he began to realize how much pain his parents must have endured in losing their firstborn son. He had always looked at the tragedy from a brother's point of view, but tonight he and Charlotte had talked about having children of their own someday. That discussion had given him an entirely different perspective on things.

Jake leaned his head back on the wall and wiped the tears from his face. *Father, please bring Your comfort to my parents tonight.* It took several minutes for their bedroom to grow quiet, but Jake remained still for as long as it took. Then, without a sound, he rose to his feet and headed to bed.

***

Annie helped Rachel fill her apron pockets full of garden seeds. "Okay, Mama, your left pocket is green beans and your right pocket is cabbage."

"But I usually have green beans in my right pocket," Rachel countered.

"Keep reminding yourself which is which. Eugene has your rows prepared just right for each one." Annie took her arm, and they headed out to the garden for planting.

At the edge of the tilled earth, Rachel stopped and turned her face toward the warm April sun. "Thank You, Lord for a beautiful morning."

"Amen to that."

"Amen, indeed," Rachel said brightly, looking down at the ground before her. "This must be the green bean row." She reached into her right pocket, then caught her mistake and laughed. "Uh oh, I just about messed up already."

"Mama, I don't mind helping you switch the seeds over if—"

"No, darlin', that won't be necessary." She pulled her wide-brimmed, straw hat more snugly to her head. "Left—beans, left—beans, left—beans. I've got it."

"Would you like me to stay with you while you plant your rows?"

"Oh no, darlin', we'd be out here all day. You go on and plant your potatoes and cucumbers. I'll be just fine."

Annie stayed and watched her mother-in-law for a brief moment just to make sure she was reaching into her left pocket. Satisfied that all was well, she moved several rows over past the carrots and turnips. The rich soil had been mixed with compost and tilled into perfect rows by her husband. He had put in several days of hard work preparing the garden, for which Annie and Rachel were grateful.

After a few minutes, Annie looked up to make sure Rachel was still reaching into her left pocket—she was. What an amazing woman. Anyone who didn't know better would think she was in her sixties or early seventies at the most. It was hard to believe that Mama was just two years short of ninety. Silver hair now crowned her beautiful features, but something about her spirit kept her young and vibrant. What a blessing for her to be able to witness the marriage of her grandson in less than a month.

When Rachel began singing "Amazing Grace," Annie joined in. Their voices blended perfectly as the morning passed quickly by.

Annie still had half a row of cucumbers to go when she heard the phone ringing inside. Thankfully, she was at the end of a row closest to the house, and she took off at a run.

"I'll be right back, Mama. Are you okay?"

Rachel rose up to her full height and waved. "Hurry before you miss the call."

Throwing her gloves onto the back porch, Annie ran through the house without bothering to take off her boots. She'd just have to clean up her tracks after the call.

"Hello?" she cried breathlessly into the receiver.

"Momma?"

The connection was horrible. Annie could barely hear through the crackling and loud humming noise.

"Jake? Where are you? I can hardly hear you."

"It's not—it's—"

She was only catching a word or two in his sentences.

"I'm sorry, sweetheart, but I can't hear what you're saying. Could you speak a little louder?"

"This—not Jake. This—Will."

Annie's breath caught as a strange fear jolted her heart.

"Momma?"

"Will?" She wasn't sure she had said his name out loud. "Will?" she screamed into the phone. "Will, is that really you?"

"Yes—in Calif—We didn't know—"

"Will!" *Oh God.* "Son, are you coming home?"

"I—soon. Can you—"

Annie's hand could barely hold the receiver she was shaking so hard. "I'm sorry, I can't hear you. Can I call you back? What's your number?"

"I love—"

"I love you, Will. I love you so much!" She realized the connection had suddenly been broken. "Oh no, no, no!" There was nothing on the line except a loud buzz, but she couldn't make herself hang up. As long as she held that phone in her hand, she held a connection to Will.

Sensing she was no longer alone, Annie glanced up to see Rachel standing motionless at the end of the hall. All of the color had drained from her face. Annie immediately let the phone drop on the cradle and ran to her mother-in-law's side, fearing she was about to faint. Both women were trembling, but Annie was able to lower Rachel into a kitchen chair. All she could do was drop to her knees in front of her.

"Who was that?" Rachel whispered. Annie could see the same fearfulness in her mother-in-law's eyes that she had felt moments earlier.

"Oh Mama." Annie let out a long, shuddering breath. Tears began to flow unbridled down her cheeks. "I think it was Will."

Rachel began shaking her head and took Annie by the shoulders. "Darlin', how can that be possible?"

"He said he wasn't Jake, and he called me Momma! I think he was calling from California."

Suddenly, Annie jumped to her feet, startling Rachel. "I'm sorry, Mama." She immediately knelt back down and took Rachel's hands firmly in her own. "I need to make some phone calls and see if I can confirm that he's truly alive and in California. The air force will know. Surely someone can help us." She rose to her feet again, more slowly this time.

Before heading back to the telephone, she filled a glass with water and handed it to Rachel. "Mama, are you going to be okay?"

Rachel had a faraway look in her eyes that concerned Annie greatly. Maybe she needed to find Eugene before making those calls. Annie's thoughts were all jumbled—she couldn't seem to make a decision on anything at the moment. She took in several deep breaths to calm her nerves and clear her mind.

Finally, she brought Rachel to her feet and led her into the front room. "Here, Mama, sit down in your chair and put your feet up." She lowered her down slowly and put the glass of water on the table beside her. "I'm going to find Eugene. I'll be right back." Annie knelt down in front of her again. "All right?"

Rachel's gaze narrowed as the two women locked eyes. "Annie, darlin', what if your mind is playing tricks on you?"

Annie felt a shiver run all the way up her spine. She wasn't sure how to respond to that query. What if her mind truly was playing . . .

No, no, no. Stop it! I know what I heard.

"Mama, promise me you'll sit here and rest until I get back with Eugene."

Rachel nodded slowly. "I promise," she whispered.

Twenty minutes later, Annie was back with Eugene. He seemed unsettled but determined to take control of the situation. When Rachel saw him, she slowly came to her feet.

"Eugene, can I talk to you for a moment?"

He nodded to her but had instructions for Annie first. "Go call the operator and see if she can tell you where the call originated from."

"I will," Annie said softly. She gave Rachel an uneasy glance, then quickly headed down the hall.

Rachel took hold of Eugene's arm. "I'm worried about her."

The crease in Eugene's brow deepened. He had already been suppressing an abundance of doubt on the way back to the house. Annie had been so sure Will had called. How could that be? He wanted to believe her with all his heart, but his mind couldn't get around the fact that the war had been over for almost a year. He worried about his wife's irrational hope that Will might return someday. On the night of Jake's engagement, she had cried uncontrollably over that very belief. He had wondered when she would ever be able to accept the harsh reality that Will was gone?

Eugene's throat tightened as he searched for words to comfort his mama. He didn't want to be critical of his wife, but he also didn't want to follow her over the edge of a cliff.

"Mama, let's try not to jump to any conclusions right now. Besides, what if she's right? Stranger things have happened, you know." He tried to give her a look of confidence, but he felt sure she could read every single thought in his head.

To his relief, Rachel's worry lines smoothed. She took in a deep breath and let it out slowly. "You're right. We need to support Annie no matter what's going on."

"Thank you," Annie breathed quietly from behind them.

Eugene and Rachel turned to face her. An awkward silence filled the space between them.

Finally, Eugene cleared his throat. "What did the operator say?"

For several heartbeats Annie hesitated. Color began to rise in her cheeks. Then, in a thick voice she told them, "The call came from California . . . it had to be Will."

Rachel choked back a sob while Eugene's heart soared. Both of them extended their arms to Annie at the very same time. Without reservation, she stepped into them. And for a very long time, she clung to them tightly, allowing hope to blossom in two hearts where none had existed before.

Chapter 51

The last week and a half had been maddening. Not only had Will failed to call home again but, inconceivably, the air force had no record of his return to the States. As far as they were concerned, his KIA status remained unchanged.

Annie looked over at Eugene as he drove to Sunday morning worship. She had overheard him lose his temper on the telephone yesterday with someone from the air force. Toward the end of the call, he had apologized for his behavior, but Annie knew his nerves were raw. He was on edge most of the time lately—they both were.

As they passed by the old church property, Annie glanced longingly toward the stone wall. Something stirred her heart deeply, and she felt an urge to visit Will's etching. But when Eugene pulled the car to a halt in the parking lot, her parents were already walking toward them.

Nathan opened the door and reached in to help Rachel out first. She was greeted with a warm hug from Claudia, and the two women began walking arm in arm toward the building.

Annie took her father's extended hand and was immediately swallowed up in his arms. "Any word yet?"

With a sigh, she let him know there had been none. "We aren't giving up though. Eugene was given a few more telephone numbers we can try tomorrow morning."

Nathan turned toward his son-in-law then. "I imagine you're racking up quite a large telephone bill. I'll be more than glad to help you with it when it comes due."

Eugene gave him a thin smile. "Thanks, Nathan, but I'm sure we'll manage."

Annie slowed her pace before reaching the door to the building. When she stopped and looked across the road, Eugene instantly put his hand on the small of her back.

"Not now, sweetheart."

She felt like arguing with him. He had no idea how strong an impulse she was fighting. But when he softly begged, "Please," she turned resolutely back toward the building. Besides, she didn't feel like explaining everything to her father.

When the service was over, the family gathered again outside. Annie strained to concentrate on Charlotte's description of the bridal bouquet she had picked out for the wedding.

"I just love daisies. They're so pretty this time of year."

"Yes, they are," Annie agreed. Although Annie and Charlotte were very different in personality, Annie knew that she would make the perfect wife for Jake. Besides the fact that she absolutely adored her son, Charlotte possessed a truly caring, compassionate spirit. She would make the perfect doctor's wife.

Jake walked up, putting an arm around Charlotte's waist. "Do you want to go by the apartment before heading out to Nana's for lunch? Dad and I finished painting yesterday."

Charlotte's face radiated excitement. "I'd love to!"

"Mom, tell Nana we'll be right out. We won't be long."

Annie smiled. "Okay, we'll see you two in a bit."

She watched as they strolled hand in hand to Jake's car.

"Honey?" Annie turned to see her mother approaching. "Roberta and Lillie want to visit Wallace's grave before lunch, but Mattie and I have a roast in the oven that needs to be tended to."

Mattie grinned widely. "We be eaten pork 'n' beans for lunch if I don't git goin'."

"Don't worry about a thing," Annie told her mother. "Eugene and I will take Mattie back to the house right away. What about Mama?"

"She wants to go with us," Claudia said. "We'll be home shortly."

Annie and Mattie headed for the car where Eugene already stood patiently waiting. Annie slid in beside her husband, making room for Mattie beside the window. All along the way, Mattie chattered about a new green bean casserole she was fixing and hoped everyone would like it.

"But Mr. Eugene, don't you worry none. It ain't too fancy for your taste."

Annie thought it nice to hear him laugh for a change. "Now Mattie," he teased, "don't you go ruining my green beans. You know I like 'em fried."

They bantered back and forth about Eugene's culinary tastes all the way to the Harrisons' gate. When Eugene turned between the stone posts, Annie leaned her head on his shoulder. She loved the drive beneath the long row of maples.

As the house came into view, Annie noticed a taxi in the driveway and wondered who on earth . . . all of a sudden, her heart jumped wildly inside her chest. She gripped Eugene's arm with incredible tenacity, letting out a heartrending sigh. There was a man standing on the porch, thin and lanky, but unmistakably Will!

Annie didn't dare take her eyes off him, fearing he would disappear from her sight. Before Eugene could put the car in park, she had reached across Mattie and opened the door. Mattie squealed with excitement and quickly got out, allowing Annie to get past her.

Annie's feet stilled as she breathlessly watched her son descend from the porch and stride toward her. His skin was bronzed and his hair nearly bleached white from the sun. Tiny lines formed around his sky blue eyes as he came out into the sun to greet her.

For a brief moment, they held each other's gaze, Annie seeing the boy and now the man she had never given up on. The deep love she had for him stole her last ounce of restraint. She reached up to cradle his face in her hands, and Will bent low, allowing her to kiss his cheeks, his forehead, his mouth, and his cheeks again. Love, pain, sorrow, and joy all blended together in her unhurried, deliberate expression of affection.

Slowly, Will rose to his full height and spoke to her in a raspy voice. "Momma, I don't deserve that. I've done nothing but cause you heartache all my life. I just want you to know . . ." He swallowed hard, tears forming in his eyes. "I want you to know that I love you with all my heart, and I plan to spend the rest of my life trying to make it up to you."

"Oh, Will," Annie breathed emotionally. "I love you so much." She threw her arms around his neck, and he held her with amazing tenderness while she wept.

After a long, poignant moment, Eugene drew them both to his chest, kissing the top of Will's head, mixing his tears with theirs. "Welcome home, Son," he managed to choke out. "Welcome home."

Eventually, the three loosened their embrace, but not their hold on one another. Annie wasn't about to let go of him—not yet. She still couldn't believe her son was actually standing here beside her after so many years and so much heartache. She suddenly thought about the grave marker with Will's name on it and let out a quiet laugh.

"What is it?" Will asked, wiping the moisture from his cheeks.

Annie brushed her hand fondly down his arm. "It's not something I can *tell* you about. It's something you'll just have to see." She was also looking forward to taking Will onto the old church property and showing him his name etched on the stone wall, the place where God had led her—her place of hope.

As the three began walking toward the porch Annie noticed, for the first time, a woman standing in the shadows. Was Will so weak that he had brought a nurse with him? The three walked up the steps together, and the young woman bowed her head as they drew near. When Will reached out to her, encircling her waist possessively, Annie's heart began racing. She knew at that moment he was intimately involved with her.

"Mom and Dad, I want you to meet Keiko . . . my wife."

The young woman humbly bowed her head lower, and Annie was touched by the gesture. She looked toward Will, whose eyes were fixed lovingly on his wife. Somehow this woman—Keiko—had played a part in bringing Will back. She knew it beyond a shadow of a doubt, and her heart was immediately filled with love for her.

Annie reached beneath Keiko's chin and gently raised her lovely face. Her almond eyes were filled with apprehension, and a lone tear streaked down her cheek.

"Oh, honey, it's okay." Annie kissed her cheek lightly. "You are welcome here."

Will let out a nervous breath and smiled at his wife. "I told you it would be fine."

The corners of Keiko's mouth tipped up slightly before she looked back to Annie. "I am so very pleased to meet you, Mrs. Wyatt." Her Japanese accent was thick, but her English was impeccable.

"And I you." Annie felt inexplicably drawn to this young woman. She looked forward to getting to know her in the days to come.

Eugene added his greeting to Keiko, then walked out to the taxi driver to let him know he needn't wait any longer. When he returned, he arranged the chairs on the porch into a close circle.

"Why don't we sit down out here and talk before everyone else gets home?" he suggested.

Will and Keiko sank into their chairs. They looked exhausted. Eugene didn't even know where to start; there were so many things he wanted to know. When he looked over at Annie, he sensed she was about to release a barrage of questions. He wasn't sure how much Will could handle.

"Son," he started, "you have no idea what a blessing this is to have you back. We thought you were . . ." Eugene paused, not wanting to actually say it. "Well, we had no idea you were still alive."

Annie moved to the edge of her seat, and it suddenly dawned on Eugene that she had been right all along. He should've realized a mother would know intuitively if her son were still alive.

Annie reached for Will's hand. "We were told your plane went down, sweetheart. How did you manage to survive?"

Eugene could tell when a soldier didn't want to talk about his experiences. He held his breath, waiting to see what his son would say.

Will looked over at Keiko who had lowered her gaze. Her hands knotted together nervously in her lap. He squeezed his mother's hand, then released it and raked his hands through his hair.

"I'm not really sure how or why I survived the crash . . . but I did." He pulled in a deep breath before continuing. "I was picked up in the ocean by a Japanese ship and taken to a camp on a small island. I got away and lived out in the jungle for a long time . . . until we found out the war was over."

Keiko's eyes locked on to her husband's. There was no doubt that Will was leaving out a massive amount of information. But before any more questions could be asked, Jake's car pulled up beside Eugene's.

Jake shot out of the car like a rocket, pumping his fist in the air and letting out a loud whoop. When Will saw him, he raised both arms above his head and shouted Jake's name at the top of his lungs. Will jumped to his feet and leapt off the porch just in time to catch his brother in midair. He lifted him off the ground, laughing exuberantly.

"Whoa, little brother, you've grown up!" Will exclaimed, lowering Jake to the ground.

Jake's face was full of emotion. He grabbed the back of Will's head with both hands and planted a big kiss on his forehead. Will laughed and mimicked his brother's gesture.

Eugene stood with Annie and Keiko on the porch, watching the reunion with a great deal of pleasure. He couldn't wait for the rest of the family to be reunited with their long lost son. *Oh God, what did I ever do to deserve this gift?*

A few minutes later, Nathan's full car pulled up the drive. Will walked out and opened the passenger door, drawing Rachel to her feet first. She held him at arm's length for a moment, "Is it really you?" she asked, tearfully.

"It's really me, Gramma."

Rachel kissed him and they embraced for a long moment.

Claudia was next, crying and laughing as she pulled Will close, telling him how much she had missed him and how deeply she loved him.

But it was Nathan's welcome that brought everyone to tears. His face was red, and he broke down in sobs when he drew his grandson to his chest. Eugene knew how special Will had always been to Nathan, but his unashamed display of emotion only proved it. Eugene held Annie close as they took in the miracle before them. He shook his head still finding it hard to believe that Will was actually home.

Roberta sweetly hugged Will's neck and then Lillie kissed him and told him, "Welcome home, Brother."

Will looked around. "What about Wallace? Where's that rascal?"

For a moment, everyone froze. Finally, Claudia gently touched her grandson's arm. "Will, honey, Wallace was sent to the Philippines . . . he didn't make it home."

Will's compassionate gaze moved back to Lillie and Roberta. He opened his arms and took them both in at the same time. "I'm truly sorry," he said in a rough voice. And then he whispered something that only the two women could hear. "It should've been me, not him."

Roberta wept quietly, and Will held her for a long time while everyone gathered around them. When she emerged from his arms, wiping her face, Roberta turned her gaze toward heaven. "The Lord giveth," she said in a trembling voice, "and the Lord taketh away. Blessed be the name of the Lord."

A hushed, "Amen," drifted among them as they turned toward the house clinging to one another. Before entering, Will introduced the family to Keiko. Eugene was concerned about Roberta and Lillie's response to Will's wife. After all, it was her people who had taken Wallace's life. But to his relief, both women welcomed her graciously into the family.

Later that evening at home, Annie and Rachel prepared Will's old room for the newly arrived couple and put fresh linens on the bed. Satisfied that everything was ready, they joined the family in the front room.

One look at Will sitting on the couch, and Annie felt a lump forming in her throat. He had an almost washed-out appearance—sickly even. How had she not noticed that earlier? He hadn't eaten much today, but Annie had thought perhaps he wasn't used to rich American food. His red-rimmed eyes, however, caused her a bit of anxiety.

Eugene and Jake were trying subtly to get a little more information from Will, but he evaded nearly every question. Keiko sat close to Will's side, softly rubbing her hand up and down his arm.

Finally, Will leaned forward and put his elbows on his knees. "Thank you all for a great homecoming. I'm really glad to be home."

"Sweetheart, this is such an answer to prayer." Annie looked around the room at all three of her men. "I never dreamed we'd all be together like this again."

Will grinned, then looked over at his wife. "Are you ready for bed?"

Annie noticed the way Keiko looked at him with complete devotion. "I am ready whenever you are," she answered quietly. Then with both hands, she reached underneath Will's arm and drew him to his feet.

Annie tried to squelch the fear that something was wrong. But at that moment, Will turned to his mother and pulled her into a strong embrace. When he released her, Annie held on to his shoulders for just a moment longer. "You'd tell me if something was wrong, wouldn't you?"

Will gave his mother a sly grin. "You worry too much, Momma." He kissed her cheek. "Nothing's wrong."

Annie let out a deep breath, trying to trust her son's bravado. Then with a wily smile of her own, she said, "You need to stop making this a habit."

His brow wrinkled for only a second. Then, realizing her meaning, he said, "I already have."

Chapter 52

Annie lay wide-awake in the middle of the night, irritated by the constant *tick, tick, tick* of the bedside clock and Eugene's soft snores. How could he always seem to sleep no matter what had happened during the day? She came to the conclusion it had to be a gift, pure and simple. She wished the gift would somehow rub off on her. Yet every time Annie closed her eyes, the rapturous reunion with Will played over and over and over again in her head.

Lord, I thank You for bringing Will home, but could You please help me stop living it the rest of the night?

A few minutes later, she quietly slipped out of bed and headed into the kitchen. Maybe a glass of milk would help her relax. But entering the kitchen produced just the opposite effect. Something was happening in Will's room that set her hair on end. It sounded like a scuffle, and she could hear a low, guttural sound, almost like a growl.

For a moment, she stood frozen in place, unsure of what to do. Should she wake Eugene? Or knock on Will's door to see if everything was all right? She moved closer to the bedroom door, not wanting to eavesdrop, but sensing something was terribly wrong. When the bedside lamp suddenly hit the floor, Annie stopped deliberating and knocked.

Silence permeated the room until she heard the soft padding of footfalls drawing near. The door partially opened, and Keiko stood in her nightgown with the eerie light from the overturned lamp behind her.

"Keiko, is everything okay?" Annie asked in a hushed voice.

Keiko bowed her head. "All is well, Mrs. Wyatt. Please do not worry yourself."

Annie looked past her daughter-in-law through the crevice in the doorway. The covers had been ripped from the bed and an overturned chair was visible beside the lamp on the floor. When Annie looked beyond the bed, her heart nearly skidded to a halt. She could see Will slumped in the corner of the room with his hands covering his head.

Keiko lifted her eyes to meet Annie's gaze. "Please, Mrs. Wyatt, there is nothing you can do. We are both fine."

There was an assurance in Keiko's eyes that told Annie this had happened before—perhaps many times before. She would just have to trust that this young woman could handle the situation, whatever it might be.

Annie hesitated, wanting to give Keiko her full support, but not knowing exactly what to say. Instead of using words, she simply pulled Keiko into a tender embrace. "I'm here for you, sweetheart, if you need anything at all."

"Thank you, Mrs. Wyatt."

"Please, call me Annie."

Softly Keiko whispered, "I will try."

"Are you sure you're okay?"

"Very sure. I will see you in the morning, Mrs. Annie."

A faint smile tipped the corner of Annie's lips. "You know where I am if you need anything . . . good night, sweetheart."

The door closed silently, leaving Annie standing in the unlit kitchen. She immediately heard the chair being set upright and the lamp put back on the bedside table. What must have gone on in that room earlier? Annie shuddered just thinking about it. She knew all too well what Eugene's night terrors had been like. But, judging by the condition of their room, Will's episodes must be of a more violent nature. There was no doubt in her mind that her son needed to see a doctor.

Annie knew it would be nearly impossible for her to sleep now, so she pulled a chair from the kitchen table and sat down to pray. Positioning her arms on the tabletop, she laid her forehead on her hands. For several minutes, she poured out her heart on Will's behalf, begging the Lord to bring healing and peace. Annie prayed for Keiko as well, asking God to give her new daughter-in-law the strength to bear her heavy burden. She petitioned the Lord until her words ran out, then she rested in the stillness of the night, letting her soul commune with the Father.

Feeling a tender caress on her shoulder, Annie slowly opened her eyes to the pale morning light. She looked up to see Rachel standing over her.

"Darlin', how long have you been up?"

Annie didn't answer for a moment, waiting for her groggy mind to clear. She tried to rub the numbness out of her hands, but they continued to tingle, almost painfully so. "I can't believe I fell asleep," she managed to say.

"You mean you slept in the kitchen last night?"

"Well, not *all* night." Annie let out a deep sigh. "I couldn't sleep, so I came in here to get a drink. I guess I never made it back to bed."

Rachel gave her shoulder a gentle squeeze. "Would you like a cup of coffee or do you want to go back to bed for a while?"

Annie closed her eyes contemplating her choices. "You know what?" she said, opening her eyes. "I think I'll get back in bed for a few minutes, if you don't mind."

"Darlin', you go right ahead. Sleep as long as you like. I'll get breakfast started since Jake will be heading to class soon."

"Thank you, Mama."

A few moments later, Annie took off her robe and slipped back into bed. Eugene turned over and cuddled up behind her. "You were up early," he said in a hoarse voice.

"I didn't get much sleep last night."

"Too excited?"

"Uh huh. How do you do it?"

She felt Eugene's warm breath on the back of her neck as he chuckled. "I don't know. Maybe there's not a lot going on up here." He thumped his knuckles on the top of his head.

They lay in silence for a while before Eugene cleared his throat. "Annie, I wanna apologize to you about everything. I know you never gave up on Will. I'm sorry for not believing you."

"Eugene, you have no reason to apologize. Nothing about it was logical. *I* can't even explain it." She turned over on her back to look at his face. "All I know is, there was something down deep in my soul that kept hope alive."

Eugene propped himself up on one elbow and traced the outline of her jaw with his thumb. "Still, I know how hard that must've been with the whole family trying to talk you into giving up."

She briefly smiled, and his thumb found the dimple in her cheek. "You know me; I embrace a challenge. But after that day you and I talked on the old church property, I decided not to say any more about it. I just had to trust that God had a plan because I couldn't live with the tension anymore."

He leaned in and kissed her forehead then the tip of her nose. "I'm so thankful for you," he whispered.

Annie brushed her hands through his disheveled hair. "And I'm thankful for you too."

When she yawned, Eugene rolled to the other side of the bed. "I've gotta get goin'. Why don't you sleep in a while?"

Annie watched him get dressed, knowing she needed to tell him about the incident last night with Will. But she knew this wasn't the right time. She yawned again and turned over on her side. Maybe later in the day, an opportunity would present itself.

Jake had already headed to the university by the time Annie made it back to the kitchen. She was still trying to shake the cobwebs out of her head. She didn't like feeling so sluggish.

Rachel had the remainder of breakfast warming in the oven. She was sitting in a chair, tugging on her boots.

"Are you heading out to the garden, Mama?"

"Yes, I thought I'd do a little gardening while Will and Keiko are sleeping. They must have been completely tuckered out after yesterday."

Annie cast a worried eye toward the bedroom door.

"What is it, darlin'?"

"Oh, nothing, Mama." She tried to erase the anxiety from her features. "I think I'll stay at the house this morning and wait for them to get up."

"That's a good idea," Rachel agreed.

When Rachel headed for the back door, Annie went with her. "Let me walk you out to the garden, Mama."

"That's not necessary, you know."

"I know, but I want to."

Despite her protests, Rachel leaned on Annie's arm all the way out to the garden. Annie made sure she had her gardening stool and all the necessary tools for her work. "I'll be back out after a bit to check on you."

"Okay, darlin'. Go enjoy your breakfast."

By the time Annie got back to the kitchen, Will's bedroom door was standing open. She glanced in and noticed Keiko neatly making the bed. Water was running down the hall, so she knew Will was in the bathroom.

"Good morning, Keiko."

"Oh, good morning, Mrs. . . . Annie." Keiko turned around, displaying a beautiful smile as if nothing had happened during the night.

For the first time, Annie wondered about her heritage. While she was definitely of Japanese descent, Keiko was quite a bit taller than most women from Japan, and her eyes were ever so slightly rounded at the corners. Annie couldn't wait to find out everything about her new daughter-in-law.

"Mornin', Mom." Will ambled into the kitchen with a towel around his bare shoulders.

"Good morning, sweetheart." Annie caught herself staring at him. She had never seen Will so thin. Even though his chest and arms were still quite muscular, his belly was almost concave—you could nearly count every one of his ribs.

He headed into the bedroom, and Annie could hear the two in hushed conversation. Unfortunately, she couldn't understand a word of it—they were speaking in Japanese. A few moments later, Will emerged from the bedroom buttoning his shirt, and Keiko inquired what she could do to help with breakfast.

Annie showed her the juice and glasses while she busied herself with the food from the oven. When the three sat down together at the table, Will nodded to his wife. "It's your turn."

To Annie's delight, Keiko bowed her head and asked a blessing over the food and over the day ahead.

While Will didn't seem to eat much, at least his spirits were high. He talked nonstop about the horses. He couldn't wait for Keiko to see them.

When breakfast was over, Annie rose from the table. "Why don't you two head on down to the barn while I clean up the kitchen? I want to check on Mama in the garden, and then I'll be down shortly."

Keiko dipped her head in respect to Annie. "I must help you first."

"No, sweetheart, that's not necessary. There will be plenty of time for that later." Annie smiled at her son. "Besides, Will's just about to bust a gut."

Keiko's brow wrinkled. "Bust . . . a . . . gut?" she repeated slowly. "Will, is your stomach hurting again?"

Will chuckled and took Keiko's hand. "Come on, kitten. I'll explain it to you on the way to the barn."

Keiko turned her puzzled gaze toward Annie. "I must go with my husband, but soon you will please tell me how I may help."

"I'll be glad to. You two have fun."

Keiko's brow wrinkled deeper, causing Annie to wonder if there was something else wrong. But hearing her daughter-in-law express concern over the size of the horses surely explained her uneasiness.

"Will," Annie called as the couple stepped out onto the back porch. "Take things slowly. It may take a while for Keiko to be comfortable around the horses."

He grinned and gave her a thumbs-up. "It'll be fine."

But several minutes later, when Annie joined them in the barn, the situation was anything *but* fine. Will had saddled Comanche and was trying to coax Keiko into the saddle. Tears already stained the poor girl's cheeks, and Annie felt drawn to intervene on her behalf. But she didn't want to cause a confrontation with Will already.

Fortunately, Eugene strode into the barn with perfect timing. "Hey, Son! I'm glad you're already saddled up. What do you say we head out into the pasture? You can help me round up some of the heifers."

Will hesitated for a moment, looking at his wife. "Do you mind, kitten?"

The look on Keiko's face was precious. "Oh, no! I do not mind. Please enjoy your horse and your father."

Annie relaxed. Her daughter-in-law's relief was palpable.

"You two go on," Annie chimed in. "Keiko and I will take some time to get to know each other."

Will nodded and kissed his wife sweetly. "Maybe this evening we can try again," he said.

"Perhaps," she said with a tenuous smile.

As soon as the men left the barn, Annie moved to Keiko's side. "Are you all right, sweetheart?"

Keiko let out a deep breath. "I am not sure." But then, her face brightened. "Please, could you help me with these very big animals?"

"I have just the thing. Come on, I want you to meet Gracie."

The two women spent the next half hour in Gracie's stall until Keiko's fear began to subside.

"She is so gentle, Mrs. Annie. I did not expect such a thing." Gracie placidly welcomed Keiko's strokes and pats.

Annie took both of Keiko's hands and moved them slowly down Gracie's right foreleg. When they neared the bottom, the mare compliantly lifted her hoof off the ground. Keiko giggled and glanced curiously over her shoulder at Annie.

"She thinks we're going to clean her hoof with a pick," Annie explained. "I'm going to let go now. You've got her."

Gracie didn't move a muscle. "She will stand like this for how long?"

"As long as you want her to."

"She is very obedient," Keiko observed, gently lowering her hoof back to the ground.

Annie ran her hands along Gracie's neck, then stepped in close, drawing her head to her chest. "Yes, my sweet girl. I love you so much."

"Maybe could you teach me to sit on a horse's back?"

"I would love to, if you think you're ready."

Annie could see a trace of fear return to Keiko's eyes, but a determination as well. "I am maybe ready."

"Come on, I'll let you sit on my horse, Josiah."

"Not Gracie?" Now there was a definite panic in the young woman's voice.

"Sweetheart, Gracie is too old to bear weight anymore. But Josiah is just as obedient. He'll be perfect for you . . . if you're sure."

Keiko's head bobbed nervously up and down. "I am sure."

After much encouragement, and arranging of Keiko's skirt, Annie was pleased to see her daughter-in-law sitting somewhat peacefully atop Josiah. And not long after that, she was leading the pair around the barn. Keiko never fully relaxed, but she had at least conquered her fear. Eugene would need to have a talk with Will and convince him not to push Keiko too soon where the horses were concerned.

Annie helped her dismount, then removed Josiah's tack while Keiko patted his neck, thanking him for the ride.

"Would you like to walk with me to the top of the ridge?" Annie asked, after Josiah had been led back into his stall. "There's a beautiful view of the farm from up there, and that will give us a chance to talk."

Keiko nodded her head. "I would like that."

As they walked up the path, Annie asked her daughter-in-law how old she was.

A pretty rose color adorned Keiko's cheeks. "I am older than your son by one year. I am twenty-five."

For the first time, Annie realized how many questions had been asked of Will and Keiko at the family gathering the day before. Amazingly, very few of those questions had actually been answered. She was dying to know every detail of their lives. *All in good time, Anne Marie.* Her intuition told her to set an unhurried pace. Just like introducing her daughter-in-law to the horses, some things couldn't be rushed.

The women sat down on an outcropping of rocks on top of the ridge, beneath the shade of a large sycamore tree. For a while, Annie drew her attention to various features on the farm. She even told her briefly about the flood of '37.

When Keiko excitedly pointed to Will riding with Eugene in the lower pasture, Annie dared to ask another question. "How did you and Will meet?"

Keiko's breathing increased markedly. She drew her hands to her lap and lowered her eyes. After a prolonged silence, she quietly said, "It is a long story, Mrs. Annie. Maybe I am not the one to tell you."

"Sweetheart, can you look at me?"

Keiko slowly lifted her gaze.

"I need *you* to tell me because Will isn't going to." Annie's eyes pleaded for her to reveal what she longed to know.

"If I am to tell you, then I must start at the beginning. It will take a very long time."

"I'll listen for as long as it takes."

Keiko lightly bit her lower lip and slowly nodded her head. "I come from a small island called Yoroshima. In the last century, a group of Christian missionaries from Great Britain came to our island. My grandmother was one who came as a child with her parents. They were very . . . I am not sure the word . . . um, very good at teaching the Bible. Soon the whole island believed in Jesus.

"My grandmother married a native man of the island and stayed to raise a family. My father was born. She taught him to speak English, just as she taught me when I was young. When he was seventeen, my grandmother sent him back to her home, Great Britain, to become a doctor. When he returned to Yoroshima, he fell in love and married a native woman named Mitsue. My mother."

Keiko's features became distressed. Annie knew she was about to share a difficult account. She silently prayed for God to give her strength.

"A terrible persecution came to our island when I was nine. When I was in the town square with my mother and grandmother, we were told by soldiers to turn our back on Jesus. Many others were standing with us. My mother bent to kiss me and whispered to me to run. I obeyed her, but I turned around when I heard screaming."

A tear slid down Keiko's cheek, and she quickly reached to brush it away. "I saw my mother and grandmother run through with a sword."

Annie let out a soft moan. Her heart was breaking for this dear girl. She reached out and gently smoothed Keiko's hair back from her face. "I'm so sorry, sweetheart," she whispered.

"Thank you, Mrs. Annie. There is more."

"I know . . . take your time."

Keiko drug in a deep breath and continued. "When soldiers came to our house outside of town, my father hid me in the jungle. He knew I would not turn my back on Jesus." A sob escaped her throat. "But God help my father; he turned his back to save our lives."

Sharing this fact caused Keiko much more anguish than even the loss of her mother and grandmother. Annie realized she was sitting beside an indomitable woman of faith. It solidified the deep connection that she was already forming with her.

"My father spent many days after that, digging a tunnel near our house. I had to live underground sometimes. It was very dangerous for me on the island. The soldiers . . ."

Color suddenly returned to Keiko's cheeks again. She gave Annie a timid look.

"I think I understand, sweetheart. They were taking the females for themselves?"

"Yes," she confirmed softly. "We wanted to leave the island and go to Great Britain, but the soldiers kept my father from leaving because he was a physician.

When the war started, they forced him to care for their prisoners. He secretly let the British and American prisoners know that he was a believer in Jesus."

Keiko shook her head in obvious grief. "He saw terrible things being done to those poor men. So terrible he cannot sleep at night."

Unexpectedly, Keiko took hold of Annie's hand and brought it tenderly to her lips. Keiko's tears fell on her hand, and Annie felt her composure slip away.

"Mrs. Annie . . ." Their eyes met and, suddenly, Annie knew what Keiko was about to tell her. She didn't know if her heart could take it. "Your Will was one of those men."

Chapter 53

Rachel had just finished making Will's favorite potato salad when Annie and Keiko returned to the house.

"Hi, you two. Lunch will be ready shortly."

"I'll clean up and help," Annie offered quietly.

Something in Annie's voice made Rachel turn and look at her daughter-in-law. She appeared to be utterly disheartened. Keiko was obviously in as low a state as Annie. *Oh dear, the two must not be getting along very well.* Rachel decided to leave the news of her phone calls until the men came in for lunch.

When Annie returned to the kitchen, she joined her mother-in-law at the counter. Rachel could literally feel a cloud of anxiety hanging over her. While Keiko was down the hall washing her hands, she hastily inquired, "Darlin', has something happened?"

Annie's hands stilled, and she pressed her lips together. Rachel was certain she was fighting to keep emotional control.

"Mama, I'm sorry. I just can't talk about it right now."

Although Rachel wanted to know what had caused such obvious angst, she was willing to wait until the time was right. And despite her pressing curiosity, this was not the time.

Keiko meekly entered the kitchen. "May I help with food preparation?"

"Would you mind putting the ham slices on the platter, darlin'?"

Keiko lowered her head in compliance and moved to the counter. At that moment, Rachel noticed a gesture that completely changed the direction of her thoughts. Keiko touched Annie's hand with remarkable tenderness, and Annie leaned her head into her daughter-in-law's. After that momentary demonstration of affection, both women continued their tasks. Rachel's heart immediately emptied of its worry concerning their relationship.

It wasn't long before Eugene and Will entered the kitchen in an entirely different mood. It was quite obvious they had shared a great morning together.

Eugene headed right for the ham, but Rachel cut him off just before he reached for a slice. "Not until you get those hands clean."

He laughed and made a move toward the hallway. But when Rachel turned her back, he snuck a piece of ham and winked at Keiko, who put her hand to her mouth and giggled.

As lunch got underway, Rachel decided it was time to announce her news. "I took two phone calls while you all were out this morning." She gave Keiko an eager smile. "Claudia called and wants to take you shopping sometime in the next couple of days. She wants to buy you some new clothes."

Will grinned at his wife. "Uh, oh. You're in for quite a day if you go shopping with Nana."

"But I cannot let her buy me clothes." Keiko looked stunned at such an offer.

"You can't turn her down, kitten. When my grandmother wants to go shopping, there's no stopping her."

Annie let Keiko know that she would come too. "My mother loves to shop for other people, and she'll especially enjoy buying something for you. Let her do it. You'll make her so happy."

"Then I will," Keiko agreed, "if you think it will help her."

Amused by her comment, Rachel smiled, and then quickly shared the news of her second phone call. "Will, a reporter from the newspaper called. He's coming out to interview you this afternoon. I guess word has gotten out that you've come home."

Will suddenly looked alarmed. "An interview?"

"Yes, and he'll probably take a picture or two. He wanted to know if we had a photograph of you when you entered the air corps. I told him—" Rachel's sentence came to an abrupt halt when Will stood up.

"No, I can't do an interview!"

The wild look in Will's eyes brought Eugene to his feet as well. "Son, relax. Everything's going to be okay. You don't have to answer any questions you don't want to."

Keiko intertwined her fingers with Will's, yet she remained silent. Rachel noticed how that simple act changed her grandson's demeanor almost immediately. Slowly, he sat back down at the table looking slightly embarrassed.

"Sweetheart," Annie said calmly, "this is big news. The war has been over since last year. For you to come home now is a miracle."

Will let out a deep sigh. "I know. It's just that . . ." He leaned back in his chair and rubbed the back of his neck. "I just don't wanna talk about it, that's all."

There was a short silence before Keiko looked at him with an intensity that surprised Rachel. "We will face this reporter together." She took hold of his hand now with both of hers. "This one thing we *can* do."

For a long moment, the two stared into each other's eyes until tranquility began to seep into Will's. Eventually, he turned his gaze back to Rachel. "What time is he coming, Gramma?"

"Two o'clock. I'm sorry, darlin', I didn't mean to cause you any grief."

Will shook his head. "It's all right. I'm sorry I got upset. It'll be fine, I promise." He gave her a grin that didn't quite make it to his eyes, but she could tell he was trying his best to regain composure.

"Well, if we're having company, I think I'll make some cookies," Rachel declared.

Annie looked over at Keiko. "Why don't you and I clean up the kitchen while Mama bakes?"

"I will be glad to help." Keiko gave Will's hand a squeeze, then began clearing the plates from the table.

At two o'clock sharp, Derek Floyd, a middle-aged reporter from the *Louisville Times*, showed up at the door. A young photographer stood behind him on the porch. Eugene opened the door and introduced himself, then made the introductions to the rest of the family.

Annie watched her son closely. He had changed into a fresh set of clothes, but patches of sweat were already showing through the back of his shirt. Bless his heart. She knew he had to be dreading the questions this reporter might ask.

"Do you mind if we go ahead and take a few shots before getting started?" Mr. Floyd asked. "Maybe one by yourself and then one with your family."

Will nodded. "That'd be fine."

A few pictures were taken inside, and then several more were taken outside. As they came back in the house, Rachel offered their guests cookies and iced tea, which Mr. Floyd readily accepted.

He patted his rotund belly. "I never turn down cookies, as you can see." Then looking at Will, he asked, "Would you mind joining me at the table in the kitchen? I prefer to have a hard surface for writing."

Will nodded once again and silently led the way. Keiko followed behind her husband, sitting down at his side. This time, Will reached for *her* hand and held it nervously. Annie, Eugene, and Rachel hovered near the kitchen door so they could listen.

The first half of the interview appeared to put Will at ease. He didn't seem to mind talking about the adventure of enlisting in the Army Air Corps or about all of his training. He spoke with great respect and admiration for his best friend, Jimmy, who had given his life at Pearl Harbor.

"So, tell me about your aircraft, The Gray Lady. What was she like? And tell me about her crew."

Again, Will had no problem describing the enormous B-17 *flying fortress*, and the close-knit crew he had the privilege of serving with. He even recounted their last mission, and how he and the radio operator were the only ones to survive the crash into the ocean.

"Byron Garrett was our radio man. I don't know how he did it, but he inflated a life raft just before impact. When I came up in the water, my Mae West, that is, my life preserver, kept me afloat until dawn. That's when I saw the raft and was able to swim to it. We had enough water and provisions for about a week on board."

Will's eyes narrowed, and he licked his dry lips. "We didn't get a chance to use much of it. A Japanese cruiser picked us up that evening." After that statement, Will fell silent.

Mr. Floyd looked up, pencil poised over his notebook, waiting for Will to continue. But Annie noticed it was almost like a chain on a lightbulb had been yanked. He sat completely stone-faced.

"So, once the Japanese had you . . . what then?" the reporter asked.

Will clasped his hands tightly on top of the table, his knuckles turning whiter by the second. When the reporter tried to prompt him once more, Will cast his gaze downward.

"Were you taken to a prison camp?"

"Yes," he responded without looking up.

The strain in her son's voice was painful to endure. Annie wanted to go to him with comfort and tell him that everything was going to be all right. This morning, Keiko had told her how the Japanese soldiers had starved him and beaten him into submission. They had ravaged his mind and body until death was but an exhale away.

Keiko laid her hand on Will's arm. "Do you wish for me to answer these questions?"

Will's nod was almost imperceptible.

"So you know what happened to your husband in the prison camp?" Mr. Floyd inquired.

"Yes, my father told me everything."

Annie inhaled a sharp, jagged breath, causing Eugene to take hold of her arm. "Are you okay?" he asked.

She fastened her gaze on his. "No," she whispered. She knew what was coming.

Before he could say any more, Keiko began painstakingly giving an account of Will's horrific treatment in the prison camp on Yoroshima. Immediately, Eugene went into the kitchen and quietly pulled a chair away from the table for Rachel, then another for Annie. He put the chairs along the wall, and both women sat down. Eugene stood beside them, the deep lines in his forehead exposing acute anxiety.

"Over time, my father got to know Will as a brother in Christ," Keiko told Mr. Floyd. "But Will became so sick that his captors thought he would soon die."

Keiko smoothed her hand along Will's arm, obviously concerned about his current well-being. He appeared to be in a trance. Annie wasn't sure whether he was even aware of what was being said.

"They threw him into a pit outside the camp with many dead soldiers, thinking he was already dead. My father passed by the pit that evening on the way home, and he saw a small movement; it was Will."

Rachel buried her face in her hands and began to weep. Keiko looked at her with great compassion. "I am so sorry for what this is doing. Should I discontinue?"

Mr. Floyd turned in his chair to face the rest of the family. "Would it be better for me to speak to her alone?" He obviously wanted this story, but he also bore a look of sympathy.

"No," Rachel answered softly. She dabbed her eyes with a handkerchief. "You can keep going." Eugene immediately brought over another chair and sat down beside his mama. He put his arm around her shoulders to give her support.

Mr. Floyd turned and made a few scribbles in his notebook. Then, in a quiet voice, he asked Keiko to continue.

At that moment, Annie and Keiko's gazes met and held. Annie was determined to give her daughter-in-law the assurance she needed to continue, despite her own tenuous composure. She nodded to Keiko, "You're doing just fine, sweetheart."

"Thank you, Mrs. Annie," she whispered.

"You were saying that your father found Will in a pit outside of camp . . ."

Keiko turned her attention back to Mr. Floyd. "Yes. Will had lost over half of his body weight. My father had no problem carrying him to our home. He had to go a very long way around the town, so no one would see.

"For weeks my father and I cared for Will, and in time, he regained some of his health. Still, he was very sick and I stayed with him always while my father's time was demanded at the camp."

Annie recalled Keiko's exact words to her this morning as they talked on the ridge. Keiko had confessed that she had fallen deeply in love with Will before she knew if he was even going to survive. She told her, "I could not leave his side, day or night."

For the first time during the interview, Keiko's eyes began to mist. "One night soldiers came to our house. We could hear them coming from far off, so I took Will to the underground hiding place. The next morning . . ."

When Keiko's chin began to quiver, Annie went to her. She sat down in the other chair at the table and drew her close. That's when Will seemed to snap out of his stupor. For a long moment, he stared at his wife and mother, then straight into the eyes of Mr. Floyd.

"We found her father the next morning outside the house. The soldiers had . . . decapitated him," Will solemnly explained. "They had found out that he was a Christian."

Mr. Floyd let out a deep sigh. "I'm very sorry for your loss," he said to Keiko. It was obvious that Derek Floyd was getting more of a story than he had bargained for, and it seemed to be affecting him deeply.

Will continued in a quiet voice. "Keiko and I gathered up provisions and headed into the jungle. I've been trained in survival skills, so that's what we did. We survived off the land for months. We had no idea that the war had ended until a native islander accidently found us. When he told us the war was over, we couldn't believe it."

Keiko sat up from Annie's arms, and Will reached for her hand again. Together, the two related how they were taken to a small port on the island and boarded a ship for the Philippines.

"From there, we made it to California," Will stated. "And with the help of God, and a lot of good people, we eventually made it home."

There was a sense of exhaustion from everyone in the room after listening to Will and Keiko's moving account. Annie hadn't even recovered from hearing it the first time. Thankfully, Will looked as though he had regained his composure, yet Annie worried about her son's fragile state of mind. She reminded herself that he needed to see a doctor—soon.

Mr. Floyd thanked the young couple profusely for sharing their story. He was anxious to get back to the newspaper office and start putting it together. He told them to look for it in Wednesday's paper, not wanting to rush Monday's five o'clock deadline. This was one piece that warranted justice.

The mood still felt heavy around the kitchen table after Mr. Floyd's departure. Annie thought it was probably time to talk about Will's night terrors, but she inwardly cringed. He had barely been here twenty-four hours. This was no light-hearted homecoming.

When Will rose to his feet, Annie knew it was now or never. "Will," she began in a low voice, "tell me about last night."

Annie felt Eugene and Rachel's eyes on her, but she steadily held her son's gaze with tenderness. Will's natural defensiveness flashed across his features, but it thankfully disappeared as quickly as it surfaced. He sank back down in his chair with a look of resignation.

Annie let out her breath in relief. "You're probably not aware of this, but your dad has experienced the same thing."

Will raised his brow and looked at his dad. Eugene appeared to be at a loss for words. The subject had obviously caught him off guard.

"I never knew you had trouble after the war, Dad."

Eugene quickly recovered his wits. "I had night terrors after the first war. You were too young to know what was going on." He shrugged his shoulders. "I guess I've had episodes on and off over the years." He leaned forward and placed his elbows on the table. "Are you having trouble at night, Son?"

Will swallowed hard. "I am."

Annie was grateful for her son's matter-of-fact confession. But now the question remained; what should they do about it? She prayed that her son would not turn to alcohol. So many war veterans were looking for relief in an open bottle. *Oh, Lord, please help Will be strong.*

Keiko quietly broke into their thoughts. "It never once happened in the jungle. It only started when we got to the Philippines."

Will nodded his head in agreement. "I think it has something to do with being around people. I know that sounds crazy, but she's right. When it was just the two of us nothing ever happened."

Annie asked Keiko, "Are you scared when it happens?"

Keiko turned her eyes to meet her husband's as she answered the question. "I am never scared for myself." Then she switched her gaze to Annie. "I am only afraid for him."

"Son, we know a good doctor," Eugene offered. "As a matter of fact, Jake went to him when he got home from Europe, and he worked for him during the summer. His name is Dr. Lindley. You need to have a complete physical, and maybe he can help you with your trouble at night."

Once again, Annie waited anxiously for her son's response. In time's past, he would've crossed swords with them at the very suggestion of help. But time and experience had produced a maturity in her son that had been lacking five years ago. Annie realized what an important part Keiko had played during the past year. This precious young woman by Will's side had truly saved his life—in more ways than one.

"I'll go," he said, his mouth tilting slightly upward.

The family let out one collective breath, and slowly the somber cloud hanging over their heads began to dissipate. Even so, Annie worried in her heart that an entire lifetime would not be able to erase the horrific deeds her son had suffered.

Oh God, help him.

The next morning after breakfast, Claudia knocked on the front door and let herself in. When she saw the women still in the kitchen, she greeted them warmly. "I'm so glad you're not down at the barn," she commented to Annie, giving her a kiss on the cheek.

"I was just about to head down. Is this the shopping day?"

Claudia smiled earnestly at Keiko. "I would love to take you today . . . unless, of course, you have other plans."

Keiko glanced quickly at Annie before reciprocating Claudia's smile. "I have no plans. But Mrs. Annie, is this a good time?"

"Absolutely! You don't mind if I tag along, do you Mother?"

"Not at all. The more the merrier. Rachel, what about you?"

"Oh, sweet friend, thank you for the invitation. I'm afraid I'd just slow you girls down."

"Nonsense, we'll take our time. There's even a new café downtown I've been dying to try out. Lunch is on me," Claudia declared.

Rachel finished putting the clean plates in the cupboard. "What about the men? Would we just leave them to fend for themselves?"

Annie laughed conspiratorially. "Why not? There's leftover ham; they can make sandwiches for lunch. Come on, Mama. It'll be fun!"

After a brief moment of indecision, Rachel yanked off her apron and tossed it on the counter. "Give me ten minutes and I'm in!"

The other three women enthusiastically cheered her decision.

Claudia took a notepad and pen from her purse. "While you three are getting ready, I'll write Eugene and Will a note to let them know they're on their own today."

Annie laughed as she headed down the hall. "I'd love to be a fly on the wall when they read *that*."

***

A little bell tinkled above the door of Fran's Dress Shop on Jefferson Street. Annie reached for Keiko's purchases to free her hands. Claudia had already bought her two skirts and three blouses, along with a new pair of shoes. Annie had even talked her into her first pair of trousers for riding. Keiko had protested over such extravagance, but Claudia had eagerly insisted on each purchase. Now she planned to help Keiko pick out a nice dress for Jake's wedding.

Annie watched with amusement as Claudia led Keiko through the shop, pulling out one dress after another and holding it up to her. She could remember her mother doing the very same thing to her growing up. Annie had never been one to enjoy shopping. It took a great deal of persuasion on her mother's part to get her into a dress shop such as this one. Many times, Claudia had to bring dresses home simply for Annie to try on.

"This would look perfect on you, honey." Claudia held up a green and white floral print dress, with gathered shoulder seams. "What do you think?"

Annie had to admit her mother had good taste. She knew the sash belt would accentuate Keiko's slim waistline.

Keiko's cheeks grew rosier by the second. "It is a most beautiful dress, Mrs. Claudia."

"You would look perfect in this at the wedding!" Claudia excitedly looked around for a sales woman to help them find the dressing room.

Almost immediately, a well-dressed, slender woman approached Claudia. "May I help you?" she asked in a pleasant voice.

Claudia held out the dress and stepped aside for the saleswoman to see Keiko. "She would like to try on this dress, please."

The woman's back straightened, and her pointy chin jutted outward. Her response to Claudia instantly went from pleasant to curt. "Is this dress for . . . *her*?"

At first, Annie was unsure of what was going on, but it soon became crystal clear as the sales woman continued. "We won't be selling the likes of *her* any of our dresses."

Claudia's mouth dropped open, but only momentarily. "May I please speak to your manager?"

The woman laughed haughtily. "No need. You're speaking to the owner, and I will not sell one scrap of material to *her*."

"Surely you can't be serious," Claudia gasped.

"Surely *you* can't be serious, bringing the enemy into my shop."

"She is *not* our enemy. You have no idea what you're saying. She has the right to try on this dress if she wants to."

Keiko lowered her head in humility, lightly touching Claudia's arm. "Please, we can go now. It is all right."

Claudia turned to Keiko, looking directly into her eyes. "Honey, it is *not* all right." Then she turned back around to the shop owner. "I'll take this dress; no need to bother trying it on."

The snobbish owner had no answer for that. Her face began to turn a light shade of red. Nevertheless, she stood her ground.

Annie noticed the other ladies around the dress shop standing like statues, staring at the face-off between her mother and the shop owner. This rude woman was bringing disgrace upon her daughter-in-law, and she could stand it no longer.

"Come on, sweetheart," Annie said quietly, putting her arm around Keiko's shoulders. "Why don't we go outside?"

Rachel had already moved toward the door, apparently anxious to get away from this situation. But just before the three could make it outside, the shop owner loudly proclaimed, "Her people killed our men. She doesn't deserve to be here."

Annie felt heat flooding her cheeks. She quickly led Keiko and Rachel out onto the sidewalk and handed them Keiko's purchases.

"Stay here. I'll be right back." Ignoring Rachel's protests, Annie headed back inside.

Without looking to the right or the left, she marched straight up to the dress shop owner. "That young woman you just humiliated saved my son's life during the war. He wouldn't be home today if it hadn't been for her. And for your information, Keiko happens to be a wonderful Christian woman—which is more than I can say for you." Annie took the dress out of her mother's hand and put it back on the rack. "Come on, Mother. You're not spending one dime here."

Claudia raised her brow and looked at the shop owner with a hint of amusement. "I guess I raised *her* right."

And with that comment, she turned on her heels and followed Annie outside. It took a while for Annie's emotions to drop from a boil to a simmer. The other three seemed to be terribly flustered by the incident. Rachel and Keiko had moved down the sidewalk away from the dress shop.

When Annie finally collected an ounce of composure, she gently took her daughter-in-law's face in both of her hands. A sheen of tears already shimmered in Keiko's dark eyes. "I'm so sorry you had to go through that, sweetheart."

Keiko shook her head, releasing the tears. "Please do not apologize. I am the one who is sorry. I have brought shame on your family."

Annie nearly choked on her reply. "You have done no such thing, Keiko. You've done nothing but bring joy to our family, and we're very proud of you."

Rachel and Claudia instantly affirmed Annie's declaration.

"What that woman said in there was wrong; it was downright evil."

Keiko lowered her head and remained silent.

Claudia spoke up then. "Why don't we drive over to the Garden Café and forget about all of this nonsense. We won't let someone's ignorant opinion ruin our time together."

"Maybe you would wish to not be seen with me," Keiko whispered.

Rachel resolutely lifted her shoulders, taking in a sharp breath. "Darlin', believe it or not, I've been where you are." She reached out and encircled Keiko's waist and started leading her toward the car. "I'll tell you all about it at lunch."

Annie stood still, relishing the moment. Who better to bring perspective to this humiliating situation? Rachel had endured years of racial abuse as a young woman. She realized that despite their gaping age difference, these two women actually had a lot in common.

Over lunch, Rachel revealed her heritage to Keiko. She told her about some of the terrible things people had uttered to her face, all because Franklin was her husband. Keiko's compassionate response was so endearing. Annie watched her new daughter-in-law with admiration, thanking the Lord for bringing this honorable young woman into all of their lives.

As lunch went on, the women were able to put the dress shop incident behind them. They determined to ban together and venture into one more shop in order to find Keiko a dress for the wedding. And by mid-afternoon, they were back in Claudia's car, cheering their success. Keiko had a beautiful green and white floral print dress, nearly identical to the one at Fran's—only lovelier.

That evening, after dinner, Annie and Keiko washed the dishes while Rachel dried. "Could you please tell me what the wedding will be like?" Keiko inquired.

Annie's face beamed with joy. "It will be small—maybe one hundred people. They only wanted close family and friends."

"One hundred is a lot."

"Not compared to some weddings I've seen. But the church building Charlotte selected is very small in downtown Louisville. It's a beautiful stone building with stained-glass windows built over a hundred years ago."

Keiko had stopped rinsing the dishes and Annie noticed her daughter-in-law's sudden discomfort. "What is it, sweetheart?"

"I do not know how to say this."

"You can tell us anything," Annie prompted. Rachel moved in close, reaffirming Annie's statement.

Keiko lowered her head. "I am afraid that Will and I are not married correctly."

"What do you mean?" Annie asked softly.

"We did not know how long we would live in the jungle . . . but we loved each other very much." Keiko turned a self-conscious gaze toward Annie. "We said our marriage vows to each other, and we were all alone."

Annie pulled in a deep breath understanding Keiko's concern. "What does Will say . . . now that you're home?"

"He says I am worrying for nothing. He believes God understands."

The three women stood in silence for a while, allowing Annie to mull over the situation. While she felt certain God truly understood, she felt just as certain that the government would not. Her heart joined with Keiko's in worry. Something would need to be done, but the thought of getting Will to talk about it caused her to cringe inwardly.

All of a sudden, the solution dawned on her. Annie excitedly clasped Keiko's dripping hands. "I think I know just the thing!"

Chapter 54

May 1946

Dressed in a black tuxedo, and looking quite dashing, Jake walked his mother down the isle of the small sanctuary. When they reached her seat in the front, he kissed her sweetly.

"Thank you, Mom, for everything," he whispered.

Annie looked into her son's deep blue eyes, trying to hold back her emotions. She could already feel the warmth of tears forming behind her eyes.

"I love you, sweetheart," she whispered in a quavering voice.

When both families were seated, Eugene took her hand and held it tenderly. He was all smiles, which gave Annie a great deal of encouragement. Perhaps she could make it through the ceremony without falling completely apart.

Just as she had determined not to make a scene, Mercy walked down the aisle, followed by Jake and Will and Sam. When they took their places up front, her sons turned and smiled directly at *her*. Annie knew she was squeezing the blood right out of Eugene's hand. Thankfully, she managed to return their smile, forcing her tears to hold off for a tad bit longer.

While Charlotte's sister Caroline and her best friend, Ellen, slowly approached the front, Annie studied Will's face. The dark circles beneath his eyes spoke of his constant inability to sleep. Thankfully, he had begun to gain a little weight after Dr. Lindley put him on an antibiotic for dysentery. It was determined that at some point during Will's time in the prison camp, he had also suffered severe kidney problems. The doctor had prescribed other medication for his kidneys and instructed him to drink water only.

While his health issues were slowly being resolved, Will had resisted psychological help. Dr. Lindley had given him the name of a very good psychiatrist, even going so far as to set up an appointment for him, but Will had canceled the appointment. He wanted to give it more time. Annie worried about how much Keiko could handle at night. She glanced at her daughter-in-law, sitting beside her, and noticed she and Will were holding each other's gazes. Her pulse quickened—excited for this day to fully unfold.

When the organ resounded with the traditional wedding march, Charlotte's mother rose to her feet, and everyone joined her. Annie could hear the small audience collectively draw in their breath. Charlotte looked stunning, walking down the aisle on her father's arm, smiling at her groom. Jake couldn't keep his eyes off her and eagerly stepped in to fill her father's spot after he gave his daughter away.

Mercy did a wonderful job with the ceremony. Annie had been thrilled to get to know this extraordinary young man over the last few days. The loss of his left hand had done nothing to hinder him physically or dampen his vibrant spirit. If Annie had a daughter, she would've encouraged her to get to know David McAllister.

As the ceremony continued, Mercy asked Charlotte to hold Jake's hands, palms up. "So that you may see the gift they are to you," he said.

Jake turned his palms upward, and Charlotte placed her hands lovingly beneath his. They gazed into each other's eyes, exchanging a smile, before Charlotte looked back to her groom's open hands. Mercy began to beautifully describe what Jake's hands would mean to her—the strength, joy, passion, and comfort they would bring to her for a lifetime.

When Mercy talked about Jake's strong hands gently holding their first child that did Annie in completely. Picturing her son tenderly cradling a little baby was all it took. Eugene handed her a handkerchief and put his arm around her shoulders.

Mercy then instructed Charlotte to turn her palms up to Jake, and he continued to paint an exquisite picture of what her hands would mean to him.

"Together, may these four hands serve God and their fellow man, for all the days that shall be given to them on this earth."

Annie noticed that she was not the only one overwhelmed by Mercy's description of their hands. This young man had sacrificed one of his own hands to the defense of his country, and yet, he had woven the entire ceremony around Jake and Charlotte's hands. The beauty of it was immense.

At the conclusion of the ceremony, a cake and punch reception commenced underneath the trees. It was a perfect day. Everything had gone exactly the way Charlotte had planned.

When it was time for the newlyweds to leave, they went back inside the sanctuary with their parents. Eugene and Annie, along with their new in-laws, Stan and Abigail, put their arms around their children while Eugene prayed a blessing over them. More hugs and kisses followed before the parents took their places outside with the other guests.

Jake and Charlotte ducked their heads amidst a shower of rice, running for the car hand in hand. Charlotte's brother, Sam, and Will had done a fine job decorating Jake's car. *Just Married* was written in soap on every window, while a dozen tin cans rattled from the back bumper.

Not long after Jake's car pulled out of sight, the final wedding guests departed for home. Abigail opened her arms to Annie. "I'm so thankful that Jake is a part of our family now."

Annie returned Abigail's heartfelt embrace, declaring her love for Charlotte. "And thank you for this." She gestured toward the church building.

Abigail smiled sweetly. "It's our pleasure. This is quite a big day for your family." She turned to her husband and said, "Come on, Stan. Let's not hold them up any longer."

Stan shook Eugene's hand. "I guess we'll be seeing each other more often."

"You and Abigail are always welcome at the house. Come on out anytime."

"We'll do that. Enjoy the rest of the day." Stan put his arm around his wife's shoulders, and they headed toward their car.

"I think everyone's waiting for us inside," Eugene said. He stuck his elbow out to Annie. "You ready?"

Annie took his arm and leaned in close to her husband. "Round two," she said with a giggle.

Eugene reached into his pocket and handed her a gold ring. "Here, stick this on your thumb before I forget."

Annie slid Will's ring onto her thumb, trying not to get swept away by her emotions. She knew it would be a difficult task, especially when they walked back into the sanctuary. The entire family was standing up front waiting for them.

Jake and Charlotte had driven around the block and snuck in the back door. They had already changed out of their wedding clothes. Annie thought Will looked a little nervous, but Jake teasingly rubbed his shoulders. "You can do it, big brother. It's not so bad."

Eugene led Annie to her place beside Keiko, then took his spot between Will and Jake. Annie thought her heart would burst with joy as she stood with all the women in her family beside Keiko, while all the men stood with Will. She recalled Keiko's timid confession to her several days ago concerning her relationship with Will. It hadn't taken long for Annie to formulate the perfect solution to their dilemma—two weddings in one day!

Mercy led them in a short, informal ceremony—just what Will had requested. And within ten minutes, they were pronounced husband and wife. Will took Keiko in his arms and gave her a quick kiss, but the family cheered and clapped when Keiko pulled him back to her, giving him a long, passionate kiss. Annie laughed through her tears, feeling Keiko's obvious relief.

That evening, the family enjoyed a leisurely conversation on Eugene and Annie's front porch. Both of the Wyatt boys and their wives had gone their separate ways after the second wedding ceremony. Jake and Charlotte headed downtown to the Brown Hotel for the night, with plans to leave for Niagara Falls in the morning. They intended to honeymoon for a week in New York, then come home to their apartment near the university.

Will and Keiko left the ceremony in Eugene's farm truck loaded with supplies for a weeklong stay at the farm in Winchester. Will couldn't wait to show Keiko their hunting and fishing lodge—including the cave beneath the house. He had purposely kept the cave a secret from his wife, wanting to see her reaction when he showed it to her.

Eugene was thankful to have Mercy with them for two more nights. He had been staying at their house since Thursday, allowing the rest of the family to see what a special young man he truly was.

Annie curled her legs up on the swing and sunk into her husband's side. Eugene slid his arm around her and set the swing in motion. "Mercy, I think you're going to enjoy our worship service tomorrow," he commented.

Mercy stretched his long legs out in front of him, feeling relaxed and comfortable with Jake's family. "I'm looking forward to it."

"You'll just have to watch out for Miss Ruby," Claudia said with a laugh. "It's possible she could hug you to death."

Mercy raised his brow. "Maybe you can give me a warning when you see her heading my way, Mrs. Harrison."

"No. No warning," Nathan interjected. "It's better not to know what's coming."

The mood remained lighthearted as they described the Oak Hill congregation to Mercy. When Rachel inquired about Mercy's church family, he spent the next several minutes describing the little church he preached for in Topeka, Kansas.

As the sun began to set on the horizon, Nathan stood and stretched out his back. "I guess we'd better head home." He held out his hand to Claudia and helped her to her feet.

Annie immediately went to her parents. First, Claudia drew her daughter close and kissed her, then Nathan held her for a long moment.

"It was a perfect day," he told her. "You raised two fine young men, honey." Nathan released her and laid his hand on Eugene's shoulder. "Both of you did a great job with those two. Better than I could've ever done."

Eugene felt his breath catch at the sudden emotion Nathan's words evoked. "Thank you, Nathan, but you and Claudia are a big part of who Will and Jake are today." He stopped there, knowing if he tried to say anymore, he would be choking on tears.

After the Harrisons left for home, Rachel hugged the remaining three on the porch. Heading for the door, she looked over her shoulder with a twinkle in her eye. "I'm going to do something to you that the devil never does."

"What's that, Mama?" Eugene asked curiously.

"Leave you alone. Good night, everyone."

"Good night, Mama."

She closed the door to the sound of laughter on the porch as Eugene and Annie settled back onto the swing, and Mercy into the nearby chair. For a while, they sat in comfortable silence, enjoying the peaceful closure of a day well spent.

Annie was the first to break the silence. "Mercy, do you have a girl back home?"

"I did," he answered matter-of-factly.

"I'm sorry; I didn't mean to pry into your business."

Mercy gave her an easy smile. "You weren't prying. It was hard at the time, but now I see it was for the best." He looked out over the front yard, now bathed in dusk. "It happened when I first got home from Europe. She couldn't seem to get past this." Mercy held up his left arm briefly, then let it drop into his lap.

"Then she wasn't good enough for you, David," Annie uttered softly.

Mercy's eyes narrowed. The lamplight from the window left half of his face in shadow. "That's what I keep telling myself." He seemed to brush away the pain from his past and looked back at Annie with a grin. "You don't happen to have a daughter hidden away somewhere, do you?"

Annie laughed. "I wish I did." She reached out and smoothed her hand down his lower left arm, all the way to the stub. "Because I would have to insist that she marry you."

Mercy held her hand briefly on top of his arm. "Thank you for that."

Annie blinked back tears and leaned into her husband again. Eugene was touched deeply by what he had just witnessed. He loved Mercy like he loved his own sons and wanted the best for him. This young man's faith had brought him back from the brink of despair. He owed him a huge debt of gratitude.

"Uh, Mercy . . ." Eugene cleared his throat. "I want to thank you again for what you did for me in the hospital in England."

"Thank *me*? I'm the one who should be thanking *you*. You're the one who gave me the courage to face life like this. You helped me walk again. You—" He stopped short when Eugene raised his hand in protest.

"You would've somehow found a way to do all of that without me. Don't get me wrong; I'm thankful to have been there for you. But, in a way, taking care of you saved *me*."

Eugene took his arm from around Annie's shoulders and leaned forward in the swing. He wanted to express his indebtedness to Mercy for his unwavering faith. So for the next several minutes, Eugene poured his heart out in gratefulness for Mercy's role in leading him back to God.

"And I want you to know one more thing."

Mercy continued to hold Eugene's eyes unflinchingly.

"It was your prayers that brought Jake back to us. For that . . ." Eugene's voice suddenly broke, and he paused to collect himself. "I will always be in your debt."

Mercy bent forward, placing his elbows on his knees. His head tilted downward for a long minute. Annie was curled up in the corner of the swing, softly crying. Eugene hadn't expected this to be such an emotional conversation, but he felt relieved that Mercy finally knew the extent of his appreciation.

Eugene stood up and placed his hand on Mercy's shoulder, giving it a firm squeeze. "I love you, Son."

Within a split second, Mercy was on his feet hugging Eugene fiercely. "I love you too," he whispered.

When Eugene finally let go of his hold, both men sat back down, seemingly unashamed of their display of emotion.

Annie wiped her hands across her face. "You two are killing me."

"Sorry about that," Eugene said with a chuckle. "I had to get that off my chest."

Mercy let out a slow, deep breath. "Well, maybe I can lighten the mood a little. I've probably got a few stories I could tell on Jake from our training days."

"Oh please do," Annie urged enthusiastically. "Tell me everything you know. I've heard so little."

Mercy cut his eyes around toward Eugene, who nodded his approval.

He rubbed his chin for a moment in contemplation. "Okay, I've got one," Mercy said. "Did Jake ever tell you about the time we *accidently* set the latrine on fire at Camp Barkeley?"

"No!" Annie squealed. "Eugene, did you hear about that?"

Eugene shook his head in amusement. "I'm afraid not." He leaned back in the swing and gave it a little push. "This should be good."

For the next several minutes, Mercy had them in stitches—and could he ever tell a story! Eugene thought that was probably what made him such a great preacher. When he started describing the look on their captain's face when he discovered the fire, all three were laughing so loud, they were afraid of waking Rachel.

"Yeah," Mercy laughed, "we gave *fire in the hole* an entirely new meaning."

Eugene thoroughly enjoyed his wife's absorption into every detail of Mercy's story. She had missed nearly three years of his and Jake's life—five years of Will's. He threw in a few lighthearted tales of his own just to see the delight on her face.

It was after midnight when they finally decided to head for bed. Eugene clapped Mercy on the back as they walked through the front door. "You need to get your rest, Son, so you'll be ready for Miss Ruby."

Annie threw her hand over her mouth, stifling an outburst of laughter. Eugene playfully shushed her, then turned to lock the door. Even though they had stayed up far too late, it had been time well spent. The war had left him with so many horrific memories, he had nearly suppressed every joyful moment he'd encountered along the way.

Eugene slid his hand into Annie's and led her through the house. Tonight had been good medicine for both of them—one more reason to be grateful to Mercy.

Chapter 55

June 1946

Summer brought with it some of the most arduous labor on the farm. It was hay season. A fairly large parcel of land on the farm was strictly used for seeding hay. It required a lot of work at cutting time, but was well worth the investment.

Eugene wiped the sweat from his brow with the back of his leather glove, then set the hook through another bale of hay. "Okay," he yelled.

Will hoisted the bale into the loft on a rope and pulley system. "Hey, Dad, we're just about out of space."

"Only five more," he called up to his son. "Can you fit 'em in?"

"Yeah, I think I can manage it."

Eugene hooked through the wire on another bale. "Here you go."

There was barely enough room for Will to walk in the loft after all the bales had been stacked. "Bumper crop this season, huh?"

"Yeah," Eugene responded. "It's been a good one."

Will started down the ladder. "I'm just tryin' to imagine Mom and Leroy taking care of all this while we were gone."

"Kind of amazing, isn't it?"

Eugene had a mighty admiration for his wife, knowing how hard she had worked to keep this place going for three years without him. She and Leroy had made a good team. There were a few times Nathan had sent extra help, especially during the hay-cutting season but, all in all, the two of them had done a commendable job.

Now that Will and Keiko were back from their honeymoon on the Winchester farm, Eugene was working with his son every day. This past month with Will had brought him a great deal of joy. Eugene had finally found the relationship with him that he'd always dreamed of.

He dipped a ladle into the water bucket, letting the cool liquid slide down his dry, dusty throat. The second dip, he offered to his son, who ambled over pulling off his work gloves.

Will slurped the water down and refilled the ladle for another long swig.

"Son, have you given some thought to my offer?"

Will let the ladle splash back down into the bucket. He ran his hand across his mouth and slowly nodded his head. "Keiko and I have been talking about it a lot."

When Eugene perceived a slight discomfort in Will's manner, he said, "It's all right if you haven't come to a decision yet. Take all the time you need." Eugene took the ladle and poured a little water on the bandana in his hand. Then he rubbed it on the back of his neck, trying to cool off a bit.

"Dad, I think we've come to a decision, but we'd like to talk with you and Mom together, if that's okay."

Eugene felt a faint constriction of his heart. He couldn't quite read Will's intention, but he respected the fact that he wanted Keiko and Annie in on the conversation.

"Okay, no problem. You wanna talk tonight after supper?"

"Yeah. Do you mind if I go get cleaned up and talk to Keiko right now?"

"No, not at all. I'll head up in a little while." Eugene clapped his son on the shoulder. "You go on."

For a moment, Will looked at his dad with a glint of affection in his eyes. It was a look Eugene had seldom seen, and it nearly did him in. If they hadn't been so dirty and sweaty, he might've hugged him.

Will's mouth turned slightly upward, and he blinked, erasing the look. "I'll see you at the house," he said.

Eugene merely nodded, not trusting his voice.

That night after supper, Eugene and Will waited on the front porch for their wives to join them. Will sat on the steps lazily tossing a baseball into the air while Eugene stood beside him leaning his elbows on the railing, talking about the weather.

"I can smell the rain coming in. I'm glad we finished with the hay this afternoon."

"Yeah, me too," Will agreed.

Annie opened the screen door and stepped out onto the porch with Keiko. "May we join you?"

Will started to get up, but Eugene pressed on his shoulder. "Sure. Why don't we all sit on the steps?"

Over the years, there had been many a family conversation on the front porch—some of the most poignant ones on this top step. Eugene felt an inexplicable comfort here—a comfort that always drew his mind back to the farm in Winchester where he had been molded by a loving man and woman of God.

With a grateful heart, Eugene sat down on the opposite side of the step from Will, allowing Annie and Keiko to sit between them.

"Supper was good tonight," Eugene commented, leaning forward to look at his daughter-in-law. "You're becoming quite the cook."

Keiko smiled delightfully. "I am learning much from Mama Rachel."

"It skipped a generation," Annie quipped. Then she elbowed Eugene in the side before he could agree.

Will leaned forward with his hands on his knees. He took in a deep breath and let it out slowly. "Dad . . . and Mom," he said, turning to look at both of them.

"Thank you for your offer of a job here on the farm. That really means a lot to both of us."

Keiko nodded her head in complete agreement. But when Will looked away and didn't say anything else, Eugene jumped in. "Well, you know your mom and I aren't getting any younger. Plus, we love having you both here with us. I think there's a lot we could do together to . . ." His voice trailed off when he noticed the expression on Keiko's face as she bowed her head.

After a short pause, Eugene said, "But that's not what you want to do, is it?"

Will turned his head slowly and locked eyes with his dad. "A big part of me does. In a lot of ways, I feel like I owe it to you to stay here and work."

"Will," Annie interrupted, "you don't *owe* us anything."

"I know," he agreed. "But that doesn't change the way I feel. You all have done so much for me over the years. I guess what I'm trying to say is, I appreciate everything . . . very much. That's what's making this so hard."

Will looked away again, and Keiko slipped her arm through his. A slow smile began spreading across his face. "I know you're gonna think this is crazy," he said, looking back. "But we were wondering if we could buy the Winchester farm from Gramma and live there?"

Eugene was completely taken aback. He hadn't even considered that possibility. At the moment, he was at a loss for words.

"Dad, you wouldn't believe how I felt there . . . how we both felt. It was like being home." Will looked at his mom, his expression full of enthusiasm. "I didn't have one night terror while we were there—not one!"

"It is true," Keiko confirmed.

Will blew out another deep breath and continued. "We're both used to a solitary life now. Keiko was raised alone; she's not used to a lot of people. When we got out there on that farm together, it just felt right. I know we could make it work."

Annie turned her gaze toward Eugene, and he could read the mixed emotions in her eyes. He felt conflicted as well, but something down deep told him that this was best for Will and Keiko. He gave his wife a reassuring nod as Will rushed on.

"We'd have to talk to Gramma to see if she'd be willing to sell it to us."

"No need to talk to Gramma," Eugene said, meeting his son's gaze. "She gave me the deed to the property a long time ago." His mouth tipped slightly upward. "You'd have to buy it from *me*."

"How much?" Will asked in a serious tone.

Eugene's grin broadened. "Four," was all he said.

Will nodded his head slowly. "Four thousand?"

"Nope. I figure a dollar for the house, a dollar for the cave, one dollar for the pond, and one more for the oak tree. That comes to a grand total of four dollars. Do you think you can scrape enough together to buy it?"

Will was so excited he stood up and took a few paces out into the yard with his hands locked behind his head. Turning back quickly, he laughed. "Are you serious? You really mean it?"

Eugene stood up and chuckled. "I really mean it," he said, sticking out his hand.

Will immediately grabbed it and shook on the deal, then pulled his dad into a jubilant embrace.

***

Rachel loved October on the Winchester farm more than any other time of year. That's when Franklin's oak tree exalted itself above all other foliage on the property. She reached out to touch the rough bark, turning her gaze upward into the sea of yellow and orange leaves, dancing cheerfully in the sun. The spreading branches caused an intense yearning for the comfort of her husband's strong arms.

"Franklin," she whispered softly, "I wish you could see this place. It's alive again." Rachel looked across the pasture toward the house, bustling with activity. "You'd barely recognize our old house. Why, it has running water, indoor plumbing, and electricity now." She laughed out loud. "We wouldn't have known what to do with such luxuries."

Slowly, she moved toward an old log and brushed it off lightly with her hand, then sat down to watch the men at work. Eugene and Nathan had painstakingly removed the front porch while Will and Jake hauled the posts and slats to a large pile behind the house. They estimated their porch project could be done in two days with so much help. Jake and Charlotte had taken off a day of school to join everyone for a three-day weekend.

Rachel smiled broadly when she saw Annie coming from behind the house in her denims and boots. She watched her pull on leather gloves and carry off several wooden slats. It was so like her daughter-in-law to be outside doing manual labor while the other women worked in the house. Oh, how she loved that woman.

Eugene jabbed the posthole diggers into the dirt and pulled off his shirt. He wiped it across his sweaty face, then threw it out into the yard. Annie snuck in close, just as he put his hands back on the digger. She yanked off one of her gloves and playfully pinched him on the side, then ran off when he tried to grab her. His laughter drifted like a beautiful melody across the pasture to Rachel's ears.

After a few minutes, Eugene dropped down onto his knees and began digging in the dirt with his hands. He called out something that she couldn't hear, and the others stopped working to join him. Rachel stood up, curious about their exuberance. All of a sudden, every one of them turned and looked toward her out at the oak.

That's when Eugene held an object up high in the air and yelled, "We found it, Mama!"

Rachel put her hand over her heart with excitement. It had to be the jar of money Franklin had buried right after they got married.

Annie met her halfway across the pasture and took her elbow. "Eugene found the jar you told us about!"

"Oh, thank heavens, darlin'. I thought I was going crazy."

Annie laughed. "He thinks we might have to break the jar. We can't get the lid off."

By the time Rachel made it to the discovery site, Eugene had wiped off the jar, but it was still difficult to see the contents. He shook it. "Definitely full of coins, Mama. The lid's sealed on tight. Do you mind if I break it?"

"No. Go ahead," she said breathlessly.

Eugene laid the jar on the cement slab of the old pump. Everyone gathered around as he raised his hammer and tapped it gingerly at first, then with a little more force. The glass broke open, and gold coins spilled out all over the slab.

Nathan gasped. "Do you know how much those coins are probably worth today? That's a small fortune." He picked one up and read the date out loud. "1871."

"There's something else," Eugene said. He carefully swept the thick shards of glass away and held up a small, yellowish envelope. Squinting in the sun he made out the faded writing on the front. "Mama, it says *Franklin* on the outside."

He held the envelope gently by the corners and handed it to Rachel. "You all should take it in and see if you can read it."

Jake began gathering all the coins. "I'll bring these in for you, Gramma."

"Thank you, darlin'."

Annie took Rachel's arm again and led her around to the back door. Rachel went inside while Annie took off her boots and left them on the steps.

Keiko and Claudia were already working on lunch preparations in the kitchen while Charlotte mopped the floor. All three women stopped their activity to join Rachel and Annie at the table.

"Here, darlin'," Rachel said, handing the envelope to her daughter-in-law. "My eyes aren't what they used to be."

Annie very carefully removed the brittle sheet of paper and unfolded it. She smoothed it out on the table and leaned in close. "Ooh . . . I may not be able to read this either. The ink has nearly faded right off the page." She narrowed her eyes and scooted in closer. "Okay, at the top it says . . . *Payment for Service Rendered.*"

Rachel sat back in her chair. "I don't understand. Franklin always received a bill of sale for the thoroughbreds he took to Samuel Hawkins. He would put the money in the cedar chest in the cave." She leaned forward again. "Does it say what services were rendered?"

Annie suddenly looked up from the paper. Her face began to turn a light shade of pink. "Mama," she said softly, "I think we need to get Eugene."

Rachel's heart fluttered in confusion. "What do you mean?"

Annie reached out and gently touched her arm. "I just think Eugene needs to be here when—"

"No," Rachel interrupted. "Tell me now . . . please." She didn't think she could stand to wait another minute.

Annie bit her lower lip then took Rachel by the hand. "Mama, Samuel Hawkins paid Franklin to . . ." She took in a shaky breath. "To take you away."

Rachel slowly sat back in her chair as the reality of that statement battered her heart. Her own father had paid one of his former slaves to take her off his hands. She had always known that Samuel Hawkins didn't care about her. He had only been fulfilling his promise to a dying lover to educate her daughter and allow her to work in his house. Rachel had known by the way he always looked at her that she was nothing but a burden to him.

She swallowed the lump in her throat and squeezed Annie's hand. "Read it to me, darlin'. I want to know what it says."

Claudia slid her hand down Rachel's arm. "Are you sure you want to hear it? This has been buried for decades, Rachel. Maybe it would be better to leave it buried in the past."

Rachel contemplated Claudia's counsel for a moment. "Maybe it would," she said, "but I need to know." She sat up a little straighter in her chair. "Please read it."

Annie cast a worried glance toward her mother then down at the paper. Slowly she read, "*On this day, 19 October 1874, I do hereby seal this agreement with one Negro male, Franklin Hawkins, to take one half-breed female, Rachel Hawkins, aged sixteen years and one month, with aforesaid agreement of payment. All rights or privilege of entitlement to any portion of the Hawkins estate are hereby dissolved for the aforementioned female. Signed: Samuel L. Hawkins.*"

Annie closed her eyes and took in a deep breath while Claudia continued caressing Rachel's arm. Keiko and Charlotte sat with stunned looks on their faces.

Finally, Annie raised her head. "I'm sorry, Mama."

Rachel knew better, but she couldn't help it; she felt like a slave again. Even though slavery had been abolished several years before this agreement, she had still been sold at a price. *Payment for Service Rendered* kept running through her head.

"Franklin took payment for me," she whispered. "How can that be true?"

Immediately, Annie pushed away from the table. "I'll be right back."

A few moments later, Eugene came through the back door. He went into the bedroom and came out after putting on a clean shirt.

"Mama, Annie told me what the paper said." He sat down in the chair his wife had vacated, taking both of Rachel's hands in his. "I'm here for you. Tell me what you're thinking."

Rachel didn't mean to cry, but Eugene's tenderness touched her heart deeply. She released his hands and wiped the tears from her cheeks, unnerved by this whole turn of events. She let out a ragged breath. "I'm simply hurt . . . I don't know what else to say."

For a long time, Eugene firmly held her eyes. She could literally see his mind whirring with activity. "You know what, Mama?" he finally said. "This just proves how much Papa really loved you."

Rachel's brow furrowed deeply. "I don't understand."

"Mama, if he had given one wit about this agreement, he would've spent that money. Don't you see? He didn't marry you and take you from the plantation for *this*." Eugene reached over and held up the fragile piece of paper. "He married you because he loved you; he wanted you more than anything else on this earth. Do you remember that time you told me about the circumstances of your birth?"

Rachel nodded her head.

"We were sitting right out there on the porch—well, what used to be the porch—and Papa told me what he told his pappy about you. Do you remember that?"

"I remember telling you about my heritage," Rachel confirmed.

"Yeah, but do you remember what Papa said?"

She racked her brain, trying to figure out where Eugene was headed with this. "Tell me."

"He said he went to sell Mr. Hawkins a colt and you answered the front door. He said you were the prettiest thing he'd ever seen." Eugene gave her a warm smile. "Papa said he ran into a table in the house because he couldn't keep his eyes off of you."

"I remember that well. He had me tickled to death over that."

"Papa told me he was in trouble when he came back here because he stayed an extra day just to be with you. Is that true?"

Rachel nodded. "Yes."

"Mama, I asked him what he told his pappy about coming home a day late. He told him that the same time next year, he was coming home with a wife."

Eugene brought the paper close to his face. "Look at this," he said excitedly. "The date is October 19, 1874. What day did you get married?"

"On that very date," Rachel said.

"Don't you see, Mama? Papa loved you with all his heart. He planned to take you away from that plantation a full year before Samuel Hawkins came up with this asinine agreement. Papa couldn't read, but he knew what it said. Why else would he have buried it deep in the ground? He didn't want you to know about it," Eugene reached for both of her hands again, "because he married you for love . . . not for money, no matter how much it was. And Mama, that's a lot of money Jake brought in."

Rachel found herself smiling at Eugene's impassioned interpretation of this *asinine* agreement. Deep down in her heart, she knew he was right about all of it. How could she have doubted for even one second how much Franklin had loved her? She felt ashamed of herself for falling into Samuel Hawkins' vile snare.

She reached up and cupped Eugene's face in her hands. "Thank you, darlin'. You just kept me from going down a shameful path."

"You're welcome," he said simply. Then he got up and went over to the stove with the agreement in his hand. He pushed a pot of boiling water over to the side and held the paper to the gas flame. When it caught fire, he took it over to the kitchen sink and let it burn almost to his fingertips before dropping the charred remains down the drain. One quick turn of the faucet and the agreement was dissolved completely.

"Well, what are we waiting for?" Rachel declared fervently. "Let's go claim the Hawkins plantation!"

That night, the men took their bedrolls out into the pasture. They let the women have all the beds in the house. Eugene sat on his blanket, staring back at the house, proud of what they had accomplished today. Tomorrow morning they should be completely done with the new porch. Not bad for a day's work.

Will leaned on one elbow as he stretched out on his bedroll between Jake and Nathan. "Dad, I still can't believe Gramma gave me all that money. Can I pay you and Gramps for all the materials you brought out for the porch?"

"Absolutely not," Nathan barked. "That porch is on us."

Eugene agreed. "He's right; that's our gift to you. Besides, now you can fence in your entire property and give your livestock more space."

"Still, I don't mind chipping in on the porch."

"William," Nathan admonished in a deep voice.

Jake reached over and punched his arm. "You'd better quit while you're ahead, big brother. Of course, if you're lookin' to unload some cash, you can always throw a little my way," he teased.

Will punched his brother back. "I should probably check your pockets. You were awfully quick to pick up all those coins for Gramma."

"What are you all laughing about?" Annie asked, as she walked up with a bedroll and pillow.

Eugene sat up. "Are you joining us tonight?"

"If you'll have me. I just couldn't stand missing out on all these stars."

"Come on," Eugene said, moving over. "Jake and I will protect you."

When she finally got settled under her covers, Will spoke up with a hint of mischief in his voice. "Mom, you didn't see Jake take any coins today, did you?"

Annie looked over at Jake. Her eyes had adjusted to the darkness, and she caught his wink. "Well, I did hear some jangling in his pockets just before supper."

"I knew it." Will raised up and started wrestling with his brother. They were acting like schoolboys again.

Annie giggled and moved closer to Eugene, so she wouldn't catch an elbow. She leaned in and whispered, "They're *your* boys." Then she kissed his ear. For a moment, Eugene considered wrestling with his wife, but when he thought about her father on the other side of their sons, he changed his mind.

All of a sudden, the tussling came to an abrupt halt, and Eugene looked over to see what had happened.

"May we join you?" Charlotte asked, in a sweet voice. "That is, if you two are finished."

Jake cleared his throat and stood up. "Uh, yeah. We were just having a little fun." He took Charlotte's bedroll and laid it out on the ground while Will helped

Keiko with hers. The two young wives immediately settled in next to each other in between their husbands.

As soon as Charlotte lay down, Annie peered over Jake. "You're in for a real treat, sweetheart. Look up."

Charlotte turned her gaze upward for the first time. "Oh my," she said. "That takes my breath away."

"How can someone say there is no God?" Keiko whispered.

Everyone agreed, including Claudia, who had just made her way outside.

Nathan immediately came to his feet and called to her. "Honey, I'm down here on this end." He reached for her bedroll and helped stretch it out between his spot and Will's.

Eugene sat up. "What about Mama? Is she okay staying inside alone?"

Claudia assured him that Rachel had no intention of sleeping outside. "She told me she was glad to have the house to herself."

He chuckled and lay back down, but not for long.

"Is there anyone out there who can help an old woman?"

All eight family members sat straight up, some already pushing back their covers.

"No, stay where you are. I've got her," Eugene said, and he was on his feet immediately.

When he got to the porch, Rachel was standing with her arms full of blankets and a pillow.

"Mama, are you sure you want to sleep in the open tonight?"

She gazed out into the inky night then back at her son. "I'm positive. A chance like this may never come along again."

Eugene could feel the warmth of her words down deep in his heart. He knew she was right; this was a memorable night for their family. All of them together, underneath God's incomparable display of majesty—a gift he would treasure until his last day on earth.

In a way, it was fitting. This is where it all began for him. The very spot where they lay in the pasture was the place where Franklin had scooped him up as a boy, saving him from the frightened horses, and even more importantly, rescuing him from a painful existence. This is where he had found love and acceptance and hope—a hope that had never let him down.

"Well, are you waiting for someone to build me some steps, or do you plan to help me get off this porch?"

He laughed and took the blankets from her arms, setting them on the porch. Then he put his hands on her waist, and gently lifted her down beside him.

When she reached for the blankets, Eugene stopped her and picked them up instead. "I've got 'em, Mama." Then he put his arm around her shoulders, drawing her close. "And I've got you too."

Epilogue

Spring 2012

"Sophie, look at this one—1852. This is it."

Twelve-year-old Sophie Wyatt ran to her father's side. "*Franklin Hawkins*," she read out loud. "*Loving husband and father.*"

"He was a slave, and so was his wife, Rachel," Scott told her.

Sophie stepped in front of the marker next to Franklin's. "*Rachel Hawkins, 1858–1957.* Dad, she lived to be ninety-nine!"

Scott noticed his wife and eight-year-old son on the other side of the gigantic oak tree. "Did you find the rest of the family?" he called.

"Yes, they're over here. There must not have been enough space beside Franklin and Rachel." Lauren Wyatt stood in front of five other graves. Each marker included the name *Wyatt.*

When Scott and Sophie walked the circumference of the oak, Lauren read the first headstone. "*Eugene Lloyd Wyatt, January 1, 1901–May 4, 1988.*" She looked at her husband. "You said Eugene was the son of Franklin and Rachel?"

"That's right."

"But Dad," Sophie interrupted, "Franklin and Rachel were slaves. Weren't they African-American?" Scott could see his daughter's mind churning with curiosity as she talked. "I thought your great-grandfather was a white man."

"He was a white man, but he was adopted by a former slave couple. They raised him from the time he was ten or eleven, I think."

"Then why doesn't he have the same last name?" Sophie asked.

"You know, I'm not really sure. There's a story I think I heard my grandfather tell one time, about Great-Grandpa Eugene having to fight in World War I before he was even eighteen. From what I recall, the army must've used the name he was born with."

Lauren stepped in front of Annie's grave, and Sophie came to stand in front of her. She looped her arms around her daughter and read, "*Anne Marie Wyatt, March 7, 1901–April 5, 1988.*"

Sophie reached up and held her mother's arms. "Look at that. They died almost exactly one month apart."

"I was fourteen when they both died—I remember it well," Scott told them. "Great-Grandma Annie passed away in her sleep, and even though my Great-

Grandpa was as healthy as a horse, he couldn't live without her." Scott gave his wife a tender look. "They always said he died of a broken heart."

The corners of Lauren's mouth turned down slightly. "Oh, that makes me sad to think about it."

"I guess when you live with someone for more than sixty-five years, that can happen."

Cameron spoke up then. "Dad, is this your grandpa? It says *Jacob Nathan Wyatt*."

"Yep, that was my grandfather. Everyone called him Jake. You were just a toddler, Cameron, when he passed away six years ago. He was eighty-two. And my grandmother, Charlotte—you all wouldn't remember her; she died of cancer twelve years before that. My grandpa was a doctor, and he always thought he'd be able to save her."

"Look at this!" Sophie exclaimed. "This grave has two headstones."

"Yeah, I wanted you to see that. This is my great-uncle Will's grave, William Franklin Wyatt. I never knew him since he died a long time before I was born. But my grandpa told me a little bit about him."

Sophie said, "It looks like he died twice."

"Well, Grandpa Jake said they were told he died during World War II, but sometime after the war was over, he just came home."

Lauren moved to her husband's side. "What's the story behind that? Do they know where he was?"

Scott shook his head with disappointment. "One of my biggest regrets is not ever sitting down with my grandparents and finding out about all of this. I never took the time to really ask them questions or listen to their stories. It bothers me now because there's no one left who knows all of the family history." He reached out and rubbed the top of his daughter's blonde head. "I'm afraid when we get back to Chicago, you're not going to have a lot to write about in your family history report."

Looking a little closer at Will's grave, Lauren commented, "He didn't live very long after the war, did he? 1955. Only ten years."

"Now that I think about it," Scott said, "Great-Uncle Will spent time in a Japanese prison camp. Some of those guys didn't live very long after their experiences in the Pacific."

Cameron walked a little farther along. "I don't see another grave that says Wyatt. I guess William wasn't married."

"Oh yes he was."

Startled by the presence of another person, the Wyatt family turned sharply. An African-American woman stood behind them, her back as straight as an arrow, yet she held a cane in her hand. She had the most lovely, expressive eyes, and her face was nearly absent of wrinkles. But her hands gave her away. Scott guessed her to be in her late eighties.

She walked up beside Lauren without using her cane. "He was married to a wonderful Japanese woman who saved his life during the war." Her gaze moved to the graves at their feet. "God wove a beautiful tapestry of your family," she said softly.

"Did you know the family?" Lauren asked.

"Did I ever," she breathed reverently. "I was part of it."

Brimming with curiosity, Scott extended his hand. "I'm Scott Wyatt, and this is my wife, Lauren, and our children Sophie and Cameron."

The woman reached out and clasped Scott's hand tightly. "So pleased to meet you. My name is Lillie, and do I ever have a story to tell *you*."

Scott's smile widened. "We'd love to hear it, that is, if you have time."

"I have time. As a matter of fact, would you like to come to my house for dinner?"

Lauren expressed her concern. "We don't want to impose."

"Oh no, it would not be an imposition. As a matter of fact, I have some photographs and letters I think you'll want to see."

With that statement, Lillie put her arm around Sophie's shoulders. "I think I can give you plenty to write about for your family history report. But before we go to my house, would you like to see where your great-great-great-grandparents Nathan and Claudia are buried?"

Sophie's excitement was contagious. "Yes, please!"

As they all turned toward another section of the cemetery, Sophie earnestly looked at the woman by her side. "How did you know we were here today?" she asked.

The old woman's eyes took on a faraway look, and then she quietly laughed. "Sometimes I just know things."

Author's Note

Dear Readers,

I am truly honored that you have chosen to read *Blind Hope*. The encouragement I've received from many of you over the past two years has been amazing. I feel blessed to share this journey with all of you. Thank you for providing me with so much cheer and support along the way. My prayer is that you have been inspired in some small way by this book.

As you may have noticed, from the first chapter of *Blinders* to the epilogue of *Blind Hope*, exactly one hundred years have passed—six generations. By the turn of the twenty-first century, much of the rich history of the Hawkins family had been forgotten. Let that be a caution to all of us. If we fail to pass down stories from one generation to the next, our own heritage can so easily be lost. That's why drawing on family stories from the past is what makes writing so enjoyable for me.

I thought you might be interested to know where I received inspiration for some of the story line. The letters that Claudia gave to Annie in chapter seven were actual letters written by my great-grandmother, Bertha Susan Gano, to my grandmother, Blanche Rollmann. You will remember these two women from *Blinders*. Claudia's tragic loss of a son during childbirth was a retelling of my grandmother's experience. It was such a treasure to find these letters among Memaw's possessions. Although her son was born in 1937, she was finally able to hold him for the first time in 1989—the day she saw Jesus face to face. This is *my* heritage of faith.

Mattie's character was based on a story my mother tells from her youth during the depression era in Pine Bluff, Arkansas. My grandmother, Gertrude Hamilton, became concerned about an African-American woman she had seen entering an abandoned house. When she checked on her, she discovered that the woman was nearly starving. Her name was Betty, and she had lost her husband and two young children. She was alone with no work and no place to live. My grandmother brought her home to help cook and clean for a household of eight. She also arranged a place for Betty to live. Although she was never paid a salary, Betty was welcomed into their home daily, fed breakfast and lunch, and then given a little food to take home every night for supper. My grandmother saved her life.

One of the pleasures in writing *Blinders* and *Blind Hope* was being able to take Eugene from boyhood to manhood. Eugene was a truly caring, compassionate man, with an extra measure of patience. Much of his personality and demeanor are based on a dear friend of mine, Matt Sills. Though Matt is nearly young enough to be my son, (for which he reminds me occasionally), I am honored to have been one of his teaching and coaching colleagues for eleven years. Even more importantly, we led some amazing mission trips together to Honduras and Mexico. Matt is God's man—not perfect, as I'm sure his wife, Sara, will tell you—but one of the most thoughtful men I've ever met, with a great sense of humor to boot!

And speaking of sense of humor—if you're wondering about Eugene's proposal of marriage to Annie, wonder no more. "How about it?" was my husband's actual question when he proposed to me. After visualizing throwing that ring box in his face, I calmly asked, "How about what?" Thirty-three years later, we're still going strong, and I'm thankful for having this faithful man of God in my life.

Please contact me at kristy.l.shelton@gmail.com with any questions or comments. I would love to hear from my readers.

Until the Lord comes again, keep the Spirit alive!
Kristy Shelton

CPSIA information can be obtained
at www.ICGtesting.com
Printed in the USA
FFOW01n1221150514
5387FF